I0665319

"I WILL SHOW YOU WHAT LOVE MEANS."

Restraining himself, Alex kissed her deeply, yet tenderly, then pressed his mouth lightly to each spot on her face where Stafford had bruised it, then to her eyes, her ears, the corners of her mouth, and her throat where he could feel a pulse beating in agitation. He raised his head and smiled at her in the darkness. "You like me a little?"

"Aye, of course, but—"

"I can bring you joy, ecstasy, feelings that you've never known before. 'Tis pleasure I want to give you, Marina," he went on in a deep, hypnotic voice, "not pain. Such sweet pleasure . . ."

Other Leisure Books by Catherine Linden:

HIGHLAND ROSE
DIAMONDS IN THE NIGHT
LOVER'S MOON

CATHERINE LINDEN

HIGHLAND FLAME

LEISURE BOOKS　NEW YORK CITY

For Ian Irvine, Laurence McNamara,
and Kevin Robertshaw, with love.

A LEISURE BOOK®

July 1991

Published by

Dorchester Publishing Co., Inc.
276 Fifth Avenue
New York, NY 10001

Copyright © 1991 by Catherine Linden

All rights reserved. No part of this book may be reproduced or transmitted in any form or by any electronic or mechanical means, including photocopying, recording, or by any information storage and retrieval system, without the written permission of the Publisher, except where permitted by law.

The name "Leisure Books" and the stylized "L" with design are trademarks of Dorchester Publishing Co., Inc.

Printed in the United States of America.

— *Youthful Folly* —

Life is but a journey
To travel how you will.
There are some who strive
Who can only thrive
By climbing to the hill,
Who will walk the sword
Or face the horde
With boldness in their blood.

There are those who will
And those who won't
Grasp life in eager hands.
Some fear to love
As they fear to live,
And the food they eat is dust.
Their souls may thirst
But never will they drink.

Northumberland,
England, 1586

At seven o'clock in the evening a small wedding party gathered expectantly in the hall of Chiltern Castle. On the gallery above, the sixteen-year-old bride, virginal in a flowing white gown and with flowers entwined in her pale gold hair, lingered with her attendants ready to make their entrance once the groom and his retinue arrived.

The bride, Marina, was pale and rather sober, but the rest of the assembly were merry and excited, except for Father Ridley who only moments before had emerged from his secret apartment behind the massive chimney to conduct the marriage ceremony—a Catholic ceremony forbidden by English law.

Only the priest was uneasy . . . at first.

Sir Guy Percy, master of Chiltern Castle, stood with his back to the fire and surveyed the scene around him. Aye, he thought, it would do well enough,

considering the haste with which everything had had to be arranged. Though frost rimed the desolate countryside surrounding his castle and there was a frigid nip in the air, the hall fire sent out a cheery blaze of warmth and the rather gloomy, dark-paneled chamber was brightened with candlelight and decorated with greenery and autumnal flowers, the air freshened with sweet-scented herbs and pine boughs.

With a glance at his priest, he thought, Would that this marriage were over with! Percy, a stout, broad-faced knight in his early fifties, was normally good-natured and hearty, but his smile was somewhat strained that evening and his manner impatient.

Feeling the bride's eyes upon him, Sir Guy glanced up to the minstrels' gallery and saw that her face was white in the dark above-stairs and the expression on her lovely face was tense and unsmiling. He knew well that his ward, Marina Dudley, had no great desire to marry young Nevil Dacre, but the silly whims of adolescent girls made little impression on a man of his station. As for the wedding itself, well . . . it was not *his* fault that it had had to be brought forward by several months and, consequently, would not now be the grand occasion they had first planned. "'Tis your own doing, you careless burde," he told her silently when their eyes met. "Mayhap now you will keep a closer check on your tongue."

Percy and his plump wife, Lady Maud, were very keen to see the girl wed and off their hands. They had raised six children of their own, and theirs had not been an easy marriage, though in later years they had reached a comfortable relationship with each other and naturally wished nothing to disturb that. It therefore had been annoying to both that their ward was rapidly turning into a dark-eyed coquette with an innocently provocative manner that had begun to

attract the attention of every worthy in the district. Strictly raised as Marina had been, *they* knew that the girl was pure and chaste, but she had a flirtatious way about her that was beginning to worry them.

"She is a ripening peach soon to be plucked if we are not vigilant," Lady Maud had fretted recently, adding darkly, "Then there is that unfortunate business at the Harvest Ball to consider. Nay, nay," she had said, shaking her head, "the thing to do is to bring forward her wedding to Dacre's son posthaste. That girl could make much trouble for herself—and us."

The "unfortunate business" that his wife had referred to had happened a few weeks ago during the annual harvest festivities. One of their guests that evening had been a man traveling from Scotland to London, a Spaniard called Sedina and an avid Catholic. He made no secret of the fact that he dreamed, along with the King of Spain, of toppling Queen Elizabeth of England off her throne and installing Queen Mary of Scotland there in her stead. Sedina, an emissary of his Spanish sovereign, had been sent to Scotland to treat with the young King and from there had slipped over the border into England with the express purpose of making as much trouble as possible.

Marina had been allowed to attend the ball that evening and had been seated next to the Spaniard at the feast that preceded it. Much wine had flowed, and the girl, unused to it, had become flushed and giddy. Sedina, like many another of late, had been captivated by the young beauty and her pert ways. He had also been intrigued by her name, Dudley.

He asked Marina brashly, not caring who overheard, "Can you be related to Queen Elizabeth's lover, Robert Dudley, the Earl of Leicester?"

She was startled, then laughed and shook her head.

"Oh, come," chuckled Sedina when she blushed, "all know how it is with them. Surely we can speak plain out here in the wilds of the North? There is scant support for the Protestant Queen here."

The North of England was predominantly Catholic and generally opposed to the present regime, but even in remote Northumberland one had to be very careful as Elizabeth had her spies everywhere. But Marina was very young and knew little about the political situation in the country. This was her first ball, and her whole intent was to seem as sophisticated as possible.

The Spaniard took his gaze from her and glanced around the candlelit hall, inquiring casually, "Where are your parents, fair Marina? Are they here among us tonight?"

"Nay," she sighed, "they are dead, I fear. Sir Guy Percy is my guardian."

"Indeed." Again the black eyes returned to her face, and this time Sedina examined her speculatively, all the while stroking his pointed beard. He had been merely jesting at first. Now he wondered if it were possible. He noted Marina's golden-blonde hair, a few shades lighter than the Queen's, and her velvety dark eyes—melting, seductive eyes of the type Queen Elizabeth was said to find so irresistible in Robert Dudley, the man who had rarely left her side since she first became queen. As he studied Marina, intrigued, several exciting ideas presented themselves to him. And how convenient, he thought, that her parents happened to be dead.

He leaned close to her and suggested slyly, "Could it be that you are one of their bastards, eh? Rumor has it that they have had several, all shunted quickly out of the way."

Marina was shocked that he would dare suggest

such a thing. The Queen and Robert Dudley! Why, the Spaniard was not only insolent, but dangerously bold as well. She had never known her parents, it was true—they had died when she was only a toddler—but she *did* know who they were, and she was certainly not a bastard! For a second, as she gazed at Sedina wide-eyed, a hazy, jumbled impression wafted into her mind from the distant past, one that, while unclear, touched her with sadness and a feeling of loss. But Marina didn't want to be sad tonight! This was her first ball and she intended to enjoy herself and make merry with everyone else.

Shrugging the feeling off, she laughed and joked, "Yea, 'tis obvious that I am one of theirs. As you can see, sir"—with a wave down at her rather modest blue muslin gown—"I am clad in cloth of gold and wear a tiara on my head, and these beads about my neck are really diamonds—"

"Marina, be silent!" thundered a man seated directly across the table. He was Clive Radcliffe, a cousin of Sir Guy's, and he had heard the entire conversation between the pair. Now, glowering at the crafty Spaniard, he warned Marina, "Guard your tongue, you foolish burde. These walls about us have ears."

When this was reported to Sir Guy immediately following the function, he felt a jolt of the greatest alarm. Fuming, he barged down the dark corridor to his ward's chamber, threw open the door, and proceeded to thrash her soundly for being so dangerously indiscreet. "See what mischief you've wrought!" Percy roared into her startled face. "That Spaniard is doubtless a spy for his King and will seize whatever means he can to try to discredit Queen Elizabeth." Shaking her, he informed her, "Do you not know, you witless twit, that Elizabeth prides herself on being a virgin? She would like her people to believe that all

her love and devotion is reserved for them. This is a difficult time for the Queen with her ministers hounding her to execute her prisoner, Queen Mary of Scotland. Should she go through with it, Elizabeth's own conduct must be above reproach. And—and for you to make such a scandalous claim at this time—!"

"I—I didn't know . . ." Marina whimpered, trying to protect herself from the angry blows raining down about her head. "I spoke in jest and meant no harm, I swear it!" At the same time she was puzzled, wondering why her guardian was so furious with her. "I thought we did not care overmuch for Protestants here and would band together with any country to bring down—"

He struck her again, harder than before. "Christ's bones, girl, how you try my patience! Dost not realize that there are informers everywhere; that we can trust no one—not even the servants in our own house?" Percy grabbed her by her long blonde hair and wrenched her white face close to his, growling, "You'd best pray tonight that nothing comes of your reckless tattle. Child though you are, you could *still* end up in the Tower of London—and us with you!"

Marina lay shivering in terror after Sir Guy left her. Never before had he spoken to her so seriously about the political situation in the country. In fact, Percy rarely bothered to speak to her at all. A busy man with many grown children of his own and a large estate to administer, he had scant interest in his young ward. As for his wife, Lady Maud, *she* occupied herself in social activities and keeping up with the latest gossip and was not above stirring up a little intrigue of her own, pitting one branch of the family against the other for her own amusement. Fat, lazy, and completely self-centered, a woman with a strong avaricious streak, Maud Percy had troubled herself little about

her own children, let alone Marina Dudley.

Growing up in Chiltern Castle, Marina had been cared for well enough and, befitting a young lady of her station, had received a classical education, but the Percys had never shown her any love or attention at all. By and large they ignored her, except when she spoke or acted out of turn, as she had that night.

Soon, she mused, she would have someone of her own to take an interest in her. That someone was eighteen-year-old Nevil Dacre, a lad she had been betrothed to since childhood, but the thought of marriage with the vague, introverted Nevil brought Marina no joy, though she knew that joy had very little to do with making an advantageous marriage. Marriage was a serious business, too serious to be left to the immature desires of young people. At least Dacre was young, and even pleasant to look upon. Surely, Marina tried to convince herself, that was something to be grateful for. She thought of poor Helen Percy—Sir Guy and Lady Maud's youngest daughter—who the previous year had been wed to a wealthy, and ugly, nobleman four times her age.

"Aye," she sighed, "it could be worse; far worse."

Oh, why had she allowed that knave Sedina to draw her into making that disastrous claim? It had only been meant as a joke, but—

Marina prayed fervently that night that there had been no informers at the harvest ball; that the Spaniard himself would not mention it when he moved on to London.

She wasn't the only one who prayed. For weeks after the ball Sir Guy lived in fear, well aware that they were living in particularly dangerous times. Though far away in the North of England, the Catholics of the area were kept informed of the situation in London by their own network of spies. Much of the intrigue—as

it had for years—centered around the figurehead of Mary Stuart, the deposed Queen of Scotland. Mary had now been incarcerated in English prisons for eighteen long years. Countless plots had sprung up to free her, schemes hatched both at home and abroad; the Pope himself was said to be actively behind many of them. The goal of them all was to knock Queen Elizabeth, thought of as a bastard by the Catholics, off her throne and place her cousin Mary there in her place. By so doing they would restore the true religion to England.

Amazingly, every rescue attempt had failed, but even so, new plots kept arising, every one of them posing a serious threat to the present monarch. Now, increasingly pressed by her ministers who were impatient to have the matter done with once and for all, they had heard that Queen Elizabeth was ready to sign her cousin's death warrant, something she had avoided doing for years.

The eyes of every Catholic both at home and abroad were turned grimly on London, causing Elizabeth to shrink with apprehension. She was especially afraid of how mighty Spain might react if she executed Mary Stuart. Worse, even some of her own Protestant subjects, for various reasons, were now taking a more critical view of their Queen, their sympathy aroused by the dire plight of Mary. They remembered that Mary had flown to England as a young woman fully expecting to receive help from her own kin—and had been locked up in prison instead. They recalled too how Elizabeth had tried to implicate Mary in the murder of Mary's husband, Lord Darnley, charging that she had been behind the plot to kill her weak reprobate of a consort so that she could be free to wed the Earl of Bothwell. This had never been proved.

Some were muttering, "Is Elizabeth herself so spot-

less? What of Amy Robsart, the former wife of Robert Dudley?" The woman had died under mysterious circumstances some years before, her death freeing Dudley to wed his royal lover. But the people of the country had howled against the idea, certain that Dudley had connived to bring about his wife's murder. Further, they firmly believed, the blood of others also stained his grasping hands. We will have no Dudley as consort, they made clear, and Elizabeth never thwarted the desires of her people—though she still kept the Earl of Leicester close to her side.

Many the world over sympathized with Mary Stuart, watching and waiting to see what her cousin Queen Elizabeth would do. It was the most delicate moment of the English Queen's reign. Now, as never before, her deportment must be impeccable, her character above reproach.

Sir Guy Percy lay awake at night sweating with fear.

"Get Marina wed at once," his wife had advised, "while we still have heads upon our shoulders to see to the arrangements. And let the ceremony be a quiet one held at night, with few there to witness it."

Percy had gone to see Lord Dacre, the father of the prospective groom, asking that the wedding be hastened. "'Tis because of my good wife," he lied. "She has been ailing of late and her condition seems to be worsening. It would be a great relief to her to see our ward safely wed."

"Then let it be done," Dacre had agreed. He had worries of his own, chiefly that his vague son Nevil might slowly be losing his mind, and once that became obvious there would be no marriage with Marina Dudley—and no dowry to fatten the Dacre coffers.

It had been arranged that the marriage should take place a week later.

Now the day had come, or rather, the evening. It was now well past seven o'clock and the small assembly gathered in Chiltern Castle were growing restive, none more so than Father Ridley.

"The groom and his party are unseemly late," the priest remarked, and bit his nails.

Percy, annoyed, strode to the window and peered out, his eyes scanning the countryside for a glimpse of the torches Dacre and his men would be carrying to light their way. He saw nothing but a vast, unrelieved darkness. Windswept hills and lonely valleys stretched between Chiltern and the Dacre fortress to the south and the Scottish border less than ten miles away to the north, some of the most desolate and potentially dangerous territory in all of England.

"What keeps them, think you?" fretted Ridley, hovering nervously at Percy's elbow. "They should have been here long since, and 'tis not like Dacre to be late for his own son's wedding." He admitted, "I—I like this not."

"Be silent, priest," Sir Guy muttered beneath his breath. "Would you alarm the others? Nay, nay, there's a good reason for his tardiness, rest assured. Mayhap some problem has arisen on his estate, or one of his party has become ill."

"There are many possibilities," Father Ridley replied dourly, thinking longingly of his secret apartment behind the chimney.

The candles guttered low and the blazing fire burned down to embers. Shadows crept out of the corners of the huge hall and moved insidiously in the direction of the small group now huddled in front of the fire, no longer gay and excited. They looked at each other uneasily, all locked in an eerie silence.

Turning from the window, Percy felt his flesh prickle when he saw a vision in white gliding down the long

curved staircase. In the preternatural aura that gripped everyone he thought for a second that he was seeing a ghost, but it was only his ward, Marina Dudley. Pointing, Sir Guy angrily ordered her back to the gallery. "Get up yonder and wait, girl! 'Tis bad luck to come down before the groom gets here."

Lady Maud, wringing her hands, spoke for them all. "What if he doesn't come?"

The Scottish Highlanders rode in stealth through the twilit English countryside cloaked and hooded and heavily armed, a tight little band of twelve determined men all bent on a single goal—to rescue Queen Mary of Scotland as she was being moved from one prison to another.

Lord Alexander Sinclair, the leader of the group, had decided that this was the most vulnerable moment to attack, perhaps the last such moment before Mary Stuart vanished into the grim fortress of Fotheringay Castle, a stronghold said to be impregnable. The conspirators were all young men from noble Scottish families, and each had embarked on the mission of his own free will, unanimously electing Alexander Sinclair to be their leader. Like them all, he was young, on the brink of his twenty-first birthday. Tall and dark but with brilliant green eyes that stood out vividly in the warm olive tones of his skin, he was a natural leader. Already he had proved that he was daring and courageous, and he came from a family with a tradition of serving the Crown as his father had done before him at the time when Queen Mary had reigned as a beautiful young woman in Scotland. It had been his sire, the Earl of Belrose, who had tried valiantly to steer Mary Stuart safely through the traps and pitfalls awaiting her when she returned from France to rule her native Scotland, but in the end the

Queen's emotional, headstrong ways had prevailed. When her nobles turned against her and she fled in search of help to regain her crown, the Earl of Belrose had urged her to go to France—but Mary turned to her English cousin Elizabeth instead, certain that she would assist her.

It had proved to be a fatal mistake.

Now, with the fiery confidence of youth upon him, Alex had eagerly picked up the gauntlet his father had cast down. That, he felt strongly, was his destiny.

Far away from the Scottish border, Sinclair and his men rode through the dusk settling over the English countryside. Three leagues from Fotheringay Castle they slowed and entered a small wood where they melded with the trees. There they waited, listening for the sound of hoofbeats approaching through the twilight. It was the most exciting—and dangerous—moment of their lives.

"What if our spies were wrong?" muttered Rab Hamilton, moving his horse closer to Sinclair's. "They might take the Queen to a different fortress."

"Nay"—Alex shook his dark head—"our contacts at Chartley Hall can be trusted. Fotheringay is definitely the place." He peered through the trees at the field beyond. "Many feel this will be her last prison. Elizabeth and her ministers are determined to have her head this time."

"And we are just as determined that they won't!" replied Hamilton with a touch of bravado. He looked at Alex hopefully. "Let us drink to the success of our venture."

Sinclair nodded. A little brandy would do them all good. He knew that his men were anxious—and they had every reason to be. If this failed and they were captured they would certainly feel the kiss of the executioner's axe. Like his friends, he was remember-

ing another rescue attempt that had recently failed, the infamous Babington Plot. The young instigator, Anthony Babington, and the others involved in the conspiracy had suffered a fiendish traitor's death on St. Giles's Field, an end so barbaric that even the spectators, though Elizabeth's loyal subjects, had been revolted at the sight, many reduced to tears.

Sinclair, like his friends, tried hard not to think about that now, and when each in turn drank from a silver flask of brandy they vowed, "Freedom or death!"

They were prepared for whatever might come, and if failure it would be—which none of them believed for a moment—they would not allow themselves to be taken alive to suffer the ignominious fate of Babington. Each had another small flask tucked away inside his jerkin pocket, a lethal dose of poison.

In the dusk Alexander looked at his friends and fellow conspirators and silently applauded each and every one of them. They were the flower and flame of Scotland, the cream of the young generation. Most were Highlanders like himself, vigorous lads who in the normal course of events would have had every reason to expect to enjoy a long, happy life—had it not been for the dream they all shared. But, he thought, a man must stand by his convictions. Queen Mary was older now, her beauty and sparkle grown dim from her long years in prison; they had heard that she was frequently ill and almost crippled with arthritis. All she had to look forward to if she were not rescued was the sharp blade of an axe.

Her predicament stirred great compassion in Alex and his friends and brought out all their chivalrous instincts. They would free this royal lady, they swore, or die in the attempt.

"Listen!" whispered nineteen-year-old Jamie Fra-

ser, and began to sweat profusely in spite of the chilly night air. "They come now . . ."

They all heard it then, the dull pounding of many riders coming toward them across the plain. Alex and his friends reached for their weapons. Success, he felt, would lie in the element of surprise.

2

The steward at Chiltern Castle was the first to spot the torches flaring in the darkness, and cried, "My Lord Dacre and his party are coming at last!"

Everyone heaved a sigh of relief—prematurely, as it turned out, because it was not Dacre and his company who rode into the courtyard but twenty strangers, agents of Sir Francis Walsingham, the man in charge of Queen Elizabeth's secret police.

To the horror and consternation of the bridal party, these men burst into the castle shouting that everyone present was under arrest. In the chaos that followed, Father Ridley vanished like a puff of smoke into his priest's hole behind the chimney and Lady Maud Percy swooned and collapsed on the floor. But Sir Guy, fighting back his terror, stepped up to the leader and blustered, "What means this intrusion? We are gathered here for a wedding. Surely that is no reason to place us under arrest?"

Norman Bellamy, the chief agent, smiled cynically. He knew that the North of England had long been a hotbed of dissent. "We have reason to believe, sir, that there's more than a wedding going on under your roof."

He turned away to order his men to block the doors and herd everyone, including the servants, into the hall. Then he looked hard at Percy. "I understand that you have a woman living here who has spread an evil lie connecting herself to the Queen. Kindly point this lady out at once."

Sir Guy went very pale, but still tried to brazen it out. "What nonsense! We have no such woman here."

"Sir Percy"—Bellamy fixed him with a cold eye— "take care how you answer. The information we have came from a reliable source or we would not have come all this way. 'Twould be better for you to speak the truth now, I assure you, than to be taken back to the Tower and have it forced out of you on the rack. Speak, man!" he suddenly thundered. "Identify the woman who made this treasonable claim."

The knight's eyes flickered to where Marina stood gripping the balustrade at the bottom of the stairs, her eyes huge in her white face. Bellamy followed the direction of his eyes and gave a start. "The bride? That—girl!"

Pointing to Marina, the agent shouted to his men, "Seize her!"

Then the interrogations began, each of them examined separately in the library of the castle, starting with Marina. Bellamy saw that she was tense with fear. She stood before him in the center of the room, a tall, slender girl with her virginal state stamped all over her. The agent felt a pang of disgust. He resented having been selected for the mission in the first place.

Now, eying Marina shrewdly, he felt angrier still. To waste his considerable talents in interrogating children! To send him into the wilds of Northumbria and risk ambush by the staunch Catholics in the region— for this! Of what consequence was Marina Dudley? For that matter, of what consequence was Sir Guy Percy in his backwater of a castle when far more important matters required his attention closer to London?

But no, he fumed, Francis Walsingham must have the claim investigated. No stone must be left unturned when the Queen's reputation was at stake. Walsingham, he thought irritably, was fast becoming ridiculous in hounding those he suspected of plotting to bring down his sovereign. Bah! Bellamy seethed inwardly, to squander my precious time like this! If indeed there was anything hatching here at remote Chiltern Castle, this young girl was certainly not behind it and no more than a puppet manipulated by Percy and his overly ambitious friends.

"Sit down." He waved Marina to a chair drawn up to the library table and seated himself across from her. For a moment he regarded her in silence. Walsingham's agent was forty years old, an intense man far more governed by ambition than emotion; the charms of women stirred him less than the lust for power. Yet when he drew the candlestick closer and her face was clearly illuminated, Marina's beauty made a strong impression on him, especially her arresting dark brown eyes very similar to those of the Queen's favorite, Robert Dudley.

Bellamy inhaled sharply. Christ's soul, he thought, staring at her, imagining now that he saw other resemblances; was it possible? For years the rumors had persisted, always strenuously denied. Yet—

"'Twill go better for you if you are truthful, mistress," he began. "Did you claim to be the Queen's daughter?"

The whole story came out about the incident at the Harvest Ball, and the instant Marina mentioned the name Sedina, Bellamy threw himself back in the chair. Sedina! How often had *that* particular name come to the attention of the secret police, always in connection with some mischief perpetrated against the Queen. They had tried and failed to find the fellow, who had proved to be as elusive as the wind, but wherever he had tarried on his journey of destruction he had left much trouble behind for those foolish enough to offer him lodgings.

"Hummm . . ." The agent pursed his lips. "Were there any other foreigners at the harvest ball?"

Marina shook her head. "N-nay, sir. Sedina was entertained here only because we have a tradition of offering hospitality to travelers here in the North. We"—she swallowed—"had no idea that the man was up to mischief."

He was inclined to believe her, experienced as he was in examining people, and he was more convinced than ever that he had come all this way for naught. It angered him, and he leaned forward suddenly and caught her lovely young face between steely fingers and looked deep in her eyes, determined to put the fear of death in her.

"Do you know, Marina Dudley, that because of the treasonable claim you made your name will be marked?"

"M-marked . . . ?"

The agent nodded. "Marked down in a special book kept by my Lord Walsingham, where the names of dissidents and subversives are noted. Such people are closely watched, and should they come to our atten-

tion again . . ." He let her imagination do the rest, certain it would conjure up a diabolical picture of what happened to these people. After a minute he waved her away. "You may go."

Sir Guy Percy's interview lasted considerably longer.

"*You* put the girl up to it," Bellamy charged. "Name the others in the plot."

Percy's broad face darkened with indignation. "I did no such thing! And there *is* no plot. The Spaniard simply stopped here on his way south from Scotland, and in these parts we never refuse food or lodgings to a weary traveler, that is all."

The agent lounged back in his chair and took another tack. "You are all Catholics here, so where is your priest?"

Sir Guy feigned surprise at the question, and lied, "There is no priest at Chiltern Castle, sir. In this house we adhere to the edicts of the Crown."

"If one is found you will be hanged."

Percy was confident that Father Ridley would never be found. At the same time he sensed that Bellamy was clutching at straws. Except for the unfortunate remark made by Marina, Walsingham's agent had nothing incriminating against him—though he was trying mightily to find something.

Percy reminded himself that he was the master of this castle, a fortress deep in the heart of Catholic England. In these parts Bellamy, rather than himself, should have a care. At this very moment, Percy doubted not, news of the visit by Walsingham's agents would have flashed over the countryside. The scouts from the various estates would have spotted them and hastened to inform their masters to be alert for trouble. The visit would by no means have passed unnoticed.

Feeling more confident, Sir Guy said, "You may search all you wish but you will find no priest here, sir. I tell you now that you are wasting your time."

The two men faced each other, and Bellamy felt the subtle change in Percy's manner. True, he was the servant of the mighty Francis Walsingham, the agent reflected, one of the most feared men in the country, but London was very far away and Chiltern Castle was in the midst of territory dominated by powerful Catholics such as the Duke of Northumberland, the Dacres, Percys, and others. These people all had large families and hordes of friends to support them; many had private armies ever prepared to do battle. He ran a finger around his ruff, beginning to sweat a little, wondering if he and his men would get away from the district safely once they finished here at Chiltern Castle.

For form's sake Bellamy kept Sir Guy in the interrogation room for another hour, trying every tactic he could think of to trip him into admitting some sort of culpability—anything! It irked him to think of having to return to London with absolutely nothing. But Percy was quick-thinking and just as determined not to be trapped.

Finally, exasperated, Bellamy snapped, "You maintain a lax household, Sir Guy. Would you have that girl lead you by the nose to the place where a noose will be put about your neck?"

The other didn't deign to reply, but he was furious at Marina.

The next morning at dawn Bellamy and his men rode away from Chiltern Castle, and by evening of that same day a messenger arrived from Lord Dacre. In silence he handed Sir Guy a sealed letter. It was brief. In light of what had happened, wrote Dacre, the marriage contract between his son Nevil and Marina

Dudley was null and void. "Few of us can afford to come to the notice of Sir Walsingham," wrote his lordship. "I could not bring such attention to my House. Therefore, it is with the deepest regret . . ."

"Bedamned!" Percy cried, and tossed the letter into his wife's lap as she sat before the fire in their private suite, Lady Maud still weak and shaken by the events of the last twenty-four hours. "This is a fine stew!" her husband raved on, stamping up and down the room in a high state of agitation. "We must get her gone from here, but I ask you, who will have her now?"

"I know of one," his lady replied with a strange smile, "though he might not be to her taste."

"Taste! What care I about her silly whims and notions?" he scoffed. "Of more concern to me, lady, is to keep this head upon my shoulders. Name the man!"

When she did so, Sir Guy burst out laughing, explosive laughter after the tension he had been under. He roared and slapped his thighs in glee until the tears ran down his cheeks, then went to his wife and kissed her, chuckling, "You are a clever lass, my Maud, that you are! Aye . . . this will be her just deserts considering the danger she has brought to our door. I will go to see the lucky groom at once."

She raised her brows. "Tomorrow night?"

"'Tis pointless to delay."

She nodded, grinning. "I think we both know what his answer will be."

In the morning Sir Guy went to Marina's chamber and broke the news to her, first, that she wouldn't be marrying Nevil Dacre after all. The girl didn't seem dismayed, and that angered Percy, so he went on harshly, "But we have found another husband for you. Edgar Stafford."

Now she *was* dismayed, and that gratified the man watching her.

"Nay, I beg of you!" Marina cried, aghast at the idea. "Not Edgar Stafford! He—he's a hard, embittered man and old enough to be my grandfather." He was also, she knew, one of the meanest men alive, even though it was whispered that he had a large horde of money hidden away somewhere in his dank hall. For all that, Stafford had never been known to spend a penny on anyone, let alone himself, and lived in a crumbling manor badly in need of repair, with few servants to attend to his wants simply because he was too stingy to pay them. But there were other aspects of Stafford's character that troubled her more. He was at least sixty years old, rough and uncouth, a fanatical Catholic who hated anyone outside his own religion—and he'd had two wives already, both deceased. These wives had died under mysterious circumstances, events that had caused much whispered gossip at the time, something to do with the fact that neither had been able to give him children.

In desperation Marina faced up to her guardian, crying, "I refuse to wed Edgar Stafford! I—I'd rather die!"

Percy strode over to her and slapped her face.

"You will wed him," he grated between clenched teeth, "for the simple reason that no one of consequence will have you now, and you can blame yourself for that, mistress. Further, my lady and I long for peace here, something we can never enjoy with you in the house, so you will marry him if I have to drag you to the altar by the hair of your head and whip the vows out of you. You've tarried under this roof long enough!"

Marina looked up at him bleakly, her dark eyes overflowing, and something made him add, "He will make few demands. 'Tis said he is impotent."

* * *

Three days later Marina left Chiltern Castle with her new husband and his small retinue of guards. Stafford's near-derelict manor lay five miles over the frost-hardened countryside, a region of craggy hills and wind-blasted moorland, territory that echoed the bleakness in the bride's heart.

As they rode along in silence, Marina reflected that her life was over before it had truly begun. Though she cringed at the thought of Edgar Stafford touching her, still it was sad to realize that she was married to an old man, an impotent man, and would never have a child of her own now, a little one to shower with all the love bottled up in her heart. She had no memory of her parents at all; both had died from smallpox before Marina's third birthday, and the little she knew of them had come from Maud Percy, whose relative her father had been. Sir Guy had never spoken about her parents at all.

At the thought of her guardian, Marina's depression was suddenly replaced by a blazing anger, and something sweet and tender in her nature was nipped and encased in ice, as the frost will petrify the flowers of autumn. She hated him! Aye, and she hated his lazy, conniving wife, for Marina had known through listening to the castle servants gossip that Lady Maud was not quite all she seemed, nor above lying and trickery. The pair seemed cozy enough together now, but in their youth, so it seemed, their relationship had been stormy, so stormy that Maud Percy had once left her husband and lived with a gentleman near London for nigh on a year. And this couple, with a past that didn't bear looking at too closely, thought to arrange *her* future!

"You are quiet, wife," Edgar Stafford suddenly remarked. "And I perceive that you look sad. A bride should not be so on her wedding day."

31

Depressed and disgruntled, Marina snapped, "A bride who is forced into marriage is never happy."

He brought his horse closer to hers and stared into her face.

Except for her sullen expression, Edgar Stafford was well pleased by what he saw. He could not believe his good luck in landing such a bride, and though he hated everything Francis Walsingham stood for, he was inclined to thank him at this moment when he beheld the girl who was now his wife. With her golden-blonde hair, smooth, firm skin, and eyes that could melt a man's soul, she stirred animal instincts in him that he had thought long dead. On this woman, Stafford felt certain, he would finally beget the son and heir that he craved and had long been denied him. Looking at her, he suddenly felt younger than his sixty-two years, young and eager and impatient as a fellow half his age to tumble his bride into the marriage bed.

He said, "Most girls must wed the man their father or guardian thinks best for them. How can they, in their inexperience, think of choosing for themselves? The idea is ridiculous."

Unhappy as she was, Marina threw caution to the winds. "And I suppose it is *not* ridiculous to link a girl of sixteen to a man over sixty," she retorted sarcastically with a haughty toss of her head.

Stafford sucked in a sharp breath and his heavily lined face darkened. With an embarrassed glance at their escort, some eight stalwarts far past their prime and because of it men who cost him little, he hissed, "Quiet, you insolent chit! 'Tis a taste of the rod you need." He lowered his brows at her. "I warn you, girl, you will not make mischief for me as you did for Sir Percy. You will show respect and obey. And you will make an effort to please me." Never a subtle man who

minced words, Edgar bluntly stated his reasons for marrying her. "I want a son and you will give me my heir."

"That," replied the bride, "will be a miracle."

They arrived at Baxton Hall, a haphazard straggle of gray stones slumped within a small wood. The manor was very ancient and had been added to by generations of Staffords through the centuries so that it could no longer claim to be any particular style except that of mass confusion. There were twin towers at either end of the building, some of the stones were chipped away in places, and malevolent-looking little slitted windows that had never been glazed allowed the chill winds ever blowing across the moor to gust inside the house. Baxton Hall seemed shrouded in gloom. As they rode into the courtyard, no cheery lights twinkled from the manor to welcome the bride to her new home, though indeed even a bonfire could not have cheered Marina at that moment.

"Tar, see to the horses," said Stafford, tossing the reins of his mount to his squire. Then with a determined glint in his eyes he grasped Marina around the waist and with a strength that surprised her lifted her down from her horse.

The moment she stepped inside Baxton Hall, Marina could see that the place had been neglected for years. In fact, it gave off an aura much like its master, one of roughness, shabbiness, squalor. There were no tapestries on the walls, no silver or painted china or color about the place as there had been at Chiltern Castle, and the only furniture—and little enough of that—was of worm-eaten black oak. Further, the hall Marina stepped into was dirty. She could not hide the look of disgust that crossed her face when she sniffed the rank, stale air—not that she needed to hide it to spare the feelings of her husband, who never con-

33

cerned himself with such delicate sensibilities. Edgar Stafford was in every way a simple man governed by basic emotions, a coarse, uncultured man with no interest in the so-called finer things in life. The finer things, after all, cost a great deal of money.

There was a small fire burning in the hall—only because it was needed to take the edge off the damp, frigid air in the chamber. The marriage "feast" served to the pair by a slatternly female servant about the same age as her master was a poor meal indeed, consisting of watery pheasant soup, hare stew, the meat grey and stringy, and chunks of rye bread, with acrid cheese to follow instead of pastries and puddings as one might have expected.

While toying with the food on her plate, Marina sent furtive glances across the table to her husband. She supposed he was remarkably hale and hearty for his age. He made her think of a gnarled old oak with his short, square body that at one time must have been very strong, and his weather-beaten face of a brownish-red hue, the large, pitted nose, grizzled hair and beard. In the past, Marina had heard, Stafford had distinguished himself as a soldier. "The man was born to fight," she had once overheard Sir Guy remarking. Even now, old as he was, he joined the young bucks of the area in their frequent raids across the border into Scotland and had kept up his ongoing battle with the Protestants in England ever since they had come to power. Many there were hereabouts who admired Edgar Stafford, but there were others, women in particular, who whispered that he was a crude beast. "One must wonder," Lady Maud herself had mused aloud, "what *really* happened to those wives of his . . ."

He made no attempt to engage his bride in conversation during the meal. All his concentration was

reserved for eating, and to watch him eat made Marina a little sick. Ignoring the knife that had been provided, he scooped up the stew with his fingers and shoveled it into his mouth, mopping the gravy with hunks of bread, then wiping his mouth on his sleeve. He ate like a dog, thought Marina, her stomach churning, but she noted that he certainly had a healthy appetite for a man of his advanced years.

The moment he was finished he hauled Marina upstairs to the marriage bed.

"Disrobe," Stafford ordered her curtly.

"Nay . . . I—"

Grabbing her, Edgar ripped off her clothes and threw her naked across the bed, the impact of her body causing a thick cloud of dust to billow up from the threadbare coverlet. Then his callused hands were all over her, squeezing her breasts, roughly fondling her buttocks, her stomach, and thrusting thick fingers between her thighs. When she choked in revulsion, desperately fighting him off, finally screaming when he began to hurt her with his coarse wooing, Stafford commenced to beat her savagely, panting, "I am your husband! I have every right! Must I knock you senseless before I can take what is my due?"

Just when Marina thought she would faint or be sick, Stafford got up off the bed and began to undress —and then she saw the reason for his impotence.

"'Twas an old wound got in battle," he muttered when he caught the direction of her eyes, "but a clever woman can overcome it, one who knows how to play the vixen." Breathlessly he threw himself down beside her on the bed, without a care that the girl he dragged into his arms was no vixen but a lass who had never lain with a man before and had no way of knowing how to please him, even had she wanted to.

The next hour was a nightmare for Marina as

Stafford panted and sweated over her while hissing
lewd commands into her ear, instructions that made
her gag, vile as they were. Each refusal earned her
another blow as her lord was made wild with frustra-
tion, lusting for her but unable to satisfy that lust in
the way he most wanted to. Finally, exhausted, he left
her and barged down the corridor to his study to drink
himself insensible.

The same thing was repeated the next night, and the
one after, and by the end of her first month of
marriage the beautiful young bride was no more. No
one at Chiltern Castle would have recognized her
now, battered and bruised as she was, all the bright-
ness and youthful confidence knocked out of her. He
had pulled out her hair by the fistful, blackened both
of her eyes, and made a red pulp of her soft mouth.
Her body ached so much that she limped when she
walked, and her right wrist, the hand he kept forcing
on himself, felt as if it had been broken. But it was
Marina's spirit that her husband *really* wanted to
break. If she would only do all he bid her, Stafford
convinced himself, then he could get her with child; if
she would do it with the proper enthusiasm.

With each indignity, each blow, something hard-
ened to stone in the young girl's heart. She blamed the
Percys for her predicament, but even more she
blamed Sedina, the Spaniard. He, after all, had been
the one to suggest that she might be the Queen's
bastard.

Thinking about that after her husband had left her
one night to shut himself up in his study to drink,
Marina—who only had the Percys' word for it that
Walter and Lisle Dudley had been her parents—
suddenly wondered if Sedina's outrageous suggestion
could be true. Imagine! she thought—the Queen of
England and Robert Dudley, the Earl of Leicester! No,

no, it was too fantastic.

Even if it *had* been true, much good it had done her!

She rose from the rumpled bed and limped to the window and gazed out hopelessly into the black night. Oh, she thought, to be free of all this! To find a way to escape before Edgar completely lost his head and killed her. How wonderful that would be!

At the beginning of December, eight weeks after her marriage to Stafford, Edgar's squire suddenly burst into the hall one evening when they were at supper.

"There be strangers arrived," Tar announced. "Scottish, by the sounds o' them."

"Holy mother!" Stafford sprang to his feet in alarm. "Warn the men."

The squire hesitated. "They say they come in peace."

The arrival of Alexander Sinclair and his party caused a great flurry of excitement at Baxton Hall. Stafford and his crew immediately scrambled for their weapons, ready to attack the instant they detected the slightest sign of hostility from the intruders. They had assured Tar, Edgar's squire, that they came in peace, but Stafford had never trusted Scotsmen, formerly their enemies. While a treaty of alliance had been concluded between Scotland and England in 1586 and they were now ostensibly at peace, old, deeply ingrained hatreds lingered on in the minds of many.

Stafford's keen eyes noted at once that the newcomers had had a hard ride and were now clearly exhausted. Though far younger and more vigorous-looking than his own aging men, they seemed in no mood to do battle, at least for the moment. He also spied a badly wounded man among them, supported by two others. Edgar took stock of their leader, a big

fellow clad in the best of riding gear, even though it was ripped and dusty; he guessed that they had recently been engaged in some fight and had come out the worst of it.

"Your name, sir?" he demanded of Sinclair. "And I would know why you came to Baxton Hall."

"Alexander Sinclair is the name, and we are lately come from Fotheringay Castle where we tried, and unfortunately failed, to free the Queen of Scots," Alex replied. Pointing to the ashen-faced fellow carried between two others, he went on, "My friend is in a very bad way and has commenced spitting up blood. We thought to rest in the woods hereabouts tonight, and came upon your manor."

"Bedamned!" Edgar whistled. He could not help but be impressed by their daring, especially following the disastrous Babington Plot and the hideous deaths suffered by the conspirators. As a rabid Catholic, Edgar was quite prepared to back the devil himself in any scheme to overthrow the Protestants, and Satan and Scotsmen were synonymous in his mind. Would that their plan had succeeded, he thought with a sigh. Though they were obviously weary and travel-worn, he felt that these men were gentlemen, not the usual rabble he encountered during his occasional raiding forays over the border, and he relaxed a little. Anyway, he reminded himself, some of his own crew were at that moment hidden on the balcony above, bows in hand, prepared for action if it were called for.

Stafford waved them over to the fire. "Sit down and take your ease. I would hear all about this plot of yours."

"First, I would attend to my injured comrade," said Sinclair. "Is there water and mayhap some clean rags?"

Up to now Marina had been ignored. She sat

huddled to the side of the huge stone fireplace trying to make herself as inconspicuous as possible. Like most people in the area, she was afraid of Scotsmen; she had heard of the terrible battles that had taken place in the past, and even today there was the odd clash between the Scots and her own people, cattle stolen, a farmstead burned, women raped. The one who caught her attention was their leader; in appearance at least he was a wonderful specimen of a man—tall, dark, exceedingly comely, the most handsome man she had ever beheld.

"You, wench"—Marina gave a start when her husband barked at her—"fetch the Scotsman water and bindings." He added in an expansive tone, "And bid Aggie bring in bread and ale."

Bread and ale! Marina's face flushed scarlet with embarrassment, thinking that it was plain to anyone with eyes in their heads that the strangers were utterly exhausted and famished. They needed good meat and wine to restore them, and all her miserly husband could offer them was the sourdough bread of the house and the even sourer ale! She was mortified. Even the poorest cotter in Northumberland could have done better than that. Here they took pride in being hospitable to weary travelers, and Edgar, she knew, was far from poor.

As she fled to fetch the water, Marina glanced back from the door to see Sinclair carrying the ailing man to the hearth, where he gently laid him down on the bare floor, there being no chairs or settles at Baxton Hall as there had been at Chiltern Castle. She felt so ashamed of their dismal, cheerless hall. Scotsmen they might be, and of course one had to be very careful, but these men struck her as being a cut above the average and not the usual rabble at all. Sinclair had treated his wounded companion almost tenderly,

which impressed Marina.

When she returned to the hall struggling with a heavy iron pail of water, Alexander Sinclair glanced up and saw her. Instantly he was on his feet, hurrying forward to take it from her hands. "This is much too heavy for a lass to carry," he said in his pleasant Northern accent. Alex wondered at the same time what kind of a man her father was to order his daughter to handle such a heavy task. He almost dropped the pail when the girl looked up and he saw the dreadful bruises and swelling on her face. "Dear Christ!" he said. "What happened to you?"

Marina hastily put a finger over her mouth, her eyes darting to Stafford. So, Sinclair thought, angered, her father was responsible for the beating, and what a beating! It sickened Alex to think what the girl must have suffered. Stafford immediately plunged in his estimation. But there was nothing he could do, so with a sympathetic smile—one that lit up his dark face— Sinclair turned his attention on Rab Hamilton while the rest of his friends looked on in concern, fearing the worst. The wounded man was delirious, his skin burning hot though even by the paltry fire it was cool in the hall. As Alex bent over him, easing back his shirt to expose a deep shoulder wound several weeks old, one that had never healed, his mind went back to that swift, fierce battle on the plain near Fotheringay Castle in September. In retrospect Sinclair supposed that they had been insanely reckless. Queen Mary had been escorted by more soldiers than they had been led to expect by their spies, but when they had struck, taking the soldiers by surprise, Alex had actually managed to get within twenty feet of the Queen's litter before the startled soldiers had regrouped and finally driven them back.

Two of their comrades had been killed outright.

Another, young Jamie Fraser, had been taken prisoner. Now they could only hope—for his own sake—that Jamie had had time to drink his flask of poison before being imprisoned in the Tower of London.

Marina watched him gently bathing Hamilton's wound with the clean cloth she had handed to him—strips she had torn from her wedding gown! She watched Sinclair's face as he performed this task and thought that he looked sad. He was thinking that while it might have been mad of them to try to free the Queen, it had probably been her last chance of freedom on this earth. Even in Edinburgh they were saying that Mary's end was near now, that Elizabeth, terrified to execute her before for fear of foreign attack, had finally allowed her ministers to persuade her to risk it.

Once Hamilton had been made as comfortable as possible and the Highlanders had partaken of the humble fare provided by their host, Alex told their story. Edgar Stafford sighed when he finished. "It bodes ill for the Scottish Queen now, but what I cannot understand is why her son, King James, does not do more to help his mother. What kind of a son is he?" he sneered.

King James had never known his mother. He had only been an infant when her rebellious nobles had forced Mary to abdicate in favor of her son. His uncle the Earl of Moray had ruled Scotland in his place as regent. Moray did not live long to enjoy his high position, but other regents followed. In the meantime, the boy king had been raised in the household of the Earl of Mar, a fervent Protestant who had poisoned James's mind against his mother. James grew up believing that Mary had conspired with Lord Bothwell to kill his father, Darnley. His advisers warned him too to keep in the good graces of Queen Elizabeth

so that one day he might inherit her crown, thus uniting Scotland and England at last.

"The King has been raised to believe that he has nothing to gain by fighting to have his mother freed, and *everything* to gain by fostering the friendship with his cousin Elizabeth," said Alexander. "Besides, Scotland is also a Protestant country as is England, so in that they are united too."

"A pox on them!" cried Stafford. "Now we have a bastard sitting on the throne of England, for I tell you this, that farce of a marriage Henry VIII went through with Anne Boleyn was no true marriage at all, nor was it legal."

Marina sat unobtrusively by the inglenook trying to hide her battered face from the curious eyes of the newcomers and especially from Sinclair. She was ashamed of how she must look to him, especially when he was so comely himself. It was pleasant to listen to his deep voice discussing the political situation, to watch his expressive face, the way his brilliant green eyes flashed in the firelight. He was no barbarian, that much Marina could tell. The Scotsman was far more cultured and well-mannered than Edgar Stafford and more compassionate too, and his bold venture dazzled her. She could have listened to him and watched him all night.

But they would be leaving at first light in the morning! Marina's heart sank. They never had guests in the house. Her husband was too mean to spend a penny to entertain them. There was no interesting conversation, as they were having tonight, no laughter, music, or merriment of any kind. Baxton Hall had a depressing, tomblike atmosphere, and all she had to look forward to was the pain and humiliation Edgar Stafford inflicted on her nightly.

Oh God, Marina thought desperately, if only she

could somehow escape!

Sinclair felt her staring at him and raised his head, and their eyes met. He saw the entreaty in those eyes and suddenly noticed their beauty. What was she trying to say to him? he wondered, feeling sorry for her and angry at her father. The mess the fellow had made of her face! He was a brute and scoundrel to treat any woman thus, especially his own daughter. Idly Alex wondered what she must *really* look like. At the moment it was impossible to tell.

The hour was growing late and Stafford stood up. With a wave to Marina he ordered, "Get above stairs, wife. I will shortly follow."

Wife! Alexander was astounded. He had assumed the young girl was Stafford's daughter, or even his granddaughter. Worse that she was actually wed to the knave, linked to him for life, the butt of his abuse. He deeply pitied her and wished there was something he could do to help her. Tied to a man like Stafford, her very life was in danger!

"Doubtless, you will be leaving at dawn?" Edgar inquired.

Alex eyed him coldly as he nodded. It was all he could do to be civil, muttering, "Thank you for your hospitality, sir." Though it had hardly been worth thanking him for! He and his men were still starving and Rab Hamilton desperately needed strong wine or spirits to revive him, also a warm blanket to cover him and ward off the damp chill now that the fire was dying down. It hadn't shamed Stafford when Alex and two of his friends had taken off their jerkins to cover the wounded man, whose skin, he had noticed, felt suddenly quite cool.

"I'll bid you farewell now," their host said. "These old bones of mine protest when I rise early." Usually he was too drunk to leave his bed before noon.

"Good eve," Alex responded curtly.

Long after the others were asleep, Alexander sat gazing into the embers of the fire thinking about their abortive mission. He found failure hard to bear. He was worried too about Jamie Fraser, the lad taken prisoner. If Jamie lived to reach the Tower he would be tortured and the names of his fellow conspirators forced out of him. As it was, the rest of them had been lucky to get away alive. Walsingham had immediately sent soldiers to comb the country in search of them, and once or twice, crossing England while making for the border, they had almost been caught. They'd had to go into hiding for several weeks until the hubbub died down, then, traveling mostly at night, had made their way to Northumberland and the border.

Tomorrow they would be on Scottish soil! Ah, thought Sinclair, how good it will be to be home at last. His roving days would then be over and he would have to settle down to the task of helping to administer the family estates. He supposed too that the time had come to start thinking about a wife. But, he had decided, there would be no cold-blooded arranged marriage for him! He had yet to meet a woman who held his interest for long, let alone one he felt willing to share his life with.

Always when Alex thought of marriage his parents came into his mind. What a love affair theirs had been! His mother, Lady Alyssa, had only been his father's mistress when she gave birth to Alex, though they had been able to marry later on. While the circumstances of his birth had made life a bit awkward for him, the love between his parents—rather rare among the nobility—had always been an example of what was possible, the kind of marriage he would strive for himself. Of course his younger brother, David, safely born in wedlock, would one day be

the chief of their clan. Alex had come to terms with the situation years ago; he felt quite capable of making his own way in the world.

He suddenly noticed that his friend Rab Hamilton lay staring fixedly at the ceiling, his eyes glazed in the smoldering embers of the fire. An icy jolt went through the young nobleman. In trepidation, his heart beating fast, Alex leaned forward and put a hand on his cheek, which was cold. A quick examination verified the fact that Hamilton was dead.

"Dear Christ!" Alex sat back on his heels, staring down at the lad who hadn't yet reached his twenty-first birthday. He felt a choking sorrow to think that his boyhood friend, one who had shared many a mischief with him while they were growing up, was no more. Gently he drew one of the jerkins that covered him over his head, musing that Hamilton had died for a good cause. He had been a lad who had always imagined himself doing mighty deeds for a noble cause.

Where would they bury him? The ground outside was frozen and they were still on English soil. Though they were close to the border, they were still a very long way away from their homes in the Highlands of Scotland.

A sudden cry from upstairs distracted Sinclair, turning his mind from his dead friend to the child-wife of their host. He could well imagine what was happening up there, and when another faint cry drifted eerily through the silent manor, Alex sprang to his feet and drew out his dagger. "By the rood," he muttered, "I can tolerate no more of this!"

Moving stealthily as a cat, he made for the stairs with the weapon in his hand and had reached the landing when the door to the bridal chamber banged open and Edgar Stafford plunged out holding a tat-

tered quilt around his nakedness. Alex flattened himself against the wall as Stafford barged down the corridor and into a room at the end. He made immediately for a keg that sat atop a tall kist, viciously turned the spigot, and filled a pewter cup with the yellow liquid that gushed out. Swallowing it, he kicked the door shut, closeting himself in the room for his nightly drinking binge.

Alex glanced around, wondering where the guards might be. He had noticed that they had drifted away while he and Stafford were talking downstairs, possibly satisfied that the Scotsmen meant them no harm. His eyes were drawn to the partially open door of the master chamber, and after waiting a few minutes, listening into the silence when the only sound he could hear was from the room Stafford had now entered, Alex warily made his way to the room his host had just vacated, bracing himself for what he might find there.

The young wife lay naked among the rumpled sheets, stunned by a blow to the head. As he stood over her, Alex saw the reddened marks of cruel fingers imprinted on her breasts, the scratches on her stomach and thighs. Furious, for her lovely young body was a mass of welts and bruises, the old mingling with the new, he felt like flying down the corridor to kill Edgar Stafford, the beast who had caused it all. But he saw that the girl was in desperate need of attention, moaning softly from lips that were puffed and bloody. Sinclair glanced around the dismal chamber and spied a pitcher and bowl on a chest. He quietly closed the door and poured water into the basin and carried it to the bed, lowering himself to sit on the edge.

Gently he drew the covers up over Marina's nakedness, then soaking an edge of the quilt in the bowl, he bent forward and very gingerly dabbed her cut lips.

She flinched, and her eyes fluttered open. Alex quickly placed a warning finger over his mouth.

At first Marina was dazed. When her wits cleared, she was astonished to find Sinclair beside her and for a few seconds thought she was dreaming. She lay gazing up at him in wonder as he gently bathed her face and sponged the blood off her lips. He looked like an angel to Marina at that moment.

Then it all came rushing back and she caught his hand, whispering, "W-where is he?" terror in her voice.

Alex bent his head to her ear. "In the chamber down the passageway—but soon to be in hell once I have finished with him!"

"Nay . . . you must not risk a battle," she warned him. "His men are hereabouts. Normally they sleep in the bothy behind the stables, but"—she drew a shuddering breath—"I think tonight, with strangers in the house, that they might be in the kitchen." Marina clung to his hand as to a lifeline. "I—I must get away from here before he kills me."

Sinclair fully concurred, and suggested, "We might be able to take you out when we go," not sure if she would accept. She was certainly in a dire position, but as some might see it, Better a devil you know than one you don't, and he and his friends were total strangers and foreigners as well. He wasn't sure she would trust them, nor would he have blamed her if she didn't. But at mention of leaving Baxton Hall the girl's eyes filled with hope. "Oh, could you?" she breathed.

"We can try." Alex wanted to ask about her family and why they hadn't done something about her desperate situation, but the moment he agreed to help her, Marina lifted his hand and pressed it to her bruised cheek. "Thank God!" she murmured. "You are the answer to my prayers, Lord Sinclair. Had fate

not brought you here tonight, I doubt that I would have been alive at Christmas."

He was touched. Flattered too that she was quite prepared to trust him. Her plight brought out all his chivalrous instincts, much the same instincts that Queen Mary had aroused. This girl too was in peril of losing her life if something wasn't done to help her, and the first step was to remove her from the clutches of her evil husband. No doubt, he thought, she had friends or relatives who would take her in.

"What is your name?" he asked softly.

"Marina, sir. 'Twas Marina Dudley until I married *him*!" There was anger in her voice and her beautiful dark eyes flashed with resentment. Alex was glad to see that her spirit hadn't been completely broken.

"Then I will call you Marina Dudley," he told her with a slight smile. "I can see that that will be more to your taste."

Marina nodded emphatically, grateful for his understanding. She looked up at the handsome young cavalier—and was instantly madly in love. Everything about Sinclair inspired great confidence in the girl—his strength and courage and air of command, his noble features, glossy black hair, and brilliant green eyes. He seemed akin to a god to her and she idolized him, and though he was a Scotsman, she knew she would be willing to follow him to the ends of the earth. No one had ever shown her such interest, such tenderness before—and he a stranger! Suddenly, in one of her impulsive gestures, Marina covered his hand with worshipful kisses. "How splendidly kind and brave you are," she told him.

Alex was moved. She was hardly more than a child and seemed quite helpless to him and, though married, strangely innocent too. Without thinking he leaned forward and kissed her on the forehead, more

49

determined than ever to get her away from Baxton
Hall. Marina's starved heart melted at the contact.
She sat up and threw her arms around his neck,
pressing herself against him as if she would never let
go. Sinclair was a little taken aback by her puppylike
affection, but his arms closed around her instinctively.
The bed covers had slipped down at her changed
position, and his hands came in contact with her bare
back, warm and soft as silk. He felt her breasts touch
his chest, smelled the clean scent of her hair, and for
an instant his arms tightened as he responded to the
warmth and emotion flowing from the girl locked
hard against him.

Alex was astounded when she burst out, "I worship
you, Sinclair!"

He pushed her away from him, his eyes searching
her face. "You know nothing about me," he reminded
her, "and should not make such remarks to a man you
do not know."

"I know that you are grand and that I adore you,"
Marina insisted.

What kind of woman was this? he wondered. Surely
like none other that he had ever met. Most that he had
encountered enjoyed flirting and playing coy games to
keep a man guessing as to how they felt about him.
Not so this one! Of course she was desperate, he
reminded himself, and a woman would say and do
just about anything in her position. He held her back
from him, his eyes automatically flicking to her
breasts. Proud and high they were and quite full for
her age, the nipples rosy and erect from rubbing
against him.

Alex, at sight of her nakedness, felt a powerful and
instantaneous hardening of his own body before Ma-
rina, blushing, grabbed the sheets and wrenched them
up to cover herself. Their eyes met and held, and in

that moment Alexander felt something stir to life deep inside him, something that went beyond mere desire. For a second he was confused at his odd reaction to the English girl. With the marks of violence on her face, Marina Dudley was far from comely, and he liked comely women. But there was that about her to appeal to a man just the same. It was a novel experience for Alex to be with a woman who did not try to hide her feelings, and flattering to find himself the object of such unabashed admiration.

He glanced at the door. "Remember," he whispered, "we are not out of this manor yet."

All Marina's fear came rushing back. "Edgar will soon drink himself into a stupor, then it will be easier to slip away. He rarely rises before noon."

"Then harken to me. I have thought of a way to take you out of here."

Their heads bent close and Alex explained his plan.

4

Nine people had ridden up to Baxton Hall the previous night and nine left it just after dawn the following morning, each bundled up in cloaks and hoods to protect them from the bitter cold. It was still not fully light and there was an inch or two of snow on the ground, but the Scotsmen galloped away fast in the semidarkness, the leader now and then glancing back.

A mile from the manor house Sinclair halted his party and looked at the smallest of the group, one almost swallowed up in a gray cloak, the hood pulled far forward so that her battered face was hidden from view. For Alex and his friends it had boiled down to a simple choice. Either they take a dead man out of Baxton Hall, one past all earthly suffering, or they take a live girl doomed to perpetual misery if she remained there. The decision had been unanimous. They must take the girl. It was what Rab would have wished them to do, they all agreed.

52

Alex walked his horse over to Marina's. "Where would you like us to take you?" he asked. Now that they had freed Marina there was no time to lose. At any moment Rab Hamilton's body could be discovered where they had left it in an upstairs chamber and Tar, Stafford's squire, would rouse his master to give chase. Aside from that, there was Walsingham's secret police to consider. The Scotsmen were, after all, still on English soil.

Alex felt a touch of impatience when Marina hesitated. "Mistress, where do you wish us to escort you?" he repeated. "We must make haste."

She bit her lip and shrugged, avoiding his eyes, then confessed, "Sir, in truth there is nowhere I *can* go."

"What?"

"My parents are dead and I have no close relatives," Marina explained, flushing when she saw them all staring at her now in dismay. "My former guardian—the couple who raised me—would never take me in. They were the ones who wed me to Stafford in the first place."

"But you said—you led me to believe . . ."

Marina shook her head. "Nay, I said nothing except that I wanted out of that house."

Sinclair was angry, and Marina supposed that he had every right to be, but she had been frantic and had grabbed the first opportunity to come along, fearing there might never be another. Alex looked at his men; they too were annoyed. She could tell that some of them, perhaps including Sinclair, felt that she had somehow deceived them.

"Leave me here if you will," Marina cried. "You have done more for me than I can ever hope to repay. But—but I would rather perish here on the moor than live another moment in Baxton Hall."

There was a tense silence, then the men muttered

their objections to the idea. Alex himself would never have considered abandoning her now. But where could he take her? He could well imagine the raised eyebrows and curious whispers if he returned home to the Highlands with the strange English girl in tow. It was out of the question.

"It grows light," one of the men pointed out nervously and they all turned to scan the wild countryside, alert for movement in the distance. Alex suddenly had an idea where he could take her—to the home of Sir Ralph Cairnmore, the kindly knight who had been married to his maternal grandmother, Alicia, during the latter years of her life. It was the only place he could think of—and fortunately a long way from his own home.

He eyed Marina coldly. "Are you prepared to go with us into Scotland?"

"Aye," she nodded at once, relief on her face, agreeing immediately without even stopping to consider the consequences. Sinclair's friends glanced at each other in amusement. One lad chuckled under his breath, "Even these English wenches are smitten with your manly charms, Sinclair," a remark that Marina overheard. A hot flush suffused her face, though it was true enough. At that moment she would have followed him anywhere.

Alex nodded. Without another word to her he spurred up his horse and they all galloped in the direction of the Scottish border. Sinclair felt as if he had been manipulated. She should have told him last night that she had nowhere to go, he thought angrily. Though he was more than willing to help her, he wasn't prepared to take on total responsibility for the English girl, one who already had a husband. What a state of affairs! Fortunately, Sir Ralph Cairnmore was a warmhearted, courtly man and very fond of Alexan-

der. Hopefully, he would understand.

At least Scotland and England were reasonably friendly now, he reflected as they rode along. It had even become fashionable for noblemen in one country to send their offspring to be educated in the other, a politically and socially sensible idea considering that King James of Scotland would in all probability inherit the crown of England once Queen Elizabeth died. Then the two countries would be united at last. It was imperative that they make an effort to understand each other, as far as traditional enemies ever could, and the best way to insure this was through the exchange of their young people, the ones most open to change.

While still a lad Alexander had spent two years as a page at the court of Queen Elizabeth. Interesting, even exciting years they had been. The ceremony, the intrigue, the jockeying for position that went on among her courtiers had astounded young Alex. But he had learned a lot during those two years, especially that, though outwardly Scotland and England were now allies, behind the scenes much of the old enmity lingered on, neither quite trusting the other.

During his time in London Alex had come to the attention of the Queen, a woman who had a keen eye for beautiful young men. "Ah . . ." she had smiled when he was summoned to her presence, ". . . I remember your noble father well." She added with a throaty chuckle, "What woman would not!"

Queen Elizabeth had studied him closely. "My cousin of Scotland had a wise minister in your sire, young Sinclair. 'Tis a pity she didn't heed him more, eh?" This with a sly glance at Robert Dudley, who happened to be with her at the time. Alex's face had betrayed surprise. How could she know what advice his father had given Queen Mary? he wondered.

Elizabeth saw his puzzlement and said, "We have those in my government who keep us well informed of events in Scotland. Tell me, Lord Sinclair, are you a loyal subject of your King?"

"I am, Your Majesty," he'd replied.

"And are you also loyal to the King's mother?" Again she glanced at Dudley, who stood watching the exchange with a smile of amusement. Alex remembered him as being a comely, though arrogant man very conscious of his position closest to the Queen. *Very* close, according to the rumors at court.

Something in the way Dudley was looking at him— and the way he felt that Elizabeth was toying with him for her own entertainment—prompted Alex to answer boldly, "One must ever feel pity for a lady in Queen Mary's position."

Elizabeth's smile vanished. The answer was not to her liking. She walked over to Alex and cuffed him on the ear, though not *too* hard. "Know this, young sir, and learn it well," she said haughtily, "that those who invite trouble to themselves are rarely disappointed. Nor should they be pitied when it finds them. You would do well to reserve compassion for where it is truly deserved."

He had gone from that interview livid, seething that the Queen had embarrassed him in front of the Earl of Leicester. He was convinced too that Elizabeth was incapable of feeling compassion for anyone. "Would that I were older!" Alex remembered thinking then. "I would find a way to free Queen Mary myself."

The idea had been born then.

But the day after his meeting with the Queen a box of sweetmeats had been delivered to his room with a brief note penned in her own hand. "You looked sour when you left my Presence Chamber yesterday. Mayhap these will sweeten you up."

Alex had been slightly disarmed, pleased enough to gobble down the bonbons. She was clever, he had thought even then, a formidable stateswoman who—unlike Mary Stuart—never failed to put her people before everything else. Her subjects worshiped her. She was their Virgin Queen. Had she not given up all others to be true to them alone, including Robert Dudley, the man who for years had been desperate to marry her?

Of course she *hadn't* given him up, though the common people didn't know that. But at least she had never gone against their wishes and married him, as Mary Stuart had done with Lord Bothwell.

Now, as they raced for the Scottish border, Alex again felt depressed when he thought about his failed mission to free the Scottish Queen. Rash and impetuous Mary might have been, too frequently ruled by her emotions, but for all her failings he was certain he would have liked her better than Elizabeth. It saddened him to think that no one—short of her son—could help her now, and to do so King James would have to be willing to break the Anglo-Scottish alliance.

They covered the last mile and galloped across the border.

All the lads cheered and those wearing caps under their hoods threw them in the air, delighted to find their native soil under their feet once more. Marina smiled at their joy, and strangely enough, though she was now in a foreign land, she too felt safe. Alex spied the relief on her face and it disarmed him. Well, he thought, she certainly had faith in us, for all that we were strangers to her.

"Best we ride on a while yet," he told her. "How do you feel?"

"Wonderful, my lord!" Marina laughed, her eyes lighting up in a way that he found entrancing. Those

eyes of hers . . . never had he seen any like them. So dark and sparkling, such a contrast to her thick blonde hair. Swollen and bruised or not, there were moments when he thought she looked almost pretty, and Sinclair couldn't help but notice how her whole expression melted when she looked at him. Failure he might be—but not to Marina Dudley!

They stopped that first night at the Four Doves, a modest little inn much used by travelers moving between the two countries. Unassuming as it was, the accommodations were a huge improvement over dank Baxton Hall. A roaring fire greeted them in the common dining room, and all about them were the sounds of conviviality. It was like music to Marina's ears.

Sinclair's friends settled themselves at a long trestle table, but Alex, who was anxious to learn more about the girl he had now become responsible for, led Marina to a small table for two drawn up to the side of the fire. He ordered a hearty meal and flagon of good wine. "First we dine," he said. "Then I must have speech with you."

"Aye." Marina nodded eagerly, ready to fall in with whatever plans he had for her. She had the utmost trust and confidence in him. Sinclair had risked his life in trying to rescue the Queen of Scots, and failing, had rescued her instead! It seemed the very essence of romance to Marina. Free now, she glowed with excitement, some of her natural high spirits and exuberance coming to the fore. Alexander Sinclair had pried her loose from her bestial husband, swept her into a new country and a new life, and dazzling possibilities opened up to her. Marina gazed across the table at Alex with eyes brimming with adoration, feelings she was too young and innocent to think of concealing.

Surely, she thought, he was the bravest, kindest, most handsome man in the entire island.

"This is the happiest night of my life," she told him candidly.

Alex was nonplussed. "You are jesting?"

"Nay," Marina shook her head firmly. "It is true."

He saw that she meant it, and was touched, thinking that she must have lived very poorly indeed, for he could find nothing special about the evening, other than that it was the first meal he had had in Scotland for months.

He waved at her plate, beginning to feel a little embarrassed at the way she was gazing at him. Alex could feel his friends watching and could well imagine the remarks they were making. "Eat up," he told her gruffly. "The wine is quite good. It will revive you."

They dined on roast venison and pheasant, vegetables and custard pies, all washed down with copious amounts of Madeira. Marina wasn't used to wine, but thirsty as she was, she drank it like water. They were ravenous and ate with gusto. Marina had not enjoyed a decent meal since the day she married Edgar Stafford; nevertheless, even hungry as she was, Alex noticed that her table manners were dainty and refined. She had obviously been raised to be a lady, even if her husband hadn't treated her like one.

Alex became conscious of other diners sending furtive glances at their table, and no wonder! The inn was well lit, and Marina's battered face with its purple-and-yellow bruises seemed to glare, advertising that she had been badly beaten. He hoped they wouldn't think that *he* had been responsible, and wished now that they had eaten in their rooms. Afraid that Marina would notice and be embarrassed, Alex scowled around the room challengingly and the others quickly looked away. But Marina hadn't noticed. All

her attention had been on him.

"Have you supped your fill?" he asked her solicitously.

She nodded. "'Twas a delicious meal." But she was a little dizzy from the wine.

Alex leaned closer. "What beautiful eyes you have," he told her, to make up for her other shortcomings.

Marina was breathless with delight at the compliment. It was one she had heard many times before, but never so sweet as when it had come from him. "Your eyes are beautiful too," she remarked in her guileless way. "They shine like emeralds in the firelight."

Alex sat back in his chair and crossed his legs. He felt uncomfortable at her wide-eyed admiration. Marina was like no other woman he had ever known. Whatever she thought and felt came spilling out, and he surmised that she had had very little contact with the opposite sex before her marriage to Stafford. There was no coyness, no subterfuge about her, and though when she smiled her eyes had a flirtatious charm, he sensed that it was unconscious, therefore all the more appealing. Behind him he could hear his friends tittering. Doubtless, he thought, they were enjoying the entertainment. He had to admit he was rather enjoying it himself, rare as it was. Females were usually so careful not to betray how they felt about a man, fearing it would place them at a disadvantage.

"How old are you?" he asked her, curious.

"Sixteen, my lord."

"And Stafford?"

Her face sobered. "Over sixty."

It was all too often done, he reflected, wedding nubile young girls to old, usually rich, men, a practice he found disgusting. He had a sudden mental picture of how Marina had looked naked, then a picture of the

gnarled, flaccid Stafford, and was revolted. How could a doddering old graybeard like that have satisfied her? He doubted that she had ever known any bliss with him at all, or had any conception of how love could be in the arms of a *young* man.

"You said that you had no living kin willing to take you in, but what of the people who raised you?" Something must be arranged, he thought. Marina certainly couldn't stay with his grandfather forever.

"My guardians were Sir Guy and Lady Maud Percy. As a babe I was brought to Northumberland from Kent, where my parents lived, though I have no memory of them at all. They died of smallpox, I'm told. My sire was a cousin of Lady Maud's, and 'twas she, returning from a visit to her family, who brought me back to Chiltern Castle." Marina added ruefully, "There must have been money behind it, otherwise the Percys would never have raised me."

"And they wed you to that scurrilous old hound?"

"Aye." She looked angry. "He has my dowry, and knowing him, he'll never let it go. Edgar had two previous wives, neither able to give him children, and he thought that with me . . ." she broke off, flushing.

Alex gave a start. "Christ's blood, you are not with young, are you?"

"Nay." Marina's blush deepened and she looked down at her plate, too embarrassed to explain why she was so certain. Alex assumed that it was because her monthly flow had appeared as usual.

"That at least is a relief," he said.

Something in his tone made Marina look at him quickly, searchingly, and she saw him frown. It brought her down to earth with a crash, all her romantic mental pictures splintering. Pride made her say, "Mayhap I could find work . . . perhaps even here at this inn."

The idea was ludicrous and he waved it away. "You are a lady and could never work here. You know, don't you, that we have committed a crime by taking you away from your husband—"

"Nothing to the crimes *he* committed while I was with him!" she shot back, her dark eyes blazing. Alex admired a woman with spirit and was heartened to see that Marina had plenty left in her yet. He chuckled, "What is one more crime after the dire one I perpetrated in trying to free Mary Stuart? One might as well be hanged for a wolf as a lamb."

"Don't say that!" Marina was a little superstitious and she shivered at the mention of hanging. "'Twas a courageous thing you did, and how I wish you had succeeded."

"I too." He looked glum and confessed, "Failure sits heavily on my shoulders, and to fail in such a good cause . . ."

She put a hand over his, distressed to see him so bleak. "They keep her so well guarded now that no one can get near her. Think of all who have tried through the years, even schemes generated by such as the King of Spain—even the Pope himself. All failures. You *tried*, my lord, and that alone marks you as one of the bravest men in the land."

He had to smile a little at her lavish praise, and chuckled, "Take care you don't swell my head."

"I but speak the truth."

He smiled at her, amused. "I'm afraid you have formed too high an opinion of me, so be warned. I'm no better or worse than the average fellow—worse, some might say," he said with a grin. "Now you must be wondering where I am taking you." When she nodded, he explained, "We are bound for Cairnmore House in Ayrshire, the home of my stepgrandfather.

He is a kind man and will make you welcome."

It seemed fantastic to Marina how radically her life had changed in the space of two days. Had anyone told her a week ago that a wonderful man would come into her life and carry her away to live in Scotland, she would have thought they were mad. As for the future, well . . . she couldn't think of that now. Instead, she wanted to hang on to this very moment, with Sinclair sitting across the table, his strong face like dark copper in the firelight; his eyes resting on her, touching her with a kind of magic. Oh, she sighed inwardly, had she only been wed to a man like Alexander Sinclair! To lie in *his* arms—hastily Marina looked away, afraid he might somehow read her thoughts.

Alex refilled her glass with wine, discovering that he liked the English girl. In a way Marina helped distract him from his bitter disappointment and worry about his captured friend, Jamie Fraser. He suddenly decided that he would do everything he could to help the hapless girl. She had nothing now. Stafford was in possession of her dowry, a grave misfortune as far as her future was concerned. But Sinclair was rich in his own right and would do his best for her. It was strange how they had met . . . mayhap, he mused, there was something of fate in that.

Robert Douglas, one of his friends, appeared at their table.

"Well," said Douglas, "we are retiring now and bid both of you a good night. We are in sore need of a bath to wash the dust of the journey from our flesh." With mischief in his eyes he informed them, "I took the liberty of ordering a tub for you also, Sinclair, and for the young lady. I trust that is satisfactory?"

Alex nodded. "You did well, Douglas."

Robert glanced from one to the other, a twinkle in

his eyes. "I can see you wish to tarry here for a while, so I won't disturb you. Have a *very* enjoyable evening—"

"Good night, my friend," Alex broke in firmly.

Douglas laughed and slapped him on the back and with the others trouped to the door, throwing many backward glances at their table, glances pregnant with meaning. Alex read them well, but Marina was gazing at him and didn't notice. He knew what they were thinking, that he would try to bed the girl, an idea that had never entered his head. But now that it had . . . he doubted not that he would do a better job of it than Edgar Stafford! Aye, his imagination raced on, he could bring her ecstasy such as she would never have tasted with her decrepit husband. And he, unlike her aging spouse, could make it last. Alex could feel his body stirring eagerly just thinking about it. It suddenly felt too hot in the room.

A serving girl came to their table to say that hot water had been taken to their rooms. Sinclair rose at once, but when Marina tried to stand, her head swam alarmingly and she had to grip the back of her chair to steady herself.

Alex laughed and took her arm. "You drank the wine too fast."

"You—you shouldn't have kept refilling my glass." Even her voice was a little slurred.

"No matter, you'll sleep all the better for it," he assured her, and steered her into the foyer and up the stairs to the bedchambers. Leaning against the wall, breathing deeply to clear her head, Marina watched Alex unlock her door and throw it open; then he pressed the key into her hand.

"You must be very weary," he commented.

It was shadowy in the upstairs hallway and the noise in the common dining room and tavern seemed

distant. There was no one about, only the two of them, standing quite close. Alexander's eyes gleamed faintly in the bracket light at the top of the stairs; they seemed to probe her, as if seeking the answer to some question in his mind. There was a strange, hungry look on his face that made Marina's knees go suddenly weak.

"Thank you—thank you for everything, my lord," she stammered, feeling breathless. The wine was making her head spin. It was overwarm in the inn. And the way Alexander was looking at her . . . a look that excited her, stirred her, made her quiver deep inside. He was so handsome, his wide shoulders thrown in shadow against the wall, his body tall and muscular, his face with that faint hint of ruthlessness because of the slight curve to his nose . . . but a face that thrilled her. Everything about him seemed strong and commanding—and he was young! Young and virile, where Edgar . . .

He pointed into the chamber through the open door.

"There is the tub. The water will be growing cold."

Marina nodded, her face hot, hating to have this wonderful night end. She blurted without stopping to think, "Will you come in for a little while? Mayhap you could tell me more of Ayrshire."

His eyes raked her now, moving from her flushed face to her heaving breasts as she sought air in the stuffy hallway, and Marina felt something blaze up deep inside her like tongues of fire. He chuckled gruffly, "Did your guardian never warn you about inviting strange men into your room?"

"I—I trust you."

Alex raised his brows. "Marina, you hardly know me. But, being the gallant I am, I would not dream of doing anything to destroy your high opinion of me," he told her, laughter in his eyes now. Turning her into

the room, he gave her a little push. "Bathe and retire," he said. "I bid you the sweetest of dreams."

The moment Alexander left her, all the sparkle and excitement went out of the evening. The very air seemed to fall flat—though it was easier to breathe. Marina undressed and got into the tub, soaping her body and hair, rubbing herself hard with the cloth provided, splashing water on her face in the hopes that it would help to clear her mind. After a few minutes she began to regret having asked Alexander into her room and wondered what had possessed her. It was just that she enjoyed his company so much, loving the novelty of being with someone a little closer to her own age.

His friends barged into his room while Alex was bathing.

"What, no girl?" Robert Douglas teased. "You would abstain when she all but begged you on her hands and knees! I ask you"—he appealed to the others—"can this fellow in the tub be Alexander Sinclair?"

"Nay, nay it cannot be," the lads mocked. One said, "The Sinclair *we* know would have had her bedded by now."

Alex ignored their remarks and pointed to a chair. "Fetch me that towel," he said, standing up.

Douglas made a sweeping gesture from Sinclair's head to his feet.

"Behold the magnificence of that manly body. Think how it could have pleasured that lonely lass down the hall, and he, the miserly knave, would withhold it from her."

"Quiet, you imbecile," Alexander growled, toweling himself vigorously and holding himself aloof from their laughter. They were all boisterous young men—

he was one himself—and he was used to their pranks and normally joined in, yet he had no taste for it tonight. In fact, it irked him.

"Bah! Who would want to bed a girl who looked like that?" said Ian Huntly. "'Tis a pity for her, of course, but—"

"In the dark her face would be hid," broke in another. "Beneath the sheets all women feel alike."

Alex stopped drying himself and swung on the youth, a lad not yet nineteen and the youngest of the group. "Keith," he said sternly, "I would expect to hear a remark like that from a tinker's whelp, not from the son of Lord Seton."

Silence fell over the group as they stared at Alex in surprise, wondering what had gotten into him. While Seton's remark might have been a little crude, it was not like Sinclair to take it so seriously. They had brought a bottle of brandy and pack of cards in with them, but one look at Alexander's face—a remote look that shut them out—told them he wasn't interested in their company that night.

They glanced at each other questioningly, then Robert Douglas, who was engaged to marry Alex's sister, Kirstin, burst out, "Bigod, can it be that the Stafford lass refused you?"

"Aye," chimed in another, chuckling, "that would account for his sour mood."

Sinclair sighed. "I am weary this night and long for sleep. We have a long ride ahead of us tomorrow."

"Sleep!" a lad with bright red hair cried. "Forsooth, since when has Sinclair been too tired for bed sport?"

Alex waved at them in exasperation. "Enough!" He strode naked to his bed and threw himself down and closed his eyes. "Good eve to you. Don't bang the door on your way out."

For a moment longer they regarded him, puzzled,

then with a nod to the door Robert Douglas led them out—and they *did* bang the door behind them.

Left alone, Alex smiled a little and quickly calmed down, wondering why he had been so grumpy with his friends. The lads meant no harm nor any disrespect to Marina, and God knows, he thought, after what they had all been through over the past few weeks, they needed a little merriment. They had had to live much like animals during their furtive journey across England to the border, their failure to rescue Queen Mary like bitter aloes on their tongues, sorrow for the loss of their comrades crushing spirits already low because of the abortive mission.

Alexander sighed. He had been churlish to the lads and now regretted it. He, unlike the rest, had Marina to distract him from his troubles. The girl had firmly attached herself to him, and doubtless the rest felt excluded. Though she was pleasant to them and laughed at their antics and attempts to forget their disappointments in jesting, Marina also—perhaps unconsciously—had made it clear that it was Alexander Sinclair who had captured her interest.

Alex threw his arms behind his head and stretched. When he considered it, Marina had been the only bright spot of the last few months; at least they'd had success in getting her away from her abusive husband. Her relief and gratitude too had been heartening. It helped to ease the sadness and depression in his heart. What a girl! Alex mused, smiling in the darkness. He had never known a woman so open in regard to her feelings before. What had been behind her invitation tonight? he wondered. There had been a moment when he had been tempted to accept and follow her into her room.

He was drifting off to sleep when he heard shouting and commotion below his window. Springing up, Alex

peered through the glass, but his view of the courtyard was obstructed by a tree. Amid the raised voices coming from the entrance to the inn he detected one that was unmistakably English.

Alex jumped out of bed and ran to his clothes and pulled on his breeches, unsheathed his sword, and hurried to the door. Phantomlike, he moved out into the corridor and headed for the stairs, wondering if Edgar Stafford could have followed them here. Now he wished that they had gone deeper into Scotland before stopping for the night, but Marina had been so exhausted, her bones sore from the long ride—and from the thrashings her swine of a husband had given her.

At the top of the stairs he paused and peered down. The foyer was packed with angry, muttering people, some waving their fists at the door. Tybold, the innkeeper, a massive man with a bald head that gleamed in the candlelight, bellowed, "Begone with you! We want nae trouble here."

Wary and alert, Alex descended the stairs with his sword in his hand, his strapping, well-muscled body, naked from the waist up, drew quick admiring glances from the few women in the foyer and looks of envy from the men. He was tall enough to see over the heads of those who stood between him and the entrance. Three men were struggling with the sentries always stationed there to keep out the rabble, but because of the hoods they were wearing Alex couldn't see their faces. One of them cried, "This be a public inn and we've good coin to pay for our ale, so you cannot stop us from entering."

Tybold whipped a pistol out of his belt and shoved his way to the front, warning, "Leave while ye can, for by God, ye'll fleece no more of my customers. I'll blast yer heads off first."

The three intruders stopped struggling and glanced up in alarm. None of them was Edgar Stafford. Alex relaxed and lowered his sword. "Who are these people?" he asked the innkeeper.

Tybold scowled and glanced at him briefly while keeping his pistol trained on the entrance. "English scum from across the border. Mind you," he was quick to add for the benefit of the Southerners then in the inn, "I've nothing agin the English. Most mind their manners. But this pack"—he waved to the door with his free hand—"slink in here to dice with my customers and trick them out of their purses, then slip away ower the border wi' their ill-begotten profits. 'Twill not happen again!"

With that he fired a shot over their heads, and, misliking their rough welcome, the three Englishmen turned and bolted away into the darkness to find their mounts, realizing that the game was up. Everyone breathed a sigh of relief and filed back into the inn or upstairs to bed. Alex turned to find most of his friends standing behind him on the stairs, all armed. "Methought it might be Stafford," said Robert Douglas, "when the English voices rang out. The lass will be sore afraid if she heard."

When his friends returned to their chambers, Alex walked outside and looked around. All was quiet now, the night frosty and bitter cold, especially against his bare skin. Eager to crawl back into the warmth of his bed, Alex bounded up the stairs and was passing Marina's door when it opened a crack and he caught a glimpse of a white face peering out from the darkness inside. She had some sort of cover clutched around her.

"Alex . . . ?" Marina's voice was thin, shaking with fear. "W-what happened?"

He hesitated for a moment; then, afraid of causing more disturbance for those anxious to get to sleep in the nearby rooms, he pushed open her door and stepped into her chamber. Neither quite knew how it happened, but the next instant Marina was in his arms.

5

Alex kicked the door closed and carried her to the bed. Marina felt astonishingly light and fragile in his arms and she was trembling so much he was afraid she would shatter. The chamber was dark and very chilly. Soothing her, assuring her that she had nothing to fear, Alex lowered her onto the bed and lay down beside her, pulling the covers up around both of them.

"'Twas only some rabble come to the inn from over the border," he explained. "Be at ease, they've gone now."

She moved closer to him. "I thought—Edgar—"

"Nay, nay." In the darkness he reached out and brushed the rumpled blonde hair back from her face. "He will never be able to find us here."

Marina shivered against him and his hand fell from her hair to her bare shoulder. "You are cold," Alex remarked, voice low. He put his arm around her and

drew her against him. "There! We can warm each other up."

"Don't leave me!" she begged, chilled to the marrow, more from fear than the rawness of the room. When she had wakened to hear English voices shouting below, Marina had been certain that Edgar had come to force her back to Baxton Hall, perhaps with a large contingent of his friends and neighbors to back him up, from all the racket going on in the foyer. Oh, the relief to find that she had been mistaken! The sheer joy to see Alex at her door, hale and hearty! Now, snuggling against him, her cheek pressed to his bare chest, his muscular arm holding her tight to the length of his strong young body, she offered up a quick prayer of thankfulness that she had been delivered from abject misery once again. No one had ever been as good to her as Alexander Sinclair, nor as sweet and kind, as understanding. Marina knew already that he was a special kind of man, far above the average. Not only was he outstanding in character, but in looks as well. She felt strongly that Sinclair was the nearest thing to a god that she would ever encounter in her life.

For a few minutes both were silent as they clung to each other for warmth. Soothingly Alex stroked her face, her neck, the silken curve of her shoulder, liking the clean, fresh scent of her, the softness of her cloud of pale gold hair under his fingers and upon his chest. When he changed position slightly, the sheet about her slipped and a jolt went through him when her breast brushed his side. He felt as if he had been burned. Instantly it was as if a blazing fire had ignited inside him, and he caught his breath. It had been months since he had made love to a woman. Desire surged through him in a hot, throbbing wave, and his

manhood was achingly rigid.

Marina raised her head slightly when she felt him tense.

"Alex . . . is anything wrong?"

He didn't answer, couldn't answer, afraid his voice would betray the lust he felt, hot and urgent and demanding appeasement. Sweat burst out on him as he sought to control his need, his loins paining him now, skin burning. Suddenly he sat up and threw his legs over the side of the bed, muttering hoarsely, "I must go . . ."

Alarmed, fearing that he had taken ill, Marina clutched his arm. "What ails you, my lord? Light the candle. Let me look at you—"

"Nay!" His voice was rough and harsh, so unlike him, but Alex cringed at the thought of her seeing the turgid evidence of his lust. "I should not have come into this chamber."

"Why . . . not?" Marina was terribly hurt and confused at his abrupt change of attitude, from tenderness one moment to cold rejection the next. Tears rose in her eyes as she asked him, "What have I done? *Why* shouldn't you have come here?"

Hearing the catch in her voice, Alex hesitated. The next moment he was leaning over her, muttering hoarsely, "I shall show you why not . . ."

Suddenly he crushed his mouth to hers and kissed her passionately, hungrily, while impatiently throwing the bed covers aside to expose her nakedness. Marina tensed with shock as his hot hands shuddered down the length of her body, cupping her firm young breasts, squeezing her hips, his fingers—then his mouth—on her nipples, her stomach, her legs. "Marina," he breathed. "Sweet Marina . . ."

She froze. Edgar Stafford and his vile lust welled up in her mind, his dirty nails raking her flesh, cruel

74

hands pulling her hair, raining blow after blow on her
when she resisted his loathsome instructions. Bed
sport—how she hated it! "Nay!" she cried aloud.
"Nay, don't hurt me!"

Alex raised his head. "Hurt you? Do you think I
ever would? I will show you—show you what love
means."

Restraining himself, Alex kissed her deeply, yet
tenderly, then pressed his mouth lightly to each spot
on her face where her skin had been bruised, then to
her eyes, her ears, the corners of her mouth, and her
throat where he could feel a pulse beating in agitation.
He raised his head and smiled at her in the darkness.
"You like me a little?"

"Aye, of course, but—"

"I can bring you joy, ecstasy, feelings that you've
never known before. 'Tis pleasure I want to give you,
Marina," he went on in a deep, hypnotic voice, "not
pain. Such sweet pleasure . . ."

Alex kissed her again, his mouth moving ravenously
on hers, his fingers flowing through her hair, his warm
hand over her body, and after a moment Marina's
tension began to ebb, her fear to slip away. An odd
languorous feeling stole over her. She felt pleasantly
relaxed, cherished. This was a world away from the
brutality that Stafford had subjected her to. It was
almost . . . pleasant. Her head began to swim, her
thoughts to spin away as Alex continued to stroke her,
his hand gradually becoming more probing, lingering
on her breast, fingers tugging gently on her nipples,
making them leap up eager and taut. Then his fingers
moved lightly over her belly, and down to the dark
place between her legs. She felt a rush of heat in her
face. Sense came back.

Marina sucked in her breath and clutched at his
hand. "N-nay . . . you must not . . ."

"Why not? Don't you like it?" His voice seemed oddly far away.

Her face was burning. "Aye, but—"

"Then what's the harm?"

Alex bent his head to her breast, his tongue slowly circling the nipple, licking her, stroking, flicking the stiff little nub, drawing it hungrily into his mouth. His burning hand moved firmly between her legs and his fingers sought and found her moistness. The firm tugging at her breast, the rhythmic motion of his fingers, made Marina gasp with intense pleasure and cry aloud as a piercing thrill raced through her veins. In a dim way she realized that Alex was right. This was ecstasy such as she had never imagined. It mesmerized her and sapped her strength to push him away. Instead, hardly aware of what she was doing, her hands rose fluttering to his muscular shoulders, the skin dewy and warm. She plunged her fingers into his curling black hair, felt the smooth tawny skin of his broad back, caught his face between her hands and brought his mouth to hers, moaning, "Oh, Alex, kiss me! I—I—" But Marina could not express what she craved at that moment, except that her whole body felt as if it were on fire, her senses clamoring, urgently demanding more, more.

Now he plundered her mouth, all restraint gone, then moved away just long enough to wrench off his breeches. He lowered the full length of his body over hers and pressed down until Marina felt the rocklike imprint of his manhood hard against her. Alex was a lusty young animal and he could tell now that the girl was as eager as he was. All his sensual instincts were fully aroused; he was burning with desire. Lifting her legs, he impatiently got between them, leaned forward, and claimed her lips in a passionate kiss, then

with a groan of release, bore down.

When Marina gave a sharp little cry he felt a vague surprise, but he was too consumed with need to pay much attention. He *did* notice that she was very tight, though the friction only increased his rapture. Powerfully, with all the youthful vigor surging through his body, he rose and fell above her. After the first stab of pain, the first soreness, Marina automatically moved to keep pace with his rhythm, and a flicker, then a burst of tingling fire swept through her body and she was drowned in a turbulent sea of intense sensation such as she had never dreamed possible. Shuddering, moaning, Marina surged against him, desperate to make the feeling last. A steamy heat enveloped both of them as they finally collapsed on the bed, locked tight in each other's arms.

For a moment or two, as they struggled for breath, neither spoke. Then Alex turned to her in the darkness and chuckled, "Well, was that better than Stafford?"

Better than Stafford! All Edgar had brought her was pain, and thankfully he had never once been able to penetrate her. Now, shattered by her blissful experience, and wanting nothing more than to lie in silence and contemplate it, and its effect on her, Marina was dismayed to hear Sinclair mention her husband's name. Edgar was the last person she wanted to be reminded of at that special moment. Thinking of him spoiled everything. It also reminded Marina that she was married; that what had just taken place with Alex had been wrong, sinful.

"Well?" he said.

Marina burst into tears.

Alex was startled. True, a virgin sometimes wept after her first physical coupling with a man, but not a married woman. "You are not sorry?" Raising himself

on an elbow, he gazed down at her in consternation, for she had certainly *seemed* willing enough. "Surely you are not concerned about betraying Stafford? The swine doesn't deserve your loyalty."

"Nay, but—"

"But what?" He sounded a little angry. Alex had thoroughly enjoy Marina and had tried to please her too. Hungry as he had been, he had managed to hold himself back until he knew she was fully aroused and ready. He found her tears insulting, a slight to his manhood. "What ails you?" he pressed.

"N-nothing . . ." There was no way that Marina could express her jumbled feelings, joy and happiness mingled with something like shame, even though, as Alex had said, Edgar didn't deserve her fidelity and it was Sinclair whom she loved. But still . . . it was wrong.

Alex got up and lit the candle, frowning when Marina's tearful face was revealed to him in the flickering yellow light, a light that emphasized the swelling and discoloration of her features. It was far from kind to her; she looked most uncomely. Staring down at Marina, Alex wondered how in the name of God he could have made love to such a plain woman. He was angry, hurt by her response, and in no mood to be charitable.

He gave a start when he saw the red spots on the rumpled sheets. For a second his eyes widened, incredulous, then his gaze jumped to Marina's thighs and he saw more of the same there. Blood—or what looked like blood!

She wrenched up the covers and turned her head away, embarrassed.

"What's this?" he demanded, pointing at the bed. Alex couldn't believe his eyes. She was a married

woman! Oh, there was something very odd about this; something that smacked of trickery. If Marina thought to splash something on the sheets to trap him in some way—

He grasped the covers and whipped them off the bed, examined the marks there, then regarded her grimly. "Where is it? Show me the stuff you put there?"

Marina didn't know what he was talking about but she was chilled at the cold expression on his face, one that transformed him from the friendly young man she had fallen in love with into a haughty, arrogant stranger. "What—what do you mean?" she stammered.

A fine show of innocence! he thought angrily. It was a common enough trick, and he should have been more alert for it. There was always that danger when a nobleman lay with a woman below his rank, the ever-present threat of entrapment. A woman's virginity was a highly prized thing, and many were the aristocrats who had had to pay dearly for that which they had never taken. His own cousin Jay Sinclair was one of them. The whore he had bedded had ended up by destroying Jay's marriage and continued to be a constant drain on his purse.

Alex held out his hand imperiously. "I would have the potion you spattered on the bed, mistress."

"Potion?"

"What was it?" His lip curled contemptuously. "Ox blood, cochineal liquid, wine? Mayhap you saved some of the Madeira from supper, eh?" he suggested sarcastically.

Marina flushed scarlet. "I—I was a virgin."

He burst out laughing, hard, scornful laughter. "And *I* am the King of Scotland! You are a married

woman," he all but shouted at her, "and you told me yourself that that husband of yours was desperate for young. Do you take me for a fool?"

"'Tis true, I swear I was a virgin."

"Pah! What man would marry a woman and be content just to gaze at her? Yours, by the looks of him, was a rutting old goat."

Alex proceeded to search the room while Marina watched him fearfully, but he found nothing that would incriminate the girl. That didn't exonerate her. The blood—as such women were wont to do—was often contained in a little pouch of cow gut, and once it was surreptitiously splashed on the bed, these women often swallowed the receptacle. Their tricks were many and varied, but it all boiled down to one thing, an attempt to sink their hooks into a man of wealth and position, trapping him into supporting them and their bastard children.

Finally Alex returned to the bed.

"There was no need for this," he said with a wave to the sheets. "I would have given you money. I always pay for what I receive."

Fresh tears surged up and spilled over onto Marina's pale cheeks, and all her beautiful illusions came crashing down. She was frightened too. Sinclair looked furious enough to strike her. He thought she had tried to trick him, she realized, but why would she play false with a man who had risked his life to take her out of Baxton Hall; who had been kind and considerate, even tender? That man, she saw, had vanished. The god had tumbled from his high place. Now another side of Sinclair had come to the fore, a darker side, and it chilled her. For him to all but call her a whore!

"I don't want your money, sir," Marina told him

stiffly, a glint of anger in her eyes. She burst out hotly, "I would rather sweep and scrub and wash tables at an inn such as this than stoop to living off men."

"Indeed?" His lip curled.

Greatly offended that Alex would be so quick to think the worst of her, she explained coldly, "Edgar Stafford was no true man. He had been wounded in battle long ago, and"—heat rose in her face—"he was incapable of performing his husbandly duties. Doubtless that was what made him so frustrated and vicious."

"I have only your word for that."

She lifted her head, insulted, and didn't bother to reply.

Alex looked at her battered face, and the marks of Stafford's brutality seemed to flare at him. Was it possible? he mused. Could this be the work of a man driven to madness by his disability, one who took out his own inadequacy on the person closest to him, as many another had done before him?

He felt himself wavering. Marina was a lady. There was no disputing that. Until he saw the blood he would never have dreamed her capable of stooping so low; perhaps he had been hasty. He could see that she felt highly affronted, and if he had misjudged her he had certainly done her a great wrong. But she was a married woman, and Stafford, though far from young, had looked remarkably fit to him.

Alex began to pull on his clothes, sorry at the way things had turned out, but men in his position were ever prey for scheming women and he had to be careful. Even his friends had been surprised at how readily Marina had been willing to go with them. Then, Alex recalled, it had only been *after* they left Baxton Hall that she'd thought to inform them that

she had no one to take her in, thus leaving them with no option but to bring her with them into Scotland. Now he was responsible for her—a responsibility thrust upon him. Irritably Alex yanked on his boots and straightened up.

Marina sat huddled in bed with the covers drawn up to her chin. In spite of everything, she looked touchingly helpless and appealing, like a lost child.

"What are you going to do?" she asked nervously, all too aware of the fact that without Sinclair's protection she would be in a precarious position indeed.

He hesitated, then sighed, "I am going to do exactly as I promised and take you to Ayrshire." He eyed her curiously. "*If* you still wish to go?"

She had no choice! "I would not want to be a burden to you."

A strange little smile touched his lips. "Then it is settled." He strode to the door and there turned to say, "We leave here at seven of the clock on the morrow. Be ready."

Marina nodded, her heart full, eyes overflowing. When he left the room she got up and locked the door and returned to bed and blew out the candle. Throwing herself face down on the blankets, she wept.

It was as if she had painted a beautiful picture and someone had taken the brush and darkened the bright scene she had created so that it wasn't so perfect and dazzling anymore, yet still the same picture. It struck her now that she had made too many grand assumptions about Alexander Sinclair—as he had once told her himself! Marina recalled him telling her the previous night, "I am no better or worse than the average fellow—worse, some might say." And she had not believed him. Fool! she thought. Fool!

He had taken her virginity, then accused her of trying to trick him, and bad enough as that had been,

had insulted her by offering to pay for her services. How could a man who behaved so chivalrously one moment turn right around and act like such a cad the next? Oh, she didn't understand him at all. But at least she knew now that Alexander Sinclair was not perfect. From now on she would be on her guard.

6

Edgar Stafford stood in the hall of Chiltern Castle and shouted abuse at the Percys.

He had spent all the previous day searching the countryside for his runaway wife and, failing to find her, came to the obvious conclusion—one he didn't want to believe—she had escaped over the border into Scotland with Lord Alexander Sinclair! He remembered that this girl, whom he had deigned to marry when Nevil Dacre refused, had come to the attention of Francis Walsingham for making serious allegations against the Queen of England. He recalled to how this man Sinclair had plotted and attempted to free the Queen of Scots, and a connection between these two things was made in his mind. Stafford, for all his miserliness, was a man of great pride, one whom people admired for his valor in battle and, in Northumberland at least, for his unflagging devotion to the Catholic religion. Failure in any form was

intolerable to this proud man, particularly his inability to beget a son—which he felt certain he could have done with Marina Dudley.

"What of this woman you wed me to?" Edgar roared at the Percys. "Methinks there was much about her that was kept from me."

Sir Guy and Lady Maud exchanged nervous glances, but Percy responded coldly, "Nonsense, Stafford! You know as well as I that she was but an innocent, untried girl—"

"Innocent!" the other roared, spittle flying from his mouth. "Nay, there is nothing innocent about that one! Did she not make treasonable claims about the Queen's grace? Did she not fall under the suspicion of Sir Francis Walsingham? And did I not deign, risking my reputation, to marry this wench when none other would have her?" He thrust his head forward, boarlike, and shouted, "You lied to me about Marina Dudley, Sir Percy! You told me that her dangerous claim to the Spaniard was but an unfortunate jest—"

"That it was."

"Nay." Stafford shook his head emphatically, his small eyes darting from the knight to his wife, both of whom stood before the great hall fire trying to keep their expressions unfathomable. "Nay, in light of her flight with Sinclair, what went before takes on a more serious implication. Forget not that this man tried to free the Queen of Scots and set her on Elizabeth's throne. Why, even a dullard could see the connection!" He struggled for breath. "I smell collusion in this," he said ominously, "and methinks you, Percy, are behind it."

Real alarm flickered in Sir Guy's eyes, though he remained remarkably calm. He reminded the furious, vindictive Stafford, "Sir, we care not for the Protestants in these parts." With a glance around the hall, he

went on in a lower tone, "You as well as any, mayhap more so, would gladly see a Catholic on the throne." When the older man compressed his lips and neither agreed nor denied it, Percy said, "Come, Edgar, the crux of the matter is not politics but an errant wife, and we are sorry for that—"

"Sorry!" All Stafford's rage and indignation came bounding back. "Aye, and *she* will be sorry when I find her!" He could have added, "She is mine, and what is mine never escapes my hands." Instead, he ranted, "You told me she had been raised to obey, but the wench denied me my rights from the first, fighting me like a—a she-cat when I would claim what was due me. Now," he choked, his eyes bulging, "I shall be the laughing stock of the county! Where, people will ask, is Stafford's young wife? And where is the child he swore to put in her belly? How can I hold up my head when there is no wife, no child to be seen at Baxton Hall?" He jabbed a finger at Sir Guy's bland face, crying, "I hold you, my lord Percy, responsible for this pass I've come to in my gray years."

Maud Percy bristled with anger. To be upbraided like this by a common, mean-hearted churl, aye, and in their own home too! She had never liked Stafford and his coarse, ungallant ways with no social graces about him. Further, she knew very well that the fellow thought little of her, perhaps having heard, when his former wives departed the scene so mysteriously, that she had discussed the matter at length with her friends and relatives, and suggested that there should be an inquiry.

Lady Maud now spoke for the first time since Stafford had barged into their hall, and it proved to be an unfortunate remark indeed. She said silkily, "Marry, but it seems you have bad luck with these wives of yours, Stafford, though in truth I have never heard of a

wife running away when she was well treated by her lord."

The vengeful little eyes swung in her direction, even as Sir Guy shot his wife a glance of stark dismay. Better to let the betrayed husband rant and rave and get it off his chest, to his mind, than to say something bound to provoke his ire still further. Ah, but Maud had never known when to hold her tongue!

Edgar stepped up to the lady and stared grimly into her face, and this time his voice was controlled, therefore all the more deadly when he said, "Lady Percy, I detect accusation in that remark, but it seems to me, knowing you as I do, that you have no right to criticize anyone." He cocked his head to the side, studying her, and went on in the same low, ominous tone, "If I remember aright 'twas you, in begone years, who brought Marina Dudley back with you from your own, ah"—mocking now—"long sojourn in London. It also strikes me, lady, that you know much more about this girl than you care to tell—"

"Stafford!" Sir Guy growled a warning. It was one thing for *him* to be angry at his wife's acid and ready tongue but quite another for Edgar Stafford to make slighting hints about her character. He glowered at the older man and asked curtly, "Was the marriage consummated?" He continued craftily, fully cognizant of Stafford's personal problem, also his grasping ways, "For if not, it can be annulled and Marina's dowry returned to us."

Stafford's grizzled head jerked from Lady Maud to her husband, and his eyes narrowed to slits. Ah . . . he thought, here one must tread warily. All his acquisitive instincts were aroused and he temporarily forgot about his missing wife when faced with the potential loss of her modest fortune, a dowry that he was determined would never be wrested from his grasp.

But Edgar Stafford was a deeply religious man, in his own way, of course, and an essentially honest man for all his other failings.

He replied cryptically, letting them make of it what they would, "There can be no annulment of this marriage."

Percy raised both hands in a gesture of helplessness. Having offered Stafford a way out, he made it clear that he had done all he could.

"It will not end here," the older man threatened, and with a signal to his squire, who had heard everything, he strode angrily out of Chiltern Castle.

Once alone in their privy chamber, Sir Guy railed at his wife. She was a gossip and a troublemaker, he shouted at her, a lazy woman good for nothing but stirring up strife and intrigue. She had no subtlety, no brains. "Dost not realize that this is serious?" he roared into her face. "Edgar Stafford can be dangerous, the more so when he loses something that belonged to him."

"Bah! Why should *we* fear the likes of him?" Maud retorted scornfully, "He's a man in his dotage and of no consequence."

"There you are wrong!" he snapped. "He's far from doddering yet. And even if *you* think little of him, there are some in this county who respect the fellow and will sympathize with him in his present predicament. They will remember that he was courageous enough to wed himself to a wife who had come to the notice of Walsingham—a wife who ran away with a Scot who had plotted against the Crown!" Breathing hard, his eyes alive with anger and alarm, he cried, "What, think you, will they make of this? And Marina, that young baggage, having come to the marriage from this house!"

The haughty arrogance vanished from Maud

Percy's face. She turned away from her worried husband and walked to the window, a plump, once pretty woman of fifty-two who, in spite of her past indiscretion with another man, had given this one six robust children, three of them lusty sons, and by so doing had made up for that lapse—so she thought—and firmly established her position as Lady of Chiltern Castle.

Maud Percy, formerly Dudley, had grown up in a rambling house in Kent within an easy ride of London. She had been one of ten children, her family prominent and ambitious, and as a young girl had spent two heady years at court. Then her father had wed her to Guy Percy who lived in faraway Northumberland, a man with no aspirations of glory whatsoever, one who was content with the rustic society to be found in his northern county when he wasn't busy managing his large estate. He had been a handsome, prosperous young man with an easygoing disposition in the early years, and Maud—who had longed for a brilliant marriage—had been slightly mollified by that, but from the start of their marriage she had sorely missed all the excitement, amusements, the color and, yes, the constant intrigue to be found in London. Whenever she could, she returned there for visits, and it had been during one of those visits that she had met the other man.

With her back to Percy she said quietly, "Stafford would not dare make trouble, considering the mischief he himself has perpetrated against the Protestants hereabouts."

"None of which ever came to Walsingham's attention," Percy snapped. "The same cannot be said for Mistress Marina!"

She shrugged. "Nor would Walsingham have bothered about that if it hadn't been for this grave decision about to be made concerning the Queen of Scotland,

when he mistrusts any slight agin Elizabeth's character. If that Spaniard hadn't gone to London and spread his lies—"

"But he did, you twit!" stormed Percy. "Think how the Queen's ministers would have taken that. For such a claim to be bruited about at just this time would have struck them as being ominous. Who, they would be bound to wonder, had put the girl up to it? They would ask themselves, 'Can there be rebellion brewing once again in the North? And who is behind that rebellion? Can we risk a Catholic uprising at the moment when Mary Stuart's death warrant is about to be signed? Nay, we most certainly cannot!'" Percy glared at his wife's stout back. "I can well imagine my lord Walsingham saying, 'We must look into the matter posthaste, Your Majesty, for we dare not disregard it, no matter how outrageous and ridiculous it may seem. This girl has announced before a large assembly that she is your daughter, an announcement that smacks of treason. I must send agents North to examine the people responsible.'"

Now Lady Maud was frightened, but she blustered, "Edgar Stafford hates the Protestants and would do naught to help their cause. Was that not why he offered hospitality to the Scotsman Sinclair, because he had tried to free Mary and bring down the Protestant regime?" She laughed shakily. "When have you ever known Stafford to offer hospitality to anyone, miserly cur that he is? But he put his hall at the disposal of this Scottish nobleman because he admired his daring deed. Nay, we have nothing to worry about from Stafford. He has Marina's dowry, forget not, and that alone will appease him. Marina herself he will forget soon enough."

Marina, Marina! The very sound of that name was enough to send the blood rushing to Percy's head,

When he thought of all the trouble that girl had caused them! Irritable and worried, he threw himself down fully clothed on the bed and mulled over the latest development, heartily wishing that he had never agreed to become the girl's guardian in the first place. His mind went back thirteen years or so to the time Maud had returned to Chiltern Castle after paying a visit to her family in Kent. She had brought Marina, a babe then, back with her.

Maud had had a sad story to relate. Her cousin Walter and his Danish wife had both perished in a smallpox epidemic, she told her husband, leaving their poor little child an orphan. Sir Guy had never met Cousin Walter, nor indeed many of his wife's countless relatives, simply because he had never had any desire to travel South, nor they any interest in coming North. He had been surprised when Maud begged him to become the girl's guardian, saying, "I have taken a fancy to her, Guy. There is something about her that appeals to me, and no one else in my family seemed much concerned about her."

It had occurred to Percy to wonder if Marina could have been Maud's own daughter, the result of her liaison with the man who had almost broken up their marriage less than three years before. Once he and Maud had reconciled, they had agreed never to discuss this affair, both vowing to put it out of their minds and pretend it had never happened. So . . . Sir Guy had generously consented to be Marina's guardian—this after his lady let it be known that there was a fair sum of money involved, with a goodly portion of it going to them and the rest to be set aside for Marina's future dowry. The money, Percy felt certain, was the *real* reason the child had so "appealed" to his wife, a woman not overfond of children.

So Marina Dudley had become his ward. But often through the years Sir Guy had found himself wondering if the story Lady Maud had told him had been true—if Marina really *was* the daughter of Walter Dudley and his Danish wife, or his own wife's bastard!

Once, slightly drunk, he had challenged Maud with his suspicions. She had taken a kind of fit, screaming, "You gave me your word never to talk about that again! Now you've broken your word, and my heart with it! Nay, the girl is not mine!" Then she had swooned and taken to her bed for a month afterwards, to the great alarm of their own children, who had loudly blamed him for threatening the health of their mother.

He never referred to it again.

But neither did Percy stop wondering. Now, with a glance at Maud's buxom figure standing at the window, he said in a quieter tone, "You did wrong to antagonize Stafford."

"Mayhap I erred in that," she nodded. "But I mislike the fellow heartily!"

"What of this pother with the Scottish nobleman?"

She snorted, "If he *is* who he says he is, which I doubt, then he is welcome to the little firebrand. I vow his heart will be roasted with her as ours was and he will not entertain her long. Then where will she be with no husband and no dowry?"

They rode through the rugged Galloway Hills, bone weary now and blind to the grandeur of nature around them, the snowy hillsides, frigid blue lakes and streams, the haunting solitude of the terrain. They had ridden in silence for a long time, and a kind of melancholy had settled over Sinclair and his friends since with each step they took closer to home the

further they left their fallen comrades behind. Alex brooded about Jamie Fraser, the lad who had been taken alive. In some ways Jamie's fate would be worse if he reached London alive to undergo the rigors of interrogation when Walsingham's agents would try to force the names of his fellow conspirators out of him, employing bestial methods to do it. If Fraser lived to talk—and could one really blame a man for talking when trapped in the rat pit with the creatures vigorously gnawing at his bones, or spread out on the rack with his limbs being torn asunder?—then Elizabeth and her secret police would have their names. They were safe enough in Scotland, Alex felt. Though King James made an effort to please his English cousin, his eye to inheriting her crown, he could hardly punish those who had tried to save his own mother. For one thing, the people of Scotland, already outraged at what was happening to their former Queen, would never allow it.

Finding himself in a doleful mood, sad at the loss of his friends, Alex glanced at Marina. She'd had a way about her of cheering him, of distracting him from his woes. But he found the girl slumped wearily over the back of her horse, her eyes fixed stoically ahead, looking as glum as he felt himself. She had been very quiet and distant since they left the Four Doves, and the others had noticed, though they'd made no comment. Alex knew that he was to blame for her changed mood. Until the night he had accused her of trying to trick him, Marina had been bubbling over with happiness—and made no secret of it—at getting safely away from Baxton Hall. The change in her demeanor was so pronounced that it made Sinclair feel uncomfortable—but he'd had good reason to challenge her! A virgin, eh? he mused, still cynical at the idea.

Yet he sorely missed her former warmth and her unabashed admiration for him, even while realizing that he didn't deserve it. He knew all too well that he wasn't the saint she had at first made him out to be. Nor had he tried to deceive her into thinking he was.

Alex moved his horse close to her. "'Twill not be long now," he told her. "You must be very fatigued."

Marina nodded, but she didn't look at him.

Alex leaned forward in the saddle the better to see her face, half-hidden from him by the hood she was wearing. Her eyes were riveted directly ahead to avoid meeting his, and her expression was sober.

"I see you are annoyed with me," he commented.

"Nay, just saddened."

"Come, Marina, there's no point in sulking. We can at least be civil to each other." When she didn't respond he went on, hoping to catch her interest, "Are you not curious to hear about where you'll be living?" At her slight nod he was encouraged, and launched into a glowing description of Ayrshire. "'Tis a bonny county by the sea, and methinks you will like Cairnmore House. It has pretty gardens and woodland trails aplenty to walk in, and a fine beach, good oak woods, with some of the best hunting and fishing in the country."

When Marina made no comment he plowed on, "Sir Ralph Cairnmore, my grandsire, is a kindly man much given to laughter and gaiety." Or at least he had been. Alex hadn't seen Sir Ralph for the past two years. "I think he will make you most welcome," he finished, and waited for her response.

"You are very kind," Marina replied woodenly.

Alex inhaled deeply, striving for patience. He cast about for some way to rouse her out of her dolor, which was making him even more depressed than he already was. With a glance at the gear she was

wearing, all the dead Hamilton's clothes, he had a burst of inspiration. "Once we arrive we must find a seamstress to make you a pretty new gown or two."

Her reaction was unexpected; most women relished new clothes. But with a cool sidelong glance at him, Marina said tightly, "I'll find work and pay for them myself."

He flushed, and threw a look around at his friends, who hastily turned away though he could tell they'd been listening.

He frowned at her stubborn face, muttering, "Until then you cannot go naked. And a lady doesn't work for a living, so be reasonable."

Marina lifted her head and steered her horse away from his, making it clear that she wasn't interested in his company, and Alexander's face tightened angrily. He said no more. He had given his friends enough free entertainment. Alex could tell that they were puzzled as they observed his relationship with Marina unfold. She could hardly be called a beauty. As he'd overheard Keith Seton say to one of the others, "The lass is as plain as rye bread." Further, she was married, with neither name, dowry, nor high connections to recommend her. But what did any of that matter to him? It wasn't as if he were considering marrying the girl— even were she free to marry. All he sought from her was pleasant company, surely not too much to ask.

Irritated, Alex spurred up his horse and galloped on ahead of the party.

Marina watched him go. Aye, she thought, he is annoyed with me. He thinks all he has to do is turn on that potent charm and I will succumb, much as I did before. Oh, but she had learned a harsh lesson since then! Now she wasn't so gullible, so easily taken in.

Since leaving the Four Doves, Marina had had ample time to take stock of her situation. It was

daunting, now that the rosy veil had been whipped off her foolish eyes. In her desperation to leave Stafford she had run away with the first man who came along, had, in essence, put all her hope and trust in the hands of a total stranger. He had seemed like the most gallant cavalier, almost like a god to her as he described how he'd tried to rescue a Queen; Alexander Sinclair had dazzled her, blinded her with his handsomeness and charm. So . . . she had gone with him, only to discover later that Alexander wasn't quite the flawless idol that she had imagined him to be.

It had come as a crushing blow, but on reflection, Marina concluded that perhaps she had expected too much of him. There was still quite a lot to admire in Alexander. She had to be fair. Anyway, here she was in a foreign country with a man she was only truly beginning to know, dependent on him in every way. She was grateful to Alex and had every reason to be, but he must be made to realize that she was a woman who demanded respect, aye, even if she *was* from a lower station in life than himself.

Finally they smelled the sea.

Exhausted as they were from their long ride, it was as if an electrical charge jolted through the men; even their drooping mounts leaped forward. On a high plateau, a body of land that Marina came to know later as the Heads of Ayr, she was thrilled out of her black mood by the stunning picture laid out before her.

There below was the aquamarine glitter of the sea sweeping away to a misty horizon with the stately grandeur of the Arran Hills rising out of the water eighteen miles from land, deep purple and capped with snow. Beneath them were tiny villages and hamlets snuggled for protection against the cliffs that

ended at the water's edge, with a picturesque harbor where fishing vessels bobbed at anchor. On a lofty promontory a castle rose proudly, black against the frosty blue of the sky, a fairy-tale setting as if cut from a picture book.

Exhilarated by the beauty of her surroundings, Marina inhaled deeply, the clean, salty air swelling her lungs and instantly clearing the dizziness of fatigue out of her head. She turned to find Alex watching her.

"Well, does it please you?" he inquired.

"'Tis the most beautiful view I have ever seen."

He was glad that there was *something* to her liking! Smiling—oblivious to the effect of that flashing white smile on the girl watching him—he pointed to the headland. "That castle yonder is Danure, home of the Kennedys, and the village below bears the same name. Mary Stuart stopped there briefly on her flight to England for help almost nineteen years ago." His face darkened as he added, "'Tis a pity she ever left it!"

Marina glanced around. "Is Cairnmore House nearby?" She assumed, since Sinclair was going there, that he shared the premises with his grandfather.

He nodded. "Follow me," and led the way downhill.

Marina was suddenly nervous at the thought of meeting Sir Ralph Cairnmore. Though Scotland and England were at peace, there were still many in both places who hated and were distrustful of the other. She worried about the sort of reception she would get. She was English, a runaway wife, and from a lower station in life than Sinclair. Alex's grandfather might blame her for involving him in her escape, which was a criminal offense. He would be bound to wonder what the young nobleman was doing with a married English woman of inferior rank to himself.

Marina fretted about that for a few minutes as they rode along, then hurried ahead and caught up with

Alex. "My lord, what shall we tell Sir Ralph?" she asked anxiously. "He . . . he might not understand."

He knew what she was thinking; a misgiving or two had crossed his own mind. But Sir Ralph had always been an easygoing fellow who never meddled in the affairs of others. Alex had always had a good relationship with the older man, and besides, other arrangements would have to be made if Cairnmore refused to shelter the lass—though he hoped that wouldn't be the case. "You have nothing to worry about," he said. "I know my grandfather."

His eyes flickered over her and he noticed that her bruises were fading more each day; with a reduction of the swelling her features were changing from lumpiness to near-delicacy. In the bright light her lustrous blonde hair shone and her eyes sparkled, her long curling lashes casting shadows on her cheeks. The girl was far from plain! Alex, glancing at her, glimpsed, as through a veil, the promise of beauty.

It struck him that soon they would be parting company, perhaps for a long time, and he realized that the thought didn't please him. Not at all! He liked Marina. Searching his soul, he realized that it went a little deeper than that. He was attracted to the girl, a fact that his friends would find surprising, but no one was more surprised than himself. Why Marina Stafford? Why indeed?

They rode through a grove of birch and oak trees and there, in a sheltered dell, sat Cairnmore House. It was a pleasant, though not grand, residence of medium size, built of solid sandstone, its warm pinkish-red color contrasting with the light covering of snow on the ground.

Alex turned in the saddle and gave Marina a long, measuring look as if trying to puzzle something out. She was caught by the grave expression on his face and

wondered what he was thinking. *She* was thinking that he looked good in the saddle; that he handled his high-spirited horse well. But then he did most things well, Marina mused with a little inward shiver that brought a rush of pink to her cheeks. He had the body of a beautiful male animal, black hair that shone like jet, and vibrant green eyes that mirrored his zest for living. Confident and commanding, active and strong and with virility in every line of his body, that was Lord Alexander Sinclair—and, God help her, she still loved him!

"How long have you lived with your grandfather?" she inquired.

"I don't. My home is roughly a hundred miles to the north."

Marina couldn't conceal her dismay and he noticed it. Their eyes met, and for that moment they were only conscious of each other, intensely conscious. Alex was the first to look away.

7

Alex was shocked when he saw his grandfather, who had recently been ill. He hardly recognized him. Sir Ralph had shrunk from a robust, hearty knight to a feeble husk of his former self.

"'Tis this clock in here," he said, thumping his chest. "It oft forgets to keep the proper time."

They were closeted together in Sir Ralph's study, seated in front of a cheery fire, goblets of brandy in their hands. The old man was very curious to hear what his favorite grandson had been up to. Ralph was well aware that Alex was a bold, somewhat rash young man. Even so, he was totally unprepared for the incredible story he listened to, a tale that filled his heart with pride, yet in spite of it, alarm.

Cairnmore sucked in his breath. "Christ's blood, Alex, the risks you take! You might all have lost your heads. Aye, and you will be in dire trouble if your friend Fraser lives long enough to divulge your identi-

ties to Walsingham. If that happens you dare never enter England again." He scratched his chin for a moment as he mulled it over, and continued worriedly, "'Tis hard to predict how King James will react once he gets wind of this, which he will."

Alex snorted, "He should applaud *any* scheme to free his mother!"

"Aye, but will he? There's the alliance to consider."

"Surely it's not worth more to him than the life of his mother?"

Ralph eyed him in exasperation. "You know well enough that it's not as simple as that. Besides, the King's mind has long since been turned against his mother. Faith, she's nothing but a stranger to him, and a troublesome one at that!"

Cairnmore admired his grandson's courage and daring, it was true, but these fine qualities must be tempered with sound judgment—if a man hoped to retain his head upon his shoulders. Yet . . . he understood and sympathized with Alex and why he was constantly driven to prove himself; his situation within the Sinclair family was a difficult one. But at the same time Ralph was afraid that Alex's recklessness would bring him grief. He wondered if Alex had stopped to consider the possible repercussions of his actions before plunging ahead, and thought not.

Sighing, Ralph turned to the next problem. "What of Marina Dudley? How does she fit into this fantastic picture?" He was almost afraid to hear the answer.

Alex told him everything he knew about Marina, and why she was with them now.

"You—you kidnapped her?"

"Nay, she came willingly."

The elderly man waved his hand impatiently. "Willing or unwilling, it makes no difference in the eyes of the law. 'Tis a serious crime to remove a

married woman from the jurisdiction of her husband, and well you know it." He scowled at the young man now, muttering, "One more crime laid at your doorstep."

Alexander's face fell. This was not the sort of reception he had expected at all. Ralph himself had had many an adventure in his youth and generally enjoyed hearing about his grandson's exploits. Disappointed, Alex felt a touch of self-righteous anger. This then was the thanks he got for trying to do the right thing; the noble thing. No ring of applause here! And to think that he had assured Marina that Sir Ralph was an easygoing, jolly old fellow!

"You cannot take the girl to Castle Augusta."

"That I know," the younger man muttered.

"Well, what means this woman to you?"

A touch of color rose in Alexander's face. How to answer that? He wasn't certain himself just what Marina meant to him, though he suspected that she was beginning to mean too much for his peace of mind. "Naturally, I feel sorry for her," he replied evasively. "She was in desperate straits."

"And you would like me to take her in, eh?"

Alex pretended surprise at the question, as if it had never crossed his mind. "Nay . . . why would I ask that of you? I only thought to stop here in passing—"

"Thought to stop in passing!" Ralph mocked. "Lad, I might be old and gray but there's nothing wrong with my mind." He eyed the younger man sternly. "'Tis high time that you weighed up the consequences before acting, not just in regard to yourself, but for the good of your family and clan as well."

This was mortifying! To come here and be harangued, criticized, and lectured! To be treated as if he were still a boy, rather than the man he was. Alex held his tongue only because he loved and respected his

grandfather, but he was shocked and hurt at the way the old man had turned on him, and so angry that he didn't trust himself to speak.

"Very well," said Sir Ralph, "the lass can bide here."

"Nay, I would not presume—"

"You would presume anything," the other said with a harsh laugh.

"I would not want you to think—"

"Since when have you cared *what* people think?"

Alexander stood up, his face tight. "I see I made a mistake in stopping here," he said stiffly. "I will leave you in peace in the morning."

The elderly knight leaned forward and caught his arm. "Sit down, lad," he said more softly. "Sit down and pour us a wee bit more brandy."

It was not easy, thought Cairnmore, to be Alexander Sinclair.

It had all started with Alicia and Angus MacKellar, the Earl and Countess of Kilgarin, more than forty years ago. Alicia, only twenty-two at the time, had been Kilgarin's second wife. His first, Magdalen, had been divorced for infidelity and she hated the young woman who had taken her place and vowed that no child of hers would inherit the chieftainship of the MacKellar clan. When Alicia gave birth to a daughter while her lord was away at war, Magdalen kidnapped the infant and bribed the midwife to destroy her. Instead, the woman gave the baby—named Alyssa— to a friend of her own family to be raised, but she never told her the true identity of the little girl.

Alyssa grew up in abject poverty unaware of who she really was, but when she was older her radiant beauty attracted the eye of handsome Blake Sinclair, the Earl of Belrose and chief of his clan. While he loved the humble village girl with a rare passion,

Sinclair was forced to bow to the pressure of his family and marry a woman of his own rank—but always he was drawn back to the beautiful Alyssa.

As long as she lived the girl was a threat to Lady Magdalen. When Magdalen discovered that Alyssa was still alive and could incriminate her, she tried to hunt her down. Fearing for her life, Alyssa rashly married Sir Simon Ogilvy, who, sniffing gain, promised to protect her. It was while she was married to Ogilvy that Alyssa gave birth to Blake Sinclair's son, Alexander.

Eventually circumstances were such that Alyssa and Blake were finally able to marry, and the chief immediately set about trying to have his son legitimated. He encountered formidable obstacles in trying to prove that Alex was his. The head of the Ogilvy clan flatly refused to allow Alexander to legally take his real father's name. The boy had been born an Ogilvy and as far as he was concerned would remain one. Neither the best legal brains in the country nor the head of the church and state could resolve the issue.

Years went by and the fight continued. By then Blake and Alyssa had several other children, and their second son, David, safely born in wedlock, was viewed by law as the heir, in spite of the fact that he hadn't been the first born of his parents. Then, when Alexander was fifteen years old, there was an unexpected development. The head of the Ogilvy clan died, and his successor, a more compassionate man, gave his permission for Alex to take his real father's name, but with the proviso that he could never become chief of the clan, long enemies of the Ogilvys.

And there it stood to this day.

Alexander's was an ignominious position to be in, though he came from a close, loving family. Some day in the future he must bow to the leadership of his

younger brother—surely, thought Ralph, a bitter pill to swallow. Just the same, the knight thought it unwise to be too soft and sympathetic with a young man of Alexander's bold temperament, as his conduct over the past few months had proved. Cairnmore felt it his duty as grandfather to point out the error of his ways.

Now, as they sat with fresh drinks in their hands, Alex looking understandably annoyed, Sir Ralph began by saying that Alex's attempt to free the Queen had been most laudable—if he had only himself to consider. But what of his family and clan? King James had severely punished others for threatening the alliance with England by confiscating their estates, attainting their titles, and either banishing them to a foreign country or sending them to the scaffold.

"Which could happen to the Sinclairs," he said, rapping his grandson smartly on the knee. "Besides, have you ever wondered why all the other attempts to free Queen Mary have failed?"

"Doubtless they were poorly planned," Alex muttered.

"Hardly likely!" Ralph scoffed. "Powerful kings of foreign countries were behind some of those plots; they say even the Pope himself. Nay, there's more to it than that. Many feel now that either consciously or unconsciously Mary sabotaged many of these conspiracies herself; that she has a deep desire to die as a martyr for the Catholic religion."

Alex stared at him. He had never considered that.

But when it came to the question of Marina Dudley his ready temper flared.

"You would have had me leave her to the mercy of her brutish husband?"

The old man shook his head. Better, he said, to have returned Marina to her guardian, or, failing that, given her over to the Church. "They would not have

turned her away with such obvious marks of violence on her face. Mayhap some place could have been found for her in a nunnery."

When Alex didn't reply, Ralph went on firmly, "And that, young sir, is as far as you should have gone with the English girl. Your first responsibility is to your own family." He leaned forward to stress his next words. "Remember this: for every action there is a reaction. Now you must wait and see what comes of the deeds you have done."

Alex felt uncharacteristically subdued when he left his grandfather's study. The old man's parting remark made him feel a little uneasy, then he shrugged it off. Sir Ralph, he thought, was old and infirm now and it had made him fretful and overcautious. Faith, he mused, nothing would get done if one first stopped to mull over the consequences. He was safely back in Scotland now and the English could not touch him.

Early the following morning his friends departed for their Highland homes, but Alex had decided to tarry another day or two to spend time with his grandfather.

The lads nodded gravely when he explained his reason for staying.

"What a dutiful grandson you are, Alexander," said Robert Douglas with a grin. "I must commend you for your attention to the knight."

"Be gone with you!" Alex chuckled, guessing what they were thinking. He slapped the rump of Douglas's horse, sending it away at a gallop, the others following. Alex watched them until they disappeared into the fog that had crept in from the sea only a few hundred yards away.

It was that hushed time of the early morning just after the break of dawn, and once his friends de-

parted, everything grew very still except for the eternal thudding of the sea breaking against the cliffs on the other side of the hill. Alex stood for a moment at the end of the long driveway leading up to the house, sniffing the morning air—though not for long. He had left his warm bed and hurried out without his cloak to bid the lads Godspeed on their long ride home. Now the ghostlike mist settled on his face and hair and shrouded the stately elms and beech trees lining either side of the driveway. There was hardly more than an inch or two of snow on the ground, but the air was frigid.

Turning, he hurried back to the house feeling chilled to the bone. The building was in darkness, even the servants still abed. With all the fires long since gone out, the atmosphere was almost as cold inside as it was without, and as Alex crossed the shadowy hall and started up the stairs, he thought longingly of the warm bed he had recently vacated. Now that bed would be stone-cold and far from inviting.

His chamber was near the end of the upstairs corridor. Passing Marina's room, he paused for a moment to listen, remembering with a touch of irritation her coolness to him ever since they had left the Four Doves—and doves were supposed to be a symbol of peace! A mischievous idea seized him. Lady, he thought, I think you would have to agree that I've done quite a lot for you. Now 'tis time that *you* did something for me.

With a swift glance up and down the silent corridor, he cautiously turned the handle of her door and stealthily slipped into the room, quietly closing and locking the door behind him. It was even darker here than it had been outside, and Alex stood still for a moment until his eyes adjusted to the gloom, his heart pounding with excitement. He had an urge to laugh as

he wondered what she would do when she woke up to find him there, but at least it would break the ice that now stood like a glass wall between them.

After a moment Alex tiptoed over to the bed.

Marina lay on her back with her long hair tumbled about her on the pillow, one bare arm thrown back over her head, the heavy quilt drawn up to her chest, the tops of her shoulders peeping out over the covers. He sucked in a breath when he realized that below the sheets she was naked, and she *would* be, of course, having rushed away from Baxton Hall with nothing but his dead friend's clothes to her name.

Alex bent down to take a closer look at her and felt a start of surprise. In the semidarkness Marina seemed almost pretty. Much of the puffiness and swelling on her face had gone down, and in the poor light her bruises were less obvious. It struck Alex that she might even be rather attractive once her features returned to normal. Aye, he thought, bending even closer, his eyes on her soft parted lips and her lashes that lay thick and dark as the fringe of a gypsy's shawl against her cheeks, she looked *very* attractive to him at that moment.

He listened intently for a minute, but the house was still. He quickly undressed and eased back the quilt and slipped in under the sheets beside her, his breath quick and ragged now. It was cozy, and the warmth closed around his chilled flesh like a cocoon. He waited a moment or two, giving his skin a chance to warm up—and it heated fast when he thought of the naked body so close to him—then moved a little nearer. Now he could smell the fresh scent of her and feel her breath whispering across his cheek, the silken touch of her hair under his skin, and in the half-light Alex stared at her profile, which he saw was quite

lovely, and asked himself, as he had done many times before, what it was that drew him to Marina Dudley. 'Twas her eyes, he decided, definitely her eyes. She seemed very young; there was a charming aura of innocence and naïveté about Marina—but there was nothing remotely innocent about her seductive dark eyes! Each time they met his, Alex felt as if he were in the grip of sorcery. Mayhap she was a witch, he mused, studying her while giving himself a chance to warm up. That would explain the strange hold she had over him. But he was hot now, and, witch or not, he had to have her!

He raised his hand and felt her firm young breast, and it seemed to fit his palm as if it had been tailor-made, her nipple like a button that triggered off a pounding desire deep within him.

Marina found herself in the throes of an erotic dream wherein a phantom lover was doing shameful things with her, touching and stroking her everywhere, slowly invading all the private parts of her body. Shameful it might be, but she had no desire to wake up, to tear herself away from sensations that swiftly propelled her toward ecstasy. A feather-light hand fondled her breasts and teased her nipples to rigid expectancy, then trailed a path of fire over her shoulders and down to her ribs, lazily tracing the slender curve of her hips, the shape of her thighs, the velvety softness of the area between her legs. She could not restrain a gasp of shock and excitement when those bold ghostly fingers gently parted her sex and began to toy with the moist female parts of her, almost casually at first, then with more focused intent.

A faint shudder ran the length of her body and her lips parted in a rapturous sigh. Soon, as the fingers began to move rapidly now, her breath came in short

little spurts and a great burst of heat fanned out over her flesh, each nerve vibrantly alert and tingling. When a hot, seeking mouth closed over her lips and she felt his tongue penetrate the inside of her mouth, there to tease and mingle with her own in voluptuous imitation of the act of love itself, the phantom lover began to assume a familiar shape and personality—one she quickly thrust aside.

"Nay!" she cried, trying to convince herself, desperate to hang on to the notion of a dream. This must be one of those strange nighttime experiences whereby demon spirits assume mortal shape for the pleasure of taking possession of living bodies. The countryside around Chiltern Castle had been replete with such tales. Soon he would depart and leave her in peace—provided she didn't open her eyes and see him, for if she did, he would return to haunt her, to pleasure her in his wicked way for the rest of her life.

Marina kept her eyes firmly closed, her mind closed also to the idea that it might *not* be a demon. She was breathless with excitement, trembling with anticipation, aware now of what was bound to come. His palpitating fingers set her aflame, and as his mouth burned down on hers, hard and urgent, Marina felt him reach for her hand and place it over something smooth and hot and so large that it made her moan in a mixture of alarm and wanton craving.

The blood rushed to the surface of her skin, her heart pounding so wildly that it made her dizzy. He didn't speak, nor did she, but Marina could clearly hear the sounds of their rising passion and feel the love-dew moistening their skin. Suddenly a shuddering wave of tingling fire blazed up from her loins, spreading until every cell in her body shrieked with desire.

She stiffened and arched against him. Instantly he mounted her, big, powerful, ready as she was, his muscular body fitting erotically to her own, hard where she was soft, unyielding where she was pliant. She felt him grasp her legs and raise them high to curve around his hips, then he slipped his hands under her buttocks and plunged deep inside her.

Oh, the rapture! The savage, lustful hunger! Alex made love to her in a kind of frenzy as he sensed her need, wild as his own. He invaded and withdrew, teased and tantalized, bringing her joy of such intensity that Marina felt as if her very bones would melt in the steamy heat of their passion. Release came in a shattering wave of ecstasy that left her limp and quivering against him.

Still they said nothing to each other, though Alex held her close, his warm hand stroking her bare back, his lips nuzzling her cheeks and ears, the arch of her throat, her skin tasting salty.

A faint shaft of sunshine brightened the room, chasing the shadows.

Marina could no longer deceive herself. A phantom lover would have departed before daylight, as his species were known to do—but here he was still beside her! She refused to turn her head to look at him, but she couldn't ignore the stern little voice of her conscience, chiding, "Marina, well you know that he is no ghost."

Alex, wondering at her continued silence, raised himself on an elbow and smiled down at her. Peeking at him through her lashes, Marina saw that he was flushed and relaxed and looked quite pleased with himself. There was no sign of remorse or contrition on that handsome face. Suddenly she was furious.

"How dare you come into my chamber thus!" she

whispered fiercely. "Do you think you can bed me whenever you like? Mayhap you've forgotten that I'm a lady!"

His brows went up and he laughed. "You wanted that as much as I did, so don't deny it. Come, Marina," he went on somewhat impatiently, "let us make up. I hope you are not of the ilk to hold a grudge or store up grievances."

"I have every right to feel aggrieved!" Her eyes blazed with resentment. "What of that night at the Four Doves when you accused me of trying to trick you? You took my virginity, then"—her voice cracked —"offered to pay. And you expect me *not* to be offended!"

Alex felt uncomfortable and looked away, conceding, "Mayhap I erred, and if so I'm sorry." He went on cautiously, "I like you, Marina, and think highly of you." He turned and caught her hand and raised it to his lips, murmuring, "My pardon for insulting you," watching her from under his brows, hoping she would accept his apology, which he meant sincerely, so that they could resume their former relationship and enjoy the short time remaining to them before he left for home. He should have gone back with the others; there would be much business awaiting his attention at Castle Augusta. Aside from that, his family would be concerned about him. Aye, he should have returned with his friends, but he hadn't been able to tear himself away from Marina so abruptly, though perhaps, he thought ruefully, that might have been the better way.

And of course she forgave him. "Oh, Alex," she said and smiled, forgetting their quarrel and remembering instead all the things he had done for her. "Alex, how much happier I feel now." Her eyes, resting on him,

were melting. The look she gave him made his heart turn over. Alex took her in his arms and kissed her deeply, tenderly, with all the depth of feeling welling up inside him, feelings he had never known himself capable of. Then—as if his tongue and mind were somehow separated—he was astonished to hear himself say, "That husband of yours is old and cannot live forever. Eventually the day will come when you will be free . . . free to take another husband, if it pleases you. Nothing can be done now," he hurried on when he saw her eyes widen, "not with that knave obstructing things. 'Tis pointless to plan, but that does not mean that *we* cannot, ah . . . enjoy each other. I will visit you here as often as I can."

She buried her face in his neck and hugged him fiercely. "I love you so much. *So much!* How I shall miss you when you leave—"

"Hark!" He lifted his head and they could both hear movement in the house, a door closing, footsteps, one servant calling to another.

Marina caught his hand. "We cannot have them finding you in my chamber! Imagine what Sir Ralph would think."

He kissed her and grinned. "Then arise so that we might make the best of the time remaining to us. You can borrow a gown from one of the housemaids until others can be made for you."

They smiled at each other, both suddenly blissfully happy.

"My Marina . . ." he said, a catch in his voice, sudden soaring joy in his heart as he beheld her face, bruised and battered as it was, so beautiful to him at that moment. Wonderingly he took it between his hands, gently, cherishingly as one might hold a wounded bird, and gazed deep into her eyes. "I love

113

you and no other. *You,* my dearest heart. And happy I am that I found you. Think not that I will ever let you go."

Alex could tarry for only two more days at Cairnmore House, and every possible minute of them they spent together. He snuck into her room at night, though out of respect for her he resisted making love to her again. They walked in the gardens, though they were bare at that time of year, and along the cliffs beside the sea hand in hand. Alex assured Marina that he had left enough funds to provide for whatever she needed, and would send more to her once he had access to his funds. He made clear that he wished her to have everything she desired and want for nothing.

Over and over again he promised to return to visit her as much as possible.

"I'd die," she said, "if I never saw you again."

Alex knew that it was going to be very hard to tear himself away. The young English lass had crept into his heart and taken it prisoner. "When I go," he told her, "the best part of me will remain here with you." And he lifted her hand and placed it over his heart.

Madly in love as they were, they had to know everything about each other. In the shelter of a cave mouth on the beach, they talked for hours. For the first time in his life Alexander was glad that he wasn't the heir to his clan. He could well imagine the roar of protest if he were to announce his intention of linking himself to an English woman, a girl with neither dowry or title or—as far as he knew—influence of any kind. His own parents were surprisingly broad-minded, but not so others of his clan. Had he been the heir, he might have had a rebellion on his hands under these circumstances, because it was vital to the good of his House that a future chief marry well.

Alex decided then that the time had come to tell his love about his background and explain his anomalous position in his family. Marina was startled to learn that Alex, though the eldest in his family, would not inherit his father's earldom and that it would go to his younger brother instead. "I was born out of wedlock, though my parents subsequently married."

When he finished telling her the story, Marina sighed, her expression dreamy. "What a romance your parents must have had!"

"Aye," he said, "and they are mad about each other still, which I suppose is unusual after all this time. She's his sweet Highland Rose—except when they have a spat," he grinned, "for my mother is strong-willed and has a temper. At such times he calls her his Wild Rose. I think sometimes he enjoys her willfulness. It gives him the pleasure of taming her."

Marina squeezed his hand. "Darling, some day that will be us."

"Would that that day were now!" Alex replied feelingly.

Marina enjoyed hearing about his family, nor was she dismayed that Alex had been born out of wedlock, since it was a common enough thing. She was glad that he didn't seem to hold a grudge, as many might have done, that he would never be the Earl of Belrose. "Nay," he said when she asked him about it, "not now, though when I was younger; when I was old enough to understand the position, I went through some turmoil and resentment. In a way . . ." he thought about it for a minute, ". . . I think it has been harder for my brother David, odd as that might sound." He leaned forward and kissed her on the nose. "Well, enough of me, what of Marina Dudley?"

Marina thought that her own background was dull and mundane after listening to Alexander's, except

115

for the part where the Spaniard had entered her life. Her lover's brows rose when she related what had happened, how her reckless claim had brought her to the attention of Sir Francis Walsingham.

"You jest?" he asked, laughing.

"Nay, 'tis true. And after that, Lord Dacre would not allow his son to wed me, so the Percys married me to Edgar Stafford instead."

"Dudley . . . ?" Alexander's mind went back to the time he had spent at the English court. He recalled all the rumors about Queen Elizabeth and Robert Dudley, also the gossip about the handsome Earl of Leicester and *other* women, because there had been others. Now, gazing into Marina's beautiful dark eyes, Alex felt a touch of excitement. "Is there any chance that it might be true? Marina, what if you really *are* their bastard daughter?"

She burst out laughing. "Nay, 'twas all a tissue of lies dreamed up by that miserable Spaniard." Then sobering, she said grimly, "Now, because of that swine, my name is marked down in Walsingham's book."

"Mine too, doubtless," Alex said with a rueful grin. "That is, if Jamie Fraser lived long enough to divulge it."

"Oh, Alex!" The thought frightened her, and Marina pressed herself into his arms. "They couldn't petition King James to have you sent back to England, could they? To stand trial, I mean, for trying to free Queen Mary?"

"Well . . . they probably will petition the King," he replied. "They certainly won't just let it drop. But the King would never send me back, nor would the people let him. Of course, I can never go back to England again."

She hugged him. "I'm afeared."

It was chilling to Marina to contemplate her sweatheart's name written down in Walsingham's book. The head of the Queen's secret police was a man who struck terror into the hearts of many. Dread stories had been circulated about Walsingham, tales of riders galloping up to houses in the middle of the night, of his agents plucking some poor unfortunate out of his bed to whisk him away into the darkness, never to be seen or heard of again. And of shrieks drifting out of the torture chambers of the Tower of London, of people being tossed into the rat pit and eaten alive by the savage creatures there, or subjected to the Scavenger's Daughter, or crippled in the Little Ease. Oh, God, Marina prayed as they walked back to Cairnmore House arm in arm, please don't let Alex ever fall into Walsingham's hands! She turned to him and said, "You must never, ever go back to England!"

He grinned, pulling her closer. "There's no need. England has come to me." And he kissed her.

When he released her, she warned, "Alex, 'tis no laughing matter."

Alex saw how troubled she was then and sought to reassure her. "My love, forget not that we are in Scotland now. Walsingham cannot touch us here. Come, be happy and forget what went before. Think of us now and in our future."

Marina relaxed a little then, but the uneasiness at the back of her mind didn't completely leave her, much as she tried to block it out. The minutes and hours winged by with astonishing speed, running through her fingers like sand on the beach, impossible to hold on to or slow down.

"Lie with me tonight," she said, the evening before

he left. "I want you to, Alex. I—I need to feel your arms around me."

He rose before daylight the next morning while Marina was still asleep, thinking it would be easier for her—for both of them. Taking care not to wake her, Alex touched his lips to hers, looked at her for a moment, and left.

8

Even before Alexander had arrived at Baxton Hall
and met Marina, there had been a grave development
in London. It had been Sir Francis Walsingham's
painful duty to inform the Queen that there had been
yet another plot to free Mary Stuart. It could not have
come at a worse time. At that very moment
Elizabeth's counselors were pressing her to sign her
cousin's death warrant, and this time Parliament
would not allow her to procrastinate.

Much as she hated the Queen of Scots, she hated
more the thought of being the one to bring about her
death. Monarchs, Elizabeth felt strongly, were above
the laws of other mortals and should not be tried and
condemned like common criminals. The idea of one
Queen sending another to the block filled Elizabeth
with reluctance and horror. Further, it could set a
dangerous example that one day might backfire on
herself.

"Tell me of this plot," she asked wearily.

It had been hatched in Scotland, Walsingham informed her. Though two of the conspirators had been killed in the fray and the leader and the others managed to evade capture, they had one prisoner. "And we have convinced that prisoner to reveal the names of the others involved."

"Ah . . . you have a way of persuading these rogues to unburden themselves. The name of the leader, if you will?"

When he told her, the Queen reared back in her chair. "What? That comely boy?"

"A boy no longer, Your Grace. Sinclair is of age and well aware of what he was about. He's a criminal like any other and deserving of meet punishment. We must petition the King of Scotland to have this scoundrel returned to us to stand trial for his crime."

Sir Francis Walsingham was a grave, meticulous man and a staunch Protestant. Like her other chief counselor, William Cecil, his whole life was dedicated to serving the Queen and guarding her interests. Keenly observant, intelligent, and not a man who was easily deceived, the black-bearded Walsingham was appreciated more by Elizabeth for his professional services than for his charm of manner. He tended to be terse and abrupt and bluntly honest, in contrast to the meeching courtiers who flocked around her, and he had one failing that often irked the Queen. Walsingham suspected everyone of scheming against her, even those closest to her—not excepting Robert Dudley, the Earl of Leicester.

Now she thought that his overzealousness had got the better of his wits. King James would hardly send one of his own nobles back to England to almost certain death for trying to rescue his own mother! Nor did she hesitate to point that out.

He stared at her, knowing how unpredictable and fickle she could be, and it was this trait in her character that he found hardest to deal with. There she sat wavering, an aging woman of fifty-two, as thin as a cane, her golden eyes now faintly sunken and surrounded by lines, her reddish hair faded and graying—though she vainly tried to hide all this with pastes and dyes. Walsingham cared nothing for her appearance. It was her shrewd, clever mind that he admired and respected, though he frequently wished that she would be more decisive.

"This nobleman is a continuing threat to your royal person," he pointed out.

"Aye," she nodded. "Nobody who conspires against Elizabeth of England can do so with impunity, but we cannot afford a repeat of that Babington fiasco. This business must be handled in secret."

Walsingham smiled. "If it please Your Grace, I think I know a way how it can be done."

Alexander left at dawn to return to the Highlands. He had said his goodbyes the night before, but Marina rose early and watched him depart from the window of her room, and as if he sensed her standing there, he turned in the saddle at the end of the driveway and blew a kiss in the direction of her window.

Then he vanished into the mist blowing in from the sea.

Marina had a sudden, terrifying premonition that she would never see him again. For a second she was tempted to dash down to the stables and jump on a horse and fly after him to warn him of the dread feeling that had seized her heart. But she knew Alex would have laughed at her misgivings and chided her about having so little faith in him. He was brave and strong and feared nothing and admired the same traits

in others, and for her to doubt him showed lack of confidence in his ability to take care of himself.

Marina tried to shake off the uneasiness without much success. She knew from talking to Alex that it was a long ride back to the Highlands, much of it over bleak moorland and rugged mountains—and she wished fervently now that he had gone home with his friends. Cutthroats and bandits roamed these remote areas, as they did in England, men on the lookout for those traveling alone. Courageous as Alex was, he was only one man, and so often brigands ran in packs, like wolves scouring the countryside in search of prey.

"God keep you, my love," Marina whispered, a hand over her heart. "And bring you back to me soon."

Until then she would wait for a letter from him, as he had promised, to say he had reached home safely.

On the first part of his journey Alex hugged the coastline with its beautiful view of the sea and the mountains of the island of Arran in the bay, white-capped against the wintry blue of the morning sky. At the little town of Monkton he turned inland, skirted the larger town of Kilmarnock, and struck out across the vast, treeless expanse of the Fenwick Moor, desolate and bare and treacherous with bogs and quicksand. Here the going was slow and tedious and would normally have been irksome for a man of Alexander's nature, but that morning he felt in fine spirits and instead of cursing under his breath at having to pick his way so carefully for fear of stumbling in the mire, he whistled cheerily and now and then said aloud, still with that sense of surprise and awe, "God's blood, I'm in love with an English lass! Aye, and not the bonniest lass I've ever seen either."

Once away from the salty air of the sea Sinclair

immediately encountered more snow on the ground and a chillier nip to the atmosphere. He pulled the hood of his cloak up over his head and wriggled his toes to stimulate the circulation inside his knee-length boots. As he rode along, Alex paid scant attention to the occasional farmhouse he passed or the hamlets and villages that thickened the closer he got to the city of Glasgow. Except for short rests and to change his mount, he pressed on steadily north and, bone-weary and freezing cold by then, stopped that first night in Stirling.

Next day he had more difficult terrain to face, the craggy Grampian Mountains, the last hurdle between him and his Highland home. Again Alex started out at dawn, bracing himself for the arduous trip ahead, and it wasn't long before he found himself struggling through deep snow in the wild mountain passes, some tracks so deep that they were blocked entirely, forcing him to make countless detours. He had hoped to be at Castle Augusta before dark. Instead, he was compelled to spend the night in the little village of Dalwhinnie and save the last lap of his journey for the following morning.

In the early afternoon, his third on the road, Alex was on a track leading directly to Augusta, almost within sight of the castle itself, when he rounded a bend to find an obstruction blocking the path ahead, a small band of gypsies in their garishly painted wagons, one of which was barring his way.

"Good day to you," Sinclair greeted a swarthy fellow who hurried up to meet him, one who, he noticed automatically, was surprisingly well armed for a tinker. Pointing at the wagon, he said, "Be good enough to pull that cart aside. I'm on my way to the castle yonder," and he pointed up ahead.

"Be you Lord Alexander Sinclair?" the gypsy in-

quired, smiling pleasantly.

"That I am."

Suddenly the tinker pulled a pistol out of his belt and aimed it at Alex's chest. "Then you are under arrest."

When Alex reached for his own weapon, the other shot his horse out from under him, the animal pinning him to the ground, and as he struggled to free himself he saw men pouring from the wagons, none of them gypsies, Alex saw at once.

9

Marina's worry about Alex persisted for a few days; then, with a great effort of will, she managed to get the better of it, telling herself that if anyone could take care of himself it was Alexander Sinclair. Had he not evaded the clutches of the Queen's men even while still on English soil? Now that he was safely back in Scotland—where Walsingham couldn't touch him— the bold Alex could well handle anything else that might rear its head; he knew his homeland and the areas to avoid, places where brigands might lie in wait for the lone traveler. So, she convinced herself, it was ridiculous to fret when she should have been deliriously happy.

Marina felt better after that; more than better. Alex loved her; he had hinted that if anything were to happen to her husband and she were free, then he might make her his wife! The thought that her dearest

wish stood a good chance of coming true brought a shine to Marina's eyes and a bloom to her cheeks. Now she lived for the day when she would see her love again. Alex had promised to visit her soon.

One day a strange little cart bounced jauntily up the driveway to Cairnmore House drawn by two fine horses. It was small, swift, a conveyance such as Marina had never seen before, one that had been designed by its female owner.

She was about to meet the indomitable Elsie Cairnmore and her husband, Garth.

The couple strode into the hall bringing a whiff of their barnyard with them. Garth had mud on his boots, and his nails, Marina noticed, were none too clean. The jacket and breeches he wore were stained and rumpled—but his wife was in her country best in a wine-red velvet cloak lined with miniver, a truly fantastic hat on her head sporting flowers, birds, and even a dangling bunch of grapes.

Marina, startled, gaped at them with almost as much surprise and curiosity as they were regarding her, for Ralph's son and his wife were nothing like she imagined they would be. It struck her too that the knight seemed a bit embarrassed when he introduced her to the couple. Upon learning who she was, and how she had come to be there, Elsie Cairnmore cried, "Imagine, an English lass living at Cairnmore House! I declare, I never thought to see the day!"

"Isn't that just like Lord Alex?" said her husband, heaving a sigh.

Both of them stared hard at the bruises on Marina's face.

Sir Ralph had been kind and welcoming from the start, but within minutes of meeting them Marina sensed that Garth and Elsie resented her being there.

The couple ran Sir Ralph's main farm at Monkwood, where they raised prize bulls as well as sheep, goats, and crops such as barley and rye. Garth Cairnmore was every inch the country squire; a big, rather loud-spoken man of forty with a florid face and booming laugh, he was a popular figure in the county, a hard drinker and always quick with a lewd joke. His helpmeet, Elsie—the mother of five lusty sons—was a strong-willed, managerial woman whose chief satisfaction in life was to organize things—her family, the finances and business of running the farm, even the community of Maybole when she could get away with it. She was a rotund, bustling little woman with very red cheeks and bright eyes the color of black currants. Those eyes were piercing and strongly disapproving when they observed the new member of the family.

"So ye ran away from your man, eh?" she asked, frowning.

"He beat me severely." Which was obvious.

"That may be, lassie. Many have to suffer the discipline o' their men. What I would like to ken is what ye intend to do now?" The small, alert eyes bored into her, alive with suspicion. "What's a' this between you and Lord Alex—"

"Elsie, let the lass be!" Sir Ralph broke in, scowling at his daughter-in-law from under his bristling gray brows. "Keep that inquisitive nose of yours to yourself."

Ralph was one of the few people able to keep Elsie in her place, mainly because he was still the head of the family and the one with all the wealth, so while she might bristle and huff and puff, while her greedy little fingers might itch to take command, Elsie was also canny and wise enough to accord him grudging respect and a certain amount of deference.

But her husband, Garth, far less acute and clever than his wife, pointed out officiously, "It's a terrible crime to break one's marriage vows. I hope no trouble comes to *us* because of this, Father."

"Bah!" snorted the elderly knight. "The lass is from England, and the English have no jurisdiction here."

Marina was pink with embarrassment. When they finally left, she said, "Perhaps Alex shouldn't have brought me here. I would hate to cause trouble for you, Sir Ralph."

He threw back his head and laughed. It would be a sorry day, he said, when he allowed Garth and Elsie to upset him. Elsie, he went on, frowning, was not the sort of wife he would have chosen for his son, but Garth had taken a powerful fancy to her and wouldn't be dissuaded, even though she was from a lower station than himself. Now he feared that some of Elsie's coarseness had rubbed off on his son.

"She's an interfering, bossy woman! She's also cunning and grasping and can hardly wait to see me in my box so that she can get her greedy hands on my money. That woman would take over the world if given half a chance!" Ralph fumed, his eyes glittering with anger. Then they softened a little when they fell on Marina's battered face. "This is still my house and you are my guest and the Monkwood crew must like it or lump it—for you are staying, Marina! Now let that be the end of it."

Marina discovered that there had been a change in the organization and management of Cairnmore House since Sir Ralph's recent illness, and though the old man struggled mightily to keep a tight grip on the reins, it was his son and daughter-in-law who really had the grip of them, at least where certain things were concerned. The couple had taken it upon them-

selves to discharge all of Ralph's old servants while he was indisposed, using the excuse that they had become lax in their duties with no one to keep a sharp eye on them. New servants had been hired, including a valet for Sir Ralph, a man called Beech who, the knight muttered darkly, had been placed in his house to spy on his activities for Monkwood.

He chuckled grimly, in some ways enjoying the power struggle. "They especially hate it when my lawyer comes to the house, and thanks to Beech, they always know when he visits me."

Ralph detested his valet and certainly didn't make things easy for him. One afternoon while he was chatting with Marina by the hall fire, Beech appeared silently in the doorway to announce that it was time for his nap. The elderly man swung around to face him, crying, "Christ's foot, leave me in peace!"

"I'm sorry, sir," replied the thin, colorless Beech, a man of about thirty with a straw-colored beard and thinning sandy hair, "but your doctor has instructed me to see that you obey orders. 'Tis for your own good," he added quickly when Ralph glowered at him.

When the valet hurried forward to help him up from his chair, Ralph shoved him aside and held out a hand to Marina instead. On the way upstairs he muttered under his breath, "To have come to this pass . . . to be handled like a babe in my advanced years. Nay!" his voice rose, "I will not have it!"

The bedchamber they entered was large and comfortable, with fine polished furniture and flowers from the greenhouse arranged around the room. A cheery fire crackled in the grate and the covers of the huge bed had already been turned down. It was a high bed, and when again Beech made to help him get in, the old knight suddenly roared, "Unhand me, you pest! What

a state of affairs this is when a man cannot get into his own bed and must be put there by a nursemaid."

Determinedly, he struggled into bed himself and fell back exhausted against the pillows. He glared up at the valet triumphantly. "See! I can manage well enough if given the chance. You tell that meddling pair at Monkwood that I don't need you. Garth can find you other employment. If and when the time comes for me to require a nurse, I shall find my own!"

Later that day Marina was reading in the library when Beech took his master's medicine up to his room. He was hardly inside the chamber when Marina heard wrathful shouting. "Nay, take it away, Beech. I'll have no more of that posset, for it tastes like cat piss."

Marina had to smile. Beech certainly had his hands full with his patient. Yet she sympathized with Sir Ralph, thinking that he should at least have been allowed to choose his own valet. The poor old fellow must know that he was losing control over his life, she mused, and Marina could well understand how distressing that was for him, since, according to Alex, Ralph Cairnmore had once been a strong, vigorous man and an excellent manager of his affairs.

Now the "Monkwood crew," as he called them, were determined to take over—and Ralph just as determined that they wouldn't!

The following Sunday Elsie and Garth sent the cart to Cairnmore House demanding the presence of Sir Ralph and Marina at Monkwood for dinner. Ralph point-blank refused to go, shuddering, "Nay, I will not expose myself to that again! Their loutish sons and all their kin will be there and the racket would deafen a miller." Then a mischievous glint came into his eyes. "But you go, Marina. You can represent Cairnmore

130

House. Besides, it will be an eye-opener."

That it most certainly was!

Monkwood was one of the best farms in Ayrshire. It had almost a thousand acres of the most beautiful land that Marina had ever seen in the Carrick Hills, with high meadows sweeping away from the sea, and bubbling streams and rivers where fish swam in profusion in summer. In milder weather plump cattle grazed the verdant green hillsides munching on the sweetest grass to be found in Scotland, according to Garth Cairnmore who proudly showed Marina around. With the coming of winter the cattle had been brought into the byres, but thick-wooled sheep still roamed the hills, food taken out to them daily. Most of the sheep, Garth explained in his blunt farmer's way, had been "put to the tup" and would lamb after the turn of the year. The lambs would quickly thrive, he told her, since by the sea the weather never got too cold and the salt in the air quickly melted whatever snow they got.

The gray stone farmhouse was stout and rambling, surrounded by the many byres, stables, and other outbuildings. The huge hall when they entered was crowded and noisy with men, women, and children in abundance, most of them members of the family. Of the couple's five sons four of them were married with youngsters. Then there were Elsie's mother and two brothers and several guests other than Marina herself.

They all stared at the English girl with avid curiosity. Her presence among them caused a great stir and a certain amount of hostility. She was, after all, English, and in this rural area many still hated and distrusted their neighbor south of the border. And worse, she was an English woman who had run away from her lawful husband, another thing that didn't set well in

131

their eyes. Marina suspected that most of them had already heard her story from Elsie, how the reckless Alexander Sinclair had helped her to escape, then dumped her into the lap of Ralph Cairnmore. She was a foreigner and a total stranger, yet the Cairnmores were expected to take care of her. All this Marina read in the inquisitive eyes that raked her over from top to toe, and it was a wonder, she thought, that she was able to withstand it and hold up her head—but she did! Fortunately, the majority spoke nothing but broad Scots, which she couldn't understand, so she was spared the details of the comments they were making about her.

The Sunday meal was served, with Elsie and Garth presiding at either end of the long hall table, and what a meal it was! Marina gazed in awe at whole joints of beef, legs of lamb, and a mountain of roast pheasants piled up on a platter. There were also smoked salmon, pickled pigs' feet, and a sea of pies, cakes, and puddings, half of which Marina was certain would never be eaten.

She was wrong. Hands, large and small, shot out in all direction toward the serving dishes, and the children yelped and sniped at each other as they fought over the choicest tasties, even as countless dogs circled the board growling and snapping as they battled and pounced on scraps tossed over careless shoulders.

Everybody talked at once in the broad Scots lingo that Marina couldn't understand. She was left feeling like a deaf woman trying to follow the action at a pantomime. They laughed, joked, argued, and shouted at each other and the din was ear-splitting. No wonder, she thought, that Sir Ralph refused to subject himself to this again.

When the meal was over, Marina was more than ready to go home, but she wasn't to be let off that easy. The table was shoved back against the wall to make room for the dancing and singing that followed. None of the dances were familiar to the English girl. The wild jigs, strathspeys, and reels made her head spin and her stomach queasy, especially following so soon after the meal, though at first no one came forward to dance with her—for which she was glad. Then she noticed Elsie bustling about among her sons, shoving them and nodding to where Marina stood alone watching the others dancing. They were all huge, burly men who towered over their mother, but they obeyed her orders and soon one after the other came forward to sweep the English intruder onto the dance floor. One even had the temerity to pinch her bottom. "No' much there fur a guid feel," he observed.

Finally, thankfully, it was time to go home. Elsie surprised Marina by saying that she would drive her back herself, "in the wee cairt I fashioned."

"You . . . you designed the cart?" Marina was quite impressed.

"Och, aye, 'twas nothing," replied the goodwife as they started off, Elsie again in her best red velvet cloak and the outrageous cornucopia of a hat perched on her head. "A' can turn my hand to anything," she boasted. "To tell the truth, I wouldna see any man standing in ma way." And with a sidelong glance at the girl, who by now looked rather pale, she said, "I ask ye, where would they be without us wimmin?"

By then it was almost dark, and Marina worried aloud, "Are you not afraid to drive out by yourself at this hour?"

"Ha! Afraid? Me? Don't be daft!" she laughed.

Then she startled Marina by whipping a pistol out

133

from the folds of her very feminine red cloak, a garment that didn't at all suit the doughty Elsie Cairnmore.

"I've got this," she said, waving the weapon about before tucking it back where it had come from. "And I've also got this." Leaning forward, she flipped a lid on a box at the front of the vehicle and jabbed a finger at a naked sword that lay gleaming inside. "Don't worry," she said, grinning at the girl's astonishment. "I ken how to use it too. Nay, lassie"—she patted Marina's knee—"you are safe enough wi' me."

Marina believed her.

But soon she discovered the reason that Elsie had jumped at the chance to be alone with her. As they jogged along the track bouncing behind the horses, darkness all around them and the night bright and frosty with a sickle moon hanging in the sky, her hostess began peppering her with questions, beginning by saying, "It's time we got to know each other better," though the ensuing conversation was all about Marina. "Now, whit about this husband o' yours?"

Marina was immediately wary. Some instinct warned her not to reveal too much to this woman, since Sir Ralph had made it clear that he didn't trust his daughter-in-law. All she said was that Stafford had subjected her to savage beatings, so vicious that she feared he would one day kill her, so when Alex had stopped at their hall and offered to help her escape she had agreed at once.

"And doubtless ye recompensed Alex well for his trouble, eh?"

The girl stared at her in the dark.

Elsie shifted the reins to her right hand and with the other pinched Marina playfully on the thigh, chuck-

ling, "Ye ken what I mean—a wee bit o' sport."

Marina flushed scarlet. Now she was glad of the dark for hiding the shameful color burning in her face, but nothing could have made her admit to this nosy woman that she and Alexander had been lovers. Her private life was her own affair.

"We are just friends," Marina replied evasively.

Then Elsie said, "Just as well. I didna think ye were his lordship's kind at all. He's always had an eye for the bonny ones, and I'm telling ye plain, he's had plenty o' them. His folks wid like to see him married and settled, but as my Garth says, why would a bull cleek himself to one cow when he can take his pick o' a whole field?"

There was nothing to say to that, so Marina kept silent, though she didn't appreciate Elsie's rustic philosophy. Yet she supposed it was natural that Alex would have had other women, even many of them. He was very handsome, very charming, also titled and rich. But that was in the past! What had happened before they met each other didn't matter. Now it was she that he loved, and Marina was determined not to let Elsie Cairnmore's gossip upset her.

"You and the old gent seem to be friends too." The older woman gave her a sly look from the corner of her eye. "But I feel it my duty to give you a piece of advice. Let Beech handle him. Beech is trained in caring for the infirm, so make sure you dinna interfere."

It was an order, no mistake about that.

Alone in her room that night Marina examined herself in the mirror. Once she had been bonny, but now her face was lumpy and lopsided, the black marks now faded to a yellowish purple—which if anything looked worse. There was a bump on her chin and a

swelling over her right cheek, and her nose was thicker than normal. It was amazing, considering what Elsie Cairnmore had told her about him, that Alexander would even have looked at her twice.

"Mayhap he's sorry for me," Marina mused aloud as she gazed dully at her reflection in the mirror. "Mayhap it's pity he feels for me, rather than love."

It was a disturbing thought, one Marina didn't want to believe, yet why would a man like Sinclair—who could have had any woman—fall in love with a girl who was ugly, penniless, even tied to another man?

She lay awake for a long time, but finally took herself in hand. There was no use anticipating trouble before it had even developed; and it *wouldn't* develop, because Alex *did* love her, as he had demonstrated in countless ways. Now she must trust him to be true to her and put Elsie's remarks about him out of her mind. The woman, as Ralph had told her, was a born troublemaker.

Christmas and New Year's came, and this time both Marina and Sir Ralph were compelled to attend the holiday celebrations at Monkwood. There was just no way to avoid it. Marina had never seen anything like it, the feasting, fighting, drinking, and dancing that went on for days, Elsie supervising everything. Elsie had also arranged to have several new gowns made for Marina by her own seamstress, from money Alex had left Marina. Elsie paid the seamstress in kind—a dozen eggs from the farm, some ox tails, a half-sack of grain—and she purchased the material cheap from a contact she had at the mill, so there was a surplus of funds left over, cash that by rights should have been returned to Marina. Without a qualm Elsie pocketed it "for her trouble."

Still, Marina was happy enough with her new

clothes, particularly the sea-green silk gown she wore
to the New Year's ball, a color that greatly suited her.
Even better, her swollen features had improved, so
much so that she received many startled glances from
the Cairnmores. The youngest of the boys, Jake,
actually asked her for several dances without being
prodded. Staring at her, he blurted, "Am no' married,
ye ken," his eyes dropping from her face to fix
longingly on the lush whiteness of her breasts rising
proudly above the neckline of her gown. Her im-
proved appearance prompted him to make her a
generous offer. "If that auld man o' yours draps deid I
might consider wedding you myself, aye, even if ye
dinna have a dowry." Jake was as huge and loutish as
his brothers, but he had the added disadvantage of
looking dim and went about with his wide mouth
hanging open. Fortunately, his amorous inclinations
were nipped in the bud when his father tapped him on
the shoulder. "My turn, lad," he said, shoving the
youth aside. Garth whirled Marina around the room a
time or two, then inquired casually, "Have you heard
from Alex since he returned to the Highlands?"

"Nay, not yet," she replied, though he had hardly
been gone for very long.

Garth Cairnmore's eyes studied her for a moment,
and something he spied in her face made him warn
her, "It could be long and weary before you do. 'Tis as
well to know that so you don't go on hoping. Alex"—
he sighed—"is not the constant sort at all. He's had
more women than you'd care to count."

Marina could not hide how those careless words
hurt her and for a minute had to struggle to compose
her face; she felt like weeping. Why hadn't he at least
written? she asked herself anxiously. Even a few lines
would have satisfied her. But feeling Garth's inquisi-

tive eyes on her, she gave herself a mental shake. She must have faith in Alex! No doubt he had been very busy since returning home, and would contact her just as soon as he could. Nay, she would not allow Garth and his wife to put poisonous doubts in her mind. Alex *would* keep his promise to her.

With the dawning of the year 1587 a period of relative quiet set in, a time when Marina and Sir Ralph got to know each other better. They quickly became close, both in a way victims of their circumstances, and it gave them something in common. The winter nights were long, and they were glad of each other's company. Ralph was very knowledgeable, and many an interesting conversation they had in front of the hall fire.

From Ralph, Marina learned much about Scottish history and politics and the folklore of his native Ayrshire. People here, she discovered, were every bit as superstitious as they were in rural Northumberland. She had noticed during her times at Monkwood that certain herbs and talismans were hung over the doors—even the barn doors—to ward off evil spirits. Ralph kept her entertained with tales about sea witches, devil crows that pecked out the eyes of the unwary, a phantom dog that on moonlight nights turned into a werewolf and roamed the Carrick Hills, and lots of other spine-tingling stories. Then there were the real-life smugglers who hid in caves along the coast, and thieving bands of tinkers who roamed the moors. An interesting tale that was based in reality concerned the Vikings who long ago had attacked and then settled along the coast of Scotland.

"That's the reason you see so many people here with flaxen hair and bright blue eyes," said the old

man. "But what you *never* want to see is King Haco's ghost ship."

"Why? What of it?" Marina asked, fascinated.

"Well, because it's a portent of doom. You see, Haco died before he could return to Norway, so his ship is destined to sail these waters forever, and to spy it sailing in the Firth is a warning that great danger is near; danger either to yourself or someone close to you."

It was fun to listen to these stories while safe and sound inside the thick walls of the house, comfortably settled before a roaring fire. They amused themselves in other ways too. Both enjoyed a game of chess—and both played to win. On Marina's seventeenth birthday on February third Sir Ralph presented her with a beautifully wrought ivory and ebony chess set, together with a length of scarlet satin for a new gown.

But she didn't receive the gift she most desired—a visit from Alex.

By this time Ralph had a good idea how it was with the young couple—or how it *had* been—though he never pried. He noticed, though, the way Marina's eyes lit up whenever his grandson's name came up in the conversation, and he found it heartrending. The old knight fumed inwardly. Young men, he thought, were so shallow, so fickle, flitting from one woman to another. He wished Alex could see the girl now. With her features returned to normal, Marina was a stunningly lovely girl with her rippling wheat-colored hair and dark eyes that would fire a man's soul. His fingers itched to wring Alexander's neck.

While Ralph was resting, Marina took to wandering the hills and seashore. Beautiful as the scenery was, she was blind to it, crushed by the misery lying heavy inside her. Oh, God, why, *why* didn't he write? It had

been weeks now. She tried not to let it, but Garth and Elsie's remarks began to take on real significance now. Surely Alex couldn't have been so busy that he couldn't at least have written a brief note to tell her that he was all right. Had something unforeseen happened with his family or clan, or, God forbid, him! Terrified by the thought, Marina flew home to question Sir Ralph, fear for her lover overcoming her pride.

"If anything had happened we'd have heard about it," the old man assured her, patting her hand. "The countess would have let me know."

"What of—of Walsingham?" Marina was pale with agitation. "Alex—"

"Nay, nay." Ralph shook his head firmly. "Alexander has nothing to fear from the English secret police here. Scotland is out of their jurisdiction and they wouldn't dare trespass here. Alex"—he hesitated, trying to think of a way to let her down easily—"has never been much of a correspondent."

"Then I shall write to *him!*" the worried girl announced.

Cairnmore frowned and shook his head. If he knew his grandson, his family would have been kept in the dark about Marina, and in a way that was best. If a letter arrived at Castle Augusta from an unknown English woman, and happened to be opened by a secretary, as sometimes happened when the person it was addressed to was out, it would only stir up a hornets' nest. Even if it was placed directly into Alexander's hands it would cause speculation among the servants . . . and quickly reach the ears of the earl and countess. They would want to know about any mail arriving from Cairnmore House—they might even worry that his own illness had worsened! But one

thing was certain, they would find out the truth soon enough. There were few secrets in the great houses, thanks to the servants.

"Hang on a little longer," he advised Marina lamely, adding irritably, "But don't worry about Alex, he's fine. That one is like a cat; he always lands on his feet."

One afternoon Marina climbed the Carrick Hills to her favorite lookout point with its magnificent view of the bay, curious sheep closing in around her. Far below, the water glittered greenish-silver, and the sky above was a cold, wintry blue—like her heart, she thought glumly. She gazed bleakly to the hills of the mysterious island of Arran; they were a soft mauve in the faint mist hanging over the water, their crests crowned with snow. Flocks of gulls followed the fishing craft that left the town of Ayr every morning in search of the great shoals of herring and cod, returning in the evening to sell off their catches at the fish auctions—if they returned at all, considering the changeable nature of these often turbulent waters.

Marina sat down for a few minutes to rest, breathing in deeply. The air was clean and salty, and a light breeze ruffled her long golden hair, sending it flying up around her head and coloring her cheeks a bright pink. Outwardly she was glowing with health, her skin soft and flawless, her eyes clear, but inside her all was dark. "Alex!" Marina cried aloud in anguish. "Oh Alex, have mercy! A few lines . . . all I ask is a few lines, my love . . ."

Suddenly she sat forward, her eyes narrowing as she detected a strange-looking ship far to the north, sailing into the Firth of Clyde from the direction of the island of Skye and the Cumbraes. There was

something peculiar about that ship, something different from all the others dotting the water as it glided in and out of the fog that hung over the sea. Marina imagined that she saw a high curving prow ending in some sort of carved ornament—perhaps a bird. She saw billowing sails and the rhythmic dipping of oars along the side, then with a start spied the figure of a tall warlord in a glittering helmet.

"My God . . ." she whispered, her blood turning to ice when she realized what it was. The next instant the Norse galley vanished in the mist.

Marina jumped to her feet and peered after it, then raced back to Cairnmore House. "I've seen King Haco's ghost ship!" she cried as she ran into the hall. "Oh, Sir Ralph, I'm not jesting. I swear I saw it sailing in the Firth." She clutched the back of the old man's chair, almost swooning. "Something awful has happened, or is about to happen. Alex! 'Tis Alex!" She burst into terrified tears.

"Nonsense!" Cairnmore gripped her hand fiercely, alarmed as all the color drained from her face as if it had been sucked out of her. "Nonsense," he repeated firmly, "'twas only a trick of the light. The tale about Haco's ship is mere superstition and not meant to be taken seriously. Get a grip on yourself!" he ordered quite harshly, afraid she was about to succumb to an attack of hysteria. "Educated people don't believe such rubbish, and you, miss, are an educated girl."

"Oh, but—"

"Listen to me, it was an illusion, nothing more. I'll tell you no more folk tales if you are going to take them seriously. For goodness sake, Marina, have you lost your wits?"

But there was something that Sir Ralph had never

told her, and he was glad he hadn't now. He himself had glimpsed the ghost ship a week before his wife, Alicia, had died. He decided he would write to Castle Augusta posthaste. Garth could mail the letter.

(faint mirrored text from facing page, illegible)

10

They had taken him out of Scotland illegally and brought him back to England to stand trial for his crime, and during the weeks he had been incarcerated in the Tower of London, Alexander Sinclair had gained the dubious reputation of being the most difficult prisoner in the fortress. He had paced about in his cell like a caged lion, rattled the bars of the window, trying to dislodge them, then pounded the door until the warden feared he would break it down. Twice he had had to be moved to more secure quarters, and on one occasion they had stripped him naked and chained him to the wall, feeding him nothing but bread and water, thus weakening him, until Alex became more tractable. And, like most of the others, he had spent harrowing times in the torture chambers, though they had stopped short of putting him on the rack. Why, Alex would never know.

For all his efforts, Alexander didn't succeed in escaping from the Tower of London. Few had, and none without outside help. No one could intervene for Sinclair for the simple reason that none of his people knew where he was. All they knew was that he seemed to have vanished off the face of the earth.

Finally, the day of his trial arrived. In a Tower courtroom Alex and his friend James Fraser faced their accusers in turn. As the higher ranking of the two, Alex was first. He stood unflinching as a list of his crimes were read out to him. He had, they charged, led a conspiracy to free Queen Mary of Scotland, a woman who herself had plotted constantly against the Crown of England. He was also accused of conspiring to depose and kill Queen Elizabeth and put the Scottish Queen on her throne, and by so doing to reinstate the Catholic religion in England.

"What say you to these grave charges, my lord Sinclair?" asked Justice Hull.

"Most of them are lies."

"Indeed? You deny attempting to free the Scottish Queen—"

"That I admit," Alex allowed. "The rest are untrue."

"Sir, that one crime would naturally lead to the others," purred Lord Hull.

"I do not consider it to be a crime to try to free a woman wrongfully imprisoned for nineteen years," Alex said loudly, his green eyes flashing with indignation. "I confess only to attempting to make right a great wrong done to an anointed Queen of Scotland, and I leave the *world* to judge if that was indeed a crime—not the biased ministers of this courtroom."

The judges looked at each other uneasily and muttered among themselves, well aware of the attitude of the rest of the world in this matter but annoyed at

being reminded of it.

The proceedings dragged on, but try as they might, the judges could not get Alex to confess to the other charges brought against him, and in the end he was taken back to his cell to await the verdict.

He was not the same man who had entered the Tower many weeks before. Rough treatment, scanty nourishment, and lack of fresh air and exercise had wrought a great change in him. His once strong, muscular body had grown thin, his face was pale and gaunt, but his green eyes were as fierce and defiant as ever, burning with indignation when he reviewed how he had been treated. He had been kidnapped from his own country and brought to England illegally. He had been allowed no counsel of his own choosing at his trial. And his family had not been informed of it nor indeed knew where he was. Everything had been shrouded in secrecy.

The verdict was brought to Alex the next morning. He had been found guilty on all counts and was sentenced to die on February twentieth.

"By what manner?" he asked.

"You are to go to the block."

When left alone, Alex lay back on his pallet. He supposed he should consider himself lucky. Anthony Babington and *his* plotters had all been hanged, cut down before death and revived, then drawn and quartered—the vicious traitor's death, though not just reserved for traitors, as Alex well knew.

It surprised Alex that he had not been condemned to that same grim fate, just as it had surprised him that he hadn't been racked in the torture chambers, as most others in his position had. The thought flickered through his mind that somebody, somewhere, had shown him a touch of mercy.

But . . . he was to die.

It was difficult for one so brimming with life to digest the fact that soon his life would be extinguished. Every cell in Alex's body shrieked in protest at the thought of being cut down in the flower of his youth—and suddenly he remembered his grandfather saying that for every action there is a reaction, a remark that assumed deadly significance now.

This then, he sighed, was where his youthful folly had led him—to the block. It horrified Alex to think that he might die for naught, if indeed, as Ralph Cairnmore maintained, Mary Stuart had been determined all along to sacrifice her life as a martyr for her religion.

He thought of his family and of Marina, the girl he loved. He considered all that might have been and was now denied him . . . because of his own actions. Alex sprang up and went to the tiny window of his cell, his hands gripping the bars until they turned white. "Dear God," he muttered, "don't let it all have been in vain!" He must go to his death believing that he would die in a good cause; that Queen Mary truly desired her freedom.

Alex was deeply worried about his family and how this might affect them. It was difficult to predict how King James might react once he learned of the plot to free his mother, a woman in essence a stranger to him and in some ways even a threat to his crown. Then there was the Anglo-Scottish alliance to consider, an alliance dear to the heart of the King, just as it was to his English cousin Elizabeth. Nay, he brooded, James might not look with favor on the rescue attempt.

Somehow he must warn his father, the Earl of Belrose. If the King took this ill, the Sinclair lands could well be forfeited, his father's titles attainted, all he possessed taken away—through the actions of his son.

Catherine Linden

A feeling of desperation seized Alex to think that his sire was totally unaware of the danger rushing toward his house. Even the whereabouts of his own son was unknown to him, since everything that had happened had been shrouded in secrecy.

He must try to bribe one of the guards to sneak a letter out of the Tower and back to his family. These men, poorly paid, were ever susceptible to graft. Alex picked up his leather jerkin and tore out the padded lining to get at funds he had hidden there, then banged on the door of his cell to attract attention, painfully aware that he didn't have much time left—and Castle Augusta was a long way away.

Eight days before, on February first, Secretary William Davison brought Queen Elizabeth a bundle of papers to sign.

There was nothing unusual about that. Davison, Secretary to the Council, frequently came with documents requiring the royal signature. Elizabeth, seeing him hesitating by the door, waved him forward and held out her hand for them impatiently, thinking that these were the last she would attend to that day. She was weary and in need of relaxation and refreshment.

Then she saw the expression on Davison's face. He stood before her white and tense, beads of perspiration gleaming on his forehead. His hand shook when he placed the folder on her desk, and when he raised his head he didn't quite meet her eye.

Queen Elizabeth's heart lurched sickeningly. Instantly she knew what he was about, and at the thought of it her face turned chalk-white, her nerves screaming. This was a game of deception, but one in which both sides knew the rules; it was a ghastly charade her ministers had decided to play out for the appeasement of Her Majesty's delicate conscience.

The Queen knew that as well as they did.

She played her part well. None of her inner turmoil showed as she gazed down at the document lying on top of the pile placed before her. Innocent enough, that one! Quickly she scrawled her signature to it and turned to the next, and the next. Midway through the stack there it was, a paper she had been dreading to see for the past nineteen long years.

Set squarely before her was Mary Stuart's death warrant.

Elizabeth hesitated, her mind reeling, the hand holding the quill turned to lead. She cried inwardly, "Could they not have spared me this hated responsibility? Could Sir Amyas Paulet, her jailor, not have taken my hint and quietly poisoned her instead?" But no, Paulet had written back in horror at the suggestion, saying, "God forbid, I could not make such a shipwreck of my conscience or leave such a blot on my posterity by shedding her blood without law or warrant."

The pompous fool! The self-righteous prig! And what of *my* conscience? the Queen fumed. What of the blot *I* would leave to posterity if I went through with this—and I a Queen!

Davison waited breathlessly, his heart thudding. The silence in the chamber was excruciating as Elizabeth sat with her head bent over the warrant, the hand clutching the quill poised. Oh, the weight of it! she groaned, the horror of having to be the one to officially sanction her execution. But . . . there could be no more delays, no more fresh plots to free her, no more turmoil in England caused by her cousin Mary Stuart—a woman who would have seized *her* crown if she could. Elizabeth firmly believed that. Now her ministers were adamant. They were no longer willing to let her procrastinate. Finally—and the Queen had

to face it at last—there was no one else prepared to take this matter out of her hands. The responsibility was hers alone.

She scrawled her signature on the death warrant.

Then she slumped back in her chair and turned her head away, ignoring the man who snatched it up without comment and hurriedly left her chamber. In the anteroom outside the other ministers were waiting, and Elizabeth could hear them rejoicing that the matter was concluded at long last. She sat on alone, suddenly hating them all. They seemed to her like carefree children while she felt so doleful and old. She could have liked Mary, she was certain . . . had they not both been Queens in the same small island, with one of them a little more entitled to wear the crown than the other, and therein lay the crux of it.

Within the hour the death warrant was winging its way to Fotheringay Castle in Northamptonshire before Queen Elizabeth had a chance to change her mind, as she was frequently wont to do. Her ministers were taking no chances, anxious as they were to dispatch with the one they considered to be England's greatest enemy.

At eight o'clock on the morning of February eighth in the year 1587, the tall, stately figure of a Queen walked courageously to her death in the Great Hall of Fotheringay Castle, condemned by another Queen who was also her relative.

Mary Stuart suffered severely from arthritis, the legacy of years spent in dank English prisons, but as she stepped into the hall she tried hard not to limp. At sight of her a hush fell over the assembly gathered to watch the proceedings. There were few Scots among them, few friends of Mary Stuart, but even so, as every eye turned toward her, many of

them were deeply moved.

Gone was the beautiful young girl who had once ruled Scotland, a vivacious girl with boundless energy who loved to dance and sing, to ride, hunt, to laugh and flirt with her courtiers. Years of captivity had changed her drastically and depressed her bright spirit, thickened her once slim body, and atrophied her limbs. But her fierce courage shone forth as radiantly as ever that morning as she glanced at the silent crowd gathered to witness her demise. Many looked down when those amber eyes touched them, unable to conceal their emotion.

The Queen was dressed in a black gown and wore a white veil on her head. She was accompanied by those of her most faithful servants and ministers who had been permitted to stay with her to the end. From the spectators the Queen glanced at the dais where the block, the axe, and the two executioners were waiting; then, her white face inscrutable, her lips moved in prayer.

In these last moments of her life the Dean of Peterborough, a Protestant, harried her to change her religion, but Mary shook her head. From the dais she spoke calmly but strongly in a voice that carried throughout the vast hall.

"I was born into the Catholic religion and will die in it. I am settled in the ancient religion, sir, and mean to spend my blood in defense of it."

Her black gown was removed and the veil lifted off her head, then her eyes were bound. Mary knelt before the block in her crimson petticoat, but in her last moment she was not alone. Her tiny pet dog had scurried unnoticed under the voluminous folds of her skirt and now lay snuggled close with his head resting on her legs, her last comfort on earth.

The axe fell and the forty-four years of her turbulent life passed into history.

William Davison, Secretary to the Council, was arrested and thrown into the Tower. Terrified after the fact at what she had done, Queen Elizabeth made Davison the scapegoat. His crime? He was charged with exceeding his authority in delivering the warrant to Fotheringay so quickly. Elizabeth admitted that she had signed it—she could hardly deny it since her signature was on the document—but now she swore that she had never intended it to be delivered to Fotheringay, or for her Scottish cousin to be executed.

In this vein she sat down and wrote a long, impassioned letter to King James, referring to the "dreadful accident" that had befallen his royal mother, insisting that she had had no part in bringing about Mary's death. "I beseech you," she wrote, "that as God and so many more know how innocent I am in this case . . ."

The King wrote back saying he hoped she could "persuade the whole world of the same," the tone of his letter heavily cynical.

Within hours of learning of Queen Mary's beheading the whole of Scotland was in an uproar. The people marched from every village and hamlet into Edinburgh, howling in fury that King James had not done more to save his mother. He should have broken off the alliance, they cried; then Elizabeth would have been forced to spare the Queen. When darkness fell, vast mobs surged through the capital brandishing torches and screaming for justice, an eerie glow lighting up the night sky, a great dull roar like thunder even penetrating the castle itself.

High above the city of Edinburgh the King trembled in his fortress.

James was twenty years old, shorter in stature than either of his parents, with reddish-fair hair and serious gray eyes. In describing him to his royal mistress the English ambassador wrote, "He is middling of aspect but his countenance is lit with the lamp of a keen mind." Now, clad in a deep purple mourning robe, James went through the motions of weeping for his mother, a mother he had never been given the chance to love or indeed even know. His favorite courtiers, who were with him, watched and waited to see what he would do.

James stalked about his room, sorely troubled, for as well as the calamity that had befallen his mother he had also learned that day that the son of one of his most important nobles was at that moment under sentence of death in the Tower of London. His crime? An attempt to free Mary Stuart!

At the window of the privy chamber the Earl of Huntly, the young George Gordon, glanced down at the street beyond the castle grounds where the angry throng had congregated to yell abuse at the King. "Their numbers are swelling, Your Grace," he said, and added with a touch of relish, for there was nothing Gordon enjoyed more than a fight, "Methinks they mean rebellion."

This chief of the Gordon clan was as changeable and unpredictable as his grandfather who had ruled their clan in the time of Mary Stuart, but the King had an affection for Huntly, even though he was a Catholic. Huntly warned, "If on top of this Elizabeth kills Alexander Sinclair, then rebellion it will be for certain."

James stopped pacing. "I dispatched a letter to Queen Elizabeth about this matter the moment I received news of it."

"A letter?" echoed the Earl of Bothwell, nephew of

the Bothwell who had briefly been married to the dead Queen. His lip curled scornfully and, pointing at the King's mourning robe, he said, "You would do well to exchange that garment you are wearing for a suit of armor and ride at the head of an army into London town, for 'tis sure that would stand better in the eyes of your people."

James eyed twenty-four-year-old Bothwell with distaste, though there had been a time that he had liked him greatly. But Bothwell had grown arrogant and overproud and fallen into the dangerous habit of telling him, the King, what to do. "By the rood, man," James said, "'tis well for Scotland that a cooler head than thine will prevail to guide us through this dark hour. Ride at the head of an army!" he sneered. "Killing and bloodshed are ever your solutions to problems. Will that undo the deed that has already been done or bring my mother back? Will it, indeed, benefit Scotland? This country has been at peace for some long while now, when in the past peace had been a stranger to it. Nay, Bothwell, for in the end my people would not thank me for plunging them into a war with England."

"What of Sinclair?" George Gordon persisted. Alex was one of his dearest friends and he himself was quite prepared to march south if the King was agreeable. He had already spoken to the Earl of Belrose, Alex's father, and promised him his full support. Gordon was the most important Catholic nobleman in Scotland with a huge clan at his command.

But the King waved his hand in exasperation. Why, he wondered, had he to be surrounded with such hotheads when his own head was so cool? He liked Alex Sinclair as much as the others, but Alex was only one man, and his duty as King was to think and act for the good of his entire country. Just the same, he asked

himself if the letter he had written to his English cousin might have been a little more forceful. Sinclair was now a hero as far as the people were concerned, while his own image was tarnished, and if Alex were to go to the block . . .

James threw himself down behind his desk and in his own hand wrote another, more ominous, letter to the English Queen; there was a threat in that letter that hadn't been in the former, but even so, James by this time better understood the nature of his English kinswoman. He knew she might well ignore it. She was a woman, he had learned, who refused to be dictated to, not even by a King. And cunning as she was, she could say that she had never received the letter at all, or that she hadn't received it in time to save Alexander Sinclair. He knew the workings of her devious mind, and that it was common practice in England to set a date for an execution, then suddenly move it forward, especially with cases that might prove embarrassing to the Crown. This had happened often enough in the past. But . . . he had done his best, or as much as it was prudent to do.

"Seal this and have it delivered immediately," the King commanded a secretary.

Huntly and Bothwell were somewhat mollified, but Maitland, who was also in the room, glanced out of a window, muttering, "How to quell this unrest?"

James suddenly had an idea.

"Arrest the Master of Grey!" he ordered.

The Master of Grey had been one of the ambassadors the King had sent to England to plead for his mother's life—which could not have been saved short of threatening to break the alliance. Grey inevitably had failed in his mission and now became the scapegoat, the same role that the unfortunate Davison was fulfilling for Elizabeth in England. He was a figure the

people could vent their fury on in place of the King.

As they left Edinburgh Castle together, Gordon remarked to Bothwell, "We must hope that letter reaches England in time to save Alex."

Bothwell nodded. He would have liked to ride at the head of an army. Steel was more to his taste in settling disputes than paper. The King was a coward! But he, his kin, would gladly have ridden in his place. Not because he had any great love for Alexander Sinclair, but because battling rather than scribbling was the quicker way to glory.

11

The Constable of the Tower himself came to Alex's cell. Alex knew immediately that he was about to hear something of great importance. For a few minutes he dared to hope. Freedom! He was going to be released! In his mind, he saw himself leaving his hated prison and riding furiously out of London and England itself, back to the beautiful mountains and moorlands of his home, to the blessed tranquillity of the Highlands— which until now he had never fully appreciated—and once there never to set foot south of the border again.

"There has been a change," the Constable informed him. "You are to be executed at nine o'clock tomorrow morning. Prepare yourself."

The door of the cell clanged shut, and again he was alone.

Alex fell back on his pallet. Prepare himself? How exactly did a man prepare himself to die, the more so a man who had scarcely yet lived? He thought of the

farewell letter he had written to his family. Had they received it? Now he would never know. He had wanted to write to Marina also, but the guard had taken everything he had, including his jerkin, as a bribe to send that one letter, and his family had to be warned of the danger they were in. Alex was confident that his grandfather would look after Marina, and that brought him great comfort. "Ah, my love," he sighed, "that I should have to leave you so soon . . ."

They came for him a few minutes before nine the next morning. Alex, as the higher ranking of the condemned men, would die first. His request to visit Jamie Fraser so that they could say goodbye was denied.

The Queen had been adamant. There would be no public spectacle made of the conspirators this time, and the fewer who knew about it the better. Sinclair and Fraser, she decreed, would be beheaded in the yard of the Tower.

Alex walked out into the courtyard with a firm step and displayed no sign of fear. To the small group of witnesses watching him he seemed proud and unrepentant, his dark head held high. He was satisfied that the speech he had written and would deliver before he died would do honor to his clan and Scotland, if not his King. Though his young face was haggard and thin, his brilliant green eyes were as bold as ever as he defiantly scanned the group assembled to see his sentence carried out. This too, he thought bitterly, would be conducted in secret.

During his captivity Alex had had little sleep and only the barest nourishment, and even that scarcely fit to eat, and as he mounted the steps to the block he suddenly felt light-headed and was forced to grip the rail and pause for a moment to steady himself.

In that instant his whole life flashed before him. He

saw, vividly, the much loved faces of his parents and brothers and sisters and scenes from his happy childhood growing up at Castle Augusta surrounded by his clan. Then into his mind came a pair of melting brown eyes, and he heard a soft voice saying, "No one could have freed Queen Mary. You *tried*, Alexander, and that alone marks you as one of the bravest men in the land."

He straightened his shoulders and continued on up the steps, thinking, Don't let that courage fail me now . . . and don't let this all have been for naught.

Alex delivered his speech in a loud, ringing voice, his eyes not on the hostile faces below him in the courtyard but on the bright blue sky above the Tower battlements, his last sight before they blindfolded him.

As he knelt before the block, his whole being shrieked inwardly, "I want to live! I want to live!"

But he said nothing.

A tense hush fell over the witnesses, and for a moment nothing happened. Alex waited, his heart pounding like thunder in his ears. Then the executioner swung high his axe.

There came sounds of a great commotion and shouting from a door leading into the Tower. Men erupted from that door and feet thudded across the cobbles and up the steps to the platform, and the executioner was thrust rudely aside. Hands reached to wrench Alex to his feet and his blindfold was whipped off. Blinking, the young nobleman stared into the red, sweating face of the Constable.

"Reprieved!" the man shouted at him, waving a document in his face. "Reprieved by this warrant signed by our most merciful sovereign."

Alex was in shock and made no response.

The Constable grabbed him by the arm and shook

him, crying, "Ye are not to die, Sinclair, can ye not understand that? Ye are not to die!"

But neither was he to be freed.

Alex was returned to his cell, there to await the Queen's pleasure. The Tower was full of prisoners awaiting the same thing, some for more than twenty years, among them many who wished they had suffered the quicker fate instead of being made to pine slowly away in captivity.

By the beginning of March the snow had vanished and the buds of new leaves swelled in the trees. Crocuses in yellow, purple, and bluish-pink massed in cheery clumps in the garden of Cairnmore House, and the birds began to preen and sing, trembling and fluttering in anticipation of the mating season. They could smell the earth stirring, and Sir Ralph's thoughts turned to spring and the new planting season. He announced at the breakfast table, "After the meal I must go down and see what's happening in the greenhouse. Now is the time for new seeds and plants to be ordered."

Marina gave him a doubtful look as they waited for the serving girl to bring in the meal. "You must take care not to tire yourself."

"I feel fit as a fiddle!" The old knight laughed with a glance out the window to the gentle sunshine, but he whispered, "Say naught to Beech about this, mind. I won't have him spoiling this bonny day with his fussing."

Fay, a rosy-cheeked table maid brought in the meal. "Good morn to you both," she said with a smile. Setting a steaming platter of mutton stew on the table, she lifted off the lid of the dish and sniffed appreciatively, "Ah . . . now that does smell tasty!"

The instant Marina smelled the food, her stomach

lurched and she knew she was going to be sick. Jumping up, she made a wild dash out of the room and upstairs to her own chamber where she hung over the washbowl vomiting until her empty stomach tightened painfully inside her and her whole body was drenched with a clammy cold sweat. Then she collapsed on her bed, weeping. She was heartbroken.

The incident might have received more attention had not Sir Ralph himself taken ill later that morning. He was puttering about his greenhouse when he suffered a stroke, which left him paralyzed down his left side. For a week he lay near death in his room, oblivious to Marina, his son and daughter-in-law anxiously hovering over him. Then, though he was still gravely ill, he rallied a little.

One day when she was alone with him he struggled to speak.

"Don't . . . leave me, Marina. Stay, won't you . . . lass?"

"Aye, of course I will," she promised, and leaned over to kiss his wan cheek. "I wouldn't dream of leaving you, Sir Ralph."

His sunken eyes were dark with worry. "They— they might try to send you away."

Marina pressed his hand, soothing, "Nay, nay, you mustn't fret. Nothing could tear me away from you, dearling. Now don't speak any more for 'tis tiring you. I'll stay beside you, never fear."

It wasn't an easy promise to keep, through no fault of her own. Garth and Elsie were constant visitors to the house now and their sharp eyes were turned to their own advantage, both determined to guard their interests. They no longer concealed the fact that they resented Marina and would have liked her out of the house. Whenever they found her in Ralph's room they coldly ordered her downstairs, reminding her that

Beech had been hired to look after the knight and she must not interfere.

On the way home from one of these visits Elsie Cairnmore worried aloud, "Your father is far too attached to that girl! What if he has already made provision for her with his lawyer? Would you stand by and see a—a foreigner snatch away what is rightfully ours—"

"Elsie," her husband interrupted with a sigh, "my father would never do wrong by us; he is not that kind of man. We will get what we are due, dinna fash yourself."

"Aye, but mayhap not *all* we are due because of that wench!"

She was driving the cart as she always did, whether or not she had a passenger, including her husband. Now, shifting the reins to one hand, she caught Garth's arm with the other, hissing, "I tell you, she must be got out of there! You listen to me; you know I am never wrong, and I have this strong feeling that we'll be diddled by that upstart." Her bright little eyes narrowed and she went on in a lower tone, "There's the powder kept in the stables. We can have Beech see to it that a wee bit of it finds its way into her food—"

"You doited fool!" It was rare that Garth challenged his goodwife, but now he felt it warranted, and he could be firm when he needed to be. Glaring at her red face, he went on, "I declare, you would see us both hanged on the Muir of Ayr, and I for one am happy with the length of my neck the way it is. We'll get rid of the wench," he stated determinedly, "but it must be done right, with no danger to us. I've already asked Beech to try to find her a post in another house."

"She's a lady," sneered Elsie. "Your father would never allow her to soil her hands."

"My father is too ill to know what's happening," he replied.

In the end it was Beech who found a way.

Sipping a mid-morning cup of ale with the staff in the kitchen, he pricked up his ears when he heard Fay remark that Mistress Marina was taking the master's illness very hard. In fact, she said, the lass was frequently sick herself and had taken an aversion to her food. "She near-fainted at the breakfast yin morning, and the color o' her face . . . !"

The housekeeper frowned. "It sounds more to me like she's pupped."

This conversation was immediately reported to Monkwood.

First thing the next morning Elsie arrived in her cart. Almost dragging Marina out of the master's bedchamber, she thrust her into the library and closed the door.

"Ye're breeding, are ye not?" the older woman challenged.

The girl's face crumbled and she turned very pale. For weeks now—though all the signs had been there —Marina had not allowed herself to believe it. Now, with Elsie Cairnmore staring her squarely in the eye demanding the truth, she could no longer delude herself. She was going to have Alexander's child! And she confronted another bitter truth then—she would never see him again. Not once had he come to visit her in all these months or even written her a letter. He had no more interest in her, that was plain. All she had meant to Sinclair was one more brief adventure.

"Well, mistress?" Elsie prompted. "What do ye have to say for yourself?"

Marina covered her face with her hands and wept. Elsie was all concern then and pretended to sympa-

thize, clucking at her and patting her hand. She said, "That husband o' yours will be sorry now, I dinna doubt. He's done himself out o' a bonny wee son or daughter. But at least," she hurried on slyly when Marina opened her mouth to tell her the truth, "the bairn will have a name. 'Twill not come into this world a bastard, thank the blessed Lord!" And she shuddered theatrically at the idea. "Now, that *would* have been dreadful."

Elsie had a very good notion of who the father was, but it suited her purpose to ignore it, to make Marina believe that she thought the child was Stafford's. Further, she was determined to convince the girl of the wisdom of that too, and went on, "The bairn will be able to hold up its head, and so will you, hen, so there's naught to worry about on that score. But listen, lass"—she leaned forward conspiratorially—"'tis best to keep this a secret for now, do ye understand?"

Marina nodded emphatically. The last thing she wanted to do was tell anyone.

"Good! Just dinna breathe a word about it, especially to Sir Ralph. The old gent would have another stroke. And never fear, I'll arrange everything for when the time comes and will help ye all I can."

Marina stared at her through her tears, terribly ashamed now for her uncharitable thoughts about Elsie. She clutched her hand, aware that Elsie was a woman who could be depended upon to get things done. "If you knew how miserable I've been! H-how can I ever thank you?"

"You just leave things to me, Marina. I'll do the right thing by you and the bairn. Leave things to me . . ."

The goodwife returned to Monkwood in great spirits and immediately sought out her husband so that she could dictate her next move. Naturally, she had it

already all thought out.

Marina felt slightly better after speaking to Garth's wife. How surprising, she reflected, that Elsie would turn out to be the one to help her. Elsie! She was sorry for having been so quick to dislike the woman, but then Marina had discovered of late that she wasn't a very good judge of character. Never, never had she dreamed that Alexander would let her down and break his promise. Not Alex! He had been all that was shining, noble, and near-perfect in her eyes and she had trusted him implicitly. "Fool!" Marina moaned aloud. "Oh, you gullible fool!" Even Edgar, for all his faults, had not pretended to be something he was not; at least he had been honest. As for Sinclair, had she not glimpsed another side to his nature that night at the Four Doves? Aye, Marina thought grimly, she had—but she'd ignored it. Well . . . she could ignore it no longer. He had deceived her in the cruelest way possible—and she hated him now. Hated him!

Sir Ralph's condition continued to be precarious, and as time passed he fretted, worrying about his grandson and why the Sinclairs hadn't contacted him. It wasn't like them, and the more he brooded about it, the stronger the suspicion rose in his mind that Garth hadn't sent the letter he had written to them. One day Ralph managed a word in private with his doctor, a man he knew he could trust, and asked the physician to write to the Highlands on his behalf, telling them of his illness and inquiring after Alexander. "Tell him," he instructed the doctor, "that I wish him to visit me as soon as possible, and that I'll accept no excuses."

When the doctor's letter arrived at Castle Augusta in the Scottish Highlands, the chief of the clan, the Earl of Belrose, was still in London trying to negotiate for Alexander's release from the Tower, so far with no

success. Queen Elizabeth told him haughtily, "You have a comely son, Sinclair. Well I remember his handsome face about my court a few years agone, though he was only a lad in his teens then. He amused me, the young rascal, strutting about, making mischief, boasting of all he would accomplish when the time came, and I laughed with the others, enjoying him." Then she had glowered. "Little did I dream that the bold deeds he meant to accomplish included snatching my crown off my head!" She went on angrily, "He came to my court for his education, and I see now that I was too lenient with him, too tolerant with the young scoundrel. Well, Earl Belrose, I am tolerant no more. Your son will now have ample time for meditation whilst languishing in the Tower, where he will remain at my pleasure. Hopefully, he will gain wisdom during his stay there."

The earl wrote back the gist of his interview with the Queen in a letter to his countess. "She is immovable, as yet," he added, "but I am, as you know, not one to give up. I could be wrong about this, Alyssa, but deep down I sense that the Queen still harbors some fondness for Alex. I think she realizes that there's no evil in him, that his deed was more one of reckless chivalry than anything else. However, my love, 'twould be wrong of me to awaken false hope in your heart. I fear there will be no early release for our son. Elizabeth has a will of iron and Alexander's crime was a grave one; he won't get off lightly—if at all."

Alyssa Sinclair was forty-two years old and the mother of four sons and two daughters. A tall, elegant woman with a light frosting of silver in her titian hair, she was still a remarkably beautiful woman, a woman with a strong will and a mind of her own. As she liked to say, she would not have been where she was today through being timid and shrinking. She had known

much turbulence and hardship in her early days, though since her marriage to the Earl of Belrose, Blake Sinclair, she had been blissfully happy—until recently. Now she was frantic with worry about her eldest son, Alexander, but at least he was alive, and, knowing her husband as she did, Blake would not rest until Alex was freed and restored to them.

Upon receiving the letter from Sir Ralph Cairnmore's doctor, Lady Alyssa set out for Ayrshire taking her oldest daughter with her. As they traveled down through the mountains with a large company of armed guards made up of their own faithful clansmen, Alyssa had a new worry—Sir Ralph. He was the man who had made her own mother's latter years very happy ones, and she would never forget him for that. They had known that Ralph was in failing health and because of it had thought it best not to inform him of Alexander's trouble, afraid it would upset him and make him worse, for Sir Ralph dearly loved his grandson. The latest letter from Cairnmore House was very distressing. Not only was the old man worse, but demanding to see Alex as well. What, Alyssa wondered, would she tell him when they met?

Sixteen-year-old Kirstin too was deep in thought as they rode along. She had a piece of information, given to her by her betrothed, Robert Douglas, that she had never divulged to her mother. It concerned the girl the lads had brought back from England with them, Marina Stafford. "Alex would want it kept a secret," Robert had warned her. "Mind, say nothing to your parents."

Lady Kirstin was troubled, thinking that the secret would be out once they reached Cairnmore House. Perhaps, she reasoned, it would be best to prepare her mother now. Better that than it coming as a shock. The girl brought her horse closer to the older wo-

man's. "I—I have something to tell you, my lady mother."

"Oh?" Alyssa smiled at her daughter. The girl was even taller than she was and had the Sinclair dark hair and eyes. Kirstin was a pretty lass and would wed her sweetheart the following year. It pleased the countess to realize that it was a love match, not just a marriage for dynastic reasons. "Why do you blush?" she chuckled when color rose in the girl's face. "Welladay, I think I am about to hear some delicious gossip! Out with it, then. I can hardly wait," she said, amused by her daughter's expression.

Kirstin gave her a sober sidelong glance. "'Tis about Alex."

Then it all came gushing out, leaving Alyssa stunned. "You say . . . you say they took this English girl out of her husband's charge and brought— brought her to Cairnmore House!" She couldn't believe it. "To Sir Ralph's?"

"Aye." Kirstin swallowed. "The woman's husband nearly beat her to death. She's only young, Mother; just a young girl; the lads felt sorry for her. You see, she was desperate to get away—so they brought her to Scotland."

Alyssa didn't know what to think. She lapsed into silence, turning it over in her mind, her first thought that Alex and his friends had committed yet another crime. One minute she was furious with her son, the next, well . . . she could almost understand. She herself had been beaten near to death often enough in her youth to appreciate what the poor English lass must have felt like, and Alex, for all his faults, had a soft heart. Something struck her then. "Kirstin, the lass must be wondering what has happened to Alex. Mayhap that was why Ralph demanded that he pay him a visit." She looked hard at her daughter as another

thought struck her. "There's nothing between your brother and this English girl, is there?"

Kirstin looked away. "I . . . how would I know, Mother?"

The one bright spot in Marina's life was that Sir Ralph was steadily improving. Even his doctor was pleased with his progress. Marina did as much for the old man as she could and read to him every day, and sometimes entertained him by singing and playing the lute. Surprisingly, Garth and Elsie no longer seemed to resent her spending time with the knight; even Beech made no objections when she ministered to his needs. There was a pleasant atmosphere in the house now, even when the "Monkwood crew" came to visit. "Och, ye do him good, lass," Elsie praised. One day she took Marina aside and solicitously asked how she felt, then said, "I'm making the necessary arrangements and have the midwife all picked out. We've a cradle at Monkwood and plenty o' baby clothes on hand. Now, do ye want to breast feed, or should we start looking for a wet nurse?"

Things could have been much worse, Marina told herself when her spirits drooped, when she cried herself to sleep at night, hating Alex, yet yearning for him too. The family, the ones who knew about her condition, were rallying around. And Elsie, dear Elsie, had been so good to her, bringing over fresh farm eggs, milk, meat, vegetables, and fresh fruit for her to eat. "You take care of yourself, now," she kept saying. "Do nothing to wear yourself out."

On a Friday night Marina and Sir Ralph were playing chess in his bedchamber when they heard a loud banging on the front door. Beech, as if on cue, flew to draw back the bolts ahead of the other servants and the new arrivals crowded into the hall. "Up

there," the valet whispered, and pointed up the stairs. "It's the second door on your right."

Then Beech scurried to hide.

Sir Ralph dropped the chess piece in his hand when he heard the sound of many feet pounding up the stairs. "Tarnation!" he cried peevishly. "If that's the Monkwood rabble come back to pester me . . ."

"Nay." Marina shook her head, her heart suddenly fluttering as she rose from sitting on the side of the bed. The Monkwood "rabble" had already visited Cairnmore House earlier that day and, since Ralph was improving, would hardly come twice. But it had to be *someone* in the family or at the very least close friends for the servants to risk opening the main door in the dark of night. Many robbers roamed the countryside and this property was secluded, so no one was admitted unless well known to the family. No, Marina reasoned, a sudden flush of excitement flooding her cheeks, whoever had opened the door to the visitors must know them well.

Alex! Who else could it be but Alexander and his friends? It was typical of Sinclair to barge into the house like this when least expected, bringing the other lads with him. So . . . he had come back for her just as he'd promised he would! Marina was deeply ashamed of herself now for having doubted him, vowing it would never happen again.

She turned to face the door, her heart thumping, desperate hope in her eyes, and instinctively put a hand on her stomach where the new life was growing inside her, wondering how Alex would react to the news that he was going to be a father. Oh, what wondrous relief to know that her love would be beside her when her time came, that her baby would have the affection and protection of a young, vigorous sire!

Marina took an eager step forward as the bedroom

door banged open—and she froze. Edgar Stafford
stood there, twelve armed henchmen behind him. At
the sight of her husband, Marina's eyes widened in
shock, a sickening lurch of disappointment almost
crushing the breath from her lungs. "You!" she
gasped, horror ballooning up inside her like a dark,
poisonous cloud, the joy and anticipation she'd felt
only a moment before instantly extinguished in her
heart. For an instant she felt stupefied wondering how
in God's name he had found her, then came a
bounding surge of terror when she realized the predic-
ament she was in.

Edgar gestured to her grimly. "Come with me,
woman. You'll pay dearly for all the trouble you have
caused me."

"Nay!" Marina screamed, even as Sir Ralph sat bolt
upright against his pillows, roaring with surprising
strength, "What means this intrusion? Get out of my
house, knave! You are in Scotland now and . . ."

But Stafford ignored the old man and marched
boldly into the bedchamber, waving for his men to
follow, ducking adroitly when Marina seized a heavy
brass candlestick off the mantel and hurled it at him
with all her strength, then fled to the other side of the
huge tester bed, placing it between herself and her
husband.

Ralph Cairnmore tried to protect Marina. He strug-
gled from his bed and made a valiant attempt to reach
his weapons rack on the wall, yelling for his servants
to come to his aid. But Tar, Stafford's squire, struck
him a vicious blow to the side of the head with the
butt of his pistol, then tossed his unconscious body
back on the bed, and Edgar grabbed his wife.

Screaming, Marina fought with him desperately,
biting, scratching, kicking with all her might as if
fighting for her very life. Death, she thought, was

preferable to returning to England and a miserable existence as a prisoner inside dour Baxton Hall. The thought of her innocent baby being born there almost drove her mad.

Even as she wrenched at Stafford's beard and bit the stubby fingers trying to grip her, Marina thought bitterly of Alexander Sinclair, the man who had used her, discarded her, and carelessly left her to her fate—aye, and her hapless baby with her. Oh, God, how she hated Sinclair at that moment. And what a senseless fool she had been to allow herself to be so readily taken in. Because of Sinclair she and her child were now at the mercy of a monster, a man who would take steps to see that she never slipped away from him again.

After a moment or two of trying to subdue her, the enraged husband caught Marina by the shoulders and banged her head against the wall, knocking her out. Then he threw her over his shoulder, crying to his men, "Let us depart," and they all hurried out of the room behind their master, even more nervous and anxious to leave this house and Scotland than he was.

The house servants cowered behind large pieces of furniture downstairs, terrified and confused at what was happening, but Beech had concealed himself at the other end of the house, closed up inside a broom cupboard. Against thirteen brawny men armed with pistols and daggers, the staff felt helpless. All they could do was peep mutely from their hiding places as Marina was carried out of Cairnmore House and tossed over the back of a horse, and in minutes the kidnappers were thundering away into the night in the direction of England.

Garth and Elsie arrived later to be told by Beech that Sir Ralph was dead. Garth gathered all the servants in the hall and issued instructions. Unbe-

knownst to them, he said gravely, they had been harboring a fugitive in Marina Stafford, a runaway wife, which could land them all in serious trouble. So, if anyone made inquiries about Marina—anyone at all, he stressed—they had to say that she had decided to return to her husband of her own free will once she discovered that she was pregnant with his child.

When Alyssa Sinclair finally arrived at Cairnmore House, that was the story she was given when she inquired about the English girl. "The lack of children seems to have been the cause of the trouble with the couple," Elsie told her with a sigh. "Now that she's pregnant, Marina feels certain that everything will be fine."

- *The Reckoning* -

12

North and South, 1590–1591

The young women sat on the fragrant grass while the children frolicked around them. In the hot July sun the air shimmered and the daisies and clover thick in the meadow blurred in a haze of pink and white, waving gently in the breeze. Downhill a silver thread of river meandered lazily to lose itself in the dark green pine woods, and in the beech trees nearby birds sang rapturously to the cloudless blue sky.

"Marina," said Gwen Porter, fanning herself with her wide-brimmed straw hat, "we really must go to the fair. 'Tis one of the biggest events in the county. Everybody goes."

"Edgar doesn't," Marina sighed.

Her friend made a face. "Mayhap not now, but I'm told he used to. Anyway, sweeting, he'll let you go with me," Gwen said confidently. "You know how he likes my Bert and thinks highly of the Porter family. He won't refuse."

Marina wasn't so sure. She glanced away to where the children were playing, her Clare, almost three years old now, and little Bobby Porter, and hoped fervently that they would never know a moment's sadness and unhappiness in their lives; that they would always be as carefree as they were today.

She had changed a lot in the last three years, outside and in. All the promise Marina had shown as a very young girl at Chiltern Castle had now come to radiant fruition. Her body was supple and shapely, her smooth skin glowed, and her thick golden-blonde hair seemed lit by pale fire in the bright afternoon sunshine. To her friend Gwen Porter she was the most beautiful creature she had ever laid eyes on, and Gwen thought it was a dreadful waste that Marina had to be tied to grumpy, elderly Edgar Stafford. To Gwen's way of thinking she should have been married to a prince, just like in the fairy tales. In a way, Gwen worshiped Marina, who was everything she herself was not—a refined lady, educated and cultured, and lovely enough to take one's breath away. As for herself, well . . . she was coarse oats by comparison, she often thought. She had been born a farmer's daughter and now was a farmer's wife, uneducated, uncultured, and far from bonny with her plump body and mud-brown eyes and hair, yet for all that quite content with her stout, good-natured husband and sturdy little boy— far happier than the tragic Marina, for all her many outstanding qualities.

Oh, it was a terrible shame and sometimes made the warmhearted Gwen quite angry. "Marina deserves so much better," she had remarked more than once to Bert. "*So* much better! If only something could be done about it . . ."

"Now, now, lass, enough of that," her husband had cautioned. "Things are what they be, and let that be

an end to it." But he added tenderly, hugging this woman he loved so much for all *her* outstanding qualities, "You are just a foolish romantic, my girl. Life is nothing like the pretty tales you used to listen to at your mother's knee, and you ought to realize that by now."

But there was a stubbornness in Gwen—her only fault as far as her husband was concerned—and she stoutly maintained, "Nay, Bert, I still say that Marina deserves a better life than she's getting now with that mean old weasel—"

"Keep your nose out of it, woman!" he warned. "We want no trouble with Edgar Stafford."

The two women had been friends almost from the time that Marina returned to Baxton Hall, and the Porters were their closest neighbors. There had been Porters at Brokenbridge Farm just as long as Staffords had resided at the Hall, and the two families had always been friendly and supported each other during times of danger or distress. Like her mother and grandmother before her, Gwen was a midwife, so it was natural that Edgar Stafford should turn to her when the time came for his wife to give birth. It astounded Marina that Edgar had managed to convince himself that Clare was his baby, and he would hear nothing to the contrary. After the child was born he said, "You have done your duty, wife, and I shall trouble you in the bedchamber no longer. But there is one thing you should know. Never think of leaving me again! If you do, it will be the last you will ever see of the little one."

Marina believed him. She was trapped.

He never hit her again or touched her in any way. To his way of thinking, he had the heir he had longed for for forty years and the birth of Clare gave him status. He basked in it, his manhood fully vindicated at last,

and in some ways it softened him a little; he also became slightly more sociable, anxious as he was to show off his heir. For the same reason he spent a little coin to improve the shabby appearance of his Hall and even permitted Marina to purchase cheap material at the mill to make clothes for herself and the little girl. Sometimes he even bought toys and sweetmeats for Clare, and he made a great show of spoiling her in front of others. But deep down, Marina was certain, he didn't love Clare any more than he loved her, the mother; he knew Clare wasn't his. Sometimes when she caught him watching her with her baby, Marina shivered. Edgar seemed to have overcome his violent tendencies, yet there was always that threat . . .

Had she not had her friend Gwen—who knew the whole story—Marina sometimes felt she would go mad.

When the children ran up demanding a tidbit, Gwen suggested, "The little ones can come with us to the fair. Think how they would enjoy that."

Marina shook her head regretfully. "He would never allow it."

"Not even if *he* came with us?" Her friend nodded in the direction of a brawny young fellow who sat perched on a fallen beech tree idly whittling a piece of wood. His name was Darby and he was Clare's bodyguard, a man who never left her side and even slept outside the door of her room at night. Stafford had also rid himself of his old retainers and hired younger, more vigorous men to watch over his property. Marina knew that her husband didn't trust her and was taking no chances.

She presented each of the children with a pear, at the same time pulling her daughter down on her knee, smiling tenderly into a pair of huge, sparkling green eyes. Soon to celebrate her third birthday, Clare was a

beautiful child with doll-like features and glossy titian curls that already tumbled halfway down her back. Now she puckered up her tiny sugar-pink mouth and gave her mother a smacking kiss.

Marina hugged her fiercely, wishing she could take the little girl to the fair, but her husband would never allow it. Soon people would be pouring into Wilton from all over the county for the annual event, including gypsies, cutpurses, and other questionable types out to fatten their own coffers from the merrymakers. Edgar had a morbid fear of losing Clare, and with so many strangers flocking into the area he would want to keep his "daughter" safely locked up behind the newly reinforced walls of Baxton Hall.

"You still have three weeks to work on him," Gwen said with a grin. She reached to touch Clare's soft curls. "Where on earth did this glorious red hair come from?"

Marina shrugged. She had never known her own parents, but Lady Maud had once told her that her father had been dark and her Danish mother as fair as she was herself. As far as she knew, there were no redheads in the family. Even Alexander had been very dark. Alexander—dear God, she never wanted to think of *him* again!

When the door of her Presence Chamber opened to admit a clerk, the Queen caught a glimpse of bright plaid garments in the crowded anteroom beyond.

"Am I never to be rid of these Sinclairs?" she cried in exasperation. "Marry, but I believe they mean to camp in that chamber yonder for the remainder of my reign."

Cecil, her Secretary of State, hid a smile. He was white-haired and stooped now, aging even faster than his royal mistress. "I fear they might, Your Grace," he

sighed. "They bring yet another petition from their King."

She had been receiving these petitions for over three years. God's blood, she railed inwardly, why couldn't they give her some peace? Had she not spared the life of that young scoundrel, Alexander? Surely they couldn't expect her to pardon him completely. Elizabeth glowered in the direction of the outer room and was suddenly awash in self-pity. She felt like rushing out to shout at them, "Let me be! Can you not see that I'm in mourning? Why should I make you happy when I, a Queen, will never be happy again?"

Elizabeth had aged drastically in the last two years, and her temper, always quick and stinging, was now at the stage where even she found it difficult to control. All the joy and zest had gone out of her life following the death of Robert Dudley two years before, and there was hardly a moment of the day when she did not think about him. Now the only person capable of lifting her spirits—even for a moment—was the handsome young Earl of Essex, but Essex, as she well knew, was of a very different caliber than Robert Dudley, and considerably less tractable. As often as he made her laugh, he made her scream with anger, but either way she felt alive only when he was in her company.

It annoyed the Queen that Essex had made friends with some of these Highlanders during the time they had hung about her court ranting and raving and having the audacity to threaten to make war on her. She would fain have had them all thrown into prison, even sent to the scaffold, had Cecil not prevailed on her to stay her hand. The situation was dangerous enough as it was, he impressed on her during the times she came close to losing her head, and they dare not provoke them in any way. Elizabeth knew this well

enough, in her sane moments, but the more she saw of them, the harder it was to keep a grip on her sanity. She especially dreaded meetings with the Earl of Belrose himself.

And to think that Essex had flouted her and made friends with them! At times the nerve of Robert (his very name had endeared him to her) oft took her breath away. He had a penchant for doing the unexpected and setting himself up as a champion for lost causes, when by rights he should have been applying himself to *her* affairs instead of frittering away his time and energy on foreigners.

And now another petition from King James! That she had not expected. The King had recently married, and she had assumed that all his attention would be directed at his bride, Anne of Denmark. The Queen's heart sank. "Did my Lord Sinclair bring the petition himself?" Though Elizabeth would never have admitted it, she had become a little afraid of Blake Sinclair and found it harder and harder to meet his burning dark eyes and took great pains to see that she was never alone with him. He was a devil! And each time they met she could feel him trying to bend her to his will . . . and each time Elizabeth found it harder to resist him. He was determined that his son would be set free. Now he was trying to tamper with her mind! Looking at him, she saw the seeds of her own destruction in his fiery dark eyes. He didn't say to her, "I beg you to set my son free," she remembered. Instead, staring at her, he said, "You *will* set my son free." Devil! Lucifer! Nay, the Queen suddenly made up her mind, she would not see Blake Sinclair again. She dare not . . .

With a start she realized that Cecil was talking to her.

The Earl of Belrose had returned to Scotland, he

said. His presence was demanded by the King on the occasion of his new Queen's coronation.

Elizabeth frowned. "But . . . that was several weeks ago. Do you mean to tell me that Sinclair has not come back here?"

Her minister nodded slowly. He seemed worried. Ominous rumors had come to his ears, he told her, which might account for the fact that the earl had not returned. "'Tis said they will be patient no longer; that other clans are fully prepared to back them up. Now even the people clamor for the King to take action, and this time they have given James an ultimatum, saying they will listen to no more excuses from England. To them Alexander Sinclair is a hero."

The Queen felt a jolt of alarm, but she was also angry. In spite of the way she felt privately, she had always taken care to treat the Sinclairs with courtesy and respect and always promised to give each petition her full consideration while stressing that she could do nothing, of course, without the approval of her Council. She managed to imply that while *she* might be inclined to leniency, her ministers might not be so disposed. In this way she had kept them dangling, taking pains never to commit herself one way or the other, yet instilling in them that element of hope. At the same time, she made it clear that any show of armed aggression would ruin Alexander's chances of freedom.

In this way she had kept the Highlanders at bay.

"I will not be intimidated!" said the Queen. "What are they but a bunch of mountain savages."

Cecil replied quietly, "Methinks they have the King and people behind them."

Outside in the antechamber Robert Devereux, the Earl of Essex, spoke urgently to the Sinclairs. He was huddled in a window embrasure with David and his

uncle, Jason Sinclair, out of earshot of all the other
people crowded into the room, waiting patiently for
an audience with Queen Elizabeth. Essex had taken a
great liking to the Highlanders, and, young and impet-
uous himself, he easily identified with the imprisoned
Alexander. Like Alex, he would far rather have been
out somewhere engaged in a challenging mission than
simpering and jockeying with the other courtiers who
clustered like buzzing drones around the Queen.
These men disgusted him. He felt nothing but con-
tempt for the outrageous lies and sickly-sweet flattery
they dripped into the royal ear. Not he! Though he
admired the Queen for other reasons, he would never,
he vowed, stoop to such base tactics to win her favor.

Now Essex was excited, as he always was when
some new challenge presented itself. He confided, "I
have thought of a way whereby Alexander might be
released. And 'tis a way that will not cause Her
Majesty to lose face." He grinned wryly, adding, "She
greatly mislikes having to back down once she has
taken a stand about something."

David and his uncle looked at each other, wonder-
ing if they dared put any stock in the rather erratic
Essex. They liked Robert, but had observed that he
attached himself to causes and just as quickly lost
interest when they showed no sign of speedily being
resolved. But on the other hand, they remembered too
that this young man had taken the Queen's fancy as no
other had done since Dudley; she was amazingly
tolerant of Essex's whims and was inclined to indulge
him.

David, tall like the rest of his family, but fairer,
gripped his hand. "If you succeed, Devereux, we will
be forever indebted to you."

"Wait here." Essex grinned, then swaggering a little,
left them and boldly entered the Presence Chamber

185

without waiting to be announced.

Cecil glanced up with a frown, marveling at Essex's impudence of barging in without waiting for leave to enter, but the Queen's glum expression brightened at the sight of the handsome young man with his waving auburn hair and dark eyes that reminded her of another Robert's. She held out her hand to him. Essex kissed it with more than his usual enthusiasm, and Elizabeth beamed. She might be fifty-six years old but she still had a great appreciation for comely men; it was a comfort to her to have this Robert to gaze upon now that she couldn't have *the* Robert. Essex had dash and flair; he sparked up any room he entered with his restless energy and brilliant smile. He drew the attention of many women. Later, he would rue the day that he had ever attracted the attention of a Queen.

He interrupted the business of the day by engaging Elizabeth in a few moments of idle chatter telling her all the latest gossip—while Cecil, who disliked him, waited impatiently. Then he brought the conversation around to the gifts that the Queen had recently sent to Scotland on the occasion of King James's marriage, and shocked her minister by tossing off lightly, "They were fine enough, I suppose, but nothing out of the ordinary."

Elizabeth's smile faded and she looked miffed. The presents she had sent to Scotland had cost a small fortune. She had chosen them with special care, anxious that hers should outdo all the others her cousin would receive, particularly those from France and Spain. Now she felt a spurt of anger to hear them criticized and made light of, but Essex didn't notice and hurried on.

"'Twould have been better to have given something more unique," he said. "Something other than the expected thing. Yours will not be much different, I'll

warrant, than those sent by Spain and France."

Cecil, listening, was appalled at his temerity. Even the royal eyes were glowering at him now, though the Queen was listening closely. How dare he suggest such a thing, she fumed inwardly, when she had taken such pains to make her gifts stand out? There were times, she thought darkly, when she wondered how she continued to suffer the slights of this impudent churl.

Devereux blithely roamed the chamber waving his hands in his expressive way, completely oblivious to the stir he had made. "'Tis the unusual that's remembered and more appreciated. If you could have found something that, say . . . appealed to the King in a more *personal* sense it would have been better, or something that would have appeased some special desire . . ."

Suddenly he swung around to face the Queen as if an idea had just occurred to him. "Your Grace, I have thought of something unique! Why not pardon the Scotsmen at present imprisoned in the Tower? Would that not bring delight to the King's heart, considering the severe pressure he has been under from his people to have these men released? What a splendid gesture of goodwill that would be, far and away above all the mundane presents James has received!"

There was dead silence in the room. Cecil almost choked in his indignation that anyone, especially this rash young upstart, should make so bold as to try to tell the Queen what to do. But Elizabeth smiled thinly, thinking, Essex, you are as transparent as glass. You will never make a good courtier, I fear. You fool, do you not realize that I'm aware of your friendship with the Sinclairs? And to try to manipulate me thus . . . !

She studied him from eyes that were hooded now, reflecting, It is well for you that I cannot find it in my heart to take offense—but take care, my incautious

young rascal, that the day doesn't come when my heart turns hard and cold.

"Well?" Essex demanded impatiently. "What think you of that idea?"

"You may leave me for now," the Queen replied curtly, snubbing him. "I have important business to discuss with my minister."

The two women wandered through the crowds who had flocked from everywhere to Wilton Fair, the largest in northern England. The fair overflowed the common into the field beyond, and in the bright afternoon sunshine the women looked about and saw a sea of gaily painted caravans, carts of every size and description, and hundreds of tents pitched far back where the field met the woods down by the sparkling water of the Tweed. Farmers had brought their livestock to be judged—cattle, sheep, pigs, and goats—and one of Bert Porter's fine bulls had taken a blue ribbon. Even Stafford had come to watch the judging and to purchase fresh stock for his estate, but once these events were over, both husbands lost interest and made ready to return home.

Gwen had no intention of going home just yet. The evening was always the most exciting time at the fair. Then all the lights would be lit; there would be games, displays of dancing, juggling, acrobatics, and sword-swallowing, and Gwen was determined not to miss it; she was equally determined that her friend would not miss it either, though Marina was too proud to ask her husband for anything.

Bert Porter glanced at Stafford and shrugged. "Ah . . . let them stay. We can leave a couple of men to protect them and bring them home. 'Tis all just harmless fun and merrymaking anyway, and Gwen knows most of the locals here."

Edgar gave in. He was even prevailed upon by Gwen to part with a few coppers so that his wife could play a game or buy a bauble or two. Stafford wasn't worried. He had little Clare behind the tough walls of Baxton Hall, his assurance that her mother would return to him. "Be home by nine of the clock," he ordered.

Once their men departed the women were gay. The plump Gwen wore her best pink silk gown, for this was an occasion! Marina was dressed in cool blue muslin dotted with gold, with blue and gold ribbons in her hair and a posy of primroses tucked into the dipping bodice of her frock. They clasped hands and laughed, delighted at the way they had "managed" Edgar, and feeling like conspirators they set out to have a wonderful time, wending and weaving among the throng, staring at everything.

There were stalls selling china and pottery, ribbons and lace, paintings and crude sculpture and just about anything one could want. They peered curiously at jars and bottles containing medicine said to cure everything from gout to toothache, and unguents for the ladies claiming to make even the ugliest face a vision of beauty. They laughed over the antics of a dancing bear, the tricks of a tiny monkey in a bright red jacket and top hat, and, shivering with delicious anticipation, ventured into a tent to see the "only woman in the world born with four breasts, two fore and two aft."

Music rang out and the hawkers had to shout to be heard over the noise of flutes, drums, clashing cymbals, and the sheer din of the crowd.

"Enter here and see a beast-man, half goat and half human!" one roared.

Another cried, "Know the future and be prepared! Madam Astra is the best in the land, consulted by kings and queens and noble folks. Come in, come in!

189

Would you stumble blindly into the future?"

Excited, Marina dragged Gwen into the tent, where a slatternly old gypsy woman sat huddled over a filthy pack of cards, the shelter reeking with sweat and alcohol. So drunk was Madam Astra that she could scarcely open her eyes, nor could they understand a word she said to them. They left in disgust and soothed their annoyance by buying a huge curling block of taffy. "I predict," said Marina, "that this sweet will make us very fat."

Giggling, they continued on, their long-suffering guards following along behind. Gwen whispered, with a glance over her shoulder, "They'll tire of this soon enough. Wait"—she fished in her basket and came out with a coin and tossed it back to them, saying, "You must be very thirsty. Buy yourselves a drink of beer."

By the time the lights came on in the evening they had lost their drunken retainers. "My, are we not clever?" Gwen laughed.

The weather was perfect for the fair, warm and still and slightly sultry, and as the torches flared, adding to the heat, both women removed their gauzy shawls and folded them away in their baskets, enjoying the night air touching the skin of their chests and shoulders which now were largely bare. Gwen in particular noticed the many masculine glances that had been directed to Marina all day, and more now that she had removed her shawl, unconsciously offering more of herself to view. Throwing a sidelong glance at her friend, Gwen saw that she looked flushed and beautiful and happier than she had ever seen her before. Her golden hair was slightly rumpled, with damp little tendrils curling around her face, and her large dark eyes sparkled in the torchlight. For these few hours, Gwen knew, Marina had forgotten the misery of her

life at Baxton Hall, and for that her friend was glad.
"If only I could help her more . . ." she thought again.
"If only she could be got out of that dismal fortress
she inhabits. Oh, why didn't Edgar Stafford die!"

They moved on through the crowd, most of whom
were strangers, Marina with a stuffed toy for Clare
tucked under her arm, drinking in the sights and
smells of the warm night and wishing fervently that
she never had to return to the Hall. And she might not
have! Aye, many was the time she had contemplated
running away once more, taking the few coppers she
had hidden and disappearing where Edgar could
never find her—but for Clare. Never, never would she
leave her daughter in the clutches of that man! Nay,
she would die first. Stafford had never touched her
again, but the threat of violence was always there, and
now it was not just herself who was at risk. He
knew—she could see it in his mocking eyes—that
Clare was not his child. Now Marina lived in dread
that one day he would explode; would try to hurt the
little girl. If that day ever came, she promised herself,
she would kill him.

The sound of lively music attracted them and they
stopped to watch a dancing display, Marina dully
conscious of time slipping away and remembering
Edgar's warning to be home by nine o'clock—and it
was eight now.

A platform had been roped off for the dancers and a
thick crowd of spectators surrounded it, the two
women wedged in among them, every eye turned
toward the stage. Almost every eye. It was Gwen who
sensed they were being stared at. Turning her head,
she met the eyes of a man standing perhaps twenty
feet away, he too hemmed in by the throng.

Yet he stood out, being far taller than those around
him. Everything about him was black—his clothes,

191

hair and beard, the shadowy hollows of his eyes—and Gwen, who feared very little, shivered at the intent way he was watching them. There was something frightening and devilish about the stranger, and Gwen was sorry now that the guards weren't with them, realizing with a pang that now they would have to go home alone.

13

The dance ended and the crowd dispersed, scattering in all directions, and though Gwen tried to keep track of the dark stranger she lost sight of him in all the people milling about. She stood for a moment scanning the common, but except for the areas lit by flares and the hurricane lamps at each of the booths, the rest was dark. Behind the stalls and caravans, under the trees that dotted the field, there were a thousand places where an evil-doer could hide, ready to pounce on two women foolish enough to travel the country roads alone.

"That man . . ." Gwen clutched her friend's hand. "I liked not the looks of him."

Marina peered at her. "What man? What are you talking about?"

When Gwen explained, Marina burst out laughing. Gwen was forever claiming that men were staring at them—at her, Marina. She seemed to think that every

193

fellow who crossed Marina's path had either amorous or evil designs on her. Marina was used to it by now and usually ignored it.

"Come on," she chuckled, "we must be getting home before Edgar sends out a search party to look for me."

But Gwen hung back. She felt safer mingling with the crowd. "Mayhap we should try to find the guards," she suggested, but again Marina laughed. It would take them hours to find their escort in a fairground still bustling with people, she pointed out, and if she didn't arrive home at the appointed time! Well, she didn't have to tell Gwen what would happen.

The two women left the common, Gwen reluctantly and more nervous than Marina had ever seen her, muttering that the stranger had had the look of the devil about him and had given them the "evil eye." She was fairly quivering with fear as they hurried along, especially once they left the lights and noise of the fair behind them and moved into the quiet countryside with its thick hedges along either side of the track and clumps of elm and oak trees, thick blackness under the swaying boughs. A half-moon like a sly, winking eye hung in the night sky and shed faint silver over their surroundings, but making the shadows where it couldn't penetrate all the more menacing.

"Dear God!" Gwen gasped and bumped against Marina when a rabbit darted out from a ditch and bounded away into a field with a flick of its white-tipped tail. Both women nearly swooned when, as they were passing along a wall, a horse suddenly put its large head over the top, almost touching Marina's shoulder. When they recovered from that shock and hurried on, Gwen constantly throwing glances behind them, they eventually came to the crossroads near an

ancient broken bridge. Marina lived a few hundred yards to the north, and Gwen about the same distance to the south. Here they stopped and looked at each other, both by now slightly breathless.

"Come home with me," said Gwen, "and Bert will take you up to the Hall."

"Don't be silly. 'Tis only up yon road—"

"What of that devil?"

Marina was a lot more afraid of the devil who awaited her at home, and shook her head. "Go." She grinned, giving her friend a little push. "I'll warrant I can beat you home."

They started off in opposite directions, both running, but as soon as she glanced back to see that Gwen had rounded a corner and vanished from sight, Marina slowed to a walk, in no great hurry to return to Edgar Stafford. Would that she didn't have to go back to him at all! It was a beautiful night, she mused with a glance about, so warm and still, the countryside bathed in silvery moonlight. The novelty of being alone, away from all the spying eyes at the Hall, filled her with a wonderful sense of exhilaration and freedom. Walking slowly, a defiance seizing hold of her, Marina sniffed the moist night air and listened to the rustling of the small wild creatures that lived in the fields and woods of the region—and fervently wished she were as unfettered as they were. It wasn't only Edgar who might explode, she thought resentfully, wondering how long she could stand to be shackled; she herself might! If only she could find a way to get Clare out of Baxton Hall; a way to support her daughter and make a home for them both, then she would be happy. Perhaps not *blissfully* happy, but well enough, far better than she was now.

The track Marina was on dwindled and led to a narrow path through a stand of birch trees, dappled

with moonlight and shadow, one that made her think of a spangled fairy glade in the quiet of the night. Smiling, she caught a fleeting glimpse of a bushy tail as a fox sped across her path, on the hunt for his supper, and there were rabbits aplenty and the scurrying and rustling of countless other small animals going about their business.

All this was natural and she had no fear, no presentiment that she was being followed. She was almost out of the woods; the path stretched before her into the moonlight, when she heard from the darkness of the trees behind her, "Marina . . ." a low voice calling her name.

She gave a violent start and spun about, peering into the woods, thinking that Bert Porter might have come after her to make sure she got home safely, or even that it could be Edgar himself. But the fine hair on her arms and the back of her neck rose quivering; her mouth had gone dry and her flesh suddenly felt cold.

Marina almost bolted when a tall figure stepped out of the shadows and walked up the path toward her, but there was something about that figure, the way he moved, the tilt of his head, that kept her riveted to the spot. Even when he came out into the light Marina didn't recognize him. The stranger was very dark and gaunt, bearded, forbidding, every inch the devil that Gwen had talked about earlier.

Then Marina saw his eyes.

"Holy mother . . ." she breathed. "Alex!"

She felt a great burst of joy. All these years . . . the wondering, the yearning, the twisting, savage knife of rejection grinding in her heart . . . yet here he was. He had come back to her! "Alex!" she repeated, taking a few steps toward him, tears rushing into her eyes. Then she stopped.

It wasn't Alex at all. It was a dark, gaunt-faced stranger who resembled him. The hope in her heart plummeted, and, peering at him in the moonlight, Marina felt the fine hairs rise at the back of her neck, thinking that it might be his ghost.

She wheeled around and bolted up the path toward Baxton Hall, too terrified to look back, even when she heard footsteps pounding behind her. She opened her mouth to scream when she heard him gaining on her, but her throat felt tight and clogged and only a choked cry came out. When Alex threw his arms around her and swept her up off her feet, Marina almost swooned, both her voice and her limbs frozen, numbed with horror. With a swift glance around, Alex picked her up and carried her deep into the trees.

Gradually, as they plunged through the underbrush, with moonlight slanting down through the branches, shafts of silvery light interspersed with darkness, Marina became aware that the hand clamped over her mouth was warm, as was the lean body welded to hers as he gripped her firmly. "Don't be afraid," he said. "I'm real enough. Are you not glad to see me?"

Alex pressed her down on a thick bed of leaves and leaned over her, smiling. "Marina! God, how I've longed for this moment. Don't be afraid," he repeated with a little laugh. "Did you think I was a ghost?"

In the cool, pearly incandescence dappling the woods they stared at each other, Alex with avid interest and joy and Marina in rigid terror. Now she knew that he was no spirit—but he still wasn't the Alex she remembered. Peering up at him, her heart fluttering, Marina saw that his face was haggard so that his cheekbones stood out and there was a bitterness to his mouth that hadn't been there before. His eyes were sunken and he looked far older and harder than the man she had fallen in love with. He seemed

197

like a stranger to her.

Waves of shock went through her. Long ago Marina had convinced herself that she would never see him again and must accept that, and though the ache had lingered on, she had resigned herself to her loss. Sinclair hadn't wanted her. She had only represented a brief little adventure in his active life. Now . . . this man, this caricature of Alexander had come back. It was cruel, horrible!

He leaned over her, his back to the moonlight. "My God, how beautiful you've become." Alex examined her flawless creamy skin, her dainty nose, unblemished mouth—all perfection where once she had been battered and bruised, potentially scarred for life. "Marina!" he breathed, his eyes hungrily roving her stiff face. "My love, tell me you've missed me as much as I have you?"

She cleared her throat. "You—you've changed," she remarked hoarsely.

"I'll explain. But now—"

Without warning, Alex bent his head and kissed her passionately, as he'd yearned to do for the last three years. Marina inhaled sharply, she pushed against his chest as she felt his hard, seeking lips ravish hers, felt his beard scrape her skin, and recoiled at the way he clutched her almost desperately, his body against hers strong, demanding. Alex hardly heard her muttered protests or felt her trying to push him away as he plundered her mouth, kissing her smooth cheeks, her throat, eyes, ears, overcome at finding her in his arms once more. After a moment he whispered, "You haven't forgotten how it was with us, surely?"

Every single day she had tried to forget! It had been the only way to save her sanity. As the shock of Alexander's reappearance receded a little, Marina was reminded of what this man had done to her. "I *have*

forgotten," she lied. "It's all in the past."

Alex chuckled huskily and kissed her again, molding her to him, desire surging as he breathed in the sweet warm scent of her, a scent he well remembered. But the moment Marina felt his desire, her anger sharpened—even as she felt something stir and leap up inside her. Changed Sinclair might be, lean and almost Satanic he looked, but his body was still young, hard, compelling, in such contrast to the gnarled, decrepit husband she was tied to, a man who could never satisfy her youthful cravings or fulfill her in any other way either. Finally Marina jerked her head away, reminding herself that Alex was to blame for the situation she was in. Had he kept his promise to her, she would never have come to this pass, nor would her baby be in the clutches of Edgar Stafford.

"Why did you come back?" There was no welcome in her tone at all. She pushed him roughly away and sat up, throwing a nervous glance around the woods. She was late coming home already. At any moment Edgar or some of his guards might appear, and if they saw her with Alex! "You must leave here at once!" she hissed, her stomach beginning to churn with fear. "Go while you can, for if my husband finds you here he will not hesitate to kill you."

When Marina made to rise, Alex caught her arm. He felt crushed by her cold reception. Perhaps, he reasoned, it had been foolish, but he had expected a warmer reception than this. He understood that Marina was very confused, and he meant to explain, though every moment he tarried here in England he was risking his life. Three years was a long time, and much had happened to both of them in the interval. Now his main concern was to ascertain if Marina still cared for him at all.

A week ago he had stopped at Ayrshire on his way

south. He had been highly skeptical when he listened to Garth and Elsie's story. But Elsie stoutly maintained, "I think the girl realized her mistake in running away from her husband. She was so anxious to go home to tell him that he was going to be a father at last. Marina seemed to feel that would change everything between them; that it would make a great difference to their marriage." Alex had not really believed Elsie, though Marina herself had told him that Stafford's lack of an heir had accounted for much of his violent behavior. But she had also sworn to Alex that she had never lain with Stafford at all; that their marriage had never been consummated.

"Why in God's name did you go back to Stafford?"

Marina tried to tug her hand away. "I must get home now!"

"You had a child, didn't you?" Alex asked her softly. "Is it mine, Marina?"

Now she knew why he had come back! Somehow, doubtless from Garth and Elsie, Alex had found out about the baby, and had come to claim her. Knowing him as she did, he was quite capable of storming into Baxton Hall to try to take his daughter, aye, even if it meant a battle with Edgar to get her. And it would. Her husband would as soon kill Clare than allow her to be taken from him.

"Edgar is the father," Marina blurted, "so you have wasted your time in coming here."

He flinched. "Then you lied to me. The marriage was consummated?"

"Obviously!" She felt a stab of guilt, one that was quickly overcome when she recalled her misery of the last three years. And there would be more than misery to bear if she didn't get home at once!

This time when Marina tried to pull her hand from his, Alex let her go.

There was a poignant moment when he turned into the light and gazed up at her, poised and ready to flee, and the moonlight was reflected in his eyes. For just that second he looked like the old Alex, and Marina felt her heart being wrenched apart, felt herself crumble, weaken; then she turned and ran away, tears blinding her.

Alex stood on the path and watched her racing away from him without a backward glance, the night breeze lifting her blonde hair to float around her slender figure, wraithlike in the moonlight. More beautiful she was, he mused, far more beautiful . . . but not the Marina he had known. Or had he ever really known her at all?

He was devastated. For more than three years, all during his time in the Tower, a dream had sustained him and kept him from losing his mind. A thousand times he had envisaged this meeting, holding her, kissing her, telling her how much he had missed her—how much he loved her. Now Marina had shown no interest in him whatsoever. Not once had she asked where he had been for the past three years. And she had lied to him about her marriage. "Go home," he told himself. "Forget."

In the courtyard of Baxton Hall Marina came upon Edgar and his men about to mount their horses, her husband shouting orders in a harsh, angry voice. When he saw her he roared across the yard, "Where have you been, woman? Did I not warn you to return before nine of the clock?"

Rushing over, Stafford grabbed her roughly and shook her. "What means this?" He glared down at her pale face, then threw a searching look over her shoulder wondering about her escort. "What happened to Ben? Why did he not return with you?"

Marina's greatest fear was that Edgar and his men would ride out in search of Ben and come upon Alexander instead, which could bring disaster to all of them.

She hated Alex Sinclair for carelessly putting them at risk.

"Ah . . . Ben became separated from us in the crowd," she stammered, shaking. "But I—I sent a lad who knows him to tell him I'd started for home . . . Gwen and I together—"

"*Late* home!" His thick fingers bit into her arm and Marina cringed, certain he was going to strike her. Instead, he thrust her through the heavy door into the hall—and in the candlelight saw her pallor.

"What has happened?" he asked suspiciously, his mean little eyes crawling over her. "You look as if you have seen a ghost."

She had, or felt as if she had. Hastily Marina made up a story about eating too freely of the cheap food at the fair and having to stop on the way home to be sick. And indeed she *did* feel ill, even Edgar could see that. The shock of seeing Alex again; the terror generated by the thought that Stafford would find them together, all of it made her feel sick and light-headed and faint. She had to grip the back of a settle to steady herself.

"Hummm . . ." Scratching his beard, Edgar examined her closely, and those eyes of his missed very little. It constantly amazed Marina that although he was now sixty-five years old, he was as fit and acute as ever, all his faculties—or almost all—still serving him well. She was so frightened by the tense, explosive atmosphere in the hall that she broke out in an icy sweat, though the room was warm and stuffy, and feeling queasy, stuffed the knuckles of her right hand against her mouth.

"Get you up to bed," he ordered finally, and waved to the stairs.

Fortunately, Edgar never troubled her in the bed-chamber, and once the door was closed and she was alone, Marina expelled a long, shuddering breath. She sagged against the door feeling too weak to take another step. Her legs were shaking beneath her and her skin was clammy, her stomach tightened into a hard knot. She felt like a woman who had just walked a tightrope and, by a miracle, managed to reach safety on the other side.

If Edgar had caught them together! If he even suspected!

After a moment Marina ran to the window and peered down into the courtyard, her heart fluttering wildly. She would not put it past Edgar to send his men looking for Ben. But there were no horses down below now, though she spied Tar and two of the others idly chatting by the stable door, so it was obvious that they were not going out after all.

"Thank God!" Marina whispered, her stiff shoulders slumping in relief.

Her eyes were drawn in the opposite direction and she scanned the moonlit countryside wondering where he might be, the shock of Alexander's sudden appearance tonight still shuddering through her in waves. But Marina had no need to wonder what had brought him back. He had made that quite clear. While in Ayrshire he had heard the news that she was pregnant—and suspected that he might be a father. She could well imagine the proud nobleman in him loathing the idea that any offspring of his should be brought up in dank Baxton Hall, another man—an Englishman!—claiming to be the father.

She went to her bed and sat down, her hands clasped tight in her lap, praying that she had managed

to convince Alex that he wasn't the father and that he would leave now and never come back.

Marina undressed and got into bed, but with scant hope of sleeping. One moment she raged against Sinclair, the next her starved senses reminded her of how it had once been between them. The touch of his lips tonight on hers, the urgent hardness of his body, brought everything back. Now she lived like a nun, the only love she knew that of her little one—but was it enough? She was still but twenty years old, and though she tried to ignore it, there were yearnings; hopeless yearnings. Marina tossed and turned, feeling them clamoring in her now, hot and insistent and desperate for release. "Why did you come back, you devil?" she moaned. "Why? Why . . . ?"

14

A somber, dark figure stood at an upstairs window in Wilton Inn, watching the people making merry in the street below, the whole town like a carnival because of the fair. The inn faced the town square and a flute player sat upon the statue of a horse, like Pan, piping madly while the people danced around him in the flare of torches, most of them very drunk. High up as he was, Alex had a good vantage point and his sharp eyes picked up a pair of cutpurses fleecing the crowd that had gathered to watch the dancers. Whores, also drawn to the town by the large influx of potential customers, were approaching men boldly, determined to make the best of the situation.

One young strumpet spied Alex standing by the window. She threw him a smile, then pulled down the low-cut bodice of her gown, brazenly displaying her wares, two large white breasts that looked moonlike in the light of the torches. She made a sign, first pointing

to herself, then jabbing a finger at the inn, offering to come upstairs if he were agreeable.

For a fleeting second he was tempted. She seemed young, at least from where he stood, and not uncomely, and he hadn't made love to a woman for more than three years. He was also tense and angry, disappointed and bitter, and to lie with a woman would have brought him some ease. But he had never had recourse to turn to a whore in his life, nor would he start now.

The urge passed and he moved back from the window and stretched out in bed, his arms behind his head, and contemplated the events of the last few weeks.

A month ago Alex had been released from the Tower. He had been let go with the warning that he must never set foot in England again. His family, indeed all who knew him, had been shocked by the change in him, but they had no conception of how ghastly conditions were in the Tower of London, nor the dire sights and sounds one heard there, or even what it felt like to live with the thought that Queen Elizabeth could again change her mind and send one to the block after all. The lady was nothing if not fickle.

No one knew better than Alex that the unconvivial hospitality of the Tower had aged and hardened him; that the carefree youth he had once been had died there. Had his character not toughened to the texture of tempered steel, he would have gone mad or expired in prison as many another had done.

His worried family had taken him back to the Highlands to recuperate, and he would have been there still had not Alex found it impossible to rest until he discovered what had happened to Marina; discovered for himself, and he was desperate to find

out if he was the father of her child.

Now, brooding about their meeting tonight, he tried to accept the fact that her feelings for him had changed with the passage of time, and that perhaps he had been foolish to hope they had not. Also, that the child she had given birth to had been Stafford's after all, proving that Marina had lied to him that night at the Four Doves.

Alex knew he should return to Scotland immediately and forget her. Every hour he spent in England was fraught with danger, though by now he could render a very good imitation of the southern accent, especially that of the North of England, which had some of the burr of his own native tongue; that coupled with his radically altered appearance—should by some chance he encounter Edgar Stafford—lent him a certain amount of anonymity, though he was still taking a grave risk. Aye, he told himself soberly, he should forget Marina; forget the past and go home. He had a full and challenging life awaiting him in Scotland. The King himself was said to be anxious to have speech with him once he had sufficient time to recover from his ordeal in England.

But the more Alex mulled over the events of the evening, the more convinced he became that there was something not right with Marina's present situation. Her reaction to his sudden appearance had been more one of terror than of loathing, though she had certainly been startled at how different he looked. Yet . . . Alex supposed it was natural enough for a woman to be alarmed at the thought of her husband finding her with another man, the more so a man who—in the eyes of Stafford—had once abducted her. If they had indeed reconciled and were now living happily with their child, the heir Stafford had always longed for, then it was understandable that Marina

would want nothing to spoil things . . . but Alex still had the feeling that something was wrong.

When he had first arrived in the area three days ago and cautiously reconnoitered Baxton Hall, Alex had immediately spotted many significant changes. First, he noticed that the wall around the manor, crumbling when he had last seen it, had now been carefully repaired and strengthened. He saw that the old guard of aging men were gone and that younger, more able fellows had taken their place and that there were more of them than in the past. Also that the downstairs windows of the house had been glazed and reinforced with iron bars. Baxton Hall now had all the markings of a prison!

Gripped by a surge of excitement, Alex sprang up and began to pace about his chamber, his mind working feverishly. Something was amiss at the manor, he felt it in his bones! That combined with Marina's almost hysterical fear when she saw him tonight almost convinced him that she was being held there against her will; she and the child both. And that baby . . . perhaps in truth a Sinclair! A Sinclair who by rights should have been under the protection of its father and clan in the Highlands of Scotland, rather than being held captive—much as he had been—in an English prison! That, Alex told himself grimly, he would never tolerate. He could not live content while a bairn of his languished behind bars.

In six days the Wilton fair would end and the town would empty out and return to normal. When that happened, strangers in the area would become much more conspicuous and questions might be asked. Then it would be dangerous to tarry; more than dangerous—foolhardy! He was not so anxious to lose his head or go back to the Tower, the more so since, and he had to recognize this, his assumption concern-

ing Marina's life now could be completely wrong.

Well then, six days, Alex promised himself, then back to Scotland.

Edgar sat across from his wife at the board and wolfed down his breakfast with his usual rude gusto. As always, he was too intent in stuffing his mouth to waste time in conversation. They were having brook trout that morning, one of Marina's favorite dishes, but she sat opposite her husband distractedly pushing the fish back and forth across her plate.

Finally, once his own plate was empty, Edgar noticed her lack of appetite.

"What's ado?" he asked gruffly, gazing at her from under his brows. "Is your stomach still uncertain?"

"Aye," she nodded. "That it is."

Shoving his own pewter dish aside, he snatched hers and quickly polished off the contents while Marina watched him uneasily. The man was incredible, she reflected. Sixty-five and he ate like a young buck a third of his age. She had once likened him to a gnarled old oak tree, well-seasoned and tough, that only improved with the years, and Edgar was that way still. He was never sick, never tired or lacking in energy, and though much of the raiding that had once taken place back and forth across the border had lessened now that England and Scotland were at peace, Stafford still indulged in the odd cattle-thieving foray to the north. In the frequent disputes over land with the next county, Edgar was always in the thick of it, always ready to do battle. He could handle a horse, sword, or pistol better than any of his men, most of whom were less than half his age.

Marina studied him covertly, detesting him, but in awe just the same. There he sat sturdy and compact, rugged and grizzled—indestructible! He was a man of

principle in his own narrow, inflexible way, and as fanatically religious as ever. That aspect of his character, she supposed, had saved herself and Alexander from even more trouble, because Edgar had confided to her shortly after he brought her back to England that, but for his principles, he would have reported both of them to Sir Francis Walsingham at the time they vanished from Baxton Hall.

"Think of it," he'd said. "You claimed to be the Queen's bastard and Sinclair attempted to free Mary Stuart. To Walsingham there would seem to be collusion in that. Be glad, woman, that I have no love for the Protestants nor would lift a finger to help them in any way. 'Tis the only thing that saved you and your Scottish lover from destruction."

He knew that the child was Sinclair's, though it suited him to pretend otherwise, and when the baby was born he named her Clare, after his mother, commenting with a sly, sidelong look at Marina, "She's a Stafford through and through, and like the beasts of the field, my kind would kill their young before they would allow others to interfere with them in any way. 'Twould be well if her mother never forgot that."

Marina never had.

Now, watching him stand up and buckle on his belt, which held a dagger and his favorite pistol, all Marina's terror of the night before came rushing back when she thought of what would happen if Stafford knew that Alex was in the area.

He threw a quick glance at her before he went out. Never ill himself, Edgar was impatient with it in others. "Take some essence of peppermint," he advised carelessly. "'Tis good for settling the belly. Or have Gwen Porter make you up one of her possets if she comes to visit."

"W-where are you going today?" Marina inquired nervously.

Stafford raised his brows, surprised that she should ask. Normally Marina showed no interest at all in his activities. He saw that she looked wan and upset and wondered if she might be sicker than he'd thought and perhaps wanted to know where he would be in case she had to reach him quickly.

"I'm off to make sure that none of the gypsy crew who came to Wilton for the fair have camped on my land," he growled, and after thinking for a moment, added, "But I'll leave Tar at the Hall. Send a message by him if you need me."

Still he hesitated, studying her. "Shall I fetch Dr. Gregory?"

The last thing Marina wanted was Dr. Gregory, he of the keen eyes and sharp intellect, a physician who had acquired an enviable reputation for excellence in the county and had a special interest in diseased humors of the mind. He it was who treated the mighty Northumberland and all the other important people in the region. He also spent time in research at the insane asylum at Newcastle.

"Nay, nay, it will pass," Marina replied quickly.

Edgar nodded and left.

Slowly Marina let out her breath, warning herself to be careful, but she was in a high state of agitation all that day wondering what Edgar and his men would find during their tour of the estate. She couldn't bring herself to set foot out of the house and refused to let Jillie, the nursemaid, take little Clare out into the sunshine to play, making the excuse that since she herself felt ill there might be bad humors lurking in the air, contamination that could hurt the child.

Marina was quivering with trepidation when Stafford returned for supper that early evening and anx-

iously examined his face when he stomped into the hall, vastly relieved when he seemed in good spirits.

"What of the gypsies?" she ventured.

Stafford roared with laughter, his small eyes glittering. He had found none on his own property, he replied, but had come upon a band of them camped in the field of a neighbor. And he had helped his neighbor chase them off.

"And a fine bit of sport we had with them too," he chuckled. "When we surrounded them and started to set fire to their caravans, their leader—a young fellow —had the temerity to challenge us. He was a proud one and eager to show off in front of his women, no doubt, but he wasn't so proud once we were finished with him."

Marina didn't want to hear what had happened to him, but Edgar told her anyway, and with relish, his tale interspersed with bursts of laughter.

"You know how the tinks like to dance?" Marina nodded, wanting to cover her ears. "Well, we forced the leader to dance a merry jig by firing shots at his feet, and Christ's blood, we thought he'd go on forever. But finally he collapsed. I put a shot through his head then to put him out of his misery, and as a warning to the others against trespassing. Then we burned their wagons and drove the rest off the property." He wiped his streaming eyes on his sleeve. "Filthy, scurvy crew. Let that be a lesson to them."

Marina was horrified. "You—you killed one of them?"

He nodded. "And I had every right, too. They were on private property."

"And . . . and there were women and children among them?"

"Aye, they are known to breed like rabbits, but they

are less than human. They manage as well in the open as the beasts of the field."

She hated him and suddenly it boiled over. Marina jumped to her feet and faced up to him for the first time since she had come back, too upset to consider the consequences. "*You* are the beast, Edgar Stafford! Oh, God, how could you do such a thing? 'Tis so heartless and cruel, so—"

"Close your mouth, woman!" he thundered, his craggy face suffused with angry color. "These gypsies bring filth and disease, they will steal whatever they can lay their hands on, including children. Do you want to see your daughter end up a slave in a tinker camp, eh?"

"They would never—"

"They would!" he roared. "And don't gainsay me, wench. They are well aware of the law against trespassing and should not have broken it, but . . ." he dropped his voice and went on ominously, threateningly, ". . . there are always those who will go too far, who *ask* to be punished severely, and rarely are they disappointed."

Later, in her chamber, Marina felt a chill at the way she had lost her head and defied him, but it was getting harder and harder to control her hatred for him all the time, though she must for the sake of her daughter, if not herself. She blamed the sudden appearance of Alexander Sinclair for losing her grip over her emotions, feelings she had tried hard to hide from Edgar ever since she returned to Baxton Hall. One thing she could now be fairly confident about—and it brought Marina some relief—was that Sinclair had left the immediate vicinity. Hating gypsies as he did, Edgar would have thoroughly scoured the estate in his hunt for them, and would have found Alex had he

been about, and God help the Highlander if he had! she thought with a shudder. God help her too!

For three days following her night at the fair Marina refused to leave Baxton Hall, turning a deaf ear to her daughter's demands to go out, preferring her mother's company to that of her nursemaid. It was more awkward when Gwen Porter tried to coax her into taking a picnic with the children by the river, but still Marina refused, mumbling that she still felt weak and unwell. Gwen walked up the track between the two properties to visit her every other day and they had become the best of friends, whispering their secrets to each other and offering mutual love and support. Both knew that they could count on the other not to betray their confidences and the women had become very close—but still Marina couldn't bring herself to tell Gwen about her visit from Alexander.

It was best, she thought, to pretend it had never happened.

Gwen fussed over her and promised to mix up a herbal medicine noted for correcting stomach upsets. "Funny," she murmured, examining Marina closely, "we ate the same things at the fair and I haven't been affected. If you are not improved by tomorrow, I should have Edgar send for the doctor. With all the outsiders in town, there's no saying what you might have picked up."

Later that day Gwen sent a servant over with the medicine and a message for Marina to walk down to visit her next day if she felt better. She proposed they spend the day making jam from all the berries that had ripened, as they had done each year since their friendship began. Edgar came in that evening smacking his lips. He had been talking to Bert Porter and heard that tomorrow was to be jam-making day at

Brokenbridge Farm. "You will go, surely?" he said with a hopeful look at her, and when Marina didn't reply, cried, "God's soul, girl, what ails you? Bigod, I weary of this mopping and sighing. 'Twill be worth giving Dr. Gregory a leg of lamb to have you sorted out. I'll send Tar with a message for him now."

"Nay! N-nay . . . I feel better." Marina looked at him directly then, her expression strained, faintly challenging. "I will go to Brokenbridge if you wish it."

A thought skittered through his mind and vanished. Stafford stared at her for a moment, puzzled at the odd way she was looking at him, then he shrugged. "And why would I not wish it? By the Blessed Virgin, you make no more sense to me than a pig in a poke."

Early the next morning Marina set out to walk the quarter mile to Brokenbridge Farm, a basket containing a sack of sugar, cinnamon, and other spices for flavoring over her arm, covered by a clean white napkin. Marina had dressed simply in a floral cotton gown of mauve, white, and green, her long blonde hair fastened at the nape of her head with a thin satin ribbon.

The bountiful lushness of full summer was upon them and the grass waved thick in the meadows, the trees heavy with shiny green leaves, all still sparkling with dew in the early morning sunshine. There was a minty freshness in the air and the perfume of wild roses from the pink and white blossoms blooming in the hedgerows bordering the lane, and under the trees, in the shadowy places, Marina spotted the damp heads of thousands of bluebells and here and there the waxen white gleam of a wood lily.

A large hare sat motionless in the field as if carved from stone, and rabbits bounced along the path ahead of her, soundless and soft as thistledown and scarcely

displaying any fear, almost as if they sensed that Marina would never harm them. From the swaying boughs of the oaks and elms she walked under burst a sweet chorus of birdsong, falling on her head like a benediction. The sun slanting down through the trees threw a shower of gold at her feet, like coins carelessly scattered across the path ahead.

Soon Marina came to the place where she had met Alexander. It was darker here and the woods were hushed. She stopped and glanced around, her heart fluttering, recalling with a shiver the way he had called her name, the ghostly sound of his deep voice coming to her out of the darkness, like the past coming back to haunt her. Then the sight of him—so different! The shock, the mixture of terror and anger, the bitter and the sweet, all clashing inside her with the force of a thunderbolt. Mayhap . . . mayhap it had only been an illusion, a trick of the mind.

With another nervous look about, Marina hurried on out into the open, glad to feel the sunshine on her face, warming her suddenly cold skin. Her mind went back to that time of waiting in Ayrshire after he left for the Highlands, but promising to return soon to visit her. He loved her, he vowed, and like a fool she'd believed him. Then, as time passed and Alex failed to appear or even write to her, hope had died a cruel death inside her and she was forced to confront the fact that he had deserted her. By then Marina knew that she was pregnant with his child.

Had Sinclair only kept his promise to her she would not be at Baxton Hall now, both she and the baby at the mercy of Edgar Stafford. Never, never could she forgive Alex for that! Marina brooded bitterly. Because of him, her little one was in the grip of a monster.

She crossed the old broken bridge over the stream, the boundary that separated Stafford land from that of the Porters, and soon reached the big graystone farmhouse itself. The kitchen was separated from the house by a kind of causeway, a prevention against fire, and there she found Gwen already hard at work surrounded by pails and baskets of berries. The heat in the room was stifling though all the windows were wide open, and the lady of the house sat at an ancient yellow deal table, flushed and sweating, her hands and lower arms stained a reddish-purple.

Gwen looked up with a bright welcoming smile. "Oh, you've come. I wasn't sure you would. Then you feel better, sweeting?"

"Aye." Marina returned her smile and set down her basket. "That medicine you sent me worked wonders." She glanced around. "Welladay, but 'tis like a furnace in here, and promising to be hot outside too. Why is it, think you, that we always pick the hottest days to make the jam?" she asked with a grin, taking a long striped apron from her basket and tying it on.

Jam making was usually a cheerful affair, though hot and sticky, and they normally laughed and chattered all the while, and to please the menfolk and children always ended by making tarts and pasties with the surplus berries, delicious when served with a pitcher of thick, fresh cream. But try as she might, Marina's heart wasn't in it that day and her mind kept wandering, so that soon she was nodding absently in response to Gwen's gossip, unable to think of much to contribute herself. Each time her friend asked her if she was sure she was all right, Marina roused herself to fresh effort, but finally, by mid-afternoon, Gwen caught Marina's hands when she tipped a kettle of bubbling jam into a row of stone jars. She pushed

217

Marina down on a stool and poured her a cup of lemonade. "Drink that," she said briskly, "then get along home. You are not fit for this work today. Nay, don't argue," she added quickly when Marina opened her mouth to protest. " 'Tis just about finished anyway and Nelly can clean up the mess. I'll stop over to see you tomorrow."

Marina nodded. "I feel unusually weary." And small wonder, she had hardly slept at all the previous night!

"Ride home on Tassel," Gwen suggested, offering her mule, but Marina shook her head, grinning ruefully.

"I'm not *that* unfit. 'Tis hardly any way."

Marina's share of the jam had to cool and set before it could be transported and Edgar would call with the cart for it later, but Gwen tucked a still-warm jam tart into her basket, carefully covering it with the napkin, chuckling, "That will sweeten him up enough for tonight."

It felt cool outside after the sweltering heat of the kitchen, and as she walked up the road some of the fuzziness vanished from Marina's head. It was four o'clock in the afternoon and the sun was working its way into the west, long pale gray shadows moving down from the hills across the ripe golden corn in Porter's fields, the woods up ahead dark against the pink wash of the western sky. Staring at the woods, Marina felt the pace of her heart quicken. Would she ever be able to walk through them again, she asked herself, without feeling that tingle of agitation, half dread, half excitement? She could feel it starting up in her now, though she still had to cross the broken bridge that separated the two properties. When she reached it, her boots unnaturally loud on the cobbles

in the quiet countryside, Marina paused for a moment, as she always did, to gaze down into the amberlike water where one could occasionally spot a fish or two. But that wasn't the reason she tarried. She needed to gather up the courage to take that path through the woods, thinking that it would be darker in there now.

Staring into the stream, her mind far away, some flicker of movement in the shadows under the arch of stones caught her eye—and suddenly she saw him standing stock-still under the bridge.

Marina sucked in a breath that rasped loud in the stillness. Her heart seemed to stop for an instant, then swelled to bursting in her chest. Terrified, she threw a glance back the way she had come, then ahead to Stafford property, and finally back at the figure waiting under the bridge.

"Blessed Jesu . . . What are you doing here?" she moaned.

"Come down, Marina."

"Nay! Are you mad?" She took a step back from the parapet, and had her legs not been so weak, would have turned and run.

"Then I will come up," Alex threatened.

"Don't! God's love . . . wait."

Panting, her legs like jelly, Marina ran off the hump-backed bridge and half-slid down the embankment in her haste, her basket with the newly baked tart tumbling out of her hand into the stream. She hardly noticed. Her feet squelched the soft mud at the edge of the water as she stumbled along the bank and plunged into the shadows to join him. Alex was all in black as before, his face whitish in the gloom and his eyes faintly gleaming. Marina stopped two feet away, quivering with rage.

"What do you want?" she demanded breathlessly. "How dare you taunt me like this! We have nothing to say to each other, Sinclair, and if you don't leave me alone I—I shall tell Edgar—"

He wrenched her into his arms and crushed her mouth in a savage kiss.

15

The touch of Alexander's lips on hers was like tinder tossed on a fire long-since tamped down. Marina felt a spark, then a flame blaze up inside her, and cool reason fell before the onslaught of intense emotion. Once she had exulted in the arms of this man, the man who had first awakened her to the ecstasy of love, only to take that love away, denying her what her mind and body craved.

For a few wanton seconds Marina felt herself carried back in time. She returned his passion, more wild now than tender. Without conscious thought her arms rose to curl tightly around his neck, her fingers plunging into his thick black hair, her grip on him frantic as she held his head firmly to hers while greedily savoring his lips. The instant she felt his probing tongue, her mouth opened to him eagerly, and when Alex rammed her against the full length of his aroused

body, Marina instinctively welded herself to his hardness.

A convulsive shudder passed through her. It was as if every cell in her body shrieked, urging her to seek appeasement, and she moved against him, her breath coming fast, a shameful desire drowning out every other consideration. For more than three long years she had lived a life of dismal sterility in Baxton Hall. Now, suddenly, her whole being was vibrantly alive. But when Alex raised his head for a moment, his gaze burning over her heated face in unconcealed triumph, Marina came back to her senses abruptly.

He chuckled, "I see you have not forgotten."

Marina lashed back and slapped his face.

Still grinning, Alex seized hold of her again and forced her down beside him on the jumble of tumbled rocks under the bridge, one arm like a vice around her, the other gripping her wrist when Marina made to raise her hand again.

"I think we have much to say to each other," he said, his eyes taking in every detail of her lovely flushed face, the smoldering dark eyes, lips moist from his kisses. "I want answers to my questions, Marina, and I warn you, I'll keep coming back here until I get them."

"You'll get nothing from me!"

"Ah, but I already have," he mocked, and swiftly, before she could turn her head away, again crushed her lips, his hot, thrusting tongue invading her mouth until she thought she would faint from the force of the violent desire it engendered. One thing hadn't changed, she thought bitterly. Sinclair *still* had the power to arouse her sexually. But that was mere lust. Mentally she hated him for the state he had left her in.

He drew back after a moment and smiled at her, then laughed softly at the fierce way she was glowering

at him. "Surely you won't insist now that you came back here willingly?" Alex sobered as he added, "If you will admit the truth, something might be done about it."

Marina tossed her head disdainfully. "What can you do here, Sinclair? This is England, not the Highlands of Scotland. I went with you once to my sorrow. You must be mad if you think I'd do so again." Her eyes glowed with resentment as all her ire came pouring out. "You made a promise to me in Ayrshire and broke it, so don't think you can vanish from my life and return whenever you please. Why would I go anywhere with a man who had once abandoned me? You are a scoundrel, Sinclair, an arrogant adventurer—"

"I was in prison," Alex said bluntly, "for the past three years."

Marina gaped at him. All her anger disintegrated. Prison! Never once had that possibility entered her mind.

"Why?" she whispered.

She was stunned when Alex explained what had happened, how on his way home from Ayrshire he had run into an ambush set up by Walsingham's agents, and had been taken back to England to stand trial for leading a conspiracy to free Mary Stuart. In growing amazement Marina heard that he had been found guilty and condemned to death, but had been reprieved at the block itself. "They didn't release me," Alex went on, his voice hollow when he spoke about his mind-destroying incarceration in the Tower. "I was held there until a month ago, when finally they let me go."

That explained the great change in his appearance! It also explained—and her heart soared—why Alex hadn't come back for her. Marina almost threw her-

self into his arms and promised to make it all up to him because, fantastic as his story sounded, she was inclined to believe him simply because of how he looked, far different from the old Alex she had fallen in love with.

But it wasn't that simple. She had Edgar Stafford and the safety of her daughter to consider, and neither by word nor deed could she encourage Alex in any way. He was too rash and daring, too impulsive and determined. If she gave him as much as a hint of the sadness and pity she felt—for both of them—she trembled to think what he might do.

Hardening her heart, and reminding herself that it was too late for them now, she said, "I cannot believe that Walsingham would have risked going into Scotland to take you illegally. Queen Elizabeth would never have allowed it. It would have put the alliance at risk." She rushed on while she still had the strength to do so, "How would King James have reacted to one of his own nobles being kidnapped on Scottish soil? Nay," she shook her head, "I cannot believe it."

"Look at me, Marina?"

Reluctantly, she did.

"Am I the same man you once knew?" A faint, rueful smile touched his lips. "The Tower of London has a way of leaving its mark on a man."

She could have wept for him then as her eyes moved over his face. Oh, he was still very attractive in a lean, hawkish way, but the marks he spoke about were very apparent. It hurt her deeply to see how he had suffered. But so had she! And if she encouraged Sinclair now, then so would her daughter! That, above all, must never happen. What good would it do them if Alex barged into Baxton Hall in his reckless way and all three of them were killed? The thought was chilling, instantly dampening the amorous feelings

she had had moments before, aye, and the ones that lingered still when his compelling green eyes met hers.

"Is the bairn a lad or a lass?" he asked her softly.

Her nervousness increased at mention of the babe, who at that moment was firmly in the clutches of her husband, and who was never allowed to go anywhere without her well-armed bodyguard beside her.

"My child is a girl," Marina replied stiffly.

"And does she look like her mother?" The gentleness had crept back into his voice, and the hand on her arm seemed to burn through the cheap muslin of her gown.

"Nay"—she shook her head—"methinks she more resembles her father."

"Stafford?"

She nodded, and almost broke down then and wept. But at mention of her husband all her anxiety came bounding back. She turned to Alex and said fiercely, "What do you think Edgar would do if he found you here?"

"I'm not afraid of Edgar Stafford," he sneered.

"Listen to me, Sinclair." Marina swallowed the tightness in her throat and made herself go on. "Whatever there once was between us is finished. Do you understand? We were both young then and—and foolish in many ways. Now I am happy with my husband and child. You must accept that and go away and never try to contact me again."

Marina had half-expected Alex to plead with her, try to coax her into changing her mind, perhaps reaffirm the love he once felt for her, which would have been gratifying. It would have been something to cherish ever afterwards, something that might have made life at Baxton Hall a little more bearable, to think that she had the undying devotion of a handsome nobleman like Alexander Sinclair.

Instead, he threw back his head and laughed.

The sound of that mocking laughter brought a deep, burning flush to Marina's cheeks and an even deeper disappointment to her aching heart. Further, it was insulting. Far from getting down on his hands and knees to beseech her to change her mind, Sinclair was gazing at her with something like contempt in his eyes.

"Well," he drawled, "if this must be goodbye, then we should part in the proper manner."

With that he jerked her hard against him and his mouth, rough now, showed her no mercy as he sought to prove to her that things were far from over between them and that the contentment she professed to enjoy with her husband was a lie. Marina angrily tried to fight him off, but it was useless. Leaner he might be, but the arms that crushed her against him were like bands of iron; she felt her back would break if she continued to hold herself so rigid, so she allowed herself to go limp with the knowledge that it would soon be over and she would be rid of him at last.

It soon proved to be a mistake.

Bending her back in his arms, Alex plundered her mouth as a man will when a raging thirst is upon him, his tongue burning a path into her mouth, his hand closing over her breast possessively, as if it had been fashioned for him alone. His experienced fingers searched and found her nipple, and soon it was peaking the bodice of her gown, eager for closer attention. Marina uttered a choked cry that was soon silenced under his hot, devouring lips, lips that tasted her mouth, her ears, and trailed a path of fire down the arched column of her throat. Then, while she moaned and quivered, hopelessly trying to free herself, Alex wrenched apart the neck of her gown and lifted one round white breast free of confinement. Bending his

226

head to it, he gave it the honeyed attention it craved, his tongue rasping and circling, teasing and tantalizing—and suddenly all the fight went out of Marina, a burning need taking its place.

Abruptly Alex let her go. Having made his point, he now regarded her mockingly, but he too had his pride and never in his life had he needed to force a woman, or even coax her. Nor were furtive moments stolen in an enemy camp his idea of wooing. Furtive skulking about struck Sinclair as demeaning.

He eyed Marina as she angrily fastened her gown and said, "I think this cannot be goodbye." Then he startled her by asking, "Do you know the ruined priory on the old Wilton Turnpike?"

She was too ashamed of her wanton response to him to answer.

"Meet me there tomorrow at two o'clock, or if you cannot get away then, at the same time the following day." He caught her chin and raised her face to his, his eyes grave now as he added, "I will wait for you until then, Marina, but no longer."

She wanted to cry that he could wait forever for all she cared, but something in his expression warned Marina that he meant exactly what he said; that this would be the last offer he would make her.

"If you come, we will decide what must be done to free you and the baby. But if you don't"—she shivered at the finality in his eyes—"I will go back to Scotland and you will never see me again."

Without another word Alexander rose and walked away, leaving her sitting alone on the bank of the stream, and when Marina finally had the strength to climb up to the bridge, he had vanished.

She stood gazing about her, a hand pressed to her lips where she could still feel the burning imprint of his mouth. Marina knew then that she had just been

given an ultimatum. "Oh!" she muttered aloud, "the arrogance of the man!" Not a word from him that he still cared, yet he brazenly expected her to follow where he led her, regardless of the risks. But then that was quite in keeping with the character of Lord Alexander Sinclair.

Slowly Marina made her way home, leaving her basket behind. It was stuck in the reeds at the edge of the stream, completely forgotten.

It was only when Edgar inquired how the jam-making was coming along that Marina remembered dropping the basket, but strangely, she wasn't perturbed. She could always retrieve it in the morning, she thought with a shrug. Strangely too, she felt detached as she watched her husband gorge himself at supper. Even the piglike sounds he made left her impassive.

In the nursery afterwards she romped with little Clare before giving her her bath and tucking her into bed, tasks she preferred to do for the child herself. They played their usual game. "Where did Clare get her beautiful red curls?" Marina smiled, winding a silky tress around her finger.

"From the fox fairy," came the prompt reply.

Marina tweaked her nose. "And where did this tiny button come from?"

"An imp."

"Aye, and her mouth?"

"I dunno, I dunno!" the child giggled, her eyes wide.

"From the sugarplum!" her mother answered and pounced on her, kissing the petal-soft lips puckered up to meet her own, the only kisses—until recently—that she had enjoyed for the past three years, and of course with Clare it was different.

As she did every night, Marina took the child in her

arms and rocked her to sleep. Clare had a nursemaid at Edgar's insistence, but it was her mother who spent the most time with her. Clare was all Marina had to love, and she loved her fiercely, protectively, possessively, trying desperately to shield her from the grimness of life at the Hall—and to make up for the lack of a father's attention. Stafford, as he had shown, had no interest in the little girl herself. He only cared for what she stood for in the eyes of his peers and otherwise hardly looked at the child. Did Clare notice his neglect? Marina often asked herself. He was, ostensibly, her father. And to coldly ignore her thus! Furious as it made her, Marina did her best to make up for it and rarely was Clare out of her sight.

When Clare fell asleep, Marina tucked her into bed suddenly wondering what her real father would have thought of her. "Oh, my baby," she moaned inwardly, torn by indecision, "what should I do?" Baxton Hall was such a cold place in which to nurture a child, and if they stayed here Clare would never know that she had a proud Highland heritage and a young, handsome father who might truly love her.

Marina straightened up to leave the nursery and gave a start when she saw Edgar standing in the doorway watching her. "You spoil that girl," he remarked gruffly. "'Tis never wise to overindulge children. It tends to ruin them for adulthood to come."

As if he were an expert on children!

Marina quietly closed the door of her daughter's room before answering him. "She is only a babe yet, Edgar, not even three years old."

"You cosset her overmuch," he persisted, his gray brows drawn together in a frown as they stood in the upstairs hallway. "All that fussing and pampering is not seemly. Forget not that you have a husband to attend to."

He was jealous! And the thought that he could actually be jealous of a mere baby sickened and angered Marina. It also made her tongue rash.

"Love never spoiled anyone!" she flared, her face reddening. "'Tis the *lack* of it that ruins a person. And while I have arms to hold her I intend to see to it that Clare never suffers from the lack of it—at least from me."

With that she swept past him and down the corridor to her room. Marina had just reached her door when he said, "I perceive that the time has come for Clare to be fostered out for her education. I will look to the matter at once."

Marina almost fell against the door, as if from a blow. The cruelest blow she could have received— and he knew it! Oh, how she hated him! Aye, and would not hesitate to kill him too if he tried to take her baby away from her. If that happened, Marina knew that she would die of a broken heart, and for a second she almost turned to beg Stafford to reconsider.

Instead, she came to a decision.

Strangely, dangerous as that decision was, Marina immediately felt better. She felt so good, in fact, that it gave her the courage to turn to Edgar standing at the top of the stairs, a satisfied smirk on his face, well aware of how he had frightened her, and no doubt expecting her to go down on her hands and knees to plead with him to change his mind, thought Marina.

She said nothing, but the look she gave him was one of raw hatred. Then, lifting her head disdainfully, Marina flounced into her room and closed and locked the door behind her.

It was not what Stafford had expected at all, and his eyes narrowed, his suspicious nature sensing some-

thing different in her attitude. "What are you up to, eh, wench?" he mused, and made up his mind to watch her more closely.

Marina was amazed at how calm she felt now that the decision had been made. She lay wide awake in bed, her mind sharp and clear, her nerves steady. All her concentration was focused on how they could get away safely. She, more than Alex, understood the situation at Baxton Hall; therefore she had no intention of leaving all the planning up to him. One scheme after another filtered through her head and was rejected. The gray light of dawn had crept into her room when a wild idea presented itself to her, one so fantastic that Marina almost laughed aloud. But it would mean taking Gwen Porter into her confidence.

"So . . . what will you be doing today, wife?" Stafford inquired at breakfast.

Marina glanced up quickly to find his small eyes resting suspiciously on her face, suspicion that Edgar lacked the subtlety to conceal.

She stifled a yawn, replying casually, "Oh, there's the jam to attend to. It will have set by now, so I suppose I must go down and fetch it back. It will mean taking the horse and cart."

"Judd will go with you."

Hiding her dismay, Marina nodded. "I'll warrant he'll be glad to help when there'll be new-made sweet stuff at the end of it."

Her husband studied her intently for a moment but he could find nothing unusual about her that morning. "You spoil the men as you spoil the child," he said. "Why should the servants have sweetmeats? Sugar is expensive."

"Ah, there's more than enough of it to go around,

and a little sweetness will improve their temper. You said yourself that they are always grumbling about the food."

Edgar studied her for a moment longer, then stood up and buckled on his belt, thinking that Marina seemed in a better mood this morning. Perhaps his threat to send the child away had done the trick, made her realize that it would be prudent to be a little pleasanter to her husband in the hope that he would change his mind. Well, he thought, all to the good, all to the good. A woman needed a fright now and then to keep her biddable, this one more than most.

Just before nine o'clock in the morning Marina rode down to Brokenbridge with Judd in the cart. "This might take a little time," she told him when they drew up in the farmyard. "You can go down to the barns to talk to the men and I'll call for you when I'm ready to go home."

Gwen was pleased to see her, as usual. "Oh, you *do* look better this morning!" she smiled.

Marina nodded. "I've found a wonderful tonic."

16

In the afternoon Alexander arrived early for his tryst with Marina at the ruined priory. He had a plan of escape carefully worked out. Two o'clock came and went, and still he waited. It was a brilliantly sunny day, but among the tumbled stones of the ruin all was shadowy and still, except for the humming of the bees around the wildflowers that had sprung up in places where the broken roof allowed light and sunshine to penetrate. A few trees had also taken root in the open patches, some grown quite tall through the years, the best of them a century-old beech with satiny, silver-gray bark that had pushed its way up through the building, its spreading branches the cause of even more destruction—a triumph of nature over stone and mortar.

To pass the time and distract himself, Alex walked about examining what was left of the priory. The stones had been cut from pink sandstone, mellow

against the green of the countryside around, and some had been carved into designs and pictures—angels, wheat sheaves, birds, and flowers. He gazed up at what was left of a vaulted window, its delicate tracery pierced with the vibrant blue of the sky. It was a hushed, haunted place, yet filled with a deep sense of peace—in contrast to the man waiting inside it.

Alex returned to the main doorway. Downhill, the town of Wilton nestled in a valley, the peak of a church spire glinting in the sun. In the stillness he could hear the noise from the fairground, the music, the shouts of the hawkers plying their wares, the occasional whinny of a horse, bursts of laughter.

The old turnpike winding uphill from Wilton to the priory was little used, except as a cattle track on market days, and when a few moments after three o'clock Alex spotted a rider approaching, his heart gave a surge of relief. She had come! He hadn't been sure she would. But he had meant it when he told Marina that he would give her only until tomorrow, Saturday, to make up her mind. Many would say he was rash indeed in coming back into England, but he wasn't quite the reckless young fool he had once been, nor had he any intention of risking his life in another lost cause. He felt that he owed Marina something and could not have rested until he discovered how she fared, but after this—if she should decide not to join him—his responsibility for her welfare would end.

Alex's eyes narrowed as he watched the rider come closer. He could see now that it was indeed a woman, and a smile touched his lips, though in truth, now that he had met Marina again, he could not have said for certain if his feelings for her were the same as they once had been. It had been more than three years ago and they had been little more than children then, filled with lofty idealistic and, he now realized, unrea-

listic notions about life. Together they had embarked on a daring and dangerous adventure, and the excitement of it had colored everything, even their perceptions about each other. All that had changed.

The figure was riding a mule. Under her dark blue gown her shape seemed stout, and though it must have been a trick of the light, her hair was dark . . .

Alex gave a start of dismay. It wasn't Marina! He ducked back inside the priory and concealed himself behind a section of tumbled wall. Straining his ears, he heard her dismount and mutter something to the mule, then her footsteps entering the building.

"My Lord Sinclair," she called out softly, peering into the gloom. "Alexander? Are you here, sir? I—I've come for Marina."

He stepped out where she could see him, and for a moment they stood facing each other in silence. Gwen Porter's heart skipped a beat when she found herself staring into the ruthless dark features of the devilish man she had been so frightened of at the fair. There was an instant when she almost turned and ran.

"Who are you?" he asked her.

Gwen moistened her lips. "I—I'm Marina's friend, Gwen Porter."

"What has happened?" His voice was harsh with anxiety. "Why didn't she come herself?"

Gwen relaxed a little when she saw how concerned he was. Looks are deceiving, she soothed herself. She threw a nervous glance back the way she had come, then waved to the rear of the building. "Best we go down there," she suggested, "then I shall tell you everything, but I haven't much time. 'Tis unsafe for me to tarry long."

They concealed themselves in what was left of the priory storehouse, seated side by side in the semidarkness. Gwen began by assuring Alexander, "She means

to go with you, my lord." Her plump cheeks glowed with excitement and her nut-brown eyes were shining, so delighted—yet scared too—was she with the role she had been cast in, that of assisting the two lovers to come together again. It was just what she had envisioned for the beautiful Marina all along! Though—she examined Alex doubtfully—he wasn't *quite* the prince she had had in mind for her friend. Sinclair looked more like a smuggler or pirate or brigand of some sort; his dark face had that ruthless hard cast to it. Still, Gwen had to concede that he had dazzling green eyes and that the Satanic aura about him was oddly thrilling. Furthermore, there was his title, his nobility to consider. That alone was worth a lot.

Gwen inhaled sharply and clasped her hands tightly together; she was breathless with the intoxication of it all, the drama that had come into her rather dull, predictable life. Aye, and she was ready and able to cope with it too, in spite of the fact that Sinclair was now gazing at her so doubtfully, even with a hint of amusement in those pantherlike eyes. Gwen was quite prepared to demonstrate that she was a person to be reckoned with, one worthy of being taken seriously.

"I will tell you of our plan," she said proudly.

Sinclair's amusement vanished. "What plan?"

"The one whereby Marina and Clare can escape."

"What!" Raw alarm sprang into his eyes. He stared at her as if she were mad. "What are you talking about, mistress? The planning will be left to *me*—"

"Nay." Gwen put a hand on his arm. "You must hear me out, sir. Consider carefully what I say, and me thinks you will not fail to see the sense in it. 'Tis beautifully simple, yet for all that, mayhap the only way this can succeed."

Alex didn't know what to make of her, though his instincts told him that Gwen Porter was a woman who

236

was game for anything. She had, after all, embroiled herself in a situation that could land her in personal danger. She had walked boldly into the priory ruins, ofttimes the lair of tramps and disreputables, to confront a total stranger. So Alexander politely listened to her, though with absolutely no intention of pursuing a scheme concocted by two women who had neither the experience nor knowledge of such things for their idea to stand the slightest chance of succeeding. But after a few minutes he began to pay her closer attention.

"You see, I'm a midwife," Gwen explained. "I have access to certain essences, certain tinctures not available to the public at large, substances used to dull the pain of labor, even to render a patient unconscious if the circumstances should merit it. 'Twas this that gave Marina the idea in the first place."

"She thought of this?" Alex shook his head. "Dear Christ—"

"Now you listen to me, sir." Gwen's hand tightened on his arm and her voice assumed a no-nonsense ring, a tone her own husband knew better than to ignore. "I presume you want to see Marina and the baby brought out of Baxton Hall with as little risk to them as possible?"

"Obviously. But—"

"Then this is the only way," she stated firmly. "Her husband is already suspicious, which is the reason Marina couldn't come here today herself. She was afraid she would lead him to you because he is having her watched." Gwen paused to study his tight, skeptical face, then warned him, "Stafford is just evil enough to kill both Marina and the child at the first sniff of trouble, so if you have a mind to go in there with pistols blazing you could end up with their deaths on your conscience."

Alex jumped up and began to pace about. He could not actually say that the proposed plan was ludicrous because it was well thought out and clever in many ways. Aye, he conceded grudgingly, and it stood as good a chance of working as any . . . perhaps better than most. In fact, he found himself admiring the women for its cunning and simplicity. But, God's soul, how could he stand by and allow these females to handle it, to take such a risk on their own? What kind of man did they think he was?

Alex turned to the woman who was watching him expectantly.

"The plan is sound," he allowed, "but I must have a hand in it. I will—"

"*Your* part in it," she cut in determinedly, "is to have horses waiting in the woods—and make sure they are swift."

He raised his head haughtily, obviously affronted to be spoken to in such an imperious manner, to be ordered about by a woman, and to be expected to take a secondary role when he had been born to lead rather than be led.

His abduracy heightened Gwen's nervousness, for Sinclair *must* be made to agree to it. It was too late now to call a halt to it. They had to act while the time was ripe.

"Sir," she said, standing up, "Marina has already taken the jam loaded with poppy juice back to Baxton Hall. It will be fed to the men tonight at supper."

His head snapped up, his heart leaping with it.

"Aye," Gwen nodded, "it cannot be stopped."

17

Marina watched anxiously for her friend from her chamber window, and when she spied Gwen approaching on the mule, she ran outside into the courtyard and the two women hurried deep into the garden where there was less chance of anyone eavesdropping. Stopping in the shade of some huge rhododendron bushes, Marina turned to her breathlessly. "Well, what did he say?"

She was not too surprised—in fact not surprised at all—to hear that Alex had been opposed to the idea of the women handling it themselves, though, said Gwen with some satisfaction, he thought the plan itself might work—if he were in charge of it.

"That cannot be." Marina brushed the notion aside. "But will he do his part in it?"

Her friend nodded slowly, and decided against telling Marina how angry Alex had been that they'd gone ahead before consulting him; but, as Gwen had

sensed, he had been far more anxious for them than anything else. With a quick glance around, she opened the flaps of a heavy bag she was carrying, and Marina's eyes widened when she peeped inside. Inside were four bottles of Gwen's homemade elderberry wine and, under them, a pistol and a dagger.

"I stopped on my way here for the wine," said Gwen very low. "'Tis added insurance. The brew is well larded with poppy juice."

"You dearest angel." Marina smiled, taking the bag. "Oh, Gwen, how will I ever be able to thank you for all you've done for me? But for you, I think I would have been in Newcastle madhouse long since."

"Welladay, hopefully you will soon be in paradise," the other said with a giggle. "I admit that at first sight of him I was not sure, but the more you study him the more you realize that there's something about that devil . . ."

They laughed softly together, as they had done so many times before, but as the shadows lengthened across the grass and the afternoon sun slid behind the largest of the barns, their mirth died slowly away. Soon the men would be riding home for supper, and both knew that Marina had things to prepare before they arrived.

It was time to say goodbye.

"I will miss you, sweeting." There was a tremor in Gwen's voice.

A gush of tears filled Marina's eyes but she struggled to hold her smile. Catching Gwen's hand and squeezing it, she said, "We will see each other again, I swear! Some day you will visit me in Scotland, and I shall come to see you when—when—"

"—when the old weasel has the grace to expire?"

Half-laughing, half-crying, they hugged each other fiercely.

Gwen kissed her on the cheek, murmuring, "God keep you and little Clare," then she hurried away.

The house servants liked their mistress. Though the master was frequently harsh and kept them on the barest rations, mostly scraps left over from the Hall table, his goodwife was always fair and slipped them an extra something when she could. But when Marina came into the kitchen and slapped down two pots of jam and even a bottle of wine on the old work table, they gaped in astonishment.

She winked at them and put a finger over her mouth, whispering conspiratorially, "Make sure not to touch this until after the master has been served his meal, then wolf the lot before he pokes his nose in the door and catches you."

They grinned, loud in their thanks.

"And Betsy"—she handed a basket to the young housemaid—"when you hear my husband step into the house, run out with this to the men, and make sure they get it, mind," she warned. "Instruct them to finish everything so that I can pick up the empty jars in the morning."

Edgar's guards ate their meals in the bothy behind the stables, and Marina could appreciate how much they would enjoy their treat since they were forever complaining about the food, or the lack of it, and with good reason. Paltry wages and near-starvation rations accounted for a constant turnover of staff—but, as Stafford had once pointed out when Marina urged that he be a little more generous, "Better to be a little hungry with a roof over your head than to be starving out in the rain."

In her chamber Marina quickly bathed and put on her prettiest gown, then sat at the spotted mirror to brush out her hair, tying it back with a pink satin

ribbon. Taking a jar of jam from the nearby table, she very carefully smeared a little at the corner of her mouth, though not close enough to be accidentally licked. Then she sat back and stared at herself—and was suddenly heart-stoppingly nervous, though up until now she had been amazingly composed.

She frowned at her reflection severely. "Marina," she told herself, "you simply cannot lose your nerve now. Blessed Jesu . . . *not now*!"

She put the cap back on the jam jar, inhaled raggedly several times, then rose and hurried down the corridor to the nursery, where she found her daughter playing "hunt the thimble" with her nursemaid, Jillie. Marina joined their game for a few minutes, then when Clare tired of it and went in search of her favorite doll, she took Jillie aside and pressed the jar of jam into her hand. It was for her, Marina stressed. Clare must have none tonight lest it upset her stomach before she went to bed, and when the girl's face fell, "Don't worry, she will make up for it tomorrow."

Jillie beamed. "Oh, you *are* kind, lady."

Marina explained about the need for it to be consumed tonight so that she could return the jar to Mistress Porter in the morning, and the nursemaid chuckled, "'Twill be gone in the twinkling of an eye."

Stafford returned to the house a little later than usual. He'd had a hard day on his estate. He stamped in muttering under his breath about the lazy serfs who worked his fields, the constant poaching of his tenants, and the fact that two of his sheep were missing, undoubtedly nicked by gypsies in retaliation for what he and his neighbors had done to their friends.

He gave a start when he turned around and saw Marina. She was seated at the board in her best pink

silk gown. A bottle of wine stood on the table, and two glasses had already been poured out. Hers, he saw, was almost empty.

Startled, he inquired suspiciously, "What's ado here?" And with a wave at her finery, then at the wine, "What means all this?"

Marina threw him one of her lazy, seductive smiles. "Good eve to you, husband. Me thought you would never come home, and the very night when I had a festive meal prepared for you. Come"—she waved to the chair opposite—"sit you down. I see you look weary this night. 'Tis a pity, for I thought we might walk down to visit the Porters after supper."

His brows came down and he fairly gaped at her. Visit the Porters? Never before had she shown any desire to go anywhere with him. And never before had she deigned to dress up for him either. It occurred to Stafford that the best thing he had ever done as far as Marina was concerned was to threaten to separate her from the child. That, he told himself, was the way to make her biddable: hint about sending Clare away. And he would, too, if Marina continued to provoke him.

"Methinks you are drunk," he said, unbuckling his belt before throwing himself down across from her at the table. "You had no right to open this wine without my permission."

She explained that Gwen Porter had made it, adding with a giggle, "Ah, 'tis fair week, Edgar, cannot we make merry a little?"

"I've had a wearisome day."

Marina held her breath when he picked up his glass of wine and carelessly tossed it back, then thumped the table shouting for the servants to bring in the meal. She pretended to eat herself while watching him covertly from under her lids, waiting tensely for the

wine to take effect, but as usual he pounced on the food and ate with gusto, displaying no sign whatever that the narcotic was having the slightest effect on him. With the main course consumed, he drew a berry tart toward him, cut it in half, and shoveled it onto his trencher, then ladled on spoonfuls of jam from the jar at his elbow.

His eyes flickered to her, and with a nod at the jam, he ordered, "See that the servants get none of this."

"More wine, husband?" Her hand shook a little as she reached for the bottle.

"Aye, but none for you, lady; you've had enough. Jam too, from that spot by your lips. I trow you are as greedy as a street urchin. 'Tis a wonder you left any for me."

Greedy! Marina was seized with a fit of hysterical laughter at the incongruity of his remark considering his own gluttony, and so tense was she that she couldn't quite choke it back. But she covered it by saying, "Oh, Edgar, what funny remarks you make. There's lots of jam, so eat your fill."

As if he needed any encouragement!

In dread fascination Marina watched him swallow three glasses of wine, eat half a jar of jam, and polish off most of the pie, and still nothing. Her hopes plummeted. It wasn't going to work! And if it failed to work for Edgar, there was an excellent chance that it wouldn't for the servants, or more importantly, his men. In the meantime, Alexander would be waiting impatiently in the woods with the horses. If she didn't meet him within the hour—plenty of time for the opium to take effect, Gwen had assured them—he might get alarmed for her safety and come to the house to investigate!

She broke out in a cold sweat, panic rising. Oh, God, she moaned inwardly, Alex would find himself

walking into a lions' den, there to be pounced on and destroyed. Realizing it had been a plot, Stafford would make her and the baby pay for it. Even poor, obliging Gwen could be hurt; Edgar was malicious and vindictive. He had never forgiven the Percys for wedding him to a girl who had run away from him—which had hardly been their fault—and had gone out of his way to strike back at them ever since.

Shaking, Marina grabbed what was left of the wine and made to pour it into his glass, but he pushed her hand away. "Nay, nay . . . had enough." Stafford tugged at the neck of his shirt. "'Tis hot—hot as Hades in here . . ."

Marina stared at him, her breath catching in her throat.

Their eyes met. His were glittering. His face had gone very red and his skin was shiny with perspiration. "You . . ." he muttered, "you . . . bitch . . ."

Then he toppled sideways off his chair, landing with a dull thud on the floor.

For a moment Marina froze. She was almost sick with terror and her limbs wouldn't function. It was as if she had been turned to stone. But gradually she became aware of the silence in the house, the only sound the ticking of the clock, and that ticking had a frantic ring to it, warning her that time was passing and that she didn't have very long. An hour, Gwen had said, before the younger, stronger ones would start to wake up—only an hour to get out of the house and leave the district!

Marina sprang to her feet as life rushed back into her limbs. With a glance at Edgar who lay snoring softly with his mouth wide open, she tiptoed down the passageway and peeped into the kitchen. Two of the servants were slumped with their heads on the table, an overturned jar of jam beside them, and the pot-boy

had collapsed near the pantry door. Darby, who ate with them, was on the floor.

Flying upstairs, she came upon Jillie in her tiny back bedchamber. To her horror the girl was not completely drugged, though she too was lying on the floor, the jam jar beside her. When she saw Marina she tried to rise, tried to speak, but her mistress had no time to listen. "'Twill soon pass, never fear," was all she had time to say before racing to the nursery to pluck Clare from her bed, snatching a blanket to wrap around her.

In minutes she was at the front door on her way out of the house.

The night was dark and still, the courtyard empty. With a wary glance around, Marina raced like a shadow across the cobbles, the child in her arms. Her breath came in quick little spurts, like a winded horse, and her flesh was clammy cold, but the gate loomed up ahead of her, and once through it, she would be free, or almost so. Then it would only be a matter of running for the woods where Alex would be waiting with the horses.

Marina had reached the gate when a figure stepped out from the bush beside it. The suddenness of it almost caused her to drop the child.

"'Tis as well I don't fancy sweet things," said Tar, grinning.

18

When Tar pounced on her, Marina went berserk, aware that she was fighting for her future—perhaps even for her life itself. Hampered by Clare in her arms, she clutched the little girl against her and kicked, twisted, bit, and did everything she could short of using her hands to free herself, and actually managed to break away from him once and stagger a few steps to the gate. Tar bounded after her and grabbed her by the hair and started dragging her back to the house, the child whimpering, Marina pleading with him to release her. "Nay," the squire panted, "'twould be more than my life's worth to let you go—"

He stopped abruptly as a shadow fell across them in the torchlight by the door. Still holding Marina by the hair, Tar started to wheel about when he was struck a stunning blow to the back of the head, so strong it sent sparks shooting before his eyes like an explosion in a

dark sky. All the power went out of his limbs and he felt himself falling, plunging headlong into a black abyss, landing with a thump at Marina's feet. For an instant she went numb. She gazed down stupidly at her husband's squire, then up into Alexander's shadowy face.

"Give me the babe!" he said, and plucked the little girl from her arms and threw Clare over his shoulders. Catching Marina by the arm, he ran with her to the gate. "Hurry!" he urged when she stumbled. "There are horses waiting in the woods."

Five minutes later they were galloping away for the Scottish border, much as they had done once before. This time, Marina prayed, she hoped she would never see Edgar Stafford again.

There was no question of stopping, even for a moment. Alex knew that Tar would recover from the blow soon enough, and though his master might not wake up so soon, the squire would be bound to rouse the sheriff to give chase. Although Alex felt confident of being able to outride a posse himself, he knew that Marina could not keep up such a furious pace.

They rode on through the night, desperate to put as much distance between themselves and Baxton Hall as possible before Tar recovered his senses, and in a remarkably short time crossed the border into Scotland. But even then it was unwise to slow down. Raiding parties from both countries had little compunction about crossing over in either direction. Stafford certainly wouldn't, Alex was sure, when he revived to find his wife and child gone. So they rode on deeper into Scotland, past Jedburgh and pushing steadily north, Alex with one arm around the little girl seated on the saddle in front of him, her tiny body held close against his, her head lolling sideways.

In their mad desire to get away, neither adult thought much of Clare's silence at first, their main fear centered on those who might be following them. It was when they reached the town of Melrose, where they spied torches glowing in the darkness, that Marina began to feel safe enough to think of other things besides possible capture. She brought her horse close to Alexander's and called to him, "How is it with Clare?" Leaning forward in the saddle, Marina felt a twinge of concern when she noticed her daughter's head sagging against her father's chest.

"Alex"—her voice sharpened with alarm—"stop over yonder by the lights. I would see how Clare is faring."

They drew up beside Melrose Inn, where a flare was burning on a bracket beside the main door. Dismounting, Alex carried the little girl to the front steps and both bent over her. Sinclair grinned. "Faith, but the bairn is a sound sleeper."

"Clare, my love." Anxiously Marina examined the little face. "Clare, wake up!"

When there was no response, the worried mother leaned closer—and saw the sticky smudges on her daughter's lips, telltale stains that she hadn't noticed in her frantic haste to get them both safely out of Baxton Hall. She raised stricken eyes to Alexander's face. "Jesu . . . she has eaten some of the jam." A wave of horror rose inside her. "She's dead! Oh, dear God, my baby is dead!" Crying hysterically, she plucked the child from Alex and crushed her limp little body against her breast, rocking her distractedly while anguished tears splashed down her face.

Alex ran up the steps to the inn and almost battered the door down to rouse the occupants. "A doctor!" he cried when a suspicious face peered out at him. "We

have a sick child here," with a wave back down the steps. "A doctor, man!" He grabbed the innkeeper by the scruff of the neck. "Where can one be found?"

There was no doctor to be had in Melrose—but a barber responded to the emergency, a man who lived up to the letter of his trade. To Marina and Alex his methods seemed barbarous indeed as he rushed Clare into a room at the inn. In his late thirties, Janton had the lean, swarthy look of a gypsy, but they saw at once that he was a fellow who totally concentrated on the task at hand; he had been highly recommended to them by the innkeeper, not that they had a choice. It was Janton or nothing. The moment the fellow established that a thin thread of life still flickered in little Clare, he ordered a tub of cold water brought to the room. In the meantime, he ripped the babe's clothes off and, ignoring the startled exclamations from her parents, proceeded to slap every inch of her body.

When two servitors struggled in with the tub of cold water, Janton plunged the child into the tub.

"Christ's Holy Mother—" Alex started to lunge at him when the innkeeper pulled him back, muttering, "Nay, nay, it looks more fearsome than it is. The wean must be shocked oot o' it, ye see. Janton kens weel how to handle opium eaters. The Laird o' Buccleugh's ain son is yin o' them and requires the barber's services frequently."

So the parents stood helplessly aside while their daughter was slapped, plunged into the water, and slapped again, Janton pausing now and then to cock an ear to her mouth or press it against her chest. "Oh, God . . ." Marina wailed when the untender treatment didn't seem to be having any effect. "Dear Lord, please spare her."

Alexander put his arm around her quivering shoul-

ders and with his hand brought her face against his chest, holding it there so she wouldn't have to watch. He knew now beyond the shadow of a doubt that baby Clare was his; the child was a tiny miniature of his own mother, the Countess of Belrose and Kilgarin. In fact, the resemblance was uncanny. And how proud Lady Alyssa would have been of her too!

A terrible bleakness struck Alexander as he watched Janton struggle to save the life of his daughter, the first of the new generation of Sinclairs. Had he met her only to lose her on the same day? Was this to be the final price he would pay for his youthful folly? He would sooner have died on the Tower Green, if *his* life could have been taken in place of his little daughter's.

He put his face against the top of Marina's head and closed his eyes—then gave a start when he heard a faint, mewling cry.

The innkeeper laughed triumphantly. "There now! Did a' no' tell ye he was guid?"

Marina and Alex rushed to the bed where Janton was bending over Clare, tapping her cheek none too gently. Dripping, her velvety skin inflamed and swollen from her rough "treatment," she looked for all the world like a kitten that had just been hauled out of a pond. They held their breaths when the long, curling lashes fluttered open to reveal a pair of dazed green eyes. "Mama . . ." she wailed weakly, and began to cry.

"Oh, thank God!" Marina wept. "Thank you, Blessed Mary."

Janton stepped back to allow the sobbing mother to take her child in her arms, but his face was grim when he straightened up and looked at Alex, who was grinning with relief, his eyes tender as they rested on Marina and his daughter. They made a beautiful

picture together, hugging, kissing, Marina murmuring soothing endearments into the tiny, wet ear. It was with a start that he turned his attention to Janton when the man put a hand on his arm, indicating that they should step outside into the hall. Once there, the barber eyed him grimly.

"The wee one should be all right now," he assured the worried father, "but had she consumed more of the poppy she would never have survived. How came she by such a substance?"

It was an impertinent question, but Alexander was too overcome with relief and gratitude to take offense, nor was he thinking very clearly at that moment, half his attention still in the other room. He would have seized the barber's hand and wrung it heartily, but the man kept his hands clasped behind his back. Then Alex became aware of the man's anger, and his own warm smile faded.

The fellow thought he was an opium eater!

During his time at Elizabeth's court and even at his own King's court in Edinburgh, he had known a few people who, jaded with other pleasures, had turned to the juice of the poppy for stimulation. The young Lord Bothwell was one of them, and there had been a bard at the English court who had written weird and outlandish verses when in the thrall of it, but in the main, opium was used by surgeons and midwives to banish pain or induce sleep.

"'Twas an accident," Alex explained. "It came from the medicaments of a midwife." Which was true enough. "I know not how it found its way into the hands of the babe."

Janton nodded; Alex couldn't tell if he believed him or not.

"'Tis a deadly intoxicant and soul-destroying if

taken regularly," said the barber. "It can also kill. Best to keep such substances well removed from the grasp of children—"

"We do not use it, man." Sinclair was growing a little angry.

Janton nodded. "That I am glad to hear, because many do, to their sorrow. Once set on that downward path 'tis nigh impossible to pull them back. Soon they leave the world behind and sink into a land of dark dreams and then into hell itself." The barber, who had two male patients in that very state—the sons of noblemen—felt it his duty to point out the effects of the poppy to everyone he met that he felt might be at risk; people with the means to procure opium.

But Alex was impatient to return to Marina and Clare, nor was he in the mood to listen to a stern lecture, regardless of how well intended. He thrust out his hand, and after a moment's hesitation, Janton took it.

"My deepest thanks to you, sir," said Alex. "You are indeed a man of rare skills." He smiled slightly. "Methinks you are wasting your talents barbering."

Janton smiled a little too. Only rarely now did he spend his time shaving customers and cutting hair. He had attracted the attention of professors at Glasgow's School of Medicine through his work with the Laird of Buccleugh's ailing son and the nephew of Baron Roxburgh, for not only did he understand that there was a dark side to medicines then in common use, but he was also an able surgeon and clever at mixing his own remedies for disease. But he had been born poor, the son of a barber, and had never had any formal education, yet for all that his natural skill had been recognized and now, urged on by Buccleugh, he had been invited to Glasgow to set up his own infirmary

ward. Janton still hadn't made up his mind whether to accept, held back by something he had overheard one eminent professor remark to another during his last visit to Glasgow. "I trow this fellow Janton is a wizard and has some evil pact established with Lucifer. How else can one explain the efficacy of his cures?"

The barber suspected he might be safer staying in Melrose.

Alexander would gladly have given him all the gold in his possession, but Janton shook his head. "My fee," he said, "is one florin."

Alex was startled. It seemed a small price to pay for the life of his child.

For what was left of the night Marina would not be parted from her daughter, who was sleeping naturally now after having supped a few spoonfuls of broth. It was sheer joy to Marina to be able to lie in bed with Clare's warm little body held tight in her arms, her soft breath against her mother's cheek, her face flushed once more with health.

Alex stood watching them for a while, thinking again that they made a lovely picture, and beautiful they both were too—his women. It pleased him to be able to admire them at leisure, now that all the frantic activity had died down and everyone gone back to bed. Clare was doll-like and perfect in her father's eyes, and though Marina looked wan and exhausted, worn out with the activity of the last few hectic hours, still . . . even fatigue could not detract from her beauty. That beauty still held him enthralled.

Finally he walked to the bed and stooped down to kiss them both on the forehead. "Sleep now," he urged softly. "We have a long ride to face tomorrow. Janton assured me that it was safe for Clare to be

moved, that the fresh air and exercise would only improve her condition."

Marina at last took her anxious eyes from her baby, and glanced up at him. It was then she noticed that Alexander too looked weary, the marks of the strain they had undergone on his face. She reached out her hand to him, saying, "Oh, my lord, are we not lucky? To have made it safely out of England, then to have weathered this crisis with Clare. I warrant that it was her nursemaid who gave her the jam. Jillie was fond of Clare and unable to refuse her anything." Her face clouded. "I should have remembered that, but in my haste to get away . . ."

"Marina," Alex said and sat down on the edge of the bed beside her, "'tis foolish to blame yourself. You did what had to be done, and I'm proud of you." He smiled. "You are brave and clever as well as being beautiful."

Marina glowed at his praise. She felt deliriously happy. And now was just the moment to give him a wonderful piece of news, though she was sorry now at having lied to him before and hoped Alex wouldn't hold it against her.

"Well," she said, "what do you think of our Clare?"

"Oh, I knew she was mine the instant I laid eyes on her," Alex said, taking her aback. "Clare is the very image of my lady mother. The countess too has that same burnished red hair and the same upward tilt to her eyes. And hers too are green."

Now, finally, Marina knew where her daughter's fiery hair had come from, something that had always puzzled her—and something she would never have known if she hadn't decided to put her trust in Alex once again. She was suddenly very curious about the Sinclairs, Alex's mother in particular. "She must be

very beautiful if Clare takes after her?"

"*Very* beautiful," he said proudly, affection in his voice.

"Alex, I'm most anxious to know how it goes with dear Sir Ralph?" Now that they were more relaxed, this was only the first of many questions Marina yearned to ask him. It came as a great blow to her to learn that her old friend had died. Tears started up in her eyes, but her voice was fierce when she said, "And 'twas that husband of mine who caused it when he barged into Cairnmore House that day!"

It all came out then, how she had become very close to Ralph while waiting for Alex to return, then how Elsie Cairnmore, upon discovering that Marina was pregnant, had promised to help her. "Then one day, out of the blue, Edgar arrived at the house with his men. There was a scuffle when Ralph tried to fight him off, but he was weak, you see, and quickly overpowered. The last I saw of your grandfather he was lying across his bed, then . . . Edgar dragged me away."

Alex brushed the tears from her cheeks and put his arm around her, then casually lay down on the bed beside her, his fingers lazily moving through her hair. "I'm sure you made the last months of his life very happy, Marina. Stafford might have hastened his end, but my grandfather had been ailing for some time."

Marina turned her wet face to his. "I cannot imagine how Edgar ever found me."

"I can," he replied grimly. "Garth and Elsie must have written to him—"

"Garth and Elsie! But . . . Elsie swore she would help me with the babe."

"Elsie is a conniving viper. I knew they were lying when I stopped in Ayrshire on my way South. Nay, Marina, they have always resented anyone, including

me, getting too close to their pot of gold—Sir Ralph
—fearing, doubtless, that he might leave them some-
thing in his will. Greed was ever the motivating force
with that pair."

Both were silent for a moment while Clare stirred in
her sleep, then Alex eyed her quizzically. "So you've
decided to trust me again, eh, Marina?"

"I am here, am I not?" She was blushing.

"Why, of a sudden, did you change your mind?"

Marina turned her head away from the probing
green eyes and lay gazing up at the ceiling, remember-
ing the exact moment the decision to go with Alex had
firmed in her mind—the night Edgar announced his
intention of sending Clare away. But . . . perhaps the
decision had been made even before that, though she
hadn't confronted it until then, hadn't been ready to
admit to herself that Alexander Sinclair still meant
something to her. The question was, what did *she*
mean to Alexander Sinclair? Had *she* brought him
back into England—or her child?

"I was miserable at Baxton Hall," Marina replied
evasively, afraid to commit herself until he did. "And
I felt that Clare should be with her real father."

"And that is the only reason?"

Her flush deepened, but Marina felt slightly an-
noyed. What did Alex expect her to say? That she still
loved him? He was asking a lot, she thought irritably,
when he kept his own feelings to himself. After all, the
fact that a man was willing and ready to bed a woman
didn't necessarily mean that he loved her, and be-
sides, they had both changed a lot during the past
three years. Lust aside, and she was quite prepared to
face up to the fact that Sinclair still excited her
physically, Marina was uncertain as to the extent of
her feelings for him—as Alex seemed to be about her.

"Is that not a good enough reason?" she finally replied diffidently. "A child needs its father."

He laughed softly, watching her, and reaching out, ran the backs of his fingers over the smooth curve of her cheek. "Well I recall when this was black and blue," he murmured, stroking her. "Now 'tis pink and soft as a rose. But you are right in saying that a child should be with its real father. I can see that you are very concerned for your daughter's welfare," he finished mockingly.

Marina glanced at him from the corner of her eye to find Alex grinning at her. Well he knew that there was more to it than that! she thought, irked that he could see through her so easily.

"Well," she said, "I perceive that three years in prison hasn't dented your confidence in yourself. You still have as high an opinion of yourself as ever, my Lord Sinclair."

His dark brows rose. "You do me an injustice, Mistress Marina." But there was laughter in his eyes. "Admit you are glad you came?"

She ignored the question and asked briskly, "Well, sir, where are you taking us now that you have us in your clutches?"

He had many choices of location—his hunting lodge near the Moray Firth, or even Kilgarin Keep, a property that had come to him nearly four years ago on his twenty-first birthday. Then there was Lynnwood, a pleasant Sinclair estate not too far from Castle Augusta itself. Alex was still unsure about the position that Marina would occupy in his life . . . but a man rarely took his mistress into the bosom of his family.

His mind, however, had been made up the moment he'd clapped eyes on Clare.

"We are going to Castle Augusta," he told her. "My daughter must meet her family."

Marina was taken aback. Somehow Castle Augusta was the last place she expected. She knew from conversations with Alex in the past that it was the seat of the clan Sinclair and she couldn't help but be nervous, wondering how they would receive her there. She was, after all, an English woman and married, and to have her foisted on them by their eldest son—of course Alexander wasn't the heir, Marina remembered. Though they would expect him too to make an advantageous marriage, it wasn't quite as imperative as it was with the son who would inherit.

"Ah . . . do you think that's wise, Alex?"

He studied her for a moment, his face sober and determined.

"Have courage, Marina, my parents will understand; they should, having once been in a similar position themselves. 'Tis amazing," he mused, "how history repeats itself."

Marina gave him a doubtful look, remembering the circumstances of his birth, but she didn't say anything, reasoning that he knew best what he was about.

When Clare turned restlessly in her sleep, perhaps disturbed by their voices, though they had been speaking very low, Alex kissed her lightly on the cheek. Then he rose, saying, "Well, I shall leave you two ladies alone. Our next stop, providing that Clare seems fit to travel in the morning, will be Edinburgh."

Clare seemed fit for anything in the morning. She jumped up bright and early asking for her breakfast, startled to find herself in a strange room, and this led to numerous questions, her quick mind as well as her body seeming none the worse for her accident.

They spent two days in Edinburgh, mainly to outfit Marina and Clare as they had fled from Baxton Hall with nothing but the clothes on their backs, and Alex was determined that they should look their best when he presented them to his family. It meant purchasing ready-made garments, which were always inferior to those specially made, but there was no help for it. Alex had no desire to tarry in the city lest he run into his friends at court, none of whom he wished to see at that particular moment. It was for a similar reason that he avoided Clairmont, the Sinclair town house in Edinburgh, and popular eating establishments such as Bell's Tavern and the Rotunda, haunts of the rich, famous, and well-connected. Above all, word must not reach King James that he was back in town, for then awkward questions might be asked. James in many ways was a peaceable, tolerant man, but Alexander felt it would be stretching that tolerance if the King discovered that he had gone back into England illegally.

Marina and Clare were delighted with their new clothes. For Marina there was a crimson riding habit in finest serge, and a billowing mist-blue satin gown with silvery tracing at the dipping neckline, a garment that Alex insisted she take, admiring the way the design drew attention to Marina's high, lush breasts. And, of course, she must have the silvery-blue ankle-length cloak that matched the gown, and day frocks in linen and muslin, in soft shades of peach and green, and boots to go with the riding habit, and two pairs of slippers, one for the evening gown and the other for the more casual attire.

"Stop!" Marina laughed when Alex kept plucking item after item off the rack, while the astonished owner of the shop stood nodding enthusiastically, a

delighted grin on her face, constantly assuring the generous gentleman, "Aye, m'lord, that's just the sort of thing they are wearing at court." Or, "If you would have the lady be in fashion, I'd suggest the lace shawl, or mayhap those ivory combs. And scent, of course; none of the high-born ladies go abroad without it these days . . ."

Staring at the pile of merchandise, including almost as much for Clare, Marina put her hands to her burning cheeks, crying, "Marry, but we shall need a cart to transport all this to Augusta! Oh Alex"—her sparkling brown eyes met his—"I've never owned so many clothes in my life!"

"Take the riding habit and one other now," he told her, smiling, thinking that she looked more like the vivacious Marina he had once known, "and we can have the rest sent on to Augusta."

They left the shop with Alex holding Clare in one arm and carrying the packages in the other, Marina hanging on to his sleeve. "I feel much like one of the pampered ladies in that castle up yonder," she said, waving to Edinburgh Castle on its massive rock high above the street. "Thank you, Alex," she said shyly.

"Thank you, Alex," little Clare echoed, and both adults burst out laughing, both thankful that the child seemed none the worse for her accident. Far from it, she seemed to thrive on the long trip north, showing an active interest in everything, constantly pointing at things and demanding to know what they were. She seemed to accept Alexander too, stranger as he was to her, and Marina thought she knew why. Because of the harsh conditions at Baxton Hall, none of Edgar's houseguard had ever lasted very long, and when one man left—or more likely, was sacked—a new one would take his place. Clare had become used to the

261

rapid turnover and constant change of faces, so that this man, big, dark, and bearded though he was, just the type who might frighten any small child, didn't seem to bother Clare.

But the first time she called him Alex, Sinclair took her onto his knee and spoke to her gravely. "A wee lass like you should not call her sire by his first name. Do you think you can remember to call me Father?"

"Aye, Alex," she'd nodded.

"Nay, my love. *Father.*"

Her big green eyes stared into his and she frowned, then twisting around to her mother, asked, "Where Father?"

The adults looked at each other, and Marina raised her shoulders helplessly, grinning. "Leave it for now . . ."

The stopover in Edinburgh was a pleasant interlude. Relieved that their child had recovered with no ill effects, and now more able to appreciate that they had made good their escape from England, both Marina and Alex were in fine spirits as he took them on a brief tour of the town. To be free of Stafford at last left Marina feeling light-hearted and almost giddy. She was bubbly, talkative, and effusive, much more like her old self. There was a rosy blush on her cheeks, a lightness to her step, and a shine in her dark eyes that made heads turn to stare at her in the street. "I am happier now," she thought, "than I have been since—since Ayrshire."

They rode past the castle, the Palace of Holyroodhouse and its beautiful park, St. Giles Cathedral, where the firebrand John Knox preached in the time of Mary Stuart—and often stirred up the people against her—and out to the ruins of Kirk o' Field where Lord Darnley, the Queen's second hus-

band, was murdered, some said by the man she married next, Bothwell. "The day she married Bothwell," said Alex, "was the day she sealed her fate—at least in Scotland. In the people's eyes she had wed her husband's killer, and only weeks after he died." He sighed and shook his head. "She was ever a rash, headstrong lady."

"Do you think she was part of the plot to murder Darnley?"

It was a question Alex had often asked himself. "I think not, nor does my father, but we will never know for certain. My sire the earl seems to think that she turned to Bothwell in desperation when so many of her other nobles ranged against her. Say what you will about the fellow, but James Hepburn was strong and courageous, if overweeningly ambitious and acquisitive. Of the Marian supporters at the time, Bothwell was the strongest—next to my father, of course," he added with a grin. "But my mother resented the time he spent away from her, so he was less at Holyrood than the Queen would have liked."

"So she came to depend on Bothwell?"

He nodded. "He cost her her crown and the love and respect of her people, a stiff price to pay for a few weeks of passion. Hardly had they married when both were driven out of the country."

Marina sighed, staring at the rubble that was now Kirk o' Field.

"And now both are dead . . ." She shivered, thinking of how close Alexander had come to following them.

There was romance and magic in the city of Edinburgh, and that day Marina fell under its spell. As they rode along the Canongate, the Lawn and Grassmarkets, through tortuous little cobblestoned

streets and wynds hemmed in on either side by ancient medieval buildings, the past in all its glory and violence came alive for her as Alexander explained historical events in detail, as told to him when a boy by his father. Though she was very nervous at the thought of meeting them, Marina looked forward to it too. But she was English—and there was no one more Scottish than a Highlander. Alex was indeed brave, she thought dryly, to think of taking her into the clan stronghold itself.

For hours Clare was intrigued by the sights and sounds of the city, her bright hair flying this way and that as her head swiveled to catch everything that interested her—the dancers and mimers with their impromptu (and not always very professional) performances at the Cross, hoping for a few coins tossed down by the passing public. The stalls at the market too caught her attention, the colorful satins and lace on display; the pretty jars and bottles containing ointments and essences; the more pungent shops selling fish, fowl, and flesh.

She was quite content to let her father hold her, and gave him a kiss and a hug when Alex bought her a poppet with wide, startled eyes and red hair much like her own, and kept her tummy filled with honeyed oat cakes and buttermilk, and as a special treat, a sticky twist of sugar taffy that managed to get stuck in her hair.

"Oh, Alex," said Marina, making a face as she carefully disentangled the copper curls from the sweet, and wiped the messy little face, "you'll spoil her. You really mustn't give in to her every whim."

Clare frowned at her mother and pushed her hands away, catching the gist of the remark, and buried her head in Alexander's chest, quickly realizing that she

had a soft mark in her father.

But eventually the little girl tired of touring and they took her back to the inn where they were staying during their brief stop in Edinburgh. It was a quaint little place called the Hare and Hound, an establishment that Alex had once heard his father speak of with great favor. Plain as it was, he couldn't quite understand his father's praise, but it had the advantage of being tucked away on a side street and Alex was anxious to avoid the more pretentious places where he might be recognized. He had rented two rooms at the Hare and Hound, one for Marina and Clare, the other for himself, but he soon hoped to switch the arrangement around.

At the inn they separated to bathe and change for dinner. Since Clare was with them, Alex proposed they dine that evening downstairs.

Clare's flagging energy revived when she sat in a tub of warm water with her mother, then was dressed in a lovely new pink organdy gown, her freshly washed curls brushed out and tied with glistening satin ribbons, finery she had never known at Baxton Hall. "There!" said Marina, smiling as she held her up to the glass. "Now you look like a little princess."

Clare laughed and nodded, delighted at the dazzling picture she made, and while her mother too donned one of the gowns Alex had bought them that day, a soft peach muslin frock with a rounded neckline, mist-green satin ribbons at her waist and cuffs, the child whirled and danced around the room, crying in a singsong voice, "Clare love Alex! Clare love Alex this much," throwing her arms wide.

Seated at the dresser brushing her own hair into a rippling cape of palest gold, Marina eyed her through the glass. "Clare would love anybody who spoiled her,

I trow. And darling, you must call him"—she had been about to say Father, but that was the way the little girl addressed Edgar, and Marina wanted the child to forget Stafford as soon as possible—"Papa," she decided with a nod. "You must call Alex Papa. Don't forget."

"Alex!" Clare called back stubbornly. "Alex, Alex, Alex!"

Marina frowned, carefully fixing the sides of her hair back with ivory combs. "Methinks you have the makings of a very naughty girl, mistress Clare. Children should be obedient to their mothers; they should never gainsay them."

"Huh?" Clare ran to the table and snatched up Marina's new bottle of scent, spilling half of it across the surface of the dresser, a mishap that earned her a light slap on the hand. Pouting, the child glowered at her mother. "Clare not love Mama no more."

When Alex knocked on the door to take them downstairs for their meal, Clare was the one to open it, but when she looked up at Sinclair her tiny mouth fell open in astonishment.

He had shaved off his beard.

Marina jumped up from her stool by the dresser, the breath catching in her throat. There he stood, tall, dark, handsome in his clean tan riding breeches, fresh white shirt, and a different kid-skin jerkin, his long, muscular legs encased to the knee in polished leather boots, his black hair newly washed and shining—the old Alex miraculously restored, or almost. The patina of maturity sat well, she thought, on his strongly chiseled features. *Very* well! Suddenly Marina felt herself blushing, a silly self-conscious smile wobbling on and off her face.

"Sir . . ." she stammered, ". . . h-how, ah . . .

different you look."

He grinned, swept Clare into one arm and held out the other for Marina, saying, "I hope your appetite is as fierce as mine is tonight."

She gave him an uncertain look, not at all sure that he was thinking of food.

19

The dining room of the inn was quite busy when they entered. Heads turned to gaze at them from other tables, admiring the attractive couple and their beautiful little girl, but before they had finished their meal that same little girl was nodding sleepily over her plate.

Marina was startled when Alex said, "I'll take her up to bed."

She laughed. "'Tis sweet of you to suggest it, but nay, I always put Clare to her bed. Mayhap when she gets more used to you . . ."

But Alex stood up and lifted Clare into his arms, and the child seemed quite prepared to go with him. She put her head on his shoulder and a thumb in her mouth and closed her eyes contentedly, and the sight of that contentment gave Marina a queer, hurtful pang. Ah, but once Clare was upstairs in the chamber

Marina was certain that her daughter would be bound to miss her and start to kick up a fuss.

She jumped to her feet. "I'll go with you."

"'Tis not necessary," Alex assured her. He put a hand on her shoulder and pushed her firmly back down in her chair. "I'll attend to Clare. You stay here and finish your wine."

Marina bit her lip. Up to this moment she had felt almost ecstatically happy. They had made good their escape from England. Clare had survived her mishap. They were free and, God willing, would never see Edgar Stafford or Baxton Hall again. But these weren't the only things to account for the warm glow and delicious excitement that coursed through her, Marina knew that well enough. Much of it had to do with Alex. Tall, handsome, and above all young!—his very nearness brought her tinglingly alive again, all her senses springing awake as from a long, deadly sleep. It pleased Marina too to notice the sidelong glances the other women in the room had directed to their table, for Sinclair was a man who would always stand out in any room. But *she* was the one who was with him! *She* had all his attention. Marina felt she was the luckiest woman in Edinburgh that night.

But still she couldn't shake that pang of resentment as she watched Alex walk away with her daughter, Clare's copper curls against her father's shining dark hair, the two of them quite relaxed with each other. Though Marina was glad about that, still . . . she felt curiously shut out, and it hurt severely. Up to now she had been closely involved in every aspect of the little girl's life. She'd had to act the part of both mother and father to her child, and it had become a deeply ingrained habit. Besides, Marina was afraid that once Clare was up in her room and realized that her mother

wasn't with her, she would feel frightened and insecure.

Marina rose and hurried after them and caught up with them in the foyer. When Alex heard her behind them he turned with a frown.

"I—I'd best go with you," Marina told him. "She's not used to anyone else putting her to bed."

He regarded her gravely for a moment, sensing the nervousness and insecurity in her manner, her strong desire to keep Clare all to herself—which was wrong, he felt.

"Marina, I would like a few minutes alone with my daughter. Go back to the table and wait for me."

Alex's voice brooked no argument, and having stated his intention, he left her and climbed the stairs, the child held firmly in his arms, leaving the mother standing in the hallway with a stricken expression on her face. Marina felt as if he had slapped her.

She was suddenly blazingly, unreasonably anger. A scarlet stain spread up from her neck into her face, and she felt like running after him and wrenching Clare out of his arms, and would have too except that it would have frightened the little girl to find herself the object of a tug-of-war between her parents.

There was nothing for it but to return to her table.

Once seated, Marina seized her wine glass and tossed the contents down, then refilled it from the bottle on their table, hoping it would still the violent agitation inside her. She was fuming, so angry she wanted to scream.

How dare Alexander come back into her life and try to take over her duties as a mother! How dare he order her around! What could he be thinking of to take her baby and shove her, the mother, away? Marina stared into her wine glass, blinking furiously to hold back the

tears, feeling terribly unwanted and bereft. Had Alex only said to her, "Do you mind if I tuck Clare in tonight?" it would have been different, she thought furiously, but of course that wasn't his way. Oh no, he was a man who always did as he pleased and wouldn't deign to ask anyone for permission. Now . . . now he was luring her baby away.

Marina picked up her glass with a trembling hand and swallowed half the contents. Well, she thought, she had much to thank Sinclair for—and she was the first to admit it—but that didn't give Alex the right to push her around; to dictate how she should conduct herself as a mother . . . or anything else, for that matter. She had no intention of exchanging one tyrant for another!

The wine had a calming effect on Marina and after a few minutes she felt a little more in control of herself, a little more reasonable. On reflection, she supposed that Alex had a right to spend some private time with his child, and though she'd had Clare all to herself up to now Marina realized that she would have to share her from then on. Very well, she thought, lifting her chin and taking a steadying breath, her eyes flickering to the door, very well then, she was prepared to accept that. What she *wasn't* prepared to accept was the arrogant way Sinclair had gone about exerting his rights.

He was gone what seemed to Marina an awfully long time. She began to fret that he might be having trouble with Clare, and no wonder! He was practically a stranger to the babe—and he had the nerve to think he could take over so easily. Nay, Marina soothed herself, Clare would soon make her preference felt when she woke up to the fact that her mother wasn't coming to kiss her good night, and to play their little

game, to hold her in her arms and rock her to sleep. Good! she thought, smiling bitterly, almost laughing aloud when she visualized Sinclair having to cope with a shrieking, angry little girl who had a pair of lungs that could be heard miles away.

Marina hastily composed her resentful features when Alex strode back into the dining room.

"She's sleeping like an angel," he announced when he sat down opposite her.

"She . . . is?" Marina eyed him skeptically. "Didn't she, ah . . . ask where I was?"

Alex had just taken a sip of his wine. Now his eyes met hers over the rim of his glass, and those eyes saw far more than Marina gave him credit for. He sensed her irritation very clearly. Alex had already noticed that Marina was totally devoted to their daughter, and that was fine up to a point, he thought. But he felt she was far too possessive, both for the good of Clare *and* herself, and it was something he intended to change. The way Alex saw it, there was more to a woman's life than mothering, something that Marina had lost sight of during her time at Baxton Hall. She seemed, he thought, a little confused about her identity, and no wonder when wed to a man who was no husband at all! Now she struck him as being confused, defensive, and lacking in confidence, as if uncertain of her own worth as a woman, something Alex was determined to remedy shortly. But there was a stubbornness in Marina, an obstinacy and stiff pride that he knew wouldn't be easy to deal with, especially as he wasn't noted for his patience.

"Clare is fine," Alex repeated, smiling. "I kissed her for both of us."

He certainly looked fine, thought Marina, glanc-

ing at him furtively when Alex called the serving
woman over and ordered more wine. There he sat,
one long leg crossed over the other, lounging back in
his chair perfectly relaxed and sure of himself.
But why shouldn't he be? Sinclair was on his own
territory now. And he knew exactly what he was
doing and where he was going, while she was still
in a state of uncertainty, mainly about her place in
his life.

Though he had changed in other ways, he was still
the same confident, commanding Alexander, only
more so, mused Marina. Aye, and even more attract-
ive in his maturity. The candlelight glinted off his
expensive polished boots, brought out the blue-black
of his hair, the rich jade of his eyes, and emphasized
the strong planes of his face and the curve of his
high-bridged nose, giving him a faintly rakish but
altogether arresting appearance.

The wine was brought to their table and Alex
refilled their glasses.

"Well!" he said with a grin when the silence grew
awkward between them. "Another inn and another
day, but still the same people."

"I wouldn't say exactly the same." Marina was in a
mood to be perverse. "How could we be when we are
more than three years older and so much has hap-
pened to us in the interim?"

He grinned. "You at least have improved with
time."

She colored as his fiery green eyes burned over her,
touching on her hair, her face, and lingering on the
twin arches of her white breasts peeping saucily above
the neck of her moderately low-cut gown—and rapid-
ly turning the same peach hue of that gown under his
bold appraisal.

Marina confessed, "I certainly never expected to be back in Scotland."

"Ah, woman, you have little faith," he teased. "There is much you have to learn about the Sinclairs, Marina. They keep their promises and take care of their own. Had you known our kind better you would have realized I'd turn up again to see how you were faring, and of course to determine if you might have something that belongs to me."

"You mean Clare?"

Alex nodded. "No Sinclair worth the name would ever allow any bairn of his to be brought up in England, especially by a knave like that husband of yours. Clare Sinclair." He turned the name over on his tongue, as if savoring it. "I misliked the sound of it at first," he admitted, "but now I think it has a bonny ring to it. 'Tis not a name easily forgotten."

Her eyes narrowed. "What if I'd refused to return to Scotland with you?"

Alex looked at her sharply. "You did, at first," he reminded her. A look of mischief glinted in his eyes as he added, "But I think you must be happy now that I managed to change your mind?"

Their clandestine—and passionate—moments under the broken bridge rushed back into Marina's mind and she burned with embarrassment remembering the shameless way she had succumbed to him—but she wasn't about to admit how much *that* had influenced her decision to return with him to Scotland. The man was far too conceited and presumptuous as it was, flattering himself by thinking that his irresistible charms had convinced her she couldn't do without him.

"The thing that changed my mind," Marina made

quite clear, "was that Edgar intended to foster Clare out, and I couldn't bear to let that happen."

For a minute the laughter and teasing died in Sinclair's eyes, and Marina felt a smug satisfaction, delighted to have brought him down a peg or two. She felt insecure and vulnerable enough as it was without Alex impressing on her how much she needed him, as if she didn't know that!

"If I'd refused to leave, would you have tried to take Clare anyway?" She had to know, to discover if it had only been the child that had prompted Alex to risk venturing back into England.

He shrugged impatiently. "You did come, so the question is a mite after the fact. Why waste time conjecturing about what might have happened? Better to concentrate on the present and future."

The future? That was her main worry. At the moment Marina had no idea where she stood. Was she in Scotland now only because of her daughter? She decided to feel him out.

"I suppose you think we can simply pick up where we left off three years ago?" Marina asked him, her heart racing, almost afraid to hear his answer.

"Nothing in this life is simple," Alex sighed, his manner falsely grave even though Marina suspected that he was laughing at her inwardly. "To pick up something that is more than three years old would be stale pickings indeed. Nay"—he shook his head, his eyes filled with amusement—"I much prefer the fresh and new. 'Tis almost always better. And the new brings more of a challenge."

Exasperation almost choked her and Marina burst out rashly, "I would know how you mean to introduce me at Augusta—as your mistress?" Then she held her breath.

Alex's dark brows rose. He was openly grinning at her now.

"Well . . . they will know that you cannot be my wife since you are already married. And they are also aware that I have no need of a housekeeper, since I already have one. So"—he lifted his shoulders—"what does that leave?"

"Oh . . ." Blushing furiously, Marina dropped her eyes to the table, her heart thudding so loud she felt certain he must hear it, all sorts of erotic images rising in her mind to taunt her, her starved flesh quivering. But after a second it struck Marina that Alex hadn't actually said he *desired* her to be his mistress, but rather that his family would assume she was. That made a vast difference.

She gave a start when Sinclair leaned across the table and put his hand over hers. "Be at ease, Marina. My family must think what they will. Only you and I will know the truth."

Her deep brown eyes rose to his, to find him smiling mysteriously, his words and manner maddeningly enigmatic.

"Only we will know," he repeated, his eyes burning into hers.

All Marina knew at that moment was that she couldn't breathe, couldn't think, couldn't gather her wits together under that dark, penetrating stare, eyes that seemed to understand her only too well, perhaps even better than she knew herself.

Hastily she looked away. "I—I must go up and see to Clare. Nay!" she added quickly when Alex too rose, "'tis not necessary that you come with me. Stay here at your leisure."

He rose anyway and escorted her out of the room and up the stairs. But when Marina would have gone

into her daughter's room, Alex caught her playfully around the waist and whisked her to the chamber next door.

"The babe needs no seeing to," he said. "But there's a matter between us that requires urgent attention."

20

The moment his door was closed and locked behind them, Alex gave her no time for sober deliberation. Ignoring Marina's tight, angry face, he said, "I see no reason to make life more complicated than it need be," and seized her in his arms, his thirsty lips swooping down to capture hers. When she tried to wrench away, to twist her head to the side to evade those ravishing lips, Alex held her firmly against him with one arm and, plunging his fingers into her hair, forced her head back so that she could do naught but glare up into his face.

He chuckled low at the sight of her wrathful, indignant expression, the outrage glittering in her beautiful dark eyes. "Downstairs you were full of questions," he said, his emerald eyes taking in every detail of her upturned face. "Now I propose to answer them *properly* in a manner that should leave no lingering doubts in your mind."

The pins and combs burst from Marina's hair as he brought her face to within less than an inch of his, then very deliberately his searching tongue teased the full outline of her mouth, his touch so light, yet so sensual that Marina inhaled raggedly, gathering all her strength to resist what she knew was to come, but even then, acutely conscious of his hardness against her, aware that she had no will to do battle with him. Almost leisurely Alex plundered her mouth with that honeyed tongue, his fingers moving more gently now through her tumbled blonde hair, his body pressing insistently against hers in a way that told Marina how much he needed her.

Her head spun alarmingly even as her famished senses leapt to answer that call, a message as clear to Marina as if he had put it into words. But no, she thought wildly, tensing herself and determined not to respond. First Alex had to make his intentions clear as far as their future together was concerned. She ached for him to tell her that he loved her; to vow that when the time came and she was widowed, then he had every intention of marrying her. Marina was driven to wring that vow out of him; to bring at least a semblance of respectability to their relationship. Then and only then could she hold her head up when she met his family.

But in moments Marina learned something that her proud spirit found difficult to digest. She was in no position to dictate! No position to negotiate or coolly haggle over terms. Shutting his ears to her cries of outrage, Alex picked her up and carried her to his bed and fell upon it on top of her, smothering her protests with his lips and tongue, with the potency of his fully aroused body. He almost ripped the new gown away, exposing her blushing flesh to the burning intensity of

the implacable eyes that gazed upon her as another might savor a feast spread out for his delectation—the lush succulence of her milk-white breasts tipped with blooming cherries, the tight plane of her stomach, the dark and secretive pelt between legs held rigidly closed against him. His fiery eyes flashed upward to her face, the full, quivering lips, silken cloud of pale gold hair scattered about on the pillow, then to her eyes, glowing as with a raging fever, and there was nothing of denial in those eyes now.

"How sweet and beautiful you are, my Marina." His voice was so deep and low that she scarcely heard it, but the emotion in his voice, if not the words, struck away all uncertainty and confusion, all the doubts and misgivings shielding her soft, vulnerable heart. "My Marina," he had said, his voice so loving, so possessive, so caring. She closed her eyes and expelled a long, relieved sigh, chiding herself for being so fainthearted.

Quite suddenly the candle he had left burning at his bedside sputtered out, nipped between Sinclair's impatient fingers. He rose then and Marina heard him undress, heard his harried breathing in the quiet room, and the darkness took on a throbbing imminence as the air will before a storm.

Then Alex was kneeling between her legs, spreading them wide, and Marina felt his fingers, like those of a blind man, tracing the shape of her features, the contours of her lips, her eyes, her ears, roving like teasing whispers through her hair and lightly down over her shoulders. She held her breath, her body trilling as each hand circled her breasts, thumbs now and then flicking nipples already ripe and clamoring for more serious consideration. She gave a start, her

lips parting, when she felt the tips of his fingers graze her stomach—taut and hard with anticipation—then sink lower to the hot, dark place between her thighs.

Board-tense, Marina felt him part her, felt a gliding finger penetrate to stroke and fondle that which had been long dead but in a flash came eagerly alive, rising like the parched head of a flower to the rain, silky, moist, beating like a pulsing heart. A great flooding heat washed over her. Instantly her flesh was drenched with dew. A mad, wanton hunger seized hold of her, driving everything else out of her mind, and voraciously Marina reached for him, thrilling when her sweating hand closed over rigid flesh.

Alex fell on her then, his lips and tongue devouring, tasting, probing, greedily sucking her breasts, ravishing her bruised, swollen lips, lapping at her ears, her throat, while his hands roved over every heated inch of her body. Everything changed then. From shrinking back from him, Marina now surged forward, unable to get close enough to quell the feverish desire shrieking inside her for release. Sobbing, she drove her fingers through his hair, her touch as ruthlessly demanding as his, clutching at the bulging muscles of his shoulders, his back, his thighs, moaning, "Oh God! Alex . . . my love . . ."

Slipping his hands under her buttocks, he lifted her onto his lap. With a delicious shock, Marina felt his burning rod plunge deep inside her, even as his mouth, hot and moist and relentless, took full command of hers. But it was she, rather than he, who had lost all control and began to move with wild abandon, faster and faster as a jockey will drive a horse to a much sought after goal. Mouths joined, her breasts crushed against his chest, her arms tight about his neck, Marina strove for that final rapture, but Alex

had no intention of allowing her to set the pace. After a moment he swept her back against the pillows and loomed over her. "Dear love . . ." he groaned, and vigorously, powerfully, drove her over the pinnacle into mind-shattering ecstasy.

Violently Marina shuddered against him, rocked to the very core of her being. It seemed as if a great hard lump had disintegrated inside her, and with the strain, the denial, of the last three years gone, she suddenly burst into tears.

Alex understood and tenderly enfolded her in his arms, his hand stroking her hair, his lips pressing soothing kisses to her wet cheeks and drenched eyes, and finally once more finding her mouth, tremulous now under his.

After a minute he teased, "Well, was the new better than the old?"

"Aye . . ." Marina admitted shakily. "And for you?"

"'Tis something I can quickly acquire a taste for."

She raised her wet face to him in the darkness. "To think we are back together again!"

"If I recall, you took some convincing. Cruel wench"—he playfully shook her a little—"you did not immediately leap back into my arms, as I might have expected. Nay, not you. It took that husband of yours to force the decision by threatening to send Clare away, then you *had* to take action. So I cannot flatter myself into thinking it had anything to do with me."

Marina was instantly ashamed. Warm and relaxed, wrapped in the security of his arms, she hastened to assure him, "Oh, Alex, it *did* have much to do with you! How can you think otherwise after . . . after what just happened between us?" She raised herself

up on her elbow and bent over him. "Do you really think I would give myself to someone if I didn't—didn't care for them?"

She felt him shrug. "I only repeat what you told me downstairs."

"But surely you don't believe it?" she queried anxiously.

He didn't, but he strung her along. "I don't know, Marina . . . as you said before, both of us have changed, I think you more than me, so I cannot presume to guess what is going through your mind. Nay . . ." he sighed and shook his head, ". . . I think you will have to try hard to convince me that you care." He reached for her hand and placed it on his thigh.

Marina realized then that he was teasing her, and snatched her hand away.

"Alexander Sinclair, you are a wicked, heathenish rascal!"

Laughing, he lifted her on top of him and kissed her passionately, and that was the last of their conversation for quite some time. But when dawn filled the chamber with a cool, white light, Alex again turned to her, asking, "Well, did I manage to answer all your questions?"

Marina lay against the damp, rumpled sheets feeling pleasantly boneless, her long-starved body completely satiated at last. It was his probing question that suddenly cut through her languor, reminding her that there was one important question that still remained unanswered in her mind, and as she thought about it—and what it meant to her—her tension came rushing back.

For a second Marina hesitated, afraid to spoil the newfound joy they shared once more. But even so, she

knew she would never have a moment's rest until she knew the truth, so she whispered, "Nay, not quite all."

Alex lifted her up to sit beside him against the pillows. Her heart fluttered at how grave he looked, all the mischief and teasing gone now. Fascinated, her heart thudding, Marina watched him remove from his little finger a heavy gold ring with a blood-red ruby at its center; then he turned to her, the expression in his eyes unfathomable.

"I may not have answered all *your* questions, Marina," he said. "But you have answered mine. You are my only love, as you ever have been, and this ring is the token of it."

Tears of joy spattered down Marina's cheeks as she watched him slip it on the middle finger of her left hand, then she threw herself into his arms.

"Alex," she wept, "you have made me the happiest girl in Scotland."

"No more doubts from now on," he said, and kissed her deeply.

In single file they rode along narrow trails beaten hard by the clansmen through the centuries, climbing steadily higher into the mountains like pilgrims on a journey to nature's shrine. So total was the silence that it seemed like sacrilege to break it, and for a long time they traveled on without speaking, the only sound the soughing of the wind through the hills, rustling in the heather, and now and then the bell-like ring of a horse's hoof striking granite, echoing like a chime through the hush of the glens.

The afternoon was sullen, the landscape a study in black, gray, and white, silver radiance bursting in the sky where the sun tried to break through the billowing clouds. Far below Marina saw the still, mirrorlike

polish of a loch, a sandy beach without a footprint, and the startled gleam of a stag's eyes watching them from a wooded gully, immobile while they rode on by. In the strange metallic light quartzite scree glittered like diamonds in the dull gray rocks. Gorse flowers hung like droplets of gold in the tangle of dark bushes, and from the black precipice high above sprayed a torrent of crystalline water, the fall vanishing into a gloomy chasm hundreds of feet below.

All about towered the mountains, marching in stately grandeur to the far horizon. Wild moorland of heather and bracken swept across high plateaus. A castle sat upon a distant cliff in lonely isolation, the only sign of man she saw in a region of dramatic beauty, desolate and untamable.

The clouds tossed and rolled in the eerie storm light, frosted with silver. Tiny pink and blue alpine flowers shivered with apprehension in the rising wind, their roots well buried in the narrow cleft between boulders, but their delicate heads vulnerable, as were all fragile things in a land made for giants.

Following Alex's horse, her eyes drawn from the scenery now and then to glance at his broad back, as if for reassurance, Marina was awestruck by the beauty of her surroundings, but also slightly nervous as they picked their way along tracks where one false move would mean a dizzy plunge into dark valleys far below. Her uneasiness increased when now and then she saw flashes of lightning and growling thunder boomed through the mountains. At such times she wanted to call to the man up ahead, to suggest they take shelter under a cliff or wait out the storm in one of the many caverns she noticed cut deep into the hillsides.

But she bit her lip and kept quiet, certain that

Highland women would not be so fainthearted, nor must she be now that she was pledged to one of the clansmen. She had the feeling that Alex would have scant patience with a jittery, high-strung woman. Fearless himself, Marina sensed that she would go down in his estimation if she showed signs of timidity.

They stopped for the night in a tiny stone cot used by herders and travelers. It was bare of furniture except for a small battered table and two stools, the only concession to comfort the massive, crude stone fireplace with a rough chimney jutting up through a hole in the smoke-darkened ceiling, stacks of peat piled up at one side. If they used some of the fuel, Sinclair explained, they were honor-bound to replace it before they journeyed on, so that the next weary traveler who stopped there might enjoy the same welcoming warmth that they would.

Soon Alex had a huge fire blazing in the hearth. It filled the dark little shelter with a bright orange glow, chasing away the cold and dampness that had Clare whimpering and Marina shivering in her boots. While she attended to the little girl, Alex, with a certain flair and obvious experience, whipped up a surprisingly tasty supper from provisions carried in their saddle bags, turning dried red meat, peas and lentils and oatmeal into a kind of stew that, while plain, was pounced on by the hungry travelers.

Their blankets were spread out before the fire. By then the heat in the small building almost made covers unnecessary, though Marina found it wonderfully satisfying to curl up against her love, the covers tucked around her back, and listen to the full force of the storm breaking ferociously over the mountains. Alex lay in the middle, cuddling Marina with one arm and Clare with the other, and for a while they lay

listening to the elements do their worst, the wind roaring through the glens sweeping lashing rain before it, bursts of lightning eerily glimpsed through the small windows, then crashing thunder so loud that Marina felt certain the world itself was being broken up and destroyed.

"I love storms," Sinclair suddenly announced. "'Tis nature's way of reminding us that she still has the upper hand; that we should not get too cocky lest she decide to test our mettle."

"Then she must test you frequently, my lord," Marina replied dryly, but hugging him to take the sting out of her words.

"Och aye," Alex nodded, grinning, "that she has. But the emblem of the clan Sinclair is an armed cockerel, and you know how fierce and intrepid they can be, ever ready for a challenge. The elements have never bested me yet, though I would not wish to be an inexperienced traveler caught unprepared in these mountains, especially in winter. This"—with a nod to the window—"is only a hint of what she can do."

Marina cuddled closer, pressing herself against the warm, muscular frame lying next to her, the babe sound asleep on the other side. Storm or not, she felt deliciously secure with Alex, suddenly certain that he could protect them from just about anything. Was this how Highland women of old felt, she mused, snug and warm in their rude little homes with the love and protection of their men and children all that was necessary to them in life? Marina felt she was one with these women at that moment as she lay warm and happy in her man's strong arms. If this was all she could expect in life, she knew with certainty, it would be enough.

"Alex."

When he turned his face to her she kissed him, and all the love, tenderness, and pride she felt in him was in that kiss.

"Are you happy, my Marina?" His voice was a soft caress.

"Wondrous happy."

"I too," he confessed.

She was drifting off to sleep with her head on his chest when Alex said, "Tomorrow we reach Castle Augusta."

An errant thought skittered across Marina's mind, one that temporarily drove sleep away. "Please, God, let nothing happen to spoil our joy in each other."

What had made her think that? Marina remembered Alex assuring her that his parents, of all people, would understand. Yet still the uneasiness persisted, and for a moment Marina wished they could stay where they were, just the three of them with no outside influence to intrude on their happiness, the only true happiness she had ever known. But she tried to take herself in hand, to still the niggling little voice now worrying away at the back of her mind, reminding herself that Alex was not the heir to the clan, which would make a difference. Less would be expected of him, especially in regard to making a brilliant marriage. But most important of all, he loved her, and he would not allow anything to come between them.

Long before they reached mighty Castle Augusta on its granite cliff overlooking the village of Lochmore, fast by the banks of the mysterious Loch Ness, they began to encounter Sinclair clansmen in their bright red-and-black plaids, the lookouts and sentries guarding clan territory.

Alexander greeted them enthusiastically in Gaelic, and though they seemed relaxed and friendly with each other, Marina noticed that these men gave Alex much deference and respect; none tried to be overly familiar, rather, they maintained a certain distance and reserve, as servants will with a master.

The importance of Alexander's position in the hierarchy of the clan, regardless of the fact that he would never be their leader, was borne home to Marina. She noticed too how the others gazed at her askance, their eyes betraying surprise and curiosity. Alex's brief introduction told them little. "The Mistress Stafford's from England," was all he said, leaving them to make of it what they would.

Immediately some galloped on ahead to warn the chief of their approach while the rest fell in behind them, keeping to a discreet distance as they continued on their way to the castle. But Marina could hear them jabbering excitedly among themselves in Gaelic, and she felt certain they were talking about her, doubtless wondering what Lord Alexander could be thinking of to bring his foreign mistress—and Clare made their status obvious—right to the door of the clan stronghold. In England few among the highborn brazenly presented their lovers to their families, and Marina could not imagine things being any different in Scotland. She quailed as she visualized their shock, the insult they would feel to have her thrust rudely into their midst whether they were prepared to receive her or not, and again she wondered at Alex's audacity.

She had taken great pains with her toilet that morning, in spite of the fact that she'd had to bathe in cold loch water. Now, dressed elegantly in her scarlet riding habit, a saucy little hat perched atop her shining blonde hair, Marina was fairly confident that

at least she *looked* like a lady, even if she had neither money, influence, nor title to her name. Aye, and she would conduct herself like one too! she made up her mind. She would not go among them with her tail between her legs or bow and scrape to win their favor. Either they would like her for herself or they would not like her at all. She was a Dudley, and Dudleys were people to be reckoned with in England. "Ah, but you are in Scotland now!" chuckled a disturbing little voice lurking inside her. "Dudleys are of no importance here."

Marina turned her head to find Alex watching her, a sympathetic expression on his face, as if he understood exactly what she was feeling. But she gave him a bright, confident smile as he rode along beside her, pretending far more courage than she felt, some instinct prompting her to take a tip from him and brazen it out.

"Proud I'll be to show off my women," he said, his eyes warm as they moved from Marina to the child sitting in front of her in the saddle. "I'll be the envy of all when they behold you, for there are none fairer in this land."

Marina realized that this was his way of conveying to her that he had no second thoughts about bringing her here, and it was the best boost to her spirits she could have had.

Then Alex raised his hand and pointed into the distance, and suddenly Marina spotted Augusta. It was huge, dark, forbidding against the storm-tossed sky, brooding down paternally on the small village of Lochmore below and the rugged territory surrounding it as it had done for over six hundred years, sheltering generations of Sinclairs within its stout, impregnable walls.

Would these same walls fall down, Marina mused, when an English *woman* accomplished what no Englishman had ever done—breach the fortress?

The outrider delivered his message to the chief and departed, and the chief in turn returned to the Great Hall to break the news to his wife. The countess collapsed into a chair and put a hand to her head, moaning, "And a child! God's love, 'tis like history repeating itself." Then fiercely, "Oh, how could he? He of all people should have known better." She pressed a clenched fist to her mouth, fighting back tears, her lovely face so pale that the earl was alarmed.

He went to a cupboard, took a key out of his pocket and unlocked it, and lifted out a cut-crystal flask of brandy and poured generous amounts into two glasses. Handing one to his wife, he said briskly, "Now listen to me, Alyssa, what's done is done and no amount of weeping and wailing will change it. Drink that," he urged with a nod to the glass, "'twill steady you."

She did, then wondered aloud, her voice breaking, "Blake, you don't think . . . you don't think this is his way of paying us back?"

The earl's dark brows flew up and he scoffed, "Nay, what nonsense! The things you get into your head! The trouble with you, Alyssa, is that you harbor guilt far more than is necessary, blowing it up out of all proportion—"

Her head snapped up as she interrupted heatedly, "Aye, I *do* feel guilty that our oldest son can never be chief one day, as is his due. And I feel guilty each time he and David squabble—"

"Brothers usually do," he said with a grin.

"We have put them in this situation, my lord, and

because of it Alex has always had a driving need to prove his worth. And now—now he has gone and embroiled himself in much the same situation with this English woman, and their child will suffer for it. By the Blessed Virgin, I—I cannot believe it."

They were in the Great Hall of Castle Augusta, the earl standing in front of a massive, ornate fireplace, his countess seated in a chair nearby, and for a moment both fell silent as they contemplated this startling turn of events. The huge room they were waiting in was very grand, the carved oak furniture glowing with a rich patina, mellow tapestries and a pastel-hued Turkey carpet on the walls, and fresh, sweet-scented rushes on the floor garnered from the banks of the Ness, with carnations and rose petals scattered among them. Vases of flowers lent color to dark niches, and there was a stunning portrait of Lady Alyssa hanging in pride of place above the mantel. Two shaggy wolfhounds lay near the earl's feet, both watching his every move while pretending to sleep.

Alyssa stared into the fire that had been lit to ward off the dampness brought about by the storm. She had known about the English girl, of course, but had supposed that the affair had been finished long ago. Now she knew that this girl had been the reason Alex had cut short his recuperation, abruptly vanishing one morning and leaving the terse message behind, "Gone to attend to business in the South." They had been under the impression that he had gone to Ayrshire to see into some property left to him by his grandfather, never dreaming that he would have dared venture into England after his recent travails there. The very fact that he had done so served to prove to her how important this woman must be to him—but the lady was already married! And the child, so Alyssa had

been led to believe, was her husband's.

She gave a start when Blake leaned down and took the glass out of her hand and set it on the mantel, then drew her up into his arms. For a moment he regarded her upturned face tenderly, thinking that she was still the most ravishing woman he had ever known, aye, even with silver threads in her flaming red hair and the faintest of lines about her eyes. She had, the earl felt proudly, the type of beauty that was nigh indestructable, that mellowed well with the passage of the years.

"If you could return to your youth, Alyssa, would you change things?" he asked her, low.

"You mean—with us?"

He nodded.

A look of horror filled her clear green eyes. "Nay, darling, never! 'Tis only that I wish . . . wish we had been wed at the time we had Alex, that is all." She hugged him tight and laid her head against his chest, murmuring, "'Tis the only thing I would change about our union, which otherwise has brought me nothing but bliss."

Remembering a recent conversation with King James in which he had brought certain matters to the King's attention, Blake raised her face to his and said, "Once, long ago, I made you a promise, Alyssa. If you remember, I told you that our son would not suffer from being born out of wedlock; that I'd do my utmost to make certain of that. Well . . ." he smiled into her curious face, realizing that nothing was decided yet in Edinburgh and that he must take care not to build her hopes up lest they be dashed, ". . . I doubt that any could say Alexander has suffered in any way through us. He lacks nothing. And, my love, he is a young man yet with his whole future before him. Depending on

293

how he conducts himself, great good fortune could lie in store for him. But for now," he hurried on when he saw that she was about to question him, "try not to worry. Remember how *we* were in our youth?"

In their youth! Alyssa looked up at him with the old flirtatious glint in her eyes. Even yet, she thought, Blake had the power to excite her—not so surprising, she supposed, since he was still a very attractive man who looked ten years younger than his fifty-three years. She chuckled softly, "Think how we are *now*!"

"Shameless hussy!" The earl pulled her very close for a moment. "Would you have our children arrive and see us behaving thus? Faith, Alyssa, but parents are supposed to be grave and dignified and . . . sexless."

They kissed again, and she suddenly decided, "We will welcome this lady of Alexander's into our home and not make a stranger of her. I would not want her to go through what *I* had to when you first introduced me to the Sinclairs. To venture among them took every ounce of courage I possessed."

So when the young couple rode into the courtyard they found the earl and countess waiting for them at the door, and a more handsome pair Marina had never seen. She was a little taken aback to see that they were holding hands, and turned to Alex quickly, whispering under her breath, "Are—are these your parents?"

He nodded, grinning, well used to witnessing demonstrations of affection between them. He could have told Marina too that his father, as far as he knew, had never taken a mistress in all the years of their marriage, which was unusual for a man in his position.

The earl himself came forward to help Marina down off her horse, and the instant she raised her face

to him, Blake realized why his son—who was so much like himself—had risked his life to bring her home to Scotland.

Setting her down, the Earl of Belrose made Marina a courtly bow.

"Welcome to Castle Augusta," he told her.

21

"And this is our daughter," Alexander said after introducing Marina to his parents. Proudly he held Clare up for their inspection.

The earl and countess stared at the child, then at each other, and suddenly realized that they were grandparents, for there was no doubt at all that the child was Alexander's babe. She was a tiny miniature of the countess, even to her flaming red hair, more like her than any of her own daughters.

For a second the new grandparents were too moved to speak. Blake's hand tightened on Alyssa's when he noticed the glint of tears in her eyes—then both reached for the little girl at once, but it was Alyssa who carried her granddaughter through the portal into the Great Hall of Augusta. Watching them, suddenly so relieved and happy that she felt she would explode, Marina felt instinctively that there was some-

thing significant in that, though she couldn't have said why.

She and Alex were given separate room in the castle, though with a connecting door. As she bathed and dressed for dinner that first evening, Marina was glad to have a few minutes to herself to absorb the exciting events of the day: Alex was with his father in the library, and Clare too had been taken off her hands by her grandmother. Now, seated at the dressing table in her mist-blue satin gown, carefully dressing her hair and anxious to look her very best that evening, Marina reflected that the meeting with Alexander's parents had gone vastly better than she had expected. She still found it hard to believe just how well, dreading the meeting as she had. They had been warm and friendly and so easy to talk to! Neither by word nor deed had they displayed any animosity toward her, or even embarrassment at her awkward position in their son's life. Clare had had a lot to do with that, Marina was certain. Their joy in being grandparents had immediately swept away any reservations they might have had, and by the time the three younger children returned from visiting their Uncle Jason and his wife, the ice had been broken and all four of them were quite at ease with each other.

Muir and young Ralph, eighteen and fifteen respectively, had recently returned from France for their summer holiday, and they were obviously startled, as was their eleven-year-old sister Alicia, to find an English woman and a small child in their home. But taking their cue from their parents, they too had been friendly, especially Alicia who cried in delight when she beheld Clare. "Welladay, now I am an aunt! Oh, wait till our Kirstin sees the babe." She glanced at Marina shyly, explaining, "My older sister has been

wed these past two years and dearly wants a baby, but"—she sighed—"as yet none has appeared. So you would do well, mistress, to keep a tight hold on wee Clare lest she be stolen from you," she finished with a grin.

All the Sinclairs were dark, Marina noticed, and well above average in height, even Alicia, a lass with a puckish grin and long black hair reaching to her thighs.

"You will meet Kirstin soon," Lady Alyssa assured Marina. "She lives not far away. Doubtless, once she learns of your arrival, she and her husband will waste no time in riding over to meet you. David too should be back from Edinburgh this eve, mayhap in time for supper." In one of her warm, impulsive gestures the countess leaned forward and squeezed her hand, adding, "We are a very close family. My lord and I have never had a remote, formal relationship with our children, such as you might find in other households. We are a candid, exuberant lot, Marina," she chuckled, "but you must not let the Sinclairs overwhelm you. For myself, I had to learn to assert myself when I first came among them. 'Tis always wise to start the way you mean to finish up."

Marina sensed that Lady Alyssa was trying to tell her something.

She liked and was impressed by the chief and his countess, and dared to hope that they would grow to like her in return. She had noticed them both glancing at Alex's ring on her finger, so they must guess, she reasoned, that they were pledged to each other and would marry when she was free to do so.

Catching sight of her glowing face in the mirror, Marina felt that her happiness was almost complete, and certainly would be once Alex made her his wife. She decided that when everything settled down she

must write to Gwen Porter and let her know how well everything had gone, but when Edgar came into her mind, Marina quickly thrust all thoughts of him aside. Marina hoped fervently that she would never have to set eyes on the man again.

When a thorough search of the countryside all the way to the Scottish border failed to uncover Marina or the child, Edgar Stafford rode to Brokenbridge Farm and barged furiously into the Porters' house, charging, "The sleeping tincture was in the jam! Only you"—he jabbed a finger at Gwen as the couple sat at the supper table with their small son—"could have acquired such a substance. So, mistress, I can only conclude that you aided and abetted my wife in her plan to leave me. Where have they gone?" he thundered, hanging over the table and glaring into her face. "Tell me now or, bigod, you'll regret it."

Bert Porter sprang to his feet, overturning his chair.

"How now, Stafford, how now?" he growled, angry that his neighbor should force his way into their home and disturb them at supper. Bert knew by now that Marina had vanished with the child, but he had no idea that Gwen had helped them leave, simply because she had felt it best—for his peace of mind—not to tell him. Bert was a simple, straightforward fellow who had old-fashioned views when it came to marriage, and though he realized that Marina was far from happy with Stafford, so were countless wives who stoically resigned themselves to accepting their fate. He would never have considered it grounds for leaving her spouse.

"I like not you coming here in this manner," Porter made clear. "And to insult my wife—"

"Ask her for yourself," Edgar interrupted. "Who but a midwife or—or doctor could have procured that

sleeping draught?"

Bert turned to his wife, who sat amazingly calm and self-composed under Stafford's tirade. "Well, m'dear, what do you have to say about this?"

She shrugged. "'Tis true I have poppy juice, but so do many who are neither midwives or doctors. I can assure you"—she raised her brown eyes and looked directly at Stafford—"that it is not so hard to come by. Look at Dacre's son, Nevil. Because of the juice, he lives his life in dreams. Aye, and many another too. Nay," she shook her head, "'tis not hard to get for one intent on finding it, and hardly evidence to accuse me."

"There!" said her husband decisively. "Now you have your answer. Now leave us in peace to finish our meal before I forget you are a friend and neighbor."

For a second the men eyed each other challengingly and there was an instant when Gwen was certain that Stafford would make a fight of it, but instead he suddenly wheeled away from the table and strode out of the house. To Tar, waiting outside, he grumbled, "There's no help to be got there, though I still say that Gwen Porter had a hand in it, and had they not long been allies of the Staffords I would not have let it rest until she spoke the truth." Edgar was no fool. He had already alienated the Percys, formerly another good neighbor, and if he were to do the same with the Porters he realized that he would stand alone in time of trouble, which could prove disastrous. Both these families were large, with hordes of kin to call upon for support. It had been this thought that had prevented Edgar from reaching across the Porters' table and seizing Gwen by the neck, choking the truth out of her if necessary.

Tar touched fingers gingerly to the large lump on the back of his head. "'Twas not a woman who near

bashed in my skull," he pointed out. "Nay, there was muscle behind that blow. Methinks her accomplice was male."

Stafford mulled that over as they rode back to Baxton Hall, then set about questioning his squire closely, demanding that he tell him of any man whom Marina had showed an undue interest in.

"'Twas none of ours," Tar assured him. "They wouldn't have dared. Besides, they are all still at the Hall now." He threw a sidelong look at his master, reminding him, "Nor could it have been an outsider. She was too closely watched."

"Well, it was *somebody*!" Edgar glared at him, and as he recalled the evening that Marina had come home late from the fair—and how pale and upset she had seemed, almost as if she had met a ghost on her way home—a dark suspicion entered his mind, one that swelled ballonlike until it burst with the force of an explosion inside his skull. "Sinclair!" he cried, reining in his horse and bringing it to a dead stop. "'Twas that bastard Sinclair! Aye, did she not run away with him before?"

"But—but that was long ago."

"Not so long," he contradicted grimly, rage boiling inside him afresh at the pair daring to thwart him once more. At the thought of it he was nearly beside himself with fury, and his squire eyed him in alarm as his face turned a deep, mottled purple. Now, too late, Edgar saw his mistake in allowing Marina to go to the fair. Taking advantage of the crowds, Sinclair must have slipped over the border to meet her, and this was the result.

"We are going to Scotland," Stafford announced.

"What?" Tar's eyes widened in disbelief.

Edgar nodded firmly. "We will leave at dawn tomorrow morning."

His squire stared at him open-mouthed, sheer horror on his face. Go to Scotland! Face the nobleman surrounded by his clan, all fierce fighters if the tales he had heard of the clans were true. Further, there was an excellent chance that they would never reach the Scottish Highlands alive, nor even get safely over the border. Finally he stammered, "Nay . . . nay, master . . . that we dare not do—"

Stafford struck him across the face with his whip.

"I give the orders here!" he shouted. "You need but obey. Do you think for a moment that I mean to accept this and do nothing? You fool, you should know by now that I *never* would. Sinclair took her to Ayrshire, did he not? Well then, he has either taken her there again or to his castle that the Cairnmores spoke about in the mountains. I will find them!" he thundered, his face purple and his eyes glittering. "And 'tis your duty to accompany me."

They rode on in silence, Tar with a livid welt crossing his face from his forehead to his chin. He had worked for Stafford for years, as no other had done, and considered himself to be a loyal servant of the old type who were fast disappearing from the scene. But . . . he was not so young as he had once been and not quite so able in battle, and if they managed to cross the Scottish border he was certain that they would have to fight every step of the way if they ventured into the Highlands, and once there, doubtless, come to a violent end at the hands of barbarians. And all for a wench who had demonstrated that she would *never* stay with Stafford, regardless of how often they brought her back. His master was mad!

When Edgar arose to start the journey the next morning his long-time servant had vanished.

A Sinclair outrider led the way through the mountains, the two young noblemen and the rest of their followers coming behind. They had left Edinburgh that morning and hoped to reach Castle Augusta before dark, but had been hampered by the weather. All were bundled up in ankle-length hooded cloaks to protect them from the howling wind that drove sheets of rain before it, making the narrow, dangerous trails even more hazardous than they normally were. They rode forward over the necks of their mounts, heads low but eyes raised to scan the wild territory surrounding them, the lair of outlaws and brigands.

When the trail broadened, Jay Sinclair fell in beside his cousin David, the future chief of their clan. Rain dripped off Jay's long nose and streamed down his weather-beaten face, with a scar running from the left side of his mouth to his chin. He was not one of the handsome Sinclairs, certainly not a comely man like David, but he had a certain roguish appeal for all that.

"What think you of all the pother to do with the King fetching his bride over from Denmark?" he said. "To hear him tell it, there have never been storms at sea such as he encountered. His Majesty is no' over-brave, I fear." There was a hint of contempt in his voice.

David laughed, nodding. "'Tis amazing he risked going over there to fetch her at all. God's soul, to think that he actually went through with the marriage! 'Tis heartrending to see how Lindsay and all his other favorites are pouting and ringing their hands now that their lord and master has proved a turncoat," he mocked. "Bothwell swears he's actually quite smitten with the Queen."

"Fy, who would not be?" Jay thought of the beautiful, golden-haired Anne of Denmark, a blushing

young virgin only recently turned fifteen, and smacked his lips. "I thought of offering my services to teach him how to work with her," he chuckled, his dark eyes twinkling. He suddenly roared with laughter, "Bigod, I would have given a pouch of gold to see them that first night in the royal bedchamber!"

David laughed too, then said, "And now all this talk about witchcraft."

"It comes from sticking his nose too closely in books."

David glanced at him, sobering, "There *are* witches in Scotland, cousin, as you well know."

Jay opened his mouth, then closed it again. He had been about to say, "And methinks your friend Bothwell might be one of that ilk," but thought better of it. At the moment Davey and Francis Stewart, the fifth Earl of Bothwell, were very thick, and Bothwell was closely related to the King through his father, Lord John Stewart, one of the illegitimate children of James V of Scotland, the present King's grandfather. Stewart's mother was Jean Hepburn, the sister of the same Bothwell who had briefly been married to Queen Mary, the King's mother, so he had a close connection to the crown. But King James loathed the man, though at first he had been generous to him and because of their kinship—and Bothwell's undeniable intelligence and bravery—had made him Lord Admiral of Scotland. But it hadn't been long before Stewart's overweening pride and ambition, his arrogance and outspokenness, had turned his sovereign against him. Though they maintained a facade of affability for appearance's sake, the inner circle at court knew how it was with them.

Jay was the same age as Bothwell, twenty-seven, and his cousin David only twenty-one, therefore through lack of experience more easily impressed. Jay had

been wilder than most in his youth, as the scars on his body attested to, but during the last few years he had calmed down and, he liked to think, matured. He could well understand David's finding the clever, boisterous, and powerful Bothwell an exciting contact in Edinburgh, and Bothwell, for his own reasons, nurtured the friendship with the future chief. But Jay sometimes wondered if it was wise. There was an unpredictability, even an instability, in Francis Stewart that Jay sensed even if David didn't, and it worried him.

The subject of witchcraft had been raised because of the violent weather Anne of Denmark had encountered during her sea journey to Scotland to join the King. So bad had it been that Admiral Munk, in charge of the fleet conducting her over, had had to take refuge in a Norwegian fjord, there to wait out the worst of the storms. This after the young Queen by proxy had almost lost her life when cannon had slipped from their moorings in the upheaval. That had been when King James, herolike, had decided to sail to Norway and bring his girl-queen back in person, but on the trip home they had again been bombarded by ferocious storms. Thereupon the good Admiral Munk declared that witchcraft must be the cause of it, that "someone" strongly desired to see the King and Queen dead at the bottom of the sea.

In a way, Jay had been surprised that a man as cultured and intellectual as James Stewart could believe in witchcraft, or at least that people who dabbled in the black arts could actually have the power to bring about the results they wished. But of course the King had the type of searching mind that carefully weighed up and considered everything before he accepted or rejected an idea, and at the moment he seemed to be seriously considering that there might be

those in his kingdom who wanted him dead. And he had determined to find out who they were and burn them at the stake.

"I mislike Edinburgh," Jay suddenly confessed. "All the scheming and intrigue ever simmering there makes my head ache. They can have it. Give me the clean, uncluttered air of the Highlands any time."

When still a few miles from Castle Augusta, they came upon the first Sinclair sentries, one of whom rode forward to tell David that his brother had arrived home. "And he has an English woman and a child with him," he added, speaking their native Gaelic.

David and Jay exchanged a look of pure astonishment.

"A—an *English* woman!" Jay fairly spluttered. "In the name of all that's holy!"

David's face tightened. "Trust that brother of mine to catch us off guard."

22

Marina had enjoyed the evening immensely—the orange glow of the fire filling the hall, the good food and wine, and Alex's eyes smiling at her in the candlelight, happy because he saw that *she* was happy. His sister Kirstin, a girl about Marina's own age, had joined them with her husband, Robert Douglas, whom Marina remembered coming to Baxton Hall with Alex following their abortive attempt to free Queen Mary. The small company had been disposed to be charming to their English guest, the piper playing discreetly in the background, and the storm outside—the real world—seemed very far away to Marina that night.

After dinner they were all seated around the fire, Kirstin strumming a lute and her husband preparing to entertain them with a song, when the huge doors to Augusta burst open and two tall men in long, dripping cloaks entered, a chilly gust of night air entering with

them, making the candles flicker and the fire emit a sudden belch of smoke. Alex stood up and thrust out a hand in greeting as David and Jay Sinclair came hastily over to the warmth of the fire, rain spattering off them onto the rushes. "Cock's bones!" Alexander laughed at the state of them. "You two look as if you've had an encounter with Nessie." Nessie was the popular name given to the monster said to reside in the depths of Loch Ness.

"'Tis an evil night," David nodded, shaking hands with his brother, at the same time throwing the hood of his cloak off his head, his thick, reddish-fair hair glinting in the light of the fire. Marina eyed him curiously. David Blake Sinclair was the only fair-haired member of the family, otherwise he was as tall and broad as the rest, she saw. Perhaps his features were a little more delicate, though he had the dark brown eyes of most of the family; Marina thought that he bore a marked resemblance to his mother. He was an exceedingly handsome man, but immediately she sensed that he was more aloof and reserved than the rest. "I heard from one of the sentries that you'd come back," he was saying to Alex. "Faith, but you come and go like a phantom."

In contrast to David's cool greeting, Jay Sinclair hurried forward and wrung Alexander's hand. "Happy I am to see you back, Cousin," he grinned. "Hopefully, this time to stay?"

Alex smiled. "That is my intention."

Then the newcomers turned inquisitively to Marina. She looked all blue and gold in the firelight, like a fine piece of porcelain, the flames etching her exquisite features and flickering in her large dark eyes. For a moment those eyes held David; bewitching they were, spellbinding. With an effort he wrenched his gaze away—to her shimmering blonde hair, then to her full

breasts above the low neckline of her blue gown—and for a second he couldn't conceal his surprise and admiration. "Well," he said, "I can see that Scotland doesn't have *all* the beautiful ladies in this island."

As was seemly considering his rank, Marina curtsied when she was presented to Alexander's brother. David took her hand and kissed it, bowing slightly. Jay seized her hand, gave it a smacking kiss, then swept her a low bow. "Charmed I am to meet you, Mistress Stafford," he said enthusiastically, his eyes bright with appreciation that he made no effort to hide.

When the two men threw off their cloaks, the servants scurried to bring them hot food from the kitchen. They stepped up to the fire and held out their hands to the blaze, and the two wolfhounds, who had been basking there, gave them an aggrieved look and slunk away to throw themselves down in a dark corner where they wouldn't be disturbed. Turning his back to the fire, David looked at Alex. "So you went back to England? 'Twould be well," he went on when his brother nodded, "if the King never hears about this."

Alex shrugged. "James himself, so I hear, risked much to fetch *his* lady home from Denmark."

"That was different."

Lady Alyssa quickly changed the subject. "How goes it in Edinburgh, Davy? What of our new Queen? Does she seem to be adapting to our ways here?"

Conversation turned to the latest developments in the capital, Jay informing them that King James had launched a witch hunt, convinced that there were those in his realm who sought by Satanic means to bring about his own death and that of his Queen. The chief laughed. "What nonsense! Surely he is not serious?"

Jay nodded soberly. "He's set on an investigation,

enraged that traitors lurk about him, and enraged that they would dare to attempt such a thing."

"If any would 'twould be the English," David added without thinking. "The King's first step should be to rout Queen Elizabeth's spies from his court. Faith, but they slink about there like hyenas, the filthy scavengers—"

"Brother," Alexander growled, "you have an uncivil tongue."

The heir flushed and stiffened at the rebuke, his eyes flashing with anger; then he realized his discourtesy. "My pardon, mistress." He bowed to Marina. "I—'tis just that I am not used to having foreigners in the castle. No offense intended."

Marina inclined her head. Her cheeks were scarlet.

There was a dreadful moment of tension as the two brothers glared coldly at each other and Lady Alyssa clenched her hands together in her lap, gazing fixedly at the fire. "Music, Kirstin," said the chief, throwing a hard look at his two oldest sons. Fortunately, the servants returned to the hall bearing steaming platters of food, and David and Jay repaired to the board for their supper.

But the evening was spoiled, though Kirstin strummed one gay tune after the other and Robby and even Jay, once he had finished his meal, obliged with a song or two. Afterwards the conversation limped off to a fresh start, and all, including David, made an attempt to be interesting and witty, but the tone of the evening was irretrievably ruined.

"Your brother doesn't like me," Marina cried the moment she and Alex were alone in her room, great disappointment in her voice. "And he hates the English."

"Nay, nay," Alex brushed it off, "you must not take it personally," but she saw that he was more than a

little annoyed. "He's only a lad yet and spoke without thinking." Suddenly he grinned. "And 'tis true that we've had few of your countrymen at Augusta."

Marina glanced at her bed where Clare was sleeping soundly.

"He showed no interest in seeing our daughter."

"We must introduce them in the morning."

Alex went to her then and slipped his arms around her waist, whispering in her ear, "Don't disturb the babe. Sleep with me this eve."

"But—what will they think?"

He laughed at that, nuzzling her cheek, her throat, his hands sliding up the bodice of her gown to her breasts. "Why, think you, that we have been given chambers with connecting doors? They know we are pledged to each other and already lovers, and that I would take you even if we'd been given rooms at opposite ends of the castle. Besides"—he turned her to face him, that lazy, sensuous expression in his eyes that Marina knew so well by now and thrilled to— "when I hunger to sleep with the woman I love I have no intention of asking others for permission."

Marina never tired of hearing Alex say that he loved her, but she felt compelled to say, "But to lie together before marriage—in their house! And Alex"—she wagged a chiding finger at him—"connecting doors are common in ancient dwellings, and they were not put there for the convenience of clandestine lovers. Nay, they were to provide an escape route for the occupants in times of trouble, and well you know it! Do you actually think your parents would aid and abet our desire to lie together?"

He laughed, his arms tightening on her shoulders. "*They* lay together often enough before marriage, and I am the proof of it."

Something in his tone made Marina lift searching

eyes to his face.

"You . . . surely you don't blame them?"

"Nay, of course not," he replied quickly. "What good would it do to blame them? They were mad for each other, as we are, and since they were in no position to wed . . ." he finished with a shrug.

Marina studied him for a moment, wondering if he resented the fact that he was not the heir; if that was what caused the friction between him and David, but she kept her thoughts to herself.

"Our situation is much the same as theirs was," Alex went on persuasively. "'Tis a fact that love does not always arrive at exactly the appropriate time, the convenient time, nor does it wait for official sanction." His eyes were warm as they moved over her face. "True enough, we are unable to wed—but by God, we are perfectly able to love each other, and I for one have no intention of stifling my feelings until some priest of the church gives me *legal* permission to show them."

He spoke with such passionate determination that Marina had to smile. She could not help but admire Alexander's forcefulness, his utter disdain for convention and rules and regulations. Had he not been, she wouldn't be in Scotland today. These were also traits in him that Marina found exciting; Alex was a man with boundless confidence in himself; he was quite prepared to go his own way if necessary, as he had proved countless times. But—it was different for a woman. Very different. Where a man might be admired and applauded for his boldness and resolution, a woman would be condemned and ostracized; she would be thought unnatural.

"Easy for you to say, sir," she said.

He gave her a direct, appraising look, admitting, "I realize it won't be easy for you, Marina, but I feel you

have enough courage and fortitude to handle it."

He threw open the door to his own room and waved her inside, saying, "I think we have need of serious speech together so that we both, ah . . . know where we stand."

Feeling a touch of uneasiness, Marina walked ahead of him into the room and watched Alex close the door behind them. Then he pulled her down to sit on the edge of the bed beside him, taking her hand in his.

"We have already lost three years," he said. "Time we could have spent together. And if we wait for that husband of yours to expire, God knows how much longer it would be. Surely you can see that the idea of holding back until everything is just right would be ludicrous?"

Marina nodded. "Aye, but—"

"We love each other"—his hand rose to touch her cheek—"and want to be together, and since we are already lovers, I want you to continue to share my bed; to live with me in a natural manner."

"As . . . as your mistress?"

Alex nodded soberly. "Until you can be my wife. There's no other way, Marina."

She recognized that much. There *was* no other way. But at least when the time came they would marry and make everything right. Marina could see that Alex was as anxious for that day to come as she was, and that knowledge made it easier for her to fill the role she must temporarily play. Otherwise—had there been doubts about that in her mind—she would never have consented to continue to live with him as his mistress.

She put a hand on his knee and cautioned earnestly, "We will have to be very discreet, to be careful not to offend—"

"Marina, there will be nothing furtive, hidden, or

apologetic about the way we live," Alex made clear. "I would not demean our love that way."

"But—but there's no need to flaunt it!" Marina protested, cringing inwardly as she visualized them being held up to public censure, contempt, and condemnation. She had been raised to be a lady; it was ingrained in her, and while Marina was well aware that many among the highborn had recourse to take lovers, since most of the marriages they were locked in were mere business arrangements, still, these illicit affairs were always conducted most discreetly and generally kept hidden in the background.

"We won't flaunt it," Alexander assured her, then added, "but neither will we live covertly, like creatures hiding in a burrow. That I could never stand!"

Her heart sank. "You—you expect me to live *openly* with you as your mistress?"

Alex nodded, saying firmly, "It is not in my nature to skulk about."

Marina bit her lip and dropped her eyes to his tanned hand resting possessively on her knee, a pale circle on his little finger where his ring had once been, the one that now gleamed proudly on hers. She *wanted* to find in herself the courage to live openly—brazenly!—as Alex suggested, and she certainly loathed the thought of acting in a way that would have demeaned their love for each other, tainting it, degrading it in a futile effort to conform to the edicts of society. But the scandal! The disgrace!

"'Tis the only way we can stay together," Alex emphasized quietly. "I will not debase what I feel for you to please others, nor," he said, "should you."

Marina flicked a quick look at him from under her lids and saw that he was determined about this. She felt a hot spurt of anger, seeing no reason why they couldn't live quietly, circumspectly, for the time being

keeping their relationship out of the public eye. There was nothing debasing about that that she could see! And it would make things much easier for her . . .

But Alexander had never been a man to take the easy way! Marina reminded herself. Now she was faced with a choice much the same as he had given her that day under the broken bridge in Northumberland, when he had told her he would wait for her decision for two days but no longer. This was one more of his impossible choices, but as with the other, he meant it. She would either live with him openly or not at all.

Suddenly—and with a sense of defiance—Marina realized that there was no choice involved. She loved Alexander, admired him for the very qualities that were causing her mixed feelings now, and certainly wanted to stay with him, aye, even if it meant thumbing her nose at society to do it.

She laughed shakily. "Well, my lord, since when have we ever gone the acceptable route? Faith, but it would seem strange to take that path now, after being used to battling our way through a thicket." Marina turned to him and their eyes met, hers as dark and fierce and rebellious as Alex had ever seen them. "I will spit in the eye of anyone who dares try to defile our love!" she declared, and meant it.

He caught her beautiful face between his hands, his look adoring. "My love," he said, "we were made for each other."

They lay naked together on the massive oak bed, arms entwined, bodies pressed close, for a few moments content just to hold each other. Secure in the warm cocoon of their love, safe behind the thick walls of Augusta and buttressed from the rest of the world by the mountains, they savored their feelings for each other while listening to the storm rampage in howling fury against the castle walls.

Alex turned his dark head, his eyes soft now, worshipful.

"There has never been another like you, my Marina," he swore. "Aye, nor ever will be. I cannot explain why, but from the first moment I met you . . . I knew, though you were a dented, battered wee creature"— he smiled into her eyes—"still, my dear one, I knew!"

"I hoped." Her voice shook with the force of her emotions. "But I could never be sure of you."

"And now you *are* sure?" His warm hand slowly caressed the side of her body as it was turned toward him, and there was reverence in that caress that went far beyond physical passion, far beyond desire or the need for quick gratification.

"I'm sure," she whispered, oh, and the wonder and joy of being so! "Did you think of me while you were in prison?"

"Aye, and nearly went mad with it." He considered a moment, then went on, "I think the worst part was not being able to contact you to let you know why I didn't come back. I realized you'd be wondering . . ."

"I thought you'd lost all interest," Marina confessed. Her expression grew sober as she remembered that awful time in her life, the waiting, waiting, then the growing despair and abject misery when she had to confront the fact that her love was never coming back; that all the promises Alex had made to her had been lies. But she had been wrong!

"Fainthearted wench!" he teased, and gave her a playful little slap on the hip that was more like a love pat. Alex hated to see the cloud of remembrance in the brightness of her eyes, and sought to bring the glow of happiness back. "Now I think you know Sinclair better than you did then?"

"M-much better." Her voice was not quite steady, for now Alex's hand lingered on her breast, his fingers

maddeningly toying with the nipple, and she felt his
need swelling against her hip, his eyes suddenly on
fire.

He kissed her mouth, her throat, her breasts, mur-
muring, "You will always be mine . . . always . . ."
And to be his—on whatever terms—seemed to Mari-
na at that moment all that she would ever desire.
Within minutes, as Alex's hands and lips scorched her
willing flesh, as he whispered how much he loved,
desired, and yearned to cherish her, Marina's passion
surged to meet his, wild as the storm that raged
beyond the castle walls. Hungrily she pressed her lips
to his smooth, tanned skin, her eager hands closing
over bulging muscles, her fingers curling in the dark
hair on his chest, then tracing the shape of him with
her hands, then her lips.

Finally they united in a kind of frenzy, and there
was a touch of rebelliousness in their union that night,
both ready to do battle with anyone in defense of their
right to love, neither doubting that they would tri-
umph in the end.

— *Demonic Pact* —

Edinburgh,
1591–1592

The violent storms of late summer gave way to a
golden autumn in the Highlands as a mellowness
settled over the land. The days were still now with soft
blue skies and warm sunshine to ripen the fruit in the
orchards of Augusta and the corn in the few arable
fields in the rocky terrain. All the colors changed in a
dramatic year-end burst of vibrant glory, the moun-
tains from dark gray to a tawny bronze, the glens
between the peaks like great fissures of fire as the trees
blazed orange, yellow, rust, and red, the streams and
lochs a sharp cerulean blue, and the moorland sport-
ing a lush carpet of royal purple heather. The air itself
had a spicy tang of summer flowers drying and
crumbling in the brief, warm sun, of apples and herbs
and freshly threshed corn. All hands on the estate,
including the villagers of Lochmore, were busy
with the harvest and setting stores aside for the long
winter ahead. Great hunting parties set out in

search of game, much of it to be smoked and dried, and the cooks at the castle were busy making jams and preserves from the fruit and berries, and apple cider, sack, and wine. Beer and ale were brewed, nuts collected from the forests, and at the end of all the activity there was the annual Harvest Ball to look forward to once the work was done.

David Sinclair was astounded when he discovered that Alexander meant to appear at the ball with his mistress. For a day or two he simmered, then, deciding that he had as much right to his say as any, he confronted his parents late one afternoon in their private quarters at the castle. His father had spent the whole day hunting stag. Now, somewhat weary and fresh from a hot tub and still in his long dressing robe, Blake was relaxing with a glass of porter before supper while Lady Alyssa worked on a tapestry by the window. When David entered he found them chatting companionably, the very picture of domestic bliss. Somehow the sight of them looking so comfortable and happy together while *he* churned with such long-standing resentment—because of them!—infuriated the young nobleman.

After a curt greeting he came right to the point.

"Well, what say you to this?" he asked angrily. "Alex means to have her stand at his side at the Harvest Ball."

The earl nodded slowly, at the same time throwing a sidelong glance at his wife, who calmly continued with her sewing, the late afternoon sunlight streaming in the window making a golden halo of her head. Alyssa winced slightly as she pricked her finger, but she didn't raise her face from the work in her lap, nor did her serene expression change. To her son she seemed completely composed, but inwardly her emotions

were in sudden chaos.

"They have decided to live openly together," Blake explained.

"*They* have decided!" David's fair skin flushed with angry color. "'Tis not for *them* to decide how they will conduct themselves here."

"Nor for you either," his father growled.

David stared at the earl, his dark eyes narrowing. "Then you mean to allow them to—to flaunt this relationship? Blessed Jesu, I cannot believe it! Have you thought how this will offend our guests, men of the Church among them? Shortly the Sinclairs will be the talk of the Highlands. Aye, and the gossip will quickly make its way to court. You know well enough how King James feels about such liaisons, especially when one of the party is married—and wed to an Englishman!"

If he'd hoped to frighten his father he was disappointed. Blake chuckled and shrugged. "The King is no stranger to scandal in his own life and"—he added pointedly—"tends to be tolerant of the affairs of others."

But his son ignored the implied rebuke and forged on. "Aye, but provided the affair is handled discreetly and not brazenly paraded before the highest in the land, as Alex means to do with his paramour."

Afraid that the conversation was rapidly reaching the explosive point, Alyssa put down her sewing and gazed at her son tight-lipped. "Alex and Marina are pledged to each other, as you know, and will marry just as soon as they can."

"Pah!" David laughed scornfully. "Alex has been involved with other women in the past and never gone so far as to wed them, so why should this relationship be any different?"

"He was not in love with the others," his mother

replied evenly.

Defeated, and aware that he was getting nowhere, David glanced from one to the other and threw up his hands. Resentment made him incautious, and he sneered, "I should have known you would support him, as you ever have. Birds of like feather always flock together . . ."

The chief stood up. His face was dark with anger. Too late, David realized what he'd said and hastily stepped back. He was appalled at the way he had insulted them, and all the hot color drained from his face as the older man strode purposefully toward him, drew back his hand, and struck him a resounding blow across the cheek.

"Now, get out!" his father ordered grimly, even as Lady Alyssa jumped to her feet with a cry of dismay. "Forget not that *I* am still in charge here and 'tis not for you to question any decision I might make, but only to stand by it. When your head is cooler I will expect an apology," Blake made clear, his tone hard and cold, "but I tell you this now—never speak to your mother or me like that again!" he roared. "Do you understand?"

David nodded stiffly; with a slight bow he turned and hurried from the room, his ears still ringing from the blow his father had given him and the chief's furious dark eyes imprinted on his brain. Never before had his father looked at him like that, his expression so chilling, so frighteningly close to hatred that the young nobleman shivered, deeply regretting the hurtful remark he had made—one he knew had hit home. Had anyone else dared to insult them thus, anyone at all, David knew they would have had to answer for it over cold steel. Many had been disinherited for less.

He clattered down the stone staircase to the ground

floor with his thoughts in turmoil and his pride in tatters, alarm, regret, and stubborn indignation seething inside him, the chief's reminder that *he* was still in charge made abundantly clear and that David had no say in the matter they had been discussing—or in any other matter either! Though the heir, he was accorded no more consideration or respect than any of his brothers or sisters—and a damn sight less than one of them, to his way of thinking! Things had been so much better when Alexander was away.

David went directly to the stables and in minutes was riding furiously for Edinburgh, where as the heir to Augusta he could expect to receive the respect he was due and a warm welcome from powerful men like Bothwell, Hamilton, Lennox, and others, men who were beginning to view *him* as their entrée into the largely intractable bastion of the Highlands. For over a year now David had been spending much of his time in the capital, carefully making what he saw as important connections for the future. When *he* became chief he had no intention of wasting his valuable time on his Highland estates; they could be left in the hands of a trusted administrator. Nay, his future lay not in the wild land beyond the mountains, of that the young nobleman was convinced, but in Edinburgh close to the King.

After a few leagues the heat of his anger cooled and he wondered idly how Alexander was doing at Cumbray, where he had gone to oversee their mother's properties. That was the role Alex had to look forward to, administrator-in-chief of the MacKellar clan, but under *the* chief, their mother. It was a very important position, one that would bring great power and prestige, aye, and great wealth too. Yet . . . for a man like his brother, born to lead, to command . . . how could Alex resign himself to never being allowed

to make the ultimate decisions?

It was a question David had often asked himself once both of them grew up and better understood the awkward situation. In a way, both of them were victims of their parents' conduct in the past. There had been a time when David, as a small boy, had adored and idolized his bold, headstrong older brother and followed him about like a shadow, trying to copy him in everything. Then they had been separated and sent to different establishments in France and England for their education, and once they parted, David's own personality had begun to assert itself. It was then that he was made to realize that one day *he* would be chief of his clan rather than his older brother, and his education was tailored with that end in mind. From the day he fully understood the true situation at Augusta, David's attitude toward Alexander subtly changed. No longer was he content to let Alex lead and direct him, and that, inevitably, brought them into conflict. But—and David had to admit this in his more reflective moments—the state of affairs at Augusta seemed to trouble *him* much more than it did Alexander. From the start, Alex had been the type to go his own way and relish forging a place for himself in the world, nor did he appear to harbor any grudges against either David or their parents. It was David himself who struggled under a burden of guilt, feeling—whether warranted or not— that he had cheated his brother out of what should rightfully have been his. It made no difference to remind himself that he wasn't to blame. The guilt still rankled, and that guilt swelled and sharpened each time Alexander was in residence at the castle, rapidly reaching the point where David avoided having to see him.

In Edinburgh he always felt better. In the capital

there were no unresolved emotional conflicts staring
him in the face and he could relax and be himself, the
acknowledged heir to the clan Sinclair. And curiously,
from a distance he always felt better about his parents
and brother, and more able to love them as he should.
Long before he reached the city, David was castigating
himself for insulting his parents and fervently hoping
that Alex would never hear about it, for if he did,
David knew that it would lead to a violent confronta-
tion between them, something he always dreaded
would happen one day.

But Alex should not have brought his English
mistress to Augusta!

Suddenly David found himself comparing Marina
Stafford to his own betrothed, Lady Elenor Hamilton.
He had been more than agreeable to be wed into the
royal house of Hamilton, with its close connection to
the Crown, and had required no urging from his
parents in his selection of a future wife; he had, in
fact, chosen Elenor himself, and counted himself
lucky that she was as enthusiastic about the match as
he was. Neither of them would go into it reluctantly,
as so often happened with others of their class, and
David was looking forward eagerly to their wedding
next spring.

Up to now, he had never given much thought to
Elenor's physical attributes. She was young and mild-
ly bonny with her fairish hair and light blue eyes, and
that had been enough for him, considering the more
important benefits of marrying one of the Hamilton
clan, a family whose head had a claim to the Crown
next in line to the King himself. Strangely, David had
never anticipated the delights of bedding Elenor.
Now, all of a sudden, he thought that odd, the more so
since that pleasure entered his mind in connection
with his brother's dark-eyed mistress, a woman who

embodied all the elements of temptation, who evoked in a man forbidden desires.

Aye, David brooded as he cantered along the narrow trails, it was as well to remove himself from Augusta for a few days to give himself a chance to cool down and grow accustomed to the new situation. He would return in time for the Harvest Ball—which Elenor too would attend—and by then have grown used to the idea of Alex's return to the family after his long absence, and the addition of Marina and their child. He must find it in himself to accept things as they were and try to make the best of it. If not, the alternative could destroy their family and split up the clan, and that must never happen.

When he returned to Augusta the day before the ball, Alexander spoke in private with his parents. For an hour they discussed business as it pertained to Cumbray Castle, his mother's seat and stronghold of the MacKellar clan, a place where she spent several months of every year presiding over her own side of the family, an arrangement that hadn't been entirely successful. During her absences, certain MacKellars had taken advantage and abused the trust of their chief, rerouting revenue into their private coffers that by rights should have gone to the countess. Alex had discovered that her commissioner, Sam MacKellar, was himself corrupt, and proposed replacing him with a manager not connected to the family, therefore with no reason to play favorites or take sides in disputes as Sam had done. It was also decided that quite soon Alex and Marina should move to Cumbray and in this way keep a tight grasp of the reins and a sharper eye on his mother's interests. David, of course, could not fill that role as he was being groomed to assume command of Augusta in the future.

After their discussion, Alexander got up to leave. He was at the door when he turned to say, "If it would make things less awkward, Marina and I shall not attend the ball on the morrow. This is your home, and neither of us have any desire to cause you embarrassment."

Alex was startled when his father replied fiercely, "You *will* attend, both of you, precisely because it *is* my home and I shall invite whom I please—and bedamned to those who disapprove!"

Though she had enthusiastically helped the countess supervise the decoration of the Great Hall with sheaves of golden corn, rye, and barley, and barrels of apples and nuts and other fruits, with scarecrows tucked into the darker recesses and a witch on a broomstick flying across a huge harvest moon, still Marina dreaded the coming ball and thought of it as a test and an ordeal to be lived through with as much tact and dignity as possible. It never occurred to her that she would actually enjoy the occasion, even as it never occurred to her to refuse to go.

Alyssa squeezed her arm as they finished bedecking the hall, which now had a delicious aroma of sun-ripened apples. "I admire your courage, lass," she said, smiling at the younger woman, then suddenly revealed something of herself. "I too refused to be hid in the background at the time I was the earl's mistress."

"Then . . . then you think we are doing the right thing?" It was the first time Marina had spoken so openly about her relationship with Alex to his mother, but now that the delicate subject had been broached she was eager for the countess's opinion.

Alyssa didn't reply right away, but finally she said, "What is right for one might be wrong for another. It

all depends on the individuals involved." She studied the English girl appraisingly for a moment, then warned, "You will have to be thick-skinned, determined, and courageous, and above all, remember to hold yourself proud so that the insults will bounce off your chin rather than your bowed forehead." They both laughed, even while realizing that it was not a laughing matter. Marina was relieved to see that the countess could find some germ of humor in a situation that must be very difficult and painful for her too.

"I'm sorry that it must be like this," she said. "I would rather hide away than bring dishonor to your Hall, but . . . Alex and I love each other deeply and mean to make things right just as soon as that is possible."

"Wear the new melon gown," Alyssa suggested, a combative glint in her green eyes. "And you may borrow my silk orchids to dress your hair. If they must crucify you, let them remember you as a bird of paradise rather than a meek little wren. Then even if they cannot like you they will at least be forced to admire your spirit."

They walked up the stairs together to the private quarters on the second floor, but before they separated Marina said shyly, "Lady . . . I thank you with all my heart for being so understanding and for welcoming me here."

Alyssa touched a hand to Marina's cheek.

"Marina, I will not deceive you. I wish that things might have been different. But," she sighed, "they are as they are, and I *do* understand." Her eyes grew serious as she added very low, "Not only will you need to be strong today in defense of your love, but always."

At that moment Marina could only think of the ordeal ahead, feeling that if she could only get through

this first step into society without being torn to shreds, the rest would be bound to be easier.

The ball turned out to be far different than Marina had imagined, largely due to the fact that Alexander's public life far overshadowed his private one in the eyes of their guests that evening. He was hailed as a hero by the hundreds of people pouring into the castle. Few among them had seen Alex since his release from prison, and all crowded around him loud in their praise and admiration at his daring attempt to free Queen Mary. "And it won't be forgotten," vowed the young chief of the clan Gordon. "Nay, not by the nobles *or* the people of Scotland. Faith, lad"—in an upsurge of emotion be threw his arms around Alexander and embraced him—"but it's grand to have you back safe and sound."

Marina flushed with embarrassment when her lover introduced her to countless Frasers, Douglases, Gordons, and others crowding the Great Hall as "the beautiful lady who provided refuge during our flight across England," a retelling of their own meeting that was highly exaggerated and embellished, but nevertheless put her in a good light, at least with their male guests, who were more impressed with feats of valor than their womenfolk. At the feast she was toasted almost as much as Alexander for providing hospitality to their native sons in their time of need. "Aye, and was so charmed by them that she could do naught but follow them back to Scotland," grinned George Gordon, winking at her from across the table, his eyes bright with admiration. "I'd say that England's loss is our gain."

Marina blushed and felt like a fraud as one blandishment followed another. Remembering the rude "hospitality" given the men at Baxton Hall, she

cringed inwardly and didn't dare glance in the direction of Robert Douglas and some of the others who had been there. But out of the corner of her eye she saw Robert raise his glass as enthusiastically as the rest, and not one of these gallent men gave the show away, for which she was deeply grateful. It was then that Marina began to relax and enjoy herself, while ignoring the cold stares of some of the women who were less disposed to be gracious to the beautiful foreigner—or fornicator, as some of them thought of her.

"Brazen strumpet!" whispered Lady Serena Grant to her daughter Magda, her eyes balefully regarding the woman who showed every sign of becoming the belle of the ball. Marina looked radiant in a gown of tissue-fine silk in a deep shade of melon, the succulent color heightening the effect of her sultry dark eyes and full coral-tinted lips, her shimmering blonde hair swept high in the latest fashion and dressed with miniature orchids the same luscious shade as her gown.

Magda Grant, who had once fostered the forlorn hope of marrying Alexander herself, whispered back, "'Tis an affront to us all for them to thrust her among us like this, forcing us to accept her."

Her ladyship snorted. "I, for one, will not! Nor will any with the slightest sense of decency."

Sir Edward, well into his cups, cast a sour eye at his wife and daughter, both of whom were so pious that he claimed they had driven him to drink. "Hold your tongue," he ordered his lady. "'Tis not for you to point the finger at anyone, considering the loins from which you have sprung."

She had "sprung" from the loins of Lady Magdalen MacKellar, a woman notorious as a witch in her day and the same woman who had done everything in her

power to destroy the Countess of Belrose and Kilgarin and rob her of her inheritance. Subsequently, there lingered deep enmity between Serena Grant and Lady Alyssa, all smothered over by a veneer of fake congeniality. Sir Edward and Blake Sinclair were cousins and the best of friends, and because of that, by the tacit consent of all involved, the old days had been allowed to sink into oblivion, at least on the surface.

The Grant women were not the only ones to whisper against Marina. The Dowager Countess of Mar too made no secret of her disapproval, nor did the wife of the Reverend Mungo Spark. Even David Sinclair's betrothed, a young lady with somewhat staring blue eyes, remarked, "I trow the magpies will be gossiping about this for weeks. To dare to bring her out into society!"

David didn't reply. He was remembering that Elenor's own mother had been the mistress of William Douglas for years, even though her husband was still alive and knew perfectly well what was going on—but then he too had a lover tucked away beyond the city wall on the outskirts of Edinburgh. In fact, it struck David that the ones most critical were those with skeletons aplenty rattling away in their own backgrounds, the very people who should have kept their mouths closed. Though he didn't approve of the way they were handling things, David couldn't help but admire how Marina was pulling it off. There was nothing self-conscious or apologetic about her manner, but neither was there brashness or indelicacy. Her innate refinement and good breeding stood out in her cultured speech and manners; she was managing a difficult situation with grace and confidence.

In some ways Marina Stafford reminded him of his mother. Both had dazzling beauty, quiet determination, and natural dignity. Quite suddenly David could

see why both his father and Alexander were prepared to risk so much for the women they loved, recognizing that they had something very special, something they would never find again.

Games followed the feast. There was much merriment and laughter as the guests took turns bobbing for apples in the great vat brought into the hall for that purpose. Then they raced about like children trying to evade the clutches of the Reaper with his fake sickle, and the Scarecrow who demanded a gold coin from the men he caught and a kiss from the women. This was followed by a ribald Harvest Pageant, deliciously lewd and shocking as these plays always were, and fools and jugglers, a magician and a fortune teller.

Then came the high point of the evening, a competition to select the King and Queen of the Harvest Ball.

Alexander—handsome in a pale gold brocade doublet that emphasized his dark good looks—was chosen at once. Then suddenly George Gordon, Bothwell, and David Sinclair rushed to Marina and swept her up in their arms, and ignoring the tut-tutting and snorting and huffing from some of the dour older women present, deposited her on the makeshift stage beside a grinning Alex.

Up to that moment Marina had managed to carry herself well. Now, suddenly, her brittle confidence crumbled as she gazed down into the hall and saw hundreds of pairs of eyes raking her over, some of those eyes burning with violent resentment; they looked as if they would have relished tearing her apart. Marina's face flamed a deep scarlet at finding herself the center of attention. She felt as if she were stark naked, hideously exposed and vulnerable. There was a moment when she took a step forward, when she would have jumped off the stage and fled—then Alexander's arm came around her waist, and in full

view of everyone he drew her close and kissed her cheek, whispering, "Don't falter now, my dear one. Don't give them the satisfaction of besmirching our love."

A cheer rang out when they kissed, though there were a few low hisses too, but when they drew apart Marina lifted her head and flashed her most radiant smile at the company, tinged with the slightest hint of bravado. The Countess of Belrose had the honor of "crowning" them, placing wreaths made of barley sheaves, nuts, and flowers on their heads. Setting Marina's firmly on her shining pale gold hair, Alyssa smiled and whispered, "Well done! I'm proud of you."

After that Marina made up her mind that she was going to have a wonderful time.

As king and queen of the ball they led their guests into the first dance, a stately number that Marina knew and far different from the ones that followed. Then came spirited jigs and reels, the music growing fast and furious, and Marina—laughing helplessly now—caught up like everyone else in the paganlike atmosphere filling the hall—found herself spun from partner to partner until she was dizzy and flushed with an excitement more heady than the strongest wine. She danced with Lord Blake, David, Bothwell, Huntly, and so many others that she quickly lost track of their names. There was great gaiety and not a little flirtation, and so many compliments lavished on her that Marina *did* feel somewhat queenly that night.

As she was whirled from one set of arms to another she suddenly recalled another Harvest Ball, and how innocently she had stepped into the trap set by Sedina, the Spaniard. Now she was older and wiser, she hoped; though in a different way, she was as vulnerable as ever, so she still had to be careful and not allow herself to get carried away or let down her

guard completely. Fawned over by the bold Highlanders, plied with goblet after goblet of wine, her pulse beating fast to the lilt of the wild music and her eyes dazzled by the blazing candlelight, it was not easy to keep her wits about her in a company that was growing less and less inhibited as the night wore on.

At some point Marina realized that she seemed to be in Lord Bothwell's arms more than any other's, including Alexander's. As a son of the house Alex was obliged to dance with every woman at the ball, even those who made no secret of their disgust at how he and Marina were living. With these women—and most of them quite matronly—he purposely danced the most hectic jigs and reels, tossing them and spinning them until they cried for mercy. Whirling the staid Lady Grant from one side of the huge room to another, and turning a deaf ear to her pleas to sit down, Alex happened to glance up as Lord Bothwell plucked a wisp of corn husk from Marina's hair, then bend down to whisper something in her ear.

Alex had never cared for Francis Stewart, Earl Bothwell, and he cared for him less now. A man a year or two older than himself, the earl was closely related to the King. Though a doughty soldier and intelligent enough, Bothwell was a notorious womanizer and had a vicious streak in his nature. He was tempestuous and overweeningly proud because of his kinship to the King, and Alex had heard while at Cumbray Castle that his unruly, arrogant behavior was causing their monarch increasing concern. His enemies at court— and he had many—thought him slightly mad. But Bothwell had his supporters too, people who seemed strangely enthralled by his peculiar brand of personal magnetism.

It worried Alex that his brother David was so friendly with the nobleman and spent much time with

him in Edinburgh and at his castle in Liddesdale. Upon his return from Cumbray Castle, Alex had tried to caution David, but he refused to listen. "Look to your own affairs," his brother had responded curtly. "They are not so immaculate that you should dole out advice to others."

Marina was beginning to feel distinctly uncomfortable in the arms of Earl Bothwell, who had consumed a great deal of wine and was growing steadily bolder. He held her too close, his lean body constantly brushing hers, his thigh pressing against her legs, his hot fingers on her bare back. He had a narrow face, hooked nose, and deep-set magnetic eyes that constantly sought and held hers. She was the most ravishing woman at the ball, he told her, looking as if he would have liked to ravish her. And she had the eyes of a sorceress. The body of a goddess. Hair like cloth-of-gold. One day soon she must visit his home in Liddesdale, he went on in that deep, mesmerizing voice, where he had many exciting revels and entertainments for his special friends, those with a taste for the unusual and different.

"And how do you know I am one of those?" said Marina, trying to draw back, hoping that someone would break in and rescue her from this outrageous flatterer who, in spite of the fact that they were surrounded by people, was almost making love to her on the dance floor.

He chuckled, his eyes dropping to the deep cleft between her white breasts, "I know; I recognize a like spirit when I see one."

Marina's brows rose and she laughed nervously; something about the man made her uneasy, even aside from the way he was holding her and taking every opportunity to touch and stroke her. Other men she had danced with tonight had flirted and paid her

flowery compliments; it was almost standard procedure at social functions, particularly the harvest celebrations that were more earthy and uninhibited than most. But with Francis Stewart it was different. There was nothing light-hearted in his banter; nothing playful. His hot hands gripped her tightly, burning through her clothes, his hungry fingers feeling the shape of her, carnal purpose in the way his body pressed hers, his eyes heavy-lidded with desire that he made no effort to conceal. It didn't seem to bother him that people were watching them or that Alexander might take offense. Marina sensed that Bothwell was the type of man who took what he wanted with a careless disregard for the consequences.

A warning bell rang then at the back of her mind, and Marina thought again of the Spaniard, Sedina. Bothwell, something told her, was every bit as dangerous.

She wrenched herself back from him and said coldly, "You know nothing about me, sir—"

"That I would like to rectify with all speed," he purred, his eyes devouring her.

Marina turned her head away and threw a desperate glance around the hall, relief flooding through her when she spied Alex pushing his way through the crowd toward them, a scowl on his face. His hand fell hard on Bothwell's shoulder, and without a word of greeting Alexander thrust him ignominiously aside, pulled Marina into his own arms, and swept her into the dance, leaving the King's proud relative humiliated and partnerless in the middle of the floor. There were a few titters from those around them who had witnessed the incident. It wasn't often that anyone dared put the treacherous Bothwell in his place.

When Marina glanced back at him she saw a look of pure venom on his face, and inwardly she shivered,

thinking that they might have made an enemy tonight and a powerful one at that. But since Alexander didn't seem in the least worried, she kept her thoughts to herself. In general the ball had gone far better than she'd thought it would, and she wanted nothing to spoil their enjoyment.

When the dance ended, Alex said, "The evening is not complete without a stroll under the harvest moon."

The idea appealed to Marina. By then she felt hot and disheveled from all the wild dancing and was more than eager when her lover led her outside for a cooling walk in the bright moonlight. They made their way downhill skirting the village of Lochmore, arms around each other, both well satisfied with their first venture into society together and inclined to dismiss those who had been against them.

The night was all black and silver as they meandered toward the steely glint of the loch. There was a pleasant tang of peat smoke in the air, the occasional cry of an owl hunting for its dinner and a faint rustling in the grass as tiny creatures like mice and rabbits raced for cover to avoid the cruel grasp of the feathered predators. The mountains loomed black against the star-spangled sky, the world about them still, cast in lunar light and shadow. From the castle behind them orange torches flared, glimmering through the trees, and the jaunty skirl of the pipes was muted now, gradually swallowed up by the great silence.

Walking softly on springy green moss, the couple reached the bank of the loch where the white face of the moon was reflected in the water, mysteriously serene. A hundred yards away a fox stood poised on a sterling shingled beach, coughed once, then vanished into a thicket. They could hear each other breathe, almost hear their hearts beating.

Alex drew her down on a mossy ridge where they lay back gazing up at the sky, his arm under Marina's head, their bodies touching, each contemplating the night. After a few minutes she said softly, "If only I could capture this moment, the feel of it, the taste, beauty . . . the joy . . . and preserve it forever."

Alex looked at her in surprise. If anything, he had expected to hear complaints, because it hadn't been an easy evening for Marina to live through with the she-wolves in the Hall baying after her blood, hissing malicious remarks, some of which she must have heard. Then Bothwell, the knave, panting and pawing her—how close Alex had come to throwing the swine out of the Hall!

He eyed her curiously. "Then you are not sorry you braved the horde to stand at my side?"

Marina shook her head. "I discovered tonight that I can face up to anything as long as you love me, Alex."

He took her hand and placed it against his cheek. "That you need never doubt, my darling."

He studied her as she lay beside him bathed in the moon's radiant light, her eyes soft as dark velvet, a blissful little smile on her lips, her hair somewhat mussed but even more attractive that way, and he thought she was the most beautiful woman on earth. Yet . . . it wasn't just her beauty that drew him to Marina. After all, she had been far from bonny when he had met her in Baxton Hall, but even then . . . even then he had felt powerfully attracted to her, drawn by some quality she possessed that he couldn't put a name to or define.

They gazed at each other in a kind of trance, spellbound with the magic of the love they shared, certain no others had ever experienced anything like it. Then Alex kissed her with passionate fervor, his fingers moving caressingly in her silken mass of

tumbled hair. His lips on her eyelids, her ears, cheeks, and throat, then gently pulling the dipping front of her gown down to uncover her breasts. Almost reverently he took them in his hands as a man will when he holds something precious, kissing the warm, creamy flesh, the hardening nipples, and felt the pounding of her heart against his mouth, the beat fast and urgent, every nerve in her body thrilling to his touch.

"Oh Alex . . . my love," Marina whispered, returning his kisses and caresses with passionate devotion. "Make love to me, darling. Here! Now!"

The serenity of the night changed in the moment before Alex took possession of her. There was an aura of expectancy in the breeze ruffling the dark water of the loch, the face of the moon reflected there shimmering and dancing, spraying shafts of silver across the black surface; in the sudden flapping of wings overhead, the cry of a wolf from a lonely mountain valley. Marina breathed moist humus scents rising from their mossy bed, and as Alex leaned over her his head and shoulders were framed by a blaze of bright stars, a canopy richer than that of any king.

"My only love," he told her. "There never has—nor ever will be—one like you."

"Nor you," she breathed. "My Alex . . ."

He kissed her deeply, and there was a tender, cherishing quality to their lovemaking that was sweeter, more completely satisfying than their usual fiery passion, each so intent on demonstrating their love to the other that they reached a new plateau that night. Never had they been closer or felt such perfect communion with each other. Both felt that they had received a wondrous gift, one that was far beyond price. Humbled by the joy they felt, savoring its rare taste, they walked back to Augusta hand in hand, content in their silence.

As they reached the huge main door Alex and Marina were completely oblivious to everything but each other. The man standing in the shadows of a great beech tree watched them through narrowed eyes, and suddenly knew how he could strike back at Alexander Sinclair for insulting him.

24

Marina stood in a field with the Earl of Belrose and watched a groom lead her daughter around the meadow on her new Highland pony, a gift from Alex's parents for her third birthday.

"She has a good seat," observed Blake as he watched his granddaughter closely, Clare proud and grinning hugely from the saddle, and very pretty in her peacock blue riding habit—a present from Alex and herself—her hands in the spanking white gloves gripping the reins tight.

"Ker, don't have her sawing on his mouth," Blake shouted to the groom. "Show her how to relax her grip. And tighten his girth a little."

When the groom gently lowered the little girl's hands and demonstrated how she should hold the reins so that she didn't injure the horse's soft mouth, Blake nodded in satisfaction. "She's a quick learner.

Alex could ride like the devil by the time he was five years old. He used to frighten his mother out of her wits," he chuckled. "But all the Sinclairs have a natural affinity with horseflesh."

The chief looked so much like Alexander that Marina had warmed to him at once, in spite of the fact that he was a rather awesome figure—very tall and dark, with strong features and riveting dark eyes that bespoke of a steely determination and great force of will, the type of man that made one think twice before crossing. Now, as she smiled at him as they stood together in the warm autumn sunshine, his delight and pride in his first grandchild heartening to the woman watching him, Marina mused that if Alex looked as virile and attractive as his father did in middle age, then she would be a very lucky lass indeed.

Blake had wings of silver in his black hair and lines on his warm olive skin, but there was not an ounce of spare flesh on his body and he held himself straight and proud, still very much the master of Augusta. It charmed Marina to see daily evidence of the love between Alexander's parents. It was quite obviously still strong and potent in the way they looked at each other, the way they touched, even when they laughed softly together, heads close. That morning, when Blake returned to the castle after a short absence, Alyssa had dashed out the door to greet him, her cheeks blushing pink as a young girl's, her green eyes sparkling, and had thrown herself into his arms the instant he dismounted from his horse.

Then they had disappeared for an hour or so into their private quarters, everyone, including the servants, discreetly leaving them alone together.

"Lovely!" Marina had thought. "Pray let it always be like that with Alex and me."

For the past week the chief had been in Edinburgh with Alexander and David but had returned that morning to settle disputes at the Highland tribunal, due to convene the following day. The two younger men remained in the capital.

"How long, think you, that they will be gone?" Marina asked the earl as they watched Ker lead little Clare around the field on her pony.

"'Tis hard to say. The King wishes speech with Alex but may keep him waiting. James is much taken up with his new Queen; he is like a child with an interesting new toy, though how long he will remain interested is debatable."

"Then he has . . . mistresses?"

Blake laughed shortly and glanced at her sideways. "Not exactly, but his favorites are akin to the same thing, if you understand me. He was raised in the company of men and much prefers their society; doubtless he feels more at ease with his own sex."

"Oh . . ." Marina blushed and looked away.

He propped a booted foot on a fallen log and leaned forward with his elbow resting on his knee, his eyes following his grandchild around the field, thinking that this was how Alyssa must have looked as a small child.

After a minute he went on, "'Tis a great surprise to all how the King has managed to work up an intense passion for Anne of Denmark, though many are certain that it will quickly fizzle out like a spent firecracker. Still . . . for the moment James seems to be enjoying playing the gallant lover with his lady, intrigued by its very novelty, no doubt. He is spending much time alone with his young Queen and is seen less about court. The only thing capable of luring him from his love nest is the ridiculous witch hunt he has set in motion, convinced that evil powers sought to

prevent him from returning safely to Scotland with his Danish bride."

"Aye," Marina nodded, "I heard tell that the sea crossing was unusually stormy and that Queen Anne almost drowned."

"'Twas the admiral of the ship who first suggested witchcraft as the cause of it, and Anne, very young and gullible as she is, firmly believes it to be true. So now the King is acting the part of the bold cavalier, bound to avenge the terrible wrong done to her. One could laugh, except that he is taking it deadly seriously, sending his agents to scour the country in search of the devils responsible."

Blake turned to face her, flicking her cheek teasingly with a blade of grass. "And Marina Stafford's impatience must needs take second place to that of the King. Who can predict when Alex will return?" His brown eyes were warm, amused when they rested on her eager face. "Alas, love must wait, but I can tell you from my own experience that it will be all the sweeter and fiercer for the waiting, all the more pleasurable to quench."

Marina smiled at him shyly, her cheeks pink.

"You are very like Alexander, my lord."

"Like him too in having the good fortune to have the love of a beautiful woman," he said with a grin.

Blake caught her face between his hands, stared down intently at her for a moment, then kissed her on the forehead. Marina's heart soared at this demonstration of affection and approval from the chief—and suddenly, for the first time, she felt at one with the clan and no longer a stranger. It was as if a great warm Highland plaid had surrounded her with its sheltering warmth and protection. I never want to leave here, she thought when Blake let her go.

Clare finished with her riding lesson and came

rushing up, all breathless and excited, to be seized by her grandfather and tossed high into the air, then carried back to Castle Augusta in his arms.

All of Edinburgh turned out to see the captured witches paraded through the streets in an open cart on their way to the dungeons of Edinburgh Castle, five women and two men of various ages, all stripped naked and exposed to the late October chill, huddled together like animals on their way to be slaughtered.

The crowd howled and jeered at them and pelted them with stones, rotten fruit, even excrement from the gutter as the wagon was slowly trundled through the town, the pace leisurely to afford onlookers a chance to gape at and vent their fury on these disciples of the devil, every foot they traveled pure hell for the unfortunates shivering together inside the cart. Though they had yet to be tried and convicted, they could see, from the screaming mob packed tight along each side of the street, barely held in check by sweating constables, that they had already been judged guilty of the vilest of crimes.

"Burn them!" the people roared. "Roast them alive!"

Hearing the noise, Alexander ran out of Bell's Tavern where he had been having an informal meeting with the Gordons, Hamilton, Fraser, and others, in time to see the wagon turning into the street. The driver, clad in red livery, sat haughtily on his high seat behind the two horses, his nose raised fastidiously as if to distance himself from what was taking place behind him while three guards with pistols kept prodding and leering at the prisoners with whom they shared the cart.

Alex and his friends pushed their way to the front of the throng. They were startled to spy two people they

recognized among the accused, Felicity MacBride, the wife of a prominent city lawyer, and Jerome Wellesley, a groom at Holyrood Palace.

"Dear Christ!" Alex cried. "Has the whole city gone mad?"

Aghast, his eyes were drawn to Mistress MacBride, still in her twenties and a comely woman, now frantically trying to cover her nakedness with her hands while constantly forced to raise them to try to protect herself from the missiles hurled at her with such force that blood streamed down her body in rivulets. They were all injured and bleeding and covered with filth, and as the wagon came abreast of them, Alexander suddenly spotted a young prisoner well along in pregnancy. For an instant her eyes met his, mutely beseeching, then she wailed, "I'm innocent! Innocent! Help me for the sake of my babe."

Shocked, sickened, and suddenly furious at the revolting spectacle, Alex drew his sword and jumped out into the road. The cart came to a sudden stop, but before Alex could take action, his friends rushed up behind him and physically dragged him back, George Gordon shouting, "For the love of God, Sinclair, stay out of this! 'Tis not a business you want meddling in."

A lump of horse manure meant for the witches struck the driver of the vehicle, almost knocking him off his perch and splattering his smart red tunic and his snooty face with dung. The watching crowd shrieked with laughter, and so comical a sight did he make as he coughed and spluttered and gingerly tried to clean himself off that others began pelting him with muck until he was forced to whip up the horses and speed away to evade his tormentors, reduced by now to almost as vile a state as his prisoners.

His name was Crockett and he was livid with fury. All the way back to the castle he turned the name that

George Gordon had shouted over and over in his mind. "Sinclair," he muttered to himself, "you are going to be muckle sorry for this. *Muckle* sorry!"

In the tavern Alexander and his friends tried to wash the sour taste from their mouths with several quick gulps of ale.

"Mistress MacBride!" Alex shook his head. "How could she have been brought into this?"

Fraser shrugged. "None are exempt from suspicion, it seems, even the highest in the land. They perhaps most of all, since they have more to gain by bringing about the King's destruction." And he named several noblemen living near the capital who had fallen under suspicion. "They are said to be a part of a demonic pact whereby they come to an arrangement with Satan. In exchange for their souls, the devil invests them with special powers which can be used for gain or to bring down their enemies."

"What nonsense!" Alex laughed.

"Aye, but many believe in it," said Gordon. "And it has a special appeal for those among the new faith, which many are said to adhere to."

In a way Alex could see how this could be. Calvinists believed in predestination, whereby a child was born either among the elect or the reprobate, their eventual fate preordained. The elect would go to heaven after death, and the reprobate to hell—and there was absolutely nothing they could do about it. If someone believed in their own reprobation, or was made to believe, then forming a pact with the devil would seem natural. . . .

"To think," he said, "that such things can still go on in this enlightened age. But that aside"—his face hardened—"'twas fiendish cruel and unnecessary to subject these poor wretches to the ire of the rabble, and one of them with child, when they have

349

yet to be proved guilty."

"Oh, their guilt is a foregone conclusion," said Hamilton. "Few will not confess under torture."

Alex remembered the eyes of the pregnant woman and felt sick.

"I will appeal to the King himself," he announced.

His companions exchanged a look of pure horror, and several chimed in at once to urge him to banish the thought from his mind. "To stand up for them would only make you seem one of them in His Majesty's eyes," warned Gordon. "Besides, it would do no good. They will all be burned—and mayhap you and yours with you if you interfere."

Alex got drunk that night, but he still couldn't get the eyes of the pregnant prisoner out of his mind. Yet . . . George Gordon was right. There was nothing he could do, nothing he *dared* do without putting his family at risk.

At the beginning of November Alexander finally had his audience with King James, who was a year younger than himself, yet in an odd way seemed older. James had grown up surrounded by adults, many of them elderly, learned men, and much of their habits and mannerisms had rubbed off on him. He was mild-mannered, clever, enjoyed good conversation and jesting with his friends, but he had never seemed young, even as a boy. Now, in his early maturity, the King had developed a paternal manner that sat well on him in spite of his youth.

"Ah, my braw Alexander!" he greeted Sinclair when he was shown into the Audience Chamber. "Glad I am to see you sprung from that English fortress, and a might of bother it was too, getting you freed."

He held out his hand to be kissed.

Alex thanked him for his effort to have him released

—and James, with one of his uninhibited gestures for which he was well known—suddenly rose and embraced him. "'Twas a noble deed," he said, "to attempt to rescue the Queen, my mother."

The King motioned for a servitor to come forward. The man carried a satin pillow on which lay a heavy chain of gold, with a medallion at its center, inscribed, and studded around the edge with diamonds and seed pearls. There was no ceremony involved. James was essentially a simple man who disliked pomp and fanfare. With his own hands he lifted the chain from the pillow and carefully arranged it around Alexander's neck, saying, "For great valor in the service of the Crown." Then he stepped back, smiling, able to be relaxed and benevolent now that the difficulties surrounding his mother's death lay three years in the past. "I would have you wear that on all public occasions," he said, anxious that others should note that the King rewarded loyal and courageous subjects. "And if ever you should have a special boon to ask of me, send me the medallion and it shall be granted."

Alexander again dropped to his knee and kissed the royal hand.

James gazed down on the proud dark head of the Highland nobleman bent respectfully before him and reminded himself that the Sinclairs had always been loyal to the Crown. The medallion was worth a great deal of money, it was true, but others less deserving had received far more magnificent rewards for pleasing their King. Alexander Sinclair would have too— were it not for some disquieting information that had recently come to the royal ear—and not from just one source, but two. The first he might have discounted, even though it had been brought to him from his cousin Bothwell, to the effect that Alex had become close friends with the Earl of Essex while in England,

and through him had been lured into working for Queen Elizabeth as a spy. Essex—and not Alex himself—so said Bothwell, had been the means of Sinclair being released, but only on condition that he agree to engage in subversive activities for England.

Then a short time ago his chancellor, Maitland, had come to him to report another unsettling piece of news. A man called Hamish Crockett, in service at the castle, accused Sinclair of obstructing him in the performance of his duties while conducting suspected witches to stand trial for their crimes. Sinclair had gone so far as to draw his sword as if to attack this man, and was prevented from doing so only by the intervention of his companions. Further, there were numerous witnesses to the incident.

James knew that Alexander had always been a reckless hothead, but until now his activities had been for worthy causes, and for the right side. His courage and fidelity had never before been questioned, and now that he had matured and, ostensibly, had learned restraint, James had planned to make him one of his most important ministers. Now . . . now the King decided to adopt a policy of wait and see, still far from convinced—as Bothwell seemed to be—that Alex was a traitor.

Wine was served and, as James liked to do, they chatted informally.

"I would like to know all that happened while you were in England," said the King, smiling pleasantly.

Alex chuckled. "I fear, Your Majesty, that it will make dull relating. Not much of interest can happen to a man behind bars."

James sipped from a silver goblet, watching him over the rim.

"You doubtless made some contacts amongst the

English nobility while in the Tower? I understand many of them languish there. They say they hail each other from cell to cell and ofttimes meet if allowed out for exercise. Firm friendships come from shared desperation."

For a while they chatted about people and conditions in the Tower, Alex beginning to wonder why the King showed so much interest, and soon James brought the subject around to Essex. "What think you of this new favorite of the Queen's?"

Alexander's brows rose. "I never met Devereux. He was not in London at the time I left the Tower."

"Ah, but a good friend of the Sinclairs nevertheless, eh?"

Alex stared hard at the King, a man of his own age but much shorter of stature, bearded, with deep-set eyes, a humorous curve to his mouth, erudite and likable, a peace lover. James was known to hate violence; even the weapons of war caused him distress, and no one ever unsheathed a blade in his presence, even to pare an apple at table. He controlled his turbulent, frequently ferocious nobles with his adroit brain rather than a sword, and had done so successfully up to that time. It was that facile mind that one had to be wary of with James Stewart.

"The Sinclairs would count anyone a friend who worked for our good," Alex replied evenly.

"Then you have friends in high places in London."

"It would seem one, at least."

"A friend *very* close to Queen Elizabeth."

"The Earl of Essex appears to enjoy her favor."

The King leaned back in his chair and crossed his legs, the gems in his garters gleaming dully; they looked dusty. The wide cartwheel ruff around his neck sagged, and a seam at the shoulder of his rich doublet

was beginning to separate. Though he was slim and compact, the upper part of his body was wide and his arms powerful and muscular, a testimony to his fondness for riding and hunting, always atop some blooded, high-spirited horse. He cared nothing for grand attire, but a fine horse always brought a shine of excitement to his gray-blue eyes, as did verbal fencing with a mind as sharp and quick as his own.

He said, "'Tis fortunate that you were never racked while in the Tower."

Alexander nodded. "Fortunate indeed."

"Unusual," His Majesty purred.

"I believe that to be true."

"And I'm told you have taken a fancy to a bonny English woman and brought her back into Scotland, leaving her cuckolded husband to wonder where she vanished to."

Bothwell! Sudden rage darkened Sinclair's tanned face and brought a dangerous gleam to his eyes. Recalling how the King's cousin had recently been humiliated at Castle Augusta—and well deserving it!—Alex knew the reason behind all this questioning. Francis Stewart had taken his revenge by putting a doubt in the King's mind regarding his loyalty!

"I confess to surprise that my Lord Bothwell would consider this matter of enough import to report it to Your Majesty," Alexander replied coldly, striking at the heart of the trouble, suddenly weary of this verbal sparring.

James was annoyed at his boldly naming the man responsible, especially when that man was related to him; he felt as if the tenor of the interview had been wrested out of his hands, and this he found irksome and insulting.

"Bothwell was not the *only* courtier at Castle Augusta that night," the King pointed out.

"But the only one with a grudge against Alexander Sinclair."

The hooded eyes narrowed. "Answer me this: Why did you obstruct a royal servant in the performance of his duties?" asked James, abruptly changing the subject. "I refer to the fellow in charge of conducting the witches to Edinburgh Castle."

The look that came over Sinclair's face sent a chill through the King. He suddenly regretted his penchant for informality, his careless habit of interviewing some of his noblemen alone, a habit his chancellor was very much opposed to. Sitting before him now was a man who feared no one, as Sinclair had demonstrated time and again. Now that man was staring at him with murderous anger stamped on his dark face, his sword within inches of his hand, a fleet horse waiting for him outside. One swift stroke and he—the King—could be cut down, nor would he be the first to die under the hands of a noble assassin, and his Highland lords were far more intractable than most. In minutes Alexander Sinclair could be galloping back to the fastness of the mountains, there to be surrounded by the might of his own clan—and well supported by other clans who were traditional allies of the Sinclairs. Once away from the capital there would be very little that could be done short of plunging the country into rebellion. Alexander was a hero to the people! That they would back him the King had no doubt. As it was, there would be many who would sneer at the poor way he had thanked Sinclair for trying to save his mother, the Queen.

Alexander leaned forward, fixing him with eyes gone flat and cold.

"Witches?" he questioned. "But I understood that the prisoners had yet to be tried, let alone found guilty."

James ran a finger around his ruff, which he realized was too tight.

"They, ah . . . would not have been arrested without there being serious evidence agin them," he countered. "All of it will come out at the trials next week."

"Next week?" Sinclair's brows rose mockingly. "Yet they have already been paraded through the streets as if they had been adjudged guilty." He paused, a pulse throbbing at his jaw as he sought to control his anger and disgust. "One of the women, not more than sixteen or seventeen years old, was far gone with child!—yet naked like the others, bruised and battered and bleeding from the abuse of the crowd. That is justice?" When the King said nothing, he announced, disregarding the consequences in his fury, "I readily admit that I tried to put an end to this woman's torment, as would anyone else with a shred of compassion and decency left in him. Aye, and I would do so again!"

James dropped his eyes to his hands, horrified at the picture Sinclair had put in his mind. He hated violence, though he recognized that at times it was necessary for his own protection and that of his Kingdom; but when it *was* necessary he had no desire to have the details thrust down his throat as they had been now.

"I—I know nothing of such a woman," he said, "but will look into the matter at once." He defended himself. "These devil worshipers cannot be allowed to swell and grow. They sought to encompass the death of my royal person and that of my Queen. Forget not that there are those in this land who would have preferred me to marry Catherine of Navarre. The Queen is aware of this and is sorely afraid that these

traitors mean to destroy her."

"I am not one of them," Alexander made clear.

No, thought the King, he didn't think he was. Sinclair was the type to scorn black magic; he was not the sort to engage in furtiveness and dark deeds behind the scenes or to subjugate himself to *any* master, whether Satan or anyone else. Alex had too forthright and open a nature, and too much confidence in himself to hide his activities in demonic cults where secrecy was imperative. James was inclined to suspect that if there was a serpent amongst his nobles, it was not Alexander Sinclair, though he supposed that time would tell.

The King eyed him consideringly.

"I sense that you put little stock in witchcraft?"

"None," came the terse response.

James leaned forward. "Aye, but there *are* such people, Sinclair," he insisted. "Those with special powers over their fellows; even, in some cases, over animals." In his extensive reading on the subject, James went on, he had learned some astounding things about demonology and lycanthropy, how in some of the remote countries certain natives had the ability to send their spirits into the bodies of wild animals such as panthers and hyenas, thereby using these creatures to kill in their stead. "Hence the legend of the werewolf." Some had the ability to cause another's death by simply casting a spell on him. "And the victim wastes away and dies."

"Because it has been *suggested* to him that he would; suggested to a believer. Sorcery cannot hurt those who don't believe," Alex maintained.

But it was obvious that the subject had caught the King's imagination, and that alone was dangerous. Whether one believed or not, he said firmly, the

demon worshipers did, and that alone could cause havoc because these people were feared and could infect others and bend them to their will. Therefore they represented a serious threat to authority, to law and order, and must be stamped out.

"Do you know," James went on gravely, "that some of my men, who would face up to anything, are reluctant to hunt down these demons? Secretly they are sorely afraid of them lest some death spell be cast over them. They make excuses to get out of the task; some simply disappear rather than face them. My own men, Sinclair!" he said angrily. "More afraid of these creatures than they are of my displeasure!"

Finally Alexander understood. The King was engaged in a power struggle and the witches were subversives like any other; *that* was why he was so intent on stamping them out. James's pet project was to bring law and order to his turbulent country, and indeed he had been more successful in that aim than any of his ancestors. Though he used less force, he had managed to achieve more, possibly because he had taken the time to understand the nature of his people, particularly the nobility. There had been surprisingly few plots against him and he was generally liked and respected—because he had taken pains to discover their weaknesses and strengths and knew how to handle them.

But there were still those few out to bring down the King. Call them witches or whatever, they still posed a threat to the monarchy. That Alexander understood, and he could see where the King would naturally be anxious to find the culprits and rid himself of them. Alex suddenly wondered if witchcraft was merely the cover for a more dangerous conspiracy against the Crown, and who might be behind it.

James saw understanding dawning on Alex's face, and smiled.

"I may have a post for you, Sinclair," he announced, thinking at the same time that it would be a good way to test the nobleman's loyalty.

Alex waited, wondering what was coming.

"I am putting you in charge of the witch hunt."

25

In early November Edgar Stafford was finally able to set out for Scotland. He had with him his new squire, Fordyce, and five of his brawniest men, all of them armed to the teeth and mounted on decent horseflesh for a change. Stafford had splurged on horses and weapons; he was no fool and knew what they would be up against. He also knew that once in the vicinity of Castle Augusta they would have to go underground and use cunning and stealth to reach Marina and the child, which was the reason he had left some of his men behind. Too many would merely make things awkward and hinder rather than help.

Fordyce was his second squire since Tar left him. The first had lasted only a week when Edgar caught him stealing. In fact, it was getting harder all the time to procure good men who were honest and willing to work, and to keep the fellows one had from being lured into better-paying jobs. None of the ones with

him now had been in his employment more than a year, and there were times when Stafford wished fervently that he had the old guard back, aging though they had been. At least they had been loyal and respectful, which was something he couldn't say about the present crew.

Take Fordyce, for instance. Edgar had had to lift the whip to him three days before when the young man, only twenty-one years old, had had the temerity to dictate to him. "'Tis overlate in the year to venture into the north of Scotland," he'd said in his cocksure, opinionated way. "We'll have foul weather to contend with as well as the savages of the North, and 'tis hard to say which of them will be worse. This venture should be delayed until next spring."

Edgar had gone purple in the face with frustration and anger, furious that such a young buck would dare try to tell him what to do. Had Tar still been with him—and how he wished he was!—Stafford was convinced that his wife and child would already be back behind the thick walls of Baxton Hall and he no longer an object of scorn and ridicule.

Edgar roared that there would be no delay as he set about the outspoken young squire with his whip, as he had done with many another before him, for a master who allowed a mere servant to domineer him would soon find *himself* dancing at the end of a string. The beating had served its purpose too. Thereafter Fordyce had been most courteous and amenable, listening respectfully as Edgar outlined the plan and promising to pass it on to his subordinates. Even the rest of the men, always inclined to be sullen, seemed more agreeable.

The only other thing Fordyce had ventured to suggest, meekly and with his hat in his hand, was that bribes might be necessary once they reached the

Highlands. "To open doors that otherwise would be bound to be shut fast against us, sir."

"I have thought of that," Edgar assured him.

Now, as they rode in the direction of the border, Stafford was very conscious of the gold carefully sewn into his old leather jerkin, gold he would certainly have to part with to get his wife and child back. "By the mass, the expense and trouble that wench has cost me!" he fumed inwardly. "Aye, and the danger she has exposed me to as well." It was one thing to slink over the border for rousing skirmishes with the natives there, then quickly gallop back into England with stolen cattle or other booty, if they were lucky. But it was quite another matter to ride deep into enemy territory far away from his homeland, with no easy route of escape should things go agin them. Marina would pay for this once he got her back. He would keep her so fast a prisoner that she would never see the light of day, except through a barred window! As for the child she was so devoted to, Clare would be sent far away for her education to a distant relative of his in Cornwall, and her mother would never know where. But at least he would have them both under his jurisdiction once more, as was right and proper. Then and only then could he hold up his head in the county and move about without having people snigger behind his back.

It was fortunate, he supposed, that it was now quite common for travelers to move between the two countries. Provided they showed no hostility and behaved in a polite, circumspect manner, it was often possible to journey on without being molested or challenged, at least in the South of Scotland. In the South they were more used to foreign traffic between England and Edinburgh, the capital, and in some districts they

were quite friendly to the strangers. But it was an altogether different story in the North, so Stafford had heard. Hideous stories had filtered back to England about the Highland barbarians, as wild and savage, so it was said, as the territory they lived in. Edgar suddenly wished he were twenty years younger, that he had his old, dependable men with him, and above all that Tar rode at his side instead of Fordyce. The new lot seemed keen enough now, but alas, their master had far less confidence in them. But, he thought stoically, they were the best that he could get.

Never once did it cross Stafford's mind to abandon the chase and let his wife go, to return to his Hall and live out his remaining years in peace, recognizing that there were some things a man just couldn't have, and to be grateful for the things he *did* have—robust good health, a few friends who admired him for his bravery, and more than enough money to last him for the rest of his days. He was no philosopher and these things didn't occur to him—but they occurred to his men. They sat around the campfire muttering while Edgar's snores rang out from his tent.

"Listen to the old dog," said one with a nod in the direction of his master's shelter. "What can he want with a young wife? He wouldn't have the stamina to satisfy her."

"He's no real man," another whispered. "He's much like a castrated bull, according to Tar, and unfit to service a woman."

"She's run before and will do so again. We are risking our lives to pander to his vanity. I tell you now, we will not get out of the Highlands alive or 'twill be a miracle."

There was a pause while they mulled this over, their faces grim in the red glow of the fire, darkness pressing

around them, then someone suggested tentatively, "Mayhap we should all steal away now while he sleeps . . ."

But one of the older ones reminded them, "'Tis not easy to find work, and a man has to eat."

Finally Fordyce spoke up, now that he had their measure.

"Stafford is carrying a small fortune in gold."

No one said anything, but they all looked at each other, and one by one they began to smile.

Alyssa Sinclair was very proud of the Lochmore Hospice, a combination hospital and orphanage midway between the village of Lochmore and the neighboring one of Blairafton. The rambling old house belonged to the Sinclairs but had rarely been used except for storage, and Alyssa had easily persuaded her husband to let her take it over to try her experiment. The near-derelict building had been repaired, and the junglelike gardens and meadows surrounding it cut back, the trees pruned, the lawns reseeded. Now, though plain and far from the grand establishment it had been two hundred years ago, it was freshly painted, clean, and above all provided a warm, comfortable shelter for the sick and destitute.

There were forty orphans in Lochmore Hospice, and almost the same number of sick people at any given time, all presided over by a director called Ben Greer, the son of a physician who had once saved Lady Alyssa's life. Greer had several assistants, and there were men to tend the fields and orchards, for Lochmore Hospice grew most of its own food and raised its own stock, with everyone old enough and fit enough to work contributing their energy and talents to make the place prosper.

Marina had never seen or heard of anything like it,

and was highly impressed as its founder proudly conducted her on a tour of the large building, where she knew almost everyone by name down to the youngest orphan. The children clustered around her with cries of delight, some running to show the countess their latest projects, from sewing to woodwork, for they were encouraged to learn crafts or trades that would help them to be self-sufficient in the future.

Marina was greatly touched to see the small hands holding up their work for approval, and the shine in their eyes when Alyssa praised their efforts or gave constructive and kindly criticism while taking pains to see that the shyer children weren't overlooked. Her patience, gentleness, and warmth were genuine, and the little ones had sensed it from the first and responded with a burst of love for their patron that brought tears to Marina's eyes. And it was the same in the infirmary on the other side of the building, where many of the patients were old people who were simply tired and worn out, with nowhere else to go.

"Some of the children were found abandoned in alleys and even in the woods," Alyssa explained as they walked around. "And most of the elderly patients, no longer able to work, were starving; some had been cast out by their own families, thus leaving them with one less mouth to feed. Many are not from this area at all—country people tend to take care of their own—but were found by the ladies who work for me in Edinburgh."

"Oh, why are there not more places like this?"

Alyssa smiled ruefully. "Why indeed. There should be; we as Christians have an obligation to help those less fortunate than ourselves. If we have luck then we must share it, or risk having it taken away."

Marina seized her hand. "I want to help, lady. You

must tell me what I can do."

"I will," Alyssa said, smiling, "and gladly. A place like this"—she waved her hand—"takes much money to maintain, for all that they make their own clothes and grow most of their own food. Money must be raised to keep it going, and that comes mainly from donations. Not always given willingly, but given just the same." She laughed, a glint in her green eyes. "Now you have witnessed the soft Lady Alyssa, but shortly you will witness the tough one."

From Lochmore Hospice they rode around the countryside stopping at the homes of merchants, landowners, lairds, and anyone the countess suspected of having money to spare to collect for the hospice. And Alyssa *was* tough, Marina noticed, when she needed to be. Though some gave generously and few cared to offend the wife of the chief, there were two or three, people like Lady Grant of Gower Castle, who donated most grudgingly and made no secret of their reluctance. Her contribution was a keg of sour ale and two scrawny chickens, duly loaded into the back of the cart with everything else, though Marina was surprised when the countess expressed her intention of having them tossed into the midden.

"You think they might have gone off?"

Alyssa chuckled grimly. "Nay. I think they might be poisoned."

"What!"

The countess shook her head. "Mayhap I am over-suspicious, but that woman's pious attitude . . . it strikes me as being false. Serena Grant's mother, Lady Magdalen, was my greatest enemy while she lived, and I suspect that Serena is my enemy too, for all her show of affability. I doubt not that she would do me a mischief if she could."

On the ride home to Castle Augusta the whole story

of Alyssa's background came out. Much of it Marina had heard before from Alexander, but his mother filled in details that painted a much more vivid picture of how her father's first wife had tried to destroy her. It was a shocking story of revenge and murder and left no doubt in Marina's mind that Lady Magdalen MacKellar had been a ruthlessly evil woman who had perpetrated heinous crimes against an innocent child, determined to cheat Alyssa out of her rightful inheritance. And she had almost succeeded too! Only Alyssa's courage and resolve to fight for what was hers had saved her.

More and more, Marina found herself admiring Alexander's mother. Though she enjoyed a high position now, her youth had not been easy, and she would never have attained her birthright had she not fought for it—nor the love of Blake Sinclair either.

Glancing at the older woman as they rode slowly home, Marina found it easy to envision how beautiful Alyssa must have been in her youth. She was beautiful now in her middle years! The forest green riding habit she wore was a perfect foil for her flaming red hair, white skin, the clear jade green of her eyes. But her beauty was not merely skin deep—that was what gave her a radiance that set her apart from other comely women Marina had known. As she had witnessed today, the countess truly cared about people, particularly those who were as helpless, as destitute and frightened as she herself had once been; and as she had once fought for justice for herself, so did she fight for others in a similar position.

Marina hoped that her little daughter, who so strongly resembled her grandmother physically, would also be like her in character. She made up her mind to help Alyssa with the hospice all she could, believing as she did that if one had good fortune it

must be shared with those less well endowed, and Marina felt that she had been privileged indeed to have met Alyssa Sinclair.

The countess broke the silence that had fallen between them.

"Did you know that Lady Grant is related to Lord Bothwell?"

Marina looked at her sharply. "Nay . . . I didn't know—but I would not trust that one either."

"She is related to him through her mother, Lady Magdalen." Alyssa's lovely face clouded and she confessed, "How I wish that David and Bothwell were not such close friends! There is something about that fellow . . ."

Marina chuckled thinly. "I know exactly what you mean!"

"Then you don't think I am being fanciful and unfair?"

Marina hesitated. She herself had no desire to be unfair, to set herself up in judgment of anyone, especially a man she hardly knew. Bothwell, after all, was not the only man to be overly familiar with women. Wrong as it was, Marina could see where he might imagine that his lofty status gave him the right to take what he wanted, and doubtless there were many women impressed by his high position and kinship to the King, and all too willing to succumb to him. She could understand that the attention he received—from men and women both—might have gone to his head.

"My instinct is not to like him," Marina replied carefully. "But then I scarcely know his lordship."

"And *my* instinct tells me that we will like him less once we know him better," said Alyssa with a sigh.

They exchanged rueful smiles, both feeling much closer to each other now that they were beginning to

understand each other better, and the last of the formality vanished between them and they became friends.

Alexander remained in Edinburgh for weeks, then returned in mid-November to tell them that he had been given an important post by the King, one he didn't seem too impressed by. "Though I can see why James would wish to stamp out traitorous malcontents, call them demons or witches or whatever you will, the names mean little."

Tongue in cheek, he showed them his reward for his efforts to save the King's mother, and they all admired the beautifully wrought medallion, the men much less effusive than the women. David was openly scornful. "James is a mean churl. He has a niggardly way of honoring the valiant. To think that that bauble is the only thing you have to show for sacrificing more than three years of your life—for almost losing your head! Bah, he has no kingly spirit in him! The man is a tight-fisted coward."

"Treasonable words, my son," cautioned his father. "I would hope you would not bruit such remarks about in Edinburgh?"

David shrugged, muttering, "All know how he is, Bothwell more than most. Even kinship cannot shame the King into generosity."

"It seems to me," said Alex, "that James has been *most* generous with Bothwell. Few would disdain the post of Lord Admiral of Scotland, nor the many castles and land—with the revenue from that land—that have come his way. Mayhap Stewart would like to be named heir to the throne."

David flushed, though indeed he sometimes wondered if that wasn't exactly what Bothwell hankered after. He scowled at his brother for bringing it out into

the open. "I see you have a mind to mock my friend."

"Nay," Alex replied pleasantly, "'twas just a thought that crossed my mind."

"You have been listening to Maitland and Moray," he challenged. "'Tis just like you to fall in with the opposition, to set yourself up as the King's sword, for bigod, James cannot handle one." His angry dark eyes looked his brother up and down and he added contemptuously, "So now he hides behind the strong arm of Sinclair, eh? Doubtless he thinks he has our clan at his disposal as well. 'Twould seem that the King has forgotten who will lead that clan one day, and it won't be Alexander Sinclair!"

A dreadful silence fell over the family seated around the blazing hall fire, supposedly taking their ease. Even the two wolfhounds looked up from their slumber, as if sensing the tension crackling around their shaggy heads.

"And it seems that *you* have forgotten who leads it now," said the Earl of Belrose, his tone ominously quiet. "Mayhap in your mind you already see me in my grave," he went on, "and yourself at the helm of the clan?"

David blanched, his throat working, shame in his eyes now as he saw the way they were all looking at him, especially his mother.

"Nay . . . I—I never entertained such a thought," he stammered, glancing beseechingly from one parent to the other. "You must not think that, for 'twould be the darkest day of my life." Then he forced himself to meet Alexander's eyes, loving him, hating him, and above all riddled with a confused feeling of guilt, and resenting the reason for his guilt. "My pardon, brother. I deeply regret that remark."

Alexander nodded. There were times when he wanted to embrace David, to soothe his troubled

spirit as he had often done when they were both small boys and his little brother was upset over something. But at other times he felt like beating sense into his head, and all the foolish notions out of it, but neither tactic would have done any good, as he had long since found out. David was exceedingly obstinate and bound and determined not to allow his older brother to influence him or advise him in any way, so different from when they had been children. Now he made a point of taking the contrary stance in everything, and it was fast reaching the ridiculous stage.

The incident led to a quarrel between Alex and Marina.

The minute they were alone in their room she chided, "You should not have provoked David by making that comment about Bothwell lusting after the Crown."

Alexander was greatly taken aback, startled at being blamed—and by Marina. "Must I now watch and weigh every word I utter to my family or risk ruffling my brother David's feathers?" he retorted irritably. "Is he so thin-skinned that he cannot hear aught but what he wants to hear?"

"He is very sensitive, Alex—"

"Pah! He is very arrogant, more like. It comes from keeping company with that scoundrel Bothwell. Stewart has put some dangerous notions in his head, methinks, ideas that want knocking out."

Marina eyed him in alarm as Alex threw off his clothes, tossing them over the backs of chairs. His dark face was grim; she could see that he was hurt and annoyed at being held responsible for starting the argument downstairs, but in all honesty Marina felt that he had been responsible, even if it was unintentional.

"Surely you would not think of knocking these

ideas out yourself?" she asked him uneasily.

Alex threw himself down naked on the bed and gave her a measuring look.

"It may yet come to that—"

"God's soul, Alex, don't even consider it!" Marina cried, her dark eyes wide with alarm. She went on heatedly, angry at him now, "Give a thought to your parents. Think how they would feel seeing their two sons battling it out. Marry, but you both act like—like children with no thought for anyone but your-selves—"

"Come to bed," Alex broke in. "'Tis too late for a lecture."

"Like you, I will say my piece," Marina snapped, adding sarcastically, "Aye, whether it ruffles your feathers or not."

He leaned over and blew out the candle, leaving her to undress in the dark. "I mislike seeing your face all twisted up in anger," he said. "'Tis most uncomely that way."

"You—you are every bit as arrogant as David!"

"I hope you will forgive me if I put a pillow over my ears. I have had little rest in Edinburgh and would like to do so now. Good eve!"

"Oh . . . !" Peering down at the bed, where she could vaguely see Alex lying with a pillow over his head, Marina felt like snatching the heavy pewter candlestick from the nearby table and hurling it at him. "Don't think that you are lily-white and blame-less," she said, giving him a hard poke in the back. "You, sir, have less excuse for your conduct, since you are older and should know better."

The only response was a loud, fake snore.

Marina finished undressing, made as if to get into bed, then instead felt her way to the door that led into the adjoining chamber, wishing that she had little

Clare to cuddle up to. But the child had been moved to the Augusta nursery weeks before and Lady Alicia's old nursemaid had been brought back to take care of her. Marina entered the empty chamber and slammed the door closed.

The air in the room was chilly compared to the one next door. Since the room wasn't being used, no fire had been lit nor any warming pans slipped between the sheets to heat up the bed. Marina gasped aloud as the cold linen came in contact with her skin; she lay down gingerly, clenching her teeth, and hastily drew the covers up to her nose. There she lay, freezing, and fuming at Alex.

She supposed, on thinking it over, that it wasn't unusual for there to be a certain amount of competitiveness between brothers. Marina had witnessed some of this between the males in the Percy family where squabbles had frequently broken out over some difference of opinion, each maintaining that his viewpoint was right. But . . . this trouble between Alex and David was more serious, though, to be honest, she felt that David was mostly to blame. Alex had told her more than once that he accepted the situation at Augusta; that he was the type of man who relished the challenge of making his own way in the world, and she could certainly believe that, understanding his nature as she did. Still . . . perhaps in some deep way—even if he himself wasn't conscious of it—Alex *did* resent the fact that his younger brother would inherit the title of Earl of Belrose and the chieftainship that went with it. Alex was a man born to lead; would it not be galling for such a man to be under the command of another? Marina brooded. As for David, he was determined to keep his forceful older brother in his place and never allow him to usurp him. Marina couldn't help but feel that their relationship to each

other boded ill for the future, when the time came when David Sinclair became chief.

The animosity between the brothers was the only blight to Marina's happiness at Castle Augusta, and she knew that it troubled their parents as well, especially their mother. And it brought something else home to Marina. She and Alex were in a similar situation with Clare, especially if any future children they might have were daughters. If they had a son, he would inherit and they would be spared the anguish the Earl and Countess of Belrose were going through now.

Alex didn't see things in quite the way Marina did. When she had brought the subject up, because it troubled her, he had said, "Marina, parents naturally want to do all they can for their offspring, but they cannot tailor their lives to suit any future children they might have. They too are individuals. Remember, we only pass this way once. So they have a right to seize all the love and happiness they can while they can, and I certainly bear no grudges against my parents for what they did. The idea is ludicrous! Anyway, 'tis better for children to grow up to observe real love between their mother and father—and to know they are the result of that love—than to be the spawn of a cold, loveless union."

When he spoke thus, Marina was convinced that he meant it, that David more than Alex had to come to terms with the situation, which in a way struck her as odd since David was the one with everything to gain . . .

Suddenly Marina saw the truth. Alex made David feel guilty! And who wants to be confronted with the object of one's guilt?

It will be better, she thought, when we move to live at Cumbray Castle. Then the brothers won't have to

see each other so much. It was sad . . . but for the good of them both, necessary.

Still shivering under the covers, Marina had a sharp longing for her little daughter, but of course Clare wasn't just hers anymore. Now she had to be shared with so many others, her grandparents, numerous aunts, uncles, and cousins. That very night the child was away "getting to know her people," as Alyssa put it. She was visiting Jason and Lizette Sinclair, cousins of the chief, and doubtless enjoying herself immensely among their many grandchildren. Aunt Kirstin too claimed the little girl frequently; Kirstin was as yet childless and poured out all her motherly instincts on her tiny niece.

Ah . . . Marina was happy that her daughter's horizons were expanding, even if it had been a painful adjustment to let her go. At least she had the assurance that Clare was with people who loved her; her own people who had her best interests at heart. Generally, they had been well-received by the Sinclairs, though there were one or two who made no secret of the fact that they disapproved and would have preferred to see Alexander properly married to a Scottish woman— one with a large dowry. "Ignore them," Alex advised. "I do."

Marina twisted and turned under the covers, unable to get comfortable. Raising herself to paw about for the extra quilt folded neatly at the bottom of the bed, she noticed a glimmer of light coming under the door from the adjoining room and took a great satisfaction in seeing that Alex too was awake.

Brute! she thought, glaring at the door, you deserve to lie awake all night for shutting me out like this when I would talk to you about something that concerns both of us. And I *will* have my say whether you like it or not! Aye, even if it means that you have to hear

something you don't like.

Suddenly the door between the rooms banged open. Alex stood there, tall and powerful, his naked body framed by the candlelight behind him.

"A cold welcome I get when I rush home from Edinburgh to see you," he grumbled. "I would have done better to stay in the city."

Marina raised herself up on her elbows. "You must do as you wish, my lord."

"I wish to jump into bed beside you. 'Tis fiendish chilly standing here like this."

She smiled and threw back the covers.

26

Alex got into bed beside her. Their cold flesh met. And quite suddenly they were tumbling together, embracing fiercely, rocking and nuzzling, each seeking warmth and comfort from each other; each eager to make everything right.

"Witch!" he teased. "For snarling and spitting at me like an adder." His hand slid down her back to her bottom and he slapped her lightly. "Do you know that I was invited to dine with the King and chose to come home to dine with you instead? I sought *your* company over that of a king. *He* treats me with respect. You with disdain."

"Must I watch and weigh every word I utter to you?" asked Marina sweetly, throwing his earlier remark back in his face. "Do I not have the right to express my feelings?"

"Indeed you do. Like this." Alex took her arms and placed them around his neck, then draped her legs

around him as he leaned over her. "Now your lips," he said, low, and bent his head close to hers. "Speak to me with your sweet lips and I promise I will listen. Say you love me, that you are glad to have me home."

Marina sighed . . . and kissed him, still slightly annoyed with him, but not as much as before; not nearly as much. The wonderful heat and strength of his naked body against hers was so distracting, lulling her mind while it woke up her senses. And it was hard to maintain cold anger when one's flesh was beginning to burn and tingle under caressing hands and lips that knew just how to fan the flames that would shortly consume her. Or to speak harshly to one who was at that moment whispering endearments in her ears. "There is no king on earth who could have kept me away from my Marina," Alex was saying, his voice so deep and tender that her heart melted and swelled with joy. "I love you and want you near me always . . ."

Now Marina marveled that she could ever have been angry at him. Oh, she thought, ashamed, how could she? She kissed him over and over to make it up to him, catching his face between her hands and pressing her lips to his eyes, his ears, cheeks, and chin, then feverishly crushing her mouth to his. "How lucky I am," she told him softly, tremulously, "to have such a wonderful, handsome, exciting man to warm my bed. Oh, Alex, how I love you! I missed you so much while you were away."

Now she had all his attention. This was the Marina he liked best, the one he had fallen in love with years ago in England. The Marina who held nothing back and told him exactly what was in her heart.

Alex crushed her to him, her full breasts pressed to the hardness of his chest, the bulging muscles of his thighs coaxing her legs to part, his swelling manhood

burning like a brand into her stomach, as if to mark her as his. With all the hungry passion building inside him, Alex plundered her soft, parted lips. His mouth moved over her upturned face as if tasting her, savoring her, and her skin and hair smelled of attar of roses, her breath fresh as a mountain breeze, her lips sweet as sugared wine. "Beautiful you are . . . body and soul," he told her unsteadily, his broad tanned hand on her belly, then curving to slip between her legs, fingers stroking her to rapture, his knowledge of her speaking through his fingertips.

Marina drew a long, shuddering breath. For a moment she seemed to float in a languid sea of sensation so that she felt drugged, intoxicated, her mouth, her breasts, her thighs, every inch of her strummed to ecstatic awareness as by a master hand. She could feel the cells of her body tingling, her breath quickening, pulse leaping as Alex's tongue traced the shape of her ear, then her mouth, her throat, the curve of her shoulder. Shivering, Marina plunged her fingers into his hair and avidly sought his mouth and tongue, moaning softly as pleasure intensified. Swiftly the drugged feeling gave way to an exhilarating excitement, a savage, desperate need, and she reached for him, thrilling at the fiery contact with the instrument that would bring her release, gasping, "I—I burn for love of you. Oh, my dearest love . . ."

In the dark room Marina could see the darker shape of him rising over her, hear his breath loud in the chamber, feel moisture breaking out on his body and hers at this supreme moment of anticipation. Then he thrust downwards and filled her with what she craved.

Powerfully he moved within her as Marina arched her body to be ravaged by his hungry mouth. Bliss, rapture, and unbearable desire drove everything else out of her mind as she felt his lips close over her

breast, bathing each in turn with a dewy heat, rasping her nipples until her whole body began to quiver and burn as with a raging fever. Wantonly, wildly, Marina clutched his wide shoulders and thrust herself against him, the deeper to take him in, bucking and writhing in her journey toward ecstasy. It came in a heart-stopping rush and she tried to cling to it, to hold it, to make it last forever, feeling so intense that she felt she would shatter.

When their pounding hearts slowed down, Alex chuckled, hugging her. "Well, I think you *are* glad to have me back."

"You—you know it well," Marina replied unsteadily.

He shoved the covers away from them. "This chamber is steamy as a jungle."

"Aye, now it is."

He turned his head to her in the darkness and, unable to see her, sat up and fumbled to light the candle.

"What are you doing?" Marina caught his arm and tried to pull him back down beside her. The moment he moved away she felt cooler, the perspiration drying on her skin making her hot flesh prickle, destroying the warm, languid feeling that followed lovemaking.

"I would look upon you in this sweet mood," he said. "A man must seize these precious moments while he can."

She slapped him, chiding, "You are not always so sweet yourself, sir! You may not realize this, Sinclair, but you have a distinctly hard, ruthless cast to your features whenever things don't go as you wish, so you have no right to criticize me."

The candle flickered into flame, and a pool of soft, golden light illuminated the area around the bed. Alexander gazed down at her as she lay back against

the pillows, one arm flung back over her head, her thick blonde hair scattered like rippling gold silk all about her, her dark eyes sultry, mouth swollen from his passionate kisses. He looked at her breasts, firm and creamy, the nipples still turgid and plummy-red, succulent as ripe fruit. Then he drew back the rest of the covers and studied all of her avidly, as a man will when something rare and beautiful comes into his possession.

"Alex—stop!" Marina laughed shakily and tried to draw up the covers, but he caught her hand and shook his head. Now his expression was grave, intent, and as his eyes moved slowly over her slender curves possessively, caressingly, Marina began to feel strangely aroused though he wasn't touching her in any way. She looked at the tanned, muscular body leaning over her, her heart leaping when she saw his maleness stir and begin to throb, pulsing with fresh desire. Marina put out her hand and touched him in wonder, amazed that Alex could be so quickly aroused but delighted and triumphant that she had been the cause of it.

He caught her hand and held it still and gazed deep in her eyes, a look that stopped her heart. Marina had the feeling that she was about to make an exciting discovery or have some mystery revealed to her.

"When a man sees before him such a goddess he must worship at her temple," Alex told her softly. Then he bent down and whispered against her parted lips, "Would you like me to worship you, Marina?"

"What—what do you mean?" Half-laughing, not sure whether he was teasing her or not, she stared into eyes that were now a dark, smoldering green. There was a singularly satyrlike look about Alex at that moment, a wicked glint in his eyes.

"I bow before you," he murmured, and lowered his head.

He swept her through a door Marina had never known existed, taking her down into an erotic world to experience a paradise such as she had never dreamed possible. Oh, the sweet torment, the pleasure, the unbearable ecstasy he was bringing her with his lips and tongue! The flaming frenzy took hold of her, lust bursting from every pore, bathing her skin in steamy dew. Desire Marina had never known herself capable of raged through her. Wild, hot blood pounded in her ears. Rational thought vanished. Only the dark and desperate craving remained.

Alexander was skilled at making it last. He knew how to drive her mad, to make her aware of her body in a way Marina never had been before, bringing her to new and rapturous heights of sensation, to the edge again and again until she was moaning, begging him for release.

Marina cried out when at last it came, sensual pleasure so strong, so powerful that it left her shuddering violently and weeping in Alexander's arms as her mind groped to understand what had happened to her. "Jesu . . ." she breathed, "I—I never knew . . ."

But if she was a goddess then he was a god and also deserved homage.

Hours later they sat up against the pillows watching the cool, opalescent light of dawn stealing into the room, toasting it with the wine Alex had sneaked up from the cellar. Both had a raging thirst after the heat of their amours. Marina felt deliciously wicked to be drinking so early in the morning, and giggled. "What will they say when we teeter down to breakfast?"

"They'll be green with envy."

Their eyes met, soft with love, and Alex kissed her tenderly.

"You make it hard for me to leave tomorrow," he said, sighing. "King James and his witch hunt! He

might at least dignify it by calling it what it really is, a weeding out of traitors."

Marina eyed him curiously. "Why were you chosen for the task?"

Alex had been selected, he knew, because the King was testing him, but he didn't tell Marina that, afraid of worrying her. Nor did he tell her that everywhere he went in Edinburgh, even in the outlying places, he was treated like a hero and feted and applauded, so much so that Alex found it embarrassing.

When Alex returned to Edinburgh and began his investigations, his first actions were hardly what James had hoped for. He ordered the release of the pregnant young "witch" from the dungeons, and also of the lawyer's wife, Mistress MacBride. Most of the male prisoners were also let go after Alexander examined them and ascertained that they were innocent, mere pawns arrested to assuage the King's sudden blood-lust, his desire to revenge the threat to his wife's life.

"I would not have let them go," George Gordon told Alex bluntly. "How will this look in the eyes of His Majesty? 'Twill fan a suspicion in his mind, mayhap lead him to think that you are in with them."

Alex shrugged. "Better that than having the poor wretches burned at the stake, as others were before them. I have no mind to live with a sore conscience for the rest of my days."

Gordon laughed grimly. "Those days could be short if James has reason to doubt your loyalty. To have to wrestle with a sore conscience is preferable, methinks, to going to the block."

King James did not hide his displeasure when Chancellor Maitland informed him that his dungeons were now almost empty. He sent for Alexander and

demanded an explanation, this in front of Maitland, Lennox, Robert Bruce, and some of his other favorites. Bothwell, though no longer a favorite, was also there standing apart from the others on the opposite side of the room.

"A marvelous turn of events," said the King. "Scotland is a country without any criminals!"

There were a few titters, though Maitland of Thirlestane's long, sober face did not crack in a smile. The King's chancellor had a serious, somewhat pedantic disposition. He was an able man, hard-working and intelligent, and had a faintly contemptuous attitude toward some of the others surrounding the monarch, an attitude he couldn't quite conceal—or didn't bother to conceal. Powerful as he was, Maitland had naturally made many enemies, including Earl Bothwell. But though he sometimes vexed the King with his sobriety—James liked people about him with a keen wit—he recognized that he had a rare and excellent servant in Maitland of Thirlestane. But the young, golden-haired Duke of Lennox, son of the man who had been the King's premier favorite while he lived, laughed openly. "Would that it were so, but alas, much as we might wish it, this land of ours is no paradise." He was girlishly pretty and fluttered his long lashes at the tall, black-haired nobleman from the wilds of the Highlands, whose expression and manner were now as forbidding as the land he came from. "God's soul, Sinclair, why did you let these fiends go to ply their evil with renewed vigor, given a nod of approval—"

"They are no more evil than you are, Lennox," Alexander interrupted curtly, leaving them to make of the remark what they would.

Lennox's fair skin flushed crimson and his eyes jumped to the King, expecting him to order Sinclair's

arrest—or at the very least chastise him—for insulting the heir to the throne. But James sat stroking his beard, his heavy-lidded eyes half-closed, his attention not on his heir but on Sinclair's hand as it rested almost casually on the hilt of his sword. There was no sarcasm in his voice when he inquired quietly, "Why did you let the prisoners go, my lord?"

Alex threw a look around the chamber at the others, his green eyes cold as ice as they lingered for a moment on Bothwell; then, dismissing him contemptuously, he fixed his attention on the King. "Only one of them was in any way suspicious. The rest had simply been caught in the net presently sweeping the land, seized by overzealous agents who had no desire to return to Your Majesty empty-handed."

"But, Sinclair"—James leaned forward in his seat —"some of these people confessed to their guilt!"

Alex laughed grimly. "Who would not confess under torture? Few have the strength and courage to resist the persuasion of the rack, or the Brakes."

"The innocent are given that strength by the Almighty," said the pious Robert Bruce. "Did you, for instance, confess while in the Tower?"

"He was never racked," muttered the Earl of Bothwell, his remark significant.

Alexander's fingers closed like iron bars over the hilt of his sword and his jaw clenched as he struggled to control his anger, all his instincts clamoring to challenge the man who had hinted that he was a Judas. Sensing his mood, and blanching at the thought of a bloody duel taking place in his chamber, James's hand shot up, the signal that no one should interrupt.

"A moment ago you said that all but one of the prisoners were free of suspicion. Name the suspect, Sinclair, and tell me why you let him go."

Again Alexander's eyes scanned the room. "I would

prefer to do so in private, Your Grace."

For a moment there wasn't a sound, but the eight men in the room were now eying each other uneasily, all except Bothwell, who cried, "You—you insolent swine! Are you questioning our fealty? Have you forgotten that you are in the presence of the King and his family? Dog!" He sprang forward, pulling a dagger out of his belt, his eyes glittering and florid color blotching his narrow face. While the King reeled back in his chair and Maitland flew to the door shouting for the guards, Alexander stood ten feet away, his legs spread, automatically balancing his body for the attack, his hand poised above his sword that was still in its scabbard. He smiled, and that smile was chilling. "You have crude instincts for a nobleman, Bothwell," he said, his voice deadly calm. "And a mouth as foul as your mind. Step hither and I promise you this, the King will have one less member of his family to worry about."

Crouching, Bothwell feinted back and forth in front of Alexander, his dagger in his hand, but the expression on his face was no longer menacing; the horrified onlookers noticed that he had gone quite pale, and he made no move to bridge the distance between himself and Sinclair. He seemed almost relieved when the guards rushed in and seized him.

Thereupon the King ordered that the room be cleared, except for Maitland and Alexander, and finally—James greatly subdued—they got down to business. Alex named the suspect, one Edward Cochrane, a tailor who lived in the region of North Berwick, a coastal area some twenty miles from the capital. The man himself was of low station, but he had important people among his clients, including several members of the nobility. The tailor had some unusual hobbies; he was a hypnotist, cast horoscopes,

and could be found roaming about at night ostensibly studying the stars. Some of the villagers where he lived were afraid of him, and the local butcher had testified that Cochrane drank the blood of an ox every day "to keep up his strength"; another informer whispered that he was a vampire with inhuman powers.

The tailor had been arrested before Alexander had been put in charge of the investigation, and he was the only one of the suspects not to break under torture. The most the interrogators had got out of him, even on the rack, were the three words "I durst not . . ."

"He is hiding something, or someone," Alexander told the King, "but was quite prepared to go to his death rather than reveal his secrets."

James burst out, "Then why in Christ's name did you set him free?"

"'Twould avail us nothing to keep the man in prison," Alex responded somewhat impatiently, "nor to execute him. And his freedom is only an illusion. Every move he makes is being watched. Hopefully, he will lead us to others."

"Aye, I see." James nodded.

"It could be nothing," Alex went on, "just mere fools dabbling in the occult, imbuing themselves with powers they don't really possess to frighten their neighbors or for gain. We shall see."

The King looked at Maitland, excitement in his eyes.

"Well," he said, "what say you, Chancellor?"

"Aye . . . a plan worth pursuing," the older man replied carefully. He didn't believe in witchcraft any more than Alex did, but of course this wasn't a witch hunt; it was a search to flush out those engaged in treachery against the King, and there were always plenty of those in any kingdom. But surprisingly

enough, there had been few really serious plots against James (the infamous Raid of Ruthven when the monarch was only sixteen by far the most grave), thanks to his ever-vigilant ministers, Maitland liked to think. Which was not to say there weren't those about him with dangerous ambitions, who might well be biding their time until the climate was more propitious for the success of their schemes. Danger was always present for a sovereign who had no children to inherit his throne. This led to various claimants to the succession, not all of them legitimate. Lennox was recognized by some as the heir, and the King himself favored him, but the Hamiltons too had a legitimate claim—though there were many who would have strenuously opposed either of these men succeeding.

Maitland could sense that the situation was coming to a head. King James had recently married. In all likelihood, children would be born from the union. Once that happened, the present claimants would have to stand aside, their chance of succeeding gone. Now was the time to strike. Which of them, Maitland wondered, would try? Like Alex, the chancellor was convinced that there was a worm near the core of the apple, and it was for this reason that he was having the Lennox and Hamilton factions watched. He also had a question about the Earl of Huntly, the most powerful Catholic nobleman in Scotland. Though the King was fond of George Gordon, Gordon—like his grandfather before him—always served his own interests first.

Unlike many of the others surrounding the King, Maitland never spoke or acted without careful deliberation, weighing up all the pros and cons. As he listened to Alexander making his report to James, he remembered that the Sinclairs were allies of the

Gordons, yet for all that he was inclined to trust
Alexander Sinclair at least, greatly admiring him for
trying to rescue Queen Mary, but he thought less of
his brother, David. David and Earl Bothwell were
very close, and Bothwell hated Maitland and took
every opportunity to discredit him in the eyes of the
King. Now he was striving to discredit Alexander—
even though he was friends with his brother. It had
come to the chancellor's alert ears that all was not well
between the Sinclair brothers, and it wasn't hard to
see why. There too the problem was the succession, in
this case to the future chieftainship of the clan Sin-
clair.

The King was saying, "This pother between you and
Bothwell must cease, Alexander. He will be banished
from court for a while for daring to draw his weapon
in my presence, as would you have been had you
unsheathed your sword. If I hear tell of either of you
trying to harm the other, the guilty party will be
arrested and dealt with most severely. Do I make
myself clear?"

"Perfectly." Alexander's voice was steely cold, but
the look of restrained violence in his eyes unnerved
James, who sat back in his chair, frowning. "I trust,
however, that I have the right to defend myself if
Bothwell should try to attack, as he did a few minutes
ago?" said Sinclair, the faint mockery in his voice
making it clear that he would defend himself whether
or not the King gave him leave.

"Ah . . . Alex, lad"—James sighed and shook his
head—"don't make things more awkward than they
need be. Expend your energies in routing the traitors
from my realm and you'll benefit from it more than
you will from seeking revenge on my foolish cousin."

Maitland's eyes went to the medallion around
Sinclair's neck, which Alex dutifully wore in the

monarch's presence, and he dropped his eyes hastily, feeling embarrassed. It prompted him to do something uncharacteristic when he saw Alex out of the chamber, for Maitland was a man who was careful never to take sides.

"Steer clear of Bothwell, for he's out to do you mischief," he warned as they stood for a moment in the corridor. Then almost as an aside, "And caution your brother against his society. 'Twill bring him naught but grief."

But when Alex tried to warn David it led to a violent quarrel between them. His brother angrily defended his friend Francis Stewart. "Bothwell is a brave man and fine soldier with the courage to speak his mind, and it shames the King to have one of his own blood make him look inferior—"

"Inferior!" Alex laughed scornfully. "The King is worth ten of his cousin. Bothwell is a vainglorious bully with a dangerously erratic streak in his nature, and treacherous to friend and foe alike—"

"Kindly refrain from trying to foist your advice on me, brother," David interrupted haughtily. "I will associate with whom I please."

27

At the end of November, while Alex was away in Edinburgh, Marina received a letter from Gwen Porter, written for her by a cousin who could read and write. She warned Marina that Stafford had left for Scotland, determined to bring her and the child back. "We have heard through channels that he has gone a little mad and vows to find you or die in the attempt. Take care, sweeting, for Edgar can be persistent and cunning as a wolf when his mind is set on something. And don't let little Clare out of your sight."

Gwen also had another piece of news for her. Maud Percy was ill with some sort of lingering disease. "We have heard that she has been making enquiries about you. Do you wish us to tell her where you are so that she can reach you? Write back and let me know."

Since Alex was away, Marina went with her news about Stafford to the chief. Blake laughed grimly. "The fellow is a fool to think of coming here. Me-

thinks his obstinacy will be the end of him. Even assuming that he reaches the Highlands alive, he will never take you out of here, that I promise you."

It was arranged that Marina should never leave Augusta without a heavily armed guard; also, the Sinclair sentries were alerted to watch for strangers and apprehend them before they got anywhere near the castle.

Sensing Marina's terror, Blake said, "Fear not, for he will never get near you. I marvel that he would even try. This only serves to point up that the man's mind has become unhinged; even his sense of self-preservation has deserted him." He squeezed her hand, advising, "Go on as usual and don't allow the knave to trouble you; refuse him even that small victory."

"I—I'll try," Marina replied shakily.

But *she* knew her husband better than any of them and though she tried not to show it, Marina was frightened, so much so that she stayed close to the castle and, as Gwen had suggested, never let her daughter out of her sight. Even walking in the gardens —and it was necessary, especially for Clare, to have exercise in the fresh air—Marina was nervous, jumping violently at the slightest sound and rushing back into the castle when anyone approached. The thought of Edgar managing to grab her and the child and forcing them back with him to dismal Baxton Hall made her ill. She knew too that this time he would keep them both close prisoners; perhaps he would even kill her as it was whispered he had done to his previous wives! With that thought in mind, Marina took to always wearing boots rather than slippers, and inside a boot was a dagger. Aye, she determined, I will kill him, or myself, before I will let him take us. Oh, God, to think of never seeing Alex again! Somehow she knew that if Edgar succeeded this time in return-

ing her to England, he would make very certain that Alexander Sinclair never set eyes on her again.

The autumn dragged on and the first snows of early winter arrived. Standing at her chamber window, gazing over the bleak mountains and moorland, Marina would ask herself, "Where is he? Can he be on his way to the castle now, perhaps disguised as a monk, or a peddler, or even a Highlander in borrowed plaids?" With the fanatically determined Edgar, anything was possible. As Blake had said, he was more than a little mad. Getting his wife and Clare back had become a sick obsession with him.

So concerned was Marina about the possible appearance of her husband that she gave little thought to Gwen's news about Maud Percy. Maud was the least of her worries at that time. The woman had been an indifferent mother to her own children while they were growing up and had shown even less interest in her ward. Then to cruelly wed her to a beast like Stafford!

Marina wrote back to Gwen saying, "Tell Lady Percy nothing. Not a hint about where I am. I have no desire for any sort of contact with the woman, nor her husband either. I would as soon forget that part of my life."

The Sinclair family moved to spend Christmas and New Year's at Cumbray Castle, the seat of the clan MacKellar. As chief of the clan, Alyssa spent every other holiday season among her own people, also several months of the year in between. Cumbray Castle was almost as grand as Augusta, and in their way the tall, red-haired MacKellars were almost as impressive as the Sinclairs. The moment they laid eyes on Clare they cried, "This one is ours through and through!" And with a glance of triumph at Lord Blake and Alexander, who came back from Edinburgh

for the festivities, Stephan MacKellar said, "The stamp of our blood has won out here, eh, my lords?"

Both Blake and his son had to concede that it had indeed. The two clans had been enemies in the distant past and it had been Blake himself who had been instrumental in bringing them together, this before Alyssa was able to claim her birthright. Now the clans were closely united, so close they were able to make teasing references to their long feud, of which all that lingered was a friendly rivalry between them. "Our next will have the stamp of the Sinclairs," Alex prophesied, and Marina blushed furiously when all eyes turned toward her questioningly.

"Aye," she nodded, reaching for Alexander's hand. "Clare, if all goes well, will have a brother or sister next July."

The announcement led to an immediate celebration, and Marina was relieved and heartened at how well they received the news, considering the fact that they were not married, that she was still locked into the role of Alexander's mistress. She had suspected her pregnancy for the past month. Alex himself had only heard about it two days before when he came to Cumbray Castle from Edinburgh. After hugging her fiercely, he had burst out in exasperation, "You must be got free of Stafford before this one is born! Christ's teeth, if I were not saddled with this commission of the King's I would go south myself and settle with the rogue once and for all. I would find him," he said grimly, "wherever he is."

That was one time when Marina was glad that Alexander *was* so occupied in the capital, because if these two men were to meet she was certain that Alex would not hesitate to kill her husband when Edgar refused to give her a divorce—as he most certainly would not.

But Marina felt better at Cumbray, believing that Stafford would never think to look for her here. Alex was with her, which always gave her a wonderful sense of security, and with the might of the two clans around them she felt that she had little to worry about. She allowed her happiness to break through and overwhelm her fear, and the holiday season was a joyous one, the entertainment boisterous and gay, the dancing lively, the food sumptuous. Here were a host of new people to get to know—Stephan and Sarah MacKellar, the elderly Lord Luke and Nan, a sweet couple and the uncle and aunt of the chief, also cousins Fiona, Mathew, Anne, and Ian and countless others, all the MacKellar side of the family. Most treated Alexander's English mistress politely and in some cases even affectionately, but when they all met for the Yuletime Ball, there were a few who sniffed their disapproval. As she had at Castle Augusta, Marina steeled herself to ignore them. I am happy, she thought, blissfully happy with my lord and living among these Highlanders and I will not allow those few to spoil it—but please, God, let Edgar never find me now, not with another little Sinclair in my belly!

Alex told her that he was sending six of his men south in search of Stafford, to investigate and report back what was happening.

At the castle there was much talk about the situation in Edinburgh where Stephan MacKellar too spent much of his time. They were curious about Alexander's job and his success with the witch hunt—of which he dared tell them little. They also examined his medallion, expressing mixed feelings about the reward. "Meager gratitude for a mighty deed," snorted elderly Lord Luke. "Had you done something of like magnitude for the King's *mother*, she would have shown the world how she honored valor—and

395

not with trinkets and baubles, bigod!"

Stephan, a member of the Privy Council, murmured, "James does naught without lengthy deliberation—"

"What need for deliberation?" scoffed David. "Even the common people know my brother was treated shabbily. Others have been given far more for far less." He glanced at Alex, who was grinning at the heated exchange and seemed not in the least put out. "Cock's bones, Esmé Lennox was handed half the kingdom for writing love sonnets to the King!"

"Mayhap I should take up poetry," Alex chuckled.

When the men discussed politics and the various power struggles going on at court, the women chatted about the latest fashions, the new innovations the young Queen had brought over with her from Denmark. She had come to her husband's capital city in a silver coach pulled by eight fine white horses. She wore a wider, fan-shaped ruff, rapidly being copied all over the nation. Only fifteen years old, she had already the reputation of being a great beauty with her round, guileless eyes and hip-long flaxen hair. Listening to this description, old Nan MacKellar sighed dreamily, "Ah, how weak with love the King must be for his lady."

"At least this time it *is* a lady!" laughed the outspoken Fiona.

There was a sudden embarrassed silence wherein old Nan gazed at the red faces around her, uncomprehending. "What do you mean, Fiona, lass?" she said at length.

Glancing at the others, who shook their heads in warning, Fiona replied obliquely, "Oh, the King has many to claim his love. 'Tis nice to find it now fixed on this one woman instead of, ah . . . scattered about."

The elderly woman nodded. "Our James is a virtuous lad, none can deny it. You'll find no bastards clinging about *his* royal robes as happened with all of his ancestors, save his own lady mother."

None of them dared look at each other for fear of laughing.

Heavy snow fell in the mountains. Fierce storms raged that obliterated everything in a sea of swirling white, leaving Cumbray Castle isolated and totally cut off from the rest of the world, a situation Marina welcomed. It meant that Edgar Stafford could not reach her, however hard he tried. It also meant that Alexander could not return to Edinburgh while the storms lasted and the tracks through the glens were completely blocked. Inside the castle all was warm and convivial, with fires roaring in every chamber, plenty of food and wine to sustain them, and pleasant company with whom to while away the long winter days and nights.

From the start Marina's second pregnancy was different. She was only sick once, nor did she feel listless and tired, as she had done with Clare. Her cheeks glowed and her eyes shone and she felt fit and energetic.

"'Twill be a lad this time," Alex predicted, examining her fondly, adding, "If I am still in Edinburgh when the time comes, I shall bring you to Clairmont, our city residence, for this time I would be at your side when our child is born. By then too, pray God, you will be my wife."

When after ten days of storms the wind died down and a tepid sun peeped through the clouds, little Clare pleaded to be allowed out to play in the snow. Marina took her out to the south lawn, the one close to the side entrance to the castle, when David Sinclair saw

them from a downstairs window. He hurried out to join them and suggested that all three build a snowman.

"Aye, Uncle Davy!" cried Clare, hugging his long legs. "But we no' have a hat to put on him."

"Right!" he laughed. "That will soon be rectified. Wait here, ladies, while I fetch the proper attire for our white gentleman."

With much laughter and a great deal of snowball throwing, their creation was finally finished—all except for his requisite garb. David held his niece up to place the hat on his head and carefully drape the scarf around his neck, the little girl squealing, "Och, is he no' braw?" her diction now heavily tinged with the Scottish twang. "Want to show nanny," she cried, wriggling to get down. Seizing her uncle's hand, Clare tugged him over to the heavy door. "Open it for me, Uncle? I bring nanny out to see him."

"Clare, say please," Marina chided. "Remember your manners."

David walked back to her, grinning. "She's a grand wee lass, the very picture of my lady mother. The MacKellars are much delighted with her because of it." He added half-jokingly, "We must take care that they don't lure her affections away. I think they gave her more toys than we did for Christmas, if that's possible."

"They are lovely people," Marina said, meaning it, but careful to add, "as are the Sinclairs."

David gave her a penetrating sidelong glance, noting her rosy cheeks and the shine in her eyes, the smile playing about her mouth. "Then you like the Highlands?"

She nodded. "And especially the people. Most of them are so open, warm, and friendly." She laughed. "I must confess that I had my doubts about coming

here, not sure of my reception, but it has surpassed my wildest dreams. What a dear family you have, David. I can appreciate them, never having had a family of my own. You have something wonderfully precious."

"Aye, I know," he responded quietly.

Clare appeared with her nurse and proudly showed off their creation.

"Walk with me a bit," David invited after the other two had gone back into the house. "I think 'tis time that you and I got to know each other better."

They strolled down a path that had been shoveled clear of snow, he in a long gray cloak and Marina in a heavy mantle of blue velvet trimmed with miniver, a loose hood pulled up over her head. She wasn't sure what to expect and, as they walked along in silence for a little while, felt a touch of tension. David had always been polite, but definitely reserved and slightly aloof, though from the first he had been good with Clare.

When they reached the back of the castle he said, "Doubtless you think I'm an unnatural brother?"

Marina swung on him, startled. "Nay! What . . . do you mean?"

He sighed, kicking at the piles of snow lining the path, his eyes roving the terrain. "You should know that I too appreciate my family. Sinclairs always stand behind their own, and I am no exception. But . . . one can defend them while not always agreeing with them. Alex and I see things very differently."

Marina didn't know what to say and judiciously kept silent.

He stopped and caught her arm, halting her. "Bothwell meant no disrespect to you at the Harvest Ball. 'Tis his way to be, ah . . . effusive." His handsome face tightened as he went on, "'Twas insulting the way Alex made such an issue of it at our harvest celebrations, demeaning a guest in our home. Then he makes

matters worse by casting a slur against Bothwell's loyalty in front of the King!" David's skin flushed with anger. "Under the circumstances, can you blame Bothwell for seeking satisfaction? Perhaps it was rash of him to do so in His Majesty's presence, but a man greatly offended does not always pause to think." He scowled. "My brother should have a care. Francis Stewart has a high position and great power. How will it benefit the Sinclairs if he makes an enemy of such a man?"

Marina stared at him in dismay and perplexity, much of what David had just told her news indeed. "When . . . when did Alex cast a slur against him?"

"At court some weeks gone." His brown eyes roved her face. "You did not know about this?"

Marina shook her head.

David explained what had happened, how close they had come to doing battle with the King and his courtiers as witnesses, and how Bothwell had been banished for it and was now completely out of favor with James and cooling his heels at his estate in Liddesdale. Alex, on the other hand, had not been punished at all.

"Naturally, Bothwell is livid at the injustice of it all, and that does not bode well for Alex," David finished darkly.

Marina was shocked and alarmed, but she wasn't surprised that Alex had not told her. He went out of his way to spare her worry.

"You can see the awkward position this places me in," David went on. "Alex is my brother, Bothwell my closest friend. Now the pair of them are enemies!" He looked down at her intently. "I don't snipe at Alex out of mere contrariness," he insisted. "He has gone out of his way to break up my friendship with a man I

admire; a man who has always been most congenial and well-meaning toward me."

Marina remembered Bothwell's behavior toward her on the night of the Harvest Ball when both his manner and the words he had said were lewd and insinuating, so much so that they had attracted the attention of others. Alex, without a word to the King's cousin, had simply taken her away from him—when he'd had every right to subject him to the thrashing he deserved. Also, if Alex had questioned his fealty, then, Marina was convinced, he must have had good reason to do so. From what she had heard about Francis Stewart since, the man was far from trustworthy and might well have an ulterior motive for befriending David, who would one day be the chief of a powerful clan and the ally of others, like the Gordons, who were even more powerful. A useful friend to have indeed!

"Alex must apologize to Francis," David blurted.

Marina's eyes widened indignantly at the remark. Never! she almost cried. Why should he belittle himself to a man he despises? But she bit the words back just in time. David, she was fast understanding, was young and inexperienced and still woefully lacking in a clear assessment of character or the behavior that motivated others. Somewhat naïve and idealistic, he tended to take people at face value. Bothwell had gone out of his way to curry his favor, and young as he was, new to life at court, David was flattered to have the friendship of such a powerful nobleman close to the King himself.

David pressed, "If all goes as planned, some day you and Alex will marry, so it would be to your advantage to urge him to set things right with Bothwell."

Marina could hardly control her anger. "David,"

she said, fighting for composure, "I would not presume to tell Alexander what to do. I know next to nothing about the situation in Edinburgh."

"But I just explained," he retorted impatiently. His fingers tightened on her arm. "Can you not understand that I am trying to avert a crisis? Since my brother won't be reasoned with, I thought to turn to you. 'Tis obvious that you can influence him as no other can."

Marina took several deep gulps of the cold afternoon air to steady herself, then faced him squarely. "Have you ever stopped to consider that your brother might be right and this association with Lord Bothwell detrimental to you?" she asked him bluntly.

His head rose haughtily. "I see that you *have* discussed this with Alex."

"Have you, David?" She went on quietly when he said nothing, "Stewart has good reason to want to form a connection with the future chief of the clan Sinclair, one closely allied to the Gordons. He is an ambitious man, is he not, a man who craves power, some say even the Crown itself! What better way to try to seize it than by having the might of the clans behind him? I am only a lass from England, one unfamiliar with the power struggles going on here—but even I can see how Bothwell might use you to his advantage. I would think about it," she urged, then turned and walked away from him and disappeared back inside the castle, leaving David Sinclair staring after her, a frown on his face.

When she told Alex about her talk with his brother once they were alone in their own room that night, he was all for barging down the corridor to confront David and whip some sense into him, furious that his brother would have informed Marina of his confron-

tation with Bothwell at court.

"Nay, leave him be," she said. "You can lead a horse to water, but not force it to drink. Now, what happened at court between you and Earl Bothwell?"

Alex's version of the incident was markedly different from the one Stewart had related to David. "I was hesitant about revealing the name of the suspect for security reasons," he explained. "There were eight men in that room at the time, and as history has proved, most with a mind to depose a monarch are from the ranks of the aristocracy. I merely stated that I would prefer to name the suspect in private. Bothwell was the only one who took offense. He, not I, drew his weapon and made to attack, hence the reason the King banished him."

"Then David had the wrong way of it . . ."

Marina looked up into his face as she lay in his arms. "Would that this job of yours be finished in Edinburgh! How pleasant it will be to live in peace in the Highlands, far away from the intrigues at court."

Alex kissed her, then smiled. "From what I've heard, those were oft the very words my mother said to my father at the time he was in the service of Mary Stuart."

"I can well understand how she must have felt!"

"Then I'll make you a promise. When this work is done, I shall refuse all other commissions and become a country squire managing Cumbray."

Marina threw her arms around his neck and kissed him.

Alexander and David returned to Edinburgh in mid-January, and at the beginning of February the Sinclair family—and Marina—made their way back to Castle Augusta. There was a startling letter awaiting

Marina from Gwen Porter.

Baxton Hall had been sacked and almost burned to the ground! Edgar Stafford had never returned from his trip to Scotland, and the men he had left in charge of his Hall had all disappeared. "The feeling is that the men Edgar took with him into Scotland were in cahoots with those he left behind to guard his manor; that the former murdered Edgar somewhere in the wilds, slipped back into England in the dead of night to plunder Baxton Hall and make off with what they could before setting it aflame," Gwen wrote through her cousin. "There's a warrant out for Lester Fordyce, thought to be the ringleader. The sheriff and his posse are searching for him now, also the rest involved, but the feeling is that Edgar is dead."

There was also more about Lady Maud Percy, who was now gravely ill. "Imagine our surprise," the letter continued, "when Sir Guy himself rode down to Brokenbridge Farm to speak to us. His lady, he said, has not long to live and has certain things she would like to tell you." Gwen added cynically, "Doubtless the woman wants to meet her maker with a clear conscience and would like to make peace with you. Shall I tell them where you can be reached? I await your instructions."

But all Marina could think of was that she might be free! Free to wed Alex at last! She felt such a surge of excitement that the letter fluttered out of her hands and she jumped up and began to pace feverishly around the room. "Oh, if only Alex were here!" she cried, desperate to tell him her news. As for Maud Percy . . . Marina would send word through Gwen that she held no grudge against her—which wasn't quite true!—but she had absolutely no desire to bring her former guardians back into her life, considering

all they had done to her. The past, as far as she was concerned, was dead, and she wanted nothing to taint her future.

She flew down the stairs to tell the Earl and Countess of Belrose her wonderful news. Then she would write to Alexander.

28

The Queen of England was in a pensive mood. She was confined to her apartments with a cold, and sickness always depressed her. Her head throbbed, her bones ached, and a sore throat prevented her from engaging in idle chatter with her ladies-in-waiting, which would at least have helped to pass the time. Even reading tired her.

There was a time when minor illness like this would hardly have bothered her; when she would have refused to knuckle under and gone on with her life as usual, throwing herself into the daily business with her ministers, seeing representatives from other lands, and at the end of her active day still energetic enough to cavort and frolic with her courtiers. Those about her had marveled at her stamina. Now they were whispering, "The Queen is growing old."

And it was true! Sitting before her mirror, gazing at herself in the glass, was no longer a pleasurable

experience. Elizabeth had always known she was not a beautiful woman—not like her cousin, Mary Stuart. Of course her courtiers had strenuously denied that, and in a surface part of her mind Elizabeth had allowed them to convince her that she was wondrous fair, even while knowing the truth at some deeper level that she rarely cared to delve into. But she had been handsome! She'd had the Tudor hair, that rich shade of reddish-gold, and fine white skin, hardly marred by her bouts with smallpox, and clear amber eyes that had shone with a lively interest in everything about her.

So when regally clad in her sumptuous gowns designed to emphasize her slender figure, and glittering with precious gems, she had been truly magnificent, a dazzling personage indeed. All that together with her quick, intelligent mind and her ready wit had drawn others to her like moths buzzing about a flame.

Oh, the suitors she had had! The princes and dukes and even kings who had desperately sought her hand —all destined to be disappointed in the end. What a rare and satisfying game it had been to keep them dangling, pitting one against the other, sometimes for years. But she had never seriously considered any of them. Only one man claimed her heart, and always had, the handsome Earl of Leicester, Robert Dudley.

She had even considered marrying him! Her people —and she had always made it her policy to bow to the wishes of her subjects—had decreed otherwise.

Ah . . . she thought, dearest, sweetest Robert. He had been a true lover, so good to look upon, so dynamic and exciting to be with, so stimulating in all ways. But also, so it seemed, ruthless, wildly ambitious, vindictive with those who opposed him, even cruel—though never with her. Elizabeth brooded about Amy Robsart, his superfluous wife, quickly

gotten out of the way. Had Robert been the means of bringing about her death as so many had whispered at the time? She would never know, nor indeed, wanted to know.

And there had been other things . . . things she was glad to shunt to the back of her mind. That had been easier to do while Dudley was alive; when her life had been too full, too crammed with constant excitement to waste the precious moments in dour soul-searching.

Now, with a dismal mood upon her, the Queen opened a locked drawer that held all her treasured mementoes—the countless gifts from Robert, not all of them costly, but dear to her just the same. These included letters and poetry he had written to her while they were apart, and which she had read over and over again. Then there were silly little things but imbued with special meaning for both of them—a pretty bottle containing the special perfume he had had concocted for her in France, now empty but the fragrance lingering on like a breath from the past. A single glove, glittering with aglets. Its partner she had lost while dallying with Robert on a terrace during a ball; she had taken it off to stroke his cheek, craving the touch of his skin against hers. Then there was a bejeweled ostrich feather—how he had loved it when she seductively tickled him with that! And a satin slipper, of all things! She had once thrown it at him during a spat, but oh, the joy of making up.

The Queen's heart throbbed painfully as her fingers touched her memories—an old program of a play, a cameo with Dudley's likeness inside, a ring he had once worn in the early days, a lock of his curly black hair inside a locket . . . so many memories. "Oh, my love . . . !" she breathed, the tears falling silently.

They had hurt others. Aye, they had, and sometimes carelessly, at other times because there was no help for it. A Queen was no common mortal. The one who held her heart must needs be uncommon too, set above the laws that governed the masses, but because of it oft required to make painful sacrifices not demanded of those of lower station. The Queen always came before the woman, the country before her personal desires, the Crown the substitute for the joy of living with a husband and children in a normal relationship that other women took for granted. No one—ever—would call her mother . . .

For a moment Elizabeth seemed to hear voices from the past—or her conscience. She was reminded that she was growing old, frail, tired, nearing her day of reckoning. Then she would account to a greater Sovereign than any here on earth. "Elizabeth Tudor," she could imagine Him saying to her, "you have been a great Queen—but a poor upholder of womanly instincts."

Elizabeth gave a start and shook her head, uneasy at the way her mind was wandering, carrying her down pathways where she was reluctant to tread and leading her in the direction of forgotten obligations. She rummaged in the drawer, suddenly wondering who she would leave these precious possessions to when she died—which would not be for a long time yet! she assured herself. Certain people came into her mind, people she had been careless about rewarding, or had long neglected. Each of these people deserved something, she thought; something that had been a part of her. Aye, and perhaps she would not wait until she died. Doubtless she could spare a few items now—now while she was still alive and could make sure the recipients showed the proper appreciation!

The Queen felt happier then. She had an important task to do.

In March, when the delicate paintbrush of spring was just beginning to touch the land with soft green and yellow and daubs of mauve and pink, Marina joined Alexander in Edinburgh, leaving Clare behind with her grandparents in the Highlands. Alexander boldly ensconced his mistress in Clairmont, the Sinclair mansion in the capital. His job claimed much of his time and he found it difficult to make the long trip back to Augusta as often as he would have liked, but short breaks were sometimes possible and those he wanted to enjoy with the woman he loved.

There was still no definite news about Edgar Stafford. Alex had dispatched even more men south to investigate, impatient to learn whether Stafford was alive or dead. In England there was a warrant out for the arrest of Lester Fordyce, Stafford's squire, and the rest of his men. Marina knew that she could count on Gwen Porter to keep her well informed from that direction.

She felt happy and relaxed with the threat of Edgar no longer hovering over her, and was delighted to be closer to Alexander in Edinburgh. True, he was not always home every night and was sometimes gone for days at a time, but she saw far more of him than she had in the Highlands. Besides, there was plenty to do in the city to pass the time, and Alex had engaged a personal maid to accompany her everywhere, a genteel woman of thirty-two who had worked in noble households before and seemed to know everybody in Edinburgh. Sissy Kenrick was a veritable treasure trove of information and gossip, and proud of the fact that her sister Jean was a tiring woman at court under the ladies of the bedchamber to the new Queen Anne.

"The Queen is most comely," she said, "but much in want of brains. One must wonder how long she can hope to hold the King's interest—though, hopefully, long enough for them to beget an heir! I fear that once that is accomplished he will soon return to his more stimulating companions. Even queens," she went on, "are mere vassals for fulfilling the ambitions of their lords."

"Not Queen Elizabeth," said Marina.

"Ha! Now there is a woman!"

Marina blinked in surprise. "You admire her?" In some ways she did herself, though she could never forgive the Queen for sending Walsingham's agent to hound her, and more especially for keeping Alexander a prisoner in the Tower for so long.

Sissy Kenrick, a plain woman with sharp features and an angular frame, a woman who had never married nor desired to be "in the yoke of another," nodded her head emphatically. "She is splendid! Had Mary Stuart been wiser she could have learned valuable lessons from her English cousin. Instead, she fell for the ploys of scheming men, but then *she* was ruled by her emotions."

Marina had many an interesting conversation with her maid. Sometimes she wondered what Sissy thought of her "living in sin" with Alexander, all too obviously ruled by her own emotions—and glad of it! But then she had been luckier than Queen Mary in selecting a worthy recipient for her love.

On Sundays her maid had the day off. This she spent with her sister, and usually returned to Clairmont in the evening with many juicy tidbits of gossip, some of it deliciously shocking.

"If she talks about others, then she must be gossiping about us behind our backs," Marina said to Alex soon after they hired the woman. "She will be filling

their ears and it will be passed on."

He grinned and shrugged. "All servants talk about their masters and mistresses; there's no way to muzzle them. But just take care not to tell her anything of real importance. She amuses you, does she not, and keeps you company when I'm away?"

The two women went out a lot now that the weather was better—shopping, to plays and the museum, and sightseeing around the royal city. Often they spied dignitaries and people of importance, and though she didn't know them personally, Sissy almost always knew who they were—and sometimes their history as well. Often they strolled the streets, stopping to watch dancing, juggling, and other impromptu entertainments. Edinburgh was a constant panoply of changing scene and color, and never dull.

One late afternoon they were in the lawnmarket when Marina, waiting for her maid to make a purchase, glanced around and spotted the Earl of Bothwell standing at a nearby stall. When their eyes met he showed no surprise at seeing her in the city, which told Marina that he already knew she had moved to Edinburgh, probably through David. He bent his head slightly in a mocking little bow, then raised his head and smiled at her.

That smile disturbed Marina. There was no warmth in it at all.

She nodded curtly, and when Sissy came back with her package, hurried off with her maid without looking at him again, but she could feel his eyes following her and they made her feel naked and somehow defiled, just from having touched her.

Sometimes the two women had the mansion all to themselves, but at other times it bustled with Sinclairs. When David, his cousin Jay, and uncle Jason Sinclair arrived a few days later, Marina re-

marked to David, "I saw your friend Bothwell in the lawnmarket on Wednesday. I thought he had been banished?"

"Aye, from court, but not from Edinburgh itself."

When after the evening meal the others went out, David took the opportunity to speak to Marina alone. "You are wrong about Francis," he insisted. "He would like the opportunity of apologizing to you for the, eh . . . misunderstanding. Why won't you give him that chance?"

"David, 'tis not necessary for him to apologize," Marina replied impatiently, weary of the subject, and knowing that nothing he could say about Bothwell would make her change her opinion about the nobleman. "I'm sorry, but I don't like him. And—"

"You don't *know* him!" he retorted hotly. "'Tis unjust to form an opinion of a person you have only met once. This hostility of yours and Alex's"—he waved his arm—"is putting a strain on my friendship with Francis." He glowered at her, warning, "You would do well to change your attitude, for your own sake if not for mine."

"What . . . do you mean?"

He walked to the window and stood with his back to her, giving himself a moment or two to calm down. David had been so sure he could influence his brother through his mistress, a woman who certainly had a powerful hold over Alex, one that had lasted for years. He felt strongly that this feud with Bothwell must be settled before others of his clan were drawn into it, and that as the future chief it was his duty to try to patch things up and act as the intermediary, if necessary. The Earl of Bothwell was a very important man, one with great power and influence—and related to the King! Though presently out of favor, he was certain to be quickly reinstated. What good would it

do to the ambitions of the Sinclairs to make an enemy of such a man? None! David was confident that the quarrel could be settled if the people involved would only sit down and iron out their differences. Since Alex never would, it might be possible to reach him through Marina.

David turned to her and asked bluntly, "Would you meet Bothwell if I arranged it?"

"Never!" she gasped, amazed he would ask. "Why should I? His behavior to us has been deplorable. He even tried to attack Alex in front of the King—which was the real reason he was banished." Angrily, Marina told him Alex's version of the incident. "Why should I lower myself by meeting such a man? And what possible good would it do?"

"It might avert future bloodshed," he replied earnestly. "Remember, it all started with you at the Harvest Ball."

"Started with me . . . ?" Marina's eyes flashed wrathfully. "*I* wasn't to blame for that. *He* was!"

David sighed and his shoulders slumped. He looked the very picture of dejection at that moment, and angry as she was, Marina almost felt sorry for him. He was young and idealistic, and, she could tell, eager to end the fray. And true enough, Bothwell was in a very strong position and to continue the quarrel would not, she supposed, benefit the clan Sinclair. Oh, if Alex were only here to advise her! But he would be gone for several days; Marina sensed—though he rarely discussed business with her—that his search was beginning to bear fruit.

In a more normal tone she said, "I dislike the man, David, and cannot imagine what good it would do for me to meet him."

His dark eyes flared with hope, sensing that she was wavering.

"I have been invited to dine with him at his manor outside Edinburgh tomorrow evening. He would be greatly honored if you would come too." He seized both her hands and squeezed them. "Please come with me, Marina." And he added persuasively, "Think of it as doing something for the clan."

She groaned, and even while loathing the idea, nodded. "Oh . . . very well."

Relieved, he embraced her fiercely.

Early the following afternoon they set out for Bothwell's country manor, which turned out to be much farther from Edinburgh than Marina had first believed. The April sun was warm on their backs as they rode through the city and into the countryside, now bursting with fresh greenery, early wildflowers dotting the fields and hedgerows with splashes of color. Marina was dressed in a jade-green silk gown embroidered with tiny seed pearls. Since all her gowns were fashionably low-cut—the way Alex liked them —and exposed more of her body than she cared to reveal to Bothwell's hot eyes, she had added a gauzy scarf delicately studded with minute brilliants, pretty and at the same time concealing. Over this she wore a mantle of the same rich jade color, but warmly lined with wool. A pert little hat sat to one side of her cascading corn-colored curls. "Ravishing!" David had praised when she was ready to leave—an unfortunate choice of word, Marina thought dourly.

David was in excellent spirits and regaled her with the latest court jokes as they rode along, clearly delighted that Marina had agreed to accompany him to his friend's house, and little realizing that as they left Edinburgh behind she had a strong urge to turn back, to refuse to go with him after all. She had no desire whatsoever to dine with Lord Bothwell, to even see him again, and though she had allowed to let

herself be persuaded for the best of reasons, Alex might not see it that way, Marina fretted. What would he think of this venture of hers into diplomacy? Back and forth her mind swung, like a pendulum gone berserk.

David, however, glowed with confidence. He seemed in no doubt about the success of the meeting. He looked very smart in his blue-and-gold doublet and matching cape, the bright sunlight bringing out the chestnut glints in his hair, his skin aglow, dark eyes shining at the coup he had accomplished in bringing both sides of the feud together. Glancing at her handsome escort, Marina found herself thinking, Well, David, you certainly have persuasiveness and tenacity. In your way you are every bit as resolute as your older brother. We must hope it is in the *right* way.

He smiled at her cheerily, commenting, "What a bonny day for a trip, eh, Marina?"

She nodded. "How much longer will this trip be?" They had already been traveling for well over an hour.

"Oh . . . about thirty or forty minutes or so."

It turned out to be quite a bit further. And at some point it struck Marina that their escort—David's squire, Boyd, and three Sinclair clansmen—had been unusually quiet during the journey. Glancing at them, she noted that they looked sober, even a little sullen, which wasn't like them at all. Even stranger, when Boyd caught her looking at him he quickly turned his head away. "What ails them?" she queried David, nodding at the men. "They don't seem too keen about visiting Bothwell's place."

He shrugged. "It comes from listening to foolish, superstitious nonsense."

"What do you mean?" Marina felt a little trill of ice scamper down her spine—and suddenly knew that

she had made a mistake in coming.

But David was waving ahead. "Here are the Hepburns!" Following the direction he indicated, Marina saw half a dozen horsemen riding hard toward them up a hill, and behind them, in a wooded valley, she glimpsed the turrets of the manor house just visible above the trees. From here it reminded her of Baxton Hall in the way it was situated.

"Welcome!" the leading rider called to them when they drew closer. "Ho, Sinclair, I like well the set of your party." Then he turned to the others behind him and, cupping a hand to his mouth, shouted back, "The lady is with him."

At that one of the others broke from the team and wheeled around and galloped back to the manor.

29

Alex and six well-trained men were hidden in the old church long before the last of the daylight left the sky, concealed in the gallery and belfry, six more waiting in the woods with the horses a quarter of a mile away. Through the narrow windows they watched night encroach, birds winging through the dusk to their nests in the trees surrounding the building. The sudden screech of an owl pierced the stillness. Downhill, in the village, lights flickered on inside the houses, and the interior of the church grew dark.

Would this prove to be yet another wild goose chase? Months of investigation, of tracking several suspects, had been illuminating, if frustrating. Alex had discovered that there were several covens of witches within a fifty-mile radius of Edinburgh alone —or people who thought of themselves as witches. Once he located their meeting places, in woods, in a secluded cove on the beach, even in a private house,

he had managed to observe a few of their services and
rituals without being detected. They were amateurs at
their craft, he had seen that at once, more enthralled
by the excitement and danger of their nefarious
activity, the wickedness and depravity of the ceremo-
ny, of tasting the forbidden, than anything else. These
groups posed no threat to King James. Their aims had
been more mundane—to cast evil spells on neighbors
and employers whom they felt had wronged them, or
make magic to "cure" a barren woman, a sick hus-
band or child. They were very disorganized, frequent-
ly squabbling among themselves over some trifle, a
rite not properly carried out, what should or shouldn't
be included in their services. So far the King's name
had never been brought up—nor had the devil, their
master, deigned to appear to grace their worship.

The chief suspect, Cochrane, had been the soul of
propriety, quietly going about his business as a tailor,
no longer prowling about in the dead of night, nor
drinking his daily cup of ox blood or in any other way
further incriminating himself—or others.

"Methinks he kens he is being watched," Captain
Turnbull had commented to Alex weeks ago. "He's a
sly one, he is, cunning as Auld Nick himself. True, he's
under observation—but, man, we canna keep oor een
on him every second o' the day! We'd need ten times
the men the King has allotted to us to manage that. In
the meantime he's carrying on his trade. Who's to say
what he's up to whilst jouking in and oot o' a' these
hooses, mayhap warning certain o' his clients to lie
low?"

Cochrane's customers too had been under observa-
tion, not an easy task when many of them were
scattered about in different parts of the countryside,
especially during the snowy winter months when it
was near impossible to hide the tracks of the investi-

gators. And true enough, King James had been typically niggardly in stumping up enough money to procure good men. Captain Turnbull was a worthy soldier as were the men in the church with Alex now—but two of those men were Sinclairs, Alex's cousins Jay and Adam! And their services would be paid for out of his own purse.

Alexander's frustration had increased over the cold winter months. Gradually he was beginning to wonder if they were chasing a myth, and the King was growing impatient at their lack of results, but no more so than Alex himself. He was anxious to complete the mission and take Marina back to the Highlands well ahead of the time when she would be confined. If this dragged on, it would be too dangerous to move her in her present condition, and he was anxious for their next child to be born at Castle Augusta. Instead of being here chasing witches, Alexander would fain have been further south chasing the almost equally elusive Edgar Stafford, desperate as he was to ascertain if Stafford was dead or alive. He wanted their next child to be born in wedlock.

Alex had been seething with impatience, thwarted in his efforts for the King, stymied at every turn in the investigation, well aware that his men, equally frustrated, were beginning to grow lax and careless—when a month ago there had been an interesting development, which had brought them to the church they were in now. A man called Digby had been arrested near North Berwick and charged with the murder of a young girl, a charge he vigorously denied. The fourteen-year-old's mutilated corpse had been found in a wood, her throat slit and strange marks cut into her body. The doctor who examined her was of the opinion that it had been a ritualistic killing, the

"handiwork of demons."

Other than to deny culpability, Digby refused to give any other information and he was condemned to be hanged. When Alex heard about the arrest he hurried to the Tolbooth to question him, trying every tactic he could to loosen his tongue, sensing that the fellow—a man in his thirties with a wife and six children—had important information that might be of use to him. The most he would say was, "If I answer your questions and am released, then I shall be a dead man anyway." Then, with a fatalistic shrug, "Hanging will be the quicker end."

Alex went to see his wife in the couple's little cottage outside the village. Immediately he saw that the woman was terrified, but not so frightened that she didn't defend her husband. "'Twas not him that done it," she staunchly maintained. "We have children of our own and Henry is a soft-hearted father; he would never have harmed that girl."

"Then who is responsible?" Alex roared, losing his temper in his frustration. "Would you see your husband hang, your children left fatherless? What will become of you, woman, with no man to support your family?" Then he added craftily, almost smelling her fear, "To protect you."

She wrung her hands, whimpering. She darted to the window of her cottage and peered out, her plump frame trembling violently. Alex was almost sorry for her as he watched her. She loved her husband, that was obvious, but some dread terror rendered her mute.

He suddenly thought of a way that might loosen her tongue.

"Give me the information I seek and I promise to protect you."

She swung around from the window, stark hope in her eyes. "Sir, could you—you move us away from here now . . . today? 'Twould have to be far away," she made clear, "where they cannot reach me. Get me out of this place and," she swallowed, "I will tell you what you want to know, though . . . I must be honest and confess that I dinna ken all the ins and outs of it."

Alex was at the stage where he couldn't afford to overlook any thread that might lead him to his quarry, and though Mistress Digby freely admitted that she knew little, still, that little might set them on the right track. But if she were suddenly to leave the area, that alone might look suspicious and tip the real culprits off, and again they would lie low. When he discovered that her parents were dead and she had a sister living in Edinburgh, he said, "Bide here another day or two, just long enough to spread word through your neighbors that you are moving to live with your family in the city. In the meantime, I'll make arrangements for you and the children to stay elsewhere."

But until then, the terrified Mistress Digby refused to give Alex her information. "Nay, sir," she shook her head when he pressed her, "I must be gone from here first."

Again at his own expense, Alexander resettled the Digbys in Dunfermline, a town north of Edinburgh, and once ensconced in her new premises the goodwife felt secure enough to talk.

Her husband had been the herdsman for an estate called The Grange, she began, and for a few extra coppers—much needed by the family—had been roped into working as a lookout or sentry for a group who met to discuss politics in various locations in the North Berwick area. Before these meetings it had been Digby's duty to thoroughly search the premises

chosen to be used that evening. "Then the group would come after dark and have their meetings," she said.

She took a deep breath and burst out, "They were a' witches!"

At this Alexander's heart sank and again he tasted the bitterness of failure. Witches! The very word had become the bane of his existence. He was disgusted.

Then she said, "They were important folks, some frae Edinburgh, but they didna want Henry to see these men, so once he finished searching the premises, Mr. Cochrane—he was the convener—dismissed him."

At mention of Cochrane, Alex picked up his ears and gave her his full attention.

Mistress Digby chuckled grimly. "But sometimes Henry hung aboot outside. He was curious, you see? That's when he found oot they were demons." The woman shuddered and hugged herself. "My man would have quit working for them, but he was sore afeared to say he wanted no part of their filthy game, frightened they would hurt him or me and the bairns. Oh, the things he heard coming oot o' them meetings! 'Twas heathenish, dreadful."

Then, she said, the meetings had suddenly stopped. Alex could understand why. Careful as Cochrane and his men had been, he must indeed have sensed he was being watched, and tipped off the others in the coven. "But they started up again in March," Mistress Digby continued, her voice shaking. "Henry knew there was something big afoot. There were more of them; he could tell they were important by the rich fur on their cloaks. Ye see, they always entered the meeting place bundled from head to toe in mantles, hoods pulled doon over their faces. They didna want to be seen, ye

ken." She sucked in her breath, adding, "Something big was underway, but I swear to you that Henry wasn't there the night they made the sacrifice to the success o' their endeavor. The . . . the lassie. My man was sick abed that eve wi' a dreadful belly distemper, so Hughie, the other sentry, took his place." She cried bitterly, "But 'twas my Henry who was blamed for killing that girl!"

By patient questioning Alexander quickly found out that Digby either didn't know the names of the "important people" attending these meetings or had thought it prudent not to divulge them to his wife. But Jane Digby was able to give Alex the three main locations where the meetings took place, a church, a barn, and a derelict house deep in the country. She also gave him another important piece of information. The other sentry, Hugh Hobart, was a young man who happened to be seriously courting a local girl, and when sent to check a meeting place he tended to go early, quickly look it over, then hurry away to see his lass in the evening. "He is no' so thorough as my Henry, but Cochrane hasn't discovered that yet or he'd knock his heid off."

It proved to be a useful tip, and turned out to be true. For four weeks now Alex and his men had monitored all three locations where Cochrane and party met—without success. But early that evening Jay Sinclair, who had been posted to watch the church, had come galloping back to tell them that a man fitting Hugh Hobart's description had entered the church, stayed inside not more than five minutes, then exited and mounted his mule to return to town.

Alex immediately set off for the church taking only six men with him, reasoning that the fewer there were, the less chance of discovery. As they waited in silence,

Captain Turnbull stationed near a front window looking downhill to the town, and Jay Sinclair by one at the back, facing across a field, Alex fervently hoped that they weren't destined to be disappointed once more. Hard facts and names were what he needed, rather than nebulous mumbo-jumbo. Alex was convinced that many in the town knew what was going on, but were too frightened to admit it; they *had* to know. The church they were in now was close to the village, and the nefarious activities of the "demonic pact" could not have escaped notice.

Whoever was behind it had power, Alex mused. The townspeople were thoroughly cowed, completely muzzled. Who was that person? He was determined now to find out his identity.

Suddenly his cousin Jay hissed, "They come now across the field!"

"How many?" Alex whispered back.

"'Tis hard to tell . . . mayhap a dozen."

Francis Stewart, the Earl of Bothwell, had spent much time in France. When he chose, the French influence was reflected in his manners. The nobleman greeted Marina and David effusively and kissed Marina's hand. He was greatly honored by this visit, he said, and delighted to be able to offer them the hospitality of his home. "I dare to hope that the rest of my company, who will join us in the evening, will meet with your approval, also the entertainment I have provided."

David clapped him on the back. "It always does, Francis. Well," he said, his eyes glinting with mischief as he glanced at the woman at his side, "here is Marina. Now, hopefully, you two can be friends."

Marina was startled and embarrassed when Both-

well suddenly dropped down on one knee, his head bowed before her. "I most humbly crave your pardon, madam, if I have unwittingly offended you," he murmured. "Please be kind enough to accept my heartfelt apology?"

"Oh . . ." she flushed, ". . . of course." Perhaps, she thought, she had misjudged the man after all.

He stood up and smiled at her, and though he wasn't a handsome man, she noticed then that he had a certain puckish charm, a smile that reminded her of Jay Sinclair.

"Now I am happy!" Bothwell announced. Draping an affectionate arm around David's broad shoulders, he went on warmly, "I would have no quarrel with the Sinclairs or anyone belonging to them." He looked Marina right in the eye, adding in sincere tones, "I truly am glad that you have forgiven me."

This Bothwell, she thought, was like a different man! And indeed he couldn't have been more gracious when he happily ushered them into his home and refreshed them with sparkling wine and dainty French pastries—the earl had the best chef in Scotland, the best pastry cook, and the wine he served was superior to that offered by the King to his guests. And his Hall—Marina gazed about her in wonder, wondering how she could ever have thought it was like Baxton Hall. The place was sumptuous, with rich velvets and priceless silken tapestries, mahogany furniture that was gilded and even set with hand-painted medallions depicting scenes from Greek mythology. There were exquisite urns and vases delicately colored and glazed and set with lapis lazuli and deep cobalt blue, and crystal that glittered in the sunlight streaming in the windows.

"Oh—'tis beautiful!" Marina gasped. She had nev-

er seen anything so opulent, so rare and splendid, and doubted that the royal palace itself was remotely as grand.

Bothwell bowed. "Thank you. I enjoy having beautiful things around me and make a point of bringing something back from my travels. If you will look at this clock . . ." He motioned Marina over to a table near the mantel where the timepiece sat. It was very old, he said, and had come from Florence. Bothwell then explained something of the history of the clock, and when his guest showed an interest he took her around the huge room drawing her attention to other unusual items and their provenance. He had an extensive knowledge of antiques which Marina found fascinating.

This was Francis Stewart at his best, the sparkling, attentive host, the more sparkling if that guest happened to be a beautiful woman. Glancing at her, but taking care not to stare as he would have liked to, Francis thought that Sinclair's fair mistress was something rather unique and special herself. Her eyes! Never had he seen such entrancing eyes, so darkly, brilliantly beautiful, the kind that immediately brought those she gazed upon under their spell. His fingers itched to pluck the pins and combs from her thick, pale gold hair, and let it spill like silk through his fingers, then take her shapely form in his arms and press his mouth to her soft lips.

David smiled to himself as he watched them indulgently, well pleased at the way things were going. He could see that Marina was still a little stiff, perhaps wary, but nothing like the way she had been when he first suggested this visit. And before long, David was sure, Francis would have her eating out of his hands. Then, all going well, they would return to Clairmont,

and when Alex came home, Marina would regale him with the pleasure of this visit and what a courteous, wonderful host Bothwell had been. He only hoped that Francis would not drink too much in the course of the evening, because he tended to become a little mischievous when under the influence, and Marina might not understand that it was mere playfulness. David also made a note to himself to drink very little. They would be returning to Edinburgh later, and it was a foolhardy fellow who traveled at night with his wits addled, prey to highwaymen and cutthroats.

Once they'd had a short rest and finished their refreshments, Bothwell led them outside to his gardens—and what a sight! The flower beds were a mass of yellow daffodils and scarlet tulips, and there were hundreds of pink and white cherry trees in full bloom. Fountains gushed silver spray into the still air. Little waterfalls had been cunningly constructed to tumble down through lush greenery into glassy pools below. Lacy humpbacked bridges spanned a stream, and an ornate bandstand took pride of place in the center of the lawn.

"This is where we have musical evenings in summer," said their host. "And ofttimes plays in which all the guests take part."

Marina could easily imagine such lovely evenings. She was enchanted with the estate, and impressed with the excellent taste of its owner. He must be very rich indeed, she reflected, to be able to indulge his lavish taste, for on top of all she had already seen, Francis conducted them to his stables full of fine blooded horses, then to his aviary of rare and exotic birds, and his duck pond where he raised birds for the table. Everything was immaculate and perfect.

Marina laughed in delight. "Lord Bothwell," she

said, "I have never seen anything remotely like it"—with a wave around—"and probably never shall again."

"You are too kind," he beamed, "and please call me Francis."

There was an instant when his penetrating eyes met hers, then he quickly looked away. "'Tis growing cooler," he said, taking her elbow. "Shall we go back indoors and partake of some hot punch? I think you will find it delicious. The spices come from the East and the wine from France—"

"Delicious, I assure you," David heartily approved. "But what else would one expect in this paradise?"

The punch *was* delicious, the conversation amusing, and Earl Bothwell faultless in his conduct. Today he was everything one would expect a cousin of the King to be. By the time the sun had started to sink into the west, Marina was completely disarmed and beginning to feel rather ashamed of herself for judging him too hastily. She could see now why David liked him so much.

The afternoon faded into evening and the first of the guests began to arrive, others coming fast behind them, more than David had imagined there would be, a host of Hepburns, some Mortons and Ogilvys, Sir Oliver Kerr—who had once insulted the King in public and spent four years in the Tolbooth because of it—and Lord White, a virulent opponent of the Lennox faction, and others, few of whom David cared for. He noticed that there were very few women among them and hoped that Marina didn't feel awkward.

Bothwell's servants sped around the large gathering serving wine, but when a servitor made to refill David's glass, he put his hand over it and shook his

head, causing the fellow to gape at him in surprise, for usually David drank heartily with all the others and spent the night at the manor. This evening would be different. David knew that Marina would never consider staying here, nor would he press her. He was grateful that she had agreed to come at all.

Dinner was served, a delectable meal, thought Marina, and the talk at table was light and amusing at first; their host had a sharp wit and kept them all laughing, but as course followed course and the wine and spirits kept flowing, the conversation—in spite of the fact that there were women present—turned to politics. First Ludovic Stuart, the young Duke of Lennox, was lambasted, then Maitland and Robert Bruce, and finally King James himself. These men were sneered at, mocked, ridiculed. "We have a King in petticoats!" declared Sir Oliver Kerr. "How, one must wonder, can he expect to put a babe in the Queen's belly?" And slyly, "Mayhap another will put it there for him, eh, Bothwell?"

There was a burst of laughter, rough and crude, one man pounding the table with his fist, another spluttering in his wine. Marina looked at their host, expecting him to be angry or at least annoyed. Instead, he was laughing as loud as all the rest.

"Aye," he chortled, "I'm ever ready to oblige my royal relative when it comes to that kind of service. After all, we cannot have poor Queen Anne pining and fretting because she's a bride untouched and untried."

Marina felt an inward start as she gazed at him. Bothwell's face was deeply flushed with all the spirits he had consumed, his eyes glittering, his courtly manner fast disintegrating into something coarse and lewd—as he had been at Castle Augusta. David too—one of the few at table still clear-eyed and

sober—stared at his friend as if he had never really seen him before. He was startled when Francis announced, "Well, good people, if things go as planned we shall all be delivered from the curse of the present regime. First business, then pleasure." His hot eyes flicked to Marina. "Our friends are working hard for us this night all over the land. Services are being conducted, success guaranteed. Oswald!" he shouted to his steward. "Bring in the document."

The steward appeared with a paper and a tray of writing materials.

Francis Stewart was the first to sign, then the document was passed to the man on his right, then the woman seated next to him, all signing until it came to David Sinclair. David read what was written there, and his eyes jumped to Bothwell. "Mother of God!" he cried. "What are you about?"

A sudden hush descended on the room, all eyes turned to Sinclair.

"Sign, Davy," Bothwell purred. "You are with me, are you not, my friend?"

"Are you mad? This is treason!"

"Sign!" Bothwell bellowed. "Christ's foot, don't try my patience." He lowered his head, glaring at Sinclair from under his brows, growling, "I would not like to think you are another such as that brother of yours, for if so—"

David jumped to his feet, his face pale, eyes bleak and disillusioned. "Listen to me, Francis, I beseech you as a friend, have done with this insanity. It has absolutely no hope of succeeding, nor would the people of Scotland ever accept you. Stop now before this goes any further. Tear up the document and forget it was ever drawn up." His eyes swept the others, all of whom were clearly hostile now. "Destroy this paper or

you are all doomed."

Bothwell leapt up, overturning his chair, and his dagger was in his hand. At the same time two men ran to bar the door.

"Sign," Francis Stewart repeated, his voice eerily quiet, "or you are the one who is doomed, Sinclair."

30

At the church door the witches halted, and the men hiding in the loft heard the scrape of a key in the massive lock and saw, dimly, candles flaring. Shuddering, the watchers hastily crossed themselves, several wishing that they were far away from here this night. The devil-worshipers shuffled into the building chanting in Latin, their voices guttural and low, their hooded figures casting weird moving shadows on the walls of the church they were about to desecrate.

There were thirteen of them led by a tall man in black robes who mounted the pulpit and turned to face the congregation, but before he threw back his hood he inquired, "Convener, is the building clean?"

"It is clean, master," Edward Cochrane assured him.

The tall man bent his head for a moment as if thinking—or listening!—though there wasn't a sound from above; Sinclair's men were well hidden.

"Look about," the leader ordered.

Cochrane knew better than to argue, though he was impatient to get on with the service, a particularly important one that night. He knew that Hughie Hobart had just returned to town from checking the premises; Hobart realized that laxity might cost him his life, therefore would have been thorough. But Cochrane dutifully hurried to the shaky wooden stairs leading up to the gallery while another man searched below. Once above, the convener paused for a few seconds, listening, sniffing the musty air like a fox after quarry. He prided himself on having superhuman instincts, and aside from that, he had made it his business to ensure that no strangers had been seen about the town that day or in the vicinity of the church itself. The people who had been watching him all during the winter months—he had sensed their presence immediately!—had given up weeks ago and returned to Edinburgh empty-handed for all their trouble. He was too clever for them, but then they were not equipped with the special instincts that *he* possessed.

Nevertheless, candle in hand, Cochrane strode about the gallery thrusting out the light to see into dark corners, for it was very dark up here, little realizing, with all his sharply honed senses, that in doing so he walked directly under the massive oaken beams where several of Sinclair's team lay prone, scarcely daring to draw breath. He passed within two feet of Alex himself, who stood stock still, dagger in hand, behind the narrow door leading up to the belfry.

After a quick look around, the convener returned to the top of the stairs, paused once more to listen; then his feet went clattering down the steps.

Thereupon the service began, all throwing back

their hoods to reveal nine men and four women, several of whom Alexander, creeping forward to station himself behind a stout pillar near the balcony rail, instantly recognized, one of them an exiled Ruthven, cousin of the Ruthven who had tried to kill King James at the tender age of sixteen. But the man acting the part of Satan was unknown to Alex, a tall, hollow-cheeked fellow with a hooked nose, black beard, and dark eyes, one who obviously looked the part he had chosen to play, and who had managed to exert great power over his followers from the homage they were paying him.

A little of Alexander's hope ebbed as he watched them going through the usual rituals he had come to expect in such services—the drinking of the blood, burning sulfur, profanely desecrating the church, voices rising as they sang their praises to Lucifer, bowing and scraping to the man leading them—chilling to watch, but all much akin to devilish services that Alex had witnessed before, and his heart sank.

A sudden hush fell over them, an expectancy in the air.

"Bring forth the prisoner, James Stewart!" their master cried in a resounding voice.

Alex felt a shiver of excitement flit across his nerves.

From her basket one of the female witches took an object about a foot long. It was completely covered, and without removing the cloth the woman handed it to "Satan," who laid it on the altar and removed the wrappings. Then seizing it—to Alex it looked like a wax doll—he triumphantly thrust it high in the air, shouting, "This is King James VI, ordained to die by me at the instigation of Francis, Earl Bothwell!"

"Die!" they all chanted. "Die!" as the effigy of the

King was passed to each worshiper in turn, touched to the candles they were holding, the wax dripping so that by the time it reached the thirteenth person there was nothing left of the tiny figure of the King.

Finally, at long last, Alexander had the name of the man behind it all.

Sheriff Roy Napier stood in the hall at Brokenbridge Farm, hat respectfully in hand as he relayed his grim news to the Porters. Both Bert and Gwen were silent when he finished, each digesting it in their own way. Gwen was the first to speak. "Sheriff, are you certain there is no mistake?"

"Very certain," he nodded. "We have Fordyce and three of the others in custody now. They confessed under torture. Fordyce gave us very detailed directions to the gravesite in Scotland, and after seeking permission from the Scottish authorities, we went to the site and exhumed the remains. I knew Edgar Stafford and 'twas him all right. He was still wearing his old tunic with his badge, though everything else of value had been stripped from his body." His lip curled slightly. "The tunic was ancient; clearly the culprits had considered it to be worthless."

The sheriff went on to say that Stafford's widow would have to be informed, and since they were close neighbors, he wondered if they knew where she could be reached. He had learned from the dead man's lawyer that there was a considerable sum of money left behind. "Folks are strange, are they not?" he said ruefully. "Stafford was rich, but he lived like a pauper. Well, at least his widow will benefit from it."

Gwen knew that Marina would have no interest in Edgar's money. It was her freedom that was beyond price to her. She gave Sheriff Napier her friend's

address in the Highlands, but the moment he left, sat down herself and wrote a letter to Marina and sent it off by express courier.

"Oh," she said dreamily to her husband, "what I would give to see Marina's face when she receives that letter."

"Sign!" Bothwell screamed when David made no move to obey him. "I ask you for the last time."

"Never!" Sinclair shouted back. "You—you traitor! And to think I held you in high esteem."

David leaped clear of the table and turned his back to the wall, his sword in his hand as the other men closed in around him. All the female guests scurried out of the room rather than watch a bloody killing, but Marina, her heart pounding in terror, glanced about frantically seeking some way she might help Alex's brother, who seemed certain to die within seconds, vastly outnumbered as he was. The sudden shattering clash of steel meeting steel, the howling of the traitors baying for blood, exploded in the room, deafening her. With a horrified glance at David completely surrounded now, fighting desperately for his life, Marina seized two heavy crystal decanters of brandy and splashed the contents of one over the tablecloth,

the other on the curtains, then hurled the candles against them, setting them alight.

As flames flickered and sped snakelike across the table and burst into a ball of orange fire on the taffeta drapes, Marina plucked a carving knife off the board and concealed it in the folds of her gown, then threw herself behind a Chinese screen opposite the door. The would-be assassins wheeled around with cries of surprise and alarm, their eyes glittering in the red glow that now filled the chamber, the fire spreading rapidly as pieces of curtain and tablecover dropped off and fell on the beautiful Turkey carpet that Bothwell had been so proud of, but one that burned as swiftly as any other.

In seconds the chamber began to reek with smoke, the men to cough and splutter, eyes streaming. Afraid of being roasted alive in a room filled with fine lace, silk, heavy velvet, and lovely—though highly combustible—wainscotting, the men made a wild stampede for the door, pushing and shoving each other out of the way in their panic, leaving only Bothwell behind with Sinclair. Choking, panting for breath, Francis Stewart thrust blindly with his dirk and caught David on the upper arm, then he too flew for the door to escape while he could. Once there, he slammed and locked it behind him—and David and Marina were trapped in the burning chamber.

David raced to the tall window and slashed down what remained of the drapes with his sword. Grabbing a heavy silver candlestick from the table, he hammered out the glazing. Thinking that Marina had run from the room with the other women when the fighting started and wondering how to reach her, he jumped violently when someone caught his arm. "Marina!" he gasped, astounded at the sight of her. "How . . ."

But she put a finger over her mouth and pointed at the window. By now her head was reeling and lungs bursting from inhaling the smoke, and she was certain that if they tarried a moment longer both of them would be overcome. She knew she had taken a mad chance in setting fire to the room, but it was the only way she had been able to think of to save David's life. Now they must get out while they could or Bothwell would get his wish after all.

David went first, the skin of his arms and face raked by jagged glass slivers still clinging to the panes, and once outside he turned around and lifted Marina over the sill. Both staggered to the nearest bushes and fell headlong onto the grass, coughing, sucking in great gulps of the cool night air, sweeter to them than the costliest perfume at that moment. As soon as their heads cleared they got up. David took her hand and they raced for the woods and kept going until they were well away from the estate, finally forced to pause for a rest on a rise of ground near an old road leading to the town of Haddington. When they looked back they could see flames shooting above the trees, and even from here could smell the smoke wafting to them on the breeze.

For a moment both were mute, then David said shakily, "I—I cannot believe it. How could I have been so wrong?"

Marina squeezed his hand; he sounded devastated, crushingly disappointed. It was a second before she felt the trickling wetness running down his arm, dripping on her hand. "You are bleeding! David—"

"'Tis nothing." He shrugged, far more upset at his poor judgment of character, hating himself too for having exposed Marina to such danger. But she ripped off a strip of material from the hem of her gown, helped him ease off his jacket, and bound the wound

as best she could. When she straightened up, David
suddenly threw his arms around her and embraced
her. "Forgive me," he said. "Oh, Marina, how sorry I
am about this . . ."

"Hush, sweeting." She stroked his hair, understand-
ing how betrayed he must be feeling, how sad to
discover that a man he had admired and defended—a
man he had idolized—had turned out to have feet of
clay. It was a bitter moment for David, but a grim
lesson Marina was sure he would not soon forget.

Suddenly he raised his head. "Listen!"

They heard the dull thundering of hoofbeats com-
ing down the hill, Alex and his men on their way to
arrest Bothwell and his fellow-conspirators. When
they reached the burning mansion they found the
place in chaos, many lying about in the grounds
outside overcome with smoke inhalation, others fu-
tilely trying to put out the fires that had spread to
other rooms. The noise—the roaring of the flames,
the shouting, the crashing of roof timbers—helped
muffle the sound of the approach of the King's men.
There had been twenty guests at the house that night
and Alex only had a dozen men with him now, but *his*
group had the advantage of surprise; they were also
well trained and far more clear-headed.

The battle with those outside the house was brief
and they were quickly bound together with chains.
Bothwell himself had been flying in and out of the
manor desperate to save as many of his valuable
possessions as possible, never realizing that the most
valuable of all—his freedom and perhaps even his
life—was at stake. When he ran out of the house
carrying a priceless T'ang vase in his arms and saw the
tall, resolute figure of Alexander Sinclair standing on
the threshold—his sword in his hand—he was so
startled and dismayed that he dropped the vase.

Horrified, he instinctively glanced down when it burst into dozens of pieces on the step, and in that moment Alex sprang forward and touched the point of his rapier to his throat.

"Lord Bothwell," he said, "I arrest you in the name of the King."

The highest in the land came to Holyrood Palace to see King James honor Alexander Sinclair and invest him with his new title of Earl of Dalraida. With the title came three castles and thousands of acres of land, and the revenue from that land, rivers and lochs and deer forests, villages and towns.

At the glittering occasion was Sinclair's wife, the new countess, Marina, his proud family, friends, and important members of his clan. The couple's two children, Clare and newborn Quinton, were too young to attend the ceremony. The countess had only two guests, Gwen and Bert Porter from England, Gwen quite overcome with tears of joy and delight when she watched Alexander receiving his earldom. "From the start I knew he was special," she whispered to her husband. "From the very start! I knew," she dabbed at her streaming eyes, "that he was destined for great things."

"To be sure," her husband murmured, patting her knee indulgently, remembering—once the whole story of her complicity in the affair came out—Gwen telling him that Alexander Sinclair looked like a pirate. But that was beside the point now and didn't seem important.

Marina, her own eyes sparkling with tears, looked from Alexander to his parents. What a moment for them too! she thought, Blake beaming with pride, Alyssa clutching his hand, smiling even while fighting back emotion that she could hardly contain, both of

them so relieved to have their two older sons of equal rank at last, David and the rest of their children sharing their jubilation.

A sumptuous banquet followed the ceremony. Alexander, the new earl, sat at the right hand of the King, and Marina, his countess, on his left, stunning in rose-pink brocade. Feeling that she was living a dream, Marina glanced down at the lower tables ranged below them at all the powerful people sitting there, dazzling in their finery, jewels flashing in the candlelight. All here today to see her husband honored, aware that he was a man who had forged his own way and mapped out his own path to glory, his triumph all the sweeter for having accomplished it himself.

King James, who had a poetic turn of mind, glanced from Alexander to Marina. "The flower and flame of Scotland," he said. "Long may the one bloom, and the other burn."

"Thank you, Your Grace," Marina murmured.

As the meal progressed, the King asked her many questions about life in England. When she told him that her maiden name had been Dudley, he inquired, "Can you be related to the Dudley who was the Earl of Leicester, once the great favorite of my cousin, Queen Elizabeth?"

Marina hesitated, then shook her head. "I think not . . ."

"But you are not sure?"

"'Tis possible, I suppose, that there might be some distant connection."

The young King loved mysteries and the English beauty intrigued him. He had discovered that her background was somewhat obscure, though certain tantalizing rumors had come to his ears through his secret correspondence with Robert Devereux, the Earl

of Essex, who had been the stepson of the Dudley in question.

"It might be possible to find out," suggested the King, gazing into Marina's brilliant dark eyes.

"Perhaps . . ."

Marina had no desire whatsoever to rake up the past. Deep down in her mind lurked a hazy impression from her very early childhood—from before Maud Percy took her to Chiltern Castle—that, though shadowy, always filled her with disquietude when she thought about it. Nay, she decided while the King watched her with interest, the past was better left alone. Her life was in Scotland now, and a wonderfully happy life it was. She was perfectly content with the way things were and some instinct warned her to leave it that way.

Dancing followed the feast, and Marina and Alexander, as guests of honor, opened the ball. When his arms went around her, Marina looked up into his face, all the pride, the love she felt for him shining in her eyes. "What a day this has been, my lord," she said smiling. "Not only the people here, but the whole country rejoicing in your triumph."

"Aye." He grinned, his eyes moving over her face adoringly. "But now what? Where do we go from here?" he teased.

"It matters not, my love, as long as we go together."

Alexander drew her close and kissed her in front of the entire assembly.

Epilogue

Late in the autumn of that year, 1592, a small package was delivered to Castle Augusta addressed to Marina. The courier left it with the steward and rode away. Later, when it was sent on to Marina at Dalraida Castle, she opened it to find a gold ring inside, a man's ring with the letter D picked out in tiny rubies on the face of it. Written on the small card enclosed with the ring was the cryptic message: "From one who loves you."

The identity of the sender was destined to remain a mystery.

Unbridled passion! Ungovernable love!
Historical Romance by

SHARON GILLENWATER

UNWILLING HEART. It was unthinkable that the dashing and impossibly handsome Earl of Beckford should have romantic intentions towards a mere servant. But lovely Sloane Donovan was no ordinary governess. She could ride a high-strung thoroughbred as well as any man, charm the most starchy dowager, and always said exactly what was on her mind. But resisting the charms of the seductive earl might be more of a challenge than even she could handle.

_____2670-8 $3.95US/$4.95CAN

HIGHLAND WHISPERS. From the sweet-scented moors of the Highlands to the elegant salons of Paris on the eve of the French Revolution, beautiful Sheridan Sinclair was pursued by a madman. Obsessed by Sheridan's uncanny resemblance to her mother, he had vowed to possess her soft body, whether she was willing or not. Only one man could save her — Jeremy Mackenzie, the brash American who had taught her the true meaning of love.

_____2783-6 $3.95US/$4.95CAN

LEISURE BOOKS
ATTN: Customer Service Dept.
276 5th Avenue, New York, NY 10001

Please send me the book(s) checked above. I have enclosed $ _____
Add $1.25 for shipping and handling for the first book; $.30 for each book thereafter. No cash, stamps, or C.O.D.s All orders shipped within 6 weeks. Canadian orders please add $1.00 extra postage.

Name _____

Address _____

City _____ State _____ Zip _____
Canadian orders must be paid in U.S. dollars payable through a New York banking facility. ☐ Please send a free catalogue.

"A STUNNING GEM OF A BOOK THAT ESTABLISHES
PATRICIA GAFFNEY AS A STAR!"– *Romantic Times*

THIEF of HEARTS

PATRICIA GAFFNEY

Beautiful young widow Anna Jourdaine feared her dead
husband's twin brother, John Brodie. His manners were
abominable, his language unbearably crude, and his
heated glances made sheltered Anna burn with shame.
But when Anna was forced to pretend to be Brodie's
wife, she found herself weakening to his seductive
appeal. In her brother-in-law's embrace, she knew that
her future happiness depended on learning which
brother was an immoral character and which was
merely a thief of hearts.

__2973-1 $4.50

LEISURE BOOKS
ATTN: Customer Service Dept.
276 5th Avenue, New York, NY 10001

Please add $1.25 for shipping and handling of the first book and $.30 for
each book thereafter. All orders shipped within 6 weeks via postal service
book rate.

Canadian orders must reflect Canadian price, when indicated, and must be
paid in U.S. dollars through a U.S. banking facility.

Name _____

Address _____

City _____ State _____ Zip _____

I have enclosed $ _____ in payment for the books checked above.

Payment <u>must</u> accompany all orders. ❑Please send a free catalogue.

SPEND YOUR LEISURE MOMENTS WITH US.

Hundreds of exciting titles to choose from—something for everyone's taste in fine books: breathtaking historical romance, chilling horror, spine-tingling suspense, taut medical thrillers, involving mysteries, action-packed men's adventure and wild Westerns.

SEND FOR A FREE CATALOGUE TODAY!

Leisure Books
Attn: Customer Service Department
276 5th Avenue, New York, NY 10001

Praise for Patricia

"Stirring scenes and dis[...]
are reminders of the true meaning of Christmas."
—*RT Book Reviews* on *Amish Christmas Joy*

"A sweet tale with well-drawn characters and a few
unexpected turns."

—*RT Book Reviews* on
Their Pretend Amish Courtship

"Davids' deep understanding of Amish culture
is evident in the compassionate characters and
beautiful descriptions."
—*RT Book Reviews* on *A Home for Hannah*

Praise for Jo Ann Brown and her novels

"The story is rich with relatable…characters."
—*RT Book Reviews* on *Amish Homecoming*

"The characters demonstrate great perseverance."
—*RT Book Reviews* on *An Amish Match*

"Readers will be pleased."
—*RT Book Reviews* on *Her Longed-For Family*

APR 0 5 2019

FIC David

Davids, P.
Amish Christmas Joy.

PRICE: $7.75 (3559/he)

After thirty-five years as a nurse, **Patricia Davids** hung up her stethoscope to become a full-time writer. She enjoys spending her free time visiting her grandchildren, doing some long-overdue yard work and traveling to research her story locations. She resides in Wichita, Kansas. Pat always enjoys hearing from her readers. You can visit her online at patriciadavids.com.

Jo Ann Brown has always loved stories with happily-ever-after endings. A former military officer, she is thrilled to have the chance to write stories about people falling in love. She is also a photographer and travels with her husband of more than thirty years to places where she can snap pictures. They have three children and live in Florida. Drop her a note at joannbrownbooks.com.

PATRICIA DAVIDS

Amish Christmas Joy

&

JO ANN BROWN

An Amish Proposal

If you purchased this book without a cover you should be aware that this book is stolen property. It was reported as "unsold and destroyed" to the publisher, and neither the author nor the publisher has received any payment for this "stripped book."

LOVE INSPIRED BOOKS

Recycling programs for this product may not exist in your area.

ISBN-13: 978-1-335-94822-9

Amish Christmas Joy and An Amish Proposal

Copyright © 2018 by Harlequin Books S.A.

The publisher acknowledges the copyright holders of the individual works as follows:

Amish Christmas Joy
Copyright © 2013 by Patricia MacDonald

An Amish Proposal
Copyright © 2017 by Jo Ann Ferguson

All rights reserved. Except for use in any review, the reproduction or utilization of this work in whole or in part in any form by any electronic, mechanical or other means, now known or hereafter invented, including xerography, photocopying and recording, or in any information storage or retrieval system, is forbidden without the written permission of the editorial office, Love Inspired Books, 195 Broadway, New York, NY 10007 U.S.A.

This is a work of fiction. Names, characters, places and incidents are either the product of the author's imagination or are used fictitiously, and any resemblance to actual persons, living or dead, business establishments, events or locales is entirely coincidental.

This edition published by arrangement with Love Inspired Books.

® and TM are trademarks of Love Inspired Books, used under license. Trademarks indicated with ® are registered in the United States Patent and Trademark Office, the Canadian Intellectual Property Office and in other countries.

www.Harlequin.com

Printed in U.S.A.

CONTENTS

AMISH CHRISTMAS JOY

Patricia Davids

This book is lovingly dedicated to the parents of special-needs children everywhere.

Whosoever shall receive one of such children in my name, receiveth me: and whosoever shall receive me, receiveth not me, but him that sent me.
—*Mark* 9:37

Chapter One

Loud pounding pulled Caleb Mast out of the first good night's sleep he'd had in a month. He squinted at the clock on his bedside table. Who was beating on his door at three-forty in the morning?

Staggering out of bed, he made his way through his condo. After four weeks on an oil platform in the Gulf, he was ready for some downtime. He'd stayed twice as long as his normal rotation to cover for an injured crewmate. The twelve-to thirteen-hour shifts seven days a week were tough. Lousy weather and a shorthanded crew made the extra two weeks a killer. All he wanted was to crawl back in bed.

If some of his crewmates were looking to celebrate on their first night in, they could have fun without him. He didn't do the party scene. Not since... He dismissed the thought without finishing it. He didn't look back. The pounding resumed.

He yanked open the front door. "If this building isn't on fire you're in trouble. What?"

A woman stood on his doorstep. She had a little girl beside her. Thunder rumbled in the distance. A fine

mist was falling, scenting the air with rain and making a shimmering halo around the streetlamp across the roadway. A yellow hatchback with a dented door sat parked beneath it.

The woman pushed back her frizzy blond hair. "You're a hard man to find, Caleb."

The voice belonged to a bad memory from his past. "Valerie?"

She gave a halfhearted smile. "You remember my name. That's something."

Was she kidding? He had turned his life upside down, cut bone-deep family ties and moved halfway across the country with Valerie Perry. A year later, she left him a goodbye note with no forwarding address and an empty bank account. Now, after nearly nine years, she was back. Why?

There were dark circles under her eyes and a droop to her full lips. She was thin as a rail. Her once-thick brown hair was bleached a brittle white-blond. It made her look cheap. Even at this hour, she wore heavy eye makeup. She licked her dry, cracked lips.

He folded his arms over his chest. "What do you want?"

"You could pretend you're happy to see me."

"If you're here to repay the money you stole, then I'm thrilled."

She dropped her gaze. "I've come for…another reason."

"Mama, I'm tired," the girl whined. She peered at him through a mop of blond hair, straight and pale as wheat straw. He was stunned to see the characteristic round face, small upturned eyes and slightly flat nose that indicated she had Down syndrome.

His Amish mother had always told him such children were God's most precious gifts, sent to special families for a special purpose.

"I'm hungry. I wanna go home." The girl's speech was slow and halting. She hid her face against Valerie's leg.

"Hush. I'm talking," Valerie snapped.

Sympathy for the kid made Caleb take a step back from the door. October in Houston was balmy compared to the crisp autumn weather of his childhood home in Ohio, but the rain was picking up. "You want to come in?"

She steered the child past him into the living room. "Lie down on the sofa while we grown-ups talk."

Talk about what? What did they have to say to each other after so long? He should have shut the door in her face. She wouldn't be here if she didn't want something.

"But I'm hungry, Mama."

No matter what Val had done, the child deserved his kindness. "I've got some cold pizza and milk in the fridge. It's not much, but she's welcome to it."

Breakfast of champions. His Amish mother would be horrified to see him feeding a kid pizza at this time of the night. Then again, she'd be horrified by a lot in his current life.

The look the girl gave him was tired, fearful and hopeful all at the same time. He crouched to her level. "It's pepperoni pizza. Is that okay?"

She nodded once. He glanced at Valerie. "Would you like something? Coffee?"

"Sure." She followed him into the kitchen. He pulled a pizza box from the fridge, placed a slice on a paper plate and stuck it in the microwave.

Valerie took a seat at the glass-topped table in the corner. "Things are such a mess. I didn't know where else to go. My boyfriend kicked us out, the jerk. My mom died last month."

"I'm sorry." Caleb had never met her mother. He shot a look toward Valerie as he spooned grounds into the coffeepot. She had a tight grip on her purse. She bit the corner of her lip and looked everywhere but at him. When the microwave bell dinged, she almost jumped out of her chair.

He checked to make sure the slice wasn't too hot, then carried it into the living room. Valerie's daughter was sitting upright on the sofa, struggling to keep her eyes open. He handed her the pizza. "I'll get your milk in a minute, okay?"

She snatched the plate from him and started tearing into the pizza. He went back to put a second slice in the microwave. Clearly, one wasn't going to be enough.

Valerie was on her feet, pacing the length of the room. "Mom's old man doesn't want the kid around anymore. Not that Joy is a problem. She's not. She's quiet as a mouse."

"Joy, is that her name?"

"Yeah, Joy Lynn."

"Nice." What else could he say?

"I thought you'd be married by now. I remember how much you wanted kids."

"I came close, but it didn't work out. She went back with her ex." And took her two kids with her. Another painful chapter of his life with a rotten ending. Parenthood didn't seem to be in the plan for him. The coffee finished dripping. He took a mug out of the cupboard and began to fill it.

Valerie sniffed and rubbed her nose with the back of her hand. "Joy is your daughter. I thought you should know."

He replaced the coffeepot with great care and set the mug down, amazed that he hadn't dropped either. "What?"

"I know I should have told you sooner, but she's your kid."

"I don't believe you." Val always twisted the truth.

"Joy, how old are you?" she asked over her shoulder.

"I'm eight, Mama."

"When is your birthday, honey?"

"You know that. December twenty-fifth. That is Christmas Day. Nana says I'm her Christmas Joy... only, she has gone to heaven, hasn't she?" Joy's voice faded away.

Valerie had left him in early summer. It was actually possible.

Unlike the last woman who claimed he fathered her babe.

He refused to think about that final, painful confrontation with his Amish family. He had to focus on the present problem. Gripping the edge of the counter, he glared at Valerie. "Is this some kind of joke?"

She took a step back. "No. Mom's death made me realize that Joy should get to know you. You're all the family she has left."

"She has you," he retorted, wondering what kind of mother she was. Hard to imagine the self-absorbed, party-all-night woman he'd known in that role. He glanced toward Joy in the living room and his heart skipped a beat. He had a daughter.

If Val was telling the truth, he'd missed eight pre-

cious years of his child's life. The knowledge made him
ache inside. Why had Valerie kept this from him? He
would have stood by her. She had to know that.

"Mama, can I have my milk now, please? I remem-
bered to say please. I'm being good."

Valerie arched one thinly penciled eyebrow. "Can
she have some milk, Caleb?"

He wouldn't get his hopes up. Valerie could be lying.
It was nothing new for her. He yanked open the fridge,
pulled out a carton and handed it to her.

She took it, filled a glass with milk and carried it
into the other room. He moved to the doorway to watch.

"Here you go. Mama left her cigarettes in the car,
sweetie. Will you be okay with your daddy while I go
get them?"

Joy jerked upright. "I have a daddy?" The kid
sounded as surprised as he was by the news.

"Yes, you do. His name is Caleb Mast."

"A real daddy?" Her wistful tone carried hope and
wonder.

"Your real daddy," Valerie assured her.

Joy's eyes narrowed. She pulled back and glared at
her mother. "Is he another uncle like Jimmy and Keith?"

"No. He's your father. You're going to love him."

"What if I don't?"

What if she didn't? He wasn't a puppy or a kitten,
something a kid liked on sight. He scratched at the stub-
ble on his cheek. He was an ex-Amish oil-rig rough-
neck with few manners and a job that took him away
half the year. He wasn't anyone's idea of a daddy. He'd
given up that dream.

He turned away to get the forgotten pizza from the
microwave and heard the front door open and close. He

carried the second slice to Joy. She smiled when she saw it and licked the milk mustache from her upper lip.

What if she is my daughter?

Did it change anything? He didn't know her. She didn't know him. How much bonding could happen in the short time he spent ashore? Besides, he was about to take a job on one of the rigs off the coast of Brazil. He stood next on the company list to transfer. He expected to get word to pack his bags any day. He'd be gone for a full year when the opening came through.

She finished the milk and handed him the plate with the glass. "I like pizza."

"No kidding."

"I like animal crackers the best. I eat all the elephants first." She rocked as she smiled.

Thunder rumbled, closer now. Her smile vanished. She glanced fearfully at the window. "I don't like thunder."

"Don't worry, it'll be gone soon."

She gave him a hard look. "Promise?"

"I promise."

"Can we have pizza tomorrow?"

Where would she be tomorrow? "You'll have to ask your mom."

"Okay." She yawned widely.

He might as well get her settled. He wasn't going to send her and her mother out into the storm. Valerie had a lot more explaining to do. He gathered the bedding and soon had Joy tucked up snugly on his sofa. She was asleep in less than a minute. He bent and brushed her hair back from her face.

A special child was given for a special reason. What reason could God have for sending Joy to him?

She was a sweet kid, but was she his sweet kid? There was testing for this kind of situation. He would insist on it. Val was up to something. He settled in his recliner and waited for her to return.

Three hours later, the storm had moved on. Morning sunlight crept in beneath the window shade. Caleb rose from the chair and opened the front door for the umpteenth time. Birds twittered in the dripping trees. The walkway and street out front were glistening wet and deserted.

Valerie hadn't come back.

He heard a noise behind him. Turning, he saw Joy standing beside the couch. "Where's my mama?"

"I wish I knew."

Fear darkened her eyes. "I want my mama."

"Hey, it's okay." He started toward her without a clue what to do next.

She backed away. "I gotta find her."

She darted around him and ran barefoot out the door toward the street, with Caleb close on her heels.

Leah Belier added a box of crayons to her basket as she shopped with her friend Joann Weaver in the small grocery store in the village of Hope Springs, Ohio.

"Are you taking up art in your spare time?" Joann asked with a grin.

"*Nee.* I noticed Emmy Chupp borrowing colors from the other students this afternoon. She loves to draw. I think she has used up the ones her mother sent with her at the beginning of the school year. I decided to get her some more."

"For Christmas?"

"That's still four weeks away. She needs them now. I'll get her colored pencils as a Christmas gift."

"That's sweet of you. How is her father getting along? I heard he broke his leg."

"He hasn't been able to work at the lumberyard for several weeks. Honestly, I'm worried about the family. Emmy didn't bring any lunch today. She told me she forgot it at home."

"Knowing you, I expect she ate your lunch, and you went hungry."

Leah chuckled. "It wouldn't hurt me to miss a meal or two, but I always bring extra food just in case."

She had shared her ample sandwich with Emmy and made a mental note to check in on the family tomorrow. As the teacher at the local Amish school, Leah kept a close eye on all her students. She was in a better position than most to see where trouble was brewing.

A new box of twenty-four crayons would cheer the shy child who liked to draw. Leah added some peanut butter and jelly to her basket. A few extra groceries might come in handy with lunches. If it looked as if they needed more help, she would let Bishop Zook know. No man's family went hungry in their Amish community. Caring for one another was a duty, not a chore.

She carried her purchases to the front of the store. The *Englisch* owner, Mr. McGregor, ran her items over the scanner. A big bear of a man with thick, curly gray hair, a wide smile and a booming voice, he and his tiny wife were longtime fixtures in Hope Springs.

"Afternoon, ladies. I hope all of you plan to come to the Christmas parade. Since this is our first year, we want it to be a success. My kids are building a float for the store. Should be grand."

"We are looking forward to it," Joann said.

"Mrs. Weaver, the printing job you did on the flyers for our dented-canned-goods sale was great. Lots of people came, not just the Amish."

Joann blushed. "Miller Press is happy to serve all those in our community, Amish and non-Amish alike. I will tell my husband you were pleased."

Joann and her new husband, Roman Weaver, both worked at his uncle's printing business.

"Good. Leah, my wife and I were just saying how much we're looking forward to your school Christmas program this year. Are the children getting excited?"

"Indeed they are. You and your wife are always welcome."

"My wife had the lights and decorations up the minute Thanksgiving was over, but it's watching your Amish students put on their plays and sing their songs so wonderfully that brings the true meaning of Christmas to my heart."

"I'm glad, for that is the purpose of our program."

"Remind your students to come to the Christmas parade. We want the kids to enjoy it, too."

"I will."

"Why, I remember the Christmas little Anna Imhoff stood so straight and tall and recited her poem with such a big grin on her face at your school. That was the year they found John Doe beaten half to death on the Imhoff farm. Course, he was really Jonathan Dresher, but he didn't know his own name for weeks. Ain't it strange the ways the Lord finds to test us?" He stopped with her last item in his hand and stared into space.

"It is, indeed." She really needed to be going. She had a long walk home before dark.

"Anna sure took a shine to Jonathan. Happy thing, him marrying her sister, Karen. Yup, that was a mighty special Christmas."

"*Ja,* it was." Joann winked at Leah. Mr. McGregor loved to recount his stories regardless of the number of times his customers had heard them.

The outside door opened, and Leah saw an *Englisch* fellow come in. There was something vaguely familiar about him. He glanced her way.

Her breath caught in her throat. It couldn't be Caleb Mast, could it?

He turned down the collar of his coat and headed to the back of the store without any hint that he recognized her.

"Leah, is something wrong?" Joann gave her a funny look.

"Did you see the man who just walked in?"

"Nee." Joann looked toward the back of the store.

"I think it was Caleb Mast." Leah was almost sure of it.

"Really? I wonder what he's doing in Hope Springs after all this time. How long has it been?"

Leah knew exactly how long he had been gone. Nine years ago this month she was to have married his brother, Wayne. Then Caleb ruined everything.

Mr. McGregor rang up the rest of Leah's order. "How did that poem go again? 'On a night so bitter and dark, in a land far, far away, a tiny child was born and laid in a manger of hay.' Is that how it went?"

Her gaze followed Caleb. He was searching for something in the cookie aisle. Why was he back? Had he come to regret his break with his family and his faith?

He glanced her way. She realized she was staring

and quickly looked down. What would she do if he spoke to her?

Nothing. Ignore him. There wasn't anything to say. The past couldn't be changed. Maybe he hadn't recognized her.

"How did it go again?" Mr. McGregor asked.

She forced her attention back to the grocer. "What?"

"The Christmas poem Anna recited. How did it go?"

"I'm afraid I don't remember offhand. I have a copy at school. I'll send it to you." She handed over her money, suddenly eager to leave the store. She grabbed her bag of groceries and rushed out the door.

Joann followed her. "Are you all right?"

In the cold air outside, Leah paused to draw a deep breath and recover from her shock. Seeing Caleb made her realize she'd been lying to herself for years.

She hadn't forgiven him. It was against everything her faith stood for.

When her racing heart slowed, she adjusted her dark bonnet over her ears. "I'm fine. Are you coming to help us bake cookies next Wednesday? Sarah and Rebecca have already said they'll be there."

"Of course. What could be more fun than a baking frolic with my friends?"

"Eating our fill, then taking the rest to the cookie exchange on Friday afternoon and getting wonderful new varieties to try in return."

Joann grinned. "My mouth is watering just thinking about it. I'll see you then." She waved as she crossed the street. The printing office was only a few blocks away.

Leah pulled on her mittens. She had a long walk ahead of her. God had allowed winter to take hold of

the land. He'd sent a dusting of snow that morning, the first of the season.

She glanced at the grocery store door. Did Caleb's family know he was coming? No one had mentioned it to her. She shivered in the cold.

She shouldn't be standing around thinking about Caleb and the harm he'd caused. She had better things to do. There was a Christmas pageant to finish planning and papers to grade, as well as chores to be done. Whatever had brought Caleb to Hope Springs, it had nothing to do with her.

At least his return would give his mother comfort. Maggie Mast would know her son was alive and well. The only contact Caleb had maintained with his family was an annual Christmas card with a brief note. A card mailed without a return address, although for the past few years the postmark had come from Houston, Texas. Leah knew Maggie cherished every one and kept them in a shoe box beside her bed.

"Mama! Daddy!" The shrill cries of a child startled Leah.

A girl in a pink sweater and stocking feet ran past along the sidewalk. She paused for a moment, turned in frantic circles, crying and calling, and then started running again. At first glance, Leah thought she might have Down syndrome. Clearly, she was distraught.

Looking around, Leah realized there was no one else about. The child paused at the corner, then ran out of sight up the block. Had she found who she was looking for? A second later, Leah heard her calling again. Apparently not.

She couldn't leave a child alone and in distress. She put her bag of groceries on a nearby bench and went

after the frightened girl. She caught up with her and took hold of her arm. "There, there, little one, what's the matter?"

"Mama's gone, and Nana's gone, and Daddy is gone, too."

Leah knelt and used her gloves to wipe the tears from her face. She did have Down syndrome. Leah was familiar with such special children. In her years as a teacher, she'd dealt with two *kinder* with the same syndrome. She knew the first thing she needed was to get the child calm enough to answer a few questions. "I'll help you find them. There's no need to cry."

The child threw her arms around Leah's neck and hung on for dear life. Leah rose with the girl in her arms. She looked up and down the street. Where were the parents? She rocked the child gently from side to side to soothe her. "Calm down, sweetheart. It will be okay. We'll find your folks in a minute. My name is Leah Belier. What's your name?"

"Joy Lynn Perry." A muffled sniff followed the tiny voice.

"I'm very pleased to meet you, Joy Perry. Do you live around here?" Leah started walking in the direction the child had been running.

"I live at one…two…one…seven Hudson Place."

There was no such address in the small village of Hope Springs. "That's very good, Joy. I'm going to guess that you came to town in a car, right?"

"No."

"Then you must have come on the bus. Did you ride the bus to Hope Springs?"

"No."

"Don't tell me you came in a buggy."

"Okay, I won't." Joy lifted her face from Leah's neck. "Can you find my daddy?"

Leah turned around slowly searching the quiet street. "I'd love to find him. Are you staying with someone in town? Are you staying at the inn?"

"No. How come you wear such a funny hat?"

"Is my bonnet funny?" Leah asked with a grin.

Joy nodded solemnly.

If she wasn't familiar with Amish dress, she wasn't staying with any of the Amish families in the area. That narrowed the number of possibilities. "If you didn't come to Hope Springs in a buggy, or a car, or a bus, how did you get here?"

"In daddy's truck."

"Ah, a truck. How silly of me. Can you show me where the truck is parked?"

Joy looked around. "No. It's lost."

Suddenly, Leah heard a man frantically shouting for Joy. "That must be your daddy. Let's go see him."

She began walking back the way she had come. She rounded the corner of the building just as Joy's daddy came running toward her. Leah said, "I have her. She's okay."

In the next instant, she was struck speechless as Caleb Mast pulled the child from her arms and held her close, his ragged gasps rising as white puffs in the cold air.

Looking straight at her, he said, "Thank you, Leah."

He had recognized her, after all. Now what did she do?

Chapter Two

Leah stood rooted to the spot. Caleb had a child. That meant he had a wife, too. He had found happiness and love in the outside world after turning her life upside down. It was so unfair. She couldn't stop the bitterness that welled up inside.

Caleb's mother never mentioned he had married or that he had children. Maybe he hadn't told her. Some outsiders were ashamed of a child who wasn't normal. Had he become one of those?

Leah quickly pulled herself together. Caleb's *Englisch* life was no concern of hers. "She's fine, only a little frightened."

Caleb set his daughter on the ground and took her by the shoulders. "What were you doing? Why did you run off?" he demanded.

"I got scared. I wanna go home." She pushed away from him and covered her ears with her hands.

"Don't do that! I'm not going to hit you."

"I'm not bad. I'm not bad." She flew back to Leah and wrapped her arms around her legs.

He pressed his fingers to his temples and exhaled sharply. "I give up. I don't know what to do with you."

Leah laid a protective hand on Joy's head. "Patience and kindness are the keys to raising a special child. All children are gifts from God, but we believe a child such as Joy is one of His most cherished gifts."

Caleb's hands dropped to his sides. He looked…defeated. "I know what the Amish believe. That's why I'm here. The only reason I'm here."

She didn't understand. He tipped his head slightly. A mocking smile lifted one corner of his mouth. "The prodigal son has returned. You don't look happy to see me."

She wasn't. She didn't care if he knew it. He had changed a great deal in the past nine years. The wild, handsome Amish boy she had known had matured into a tall, rugged-looking man with a muscular frame and deeply tanned skin. He wore his dark hair cut short in the *Englisch* way, not in the bowl-cut style the men of her community wore. She didn't remember the small scar that cut through his right eyebrow. How had that happened? It was a faded white line now, not like the jagged red scar that still marred her sister Rhonda's face.

An accident, caused by Caleb's recklessness during their teenage years, had cruelly marked her beautiful sister, but it was his later actions that had truly scarred her.

Leah realized he was studying her, too. Watching her with hard, piercing gray eyes that gave away little of what he was thinking. A shiver of awareness raced through her and brought a rush of heat to her face.

His mocking smile widened. "It's good to see you,

Leah. Did you marry my brother, or did you come to your senses in time?"

She stiffened. The hurt was old, but it had never healed. "Your brother married Rhonda."

"Wayne married your sister? Wow, I didn't see that coming. Funny how things turn out, isn't it?"

"Funny? It is far from funny." She kept the rest of her angry reply bottled inside only because of the child. How dare he mock that terrible time? He'd left her sister unwed and pregnant when he ran off to start a new life among the *Englisch*.

"Bad choice of words. I'm sorry."

"Your brother is a man of honor," she said tartly.

He tensed. "And I'm not, is that what you're saying? Oh, if only you knew the truth about my brother and his honor."

"Your deeds speak so loudly that I can't hear what you're saying."

"An Amish proverb for every occasion. I see your quick wit hasn't changed. I do remember that about you."

"And I have not forgotten the way you denied your own child. The way you called my sister a liar to her face. You shamed us all."

Caleb had held only a faint hope that Rhonda Belier would have admitted the truth sometime during the past nine years. Clearly she hadn't. He wasn't the father of her child. They had dated, but they had never been intimate. He had no idea who the father might be.

That Wayne had fallen on the sword of family honor and married her came as a shock. Had his guilt driven him to it? Had Wayne owned up to his past sins, or

was he still using Caleb as a handy scapegoat? From Leah's reaction, Caleb figured he himself still bore all the blame. He struggled to suppress those unpleasant memories. Nothing hurt as much as knowing his family and friends had turned their collective backs on him. No one had believed his side of the story. Not his parents, not even his brother, and that hurt most of all.

Caleb had always been the wild one, the one in trouble, the one eager to rebel against the constraints of their closed community. He had badgered and baited his brother into going to a party where he knew there would be drinking that night. He'd thought Wayne deserved one night of fun before he settled down to marry. Caleb had owned a forbidden car. He'd goaded his brother into driving it. Hours later, when Caleb had learned that Wayne had crashed into Rhonda's buggy, he had been sick with remorse.

Wayne had managed to make his way home, terrified, almost incoherent with fear and shame. He thought he had killed Rhonda. When Caleb realized that no one knew about the accident, he had quickly gone to the crash site. He'd discovered Rhonda was alive but injured and had summoned help for her. He'd allowed everyone to think he had been the one driving. He had stoically endured the shame heaped on him by his family and the community. He knew he deserved it even if he hadn't been behind the wheel. He had done it to shield his big brother, the one who could do no wrong in their father's eyes.

Months later, when Caleb begged Wayne to believe he hadn't fathered Rhonda's child, Wayne refused to accept Caleb's word. It had been the final blow in their relationship.

Caleb shrugged off his resentment. He'd made a choice to come back. Now he had to face the consequences of that decision. Hopefully he wasn't going to be here long. Leah's brown eyes fairly snapped with anger. He could see she wanted to say a lot more. He figured the only reason she wasn't reading him the riot act was because Joy was listening.

He remembered Leah as a skinny girl with wide brown eyes and a tendency to speak her mind. She'd been someone who found the world and everyone in it of interest. She'd seemed an odd pick for his self-righteous brother back then. He'd found it hard to imagine her in love with Wayne.

She certainly wasn't a skinny kid anymore. Even under her long coat, he could tell she had filled out in all the right places. A black bonnet covered all but the front of her honey-blond hair. Like all Amish women, she wore it parted in the center and coiled into a bun at the back of her head. Amish women never cut their hair.

Her plump cheeks were pink with cold or perhaps her anger. He wasn't sure which. Had she married? The Amish didn't believe in jewelry of any kind, not even wedding bands, so he had no way of knowing. What did it matter anyway?

"I don't know why your sister lied about me. I'm sure she thought she had a good reason." A lie told for any reason only led to more lies and heartache. He had learned that bitter lesson well.

He turned his attention to his daughter. "Come on, Joy, we should get going. You didn't put your coat or your shoes on. You're going to freeze out here." He reached to pick her up.

She jerked away and hid behind Leah's skirt. "I don't

wanna go with you. I wanna go to Nana's house. I don't like you anymore."

Leah's eyes narrowed. A frown creased her brow. He shook his head. Trust Joy to make him look like a bad parent. Leah would have no trouble believing her.

Well, he *was* a poor excuse for a parent. If he'd learned anything in the weeks since Valerie's vanishing act, it was that he had no idea how to be a father.

"We've had this talk, honey. You can't go back to Dallas. Nana isn't there anymore. She's gone to heaven." He tried to reason with Joy although he knew it wouldn't do any good when she got in one of her moods.

"Go away. I want *Mama* to come get me."

He threw up his hands. "So do I, but it looks like that's not going to happen."

He pressed his lips shut. It wasn't Joy's fault Valerie had dumped her like an unwanted dog. He understood how difficult all the changes must be for her, but what choice did they have? "It's not far to your new grandma's house. You want to meet her, don't you?" he asked calmly. He tried again to catch hold of her.

"No!" She pulled away from him and looked up at Leah. "I wanna go home with you."

He shoved his hands in his coat pockets. "Fine! Guess I get to eat the animal crackers that are in the truck. I'm going to bite the heads off all the elephants."

Joy glared at him but didn't rise to his bait. The mulish expression on her face did not bode well. He sighed. No matter what he did, no matter how hard he tried, he couldn't make a connection with her. She hated him.

"Please, Joy. We need to get going. Say thank-you to Leah and come on."

"No, no, no!" She dropped down on the sidewalk, screaming and kicking her legs.

Now his face flushed with embarrassment as people coming out of the store stopped to stare. He glanced at Leah. What was she thinking? Perhaps it was best that he didn't know. He shook his head. "I'm sorry."

Her gaze softened slightly. "I've seen a temper tantrum or two in my time."

"Any suggestions on how to deal with them?" He was willing to take any help he could get. He kept a close eye on Joy so she didn't hurt herself.

"I'm sure as her father you know what's best for her."

He ran a hand over his hair. "I've been her father for a total of six weeks and three days. Believe me, I have no idea what's best for her. Pick her up. Don't pick her up. Let her cry it out, put her in time-out. Ignore her. Distract her. Reason with her. I've had all kinds of advice from the two nannies who both quit within a week, from the principal of an expensive private school that wouldn't take her after the first day, and from her step-grandfather, who said to throw water in her face, it worked for him."

"Did you?"

He glanced at Leah and saw her regarding him intently. She hadn't scurried away and left him to deal with the situation alone. His respect for her jumped considerably. Joy continued to kick and scream.

"No. I almost threw water in *his* face, but I left before I did something I knew I would regret."

"Very wise. Very Amish. Where's your truck?"

"On the other side of the store." He tipped his head in the general direction. He was ex-Amish, not Amish.

Leah bent down and lifted Joy. His daughter wasn't

a lightweight, but Leah had no trouble carrying her. She held the screaming child close and started walking. "We're going to the truck now, Joy. It will be warmer there. As soon as you calm down, we will talk about what's upsetting you."

Caleb followed, happy for once to have someone else take charge. When they reached the truck, he stepped ahead to open the passenger-side door. To his surprise, Leah didn't deposit Joy inside. Instead, she climbed in and held Joy on her lap.

He walked around to the driver's side and rescued his scattered groceries from the sidewalk where he'd dropped them when he discovered Joy was missing. Opening his door, he set them behind the driver's seat on the king cab's rear bench seat. He climbed in behind the wheel, at a lost as to what to do next.

He wanted to take Joy from Leah, but he was afraid it would make things worse. He started the engine. After a few minutes, warm air filled the cab. He noticed the soothing way Leah rocked Joy and consoled her. Joy's sobs were growing less dire.

He gripped the steering wheel. His parental short-comings were laid bare once more. Joy would take comfort from a stranger before she took it from him. At least Leah seemed to know how to handle his daughter. He glanced her way. "Thanks for your help. Again."

"I do it for the child," she said primly.

He got the message. "Not for the father who strayed from the Amish fold."

She looked directly at him. "*Nee,* not for you."

Leah continued to hold and rock Joy until the child calmed down. Spent by her outburst, she rested in Le-

ah's arms with only occasional hiccupping sobs to break the awkward silence. Leah brushed Joy's fine, soft hair away from her face and glanced at Caleb. Did he know how blessed he was to have this child?

She was forever comforting, caring for and teaching children who belonged to others. Her profession was a labor of love, a sacred duty, but it wasn't like having children of her own. The unfairness of it cut deep. She longed to hold her own babe. She didn't understand why God had chosen this path for her. She could only travel it as best she could and trust in His mercy.

After a few minutes, Joy sat up. She looked at her father. "Can I have an elephant now?"

Caleb reached behind the seat and brought out a red-and-yellow box made to look like a circus wagon, with colorful animals printed on the sides. He handed it to her. There were several similar boxes on the floor of the truck.

He must have noticed Leah's gaze. "Sometimes they keep her from having a meltdown like the one you just witnessed. I stopped to stock up before heading out to the farm. She was sound asleep when I went in the store. I couldn't have been gone more than five minutes."

Leah didn't want to feel sorry for him, but she couldn't help it. It was easy to see that he didn't know how to handle his newly acquired daughter. What was the story behind his cryptic comment about only being a father for six weeks? Had he adopted a special-needs child? Curiosity, often her downfall, prompted her to remain in the truck and learn more about Caleb and Joy.

Joy opened the box and picked out two elephant-shaped cookies. She looked at Leah. "Do you want one?"

Leah held out a hand. "May I have a lion?"

"Okay, sure." Joy extracted two of them, laid the pair in Leah's palm and gave her an endearing grin.

Children with Down syndrome were normally happy, gregarious individuals. Leah loved that about them. "What shall we give your daddy?"

"A bear," Joy said quickly.

Leah glanced at him from the corner of her eye. His daughter's remark caused a reluctant grin to tug at one side of his mouth. "Is that your way of telling me I'm as grumpy as an old bear?"

Leah leaned over to see Joy's face. "Is your daddy grumpy?"

"Sometimes." Cookie crumbs sprayed from her lips. She handed him three bears.

"I get grumpy sometimes, too," Leah admitted. "So do you. What made you so upset a little while ago?"

The child bowed her head. "I don't know."

"I think you do. Your daddy can't fix things for you if he doesn't know what's wrong."

"He wants me to go away."

"That's not true," Caleb said quickly.

"I wanna go home and be with Nana. I want Mama to come get me and take me home. She'll never find me here." She laid her head on Leah's shoulder and closed her eyes.

Leah glanced to Caleb for an explanation. He shook his head slightly. Whatever the story was, he didn't want to recount it in front of the child. Another awkward minute of silence passed.

Joy sat up and cupped Leah's face with her hands. "I'm sorry I was bad."

Leah's heart turned over. What a sweet child. "You

are forgiven. You will like your *grossmammi* when you meet her, and she will love you."

Joy tipped her head to the side. "What's that?"

"*Grossmammi?* It's the Amish word for grand-mother."

"Oh. What's an Amish?"

Leah chuckled. "I am Amish. We are a Plain People who believe in remaining separate from worldly things and living a simple life so that we may live close to God and each other."

"You're not plain. You're pretty."

"So are you." Leah gave her a quick hug. "But I need to be going. It's getting late. I have a long walk home."

"Don't go!" Joy threw her arms around Leah's neck and held on tight.

"Joy, stop that. She has to go." Caleb tried to pull her arms loose.

"No," she sobbed, and held on tighter.

"Stop. You're hurting me. Let go and we will talk about it," Leah said firmly.

Joy slowly released her grip. "I'm not bad."

Leah waited for Caleb to say something, but he seemed at a loss for words. She took Joy's hands and met her gaze. "No one said you are bad. However, your behavior just now was not very nice."

"I want you to be my friend. I don't want you to go away."

"I am your friend, but I have to go home. You have to go meet your grandparents."

Caleb spoke at last. "Let me give you a lift home. It's the least I can do after all your help."

Leah could see Joy was on the verge of another breakdown. She hated giving in. It wouldn't teach Joy

self-control if she got her way with her tantrums. Still, Leah didn't want to be the cause of another episode. She hadn't forgiven Caleb for the way he had treated her sister, but ignoring someone in distress, especially a child, wasn't something she could do. Allowing Joy a chance to calm down might make their parting easier. "That's kind of you to offer, Caleb. *Danki.*"

"Great." His relief was almost comical.

Leah put her hand on the door handle. "I left a bag of groceries on the bench in front of the store. Could you get it for me, Joy?"

"Okay. You won't go away before I get back, will you?"

"I will wait right here."

"Put your shoes and coat on first," Caleb said.

Joy climbed in the backseat, pulled her sneakers and jacket on, then climbed over Leah to get out.

Caleb relaxed as he watched his daughter run to pick up the grocery bag. "You're very good with kids, Leah. How many do you have?"

"An entire school full."

He scowled for a second and then smiled. A warm and genuine smile that smoothed the lines of worry from his brow. He was handsome in a rugged way that many women would find attractive. She refused to be one of them. A kind heart was more important than a handsome face.

"I assume that means you're a teacher?"

"*Ja,* at Walnut Valley School."

"The same one we attended as kids? That's got to feel strange."

"Not so much. Do you mind if I ask what happened to Joy's mother?"

His scowl reappeared. "To make a long story short, Valerie and I were together for a year after I left here. One day, I came home and found a note telling me she was leaving. It wasn't until the next day I found out she had cleaned out our bank account and left me with a pile of debts that took me three years to pay off."

His life hadn't been easy out among the *Englisch*. Leah found small comfort in the thought. Her life hadn't been easy, either.

"I didn't hear from her again until she turned up at my door in the middle of the night a month and a half ago. She had Joy with her. She told me I was Joy's father. She went out to smoke a cigarette and never came back."

He had been abandoned the same way he had abandoned her pregnant sister. The irony wasn't lost on Leah, but she saved her pity for Joy.

She looked out the window to see what was keeping her. A horse and buggy had pulled up in front of the store. Joy stood transfixed by the sight. A woman and a young girl got out. Leah recognized Karen Dresher and her young sister, Anna Imhoff. Anna was eleven and one of Leah's brightest students.

Caleb continued speaking. "My attorney helped me track down Valerie's stepfather. I learned Joy's grandmother raised her until her death a few months ago. Valerie came and went over the years. She took Joy with her a few times but always brought her back. The kid's had a rough life."

"No wonder she was terrified when she woke and you were gone. She needs stability, a sense of home and security. You are right to return to your family. Among us you will both find acceptance and peace."

Leah meant her words, although she knew it would be difficult for everyone involved, particularly her sister, to accept Caleb back into the family.

Outside, Karen and Anna were talking to Joy. Anna was encouraging her to pet the horse's nose. Leah smiled and waved to them. Karen waved in return.

"I'm hoping Joy will find acceptance here, but the Amish life isn't for me," Caleb said.

Leah whipped around to stare at him in shock. "After all your child has been through you mean to abandon her, too? How can you be so heartless?"

To think she had spared one ounce of pity for him. She fumbled for the door handle, determined to leave before she said more. He leaned across the seat and grabbed her arm to stop her.

Chapter Three

"It isn't like that. I'm not dumping her off the way her mother did."

Caleb needed all the help he could get. He couldn't let Leah leave thinking less of him than she already did. If that was possible.

As a teacher, Leah would be an important part of Joy's life in the Amish community, second only to his parents if they agreed to raise her. He wanted Leah on his side. On Joy's side.

Leah stopped trying to open the door and glared at him. "What is it like?"

He let go of her arm. "I put a great-paying job on hold when Joy arrived in my life. I've tried to give her what she needs, but my one-bedroom condo isn't exactly set up for family living. I've come back where I know I'm not welcome because I want Joy to have a home. A place she will always belong. A place where she will be loved and valued.

"Yes, I'll be leaving, but not until I'm certain she can be happy here and that this is the best thing for her. If

that takes two months or twelve months, I'll stay that long. Honestly, I doubt she'll even miss me."

"How can she have such happiness without her father or her mother?"

"I'm her father in name only. She barely knows me. Her mother… I can't even talk about Valerie without getting angry."

He drew a deep breath to calm down. After a few seconds, he said, "I know Val had it rough. Joy can go from sweet to those horrible tantrums in five seconds flat. I didn't know kids with Down could be that way. I thought they were always happy and loving."

Having a special-needs child had been a rude awakening for Caleb. He'd had no idea what to expect. As he struggled to adjust, he found himself wanting to shout at the people who looked away when they saw Joy was different, as if seeing her somehow disturbed them.

Her step-grandfather had talked about her as if she wasn't in the room with him, calling her stupid and a pain. Even in the few weeks she had lived with Caleb, a dozen people told him how sorry they were that he had a retarded child. Joy deserved better. He didn't know how else he could give her a chance to be accepted for who she was.

Leah didn't say anything so he went on. "Joy has learned not to trust people. Especially men. Her step-grandfather is a prime example. My attorney uncovered reports of abuse in the home. Her life when she was with her mother wasn't any better. Val has a drug problem. I believe she tried to be good to Joy, but she couldn't even take care of herself, let alone a kid."

"I'm sorry Joy has known such unhappiness."

"Do you see why I know she'll be better off here?

You'll be her teacher. You'll see her nearly every day. With your help, Joy can learn to trust again. She'll be cared for and loved by the Amish community her whole life. She'll never be made to feel inferior. I want her to have that."

He'd tried to give Joy that kind of life in Houston, but he had failed miserably. He'd thought leaving the Amish was hard. It was nothing compared to the changes he had to make in his life when Valerie dropped Joy in his lap without so much as a toothbrush. Could he make Leah understand that?

"Joy can be a charming child, but she doesn't adapt to change well. Her way of coping is to fall down and have a screaming fit or simply run away, which she did numerous times in the first four weeks with me. She wanted to go find her mother. She had it in her little brain that her mother would come get her if she went back to Nana's house.

"The police officers in my part of town knew us on a first-name basis. I lived in a constant state of fear. I couldn't take my eyes off her. The last time, when Joy was found walking along the middle of a freeway, I reached my breaking point. Something had to give."

Leah looked down and smoothed the front of her coat. "If you think so highly of our community, why haven't you returned to us before now?"

He didn't care to explain the complex reasons why he'd left and why he'd stayed away. "This isn't about me. It's about Joy. Do you honestly believe she is better off with me? I don't think so. You believe she'll be better off as part of the Amish community, too. Will you help her?"

Caleb studied Leah's face as she considered his

question. If only he knew what she was thinking. She looked out the window toward his daughter. Joy was grinning from ear to ear as she patted the horse. She took a step back and clapped her chubby hands together, then reached up to touch him again.

"The school board will have to approve her transfer to our school," Leah said at last.

He hadn't considered that. "Do you think it will be a problem?"

"Perhaps. She is *Englisch,* after all. They may feel she should attend the *Englisch* school in town. Your parents may need to plead her case and state their desire to raise her in the Amish way. Will they do that?"

"All I can do is ask."

His mother would welcome Joy with open arms. He wasn't so sure about his father. He had to believe they would agree with his decision to bring her here. If not, he didn't know what he would do. Joy needed more than he could give her.

"I should tell you that Wayne is on the school board."

"I see." Would his brother block his efforts?

"No matter where she continues her education, you'll need her records from her last school. Do you have them?"

"She was homeschooled by her grandmother."

"Can you get copies of her curriculum and any test scores? Each state has different requirements. I'm not familiar with what Texas requires."

"I'll have my attorney get what he can and send it to me." Caleb had already paid the firm a big chunk of his savings to gain temporary custody of Joy. Whatever it took, he was willing to do. His one overriding

fear was that Valerie could get Joy back and all of this would have been for nothing.

Leah stared at him for a long moment. "What happens when Joy's mother returns for her and wants to take her away?"

He shifted his gaze to his hands on the steering wheel. It was a question he couldn't answer. He wanted Joy to know security and happiness. His attorney was working to sever Valerie's parental rights on the basis of abandonment, but Caleb wasn't sure what would happen if she returned to fight for custody.

"I left a letter for Valerie with her stepfather and one with my attorney if she should come looking for us. I let her know I was taking Joy to my folks. She knows they're Amish. I'm hoping she'll realize that Joy is better off with them and stay out of her life."

"Shouldn't you pray that she sees the error of her ways and wants to reunite with her daughter?"

"You can pray for that if you want. I won't waste my time. God doesn't listen to me." Caleb had stopped praying a long time ago.

Sadness filled Leah's eyes. "God hears everyone's prayers. Perhaps you are the one who has stopped listening for His answer."

He tipped his head to the side and tried for a lighter tone. "Maybe you should pray for me, then."

Her chin came up a notch at his challenge. "I will, Caleb Mast. I will do just that."

Joy finished petting the horse, picked up the grocery bag and came running toward the truck. He got out and held open the door as she raced around the hood.

"Did you see me? I touched a horse, a real horse.

Not a pretend one. His name is Benny. He belongs to Anna. I want a horse."

He smiled at her excitement. Taking the bag of groceries from her, he handed them to Leah and then lifted his daughter into the truck. "You'll meet lots of horses at your grandpa and grandma's farm. Cows, too, and chickens and ducks, but no elephants."

"Do they have a dog?"

Caleb glanced at Leah. "Do they?"

"They don't have a dog, but I do. Her name is Trixie, and she is going to have puppies soon. I've been trying to think of some names for them. Have you got any suggestions?"

Caleb breathed an inward sigh of relief. Leah seemed to be on board with his plan. While she might not like helping him, he had to trust that she would do what was best for Joy.

He drove out of town with a renewed sense of hope. This might actually work. If Joy was happy and safe, he couldn't ask for more.

"If your dog has a girl puppy, you can call it Princess," Joy said from the backseat.

Caleb smothered a grin and waited for Leah's reply. She tilted her head slightly. "I think Princess is much too fancy a name for an Amish dog. She will be a working dog."

"What kind of work can a dog do?" Joy asked.

"My puppies will grow up to herd sheep and cattle, just like their mother and father do."

Caleb glanced at Leah. "Are they border collies?"

"English shepherds."

The breed wasn't well-known outside farming communities. Similar to the border collie in size and coat

texture, they were often sable and white or tricolor. Unlike many herding dogs, English shepherds were used to guard as well as herd cattle, sheep, goats, pigs and even fowl. They made excellent farm dogs.

"Pete would be a good name," Caleb suggested.

"Not for a girl dog, Daddy," Joy said in disgust.

"Right. Not for a girl dog," he conceded.

Leah half turned in the seat to speak to Joy. "Can you think of another name?"

Joy was thinking, so Caleb ventured a second suggestion. "Matilda."

"No." Joy shook her head. "I don't like that name."

"Okay, how about Tilly? It rhymes with *silly*," Leah said.

He glanced at his daughter's face in the rearview mirror. She grinned at Leah. "No, not Silly Tilly. I like Pickles."

"*Ja,* I like pickles, too. Dill pickles, sweet pickles, even bread-and-butter pickles. Do you like pickles, Caleb?"

"I do. I like pickles on sandwiches and on hamburgers. I like to eat the little crispy ones right out of the jar."

Joy shook her head. "Not pickles to eat. Pickles for a name. I want to call the puppy Pickles."

"*Ach,* I see." Leah nodded solemnly. "Pickles is an excellent name. If my Trixie has a girl puppy, her name will be Pickles."

They'd gone only half a mile down the highway when they came upon a buggy traveling in the same direction. Caleb slowed to a crawl, unable to pass on the hilly road.

"Does your family know you're coming?" Leah asked.

"I wrote. I wasn't sure when to tell them to expect us." He hadn't mailed the letter until the day they left. Up until the moment he dropped the letter in the mailbox, he'd hoped he could find a way to manage his life with Joy in Texas. Admitting that he couldn't was a bitter pill to swallow. He simply didn't know where else to turn.

Leah lapsed into silence until he had the chance to pass the buggy. As they went by, she sat back and muttered, "Oh, no."

"What?" He looked in his rearview mirror but didn't see anything amiss.

"That was Esther Zook."

"The bishop's wife?"

"The same."

"Has she changed any in the past decade?"

"*Nee,* she has not."

"So gossip about you riding with an *Englisch* fellow will be spreading before the sun sets tomorrow. Good to know some things never change. Will it be better or worse for you when she learns it was me?"

"You were not baptized. No one must shun you."

"Some people will think I should be."

"Not everyone has a forgiving nature, in spite of what we are taught."

He glanced at her. "Do you?"

"Have a forgiving nature? I thought so, but I find it is something I must work on."

It wasn't the answer he wanted. For some reason, he wanted to know that she had forgiven him for leaving the Amish, for straying so far from the path laid out from his birth. It was a foolish thought. He was grate-

ful she was willing to consider teaching Joy. That was enough.

"I live in the same house. It's past the next hill on the right-hand side of the road, a short mile after the school."

"You still live with your folks?"

"*Nee,* they are gone now."

"I'm sorry." He slowed as he topped the rise. The school building and schoolyard were just as he remembered them. He would have to tell Joy to look for his name carved under one of the desks. The lane to Leah's home came all too quickly. He turned in and hoped Joy would say goodbye without making a fuss.

Her face took on the mulish pout he dreaded, once Leah opened the door to get out.

She held out her hand to Joy. "It was wonderful meeting you. I look forward to seeing you at school."

"At school?" Joy gave her a puzzled look.

"Your father wants to enroll you in my school. If it works out, I'll be your new teacher. Wouldn't that great?"

Joy folded her arms over her chest and stared at the floor of the truck. "I don't like school. Other kids make fun of me."

"My students won't do that. Besides, even if you don't come to my school, I'm sure your father will bring you over to see the puppies when they arrive."

Joy looked at Caleb. "Will you?"

"Sure, kiddo."

Joy clapped her hands and rewarded him with a beaming smile that crinkled her eyes closed. He smiled in return. It was amazing how fast he was growing to love her. That was one more reason to get her settled

quickly. Another painful upheaval wouldn't do either of them any good.

He glanced at Leah. She was smiling at Joy, too. As their eyes met, his heart gave a funny kick. She really was a pretty woman. He liked the way her eyes sparkled when she smiled.

The last thing he expected to find in Hope Springs was an Amish woman who caught his fancy.

If only things had been different.

And that was the story of his life.

Leah looked away first. "Goodbye, Joy. Be sure and tell your *grossmammi* I said hello."

"I will." Joy waved.

Leah waved, too, and closed the door.

Caleb sat and watched until she entered the house. After a few minutes, the soft glow of lantern light lit the windows. He couldn't put it off any longer. It was time to go home. He shifted the truck in Reverse and began to back up.

"Daddy, stop!"

He hit the brakes. "What?"

"Leah wants you."

He looked toward the house. She stood on the porch motioning to him. He put the truck in Park. Was something wrong? He looked around the cab. He didn't see anything she might have left behind.

"Stay here, Joy." He opened his door.

"But I want to come in."

"We're not staying. I'm just going to see what Leah wants." He stepped out of the truck. The light layer of powdery fresh snow muffled his footsteps as he crossed the yard to her porch.

Leah's eyes were bright with excitement. As he

neared, that excitement faded. She bit her lower lip and clasped her hands together nervously. When she didn't speak, he asked, "Is something wrong?"

"*Nee*. It's only that Trixie has had her puppies. I thought perhaps Joy would like to see them."

Bemused by her unexpected offer, he hitched a thumb toward his truck. "I'm sure she will. I'll go get her."

He was happy to put off going home for a bit longer. The real upside was spending more time in Leah's company.

What was she thinking?

Leah couldn't believe she had just invited Caleb Mast into her home. She had been so excited to find the puppies had arrived that she had simply stepped out and beckoned Joy to come see them, not thinking that Caleb would come, too. She could hardly ask him to wait outside while she took his child in. She prayed her sister wouldn't find out.

Leah watched as Caleb lifted Joy out of the truck. He spoke to her quietly and then held her hand as they approached the house. Leah stood aside and let them enter.

She had placed the whelping box in the kitchen, near the stove for warmth. Trixie lay on an old quilt in a corner of the box with three tiny black, brown and white pups nestled against her belly. She pricked up her ears and gave the newcomers a guarded look.

Trixie was a medium-size dog with long black fur and a white blaze that went down her face and chest. Over her eyes and upright ears, she had brown points, which gave her an inquisitive look. Two of the puppies were marked like their mother. A third was as pale

brown as winter grass, with a white blaze and chest and four white feet.

Leah spoke quietly to reassure her. "It's okay. They want to admire your babies."

Joy knelt beside the box with Caleb at her side. "They are super awesome. Can I touch them, Daddy?" Her voice squeaked with excitement.

He brushed a lock of hair away from her eyes. "You have to ask to Leah. Remember, I said we have to talk very quietly so we don't disturb them."

She nodded and looked up at Leah. "Can I touch them?" she whispered.

"I think Trixie will allow that." She reached into the box and lifted a tiny ball of fur. The puppy mewed at having its sleep cut short. Trixie rose to her feet and stood close as Leah handed the pup to Joy, showing her how to hold it properly.

Joy raised the puppy to her face. "Oh, it's so soft. It this Pickles?"

"Let me see." Caleb took the puppy from her and checked the gender. "Yup, this is Pickles." He handed her back to his daughter.

Joy pressed her close. "I love you, Pickles."

The puppy started crying, making Trixie whine with concern. Leah said, "We should put Pickles back with her mother now. She needs lots of rest so she can grow up to be a wonderful helper on someone's farm."

Joy handed her back to Leah. Trixie nosed her pup and licked her as Leah replaced her with her litter-mates. Joy looked at Leah. "Pickles's mommy will take good care of her. She won't run away and leave her to be scared."

Leah exchanged a poignant look with Caleb. They

were both thinking the same thing. Joy was referring to her own mother's actions. Caleb put an arm around her. "No, Trixie is going to take good care of all her puppies."

Joy pushed his arm away and looked around the kitchen. "Where is their daddy?"

Leah knelt beside her. "His name is Duncan. He lives on a sheep farm not far from here with his master."

Joy frowned. "Does he ever come to visit his kids?"

Leah smothered a smile. "They were only born today. I'm sure he'll be by when he hears the news."

"He better come. He shouldn't be a deadbeat dad. My friends Jenny and Kala have deadbeat dads."

Puzzled, Leah said, "What does that mean?"

Caleb rose to his feet. His demeanor changed as he squared off, almost as if he expected a fight. "A deadbeat dad is a man who doesn't take responsibility for his children, doesn't visit them or help support them."

She rose, too, as the past came rushing in to spoil the moment. "Your *Englisch* world must be a sad place if such a thing is common there."

Caleb took Joy's hand. "It can be sad. It can be wonderful, too, just like here. Say goodbye to the puppies and thank Leah for letting you see them. We have to get going."

"Thank you. Take good care of Pickles. I like her the best."

Leah spoke before he made it out the door. "The school board is meeting next Thursday evening at Eli Imhoff's home. You are welcome to come and speak with them."

"All right." He didn't say anything else.

Leah closed the door as the pair left, and watched

through the kitchen window as they got into Caleb's truck. Rarely had she been so torn about what her course should be.

If she aided his daughter to become Amish, was she helping him avoid responsibilities to a child for a second time?

He genuinely cared about Joy. She saw it in the way he touched his daughter and in the way he spoke to her. He was trying hard to do the right thing.

Why hadn't he given that kind of care and attention to her sister and their unborn child?

Could a man change that much?

With God, anything was possible. If Caleb had changed, why continue to deny he was David's father? He no longer had an obligation to marry her sister or take care of David. Admitting the truth wouldn't change anything except to free his soul from the burden of his lie. It didn't make sense.

Perhaps he was too prideful to admit the truth. That she could believe, yet it was too simple an answer. There had to be more. Something was holding Caleb apart from the Amish community and from his family. Something painful. What was it?

Chapter Four

Caleb turned his truck onto the narrow dirt lane lead-
ing to his childhood home and stopped. It was almost
dark. A crimson band of clouds in the west marked the
end of the day and a new start to Joy's life.

Up ahead, a large two-story white farmhouse stood
nestled into the slope of a hill. It was backed by a thick
stand of trees. Their branches were bare now, a mat
of dark lines scratching against the bloodred sky. His
mother's laundry hung freeze-drying in the winter air
from the clothesline at the side of the house. White
sheets, blue dresses, blue work shirts, black aprons and
dark denim pants. The color palette was the same as it
had been throughout his childhood.

He'd thought he was prepared to come back, but he
wasn't. A rush of emotions and memories hit him like
a truck and then parked on his chest, making it hard to
breathe. Scenes from the wonderful years of his youth
and the heartbreaking months before he left flickered
through his mind like old movie clips.

Working in the fields with his father, driving a team
of mules for the first time. Hot summertime days spent

shucking corn, followed by a dip in the cool river with his brother. His mother, calling everyone in to eat the most wonderful meals. His father, bowing his head in prayer. They were good memories.

Then there were the not-so-good memories. The wreck that scarred Rhonda. The bitter arguments with his parents during his *rumspringa,* his teenage years, when he tried to sample all that wasn't Amish. He was introduced to Valerie during that time at a friend's house in Cleveland. She was quite simply the most exciting woman he'd ever met. To remain Amish or to go out into the English world became a real question in his mind for the first time.

Then Rhonda Belier's accusation that he was the father of her unborn babe changed everything. No matter how he denied it, his family expected him to do the right thing and marry her. Nothing he said made any difference until the night he flatly refused to marry her in front of both their families. Leah had been there, but he'd barely noticed her in the room. How did she remember that night? He kept begging Rhonda to admit the truth, but her silence had condemned him. It was the worst night of his life.

What followed was an unofficial shunning by his father. For days, Ike Mast acted as if Caleb wasn't present. He was waiting for a confession that his son couldn't make. Caleb wouldn't take the blame. Not this time. As painful as his father's shunning had been, it was Wayne's refusal to believe Caleb that had finally driven him away.

He shook off the disturbing images from his past and looked around. This stretch of farmland amid the

gentle rolling hills of Ohio was, and always would be, home. Too bad it wasn't where he belonged.

What would his life have been like if he had stayed? He couldn't imagine bending far enough to fit into the mold he had been expected to fill.

If he had married Rhonda, Leah would be married to Wayne and not teaching school. She might have children of her own by now. She would make a good mother. She certainly had a way with Joy.

Why hadn't she married? Was her love for Wayne so strong that she couldn't care for another? He hoped that wasn't the case. Watching the man she loved marry her sister couldn't have been easy. What was their relationship like now? Did Wayne love his wife and the child that wasn't his? What must that be like?

Caleb rubbed a hand over the stubble on his cheeks. His actions had affected far more people than he knew. Leaving had seemed like his only option, but had it been a mistake?

Joy, on the front seat beside him, stretched to see over the dashboard. Was he making another mistake bringing her here? He could turn around now and find a job somewhere, working on an oil rig that wasn't a hundred miles out in the Gulf. He could be home every night. There had to be someplace they could belong and make a go of it.

Even as the thought came to him, he realized Joy hadn't been happy since she had come to him. This was his last hope.

She pointed off to the side. "I see tepees. Lots of them."

The field on the left-hand side of the lane had shocks of cornstalks stacked to provide winter feed for the an-

imals. The long lines of bundles stretched in straight rows across the twenty-acre field. It was hot, itchy work in the summer, piling the stalks together and tying the tops so they would cure properly and not blow over in the wind. He didn't miss that job.

"They aren't tepees, but they do look like them. They're cornstalks."

"They don't look like corn."

"They don't?"

"No, corn is yellow and it comes from a can."

He smiled. She had a lot to learn about living on a farm. He hadn't prayed much in the past nine years, but he silently sent up a plea now. *Please, Lord. Let this be the right decision for her.*

He drove down the lane and stopped in front of the house. A buggy with a black horse in harness stood at the front gate. Did it belong to his folks or did they have company?

For Joy's sake, he didn't want his reunion to occur in front of strangers. He considered driving away, but the front door opened and his mother came out. She stood on the steps, watching him.

He looked at his daughter. There had been so much upheaval in her life. Was he doing the right thing by bringing her here? He couldn't manage on his own. He had tried and failed miserably. He had to believe this was the right thing. "Are you ready to meet your grandparents?"

She shrank back in the seat. "What if they don't like me?"

"They will love you."

"What if they laugh at me or call me stupid?"

He took her chin in his fingers and tilted her face

toward him. "I know this is very hard for you. I wish things were different, but they aren't. Do you see that woman standing in the doorway? She is your grandma. I'm one hundred percent certain that she will never laugh at you, never make fun of you. She will love you with her whole heart and soul."

"You promise?"

"I promise. She's waiting to meet you. Are you ready?"

"I guess."

"Then I guess I'm ready, too." That was a lie. Petrified was closer to the truth.

Opening the truck door, he stepped out. His mother came rushing toward him. Behind her, he saw his father looking on from the doorway. Ike Mast did not rush out. He turned away and went back inside. Caleb swallowed the hurt. It was what he had expected.

His mother's steps faltered as she drew near. Her hands were clenched tightly together in front of her. Her eyes searched his face. "Caleb, is it really you?"

He was stunned to see how much she had aged. A black prayer *kapp* covered her gray-streaked hair. She wore a black apron over a blue dress like the ones on the clothesline. She hadn't bothered to put on a coat.

"*Ja, Mamm,* it's me." His throat closed with emotion. He couldn't say another word. None was needed. With a glad cry, she launched herself at him and threw her arms around him.

"*Mein sohn es* home. *Gott* be praised."

He held her for a long moment as he struggled to regain his composure. She was happy to see him now, but he was going to break her heart all over again when he left. He choked back tears and pulled away.

"*Mamm,* I have someone who wants to meet you. This is my daughter, Joy. Did you get my letter about her?"

His mother dabbed her tears away with the corner of her apron. "*Ja,* I did. Welcome to our home, Joy. My name is Maggie, but you can call me *Mammi.* I'm so happy to meet you."

"Are you really my *grossmammi?*"

His mother's eyes brightened. "So your father has taught you some Pennsylvania Dutch. That's *goot.*"

"He didn't teach me. Leah taught me."

He caught the worried glance his mother flashed him. "You have spoken with Leah?"

"We met in town." He looked down at his daughter. "She's looking forward to having Joy come to her school."

"Leah is a kind woman. Your brother and his wife are inside. I thought you should know that."

He shoved his hands in his pockets. "Then it really is a family reunion."

"I have not told Wayne that you are returning. He doesn't know about Joy, either."

"Did you tell Father?"

"*Ja.*"

Caleb straightened and took Joy by the hand. "Then we should go in."

His mother nodded and walked quickly back to the house. He followed more slowly. As they reached the door, Wayne blocked their way. A thunderous expression darkened his face. "There is nothing here for you. Go back where you came from."

"Wayne, please." Maggie's gaze darted between her sons.

"Shame on you, Mother. How could you do this to us? Rhonda, David, we are going home." He stood aside. His wife and son hurried out the door. The boy stared at Caleb with wide, curious eyes. Rhonda didn't even look. She kept her face down as she rushed past him, one hand covering her scarred cheek. Wayne followed close behind them.

Caleb caught his brother's arm and pulled him to a stop. He whispered, "Have you told her the truth?"

Wayne pushed him away. "There is nothing to tell. You are not welcome."

Caleb stepped aside. Joy clung to his leg, hiding her face. He placed a reassuring hand on her head. "Wayne, can we at least be civil to each other? For Mother's sake if not for our own."

Wayne stood at the gate as his wife and son climbed in the buggy. "'Be ye not unequally yoked together with unbelievers: for what fellowship hath righteousness with unrighteousness? And what communion hath light with darkness?' *2 Corinthians* 6:14."

"I remember the passage."

"Do not trouble me or mine. We do not know you." With that, he strode to the buggy, climbed in and quickly drove away.

"What did you expect, Maggie?" Caleb's father asked from the doorway. "You should have told them Caleb was coming. You should have given them a chance to prepare."

"*Mamm* didn't know I would arrive today."

"I planned to tell Wayne and Rhonda tonight, that's why I asked them to come over, but then it was too late. Caleb was already here."

Ike stepped back from the door. "Come inside. We're letting all the heat out."

Maggie went in. Caleb picked up Joy and followed her. His father closed the door behind them.

The warmth of the kitchen was a welcome relief from the chill outside. The smell of the evening meal lingered in the air. His mother had been baking bread. There were five loaves lined up on the counter. The delicious aroma was enough to make Caleb's stomach rumble. Three animal crackers didn't make for a substantial supper.

Ike looked at Joy. "Who have we here?"

Caleb braced himself. "This is my daughter, Joy."

"And where is your wife?"

He met his father's steely look without flinching. "I'm not married."

Ike's lips thinned with displeasure. He gathered himself and managed a smile for Joy. "Welcome to our home, Joy. I'm Ike Mast, your *daadi,* your grandfather."

She looked at Caleb and whispered, "Is he like Nana's Jake?"

"No, honey, he's your real grandfather. He's much nicer than Jake."

Caleb set her down. She gave Ike a tentative smile. "Your house smells good."

He chuckled. "I reckon it's your grandma's cooking that smells good. Are you hungry?"

She nodded. He tipped his head toward the large wooden table. "Have a seat and Maggie will fix you something to eat."

"You mean *Mammi,*" she corrected him as she climbed on a chair.

"*Ja,* your *mammi.* You know some of our speech. That is *goot.* Good."

"What is *ja?*"

"*Ja* means yes," Caleb explained.

"*Ja* is yes. Good is *goot.*" Joy nodded vigorously, making her straight blond hair swish across her face. She pressed it back with both hands.

Ike looked Caleb up and down. He nodded toward the table. "You look like you could use some of your mother's cooking. You're skin and bones."

The tension holding Caleb upright drained away, leaving him weak and shaken. To be invited to sit at the table with his father was more than he'd hoped for. He had to clear his throat of a lump the size of Texas before he could speak. *"Danki."*

Joy held out her hand. "Sit by me, Daddy."

Maggie was grinning widely. "He can't, child. This is the women's side of the table. He must sit across from us. I will sit by you as soon as I get some food on. Husband, would you like something?"

"A slice of your fresh bread with butter."

"*Kaffi,* too?"

"*Ja.*"

As his mother went to the counter and began cutting a loaf of bread, Caleb rounded the table and pulled out the chair on his father's right-hand side.

He had almost forgotten how fully Amish traditions permeated every aspect of life. His father sat at the head of the table, with his wife on his left. Sons sat on his right-hand side, from youngest to oldest down the table; daughters sat beside their mother in the same fashion. Caleb knew without a doubt that his chair had

been empty since he left home. An empty chair was a pointed reminder to everyone about who was missing.

"Bread and butter will be fine for me, too, *Mamm,* but no coffee."

"Lemonade, then?"

"Sure." She wouldn't be satisfied until she had made a special effort to please him. If he let her, she would cook a feast. It was late, but he knew that tomorrow mounds of food would be set in front of him. Cooking was his mother's way of showing her love.

She soon had thick slices of fresh baked bread slathered with peanut-butter spread for Joy, and butter for him and his father. She gave Ike his coffee and Joy a mug of milk, then she set two glasses of lemonade on the table. Still smiling, she took a seat beside Joy.

Her hand shook slightly as she tucked a strand of Joy's hair behind her ear. "I have wanted a granddaughter for a very long time. I am so happy that *Gott* brought you to us."

Joy gave her a beaming peanut-butter-smeared smile. "Daddy said you would like me. I like you, too. I had another *mammi.* I called her Nana. She went to heaven."

"I'm sorry to hear that. You must miss her. She is with *Gott* now, so we must be happy for her."

"Who is *Gott?*" Joy asked around a mouthful of bread.

"God," Caleb translated.

"Tomorrow, you can tell me all about her. It's getting late. It's time for a little one like you to be in bed," Maggie said.

"Can I sleep here?"

Maggie nodded. "I have a room upstairs that's just

for you. Finish your bread and your milk. I will show you the way."

Caleb rose from his place and headed for the door. "I'll get our suitcases."

Outside, he paused to watch his breath fog in the cold evening air. He missed the warmth of the Gulf breezes. He'd forgotten how hard the cold could bite his face and make his eyes water. How long would he have to stay? How soon would Joy adjust to life among the Amish? Would she adjust? Was he expecting too much? Even with Leah to help guide her, it was going to be a difficult transition.

Hunching against the cold, he hurried down the steps and gathered enough of their things to make it through the night. Tomorrow would be soon enough to unpack the rest.

He unplugged his cell phone from the car charger and put it in his pocket. His truck battery would be the only source of electricity for keeping his phone charged while he stayed on the farm. His parents wouldn't like the fact that he was bringing a phone into their home, but he needed it to maintain contact with his attorney.

Back in the house, he saw his mother had already taken Joy from the room. His father was sitting quietly at the table. A troubled frown marred his brow. "I'm afraid to ask because I think I know the answer, but I must hear it from you. Are you here to stay, *sohn?*"

"*Nee, Daed.* Only for a while."

"It breaks your mother's heart to see your place at the table empty."

"Perhaps having Joy here will ease some of her pain."

"Your child cannot heal what is broken in this family."

"I'm sorry. I couldn't stay."

"We have forgiven you. Rhonda has forgiven you. Wayne will forgive you in time."

"That would be nice if there was anything to forgive. I'm not the father of Rhonda's child. I don't know who is, but it isn't me."

"Why would Rhonda maintain such a lie?"

"I wish I knew. I wish that you believed me."

His father's frown deepened. "You come to my door with another child born out of wedlock and ask that I believe you are innocent?"

"I knew there'd be no point going through this again. Look, Joy needs a stable family life. She hasn't had that. I can't give it to her. I'm hoping you can. I know it's asking a lot, but will you consider raising her?"

His father was silent so long that Caleb started to think the whole trip had been for nothing.

"You think her life will be better, will be happier, with us but without you, her father?"

Leah had asked him the same thing. "I hope so."

"Where is the child's mother now?"

"I have no idea. She went out to smoke a cigarette and never came back. I turned the city upside down looking for her."

"Then you understand a little of what we felt when you left."

Facing the truth was hard. Caleb saw his actions in a different light now. "I admit I didn't go about leaving in the best way, but I felt it was my only option."

Ike banged his hand on the table. "Running away from a problem never fixes it."

"Some problems can't be fixed!" Caleb struggled to

control his temper. This was his father. Ike deserved respect.

"Can't I leave you two alone for ten minutes without an argument starting?" Caleb's mother asked from the doorway.

"It wasn't an argument," Ike said gruffly.

She gave him a sympathetic look. "We all need a good night's sleep. In the morning, things will look different."

No, they wouldn't, but Caleb didn't say that. Ike rose from the table and went through the door that led to their living room and their bedroom beyond.

Maggie came and stood in front of Caleb. "I am so pleased that you are here. I'm glad, too, that you have brought this child with you."

"I didn't know what else to do. I didn't come back to make trouble."

She laid a hand on his cheek. "All of life is made up of bits of happiness and bits of trouble. In between, there is prayer and hard work and if we are blessed, sometimes wondrous joy. This is the way of the world."

"All struggle and no reward," he said dryly.

"Our rewards come in God's own time. You need rest. I see how weary you are. I made up the bed in your old room. Joy is waiting for her nightclothes in the bedroom over the kitchen."

"Thanks." Without central heat, the room over the kitchen was always the warmest one on the second story. He picked up their bags and started toward the stairs.

"Caleb?"

He glanced over his shoulder, waiting for his mother to say more. She hesitated, then said, "Don't be too hard

on your father. He doesn't know how to bend without breaking. The two of you are more alike than you think."

He nodded. "I was wrong not to keep in touch. A card once a year wasn't enough, was it?"

Tears filled her eyes. "It wasn't enough, but it gave me joy every Christmas to know that you were all right and thinking of me."

"I'll do better in the future. I promise."

A frown creased her brow. "You will not be staying?"

He heard the pain in her voice, but she deserved the truth. "Only for a while."

Tears filled her eyes. She dabbed at them with the corner of her apron. The last thing Caleb wanted was to upset her. "I'm sorry. I came because I want the two of you to raise Joy. I know what I'm asking won't be easy. I will help financially, so you don't have to worry about that. I have a good job, but it takes me away from home a lot. I may even be leaving the country soon."

Maggie shook her head. "It is not about the money."

"I know that. Will you consider my request?"

"How long can you say?"

He noticed she hadn't given him an answer. She wouldn't. It would be his father's decision.

"Until I'm certain that this is the right move for Joy."

She came and cupped his face between her hands. "Then I will treasure every minute and pray you have a change of heart."

"That's not likely."

"*Ach,* but it is not impossible. *Gott* may yet answer my prayers."

Chapter Five

Early the following morning, Caleb dressed quickly in his room, having slept better than he had in years. There was something comforting about huddling under a mound of quilts in a chilly room. However, getting dressed in the cold was a good reminder of why he liked living in the South. He might need to invest in a couple pairs of long johns. Joy would need some for sure.

He checked on her and found her bed empty. He rushed downstairs in a panic. Thankfully, she was seated at the kitchen table, enjoying scrambled eggs, bacon, biscuits and fried potatoes. The aroma of his mother's cooking made his mouth water and his stomach rumble.

Mamm came in from the other room. "Ah, *goot,* you are up. I must go into town and get some fabric for Joy's new dresses. I'd best hurry if I'm to get there and back in time to fix your *daed* his lunch. There is a plate in the *offa* for you."

"That means oven," Joy said with a grin. She had a streak of his mother's homemade apple butter smeared on her cheek.

He winked at her. *"Mien meiya eems es in da offa."*

Her eyes widened. "You speak Pennsylvania Dutch?"

"Pretty *goot, ja?*"

"What did you say?" she demanded.

"I said, 'My morning meal is in the oven.'"

"That is…way cool."

He had finally impressed his eight-year-old daughter. The morning was looking up.

His mother moved to stand behind Joy. She stroked her hair with a look of tenderness in her eyes. "Finish your breakfast. Your *daed* can teach you many words while he shows you around the farm today."

"Okay." Joy started forking eggs in her mouth. It was the first time he'd seen his child relaxed in weeks. His mother and her comfort food had that effect on people. It was exactly what he wanted for Joy.

Caleb used a hot pad to pull his heaping plate from the oven. After he finished his breakfast, he made sure Joy was well bundled up in a new coat, snow boots and mittens they had purchased on their way north. Together, they set off along the same path he had used countless times when he walked to school. It felt familiar and strange. Joy ran in front of him, kicking up clouds of powdery fresh snow that had fallen in the night.

As they got deeper into the woods, she drew close to him and took his hand. "I don't think I like this place."

"You don't like the woods?" He tried to see their surroundings through the eyes of a child who had grown up in a run-down trailer park on the outskirts of Houston. The two places were worlds apart. Trees pressed in around them. The bare branches creaked and clacked in the cold breeze.

"I think something might get us," she whispered, her hesitant voice wobbled with fear.

"I walked through these woods every day from the time I was your age until I was grown. I never saw anything that could get me. Shall we check and see who else has walked along this path?"

"How can we do that?"

"Everyone who walked this way or crossed this path has left their signature in the snow. Turn around and look where we've walked. What do you see?"

She stopped and looked back. "I see our footprints."

"That's right. Now look in front of us. What do you see?"

She scanned the area. "I see funny marks in the snow."

"Let's take a closer look." He crouched beside the dots that crossed the path in front of them.

She imitated his position and propped her chin on her hand. He almost laughed at her serious expression but quickly controlled himself. It was important that she learn to be at home in the outdoors. "If you look closely, you'll see two tiny paw marks in the snow and two drag marks behind it."

She looked up at him. "Are they puppy tracks?"

"That's a good guess. Puppies have little feet, but this was made by someone who hops along."

Her eyes grew round. "A rabbit?"

"That's right."

She jumped up and rushed toward the edge of the path. "Can I see it?"

He caught her by the shoulder. "Whoa. We might see a rabbit later, but we can't follow him. We have to stick to the path."

"Why?"

"Because rushing into the woods without knowing your way around is how you get lost. You must never do that. Let's keep walking and see who else has shared our path."

She gazed longingly toward the rabbit tracks but allowed herself to be led away. After a few dozen yards, she pointed ahead of them. "I see more tracks, Daddy. Who made those?"

"Those were made by a big deer. Can you see how they are split in two and pointed?"

She ran ahead of him and stopped, pointing at her feet. "Who made these?"

"That's the footprints of a raccoon. See how the paw marks are like little handprints? Mr. Raccoon has hands a lot like you and I for gripping things. He has a face like a bandit with a black mask around his eyes and a short snout with sharp little teeth."

She took a step back and pulled her hands to her chin. "Does he bite?"

"He would bite you if you tried to pick him up. If you let him mind his business, he will let you mind yours and everyone will stay happy."

"Did you walk to school by yourself? Grandpa says I'll have to learn to walk to school by myself. When I'm grown up I can drive a buggy."

So his father was considering letting Joy live with them. "You won't have to go by yourself until you feel good about doing it. I didn't walk alone. I walked with my brother until he got too old for school."

"Uncle Wayne? I don't like him."

His first impulse was to say that he didn't like Wayne, either, but he held his tongue. He loved his

brother. He didn't like the way things had turned out between them. Joy was going to be living here. She would have to learn to get along with everyone in the family.

"Your uncle Wayne can seem gruff, but he is a good man. I think you will come to like him in time. His little boy is almost the same age as you."

They heard the sound of crashing in the underbrush. Joy threw her arms around his leg and held on tight. "What's that?"

They had their answer as a black-and-white dog bounded out of the woods and came loping toward them. Caleb's heart gave a glad leap when he thought it was Trixie, but he quickly saw he was mistaken. This dog shared similar markings but was taller and heavier with more brown on his legs.

"Duncan won't hurt you." They both turned as Leah walked up beside them.

Caleb hadn't forgotten that she and Rhonda used to take the same shortcut through the woods on their way to school. Had he subconsciously come this way in the hopes of meeting her? Maybe.

In any case, he was pleased to see her again. Very pleased.

"Leah!" Joy shouted and waved.

"Hello." She smiled brightly at his child.

The tug of attraction was strong, but it was foolish to dwell on it. He'd be leaving in a few weeks. Still, something about her made the morning brighter. If things had been different, if they had met in another time and another place, he would have followed the urge to know her better, but she wasn't for him.

To her, he was an outsider. The man who'd dishon-

ored and abandoned her sister. He should be thankful she had taken an interest in helping Joy.

"I'm so happy to see you." Joy ran to her and wrapped her arms around Leah's legs. Duncan joined the game and jumped up, too. The impact of the child and the big dog together knocked the teacher off balance. Caleb lunged forward to catch her.

Leah staggered into Caleb. His strong arms closed around her and kept her upright, saving her from a tumble in the snow.

She looked up and saw a slow smile curve his lips. Her heart skittered wildly for an instant before she remembered who was holding her. Struggling to regain her composure, she moved away from him.

"I wasn't expecting to see you this morning." Her voice sounded breathless. She stopped talking and pressed her lips together.

Caleb thrust his hands in his coat pockets. "Joy and I are exploring. So this is the proud papa." He bent to scratch Duncan behind one ear.

"He showed up outside my door today. I guess he knew something was up."

"Did he like Pickles?" Joy asked.

"*Ja.* He looked over the litter, and I think he liked Pickles a lot. Trixie normally walks with me to school in the mornings, but she's too busy with her puppies. Duncan occasionally joins us."

Joy was still hanging on to her leg. "Does he bite?"

"Never," Leah assured her in all seriousness. "Duncan, sit."

The dog promptly sat. "Now shake hands with Joy." He raised his paw. Joy let go of Leah's leg and tenta-

tively shook the dog's front paw. Duncan added a quick lick to Joy's fingers, making her squeal.

"Did you see that, Daddy? He kissed my hand."

"I saw. He's a very polite pooch."

"It was nice seeing you again, Joy. I must be going. The teacher can't be late to school. Come, Duncan." There was always plenty to be done before her students arrived.

"I thought I would show Joy the way to the school. Mind if we walk with you?" Caleb waited for her reply, watching her intently.

"Of course not." She had to be polite, didn't she?

"Duncan's owner must not live far away," Caleb said.

"He belongs to Carl King. He works for Joseph Shetler on his sheep farm just over the next hill."

"I remember Woolly Joe, but I don't remember a man named King."

"Carl is a newcomer. He has *Englisch* ways, but some people wonder if he isn't ex-Amish from another place. He and Woolly Joe keep to themselves. I think Duncan enjoys visiting the school for a dose of company."

Joy, more confident now, ran ahead a little ways with the dog dancing at her heels. The path was wide enough for a few hundred yards, but it narrowed, forcing Leah and Caleb closer together. The bare branches of the trees laced together overhead and gave Leah the feeling of being sheltered. Snow crunched under their boots. Occasional clumps of it fell from the trees and scattered in the breeze, leaving sparkling showers in their wake. It was a beautiful morning. Caleb walked close beside her in silence.

She glanced at him and wondered what he was thinking. His gaze was on Joy and the dog. A sweet smile

curved his lips. It would be good for both of them if he changed his mind and stayed, even if he didn't give up his *Englisch* ways. Could Leah help him see that?

Joy stopped and pointed to the ground. "I see more rabbit tracks."

He squatted beside her. "You're right. A rabbit went this way not long ago. Keep your eyes peeled for more tracks."

Joy patted Duncan's head and grinned at Leah. "Daddy is teaching me about animal tracks. This is a rabbit track, and I know a raccoon track and people tracks and now I know dog tracks. Duncan is making big tracks in the snow."

The dog had his nose down investigating the new trail. After a few seconds, he took off at a trot back the way they had come.

Joy frowned. "Where's he going?"

"Home, I reckon," Leah said.

Joy's frown turned into a pout. "I wish he would stay with me. I miss him."

Caleb lifted her chin so she would look at him. "He has work to do. If you ask Leah very nicely, she might let you visit Trixie and her puppies again after school one of these days."

Joy's beaming smile returned. "Could I? Please?"

"I'd like that," Leah replied and spared a sidelong glance at Caleb. He wasn't as she had imagined him all these years. He wasn't indifferent to his child or harsh. She had pictured him living in a perpetual *rumspringa,* doing all that was forbidden to the Amish, drinking, going to parties and movies and driving fast cars.

What had his life been like? And why did it matter? If only she could quell her curiosity about him. As they

kept walking, she tried, but it seemed that she couldn't give up the need to know more. She finally blurted out, "What kind of work do you do in Texas?"

He seemed surprised by her question. She was a little surprised herself at her boldness.

"I'm a roughneck. I work on oil rigs, mostly off-shore rigs. The pay is better."

"Out in the ocean?" Her secret dream had always been to travel. To see the mountains and the oceans, to view and admire God's handiwork beyond the hills and fields of her small community.

"Yes, out in the ocean or rather in the Gulf of Mexico."

"Was it wonderful? Was it frightening?"

"Mostly it was noisy, hard work for very long hours. At times, it could be too beautiful for words. Then again, during some bad storms, I only wanted to get my feet back on dry land."

"To look upon the ocean must be a wondrous thing." She couldn't help the longing that slipped into her tone.

"You should go."

She looked down. "I have no reason for such a journey."

"Travel isn't forbidden. Many Amish visit the seashore."

"I couldn't go alone, and I don't know of anyone who would go with me." Outside of her friend Levi Beachy, she hadn't spoken to anyone who wished to see more of the world the way she did. Levi had planned to move to an Amish settlement in Colorado, but then he had married her friend Sarah and they were both happy to remain in Hope Springs now.

"Don't some of the older couples around here travel to Florida for the winter? I've heard it's a popular destination for Amish snowbirds."

"Some do. Not many."

"If the chance comes up, you should go along."

"I teach school through the winter, so that won't work."

"I guess not, but you won't always be teaching."

"True. Someday I'll be too old to keep up with the children."

"The ocean will still be there for you."

She hadn't expected him to be understanding and sympathetic. Under other circumstances, he was the kind of man she could like.

Caleb was sorry when they arrived at the school. For a while, he had forgotten that he didn't belong here. Leah was responsible for that. He wanted to ask if she had found forgiveness in her heart for him, but he knew it didn't matter. He would leave again anyway.

She went ahead of him up the steps. He and Joy followed her into the school building. Immediately, the smells and the sight of the interior filled him with nostalgia. Nothing had changed in the years he'd been gone.

The floor was the same wide planking, scuffed but clean. Light poured in from the large windows along both sides of the single room. A blackboard covered two thirds of the front wall. Above it, student artwork was still displayed. The childish drawings were much the same, even if they had been done by different hands.

Squarely in the middle of the front sat a large stove. It could burn wood or coal, depending on how much

heat the building needed. Slightly off to one side was Leah's desk. Books and stacks of papers were arranged neatly on the shelves behind it. Old-fashioned wooden student desks were arranged in four rows, two on either side of a wide center aisle.

He could remember hiding behind the open lid of his desk near the back and sharing a laugh with his friends. The teacher would eventually come by and silence their conversation with a pointed look. Lidia Yoder had been a stern but fair teacher who had no trouble quelling the occasional rowdy student.

"What happened to Lidia Yoder? Is she still around?"

"She lives in a little house in Hope Springs. You should go see her."

"I might do that."

He tried to remember where Leah sat in the old days, but he couldn't recall. He hadn't had his eye on girls at that stage of his life. Mostly, he'd wanted to be out playing Duck, Duck, Goose, softball or sledding when the snow was deep enough.

Leah went straight to the stove and opened the fire-box door. It was the teacher's job to arrive early and get the stove going so the room would be warm by the time the children arrived. He said, "I'll bring in some coal for you."

"*Danki.* That would be nice. I'll get the kindling ready."

He picked up a large black metal bucket from the side of the stove. His daughter had gone to gaze at the blackboard. "Joy, why don't you come with me? I'll show you the coal shed."

She picked up a piece of chalk from the tray that ran the length of blackboard. "Can I draw instead?"

He glanced at Leah. She nodded. He said, "Sure. Just do what Leah tells you. I'll be back in a few minutes."

Suddenly, Joy spun around, a worried look on her face. "Promise you'll come back?"

His heart contracted painfully. That was exactly what her mother had done. Said she'd be back in a minute and then pulled her disappearing act. He crossed the room and dropped to one knee in front of Joy. He knew Leah was listening although she pretended to be busy with the stove. "Honey, I promise I won't ever leave without telling you where I'm going and when to expect me back. Okay?"

"Okay." She didn't sound convinced, but the panic was gone from her eyes.

"Good."

"You mean *goot*."

Grinning, he nodded. "*Ja, goot*. Can you draw me a picture of Pickles?"

"Okay. How do you say *dog* in Pennsylvania Dutch?"

"*Hund*." He stood and picked up his bucket.

"How do you say *cats?*"

He was already halfway to the door. "*Katz*."

"Daddy, that's the same."

"Many of our words are the same or very similar," Leah said. "In school, my students only speak English, while at home they speak Pennsylvania Dutch. While you are trying to learn our language, I am teaching my students your language."

"That's just weird." Joy turned back to the board and made a large oval.

Caleb paused in the open door. "She has a point. It is weird."

He ducked outside before Leah could reply, but he

caught a glimpse of her engaging grin before he closed the door.

Wouldn't it be nice if he could make her smile more often?

Chapter Six

"Why are we stopping, Daddy?"

Late on Sunday morning, Caleb parked his truck at the end of the lane leading to the Sutter farm. The three-hour service would be ending soon.

He hadn't wanted Joy to spend the entire time sitting on a hard bench and listening to preaching in a language she couldn't understand. Not yet. He wanted to expose her gradually to the things an Amish life would include. Bringing her late to the preaching was a step along that path, although he knew not everyone would approve.

"I'm stopping here because it wouldn't be polite to arrive at a church meeting in an *Englisch* vehicle."

"Why?"

"Because Amish people come to the church services on foot or in a buggy."

"Why?"

He sighed heavily and repeated the phrase he'd heard a hundred times during his childhood when he questioned why things were done. "Because that is the way it has always been."

"Okay."

Surprisingly, the answer was enough for her. It hadn't been for him. She pushed open the door on her side and stepped out. He reluctantly joined her. An Amish Sunday service was the last place he wanted to be. Maybe he should have let her come with his folks. He would have been home when she came back.

This time.

Thinking about the day he wouldn't be around when she came home made him squirm. He couldn't stay. His life wasn't here, but Joy's could be. He had to keep what was best for her at the forefront of his mind and not dwell on how much he was going to miss having her around. She appeared to be settling in well with his parents. Much better than he had expected. She hadn't pitched a fit or talked about her mother in days.

She held open her jacket and made an awkward twirl in front of him. "Do you like my dress, Daddy? It's the very first dress I ever owned. *Mammi* made my dress and my *kapp*." She patted the white head covering that marked her as Amish.

"*Mammi* made me two white *kapps* and two black ones."

"You look very Plain in it, honey."

She scowled and stared at the ground. "I know I'm not pretty like other girls."

His heart twisted with pain. She'd never been made to feel good about herself. He crouched in front of Joy and smoothed the creases from her white apron. "Looking Plain means you look very Amish. The blue color of your dress makes your eyes as bright as the sky."

"I'm still ugly."

He lifted Joy's chin with his finger. "Never think that. God made you pretty in a very special way. He

made you pretty from the inside out, not just on the outside like some girls."

She looked up with uncertainty in her eyes. "He did?"

"Yes, He did. Do you know what I see when I look at you? I see the prettiest girl in the whole world wearing a brand-new dress made by a grandmother who loves her."

Her frown vanished. "And a new *eahmal shatzli*."

It meant *long apron,* and it was part of a young Amish girl's traditional dress. "Someday, when you are grown-up enough, you will put off wearing your long apron and wear a matching cape and short apron like your grandmother."

It was a huge milestone in an Amish girl's life. Another one he wouldn't be around to see. The thought brought a funny ache to his chest.

Joy held her apron out and flapped it. "I don't have to take it off today, do I?"

He smiled. "No, not today. Today, you're going to your first Amish church service in your brand-new dress."

"I hear singing, Daddy."

"I hear it, too." The slow cadence of Amish voices rose and fell as each word was drawn out over several notes. There was no music, only voices raised in worship.

"I don't know that song. It sounds sad."

He knew it by heart. He'd sung it countless times while seated on hard wooden benches, eager to have the service end so he could get out and visit with his friends and get up a game of volleyball or horseshoes.

"No one expects you to know it, Joy. You will learn

that song in time, and many the other songs, too. Are you ready to go?"

"Yes. I mean, *ja*."

"*Ja* is *goot*."

She pressed her hands to her mouth and giggled. "You sound just like grandpa when you speak Amish, Daddy."

"Do I? I reckon that's not a bad thing." He deeply admired his father. If only the feeling could be mutual.

They walked up the dirt drive, taking care to avoid the slushy snow melting in the sunshine. When they reached the house, he stopped and looked down at Joy. "Amish men and women don't sit together at the preaching. You will have to go in and find your grandmother."

"Aren't you coming in?"

"No." He wouldn't be welcome. Wayne would have seen to that. In a way, he felt sorry for his brother. It couldn't be easy living with so much guilt and fear.

"What if I can't find Grandma?"

"You will, but if you don't see her, it's okay to ask where she is. You'll have to sit still and be quiet until the service is over, but then you can play with the other kids and there will be lots to eat."

"What if the other kids don't like me?"

"They will. But if you want, you can stay with your grandmother, okay?"

"I guess."

"Go on inside."

"You won't go away and leave me here, will you?"

She couldn't shake the fear of being left alone. Who could blame her? He pointed to a stump by the corral fence. "I'll be waiting right over there."

"Promise?"

"I promise."

She studied him for a long moment, trying to decide if he was telling the truth, then she nodded and walked up the steps and inside the house. He waited by the door, expecting her to come running back out, but she remained inside. It was a small victory for him and for her.

Half an hour later, the final hymn faded away and Caleb knew the service had ended. He waited out at the stump with his hands pushed deep in his coat pockets. It was sunny but still cold. He saw Joy come out with his mother. Joy darted across the yard toward him.

"I was good, Daddy. I sat real still, and I prayed for you because *Mammi* said I should."

If God listened to anyone, surely He would listen to this child. "Thank you. I'm glad you were good."

"Don't you mean *danki?*"

"I do. *Danki* for your prayers." Caleb lifted a hand to wave to his mother and let her know he would keep Joy with him. She nodded and went back inside to help prepare for the meal.

Caleb saw his brother come out with their father. He met their gazes before they both turned away without acknowledging him. It hurt to be ignored in front of others, but he steeled himself to endure it. He hadn't taken the vows of baptism, but his actions, so far outside of what was expected of an Amish person, made his presence unacceptable to many.

Joy was chattering about the funny man with a beard who spoke during church when Caleb caught sight of Leah as she came out with her sister. Rhonda saw him

and quickly averted her eyes. She pulled at Leah's arm, but Leah ignored her. In front of everyone, she crossed the yard toward him.

Leah knew what she was doing would set tongues wagging, but she didn't want Joy to see her father being ostracized by everyone in her new community. He'd made the effort to bring his daughter to church. Leah reluctantly admired his courage in doing so. If only he had found the courage to marry her sister instead of running away from his responsibilities all those years ago. All their lives would have been different.

And Joy wouldn't be among them.

The child ran to greet her. "Leah, I didn't see you inside."

She smiled at the child, so full of happiness today. "I was there. I saw how well behaved you were."

"Danki."

Leah let her smile fade as she looked at Caleb. "Good morning."

"You mean *guter mariye,*" Joy said with a bright smile. She was such a charming child. She seemed eager to learn all things Amish.

"Are you sure you know what you're doing?" Caleb stared past Leah. She knew all eyes were on them.

"I wanted to ask if you were able to get Joy's school records."

"I had my attorney fax them to the local public library, since I don't have access to a printer. I picked them up yesterday. They're in the truck. I left it parked at the end of the lane."

She hesitated. Walking off with him alone, even for a short trip, would put her in a tenuous position.

He seemed to sense her reluctance. He gestured toward the highway. "I'll go get them. Would you look after Joy until I get back?"

"Of course."

"Joy, mind Leah. Would you like to go home with me or ride home in the buggy with *Mammi* and *Daadi*?"

She squeezed her eyes shut. "The buggy!"

His gaze remained on Leah. "I wouldn't trust her to just anyone, but I've seen how well you can handle her. I'll be back in a few minutes. Do you want a box of *a-n-i-m-a-l c-r-a-c-k-e-r-s?* I have some in my pocket just in case."

"We'll be fine." He trusted her to look after Joy. The thought filled her with warmth. She watched him walk away with long, sure strides.

And why shouldn't he trust her? Looking after children was what she did. Other people's children—never her own. Because of him.

She accepted it as God's will, but sometimes she wondered why she was the one left without love in her life. She loved her students and they loved her, but it wasn't the same. That love couldn't hold her with tender arms or kiss away her fears in the darkness. She longed for the things marriage would bring—companionship, shared laughter, a sense of belonging to something important. But it wasn't to be.

Rhonda came up to stand at her side. "You shouldn't be talking to him."

"He isn't under the ban. We have no cause to shun him."

"How can you say that?"

Leah gave a tiny shake of her head and glanced toward Joy. This wasn't a conversation the child should

hear. Fortunately, Anna Imhoff came up to greet Joy. "Anna, why don't you take Joy and introduce her to some of the other children?"

As they walked away, Leah turned to her sister. "It happened a long time ago. Nothing can change it. Maybe it's time to forgive Caleb."

"I have forgiven him, but I'd rather you didn't talk to him."

"He wishes to enroll his daughter in our school."

"Is he staying in Hope Springs?" Panic flooded Rhonda's face.

"No. He knows the school board must agree to allow Joy to attend Walnut Valley. I told him what records we would need. I owe Caleb the same attention I owe any parent. Nothing more."

"I wish he would leave and be done with it. Is he eager to rid himself of his daughter?"

"I don't think he is eager to leave her." She sensed a conflict in him. Was it because he didn't want to leave his child or because he didn't want to leave her with his Amish family?

Rhonda huffed. "I see. You've taken one of your broken-winged fancies to him, haven't you?"

"I haven't taken a fancy to him. I have taken a fancy to his daughter. Joy can be a trial, but she has a big heart."

"She'll be better off without him."

"I think they belong together." Joy needed her father in her life. And maybe her father needed her more than he knew.

Maggie came out of the house. She stopped short and looked around with a worried frown. "Leah, did Caleb leave?"

"*Nee*. He will be back in a few minutes."

"Where is Joy?"

Leah pointed toward the barn. "She is playing with Anna and meeting the other children."

Maggie relaxed. "That's fine. I want her to make friends."

"Speaking of friends, that reminds me. Did Rhonda tell you I'm having a cookie-baking frolic at my house on Wednesday evening?"

"I forgot to mention it," Rhonda said quickly. She stared at her feet. "So much has happened."

Leah and Maggie shared a sympathetic glance. They knew Caleb's return had been hard on Rhonda. Leah tried to lighten the mood. "You're welcome to come, Maggie, and bring Joy, too. I'm sure she would enjoy that."

"I'm not sure, but thank you for the invitation. I'd better get back inside and help Nettie clear plates so the next group can eat. It was good of you to let Bishop Zook know the Chupp family is struggling. The community will make sure they have all they need until William is back on his feet."

"I noticed some bare cupboards when I visited them on a school matter. I did nothing special."

Maggie hesitated, glancing between Rhonda and Leah. "I must thank you, too, for being kind to Caleb and to Joy. You've made a good impression on the child."

"She is sweet."

"She truly is." Maggie went back inside.

Leah placed a hand on her sister's shoulder. "It's going to be okay."

"I don't see how. Maggie wants Caleb to stay. I can't

imagine facing him at every family gathering, every church or school function."

When Caleb came back into sight, Rhonda pressed her hand to her scarred cheek and hurried inside the house. Leah waited until he approached. He looked after her sister. "I'm sorry my being here upsets Rhonda."

"Do you blame her?"

"That is a loaded question I choose not to answer. Here are Joy's records." He handed over a manila envelope. "*Danki*. I must get back to the house."

He frowned slightly, as if he were aware of her discomfort and knew he was the reason for it. He shoved his hands deep in his coat pockets. "Will you be at the school-board meeting?"

"I'll be there."

"Until Thursday, then."

She watched him walk back down the lane, with his shoulders hunched against the cold and against the stares that followed him. He looked so alone.

Leah wasn't surprised when her sister came over that evening. Although they made a habit of visiting each other at least once a month, the closeness they once shared was missing. Leah knew part of that was her fault.

"Do you know what you are doing?" Rhonda demanded.

"Good evening, Rhonda. Won't you at least let me take your coat before you start scolding me?"

"I can't stay. Why are you befriending Caleb Mast?"

"We talked about this at church. I don't believe I have befriended him. He wants to enroll his daughter in our school. She has special needs. It's important that

I know what those are. I'm sure the school board will ask for my input on his request. I take my job seriously."

Rhonda paced the small kitchen. "I don't know why he had to come back."

Leah softened her tone. "He doesn't intend to stay long. He'll be gone and things will get back to normal, except Maggie and Ike will have another grandchild in school, and David will have a new cousin."

"I don't want David to have anything to do with Caleb or his *Englisch* daughter. Wayne won't tolerate it."

"I'm sorry he feels that way. Joy is a wonderful child who has led a very sad life. I think she can be happy here. I think she can learn our ways and become a productive member of our community. I hope he can see that. As a member of the school board, his acceptance of her is important."

"What if her father changes his mind and comes to take her away?"

"Is that what's wrong? Are you and Wayne afraid Caleb has come back to claim his son?"

"I wouldn't put it past him."

Leah drew her sister close. "He gave up any right to David when he denied him years ago. Wayne is David's father in every sense of the word."

"In every sense but one, and that is the most important."

"That is the least important part of being a father. Wayne loves David. He could not love him more if he tried."

"I know." Suddenly there were tears streaming down Rhonda's face. "But every time he sees my son he is reminded of my sin. I can tell by the way he looks at me.

He can barely touch me. He is so angry now that Caleb is back. I don't know what to do."

Leah led her weeping sister to the sofa and sat beside her. She had always suspected that things weren't good between Rhonda and Wayne, but her sister had never spelled it out so plainly. Nor had Leah asked.

Rhonda looked up with pain-filled eyes. "You hate me, too."

"Oh, Rhonda, I don't hate you."

"I ruined everything for you."

"You did what you thought was best for you and your child."

"We don't talk like we used to. Remember when we were girls, we would huddle together under the quilts at home and talk about the boys we liked and the kind of lives we wanted to live? We used to laugh so much. We never laugh anymore."

Leah had been deeply hurt when Wayne broke their engagement to marry Rhonda. As the youngest child, Rhonda had always seemed to end up with the best of everything. She had been the prettiest girl in Hope Springs. Everyone said so. She was smarter, more popular, more outgoing—she was everything that Leah wasn't.

Rhonda could have told Wayne no. She could've gone to stay with their childless cousin in Indiana. The couple would have welcomed her and raised her baby as their own. It seemed to Leah that Rhonda was intent on spoiling her life, too, since she had ruined her own.

Leah had let her bitterness simmer, and it had tainted her relationship with her sister. It wasn't right.

"I remember how it was. We used to laugh all the time. You must come and stay with me for a few days.

Wayne and David can manage without you. Who knows, Wayne may realize how much he misses you, for I believe he loves you, even if he has trouble showing it."

Rhonda pressed a hand to her scarred cheek. "If only I wasn't so ugly."

"You are not ugly, and you must never say so again. That is prideful and vain. We are all as God has made us, and we must accept that, flaws and all. True beauty shines from the heart, not from our faces."

"I try to accept it as God's will. You would think by now it wouldn't cross my mind, but I can't help how I feel."

Leah hesitated and chose her next words carefully. "Acceptance follows forgiveness. Have you forgiven Caleb for the accident that injured you?"

"Of course I have," she said quickly. Too quickly. There was no sincerity in her voice. "I just wish he would leave. It was better when he wasn't around." She started crying again. Leah held her tight and let her weep out her unhappiness.

The inability to find forgiveness was a trait both sisters shared. Leah thought about Caleb and Joy and about his struggle to do what was right for the child. He wasn't a cruel or careless man. Perhaps he hadn't been cruel and careless in the past. Maybe he had only been a frightened boy who couldn't face a man's responsibilities.

No matter what he had done or why, the Savior had died on the cross for his sins. Who was she to say it wasn't enough?

Caleb was at home when his parents returned with Joy late in the evening. He walked out to meet them.

Joy climbed out of the buggy. "I have a new friend, Daddy. Her name is Anna."

"That's good. Did you meet lots of new kids?"

"They didn't make fun of me, not even once."

"And why should they?" Ike asked as he helped Maggie out of the buggy.

"'Cause I'm not smart. I'm not good at games, and lots of times the kids call me stupid and other bad names."

The memory of such times took the light from his daughter's eyes. Caleb exchanged a speaking glance with his father. Maybe now he would understand why he had brought her here.

Ike pulled a large basket with handles from the backseat. "There will be no name-calling from the children in our church. If this should happen, you must tell me at once so that I can speak to their parents. Now, take this inside and help your grandmother put our lunch things away.

Joy took the basket. It was almost bigger than she could manage. She hefted it higher and followed Maggie into the house.

Caleb took hold of the horse's bridle. "I'll put Bobby away."

To Caleb's surprise, his father didn't go inside. Instead, he stood by and watched as Caleb unhitched the black gelding. As he led the horse to his stall, his father followed and stood outside the pen. Once Caleb had unbuckled the bellyband and the collar, he lifted the harness off Bobby and set it on the boards.

Ike took it and hung it on the pegs made to hold it. "Your daughter seems to like it here. The place she came from, it sounds like she was unhappy there."

Caleb picked up a brush and began to rub down the horse. "I don't think Joy has met with much kindness in her life. Handicapped children are not always welcomed in the *Englisch* world. Some see them as a burden."

Ike stopped working and stared at Caleb. "And how do you see her?"

Chapter Seven

Caleb stopped brushing and looked over the animal's back at his father. "You mean do I see Joy as a burden?"

Ike began to wipe down the harness pieces with an oiled rag. "You bring her to us and say you intend to leave. What are we to think?"

"I'm sure it looks like I'm trying to get rid of her. I don't know. Maybe that is what I'm doing. I wasn't prepared to have a child, let alone one with Joy's special needs. I tried to manage, but the harder I tried the more difficult she became. She hid from me. She ran away. She kept trying to go back to where her grandmother lived because she thought her mother would come find her there. I lived in constant fear that she would disappear and I wouldn't be able to find her."

"This fear I know well. I have lived with it for many years."

Shame welled up in Caleb. "I have done some things that I'm not proud of in my life, but what I did to you and mother was cruel. I'm truly sorry. I hope you can forgive me."

"We forgave you long ago."

"*Danki,* Father. If Joy can't stay here with you, I don't know what I will do."

"Our ways are the best ways. *For us.*" He patted his chest for emphasis. "They are not best for everyone. You have chosen an *Englisch* life. This I cannot like, but I know a man must find his own way. Until you are certain why you brought Joy to us, I cannot say that she may stay."

"You want to send her back into a world that is cruel and unjust to her?"

"It breaks my heart to say this, for she is flesh of my flesh, my own granddaughter, but you are her father. She belongs with you."

"You sound like Leah. I can't give Joy what she needs. She needs stability, a sense of belonging, a place where she can feel safe."

"What she needs, what all children need, is love. If you give her that, all else will follow."

Caleb started brushing Bobby again. "It's not always that simple."

"Which commandment did Jesus say was the first of all?"

"*Mark* 12:28–31. 'The first of all the commandments is, Hear, O Israel; The Lord our God is one Lord: And thou shalt love the Lord thy God with all thy heart, and with all thy soul, and with all thy mind, and with all thy strength: this is the first commandment. And the second is like, namely this, Thou shalt love thy neighbor as thyself. There is none other commandment greater than these.'"

Ike smiled. "You have not forgotten all I have taught you."

"No, not all."

Ike grew solemn again. "Your brother doesn't think I should allow you to stay here. He says you are unrepentant for the shame you brought on our family. Others in the church will agree with him."

"Good old Wayne. Always the upstanding one. The one that never got into trouble." He wasn't proud of the bitterness that seeped into his tone. Leah had said not everyone had a forgiving nature. Like her, it was something he needed to work on.

Strange how often his thoughts turned to her and how much weight he gave to her words.

"You once looked at your brother with admiration and love, and he looked at you the same way. What came between the two of you?"

Caleb began putting away the grooming gear. "You know the story."

"I know what you both have told me. What haven't you told me?"

Caleb struggled with how to answer his father's question. The barn was quiet; only the rustling of the animals in the nearby stalls broke the stillness. As much as he wanted to clear his name and mend his relationship with his father, he couldn't do it. It wasn't his secret to share. He had given his promise to Wayne and he wouldn't go back on it.

"I wish I could tell you, *Daed,* but it's between Wayne and me. Can you accept that?"

"It seems that I must," Ike replied wearily.

"Do you want me to take my daughter and leave? I will. I don't want to cause trouble for you."

"What child doesn't cause a father trouble? *Nee,* you may stay awhile longer. Your mother hopes you will stay until Christmas, at least."

"I won't leave before then unless you ask me to."

"*Goot.* That will make your mother happy."

The two walked back to the house side by side. Ike stopped and looked up. "It will snow soon."

Caleb saw only clear blue sky. "Are your bones telling you that?"

"*Nee,* I heard the forecast on the radio at the feed store yesterday."

Chuckling, Caleb shook his head. "I've forgotten how much of the outside world actually seeps into this community."

"As long as we do not seek the things of the outside world for ourselves but keep *Gott* at the front of our lives, there is little harm in listening to the radio once in a while."

"Especially when the Cleveland Indians are playing. How did they do this year?" His father, like a lot of Amish, loved baseball and followed local as well as national teams in the newspaper.

"Not as well as some, but there is always next year. Hope Springs had a *wunderbaar* girls' softball team this year. Those Miller twins can sure hit a ball. They went all the way to the state championships, but they didn't win. Reminded me of the time you and Wayne played for that team over by Berlin. You boys were *goot.* You made it to the state tournament, too."

"And we didn't win, either, but we had a great pitcher. Roman Weaver should have gone on to play pro ball. Is he still working with his *daed* at the sawmill?"

"*Nee,* Roman's arm was crushed when a car hit his buggy. He is slowly getting better, but he has taken over his uncle's printing business."

By this time, they had reached the house. Caleb held

the door open for his father to go in. His mother was already at the stove getting started on supper. Joy knelt on a chair in front of the sink, washing the dishes they had brought home from lunch. She grinned at him. "Look, *Daed,* I'm helping."

"So you are." He'd never seen anyone so excited to be washing plates.

"Nana never let me wash dishes 'cause Jake said I was too clumsy. I only dropped one glass and broke it so far. *Mammi* didn't even get mad. She broke one, too."

"Did she?" Ike looked to his wife for an explanation.

Maggie shrugged. "I told her it could happen to anyone and not to fret. Then it happened to me. We are keeping score. The one with the fewest broken dishes at the end of the year wins."

Ike huffed. "I reckon I'll be buying new plates before spring."

Maggie grinned. "A new set for Christmas would be nice. These are old and chipped. What were you two talking about?"

She was still hopeful that Caleb would change his mind and stay. He read it in her eyes.

Ike gave a slight shake of his head. She turned back to the stove, but her shoulders drooped ever so slightly.

"I was telling Caleb about Roman Weaver's accident."

Maggie stirred a pot of stew. "He sure surprised us all when he married Joann Yoder last month. I thought she would stay a spinster forever. Would you like some *kaffi,* Ike?"

He shook his head. "Maybe later. I think I'll read the Good Book for a while."

Joy slid off her chair. "I'm finished."

Ike looked over her work. "You've done a fine job. Would you like me to read you a story from the Bible?"

"I guess, since there isn't any TV."

Caleb slapped his palm over his mouth to keep from laughing out loud. His father scowled at him but extended his hand to Joy. "I will read you a story about a great flood and how *Gott* saved Noah and all the animals."

As his father and Joy left the kitchen, Caleb said, "I'll take a cup of coffee if you have it ready."

"Help yourself."

He fetched a mug from the cupboard and filled it from the pot simmering on the back of the stove. "Speaking of spinsters, I'm amazed that Leah never married."

He wasn't sure he should broach the subject, but his mother was in a position to know Leah pretty well.

"It wasn't from a lack of suitors. There were plenty of young fellows who wanted to walk out with her, but she never took to anyone after..."

"After Wayne married Rhonda."

"Ja."

"She must have loved him a lot." Was it any wonder she hadn't forgiven Caleb for his part in wrecking her dreams of a home and a family of her own?

His mother turned to him. "All things happen for a reason, Caleb."

"I can't imagine the reason for so many messed-up lives." All because of him.

"Nor could I, but look into the other room. What do you see?"

He glanced over and saw his father in his favorite chair with Joy parked on his knee, listening intently as

he read to her. "I see a little girl who is opening up, becoming the happy child I knew she could be."

"*Ja. Gott* sends such special children to a family for a special reason. He sent her to you. He has a reason. I, for one, am very, very grateful for His gift. You should be, too. Now, I must get some plums from the cellar. Your father loves to have plums for dessert on Sunday night." She opened the door at the back of the kitchen and took a lamp with her as she went downstairs.

Caleb sipped his coffee as he listened to the story his father was reading. He hadn't thought of Joy as a gift. He'd only seen the problems she presented. He was guilty of seeing her disability and not her abilities as surly as the people who'd made him angry when they looked away from her or called her retarded.

No more. From now on, he would focus on the positive things his daughter brought to him.

Coming here was meant to benefit Joy. It turned out that he was also reaping the benefits of his parents' wisdom and faith. He had let an important part of himself wither away when he shut God out of his life.

A special child given for a special reason. Maybe his mother was right. Without Joy, he might never have come back to his family and to God.

He took his coffee into the living room and sat on the sofa next to his father and Joy. He listened to his father read the Bible and watched a whole new world open up for his child.

"I want to see the puppies. Pickles is missing me, I know she is. You don't want her to be unhappy, do you?"

Joy had been bugging Caleb for the past three days to visit Leah. He was running out of excuses. They were

sitting on the back step, shelling black walnuts for his mother. She intended to bake black walnut cookies for an upcoming cookie exchange. The snow that had fallen on Sunday night was melting in the bright sunshine. His mother was doing her laundry at the propane-powered wringer washer on the back porch.

He cracked another shell and handed it to Joy to pick out the nut meat. "Honey, Leah may not be home."

"Call her and see."

"I can't call her. She doesn't have a phone. The Amish don't use telephones in their homes."

"That's just silly."

"It may seem silly to you, but it is not silly to Leah, or to grandpa and grandma. You can write her a letter and ask if you may come visit Pickles. In a few days you will have your answer."

"But I don't want to wait a few days. I want to see Pickles today."

"Not today. I'm sorry. I will help you write your letter." He was learning to be firm with her. She hadn't had a meltdown since the one when they arrived in Hope Springs, but he knew it wouldn't take much to trigger another.

His mother came through the screen door with a basket of laundry in her arms. "Why the long face on such a beautiful day, Joy?"

"Daddy says I can't go see my puppy, and I'm sad."

Maggie looked to Caleb for an explanation. "Leah showed Joy her puppies the first day we came to town. She allowed Joy to name one. Since then, this kid has been bugging me to take her back to see them again."

"There's no reason you can't go visit Leah this evening."

A rush of eagerness filled Caleb at the thought of seeing Leah again. He was being foolish, but he couldn't help it. There was something special about her. It was more than the way she treated Joy. It was something he couldn't define. Simply being in her company made him happy. Did she feel the same way? Would she miss him when he was gone?

"Joy, can you help me hang the clothes on the line so they will dry?" his mother asked.

"Sure, but why don't you just put them in the dryer?"

Caleb put aside his hammer and followed them to the clothesline. Maggie set her basket down and raised her hands to the sky. "This is my clothes dryer. The good Lord has given me sunshine today. My clothes will be dry enough in no time. Didn't your Nana have a clothesline?"

"We took our things to the Laundromat."

"I think you will see that this way is better. The clothes will smell so nice and fresh. Can you help me pin these pants to the line?"

Joy stretched her arms above her head. "I can't reach it."

Caleb wrapped his arms around her waist and lifted her to the proper height. "Now can you get it?"

Joy giggled. "I'm as tall as you are."

"And almost as heavy. Get to pinning."

His arms were starting to ache by the time they were finished, but seeing his mother and his daughter working happily together was worth the discomfort.

When he put Joy's feet on the ground, she clapped her hands together and bounced up and down. "Can we go see the puppies now? Can we?"

His mother shook her head. "School doesn't let out

until three-thirty. Then we must give Leah time to get home. You should go at four o'clock. I have another basket to hang. Don't run off."

As his mother went back up to the porch, Joy turned to him. "What time is it now, Daddy?"

"It's not time to go yet."

"Will you tell me as soon as it's time?"

"I will."

"Promise?"

"I promise. Do you believe me?"

She looked at him intently, then gave him a great big grin. "*Ja!* You always keep your promises."

"That's right, I do." No matter how painful it was to do so.

He shook off the thought. "Here comes your *gross-mammi* with another load. Let's help her hang up the clothes." He picked up Joy again.

"Someday I'm going to be big enough to do this by myself," she declared, struggling to place a clothespin on one end of the sheet his mother hung over the line.

Someday she would be, and he wouldn't be around to see it. The thought was a sobering one. He wanted to see her grow up. He wanted some part in who she became.

So, why couldn't he come back to visit? Now that he had faced his parents and gotten over that hump, was there really a reason he couldn't? Just because he couldn't live Amish didn't mean he had to cut himself off from Joy completely. Would his parents agree to his visits? He was sure his mother would.

Cheered by the idea, he started thinking about annual or semiannual trips home. He'd write and let his folks know he was coming so Wayne and Rhonda could

avoid seeing him if that was how they wanted it. Perhaps in time, that rift could be mended, too.

He wanted to see Joy grow up. He wanted to be a part of her life, even if it was a small part. Until now, he'd only focused on the crisis in front of him. He'd been unable to look ahead. Now that he could, coming back for visits was a great idea.

He would tell Leah of his decision tonight. What would she think of it?

Trixie's barking alerted Leah and her friends Rebecca, Sarah and Joann to more visitors. Leah was surprised to see Caleb and Joy on her front porch when she opened the door. *"Gutenowed."*

Caleb looked ill at ease. "Good evening. I see by the buggies out here that you have company. I hope we're not imposing."

"I want to see Pickles. Can I, please?" Joy bounced beside him.

"Joy has been bugging me to let her visit the puppies again. My mother thought it would be all right if we came after you got home from school tonight."

Leah had mentioned tonight's baking frolic to Maggie and Rhonda at church. Maggie must have sent Caleb today because she knew Leah would have company. It eased the awkwardness of allowing Caleb into her home. Bless Maggie for being so considerate, but why hadn't she brought Joy?

Joy folded her hands together. "Please, can I see Pickles? I know she's missed me."

Grinning at the girl's excitement, Leah nodded. "I think she *has* been missing you. Come in."

Caleb, his shoulders hunched against the cold, said, "I can wait out here."

An outsider coming to visit a *maedel* who lived alone could be cause for talk. He was being protective of her reputation. That surprised her. It was odd how many things about Caleb Mast had surprised her in the past few days.

"You may come in. I'm sure you will remember most of my friends." She stood aside as he entered. He stopped only a few feet past the doorway as he took in the women seated around her kitchen table. Joy, when she realized there were more people in the room, became shy and hid behind her father.

Leah made the introductions. "Caleb, this is Joann Yoder, now Joann Weaver."

"I remember you from school."

"It is *goot* to see you again." Joann gave him a welcoming smile.

"Joann married Roman Weaver a few weeks ago."

"Congratulations. I heard about Roman's accident. I hope he makes a full recovery. Tell him I said hello."

"I will."

"Next is Sarah Beachy. She is married to Levi Beachy. I don't believe you have met Rebecca Troyer. She moved to Hope Springs a few years ago from Berlin. Her husband is Gideon Troyer, a cousin of Adam Troyer. This is Caleb Mast. He is Maggie's youngest."

He nodded to each of them in turn. "I'm sorry to crash your party."

He gently coaxed Joy forward. "This is my daughter, Joy. She is the one on a mission."

"'Cause I've been missing Pickles and she has been missing me," Joy declared.

Leah grinned at her friends. "Joy was here the day the puppies were born. She named the blond one."

"Pickles is a marvelous name," Joann said.

"Are you going to name the others?" Rebecca asked.

"Yup. They are Peanut Butter and Jelly."

Sarah was trying hard not to laugh. "Pickles, Peanut Butter and Jelly. I'd say those are some unusual but tasty names for puppies."

"If there had been a fourth one, you could have called it Church Spread," Joann added in all seriousness.

"What's that?" Joy asked, looking up at her dad.

Caleb smiled at her. "Church spread is peanut butter mixed with marshmallow cream."

"I had that Sunday. It was yummy." Joy closed her eyes, grinned big and rubbed her tummy, her shyness forgotten.

"My grandfather loved to eat his church spread with dill pickles. I don't have church spread, but I do have oatmeal raisin cookies. Would you like some?" Leah picked up a plate from the counter and held it out to Joy.

Joy glanced up at her father. He nodded. She quickly took two and rushed to the corner where Trixie lay with her pups.

Leah was left standing beside Caleb. She realized her friends were all watching her closely. She held the plate toward him and tried for a casual tone. Anything to hide the fact that her heart was racing as it always did when he was near. "We are getting ready for a cookie exchange at Rebecca's home on Friday. Would you like to sample some?"

"Oatmeal raisin is my favorite. How did you know?" He winked at her friends, as if she had made the cookies just for him.

Her smile turned chilly. "Your brother told me."

That took the grin off Caleb's face.

Instantly, she was sorry. No one at the table knew the full story about Leah's broken engagement. They only knew that Wayne and Rhonda had had a hurry-up wedding. They certainly weren't the first young couple to have a babe arrive early. Only Sarah knew Leah had been serious about Wayne. It was never mentioned after the wedding took place. As upsetting as it was at the time, Leah realized now that she hadn't truly been in love with Wayne. She had been in love with the idea of marriage and starting a family of her own.

Would she have grown to love Wayne the way a wife should? She honestly didn't know.

She set the plate aside and joined Joy where she knelt by the puppies. "Would you like to hold Pickles?"

"Yes, please. Daddy said I wasn't to bug you about it. I was just to look at her."

"Then you have done very well to obey him." Leah lifted the pup from the blanket.

Joy took the puppy from Leah. "Has their daddy been here?"

"*Nee,* he has not come by again," Leah admitted.

"But it's almost Christmas. Pickles wants to see her daddy for Christmas."

Caleb said, "She has her mother and that's all she needs right now."

"No, she wants them both. See how unhappy she is. It's all right, Pickles." Joy hugged the puppy to console her.

Leah met Caleb's gaze. What was sad was the way Joy gave the puppy her own wants and needs.

Joann joined them. "May I hold a puppy?"

"Of course." Leah handed her friend the largest male.

"What do you think, Joy? Is this Peanut Butter, or is this Jelly?" Joann asked with a grin.

Joy gave the question careful consideration as she held Pickles next to her cheek. "I think that one is Peanut Butter. He has brown feet."

"Have you come home for a Christmas visit?" Rebecca asked Caleb.

"Something like that."

"Then you must bring Joy to our cookie exchange. I know she will enjoy it. There will be many children her age there. My husband would be delighted to meet you. He was out in the *Englisch* world for years before returning to us. He enjoys talking about cars and airplanes and all the things that he used to know."

Caleb shot a quick glance at Leah and then looked down at his boots. "Thank you for the invitation, but I'm not sure I can make it."

Sarah said, "We hope you can. We won't even require you to bring a pail of cookies, for I'm sure your mother will bring plenty. There will be more than enough for everyone. Leah, I think your last batch should be about done."

Leah glanced at the clock and hurried to her oven. The cookies were a little browner than she liked but thankfully not burned. She set the baking sheet on top of the stove and began removing the cookies. Caleb went to crouch beside Joy and admire the puppies. "They are getting bigger already."

Leah watched their interaction. It would be a good idea for Joy to interact with the other children on a fun occasion. Caleb would be reluctant to come if his brother and Rhonda were there. Maggie could bring the

child, of course, but Leah found herself wishing that Caleb would come, too. The more he became involved in the community, the greater the chance was that he would change his mind and stay.

She transferred the last cookie and set the sheet aside to cool while she spooned more dough onto a second sheet. "Joann, have we heard who all is coming to the exchange?"

Joann's work at the paper left her privy to all the local goings-on. "I don't think there will be as many families there as last year. We're having it a week earlier, and it turns out Esther Zook is hosting a quilting frolic for her niece on the same night."

Sarah moved to snitch a warm cookie from Leah's plate. "That means Grace and Henry Zook won't be there, but Levi and the twins are coming. What about Rhonda and Wayne?"

Leah resisted the urge to see if Caleb was listening. She bent and put a new tray of unbaked cookies in the oven. "Rhonda will go to the quilting bee. She mentioned that Wayne plans to visit with Bishop Zook about a church issue, so they won't be at the cookie exchange."

Joann replaced the puppy she was holding and returned to the table. "If our turnout is small, we can hold another one closer to Christmas."

Sarah said, "We should hold one when the twins are away visiting their grandmother. Then everyone can be assured that they will get home with cookies and not empty pails."

The women laughed. The twins, Moses and Atlee, were notorious pranksters.

Caleb stood and said, "Joy, it's time for the puppy to go back with her mother."

She replaced the puppy and gave Trixie a pat on the head. "Your baby likes me, but she needs you more. You are a good mommy."

"That's right," he said and took her hand.

Leah turned away from the stove with a dozen cookies wrapped in a blue-and-white-checkered napkin. She handed them to Joy. "A few for the road."

"Yum." Joy gleefully grabbed the offering.

"What do you say?" Caleb prompted.

"Thanks. I mean, *danki*."

Leah propped her hands on her hips. "Your *Deitsh* is getting better all the time."

"*Mammi* is helping me. Can I have a cookie now, *Daed?*"

"When we are in the buggy. Leah, will you walk us out?"

She hesitated and glanced at her friends, but they were busy looking through her recipe book for a new sugar cookie. She followed Caleb outside. He opened the door of the buggy for Joy and she hopped in. He said, "Now you can have one."

"Two?"

"One."

"Okay."

Leah grinned at Joy's dejected tone. Caleb turned to face her. "You don't have to do that."

"Do what?" she asked, even though she knew what he meant.

"You don't have to put yourself between my brother and me."

"I have no idea what you're talking about." She didn't want him thinking she had his interest at heart. Maybe

she did, but she wasn't ready to admit it. Certainly not to him.

"You wanted me to know Wayne wasn't coming to the cookie exchange so that I could come. I don't want you to feel you have to take sides."

"I'm not."

"Then I'm glad you invited me. I'll be there." His voice grew warm and her pulse sped up.

She clenched her hands together to hide her growing jitters. "Joy will enjoy it."

"I will, too, if you are going to be there."

She stared at him in speechless shock.

He seemed to realize he'd gone too far. "Thanks again for being kind to Joy and including her. It helps knowing she will have a friend in you when I'm gone."

She gathered her scattered thoughts. "I wish you would reconsider that decision."

"Do you?"

He took a step closer. She didn't back away. His gaze softened. "Do you really want me to stay, Leah?"

Chapter Eight

Caleb's low, husky voice caused Leah's breath to catch in her throat. His nearness sent her pulse racing. Thick tension filled the air. His eyes held an emotion she didn't understand, but it pulled at her, making her want to move closer to him.

She had an overwhelming desire to lay her hand upon his cheek and study him until the riddle was solved. What would his skin feel like? She could imagine the rough texture of his whiskers, the heat that would warm her palm and spread through her body.

His lips were slightly parted as he gazed at her. When he kissed, would they be soft and inviting or hard and demanding? If she moved a step closer, would she discover the answer?

The boldness of her thoughts shocked her. She came to her senses and looked away to break the attraction growing between them. "I'm only thinking of Joy. She needs you to stay."

He moved back a pace. She sensed his disappointment. "Fair enough. Don't let your cookies burn."

He climbed into his father's buggy and gathered the

reins. She took a step toward him, wanting him to stay longer, but she didn't know what to say.

Why did he confuse her this way? She was a level-headed person. She never flustered easily. So why was she flustered now?

He gave her a wry smile, as if he understood something she didn't. He clicked his tongue to set the horse in motion and drove away. She stood staring after him until the cold made her shiver.

She returned to the house to find her friends watching her with wide eyes. No one said anything. Finally, she asked, "What?"

"Caleb Mast has grown into a *gutguckich* fellow." Joann went back to studying the recipe book.

"A very good-looking man, indeed," Sarah agreed. "I liked him and his darling daughter."

"Do you think he means to stay among us?" Rebecca asked.

"I don't think so." Leah closed the door. She didn't feel right sharing Caleb's plans with her friends. They might not look so kindly upon him if they knew he intended to leave Joy with his parents and go back to his *Englisch* life.

Although why she should wish to protect him was a mystery to her. One she didn't care to examine too closely. Not with so many prying eyes watching her.

Rebecca smiled softly. "My Gideon did not know he wished to return to us until he came for my quilt auction."

Two years ago, the community had come together and held a quilt auction to raise money for a surgery that would restore Rebecca's sight. Gideon learned of his lost love's plight and returned to help. Leah was

happy to stop talking about Caleb. "You mean Gideon didn't know he wanted to return until he saw *you* at the quilt auction."

Rebecca shrugged. "If I was the tool used to nudge Gideon back to God, I'm happy I was part of His plan. God moves in mysterious ways, you know. We all have a part in His wondrous design though we may never know what that is."

Leah went to the stove, picked up her hot pad and opened the oven to check on her cookies. They needed another minute or two. She closed the door and put the hot pad aside. Was she part of some plan to help Caleb return to their community? It was hard to imagine a more unlikely scenario.

"Let's try this recipe for macaroons." Joann stabbed the page she was studying.

"Do we have all the ingredients it calls for?" Sarah leaned over to read it.

Joann looked at Rebecca. "I think I put a can of sweetened condensed milk in with the things I brought. Would you check and see if it's in that box on the counter?"

Rebecca came to stand beside Leah. She glanced into the box and said, "Yes, we have some."

Leah looked down at the oven. "They aren't ready yet."

"I guessed as much." Rebecca lowered her voice. "When I was blind, I spent a lot of time listening to people and reading what they thought in the tone of their voices. Now that God has seen fit to restore my sight, I spend a lot of time watching people."

"And?" Leah shifted uncomfortably.

"I see and hear something between Caleb Mast and you."

"You are mistaken." Leah opened the oven door again. The cookies still weren't ready. She closed the door with a bang.

"If you say so, I must accept that. Just remember that lying is a sin."

Leah yanked open the oven door and pulled out the cookie sheet anyway. "He's not one of us. He turned his back on his family and cast aside his faith. How could I have any feelings for a man like that except pity?"

The hot tray of cookies slipped sideways and she burned her fingers when she tried to save it. The pan clattered to the floor, sending cookies tumbling across her kitchen. Dropping the sheet, she brought her stinging finger to her mouth.

Her friends rushed to help. Sarah and Joann cleaned up while Rebecca pulled Leah to the sink and ran cold water over her hand.

The pain was just punishment for her lie. It wasn't pity that made her heart race when Caleb was near.

What was wrong with her?

Caleb slapped the reins against the horse's rump to speed him up. No matter how fast Bobby trotted, he couldn't outrun Caleb's humiliation. He had made a fool of himself. There was no way around it.

Had he really expected Leah to say what he wanted to hear? That she wished he would stay for her?

Of all the women in the world, why did it have to be Leah Belier who turned him inside out? When he was close to her, his brain shut off and his emotions took

over. She made him feel breathless, like a love-struck kid with his first crush.

Caring about her wasn't the problem. The consequences of pursuing her would be disastrous. For both of them. He had to get himself in hand. There couldn't be anything between them. She would never leave the Amish, and he couldn't stay.

Besides, Leah wasn't interested in him. Her interest was in Joy, not in Joy's wayward father.

"Do you want a cookie?" His daughter held the napkin toward him.

"Thanks." He selected one and took a bite. It was delicious. Of course Leah had to be a good cook, too. Good with kids, good with dogs, the only thing she wouldn't be good with was having Caleb Mast as a suitor.

He sat up straight. *Suitor* was a strong word. Was he really contemplating a relationship with her? He had to be out of his mind.

Joy sighed heavily. He glanced her way. "What's the matter, kiddo?"

"I'm tired. Why can't we drive places in the truck? We could be home by now."

"I thought you liked riding in the buggy. I'm using it out of respect for my parents. They believe that cars are worldly things. While we are staying with them, it's only polite to honor what they believe, even if I don't think that way myself."

"Are we going home to Texas soon? Mama might come see me for Christmas. She did last year."

How long would she hold on to that wish? Was it wrong for him to hope she would forget about Val and her life before coming to Hope Springs? "Your mama

can come and see you here if she wants. I left word with Jake so she knows where we're staying."

"I don't think she can find me here. I don't think she likes me anymore."

"Your mother loves you and she always will." He hoped it wasn't a lie.

"Are Grandpa and Grandma really poor?"

That was an abrupt change of subject. "No. They just believe in living a simple life."

"Is Leah poor?"

"I don't know. Why?"

"Grandpa, Grandma and Leah don't have any Christmas decorations up. They don't have a tree or stockings hung. Nana said that sometimes poor people can't afford a Christmas tree."

How did he explain Amish reasoning to an eight-year-old who couldn't grasp complex ideas? "That's not the reason my parents and Leah don't have a tree. They believe in celebrating the true meaning of Christmas, which has to do with the birth of Christ."

"The baby in the manger. I heard that story."

"Good. I'm glad." At least she'd had some exposure to the faith that was so important to the Amish community he hoped she could join. He should have explored the topic sooner.

"Do you think Santa Claus is going to be able to find me way out here?"

He hadn't given a single thought to how he should celebrate Christmas with her. Add another item to the list of things that made him a lousy parent. How would she react to the customs that were so very different from the ones she had grown up knowing?

"Joy, Santa Claus doesn't come to Amish homes."

"Why not? Are the Amish bad?"

"Of course not. Santa Claus doesn't come to Amish homes because he knows that the Amish don't need him to help celebrate the birth of Jesus."

"But I'm not Amish. I've been good. He's going to bring me presents, isn't he?" She sounded worried.

He quickly sought to reassure her. "There will be presents for you, Joy. They won't be fancy presents, and Santa won't bring them. Your grandpa, grandma and I will get them for you."

"How will you know what to get? Santa always knows and picks just the right presents, even if I don't tell him."

Was now the time to tell her that Santa was a myth? He decided that could wait. The poor kid was already being inundated with changes. Once she was older and came to understand the true meaning of Christmas, she would set aside her childish notions.

"We'll manage. Trust me. You're going to have a wonderful Christmas season full of all kinds of new things. Why, we are going to the cookie exchange in a few days. We'll take a pail with us and fill it up with all kinds of yummy cookies. Doesn't that sound fun?"

"I guess, but what about our Christmas lights? Nana always put lights around the porch on our trailer."

"We won't have lights at the farm, but we'll go to town one of these nights to look at all the Christmas lights that are up there. If it snows enough, we'll go for a sleigh ride. Would you like that?"

"Is a sleigh ride fun? Is the sleigh pulled by reindeer?"

"It will be pulled by Bobby or maybe Grandpa's big

draft horses if the snow gets real deep, but it's a lot of fun."

Sleigh rides were some of the best Christmas times in his memory. His family and friends piled under quilts as they raced over the snowy fields to have hot chocolate or hot spiced cider after caroling at neighbors' homes along the way. It didn't matter to them if the neighbors were Amish or *Englisch*. The season was for spreading joy to all.

He glanced sideways at his daughter. It wasn't like a trip to a fancy mall. Would she enjoy it? He hoped so.

She shook her head. "I'm not sure it can be Christmas without a Christmas tree, Daddy."

Maybe he was asking her to make too big of an adjustment. Just because he thought this might be the best life for her didn't mean she would feel the same way. "Let's try it this year and see how you like it."

"I'm gonna tell *Daadi* and *Mammi* that I want a tree. They will get one for me."

"I'm sorry, honey. They won't."

"But I want a Christmas tree! I want one. Pickles wants a tree, too. Mommy will have a tree at her place. I know she will. I want to go live with Mommy!" She threw her napkin on the floor and began kicking the front panel of the buggy.

The horse, startled by the sound, veered sideways, pulling the buggy into the wrong lane.

Caleb reined the horse back into line and made a grab for Joy. "Stop that!"

She screamed, and to Caleb's horror, she bolted out the door of the moving vehicle. He pulled to a stop as quickly as he could. "Joy! Joy, are you okay?" He looked back but couldn't see her.

A second later, he heard her crying. He dropped the reins, got out and ran to the back of the buggy. Joy was sitting at the bottom of a ditch, with blood smeared across her face. She had her hands cupped over her nose. He dropped to her side. "Hold still, kiddo. Where does it hurt?"

"I hit my nose," she mumbled through her fingers.

"Let me see." He pulled her hands aside and checked her over carefully. A bloody nose appeared to be the extent of the damage. Pulling a handkerchief from his hip pocket, he pressed it to her face. "You could have been hurt very badly. Never do that again."

Her tantrum forgotten, she struggled not to cry. "Are you mad at me?"

He pulled her into his arms. "*Liebschen,* you scared me out of ten years of my life, but I'm not mad. Please don't scare me like that again."

"You're squishing me."

He loosened his hold and looked at her face. "I'm sorry. Is that better?"

"Yes. What does *liebschen* mean?" Her voice was muffled beneath the cloth she held to her nose.

He chuckled as his fright faded, leaving him shaking like a leaf in the wind. The cold wet ground was seeping through his pants, but he didn't care. She was safe. "*Liebschen* means sweetheart."

"Am I your sweetheart?"

"Yes, you are. Let me see that nose." He took the cloth away. The bleeding had stopped.

"It still hurts."

"I'm not surprised. Joy, if you are upset about something, running away won't help. You need to talk to

me about it or to Grandma or Grandpa. Do you understand that?"

"I guess."

Did she? Would she ever outgrow the habits that seemed so ingrained in her?

A car coming from the other direction stopped beside them. A gray-haired man rolled down his window. "Is everything okay?"

Caleb raised a hand and waved. "I think so."

The man put his flashers on and got out. "What happened?"

Caleb picked up Joy. "She jumped out of the buggy while it was moving and got a bloody nose for her trouble."

"Better let me have a look at her. I'm a doctor."

Caleb recognized Dr. Harold White. The elderly physician had managed a clinic in Hope Springs since before Caleb was born. He was well respected by the Amish who used his inexpensive services. "I remember you, Dr. White. I'm Caleb Mast. This is my daughter, Joy."

"Would you be Ike's youngest son? The one that moved away?"

"I am."

"I heard you were back in town."

It wasn't surprising. News traveled fast in the small community even though most residents didn't own phones.

Dr. White smiled at Joy as he carefully felt her head and neck and checked her over. "I put eight stitches in your daddy's foot when he was about your age. He cut himself on a piece of broken glass at a picnic."

Caleb stared at him in astonishment. "You have a very good memory."

"I never forget a patient. Well, young lady, you look just fine to me."

She shook her head. "I'm not fine. I have Down sindome."

Dr. White leaned back. "You mean Up syndrome, don't you? That's what I call it. Because the people with Up syndrome who I know are happy, not down and sad. My professional diagnosis is that you have Up syndrome."

She smiled at him. "*Ja,* I have Up sindome."

"Yes, you do." He looked at Caleb. "Keep an eye on her for behavior changes. If she develops a headache, bring her in to see me."

"I will."

Dr. White touched a finger to Joy's nose. "From now on, I want you to wait until the buggy isn't moving before you get out."

Caleb shifted her in his arms. "I think she has learned her lesson."

He carried her to the door and put her on the front seat. He turned and held out his hand to the doctor. "Thanks for stopping."

"Happy to do it. I was on my way home from seeing a patient who has a broken leg out this way."

"I didn't think doctors made house calls anymore."

"I do for some of my elderly or Amish patients if it's a hardship for them to come to me. I enjoy it. I'm glad you had a better outcome than the last time we met at an accident site."

Caleb felt his skin grow cold. "You were there?"

"I was. I've always been sorry that Rhonda's par-

ents didn't allow her to have a repair on her face. With a little plastic surgery, her scars would have been much less noticeable."

"You know the Amish. It was God's will."

"Many Amish accept modern medical care, but I had to respect her father's decision even if I didn't like it. I never understood how you got out of that car without a scratch."

Caleb, uncomfortable with the way the conversation was going, climbed in the buggy with Joy. "It must have been God's will."

Dr. White didn't take the hint. He stood with his hand on the door, preventing Caleb from closing it. "God must have blessed you, indeed. I saw blood all over the door panel. I was sure you had been cut by the broken glass. You didn't have mud on your clothes, either. I remember thinking that was odd because, with the car upside down, you would have had to crawl out the window on your belly, and that field was very muddy that night."

"You must be mistaken. I recall being muddy."

"You know, in my mind, the investigating officer did a poor job that night."

"He sure hit me with a slew of tickets and a hefty fine. No driver's license, no insurance, no tags and reckless driving."

"And he came to collect your fine in person, didn't he?"

"He did." Caleb had been surprised when the young sheriff's officer with auburn hair and a superior attitude showed up at his home the next day. He demanded the fine be paid or Caleb was going to jail. Caleb's father

handed over the money in silent disapproval. It took Caleb almost a year to pay him back.

Dr. White shook his head sadly. "Drake Colburn has engaged in some questionable behaviors. The Amish are easily taken advantage of because they don't report crimes. They pay their debts without question. I was glad when Nick Bradley, our current sheriff, fired Drake. Unfortunately, he's working for a neighboring county now. There are a lot of Amish in his new territory. I have encouraged several of my patients from the area to report his behavior, but I don't believe any of them have."

Dr. White took a step away from the buggy. "I'm keeping you with my long-winded ways. Sorry. Take care, Joy, and come visit me sometime."

"Okay." She sat quietly on the seat beside Caleb, her outburst forgotten.

"It was good seeing you, Dr. White. Thanks again for stopping to help." Caleb closed the door, set the horse in motion and tried to relax.

Thinking about the night of the crash that injured Rhonda was something he didn't do. Ever. But hearing Dr. White's descriptions brought it all back as if it had happened yesterday.

The doctor had a good memory for details. Details that had been overlooked by everyone else. How strange that only an outsider had questioned Caleb's story.

Not that it mattered.

Caleb sighed heavily. He had lied to protect the brother he loved from shame. That lie, told for the best of reasons, had become a haunting, foul thing that hung between the brothers. Wayne, always the good son,

hadn't been able to admit what he had done. He made Caleb promise never to reveal the truth.

Until Wayne released him from his promise to keep the events of that night a secret, the people who mattered, including Leah, would always believe the wild and reckless younger Mast brother had been behind the wheel the night Rhonda Belier was run down on the road near her home.

Caleb turned the buggy off the highway and into the lane that led to his father's house. Joy, exhausted from her ordeal, had fallen asleep on the seat beside him. If Leah knew the truth, would it change how she felt about him? Probably not, unless Rhonda admitted her lie, as well.

Why had she named him as the father of her child? What did she hope to gain besides a reluctant husband? He had never understood. It was likely that he never would.

No matter how much he might enjoy Leah's company, their relationship was doomed.

Chapter Nine

On Thursday evening, at his mother's insistence, Caleb hitched her gray mare to her two-wheeled cart for the short drive to the Imhoff farm. He led the horse to the front gate and waited. His mother came down the walk with a large brown paper bag in her arms and handed it to him.

"What's this?" he asked.

"A rhubarb cake for the board to enjoy."

"Sounds delicious."

"Well-fed men are happy men."

"You'll get no argument from me on that score."

She climbed in the cart. After making certain that she was bundled against the cold with a thick lap robe, he hauled himself up beside her. "Are you sure you wouldn't rather take the buggy? It would be warmer."

"I enjoy being in the open. It's not that cold. You've grown soft in your years away."

He could see his breath in the air. It was cold. He glanced at the house. "Do you think *Daed* will be okay with Joy till we get back?"

"He managed with you and Wayne when you were that age."

"Yes, but Joy can be...difficult at times." He was thinking about the way she jumped out of the buggy yesterday. What if she took it into her head to run away again?

"They'll be fine. Stop fretting. I will drive if you don't care."

He handed her the reins. "Maybe I should stay home and let you go alone."

"*Nee.* As Joy's father, you should be the one to ask permission for her to attend school here."

He wasn't too sure about that. His presence could just as easily turn the board against his petition, especially since Wayne was a member. If they said no, he would go on to plan B. As soon as he figured out what that was.

It would take about fifteen minutes to reach the school. The Imhoff farm was two miles farther down the road. Caleb glanced at his mother as they turned out onto the highway. "What do you think they will do?"

"Eli Imhoff is the school-board president. He is a fair man. He will give our request due consideration."

"But he's not the only one on the board. What about the others?"

"Adrian Lapp is the secretary. He won't have a problem with Joy attending school at Walnut Valley. His adopted son, Kyle, was *Englisch* before coming to live among us."

"I hadn't thought of that." Was adoption plan B?

"Thought of what?"

"Letting you and *Daed* adopt Joy."

His mother scowled at him. "Would her mother agree to that?"

"If her parental rights are severed, she won't have a say."

"As much as I love Joy, I can't see taking her from her parents. The *Englisch* may have a law that allows it, but we do not."

So much for plan B. He didn't really care for the idea anyway. He wanted to be more a part of her life, not less. He returned to the subject of the school-board meeting. "What position does Wayne hold?"

He sensed his mother's hesitation. "Wayne is the tax collector. Samuel Stutzman is the treasurer."

"Great. Samuel Stutzman never liked me. We might as well go home. This is a waste of time." Between Samuel and Wayne, Joy didn't stand a chance of getting into school.

"This is what you wish for your daughter. You can't give up so easily. Samuel is a contrary soul, to be sure. He rarely sees the bright side of things, and he is very set in his ways."

"You're not making me feel better."

"If something is his idea, then it is good idea. I have helped him see this was his idea."

Caleb looked at her in surprise. "When did you do that?"

"When you went to see Leah last evening, I went to visit Samuel and his wife. I took them a few jars of my rhubarb. Your father doesn't care for it and I know Samuel does. I simply told him how I wished Joy could come to know and love our ways as his children and grandchildren do. When I mentioned your plans to have Joy live with us, his wife said I should send her to an Amish school instead of sending her to the *Englisch* one."

"Okay, but how is that Samuel's idea?"

Maggie laughed. "Every husband whose wife has a *goot* idea soon believes it was his thought in the first place."

"I hope you're right."

Caleb pressed a hand to his stomach. He hadn't had butterflies like these in years. They weren't even butterflies, more like overgrown pigeons. As they approached the turnoff to Leah's home, he wondered if she was already gone. The monthly school-board meeting was when teachers received their salaries. He was surprised when his mother slowed her mare.

"What's wrong?"

"Nothing's wrong. Before we left the preaching service last Sunday, I offered Leah a ride, since I knew we were going right by her place."

"And she accepted your offer? Did she know that I was going to be with you?"

"Of course. She thought it best for us to present a united front. The board may grant our request more readily if they know she is in favor of it."

He remained silent. His mother glanced his way. "Leah is an upright and caring woman. Joy is quite taken with her and speaks fondly of her."

Where was his mother going with this? "Leah has a dog with three puppies. Of course Joy is taken with her."

"It's more than the puppies. Joy truly likes her. Leah would make a wonderful mother, don't you think?"

"I'm sure she would. I hope you aren't thinking of matchmaking for us."

"Why would you say such a thing?" She pulled to a stop in front of Leah's gate.

He noticed she didn't deny the charge. Did she think

a woman would keep him in Hope Springs? "I'm not going to stay, *Mamm*. Please don't get your hopes up."

She patted his knee. "A mother has many hopes for her children. You cannot change that with a few words."

Leah's front door opened, and she came out bundled up against the cold. She carried a large basket over one arm. He got down from the cart. "Let me help."

"Danki." She handed over her burden.

He set it behind the seat with his mother's cake and took Leah's elbow to help her up into the cart. When he got in after her, there was very little room for him to sit. She scooted over as far as she could. Easing into the space left, he had no choice but to put his arm along the back of the seat behind her. He practically had his arm around her. With his free hand, he arranged the lap robe over both of them. His mother should have taken the buggy. This cart was too small for three adults.

"Is everyone cozy?" his mother asked with a bright smile. Before anyone answered, she set the horse into a brisk trot.

Leah had spent the past hour mentally preparing to spend a brief buggy ride to the meeting with Caleb in the same vehicle. She hadn't prepared for this.

Sandwiched between him and his mother, she was pressed against his side from shoulder to hip. She could feel the warmth of his body through her coat. She clutched the lap robe with both hands. "Maggie, was there something wrong with your buggy?"

"Nee. It's a fine evening, isn't it?"

"She likes to drive in the open," he muttered between clenched teeth.

"I do. It reminds me of the times Ike took me driving

in his courting buggy. *Ach,* what a fine courtship we had. Your father was a romantic young man. He always brought some small gift that would make me smile."

"It sounds as if you were made for each other." Leah tried to edge away from Caleb, but it was useless. She had nowhere to go unless she moved onto Maggie's lap.

"I knew it from the first day I saw Ike at my cousin's wedding. What a handsome fellow he was. My parents didn't think much of him. He was too wild for their liking."

Caleb leaned forward to look at his mother. "*Daed* was a wild fellow?"

"*Ja.* So much like you when you were a boy, but I knew he would settle down and become a *goot* husband and father, and I was right."

Leah wondered what Maggie was trying to tell her. Was she hinting that Caleb would become a good husband and father, too? It might happen, but not unless he changed a great deal.

He leaned close and whispered, "I'm sorry about this. Are you comfortable?"

"Well enough."

"It isn't much farther. I can walk home when the meeting is over."

"So can I."

"But you shouldn't have to. What's in the basket?"

"Cookies and brownies. Hungry men are cranky men. I thought I would sweeten them up before the meeting got started."

He laughed. The rumble from deep in his chest vibrated against her shoulder and arm. It sent a tingle of warmth through her. He had a nice laugh. Her discom-

fort forgotten, she gave him a quizzical look. "What's so funny?"

"You and my mother think alike."

"How so?"

Maggie chuckled. "I brought rhubarb cake."

Leah met Maggie's glance and they both laughed. The tension in the air eased and the rest of the ride passed quickly.

A large hand-painted sign depicting an anvil marked the lane of Eli Imhoff's farm. He was a blacksmith by trade and a horse breeder by choice.

The Imhoffs lived in a two-story white farmhouse with a smaller *dawdy haus,* a second home for elderly family members, connected to the main building by a covered porch with white railings and wide steps leading up to it. Three large birdhouses sat atop poles around the yard. The flowerbeds were empty now, but Leah knew they would be loaded with blooms from spring through fall. Nettie had a green thumb. There was already one buggy parked in front of the house.

Across a wide expanse of winter-brown grass stood a large red barn and several outbuildings. In the corrals, a pair of enormous caramel-colored draft horses and a dozen Standardbred horses munched on hay bales. Eli was known far and wide as a breeder of fine trotters. Some of his horses, sold to *Englisch* trainers, had gone on to win major races.

Maggie pulled to a stop in front of the main house, and Caleb hopped down and offered his hand to Leah. She placed her fingers in his. Even through her gloves, she could feel his strength. He let go of her as soon as her feet touched the ground. Rounding the cart, he helped his mother down, too. Leah fetched her bas-

ket from the rear of the cart and followed Maggie to the front door. Once Caleb secured the horse, he came after them.

The door opened as they reached it. Nettie Imhoff stood aside. "Come in. Maggie, what were you thinking to travel in an open cart in this cold? I'll heat some bricks for you to use on the way home. No sense getting frozen toes."

"*Danki,* Nettie." Maggie stamped her feet. "It is a bit chilly out today. This is my son Caleb. I don't think the two of you have met."

Caleb nodded to her. "I don't believe we have."

"My son and I came to Hope Springs a few years ago from Pennsylvania after my husband passed away. Elam was hoping for a new start in a new place. We certainly got it. He married a fine girl, and I was blessed to find a man willing to put up with me and my set ways."

Eli walked into the room. "Don't let her fool you. She's the one who puts up with me and mine. Hello, Leah. I hope we can have a short meeting tonight. I've got a sick mare down at the barn."

She glanced at Caleb. "We do have a few things to talk about, but first, we brought some desserts."

"How nice. I'll get some plates." Nettie opened the cupboard door.

Eli grinned. "Dessert sounds wonderful. Don't marry a pretty woman, Caleb. Marry a good cook. Looks fade, good cooking doesn't."

Nettie stopped and turned around with a plate in her hand. "Are you saying my looks are gone?"

Eli realized his mistake. "*Nee,* you're a fine-looking woman, Nettie, and a *wunderbaar* cook. I'm a doubly blessed man."

She shook the plate at him. "You are, and don't forget it."

The outside door opened and a tall Amish man with a thick reddish-brown beard entered the kitchen. He carried a black notebook. His wide smile included everyone in the room. *"Gutenowed."*

Eli said, "Good evening, Adrian. You've come just in the nick of time."

Adrian hung his black hat on a peg beside the door and then scanned the room. His eyes widened when they settled on Caleb. "Caleb Mast, is that you? It's been many a year since I laid eyes on you. How has the *Englisch* world been treating you?"

"Well enough, Adrian. Good to see you again." Caleb was heartened by the reception he was receiving. Maybe Wayne hadn't turned everyone against him.

The door opened again and Samuel Stutzman came in. He hung his hat beside Adrian's. He stared at Caleb without greeting him, and then he nodded to all the others. "Blessings be upon this house."

Acceptance by everyone was too much to hope for.

Eli laid a hand on Samuel's shoulder. "Why don't we get out of the kitchen and let our women have their space? Come into the living room and have a seat."

Caleb glanced at his mother and Leah. They both gave him an encouraging nod. He left his moral support in the kitchen and followed Eli. Chairs had been arranged on both sides of the living room. They must be expecting a fair number of parents to attend.

Eli settled in a winged-back chair near the fireplace. "So, what brings you to our school-board meeting?"

Apparently, Eli didn't believe in beating around the bush. Adrian and Samuel took a seat on the couch but

didn't say anything. Adrian opened his notebook and pulled a pen from his pocket.

Caleb cleared his throat. "I have a daughter who is eight years old. Her name is Joy. She has Down syndrome."

"I met her at the church service. My daughter Anna introduced us. You are blessed to have such a special child."

Caleb drew a deep breath. "In the *Englisch* world, a child such as Joy is not always treated as a blessing."

Eli nodded. "I understand that this is so. It is a sad thing when people cannot see the beauty in all God's creations."

"Joy's life has not always been happy. It is my wish that she grow up here."

Eli laced his fingers together over the slight paunch of his belly. "Both you and your daughter will be welcome if you are accepted back into our faith. You should speak with Bishop Zook. He can guide you in this matter much better than I."

"That's the thing. I don't wish to live Amish. While I believe it is the best thing for my daughter, it is not the life for me."

A troubled frown marred Eli's jovial face. He shared a speaking glance with Adrian and Samuel, and then said, "Such an arrangement will be very confusing for your child. Our ways are not easy. It is the solemn duty of a parent to teach by example. If you do not live as we do, how can you expect your daughter to learn, respect and adhere to our ways?"

"Joy will live with my parents, not with me. I'm here tonight to ask that she be allowed to attend Walnut Val-

ley School even though I am no longer Amish." Caleb
fell silent as Leah came in with a plate in each hand.

"Eli, would you like a brownie, rhubarb cake or
both?"

"Cake will be fine." He accepted the plate she handed
him. "Did you know about this?"

She flashed a scowl at Caleb. He should have waited
until after the cake to make his request. "I learned of
Caleb's plan last week."

Eli raised an eyebrow at her admission. "Perhaps
it would have been better to discuss it with me before
now."

"I'm sorry. I thought it would be better to present the
idea to the entire board."

"I see. What do you think of allowing an *Englisch*
child to attend your school?" Eli took a bite of his cake.

She handed a plate to Adrian. "Joy will be a wonder-
ful addition to my classroom, just as Kyle has been."

Lifting his fork, Eli pointed at her. "Who will you
go to if there are problems with the girl?"

"Caleb, of course. Also Maggie and Ike, since she
will live with them."

Adrian spoke up. "Where will you live, Caleb?"

Caleb hesitated. This was going to be the tricky part.
"Texas for now, but I plan to spend a year in Brazil. I
work on off-shore oil rigs. My parents will make all
decisions about Joy while I'm away."

Samuel said, "I think the child should be allowed to
attend school. I said as much to Maggie just the other
day. Maggie and Ike have always supported our school.
So does Wayne. I see little reason why we should deny
this request."

"What does Joy's mother think of this arrangement?" Adrian asked.

"She isn't in the picture. She left Joy in my care and took off. I don't know where she is."

Eli clearly wasn't pleased with the information. "And now you will leave Joy in the care of your parents and take off."

"No one can do a better job of raising Joy than my parents. I wish I could be the one to raise her, but my job takes me away for long periods of time."

Caleb heard the outside door open again. A small group of parents entered. Greetings and chatter filled the kitchen. Wayne entered the room and stopped short at the sight of Caleb. His face grew red with agitation and he looked to Eli. "I can have no part of this meeting with this man here."

Turning on his heels, he started to leave, but Caleb shot to his feet. "Don't go. I've finished all I came to say. Please continue your meeting. Eli, thank you for hearing me."

Caleb walked into the kitchen, where Rhonda stood beside his mother. She averted her face. He spoke to his mother. "I'll walk home. See you there."

He went out the door and stopped at the gate as he waited for the cold air to cool his temper. If his brother couldn't manage a single civil conversation, what hope was there for them?

"Caleb?"

He turned at the sound of Leah's voice. "I'm fine. Go back in."

She came down the steps and stood beside him. "I will plead Joy's case to them."

Did she have any idea how much her kindness meant

to him? He gave a slight nod. "I know. Thanks. I wish…
Never mind what I wish. Do what you can. If they say
no, I'll enroll Joy in the public school in town. They
might change their minds in a year or two with me out
of the picture."

Her chin came up. "I will see that they do."

Her bravado made him smile. "Joy couldn't have a
better champion. Good night, Leah Belier."

"*Guten nacht,* Caleb Mast. Take care."

The following afternoon, Leah had only been home
from the cookie exchange for a few minutes when she
heard a buggy come into the yard. Eli and Nettie Imhoff
got out of it. The school-board meeting had adjourned
without making a decision about Joy. They had planned
to meet again at Wayne's home this afternoon. Had they
come to a decision?

Leah had been disappointed, but not surprised, when
Maggie and Joy came to the cookie exchange without
Caleb. Joy had had a good time playing with Anna and
Emmy Chupp. It gave Leah hope that she would as-
similate into the community and form lasting bonds.

Leah invited Eli and Nettie in and waited impatiently
for them to get settled. She was eager to learn the ver-
dict, but she couldn't neglect her duties as the woman of
the house. When they were situated in her living room
with cups of steaming coffee in their hands, she took a
seat in her rocker and waited for Eli to speak.

He took a sip of his coffee. Nettie, brimming with
excitement, said, "They have decided that Joy can at-
tend our school."

Leah breathed a prayer of thanks. Eli gave his wife a

sour look. She sat back with a grin on her face, not the least bit intimidated, and blew on her coffee to cool it.

He said, "That was our decision. Joy Perry may attend Walnut Valley School. Although her father does not follow our ways, the majority of us believe it is good that he wishes his daughter to do so. We wanted you to be the first to know, since the responsibility for her education will fall directly on you. If you have any concerns that you felt you could not express in front of Maggie and Caleb, I would hear them now and hold them in confidence."

Did she have reservations? No. Teaching was the path God had chosen for her. Providing an education for Joy was what she was meant to do. "I'm delighted with the decision. I'm sure that Maggie and Ike will provide all the support I need if there are problems. When can she start?"

"On Monday if you and her father agree."

It was Friday evening. "That won't give Joy's family much time to purchase the supplies she will need for the rest of the school year. I do keep a stash of extra supplies for emergencies here at home."

"A sound idea after what happened last summer," Nettie said sadly.

Last summer an arsonist had set fire to the school. By the grace of God, the building had survived with only moderate damage, but all the children's books and records had been destroyed. Although it was an event that was unlikely to be repeated, for the arsonist had been arrested, Leah now made sure she kept only part of her records and supplies there.

Eli said, "I spoke privately with Caleb before the board met again. He has agreed to pay his fair share to

the school district just as any parent would. Although he will not live in the area, he has expressed his intention to return several times a year to help with the physical upkeep of the school. I saw that as more than fair."

"He intends to return?"

Eli nodded. "That's what he told me."

It was the first Leah had heard of such a plan. She had heard him express only his intention to leave and allow his daughter to live an Amish life with his parents. When had he had this change of heart? Perhaps his attachment to Joy was growing.

When the couple had finished their coffee, Leah took their cups and carried them into the kitchen. Eli and Nettie followed her, stopping beside Trixie's box to admire the puppies. Nettie picked up one of the boys. "Elam was just saying the other day that he'll soon need a dog to help control his flock."

"Trixie is very good at gathering in the geese and ducks. I'm sure her puppies will be, too."

Nettie laughed. "He has neither geese nor ducks. What he and Katie need help with is their gaggle of children. They have three now, and I reckon that's not the end of it."

"*Nee,* not the way he smiles when he looks at her," Eli said with a grin.

Nettie laid a hand on his arm. "He smiles at her the way you smile at me."

The widow and widower had wed two years ago, and it was clear they were every bit as much in love as the youngsters in the family. Leah knew a moment of envy. Why wasn't there someone for her to love?

Nettie reached for her coat. "We are on our way

to see Maggie and Ike and let them know the school board's decision. Would you like to come with us?"

There was no real reason for her to go, but Leah pulled her own coat off the hook, excited at the idea of seeing Caleb again. And Joy. "I would. In case Maggie or Ike has questions for me. And I can deliver the supplies to Joy. It will only take me a minute to get together what she will need."

Twenty minutes later, they pulled up in front of the Mast farmhouse. Maggie opened the door and invited them in. Ike came in from the living room. Eli said, "I would speak with you about the education of your granddaughter. Is her father about?"

"He and Joy have gone down to the barn to feed the horses. I will get him." Ike reached for his hat.

Leah said, "I'll go."

"Very well."

Outside, Leah hurried across to the old red barn. The wind was cold as it blew down from the north, pushing a flurry of snow with it. Inside the relative comfort of the barn, she pushed her bonnet back and adjusted her *kapp*. She located Caleb by the sound of his voice coming from the hayloft. He was talking softly to someone, most likely to Joy.

Leah pressed a hand to her heart to still the sudden rush of pleasure that raced through her at the sound of his voice. In spite of her misgivings, she had come to care a great deal about him. Much more than was wise. How could she have allowed this to happen?

Recognizing the attraction for what it was, she knew the best thing for her was to turn and walk away.

Chapter Ten

Leah's common sense told her to call out to Caleb and Joy and then return to the house. She opened her mouth but heard the sound of Joy's giggle and remained silent. Maybe she was being foolish, but she adored spending time with Joy. Whatever they were doing sounded like fun. She would guard her heart against becoming more involved with Caleb now that she understood what was happening.

She climbed the ladder to the haymow and followed the sound of Joy's giggles. She found father and daughter lying in a pile of hay, staring at the rafters. Joy spied her first. She held a finger to her lips. "Shh."

Caleb rose on one elbow. A piece of straw dangled from his lips. He whispered, "We're watching a barn owl."

Leah looked up. "Truly? They're an endangered species in this state. Where is it?"

"On the rafter near the center of the barn, just slightly to the left. It looks as if he's been roosting here for a while."

"I still don't see him."

Joy said, "If you lie down, you can see him better and your neck won't get tired. What's *endangered?*"

Leah stepped across the hay and sat down beside Joy. She wrapped her arms around her knees, conscious of the fact that Caleb was stretched out on the other side of his daughter. The classroom wasn't the only place to share knowledge. Times like this were perfect to teach children about nature and the gifts of God. "Endangered means there aren't very many of them anymore. Barn owls love to live in barns and old silos, but many of those have been torn down to make way for houses and towns, so the barn owls don't have places to live anymore."

"That's sad."

"It is. Did you know they are sometimes called a flying mousetrap because they eat so many mice? They truly are a farmer's friend. I still don't see him."

Caleb removed the piece of straw he had in his mouth. "Give your eyes time to adjust to the dark. I assume you are here because you heard from the school board."

Leah lay back beside Joy and closed her eyes. "I did. Eli and Nettie brought me over. They are inside speaking with your parents."

"Let me guess. Wayne got them to vote against me."

She opened her eyes and turned in his direction. The worried frown on his face put a crease between his brows. She was happy to give him the good news. "*Nee,* he was overruled by the others. She can start on Monday."

Caleb sat up. "Are you serious?"

"I am."

Joy pointed overhead. "He's looking at us. He can turn his head all the way around. Cool."

Leah leaned close to follow Joy's finger. "I see him now. His face is so pretty and white. Doesn't he have huge eyes? They help him see at night. Maybe he thinks we are giant mice here in the straw."

"That's silly. We don't have big ears, and we don't have tails."

"Very true. Joy, how would you like to come to school on Monday?" Leah asked.

"I don't know. Would I have to go alone?"

"There are twenty-seven other children in my school, so you can't possibly be alone."

Caleb stretched out in the hay once more. "You wouldn't have to walk to school alone, if that's what is worrying you. I will go with you and spend the day. How would that be?"

"I guess that would be okay. Are the other kids going to think I'm stupid?"

"Nee," Leah answered quickly. "They are going to see what a very special person you are. You can be a big help to me at school, you know."

"How?"

"Just by speaking English. It helps the younger children learn the language when they hear it spoken. Anna Imhoff is very excited that you will be in our school."

"I like Anna. She's really nice to me. Oh, look. The owl is gone. Where did he go?"

Caleb sat up and tickled her chin with a piece of straw. "He went out to hunt for his supper. He doesn't have a *grossmammi* to cook for him. He has to go find food himself. Shall we go in and see what *Mammi* has cooked for us?"

"I want to stay out here in case he comes back." She folded her arms over her chest.

"Nope. No arguments. Leah and I are going inside. If you stay out here, you will make your grandmother worry about you. She'll be mad at us for leaving you out here alone. Do you want to get us in trouble?"

She mulled over the idea and shook her head. "No."

Each time Leah saw Caleb with Joy, she was amazed at the difference in him. The frantic, frazzled man she first met outside the grocery store had become a caring and compassionate parent. He was making an effort and making progress at becoming a father. She could see the love for his child growing stronger every day, and it pleased her.

He helped Joy to her feet and began brushing away the bits of straw stuck to her coat and bonnet. "You had better brush me off, too. I don't want to carry all of this into Grandma's clean house."

Joy energetically brushed the back of his pants and as high as she could reach on his back. "I can't get it all. Leah, can you help me?"

Leah rose to her feet and shook out her skirt. Caleb held his arms out to his sides. She moved close and set to work picking the straw off his coat, ignoring the way her insides fluttered at his nearness. She smoothed away the loose bits from across his shoulders. Even through the thick material of the coat, she could feel the firmness of his muscles. She could tell he was used to hard physical work. Slowly, she brushed down each arm. Finally, all that was left was a few pieces of straw in his hair.

Without thinking, she slid her fingers up the nape of his neck. His hair was short but thick. It felt like soft fur

beneath her fingers. When she realized what she was doing, she stepped away quickly. "Clean as a whistle."

He cleared his throat. "Thanks. We should go."

"*Ja*. Eli and Nettie are probably wondering what happened to me." She started toward the ladder, but he stopped her by grasping her arm.

"They will think you've been rolling in the hay. Hold still a second."

Standing behind her, he gently brushed at her back. He kept one hand on her shoulder to steady her. In the space of a few seconds, it went from a friendly gesture to an intimate experience. She could feel his breath on the back of her neck. His hands stopped moving and rested on her shoulders. Her own breathing became ragged. If she turned around, would he kiss her?

"Come on, guys. I'm getting hungry."

Embarrassment sent a wave of heat to Leah's face. She'd completely forgotten about Joy. "We're coming."

Caleb watched as Leah quickly followed Joy down the ladder. Once again, he had let his growing desire override his common sense. Yet Leah hadn't rejected him outright. She'd tolerated his touch, but what did that mean, exactly?

She kept her attention on Joy and held her hand as they crossed the yard. "I've brought your books and some supplies. Pencils, crayons, paper and such. You have all you need to begin school."

She stopped at the buggy and drew a bag from the backseat. She handed it to Joy. "Don't forget to bring it to school on Monday."

"I won't." Joy gazed up at her with admiration shin-

ing in her eyes. Caleb knew exactly how she felt. Leah always seemed to know what Joy needed.

Inside the house, Nettie and Maggie were busy at the stove. Maggie said over her shoulder, "Ike and Nettie are staying for supper. I hope that is okay with you."

Leah smiled, but it was stiff. She cast a sidelong glance his way and then quickly looked at his mother. "What can I do to help?"

"You and Joy may set the table."

The meal was one of the longest that Caleb had ever endured. Leah sat across from him and spent the entire time trying not to look at him. It was a relief when everyone finished. The men went into the other room while the women began to clean up.

Eli moved a small round table and positioned it between two chairs. "How about a game of checkers?"

Ike pointed to Caleb. "Better warm up with the boy before you take me on."

Eli snorted. "It will be a rare day that I can't best you, but take a seat, Caleb, and give your father a short reprieve. Will you be black or red?"

"Red." Caleb sat down and put his pieces on the board, but his mind wasn't on the game. It was on Leah. What was she thinking? Did she find his touch repulsive? If not, where did they go from here?

The short answer was nowhere.

Eli beat him soundly in record time. Caleb looked to his father. "*Daed,* why don't you have a go at him? You always were a better player than I was."

Ike rose from his chair. "Are you ready to take your beating, Eli?"

"Ha! You can try."

Caleb watch them set up a new game and then wandered to the doorway that led to the kitchen.

Joy sat quietly at the table with her chin propped on her hands. She had been quiet throughout the meal. Was she feeling okay?

"What's the matter, Joy? Do you have a headache?" he asked. It was something Dr. White had told him to watch for.

"No."

Maggie pressed a hand to her forehead. "You aren't warm. Do you feel sick?"

"*Mammi,* your house isn't very Christmassy."

She still wanted a Christmas tree. Caleb wondered how his mother would handle the request.

Maggie looked around the room. "I reckon you're right. Do you want to help me fancy it up?"

Joy brightened. "Sure. Can we put up a Christmas tree?"

"*Nee,* child, for that is a worldly thing. It is not permitted. I know something we can do. I've been getting Christmas cards from my friends and family for the past few weeks. I keep them in a box in my bedroom. Wait a moment and I will get it."

She returned shortly and set a shoe box on the table. "Let's put them up so everyone can enjoy them. Leah, would you get me a ball of yarn from my knitting basket by the fireplace?"

"Of course." While Nettie, Maggie and Joy began sorting through the cards, Leah approached Caleb. He was blocking the doorway. She paused in front of him but kept her gaze on the floor. Softly he said, "I didn't mention how nice you look tonight."

Color bloomed in her cheeks. She smoothed the front

of her dark green dress with its matching apron. "This is only one of my school dresses. It's not new. In fact, it's a little stained and worn."

"Actually, I hadn't noticed your dress."

Her eyes flashed up and locked with his. He didn't flinch from her gaze. He wanted her to know that he saw her, and he liked what he saw. He stepped aside. She rushed past him. Quickly, she came back with a ball of yarn, but she avoided looking at him. Caleb followed her into the kitchen and took a seat across from his daughter at the table.

"What do we do now?" Joy asked.

Maggie glanced around her kitchen. "I reckon we have to decide where we want to hang our cards. Then we will put up some yarn and hang the cards on it. Where do you think they should go?"

Joy looked around. "I'm not sure."

"You used to hang them across the windows when I was little." Caleb began reading some of the cards. A few of them were store-bought cards, mostly from the English neighbors and shopkeepers in the town. The others, from family and Amish friends, were homemade and decorated by hand.

"All right, we'll start with the windows." His mother opened one of the kitchen drawers and pulled out some thumbtacks.

With Nettie's help, she stretched three strands of yarn across the large windows that looked out onto the front porch and then stood back with her hands on her hips. "Do those look straight?"

"They look fine," Caleb said. "Joy, why don't you pick out the ones you want to hang up?"

"Okay." She began sorting through the box. "I like

this one, and this one." She handed them to Leah, who was seated beside her. Leah took them to the window.

"Daddy, you hang up these." She handed him a small bundle.

Caleb worked silently beside Leah until Nettie began to hum a Christmas song. Leah started humming, too. Soon Caleb began to sing the well-known hymn, "O Little Town of Bethlehem," and Leah, Maggie and Nettie all joined in.

Still singing, he went back to the table and picked up Joy. He carried her to the window so that she could hang the rest of the cards she had chosen.

When the song was finished, Joy clapped her hands. "Now it looks more like Christmas."

Eli and Ike came to the doorway. Ike said, "I reckon I could bring in a little greenery for the mantel tomorrow."

Maggie smiled at him. "*Ach,* that would be *wunderbaar.* I love the way the pine branches make the house smell."

Caleb reached for his coat. "No reason to wait until tomorrow. I can go cut a few now."

"But it's dark outside already," his mother said.

"I've got a flashlight."

Maggie turned to Ike. "Go with him and hold the light."

"These old bones don't want to go back out in the cold."

Caleb saw his chance. "Leah, would you come hold the flashlight for me?"

"That's a good idea. Thank you, Leah." His mother smiled at them both.

His father came to the table. "Joy, would you like

to make some Christmas cards to send to your friends back in Texas?"

"I don't know how."

Ike sat down at the head of the table. "I will help you. Mama, do we have some colored paper?"

"We do. I have cutouts of flowers and birds and butterflies. I collect them all year for just this reason. I have glue, too."

"Leah brought me colors. Can I use them?"

"*Ja.* We will make some lovely cards to send to your friends." Maggie left the room and returned with another, larger box.

The adults all took a seat at the table to join in on the card making. Nettie began another song and soon everyone was singing along.

Caleb put on his coat and held Leah's for her. She slipped into it and quickly stepped away. He took a flashlight from the cabinet and held it out to her as he opened the door. She took the light and walked out ahead of him.

The clouds had moved on and a clear, star-filled sky arched overhead. The moon was a slim crescent rising in the east.

She turned the flashlight onto his face, making him squint against the brightness. "What did you want to talk to me about?"

He turned his face away. "I don't know what you mean."

"I assumed you wished to speak to me privately, since you asked me to accompany you outside."

"Can you shine that light somewhere else?"

"Sorry." She aimed it at the ground.

"Thank you. I didn't have anything special I needed

to tell you. I just wanted your company. I'll get the saw from the shed. Mind if I use your light?"

"Not at all." She sounded confused. He didn't blame her.

His ulterior motive was to spend time alone with her, but he did have questions about Joy. Perhaps it was better to get on a safe subject.

"I know you've had a chance to read Joy's records. Do you think she is ready for the second grade?"

"I don't think so. Her grandmother kept very poor records. I don't believe she put a lot of effort into educating Joy. I could be wrong. I can evaluate her and make a better judgment in a few days."

"I don't want her to feel bad about not keeping up with the kids her age."

"I think I will be able to manage that part of it. As long as she feels included and comfortable, I don't think she'll realize that she is behind others her age. This will be her first public school. She won't have anything to gauge it against."

"She ran away from the private school I enrolled her in."

Leah shrugged. "She may do the same at Walnut Valley. We won't know until we give it a try."

He collected the saw from inside the shed, and by unspoken consent, they began walking into the woods along the path that led to the school. "I'm sure you'll make her feel comfortable. You have that effect on people. Will my being at the school make you uncomfortable?"

"*Nee,* parents visit our classroom often."

"I'm not exactly your run-of-the-mill Amish parent."

She tipped her head slightly to study him. "You are

getting there. I see a little pine tree that looks eager to donate some branches to help celebrate our Lord's birth." She pointed the flashlight to the side of the trail.

Caleb walked up to the small fir tree. It was only about six feet tall and shaped like a perfect Christmas tree. "It's a shame I can't take the whole thing back for Joy. She wants a Christmas tree so badly. I didn't realize how hard it would be for her to give up all the English trappings of the season."

"Are they hard for you to give up?"

"Me? I never bothered with a Christmas tree. My condo was too small. Christmas was just another day for me."

"Then it is a good thing that Joy has come into your life to make Christmas meaningful again."

He smiled softly as he remembered meeting his daughter for the first time. "She told me her nana used to say she was her special Christmas Joy because she was born on Christmas Day. I think Joy believes the holiday decorations are there to celebrate her birthday.

"Mom intends to make her a special birthday cake and have a small family celebration on Christmas night. You're invited to come."

Leah grinned. "I will. We want her to know her birthday is important to us, too."

He trimmed a few of the lower, longer branches to take back to the house. Hopefully it would be enough to give Joy the sense of Christmas that she craved.

Leah walked all around the small tree. "I see no reason why Joy can't have her Christmas tree. It wouldn't be right to cut it down and bring it into the house. That would be worldly. But to put a few homemade decora-

tions on this little tree out here for just the two of you would be an acceptable thing.

"We can make decorations that will look pretty and feed the birds, as well. Stale popcorn strands with dried berries. Perhaps some orange slices or apple slices smeared with peanut butter and coated with birdseeds. No one would object to such a useful tree."

It was the perfect solution. Why hadn't he thought of it? He looked at her in amazement. "How do you do it?"

"How do I do what?"

He stepped closer and spoke softly. "How do you see what others need and find a way to give it?"

She gazed at his face. He could see the starlight reflected in her eyes. Her white *kapp* outlined her face with a circle of brightness in the dark.

"I don't do anything special."

"Yes, you do. You do something special for my child every time you see her. You calm her, you teach her, you encourage her and you bring her joy. You have a very special gift."

She looked away. Was she uncomfortable with his praise? "The Lord gives us what we need to follow the path He has chosen for us. Teaching is my calling. Any gifts I possess are given by Him."

Caleb placed a finger beneath her chin and lifted her face until she was looking at him. "Then for the first time in a long time, I give thanks to Him for what He has brought into my life. You."

Caleb ached to kiss her. He wanted it more than he wanted his next breath. They were cocooned by the night. The scent of fresh-cut pine filled the air. He leaned toward her slowly, waiting to see if she would reject him or welcome him.

He didn't get the chance to find out. His mother's voice broke the connection between them as she called their names.

Leah stepped back quickly. "We must return to the house."

"I'd rather stay out here with you."

She turned and raced away, leaving him standing alone in the darkness.

He curled his cold fingers deep in his pockets. Something told him that Leah was the woman he'd been waiting his whole life to find. Did she feel the same? He longed to know.

Yet even if she did, how could they make a life together?

Chapter Eleven

"I'm so excited. Were you excited on your first day of school, Daddy?"

Joy swung her red-and-white lunchbox from one hand as she walked beside Caleb on Monday morning. She wasn't exactly walking, more like bouncing. She wore a simple blue dress and a black *kapp* beneath her black coat and bonnet. She had gray snow pants on under her dress to keep her legs warm on the walk to school. The pants would come off once she was at school and would be put back on for recess outside and the walk home.

"I was about as excited as you are."

Almost as excited as he was now at the thought of seeing Leah again. Their moments together on Friday night replayed in his mind. If his mother hadn't called to them, he would have kissed Leah.

He was almost sure she would've let him.

He intended to test his theory at the first opportunity. Better to know than to spend another sleepless night wondering. She had been on his mind constantly even though he knew nothing could come of their re-

lationship. He wasn't going to stay in Hope Springs and Leah would never leave the Amish. Or would she? Was it wrong to hope she might consider a life outside the Amish?

A small voice at the back of his mind reminded him there was another choice. He could stay and resume his Amish life.

Was that really a possibility? Two weeks ago he would have said no. Now the idea didn't seem so far-fetched. Wasn't he happier now than he'd ever been in the English world?

"I know my ABCs, Daddy. Do you want to hear them?" Joy looked at him hopefully.

"Sure."

"A. B. C." She smiled brightly.

"So far so good. Can you say the rest of them?" He scanned the woods, hoping to see a glimpse of Leah. She was probably already at the school.

"A. B. C. That's the ABCs."

"What if I asked you to say the alphabet? Could you do that?"

Her happiness faded. "I don't think so."

"I happen to know the entire alphabet. I'll help you learn it."

"For real?"

"For real."

"What will I do in school?"

"Oh, lots of things. Leah is going to help you learn to read and write and to do your sums. You're going to learn history and geography. You'll learn things like how to drive a buggy and share the road with cars."

"It's gonna be so fun."

"I hope so," Leah said. She was sitting on a fallen

log off to the side of the trail. In her dark coat and bonnet, she had blended into the pines behind her. If she hadn't spoken, he might've walked past her. She was waiting for them.

"Good morning. I was afraid we had missed you." A surge of pleasure filled him when he saw her shy smile.

She rose to her feet and joined them. "I didn't want to miss walking to school with Joy on her very first day at Walnut Valley."

"Am I really going to learn to drive a buggy?" Joy asked.

"Not today, but you will learn many practical things at school."

"How is Pickles? Has her daddy come to see her?"

"No, Duncan hasn't been over."

"He's not a very nice daddy," Joy declared.

"I'm sure he's just been busy taking care of all Woolly Joe's sheep."

"I miss Pickles."

Leah glanced at Caleb. "You must ask your father to bring you over to see her again. She's becoming a little butterball. She is bigger than both her brothers."

Joy said, "I wish I had a brother. Dad, can I have a brother one of these days?"

The light mood of the morning vanished. Caleb knew exactly what Leah was thinking. She was thinking that David was Joy's half brother. What would it take to convince her it wasn't true?

He said, "I think you should stick to wishing for a dog."

Joy continued talking nonstop, but the adults walked in silence. When they finally reached the school building, Leah set about her work and got the fire going.

Caleb brought in two buckets full of coal and then took a broom to clear the snow from the front steps.

Joy spent the time exploring the room and chatting away. Leah showed Joy her desk in the first row and helped her unpack her supplies and stow them. When it was warm enough, Leah had her put her coat and bonnet in the cloak room. Together, they made a sign with Joy's name on it and hung it over the hook so that she would be able to find her things later.

The other students began arriving in family groups thirty minutes later. They were noisy as they filed in, calling greetings to each other and to Leah. Joy, overcome with shyness, moved to stand beside Caleb.

Some of the children brought out potatoes wrapped in aluminum foil and placed them on a ledge to roast inside the furnace door. Two brothers brought out soup in a glass jar and set it on top of the stove. Leah filled a kettle with water and placed it on top of the stove, as well, to provide moisture in the air.

One excited little girl with blond pigtails ran up to Leah. "*Teetshah, Mamm* has a *nei boppli.*"

"That's wonderful, Ammia, but you must remember to speak English when you are at school."

Ammia concentrated a moment and then said, "Teacher, my mama has a new *boppli.*"

"A new baby."

"*Ja,* and it's a girl. Her name is Mary. I have a *shveshtah.*"

"You have a sister. I'm so glad for your family. Your mother and father must be very happy. Now, you should take your seat. We have a lot to do today."

Caleb moved to a wooden bench at the back of the

room. Joy followed him. He sat down and pulled her to him. "Are you okay?"

"There are a lot of kids here." She chewed her thumbnail.

"I know, but soon they will all be your friends."

"I don't know." Uncertainty colored her shaky voice.

Anna Imhoff came in the door. She spied Joy and waved. Joy waved back. Caleb said, "See, you have one friend here already. Go and take your seat like the other children are doing and listen to Leah. If you have a question, be sure and raise your hand. I'll be right here if you need me."

"Promise?"

"I promise."

Joy walked reluctantly to her desk and sat down. Leah went out and rang the school bell. The last students to come in were the older boys who had been having a snowball fight outside. Tagging along behind them was David. He cast a curious look at Caleb and then raced to his seat.

When the clock at the front of the room reached eight-thirty, Leah tapped her desk bell with a pencil. The room instantly became quiet.

Leah scanned the room and recorded each of her students in her attendance book. Everyone was present.

She moved to the front of the classroom and smiled at all their bright and shining faces. "Good morning, boys and girls."

"Good morning, Leah," they replied in unison.

Walking to the blackboard, she wrote out the date followed by the arithmetic assignments for each of the

classes as she did every morning. When she was finished, she returned to her desk and picked up her Bible.

Each day the teacher in an Amish school chose a passage to read. This morning Leah chose *Matthew* 5. When she finished reading the Sermon on the Mount, the students all rose, clasped their hands together and repeated the Lord's Prayer in unison. Joy, looking uncertain, stood, too, but she didn't know the words. It was another thing she would have to help her learn.

The Bible reading and prayer would be the only religious part of the day. The Amish believed that the instruction of faith was a sacred duty. Religion was taught at home and in their church services, not at school.

After everyone took their seats again, Leah glanced toward Caleb and gave him a tentative smile. She could see he was nervous about Joy's behavior. Neither one of them wanted to see Joy upset enough to have a tantrum.

She said, "Children, we have a new student joining us. This is Joy Perry. She is the granddaughter of Maggie and Ike Mast. Her father, Caleb Mast, is also with us today. I want everyone to say good-morning to him."

The class turned in their seat and a chorus of greetings filled the schoolroom. He nodded to them. "Thank you."

Leah beckoned Joy to come forward. She rushed eagerly to Leah's side. It was a blessing that Joy had taken such a liking to her. It would make her transition into the community that much easier.

Leah said, "Joy comes to us from Houston, Texas. She grew up in an *Englisch* home. She doesn't speak our language, so please remember to speak English when you talk to her. I know everyone will make her feel welcome."

Joy smiled shyly at her new classroom and raised her hand in a quick wave. "Hi."

"Welcome, Joy." Anna Imhoff waved from her seat in the middle of the girls.

Leah leaned forward to see Joy's face. "Why don't you tell the children something about yourself?"

Joy looked up and whispered, "Like what?"

"Anything. You could tell them about Pickles."

Beaming, Joy said, "I have a puppy and her name is Pickles. She lives with her mommy at Leah's house, but when she is big enough, she will come live with me and she'll never, ever go away. Oh, and Dr. White says I have Up sindome, not Down sindome."

Leah nodded. "Very good. Anything else?"

Joy shook her head quickly, making the black ribbons of her *kapp* wiggle. She looked very Amish in her blue dress cut in the same style as the other girls. The Amish were all about uniformity and not standing out. The only difference between Joy and the other girls was that Joy's hair wasn't long enough yet to put into a braid or bun.

Leah picked up a copy of *Unpartheyisches Gesang-Buch*, their German songbook, from the corner of her desk. When she realized that Joy wouldn't know any of the hymns, she laid it aside and picked up a collection of Christmas songs.

Singing was a normal part of each school day. Without being told, the children filed to the front of the room and lined up in their assigned places.

Joy stood to one side, not knowing where to go. Leah came to stand by her. She slipped her arm across Joy's shoulders. "It's Monday, and on Monday, Wednesday and Friday we normally sing German songs. The chil-

dren take turns picking which songs we sing. Because it's your first day, how would you like to choose some Christmas songs to sing? Do you have a favorite?"

"'Up on the Rooftop.'"

"I'm afraid we don't have that one. What else do you like?"

"'Jingle Bells.'"

"We sing a song to that tune, but the words are different. I'm afraid you wouldn't know it." Leah realized it wasn't going as well as she had hoped.

"You pick a song." Joy was beginning to get frustrated.

"How about 'O Little Town of Bethlehem'? You were helping us sing it at your grandmother's house last Friday." Leah glanced toward Caleb and saw his tender smile. He remembered the evening, too.

Singing without accompaniment, the children blended their voices together in a spirited rendition of the chosen work. When the song was done, Leah helped Joy select two more. After they finished singing, she said, "Now I would like to run through the songs we have planned for the Christmas program. We will have a full rehearsal on Thursday after school, so everyone practice your parts for the plays and skits at home and be ready."

The songs included traditional Christmas hymns and popular secular songs that expressed the true meaning of Christmas. There was nothing about Santa or reindeer. Only the first-and second-grade children had trouble with their song and had to repeat it several times. Joy listened but didn't join in. When they were done, Leah sent all her students back to their seats. They began working on their mathematics without urging from her.

With the upper grades working quietly, Leah gathered the first graders and Joy in a small group beside her desk where she could work with them on oral reading skills.

Like all Amish children, these first graders came to school speaking only Pennsylvania *Deitsh,* a German dialect outsiders called Pennsylvania Dutch.

English was the language of business and life outside the Amish home. It was essential that children learned to speak and write it. While the Amish strived to live separate from the world, they had to live in it. To that end, only English was spoken at school. Leah spoke Pennsylvania Dutch only when one of her young pupils didn't understand the meaning of what she was trying to express.

As Leah had suspected from Joy's sketchy records, the child couldn't read or write, but she seemed eager to learn. If she noticed that she was older than the other children, she didn't mention it. After they were finished, Leah had the first graders return to their seats and take out their workbooks to do the pages that corresponded with their reading lesson.

All the older students were working quietly, so she returned to help Joy copy the alphabet in her tablet. When the hour for arithmetic was up, the older students exchanged papers and graded each other's work. When each student had a chance to see their mistakes, the papers were passed to the front, where Leah collected them.

At ten o'clock, she said, "All right, children, it's time for recess. Go to the bathroom, get drinks of water and sharpen your pencils now so that you don't have to do it later."

The room dissolved into a beehive of activity as the children put away their work and grabbed their coats to play outside.

Anna brought Emmy Chupp to Joy's desk. "This is Emmy. She wants to play Bear with us. Do you want to play?"

Joy looked eager to join them, but she held back. "I don't know that game."

"It's easy," Emmy said. "One of us is the bear and we try to catch someone else. Then they are the bear. It's fun, come on."

Caleb came forward. He said, "Don't forget to put on your coat."

"Will you watch me play Bear, Daddy?"

"That was my intention. Go on outside. I need to speak to Leah for a minute."

He waited until the last child was out the door before he spoke. "It seems to be going well, don't you think?"

"Did you expect it to go badly?"

"I had visions of screaming and temper tantrums. I'm happy to see I was wrong."

"The day isn't over yet." She walked to her desk and he joined her.

"What is your assessment of her learning readiness?"

She looked at him in surprise. "Don't you sound like a teacher?"

He flushed with embarrassment. "I'm doing my best to be an informed parent."

"I'm happy to see that. By this age, she should be in the second grade, but she is below the first-grade level in reading and comprehension. I don't believe her grandmother devoted much time to actual instructions.

Joy is eager to learn, but she has a lot of catching up to do."

"What can I do to help her?"

"Work on reading. Read to her every night. Let her follow along with the words and repeat them after you. You may want to teach her some of our German songs. That way she won't feel so left out during our morning singing. I'll give you a list of the ones that are easy."

"Good." He gestured toward the door. "I'd better get outside before recess is over. I don't want to miss seeing her be the bear."

Leah called to him before he reached the door. "Caleb, you are doing a good job with her. I see a lot of improvement in her behavior."

A wry smile pulled the corner of his mouth up. "You weren't with us when she jumped out of a moving buggy on the highway. She has a long way to go."

Leah hesitated to ask, but she wanted to know. "Does that mean you'll be staying longer than you thought?"

His smile widened. "I've found more than one reason to stick around."

He went out the door and Leah drew a sharp breath. Did he mean her? Had she given him the impression she would welcome his attentions? Her head told her no, but her heart disagreed.

At ten-fifteen, Leah rang the bell to bring the children back to class. Her grades four to eight had reading classes. Each student came and stood beside her, then read from their assignment and answered her questions to determine their comprehension of what they had read. All the time she was listening to her students, she was aware of Caleb sitting at the back of the room, watch-

ing her every move. She hadn't been this flustered since her first day as a teacher.

Eleven-thirty finally rolled around. She stood in front of her desk. "Children, you may go wash your hands, get your lunch boxes and return to your desks. Please go by rows. If any of the younger children need help, older brothers or sisters may go with them."

Joy fetched her lunch box and carried it to her father. "Can we go home now? I'm tired."

"School isn't over, Joy."

"But I want to go home now."

Caleb glanced at Leah. She came to sit beside him on the bench and spoke to Joy. "Are you feeling okay?"

Her lower lip stuck out. "I want to go home."

Leah met Caleb's gaze and raised her eyebrows. There wasn't any point in pushing the child to remain. He nodded in resignation.

Emmy ran up to Joy. "Don't go home yet. We're going to have another recess after we eat, and we can play on the swings. After that, we'll have story time and then we can color something. I'll let you use my crayons."

"You will?"

"*Ja,* I have lots of colors."

"Okay."

"What did you bring for lunch? My *mamm* sent me a roast beef sandwich and a big slice of carrot cake."

"*Mammi* gave me a peanut butter and jelly sandwich. I named Leah's puppies Pickles, Peanut Butter and Jelly." The two little girls walked back toward their seats.

Caleb blew out a breath of relief. "Crisis averted

by crayons. Who knew they worked as well as animal crackers?"

They shared a smile, which sent a burst of happiness through Leah. He had a sense of humor, and she liked that about him. She liked a lot of things about Caleb Mast. But she couldn't sit here and flirt with him. She had a class to teach.

"Everyone back in your seats."

Joy opened her lunch box and was unwrapping her sandwich when Emmy stopped her. "We have to pray first."

Leah walked to the head of the class and clasped her hands together. The students repeated a prayer in unison and then quickly ate lunch. When they were done, they hurried outside. Caleb followed them out.

Leah made two cups of hot tea from the water in the kettle and carried them outside along with her sandwich. She sat on the steps to keep an eye on the children. And on Caleb.

Caleb pushed Joy and Emmy on the swings, but the two girls soon decided they wanted to play on the tee-ter-totter. He saw Leah had come out of the building, and he crossed the schoolyard to join her on the steps. She inched a little farther away. He'd forgotten for a moment that there were many eyes on them.

He found her attractive, but he was beating his head against a closed door. They were separated by her sister's lies and so much more. Any feelings they had for each other were doomed before they could have the chance to explore them. She knew it as well as he did.

"I made you a cup of tea." She held out a mug.

"Danki." A strange yearning pulled at his insides.

What would it be like if he wasn't *Englisch?* What if they could put the past behind them and start fresh? What if he made a home here with Joy? An Amish home. The image pulled at his soul and forced him to admit that he had been wrong to leave his faith behind along with his family.

The sun was bright overhead. It reflected off the snow in a million sparkling pinpoints of light. There was a chill in the air, but he endured it without complaint. For a little while, they sat quietly and watched the children on the playground. He was acutely aware that she was only inches away. He beat down the urge to reach for her hand.

She broke the silence first. "Joy seems to be doing better now."

His daughter was laughing as she rode up and down on the wooden teeter-totter. Anna was standing beside her. "I see she has made a friend. I've met Anna. Who is the other one?"

"Emmy Chupp."

"I don't think I know the family."

"The Chupps moved here last year. Her father works at the lumberyard. He fell and broke his leg a few weeks ago."

"I'm sorry to hear that. His daughter has taken quite a liking to Joy."

"Is that surprising?"

"Not at all. Even with the language barrier, she seems to be interacting well."

"Both Emmy and Anna have more experience speaking English. Emmy helps her mother and older sister in their soap-and-candle shop in town, so she speaks to many tourists. Anna's sister, Karen, married Jona-

than Dresher, a convert to our faith. He credits Anna with teaching him our Pennsylvania Dutch language."

Caleb leaned back on his elbows and crossed his boots. "I've never known an outsider who chose to become Amish."

"You must ask him to tell you his story someday."

"I hope I have the chance to hear it."

She turned her head to frown at him. "You're not leaving yet, are you? Joy is not ready for that."

He wasn't ready for it, either. What he really wanted to know was Leah's feelings on the subject. "Will you miss me when I'm gone? Should I stay?"

He could tell he had flustered her. She stared at her hands wrapped around her mug of tea. When she wasn't looking, he had a chance to study the delicate curve of her neck and the rosy color in her cheeks. Did she have any idea how beautiful she was? He was glad she hadn't married his brother. He took a sip of tea and waited for her answer.

"I'm not sure that my opinion matters one way or the other."

"It does to me."

She sighed heavily. "What would you have me say? I am Amish, Caleb. You are not. I have taken my vows. If nothing else stood between us, that would. I urge you to think of Joy. She has already lost or been abandoned by everyone she knows and loves. You're her father. She belongs with you."

"I am thinking of her. The longer I'm with her the less I want to go away and leave her here."

Leah placed a hand on his arm. "Then stay."

Chapter Twelve

Leah realized that Caleb was waiting for more encouragement from her. She was flattered that he cared for her. She cared for him, too. Perhaps more than she should, but she couldn't give him what he wanted.

She turned sideways on the step so she was facing him. "Caleb, if you stay or if you leave, it cannot be because of me. Would I like you to remain and become a part of our community? Of course. Your parents would, too. Many of your old friends would rejoice to know you have returned to us, but such a decision is too important to be made for one reason only. Pray for guidance. I will pray that you follow the path our Lord has chosen for you."

"Wise and kind as well as pretty. It's no wonder you are such a good teacher."

No man had called her pretty in a long time. His smile brought a warm glow to her heart. He truly had changed from the wild and reckless boy she once knew.

"Daddy, I found a cousin. I didn't know I had a cousin, did you?" Joy headed toward them, pulling David along by the hand.

Leah saw the sorrow that filled Caleb's eyes before he turned from her and gave his attention to the children. "I knew there was something I forgot to tell you."

She threw her arms around David in a bear hug. "This is David. His daddy is your brother, and that makes us cousins. I always wanted a cousin."

"Hello, David. It's nice to meet you."

David pulled away from Joy. "*Mamm* says not to speak to you."

Caleb nodded in resignation. "You are right to do what she tells you."

Leah rose from her place beside Caleb and took both Joy and David by the hand. "Did your *mamm* say you couldn't speak to Joy?"

"*Nee.*"

She began leading them toward the swing set. "Then you two must get to know each other. Why don't you push Joy on the swing and tell her all about your family and your home. David's father is your daddy's brother, but his mother is my sister. That makes David my nephew."

Joy tipped her head sideways as she gazed up at Leah. "Does that make you my aunt?"

"*Nee,* it makes me David's aunt. We say *aenti.* You and I are not related at all."

Joy looked disappointed. "I never had an *aenti* before."

David brightened. "You do have one. My *mamm* is your *aenti.*"

"She is?"

Leah nodded. "Rhonda is your *aenti,* and her husband, Wayne, is your *onkel,* your uncle."

Joy's face grew troubled. "Mama used to tell me her

boyfriends were my uncles. I didn't like them. Some-
times they were mean."

"My *daed* is not mean. You would like him. He takes
me sledding and ice skating in the winter, and he lets me
help him drive the team of horses during the summer."

"He doesn't sound mean. I might like him."

David pointed toward a farm in the distance. "That's
our *haus*."

"What does that mean?"

Leah translated. "It means *house*. That's where
David and his parents live."

Joy shaded her eyes to look into the distance. "That's
not so far."

"It only takes me ten minutes to walk to school. I
have a brown-and-white pony named Budget. He's re-
ally fast."

Joy grinned. "I like horses. Can I meet him?"

"I don't know. Mom doesn't like your dad."

Leah looked over her shoulder. Caleb rose from his
seat and entered the school. Once again, she was struck
by how alone he seemed to be. She prayed God would
show her the way to heal the breach between their fam-
ilies.

Caleb had come to school to make sure that Joy felt
comfortable in the new surroundings. Although his
main reason for being in the building was to keep an
eye on his daughter, he found his gaze constantly drawn
to Leah. He watched the way she moved, the way she
gestured with her hands when she spoke, the way she
seemed genuinely interested in every student in her
classes. It was clear that her students adored her in re-
turn. The entire room was well behaved and respectful.

After their conversation on the steps, he was pleased to know she wasn't indifferent to him, but he also knew their relationship wouldn't go forward until he made a major commitment.

He wasn't sure he could do it. Coming back to the Amish had not been on his to-do list. But then, neither had becoming a father to Joy. The Lord's path for him was taking some strange twists and turns. Leah was right. Remaining in Hope Springs wasn't something he could decide on his own. He needed divine guidance. He might be rusty at praying, but he still knew how to do it.

Please, Lord, show me the path You would have me take and give me the courage to follow it.

At three-thirty, Leah addressed the school. "On Wednesday, the day after tomorrow, we are going to do a special project. We are going to make a feast for our feathered friends. When the snow is deep, the birds have difficulty finding food. Since Christmas is just around the corner, I thought we should lend them a helping hand. I have made a list of things I would like you to bring to school."

She moved down the rows, handing out note cards. When she reached the back, where Caleb was seated, she handed him a card, too. He turned it over. It said, *This way, you will have many hands to help make your decorations.*

She walked back to the front of the room. "You are dismissed. I will see you all tomorrow."

Caleb walked forward through the stream of children headed out the door. He helped Joy gather her things and stow them in her desk. "What did you think of your first day of school?"

"I like recess."

"That was my favorite part of school, too." He was grateful that she had managed the entire day without a meltdown and had made a few friends in the process.

Leah straightened up the classroom and erased the problems from the blackboard. "Tomorrow will be even more fun."

Joy gaped at her. "I have to come here *again?*"

Caleb laughed. "Only until you finish the eighth grade."

She shut her desk. "I hope that doesn't take very long. Leah, can you walk home with us?"

Bless you, child, you took the words right out of my mouth. Caleb waited with bated breath for Leah to answer.

"Since we both are going in the same direction, I don't see why not."

"Cool."

Caleb made sure Joy was bundled up against the cold and that he had his rising excitement in check. Just because Leah agreed to walk a little ways with Joy didn't mean she wanted to walk out with him.

Leah closed the school door behind them and tied her bonnet under her chin. "I think we are in for more snow."

Caleb glanced at the low gray clouds scuttling by. "You may be right."

They fell into step together as they started down the path through the woods. It would have been almost as easy to reach Leah's house by walking along the road, but the quiet stillness of the trees offered privacy and a feeling of intimacy.

When Joy ran a little ways ahead of them along the

path, Leah asked quietly, "Are you seriously considering staying in Hope Springs?"

He wished he could tell what she was thinking. "I have started to think that it might be an option."

"What has changed your mind?"

He wanted to say she had, but he didn't. "Many things, but mostly it's because I have missed all of Joy's life up until now. I don't want to miss more."

"I can understand that. It won't be easy if you do stay."

"I know. I have to find a way to make it work, if that exists. Wayne and Rhonda are dead set against my staying."

"Perhaps they will come around in time."

"Maybe. Do you think they will? You know them better than I do." He took a huge leap of faith and reached for her hand.

Startled, Leah almost pulled away, but she didn't. He slowed his steps and so did she. She wasn't in any hurry to reach the place where they would part ways.

Remembering Rebecca's words about how God had used her as a tool to bring Gideon back to his faith, Leah wondered if God wanted to use her in the same fashion to help Caleb.

It was a fine line to walk. She would have to guard her heart against caring too much for a man who was forbidden.

She thought about his question and finally said, "Rhonda carries so much bitterness in her heart. I don't know if she will ever be able to see past that."

"Can you?"

"The past can't be changed. It is what we do in the

present that matters. Can you leave the English world and all its temptations behind?"

"Can I live Amish again? Maybe."

"I fear there's not much conviction in your voice."

"You're right. I have doubts, but I'm open to the idea. I couldn't have said that two weeks ago. I'm praying about it, and I couldn't have said that two weeks ago, either."

"Then I will pray you make the right decision."

Joy came running up and squeezed in between them. She took each of their hands. Leah shared a smile with Caleb as Joy began to chatter about the things she enjoyed doing with her new friends at school.

Leah tempered her rising happiness with a heavy dose of practicality. Many things stood between them, and she wasn't at all sure of what God wanted from her.

"Joy, is your daddy taking you to see the Christmas parade in Hope Springs on Saturday?"

Joy grinned at her dad. "Can we go to the Christmas parade? Please, please, please?"

Caleb rolled his eyes. "Now that Leah has mentioned it, I'm pretty sure that you will bug me until I do. Since when has Hope Springs sponsored a Christmas parade?"

"This will be our first annual Christmas parade. It was the brainchild of the new mayor. Tourism falls off in the winter months. He thought a Christmas parade might bring more people to town and give a boost to the local economy."

"It's a good idea, if the weather cooperates. What is the forecast for Saturday?"

"The paper said it will be sunny but cold. Still, it

could be worse. Everyone is looking forward to the event."

"Are you going to be there?" Joy asked.

"I am going with my sister and her family."

"Oh." Joy's lower lip stuck out as she pouted. "I wanted you to go with us."

"I am sure that we will see each other there."

"That's not the same. You don't like me anymore." Joy let go of their hands and ran toward home.

Leah called after, but she didn't look back.

Caleb said, "Don't worry. She gets cranky like this when she gets tired, and she has had a long day."

Leah felt terrible for upsetting her. "I will remember that and make sure that she takes a rest break at school."

"I should keep her in sight so she doesn't get lost. See you tomorrow." He followed his daughter, leaving Leah watching them and wondering if Joy would ever gain the sense of security and confidence that she needed.

The following morning proved to be a difficult one for both Leah and Joy. Emmy Chupp's mother arrived for a visit and brought fresh baked cupcakes for the class because it was Emmy's birthday. She sat quietly at the back of the room just as Caleb was doing. Joy became increasingly restless throughout the morning and had trouble staying on track.

She frequently got up from her desk and disrupted the other children who were trying to work. At recess, she refused to play with the other children and remained at her desk. Emmy's mother went home after she distributed the cupcakes at lunch. When she was gone, Joy went out to play, and Leah held a short conference with Caleb.

"What am I doing wrong?" She was seated behind her desk, feeling worn-out and frustrated.

He rested his hip casually against one corner of the desk. "I don't think we're doing anything wrong. Joy has trouble adjusting to change. I think once she becomes used to a routine, her behavior will improve."

"The teacher is the one who is supposed to be encouraging the parent, not the other way around."

"We are both finding our way with her. My one consolation is that her life here is so much better than when she was with her mother."

Leah moved a set of papers from one side of her desk to the other. "Have you heard anything from her mother?"

"Not a word. My attorney let me know that my petition for full custody has been granted. It will take more time to have Valerie's parental rights severed permanently."

"Has Joy spoken about her?"

"Not since the evening we left your place and she jumped out of the buggy on the way home. Do you think I should talk to her about Valerie?"

"I don't know. On one hand, I think it would be good for her to share what she's feeling, but on the other hand, I don't want to upset her more than she already is."

"I feel the same way. If she continues to misbehave this afternoon, how would you feel if I took her out of school and took her home?"

"You are her father. You are the best one to make that decision."

"You are forgetting that I've only been a father for two months. I'm not sure you can make a case that I'm the best one to make decisions for her."

"Who else is there?"

"Good point. Honestly, Leah, if you see me taking the wrong track with her, let me know."

He was deadly serious. She had an overwhelming urge to wrap her arms around him and tell him that he was doing a fine job. He had been given a difficult task, and he was trying his best to do the right thing for his child. "It's good to know that you are open to suggestions. Not all of my fathers are."

He glanced at the clock. "Time to round them up."

"Let us pray that the afternoon goes better."

He stood up. "Amen to that."

Their prayers were answered. Joy came in from playing outside, hung up her coat and mittens, and calmly took her seat. For the rest of the afternoon, she was a model student. Leah exchanged a puzzled glance with Caleb. He simply shrugged his shoulders. Neither one of them knew what had changed.

On Wednesday, Joy was up early and dressed for school by the time Caleb came down for breakfast. She had finished setting plates on the table. "What should I do now, *Mammi?*"

Caleb took his place at the table. His father had already eaten and had gone out to do chores. His mother smiled at Joy. "You can fetch the butter from the refrigerator and then we are ready to eat."

Joy did as she was asked, and then took a seat at the table and folded her hands. "I am ready to pray, Daddy."

He shared an amused look with his mother, then said, "We normally say our prayers silently, but since you do not know them, I will teach this to you."

He bowed his head and closed his eyes. Joy did the

same. "This is the *Gebet Nach Dem Essen,* the Prayer Before Meals. Lord God, heavenly Father, bless us and these Thy gifts, which we accept from Thy tender goodness. Give us food and drink for our souls unto life eternal, that we may share Thy heavenly table with Thee, through Jesus Christ. Amen."

He then recited the Lord's Prayer as was done before every meal. When he finished, he opened his eyes and looked at Joy. She still had her eyes scrunched closed and her hands folded.

Caleb's mother came up behind him and placed a kiss on the top of his head, something she hadn't done since he was seven years old. "You may eat now, both of you."

Joy's eyes popped open and she grabbed her fork. "*Goot,* because I'm hungry. We're going to do something fun in school today. We are going to make things for the birds to eat."

Caleb's mother dished up the food and then took a seat beside her granddaughter. "So you like school, do you?"

"Mostly. I like recess the best. I like my teacher, and I like Emmy, and Anna and David. They are my friends."

She cocked her head to the side and looked at her grandmother. "It's okay to be friends with my cousin, isn't it?"

"It is most definitely okay," Maggie assured her.

Joy finished eating in record time and waited impatiently for Caleb to get done. When they were finally on the way to school, he tentatively broached the subject of her mother.

"Have you mailed all the Christmas cards that you made the other night?"

"Yup."

"Did you make one for your mother?"

"Yeah, but I don't think she'll get it. I don't know where she lives now. *Mammi* wrote Nana's address on it."

"Maybe your step-grandpa will give it to her."

"I don't think so. He didn't like her. He called her a junkie."

"Do you know what that means?"

"It means she gets sick, and she has to take really bad medicine, but it never makes her better."

"I guess that's about right."

"She could get better if she wants to. Nana said that. But I don't think Mama wants to."

"From now on, when we say our prayers at night, we are going to ask God to help her get better."

"Do you think He can do that?"

"Yes. I believe He can."

The rest of the morning went off without a hitch. Joy repeated much of the Lord's Prayer with the other children and joined in singing some of the songs she had learned. She wrote out all the letters of the alphabet and happily showed them to Leah. She was behaving so well that he began to think they were over the hump at school and she could do without him. When the children went out for their first recess, he mentioned the idea to Leah. She agreed it was worth a try.

He waited until the children were going out for their lunch recess before he pulled Joy aside. Leah came to stand beside them. He was grateful for her presence.

"Joy, I want to talk to you."

"But, Daddy, it's time for recess."

"You can go in a minute. Remember I told you I

would always let you know when I was leaving and when I would be back?"

"Kind of." She tipped her head slightly as she stared out at the children playing in the schoolyard.

"Okay. I wanted to let you know that I'm going home for a little while this afternoon to help Grandpa. I will be back before school lets out so we can walk home together. Is that okay?"

"Sure. Can I go play now?"

So much for the meltdown that he had been expecting. He exchanged glances with Leah. She looked as relieved as he felt. "Okay. Have a good time. I'll see you later."

She ran out to join the circle of children getting ready to play Duck, Duck, Goose. Anna Imhoff and David made room for her between them.

Caleb blew out a breath and walked to the door. "That was easier than I thought it would be."

"She seems to be adjusting well. She's a different child than the one you brought to school yesterday."

"I think so, too."

They stepped outside and stood close together on the steps of the school. He was reluctant to leave. If Joy did well, he would lose his excuse to spend time with Leah.

"I will keep a close eye on her," she assured him.

Caleb allowed his gaze to linger on her face. "I know that. I couldn't ask for a more capable or compassionate teacher for Joy. You've been good for her. And for me."

A blush stained her cheeks and she looked away.

Realizing he had said too much, he walked down the steps and started toward home.

Leaving Joy at school was much harder than Caleb had expected. At the edge of the woods, he stopped

and looked back. Leah still stood on the steps, watching him. He lifted a hand in a brief wave. She did the same. It wasn't much, but somehow it raised his spirits immensely.

When he reached the house, he saw a buggy tied to the gate and recognized Wayne's horse. He half hoped that Rhonda had come to visit his mother. Maybe he could convince her to tell the truth now.

He was disappointed to see his brother come out the front door. Wayne folded his arms over his chest. "I would speak with you."

"Fine. Say what you have to say. I'm listening."

Wayne looked over his shoulder toward the house. "Not here. Get in the buggy."

Caleb extended his arm. "After you."

Both men climbed into the buggy. Wayne picked up the reins and sent the horse trotting out of the yard. Caleb waited until they were at the end of the lane before he spoke again. "I want to thank you for agreeing to let Joy attend school at Walnut Valley."

"My wife insisted."

"Then please give her my thanks."

"You have what you came for. Why are you still here?"

"I came because I wanted to see Joy settled and happy. The longer I'm around her, the less anxious I am to leave. She is my daughter, after all."

"There are people in the church who believe our parents are wrong to allow you to stay. There's talk of shunning them."

"Is that why we're taking this little ride? So you can guilt me into leaving. Again."

Wayne turned the horse into a cornfield and pulled

to a stop. "We all know you left to be with your *Englisch* girlfriend."

"You don't really think I left because of Valerie, do you? I will admit that Valerie made leaving easier, but she wasn't the reason I couldn't stay."

"You left because you couldn't face what you had done to Rhonda. She is a good woman. She deserved better from you."

"She did deserve better from someone. Just not from me. I dated her for a while because I felt sorry for her after the accident, but I was never with her in that way. I left because no one believed my side of the story. Not even you. After what I did for you, how could you turn your back on me that way?"

"Lying comes easy to you."

"And silence comes easily to you. A lie doesn't have to be spoken to be a lie. Why haven't you told Rhonda that you were driving the car that hit her that night? I can understand why you never admitted it to our parents. Dad thinks the sun rises and sets on you. You were always the good son. I knew it would break his heart to find out you ran away and left an injured woman trapped under that car."

"Your car! The forbidden thing you kept hidden in the woods. You made me drive it. It was all your fault," Wayne shouted. "I never would have gone to such a party without you egging me on. Laughing at me, poking fun at me, calling me a coward. You led me astray. God forgive me."

Caleb stared down at his hands. "I know I did. That's why I let everyone believe I was driving. They were shocked but not surprised. They expected trouble from me."

"Go away. Haven't you done enough?"

Yes, and I've suffered enough, too, brother. I want a new start. You owe me that.

He didn't say what he was thinking. Instead, he looked at Wayne. "You have been married to Rhonda for nine years. How can you look at her every day and not tell her the truth about that night?"

Wayne seemed to shrink in on himself. "At first, Rhonda said she forgave you. I thought things would be all right for her. Then she became pregnant and you refused to marry her. She was crushed. She changed. She became a different woman.

"It was only after we wed that I saw how much she hates the way she looks. She can't bear to have people stare at her. She has never forgiven the person who scarred her. To this day, she carries that bitterness in her heart. How could I admit that I am the one responsible after she believed it was you for so long?"

Caleb realized he wasn't the only one suffering because of the deceit they had carried out. He didn't want to feel sorry for his brother, but he heard the despair in Wayne's voice. Was there any way to help?

He laid a hand on Wayne's arm. "Swallowed alive by guilt and bitterness is a terrible way to live. Have you thought about getting some professional help? Dr. White is a good man. He can find someone that you can talk to. Someone who can help Rhonda find a way to accept her disfigurement."

Wayne stiffened and shook off Caleb's hand. "We will not air our dirty laundry in public. We did well enough until you came back. We will do well enough when you are gone." He slapped the reins against the horse's rump, drove back out onto the highway and headed toward the farm.

"And if I decide not to leave?" Caleb asked.

Wayne looked shocked. "What are you saying?"

"I'm considering returning to the Amish."

"No!"

"You don't get a say in how I live my life from now on."

"The church congregation must vote to accept your return. They won't. Not if I can help it. There is no repentance in your heart. I will say this to all."

Caleb struggled to control his temper. "There are other congregations in the area. You can't keep me out of them all."

Wayne pulled to a stop in front of Ike's house. "Have you come back to torment me?"

"No, I came home because I have a daughter with Down syndrome. She needs a loving home and a welcoming community to live in. I thought I would find that here. You have son. You know what I'm talking about."

Wayne's anger drained away. "My wife is afraid of you. Somehow, she believes you can hurt David."

"I won't. I promise you that."

"I know what it is to love a child. I could not love him more if he were mine."

"Then for the sake of our children and our parents, let us find a way to be civil to one another."

Before Wayne could answer, a teenage boy came running up to the buggy. He leaned on the wheel to catch his breath. "Teacher sent me to find you, Caleb Mast. Joy has run away."

Chapter Thirteen

Leah went weak with relief when she saw Caleb leap out of the buggy that came tearing into the schoolyard. The feeling was quickly followed by shame. She ran toward him and threw herself into his arms. "I am so sorry."

He hugged her close. "Have you found her?"

"*Nee.* I have the older children scouring the woods. They are to listen for the school bell. If it rings, they are to come back."

"What happened?"

"I don't know. Everything seemed to be going fine. She was happily playing with the others. I went inside to write out the history assignment for the upper grades. I was only gone a few minutes. I rang the bell to call everyone inside, and that's when I noticed she wasn't with the other children."

Leah was shocked to see Wayne get out of the buggy, as well. "Is there someplace she might go?"

Caleb turned in a circle as he raked a hand through his hair. "She's not familiar with anything but the way

to get to school and the way to go home. Leah, is it possible she went to your house to see the puppy?"

Leah hated the look of fear on his face. She hated knowing she was responsible. "I sent two of my girls to check. They aren't back yet."

"If she's not there, I have no idea where she can be. Are you sure none of the children saw where she went? Were there any cars that stopped on the road?"

Leah shook her head. "The children saw nothing out of the ordinary."

"She couldn't have vanished into thin air." His frustration was breaking through.

Leah saw the girls she had sent to her house running toward her. They didn't have Joy with them. They stopped beside her. "We didn't see any sign of her."

"*Danki,* please go inside and help watch the little ones."

Wayne said, "We can organize a bigger search party and get some men on horseback to cover more ground. Ring the bell, Leah, and call the children back. We will send them home and have their fathers meet us here."

"Please, God, let her be all right." Caleb walked away from the school and began calling her name. Leah had been doing it to no avail.

She hurried to the school bell and began ringing it. One by one, the children returned from the wooded area and fields next to the school. As the last one came in, Leah noticed a pony cart coming down the road. She recognized her sister. A moment later, she realized Rhonda wasn't alone. Joy sat beside her.

Leah screamed to Caleb, "We found her."

He ran to her side. "Where is she?"

Leah pointed toward the road. "She is with my sister."

Rhonda turned her pony into the schoolyard and stopped. Caleb snatched Joy off the seat and held her tight. "Thank God you are safe."

"Daddy, you are squishing me."

He dropped to one knee and set her on her feet in front of him. "You have to stop scaring me like this. Why did you run away?"

"I didn't run away. I went to David's house to meet my *aenti* and to see his pony. Can I have a pony, please? I'll take good care of it."

Leah knelt beside them. "Joy, you can't leave school without permission."

"I can't? Why not?"

"Because that is the rule," Leah said.

"That's just silly."

Caleb stood and looked down at her. "It is not silly. It is the rule. And you are never again to leave without permission. Do you understand?

Her lower lip stuck out. "Yes, Daddy."

Caleb offered his hand to Leah and helped her to her feet. He turned to Rhonda. "Thank you for the care you have shown my daughter."

She looked away. Without a word, she turned the pony and drove away. Wayne went inside the school and returned a moment later with David. "Get in the buggy, *sohn*."

Joy waved at David. "I like your pony."

Leah met Caleb's glance. "Why don't you take Joy home, too? I'm letting school out early. I think we have all had enough excitement for one day."

"But what about the bird treats we were going to make?" Joy asked.

Leah smiled at her. "We will make them first thing tomorrow morning. How will that be?"

"Goot!" she shouted.

Caleb gave his daughter a small push toward the school. "Go get your things."

As she ran up the steps, Leah turned to Caleb. "I am so sorry that this happened. Please forgive me."

He drew her close and wrapped his arms around her. "There is nothing to forgive. I have the feeling that life with Joy is always going to be an adventure. I just thank God that she is okay."

Leah knew she should move out of his embrace, but nothing had ever felt so right or so comforting. "I shouldn't have let it happen. I should've kept a closer eye on her." She pressed her face against his neck.

He cupped her cheek with his hand. "You were as frightened as I was. I see how much you care for my child. I hope you know how much she cares for you. Almost as much as I do."

Leah raised her face and looked into his eyes. They were filled with tenderness. She knew that he was going to kiss her. She knew she should stop him, but she didn't.

The gentle touch of his lips sent a thrill straight through her. The moment was everything she had dreamed it would be and more. Her heart skipped a beat and soared with happiness.

He drew away suddenly. "I have wanted to do that for a very long time."

She stepped out of his arms as reality brought her crashing back to earth. She hoped none of her students

had been watching. "It doesn't change things. You know that."

"It does for me. You are making a hard decision much easier. Bless you, Leah, you are a rare treasure."

The schoolhouse door opened and Joy came out with her lunch box and the paper she had finished that day.

"Look what I did, *Daed*. I want to show *Mammi* I got 100 on my math paper."

"That's great, honey. Say goodbye to your teacher, and let's go home."

As they walked away, Leah realized she had been wrong. The kiss did change things. She could never look at him again without remembering it. It was a memory she would hold close to her heart.

"You look happy today, teacher."

Leah realized she was grinning foolishly and schooled her expression into something more appropriate for the classroom. Anna, Emmy, David and Kyle were gathered in front of her desk. "I'm happy because Christmas is almost here."

And because Caleb Mast had kissed her yesterday.

It had been all too brief, but that hadn't detracted from its impact. She started smiling again just thinking about the tender way his lips brushed hers. She would remember forever the sweetness of the moment.

Anna said, "Christmas is what we wanted to talk to you about. Actually, about our Christmas program."

"What about our program?" The rehearsal had gone quite well. Only one child had forgotten his lines.

"Joy doesn't have a part in it," Kyle said.

Everyone but Joy had remained after school for the

rehearsal. She had gone home with her father after having an entire day that was crisis-free.

Leah frowned slightly. "Joy started school so late that I didn't think she would have time to learn our songs or a part in the play or the skits you children are putting on. I don't want to make her feel uncomfortable. I thought it would be best if she watched the program with her family this year. I promise that next year we will include her."

Anna looked at her friends and then said, "We have written a play for her. I know that it's your job to choose the songs and plays, but maybe this once we could do one?"

What wonderful children they were for wanting to include Joy. "I'm pleased that you have thought of this. But the programs have already been printed."

"Couldn't you just announce that we have added one more play?" Anna handed Leah a piece of paper.

Leah opened it and read the short play. She looked at the children standing in front of her as her heart swelled with happiness. "Are you sure you want to try this?"

They all nodded vigorously.

"All right. I will talk to Joy's father and grandmother and find out if they can help her learn her part."

"*Danki,* teacher. We will help her, too," Kyle said. He knew how hard it was to be an outsider coming into a small Amish community. It was generous of him to help make Joy's transition easier.

The children finished straightening up the desks and went home. Leah stayed behind to finish her own work. Picking up an eraser, she began to clean the blackboard. Now that she was alone, she was free to think about "the

kiss" and what it might mean for her if Caleb stayed and joined the church.

Laying down the eraser, she picked up a piece of chalk and wrote *Caleb Mast* in large letters across the board. Then beneath it she added *Mrs. Caleb Mast,* then *Mr. and Mrs. Caleb Mast.*

She stared at the board and started to giggle. She wasn't any better than the boy-crazy girls in her eighth-grade class. The possibility of marriage and family made Leah's heart sing, but she was a practical woman, not a teenage girl. One kiss did not mean a lifetime to-gether.

Caleb hadn't said anything about love or marriage. Although he was considering returning to the Amish way of life, he had not yet made that commitment. A kiss was just a kiss without it. But if he chose not to stay, her heart would break in a million pieces.

On Saturday, she would spend the day with her sister and her family. While Caleb had made strides in repair-ing his relationship with his parents, he hadn't made any progress in gaining her sister's forgiveness. Although Caleb was a touchy subject, Leah hoped that she could find a way to help Rhonda accept, if not welcome, his return to the community.

She stared at the blackboard and sighed. She was letting her foolish heart put the cart before the horse. She picked up the eraser again and wiped away her daydreams.

If the new mayor's goal was to bring people to Hope Springs for the Christmas parade, the plan was a whop-ping success. Caleb held Joy's hand as they made their way along Main Street. His parents walked behind

them. The parade wasn't due to start for another half hour, but already there were crowds of people seated on lawn chairs lining the street. The mix was equally Amish and non-Amish. There were sheriff's deputies and town police officers directing traffic away from Main Street to keep it open for the parade vehicles. Caleb had left their buggy at the parking lot next to the Wadler Inn, near the edge of town.

"Where are we going to sit, Daddy?" Joy tried to see around the people in front of them.

He was searching the crowd for Leah, but he hadn't seen her or his brother. He looked over his shoulder. "Where do you think, *Daed*?"

"Down by the park. There is more space and we will be able to see more than just this narrow street."

"The park it is." Caleb moved ahead quickly. If Leah was here, he wanted to see her. He didn't have to speak to her, although he would like that very much. But just to see her would be enough today.

It was hard to stop thinking about her. About the kiss they had shared. Did she regret it? Had he embarrassed her? Would she let him kiss her again? They were questions he was afraid to ask. He knew if they saw each other, he would read the answers on her face.

His father was right. People were more spread out along the edge of the park. A number of children were making good use of the playground. He and his father set out their canvas folding chairs while his mother unpacked food from a small basket. As soon as they were settled, she handed out whoopee pies and bottled drinks.

Caleb was amazed at the number of people who stopped to say hello and to meet Joy. He had dressed Plain that day, with the dark coat, dark pants and black

wide-brimmed hat borrowed from his father. They had been sitting for about ten minutes when Joy suddenly bolted out of her chair and ran toward an English family. He rushed after her as she grabbed a little girl about her own age and squealed with glee.

"I'm sorry," he said to the startled father.

"Look, Daddy. She's just like me."

It was then Caleb realized the other child also had Down syndrome. Her father extended his hand. "I see you are blessed with a special child, too. Aren't they amazing children?"

"Yes. I hope she didn't frighten your daughter. She doesn't normally grab people. Joy, let her go, honey."

"Melissa hugs everyone. I'm Gerard Franks. Do you live in the area?"

"Joy and I recently moved to Hope Springs. I'm Caleb Mast."

"Nice to meet you. We live near Millersburg. Not too far away. Maybe we can get together for a playdate with our girls one of these days."

"I think Joy would like that."

Gerard pulled out a business card. "I'm the treasurer of the local Down syndrome support group. We meet once a month so that our families can get together and enjoy each other's company."

"I didn't realize there was a support group for children like Joy."

Gerard looked surprised. "There are local as well as national chapters. If you're interested, drop by one of our meetings. We're working to change the world's perception of our children and give them the future they deserve. We also help new parents face the special chal-

lenges our blessings bring. We have many Amish fami-
lies in our group. Joy won't feel out of place."

He took his daughter's hand and they walked away.
Joy turned to Caleb. "She has Up sindome just like me."

"I see that."

He stared at the card in his hand. It felt strange to
know other people were dealing with the same is-
sues that he faced. That they were working to ensure
the same kind of future for their children that he was
seeking for Joy. Somehow, he thought such acceptance
only happened among the Amish. It seemed that he
was wrong. If things didn't work out, if he found he
couldn't accept the Amish way of life again, he and Joy
wouldn't have to face life alone.

He walked back to his parents and held Joy on his lap
so that she could see better. The shrill siren announced
the beginning of the parade. Leading the way was the
county sheriff's SUV with all its lights flashing. As it
rolled down the street, the siren would sound every few
minutes. Joy got off his lap and raced to the edge of the
street. She covered her ears and grinned each time the
siren sounded.

Walking behind the sheriff's vehicle was a color
guard made up of veterans. They held their flags stiffly
in front of them and marched with precision. Some of
them were older than Caleb's father.

After that came the high school marching band, a
saddle club with all the horses sporting red-and-white
ribbons braided into their manes and tails, and numer-
ous homemade floats from the local merchants and
churches. Some of the car dealerships from as far away
as New Philadelphia had convertibles and trucks decked
out with holiday lights and Christmas trees. They threw

candy toward the children gathered along the edge of the street as a fellow dressed like Santa Claus rode up and down and all around on a small motor scooter.

When the local ambulance passed by, Caleb caught sight of Leah and her family on the other side of the street. David saw Joy at the same time and darted out into the street toward her.

He didn't see the motor scooter bearing down on him. Santa was waving to the crowd and didn't notice the boy in his path.

Caleb shot into the street, but a sheriff's deputy had already grabbed David and hauled him out of harm's way.

Caleb and Rhonda reached him at the same time. There was something familiar about the man, but Caleb couldn't place him. The officer tipped his hat toward Rhonda. "Long time no see, Rhonda."

The color leached out of her face. She reached for David, but the officer held on to him. The officer's eyes never left Rhonda's face. "You've got a nice-looking boy, Rhonda."

She reached out and yanked her son away from him. He smiled as she hurried back into the crowd. Caleb had a chance to study him. The uniform was different from those of the officers he had seen directing traffic. The patch on his arm bore the logo of the county to the south.

When the man turned toward Caleb, he realized who it was. Drake Colburn, the deputy on the scene the night of Rhonda's accident. He looked Caleb up and down. "What do you want?"

"Just to add my thanks. How do you know my brother's wife?"

"That's my business and none of yours. Have a nice day." He walked away along the parade route, motioning to people to move back out of the street.

Caleb returned to his family. The parade was soon over and they joined the flow of the crowd as they headed out of town. He scanned the area for Leah but didn't see her. She would be at the church service tomorrow. It was unlikely that they would find time to be alone together, but tomorrow night they had something special planned for Joy. He knew he'd have the chance to repeat their kiss or discover if he was wasting his time. He walked on, disappointed but more than a little curious about Rhonda's reaction to Drake Colburn.

On the way to the buggy, Joy stopped to stare in the window of a shop with a white flocked tree on display. She pressed her nose to the glass. "It's a pretty tree. Mama said we would have one like this someday."

He didn't know what to say. He took her hand and gently led her away. "Did you like the parade?"

She looked over her shoulder. Another family had stopped in front of the window to admire the display. "Christmas is for families to be together."

"Yes, it is. And I'm glad I have you with me this Christmas. You are making it very special. You are my very own Christmas Joy."

She smiled at him then, and he hoped the tree and thoughts of her mother would be forgotten.

Caleb had made up his mind, but he was still nervous as he rode in the buggy with his parents and Joy on Sunday morning. If he was coming back to the Amish community, and back to God, attending church was the

best place to start. Then a job would be next on his list. He couldn't live on his savings forever.

"It will be *goot* to have our son and granddaughter listen to the Lord's words with us." His mother could not have looked more pleased. Even his father was in a happy mood. He let Joy take the reins for a while as they trotted along a deserted stretch of country road.

It didn't take long to reach the Yutzi farmstead, where the services were to be held. Caleb unhitched the horse and led it to a nearby corral where two dozen other horses were lined up in their harnesses, munching on hay and waiting to make the return trip with their families. When he approached the barn where the preaching was to take place, he saw that his parents and Joy had already gone in.

He stepped inside the cavernous opening. Tarps had been used to cover the hay bales stacked along each side. The benches had been set out in rows with a wide center aisle. The men sat on one side and the women sat on the other.

Caleb walked to the last row. A pair of teenage boys scooted over to make room for him. He was prepared to spend three hours sitting on a hard wooden bench. What he wasn't prepared for was the swelling emotion that engulfed him when the first familiar hymn began.

The slow and mournful chanting rose in volume as many voices blended in the ancient German song that had been passed down through the generations. No music accompanied the singing. Only the voices of the faithful poured into his ears and into his heart.

Listening to the words of sorrow, hope and God's promise of salvation, Caleb felt a stirring deep within his soul. Why had he stayed away from God so long?

His life had been empty without faith, but God was filling him again.

He quietly added his voice to the chorus. When the song was done, he listened intently to Bishop Zook as he spoke about the hardship of the journey that Joseph and Mary had undergone on the way to Bethlehem and the great joy that awaited them at journey's end.

When the second hymn began, Caleb opened the hymnal beside him on the bench and joined in the song. He looked across the aisle and saw Leah looking his way. She smiled at him, and it turned his heart inside out. He suddenly realized he didn't just like her. He was falling in love with her. With her kindness, her wonderful bright mind and her adorable smile.

God had given him a special daughter, and Joy had led him home, to his family and to his faith. Had God used Joy to bring him love, too? Did the Lord have more blessings in store for him?

Caleb opened his heart and prayed that Leah would be one of them.

Much later that afternoon, Caleb sat at the kitchen table and motioned to his parents that he was leaving the house. They smiled and his father winked at him, as happy as a kid to be in on the secret.

Caleb said, "Joy, I have a surprise for you."

"What is it?"

"If I told you, it wouldn't be a surprise. Put your coat, snow pants, boots and mittens on."

"Why?"

"Because your surprise is outside."

She took her coat from the peg and buttoned it. "Is it big? Is it a pony? Is it a sled?"

"It's not a pony or a sled. Stop asking questions and

hurry up." He opened the door. She pulled on her snow pants and boots and joined him. He led her along the path they took to school.

When they were at the place where the path made a small bend, he said, "Cover your eyes and no peeking."

She placed her mittens over her face. "I can't see."

He picked her up and carried her the rest of the way. "Can I look now?"

"No. Keep those peepers shut." It was a bit of a struggle to walk through the thick snow, but he trudged ahead.

She waited another minute. "Can I look now?"

"I guess so." He was standing in front of her tree.

Her eyes opened wide with shock. "A Christmas tree." Her voice was hushed with wonder.

Leah stepped out from behind it. "Surprise. Do you like it?"

Joy threw her arms around Caleb's neck and squeezed hard as she pressed a kiss to his cheek.

His heart swelled with love. "I guess that means you like it."

"It's beautiful." She struggled to get down. He set her on her feet in the deep snow. Leah had tied red bows of yarn to the branches. With the newly fallen snow clinging to the needles, it looked sparkling and bright. Joy walked around the tree and clapped her hands.

Leah smiled at him. The sight of her warmed his heart. Would she consent to share his life? It was too soon to ask, but he knew he wouldn't be able to wait much longer.

Picking up a basket, Leah said, "I brought more decorations. These are the ones the children made at school."

For the next half hour, they hung slices of oranges and apples around the tree, along with pinecones that had been smeared with peanut butter and rolled in birdseed. The brightly colored yarn would supply the birds with soft nesting material come spring. When Joy couldn't reach the higher branches, Caleb lifted her and held her as Leah handed her more decorations. When they were finished, he put Joy down and she stood back. "Where's the star?"

"I have it right here." Leah produced a large gingerbread cookie shaped like a star and frosted white. She handed it to Caleb. He raised one eyebrow. "It's a little worldly for the birds, isn't it?"

"I think it's nearly perfect."

He propped the cookie in the upper branches and took a step away. Joy, her cheeks red from the cold, turned to Leah. "Can I show it to Pickles? She's never seen a Christmas tree."

"When she's a little older. Her eyes are open now. You must come and visit her soon."

"Can I, Daddy?"

"How about going there tonight?"

"Yeah!" She threw her arms around his legs. "This is the best surprise I ever had."

Emotion choked off Caleb's voice. What a true blessing this child was. If she had to go back to Valerie, he didn't know how he would face it.

"You are going to make many, many birds happy with your Christmas gift to them," Leah said.

Caleb cleared his throat. "Are you ready for another surprise?"

"Yes!" She jumped as she shouted.

He pointed toward the lane. "Go right through there. *Mammi* and *Daadi* are waiting for you."

As Joy took off, he turned to Leah and moved to stand directly in front of her. "Thank you for making my child so happy," he said softly.

"It was a joint effort." Leah's heart fluttered wildly. She had waited for days to be alone with him. They didn't have much time. People were expecting them. Would he kiss her again? Should she let him?

"It means a lot to me the way you've taken Joy under your wing. I was wondering…" He gazed into her eyes.

"Wondering what?" She licked her suddenly dry lips.

"I was wondering if I could kiss you again."

Chapter Fourteen

Caleb didn't wait for Leah's answer. She didn't have one anyway. He closed the space between them, wrapped his arms around her and pressed his mouth to hers. Leah closed her eyes to savor the tender excitement that made her slip her arms around his neck and pull him closer still.

His kiss, tender and tentative at first, deepened at her response. His firm lips drew forth an ardent desire that left her breathless and yet wanting more. When he pulled away, she was reluctant to let him go.

He raised his face to the sky as he drew a shuddering breath, then he cupped her head and pressed her face against his neck. He smelled like pine needles and the crisp outdoors, yet underneath it all was a wonderful earthiness that was uniquely his own scent.

He said, "I wish Christmas was over."

"Why?"

"Because then my parents wouldn't be waiting for us to join them and I could keep you to myself for a lot longer."

She gave a sigh of her own and stepped away. He re-

leased her, letting his hands slide down her arms slowly, as if he couldn't bear to let her go.

She had to know for certain what his intentions were before she could let things go any further. "Caleb, does this mean you are staying? That you will become Amish?"

"Yes. I've thought about it and prayed about it. This is right for me. I know it."

Tears blurred her vision. "I'm so glad."

"Hey, don't cry."

"They are tears of happiness. You promised Joy she could visit the puppies. I see no reason why the two of you can't come over whenever you'd like."

He chuckled. "Don't give me an open invitation. I'll be outside your door every day when you get home from school."

"And what makes you think I would object to that?" She gave him a saucy smile and began walking toward the lane.

He quickly caught up with her. When they came out of the woods, she saw his parents were waiting for them in the sleigh. The big draft horse stomped one foot and shook his head, making the bells on his harness jingle.

Joy was already in the front seat between Maggie and Ike. "We're going for a sleigh ride. We're going to sing songs for our neighbors. And then go to town to see all the pretty lights."

Caleb spoke softly in Leah's ear. "Looks like we get the backseat to ourselves."

She quickly became the prim schoolteacher. "Where you will behave yourself, Caleb Mast. Or else."

"Or else what?" He helped her into the sleigh.

"Or else you will find yourself walking home. Ike, I think everyone should be at my place by now."

"We'll be there in two shakes of a lamb's tail. I reckon it's time I met this puppy I have heard so much about."

"You will love her," Joy assured him.

When they pulled into Leah's yard about twenty minutes later, they found four sleighs gathered there. Ike helped Joy down from the seat. When they entered the house, she stopped. "What are all these people doing here?"

Leah said, "We are going caroling. Won't that be fun?"

Elam Sutter and his wife, Katie, along with their children, had arrived. Marvin Chupp sat at the kitchen table, with his cast stretched out in front of him and his crutches at his side. His wife stood behind him with her hands on his shoulders. Levi Beachy and Sarah each held a cup of the spiced cider that Leah had left simmering on the stove for everyone to enjoy. Levi's lanky twin teenage brothers flanked them. Jonathan and Karen Dresher were seated on the sofa with Nettie and Eli. The rest of the children were gathered around Trixie and her puppies. Leah was happy to see David in the group.

She looked around. "Are Wayne and Rhonda here?"

Sarah shook her head. "Wayne brought David, but he couldn't stay."

Leah tempered her disappointment with the knowledge that it was a small step for Wayne to allow David to join Caleb and Joy on the outing. She wondered if Rhonda knew that Caleb would be joining them.

"*Daadi,* come meet Pickles." Joy led the way to the

box in the corner of the kitchen. The children gathered around it made room for them.

Joy greeted her friends. "Hi, Anna. Hi, Emmy. This is my grandpa. And this is Pickles." She carefully lifted the puppy from the box.

Ike admired Pickles and agreed that she looked like a very good farm dog in the making.

Leah said, "I think we are ready. Where shall we go first?"

Elam Sutter rose from his seat. "I know my neighbors the Zimmermans always enjoy hearing the children sing."

"So do Mr. and Mrs. McGregor," Katie added. "If we make a loop around Pleasant View Road, we will end up in Hope Springs and we can give them a surprise concert."

With the route agreed upon, everyone went outside. Jonathan helped his pregnant wife into the backseat of Eli's sleigh. "This reminds me of the first time I rode in a sleigh with you, Karen. We were on our way to the Christmas program at Leah's school."

"I remember," Anna said. "You kissed my sister that night."

Karen frowned at her in surprise. "And how would you know that?"

"Jonathan told me that was the night he fell in love with you."

Karen tried to scowl at Jonathan, but she couldn't keep the smile off her face. "Should I know what else you have told my little sister about us?"

"Nope. Are you warm enough?"

"I will be when you get in."

Caleb spoke to Leah. "Will you ride with us?"

"Of course."

Jonathan called out, "Be careful, Caleb. Look what happened to me after one sleigh ride with the pretty Amish *maedel*."

Leah blushed. "Ignore him," Karen said. "I do. You're in for a delightful night, Leah. Enjoy it."

Eli slapped the reins against his horse and drove out of the yard with Karen and Jonathan laughing together. Leah smiled at Caleb and got into the sleigh with happy anticipation coursing through her veins.

Maggie said, "It is hard to imagine that Jonathan was once an *Englisch* fellow. He is so at home with us. Caleb and Leah, get in so we can get going. This little girl wants to do some singing."

Caleb joined Leah in the backseat of the sleigh. He carefully tucked a blanket around them both. As Ike followed the others out onto the road, Caleb realized that Karen was right. There was definitely something delightful about the night.

The fields they passed were blankets of white dotted with farmhouses and barns. The woods along the way were dark and gloomy. The light from the lanterns on the sides of the sleigh couldn't penetrate their depths. Overhead, the stars looked close enough to touch in the clear night air.

The cold stung his cheeks and made him wish he had a scarf to wrap around his face. The jingle of harness bells and the clip-clop of the horses' feet on the roadway were the only sounds. The glow of the lanterns on the other sleighs guided them forward.

Leah pulled the blanket higher. "I hope you didn't take offense at Jonathan's teasing."

"No. He is a good-natured fellow. I had forgotten how much fun it was to do simple things like this."

"I'm glad you have remembered."

In an hour's time, they visited four homes and stood in a semicircle around the children as they sang. Joy was off-key and a little slow, but her enthusiasm made up for her lack of talent. At each house, they were treated to baked goods and hot drinks before they climbed back in the sleighs and drove on.

They were nearing the end of Pleasant View Road when a dog darted out onto the road and began barking.

"Grandpa, stop. It's Duncan," Joy shouted.

Ike pulled over to the side. Duncan jumped into the sleigh and proceeded to lick Joy's face.

"*Ach,* get down, you silly mutt," Maggie scolded.

He scrambled off the seat and jumped down. Joy leaned over the side. "You need to come visit your babies. They need their daddy and their mommy."

He barked once and ran back the way he had come. Joy looked at Leah. "Is this where he lives?"

"*Ja,* it is Woolly Joe's farm. Duncan's owner, Carl King, lives in the shepherd's hut just beyond the fence."

"You should tell him to bring Duncan to see Pickles."

"I will mention it to him as soon as I see him." Leah exchanged an amused glance with Caleb.

He lowered his voice and leaned close. Beneath the quilt that covered them, he threaded his fingers between hers and held her hand. "Joy is a little like her father. When she gets an idea in her head, it's hard to make her let go of it. Duncan had better get his tail over to your place and wish his puppies a merry Christmas."

"And what idea do you have that you can't let go of?"

"At the moment, the only thing I don't want to let go of is your hand."

It was a night that Caleb would never forget. As they returned to Leah's home, he saw the way his life could unfold in Hope Springs. He and Joy would always be surrounded by his family and friends. The simple things—prayer, hard work and the company of men and women who sought to put God first in their lives—would fill the void that existed in his heart. If that life included Leah, it wouldn't be merely plain—it would be priceless.

The depth and intensity of his feelings for this woman frightened him. He wanted it to be real. He thought he had been in love before, but those emotions were nothing compared to this need to have Leah be a part of his life.

He didn't want to mess this up.

He gave her fingers a squeeze and then let go of her hand. He wouldn't rush her. He wanted her to be as certain of her feelings as he was.

Now that he was home, they would have plenty of time to discover if they were right for each other. Even if they were meant to be together, one huge issue remained unsolved. Rhonda's accusation.

If Leah couldn't accept his word over her sister's, how could he consider a life together? If she believed he was lying about something so important, would she ever be able to trust his word?

He glanced at the woman seated beside him. Somehow, he had to make her believe he wasn't David's father. He prayed God would show him how to do the impossible.

* * *

For Leah, the following week was a whirlwind of activity. There was so much to do to get her students ready for the Christmas pageant, make her own Christmas preparations and still maintain the class work the children needed. Each day, they practiced their songs and rehearsed their parts after school.

Joy blossomed when she learned she would be included in the school program. For the entire week, she worked so hard it was almost painful to watch, but each success made Joy that much more determined to master her part.

It wasn't until Friday evening that she and Caleb came over to visit the puppy. Joy proceeded to tell Leah that she didn't need her daddy to walk her to school anymore.

Leah glanced at Caleb, who was sitting at her kitchen table. He shrugged. "I told her I didn't think it was a good idea for her to go by herself."

"I'm not going by myself. David is gonna walk with me. He is gonna walk to Grandma and Grandpa's house, and then we are gonna go to school together just like you and your brother did when you were little."

"That sounds like a very good plan," Leah said.

Caleb slowly shook his head. "I don't think so."

"It will make David walk an extra quarter of a mile each day both to and from school, but if he wants to do it, I don't see why you should object. He does walk over to visit your parents on his own."

"He's only nine years old."

"He is a levelheaded boy. You roamed the countryside when you were his age. No one gave it a second thought. It's nice that he and Joy can be friends and

playmates. It will be good for both of them. For the whole family."

Joy folded her hands together. "Please, Daddy, I want to walk with David. He's my real friend."

He hesitated. Leah gave him a sympathetic smile. "You can always follow behind them and make sure they get where they're going."

His sheepish grin told her that was exactly what he had been thinking. "All right, you can walk with David. If it's okay with his parents."

"Cool." Joy returned to playing with the puppies. They were getting big enough to waddle around outside their box. Joy giggled as all three of them tried to climb into her lap.

Leah took a seat across from Caleb at the table. "She will grow up no matter how hard you try to prevent it."

"You're right, but I'm not ready for it."

"How is your job search going?"

"Not well. I'm tired of freeloading off my parents."

"I'm sure they don't consider it freeloading. I know you help your father with his chores."

"Sure, but it's nothing that he can't do himself."

Suddenly, she heard a buzzing noise. Caleb reached into his pocket and pulled out his cell phone. She was disappointed that he hadn't given up all of his worldly things.

He folded it shut and put it back in his pocket without answering it. "I'll let it go to voice mail. It's my old boss. I'd like to get rid of the phone, but my attorney says I need to be easily accessible until the custody issue is resolved."

She glanced at Joy to see if the child was listening.

Assured that her attention was on the puppies, Leah asked, "Have you heard anything new?"

"They are still trying to locate Valerie. She can fight it if she wants."

Leah watched Joy putting the puppies back inside the box. "If she knew how happy Joy was now, I think she would agree that you have done the right thing."

Joy came to stand beside them. "Has Duncan been here to visit?"

Leah shook her head. "If he has, I haven't seen him."

Joy propped her hands on her hips. "That dog is a deadbeat dad. I'm gonna have a talk with him."

Leah and Caleb exchanged an amused glance as they struggled not to laugh.

He stood and said, "We should be getting home, Joy. Thank Leah for letting you visit with Pickles, Peanut Butter and Jelly."

"I enjoy watching her as much as she enjoys playing with them. I'm sorry I've been so busy that you had to wait until now." It had been almost a week since the caroling party. Nearly a whole week since the last time he had kissed her.

Caleb smiled in understanding. "After Christmas, we will all have more time to spend together."

"I look forward to that," she said with a tender smile.

Joy pulled on her coat. "*Danki,* Leah. See you at school. Our program is three days away, and Christmas is the day after that and it's my birthday, too. I'm gonna have so much fun. Come on, Daddy, we have to check my Christmas tree on the way home. Those birds are eating everything."

She charged out the door, leaving Caleb and Leah

alone for a moment. He crossed the room and gave her a quick kiss. "Until after Christmas."

She closed the door behind them and leaned against it. It was all happening so fast. Only a month ago, she had been horrified to see him return to Hope Springs. Now she never wanted him or his daughter to leave.

It was snowing again. Large light flakes floated down like feathers. Caleb listened to the message from his former boss on the walk home. "Mast, I know you're still visiting your family in Ohio, but if you want that transfer to Brazil, we got an opening. I can't hold it for long so let me know soon as you can."

Caleb closed his phone and put it in his pocket. A month ago, he would've jumped at the chance to rake in a bigger salary and see a bit of the world. None of it seemed important now. He glanced at his daughter. She had changed everything.

His phone rang again. Caleb already knew what he would say when he talked to his boss. He opened the phone, but the name on the screen wasn't Sanford Limited. It was his attorney. He pressed the button to talk. "This is Caleb."

"Mr. Mast, I'm glad I reached you. We found her."

Caleb stopped walking. "And?"

"She relinquished all rights. You have sole and permanent custody of your daughter. Congratulations. We'll get you copies of the paperwork as soon as we can."

Caleb didn't hear anything else his attorney said. His relief was overwhelming. He bent forward and braced his hand on his knee. He never had to worry about losing Joy again. Until this moment, he hadn't realized

how heavy that worry had been. He felt as if he could float up off the earth.

He walked back to the house with Joy and marveled at the journey the Lord had taken them on. At the front steps, he said, "Go on in and tell my folks I have something I need to do. I'll be home later." Once Joy was inside, Caleb turned and jogged toward Leah's house. He needed to share this with her as soon as possible.

Leah was surprised when Trixie alerted her to another visitor. She looked out her window and saw Caleb standing just off her porch. Why had he come back so soon? Snowflakes swirled around him. He had his hands in his pockets. He looked uncertain and alone.

She happily opened the door. "You should come in before you turn into a snowman."

He managed a smile. "It is a little cold out here."

She stepped aside and let him in. Her foolish heart was about to jump out of her chest. "Would you like some coffee?"

"That would be great."

She set about filling the pot with fresh water and spooning the grounds into the basket. "Did you forget something?"

"No."

"Joy is so excited about Christmas."

"Joy is the reason I'm here. No, that's not exactly true. I'm here because of you."

She wiped her hands on her apron. Suddenly he crossed the room and grasped her hands. Startled, she stared into his eyes. They were dark with emotion. "When I first arrived, I never planned to stay here, but

from the moment we met, I haven't been able to stop thinking about you."

"Nor I about you."

"I'm not very good at this. I know this is too soon, but I want you to know that I have fallen in love with you, Leah Belier. I never intended to. I tried not to, but you are an overwhelming force of nature."

"I'm not sure whether to be flattered or not."

"I just learned that Valerie has relinquished all rights to Joy. She and I are free to stay here."

"How sad for her, but how wonderful for you."

"There is something I have to ask you."

She laid a hand on his lips. "Before you say anything, I must speak. I have forgiven you for everything in the past. It took me a long time to let go of my anger, but you have made me see that people really can change."

He smiled sadly. "In all the years I was gone, I never belonged anywhere. I blamed that on the events of my life. I tried to find a place where I could be happy, but I always came up short. Until I came home. I want to stay now. I want you to want me to stay."

"I do. Caleb, you and Joy have come to mean so much to me. I can't imagine my life without you. You have my forgiveness. We will never mention the past again."

He caressed her cheek with the back of his knuckles. "I treasure the fact that you forgive me, but I'm not the father of your sister's child."

She turned her face away from his touch. "Caleb, please."

He took a step away from her. "I wanted everyone to know the truth. I wanted to hold my head up. Most of all I wanted my family to believe me. It doesn't matter

anymore what other people think, but I need to hear it from you. I need to hear that *you* believe me."

"Caleb, you're asking me to call my sister a liar."

"Yes, I am."

Leah pressed a hand to her forehead. This was her worst nightmare. "Don't do this. Don't make me choose."

The light went out of his eyes. Grayness settled over his face. "I guess that's my answer, then, isn't it?" He turned toward the door.

"Caleb, wait."

He paused with his hand on the door, but he didn't look at her. "Wait for what, Leah? What will change your mind? A DNA test? Rhonda won't consent to that because she knows I'm not the father. I asked you for too much. I'm sorry. How can there be anything between us if you think I'm a heartless liar?"

She crossed the room to lay her hands on his arm. "I want to believe you, Caleb. I want to believe my sister, too. All I can do is say the past is the past. I know you aren't like that now. You're a fine, caring man and a good father."

"Maybe it's in the past for you, but not for me." He opened the door and walked out.

Leah put a hand behind her to search for the table, and staggered on trembling legs until she ran into it. She didn't have the strength to stand up. She collapsed onto a chair and put her head in her hands. How could such a wonderful night have turned out so horribly wrong?

"Oh, Caleb, what have we done?" She buried her face in her arms and wept.

* * *

Caleb wiped the tears from his cheeks before he entered the house. Thankfully, his parents had already gone to bed. He climbed the steps to his room and paused at Joy's door to check in on her. She was sleeping peacefully. His tears started flowing again.

He shut her door, sat on the edge of his bed and tried to figure out what to do now. Now that his precious dream had crumbled to dust. He couldn't blame Leah for supporting her sister. The fact that Wayne hadn't believed his side of the story had cut like a knife.

At least Joy was safe and happy now. That part of his plan had worked out. He lay back and covered his eyes with his arm. Where did he go from here?

He didn't get much sleep, but he eventually came to a decision. When he heard his parents stirring downstairs the next morning, he rose and went down, too. His mother took one look at his face and knew something was wrong.

"Caleb, what is it?" She clutched her apron in her hands.

He tried to smile and allay her worry. "I had a call from my attorney yesterday."

"It's bad news?"

"No, it's good news. Valerie has relinquished her rights. Joy will be able to stay here forever."

"It is sad for the child's mother but *wunderbaar* for us." His mother turned back to the stove.

Caleb's father read between the lines. "Joy will stay with us, but you will not."

His mother spun around. "Why do you say that?"

"I have to go back to Texas for a while. There is paperwork that needs to be done. I have my place to put

on the market. It may take a few months, so I'll be taking a job down there."

"Months? So long?" She glanced at her husband.

Ike drew a deep breath. "We will take *goot* care of Joy until you return."

"I knew you would."

"Where are you going, Daddy?" Joy stood in the doorway with a look of panic on her face.

He forced a bright smile. "Good morning, kiddo. Come here, I have something to tell you."

She crossed the room slowly. He sat in a chair and lifted her onto his lap. "Do you remember when I said I would never leave without telling you where I'm going and when I'll be back?"

"Yes."

"Joy, I have to go to Texas for a while. You know I've been looking for a job and I can't find one here, but I have a job waiting for me in Houston. I'll need to stay there for several months, so I can't tell you exactly when I'll be back."

He wasn't lying. He would be back. To visit, but not to stay and build a life as he once thought. He couldn't bear facing Leah time and again, knowing his love for her was hopeless.

"When are you going?"

"Tomorrow."

His mother started sniffling and left the room.

Tears formed in Joy's eyes. "But you will miss my program and my birthday."

He hated to disappoint her, but wasn't it better to make a quick clean break? She would be so busy she wouldn't even miss him, but he was going to miss her.

It wasn't for her sake that he was leaving so soon.

He was a coward. He couldn't bear to drag out the parting. He couldn't stand to face Leah again knowing how much he loved her and knowing she would never believe his side of the story.

"I'm sorry about that, but you can tell me all about your program and Christmas when we talk. Grandpa will take you to use the phone at the neighbor's house so we can stay in touch. You can call me anytime. He and Grandma will be there for your program, so you won't be alone. Okay?"

"I guess." She got off his lap and left the room.

His father said, "Caleb, you are making a big mistake."

"Mistakes are what I seem to do best, Dad." He rose and went to his room to pack.

Chapter Fifteen

Leah didn't leave her house on Saturday. All she did was cry and ask God why He had allowed her to fall in love with someone who broke her heart. If she indulged in self-pity, there was no one but Trixie to see. No one to tell her she was better off without Caleb. No one who could lend her a shoulder to cry on. She was a foolish spinster who lived with a dog. If she had been content with her lot, she wouldn't be grieving now.

It wasn't until Sunday evening that she finally got a grip on her tattered emotions. She began to analyze her last conversation with Caleb without the hurt and anger clouding her judgment.

Caleb had asked her to believe he wasn't David's father. After years of thinking that was the case, she repeated what she believed was true. Rhonda said he was the father. Rhonda wouldn't lie.

Or would she?

Caleb had been sincere. He desperately wanted Leah to believe him even if she was the only one who did. It would have been much easier for him to accept her forgiveness and let it go at that. They could have been

happy together, for she'd meant it when she said she forgave him. She never would have mentioned it again. Had he cast her aside out of false pride?

He'd said he loved her. She believed that. If she loved him, and God help her, she did, then she had to believe in him. Caleb was telling the truth.

So why had Rhonda lied?

It was time to find out. Leah wouldn't leave her sister's house until everything was out in the open.

It was late by the time Leah drove up and stopped in front of her sister's gate, but there was a single lamp burning in the kitchen. Through the window, she could see Rhonda scrubbing the kitchen floor, always the last chore of her day. She looked up in surprise when Leah walked in.

"Sister, what are you doing here? Is something wrong?"

"Where's Wayne?"

Rhonda propped her mop against the wall. "He's out in the barn. One of the horses has foundered. What's going on?"

"Where is David?"

"He's outside with Wayne. Are you going to tell me what you're doing here?"

"You lied about Caleb being the father of your child. Why?"

Leah waited for her sister's reply. She couldn't believe she was questioning her sister's honesty, but either Caleb was lying or her sister was. In her heart, Leah wanted to believe both spoke the truth, but that wasn't possible.

Rhonda turned away. "How can you say such a

thing? Do you think I would lie about something like that?"

The hesitation in her sister's voice told Leah the truth. Her legs buckled. She sat down at the kitchen table. "Oh, Rhonda, why did you do it?"

If only she'd had the courage to believe Caleb. Would he forgive her for doubting him?

Rhonda spun back, her eyes snapping with anger. "How can you believe that outsider over your own sister?"

"You ruined his life."

"He ruined my life. Look at my face."

"Who is David's father?"

"Caleb."

Anger gave Leah a strength she never suspected she possessed. Springing to her feet, she grabbed her sister's shoulders and shook her. "Do you even know how to tell the truth?"

Rhonda pushed her away and folded her arms tightly across her chest. She seemed to shrink into herself. "Why can't you leave it be?"

"Because I'm in love with Caleb and because I don't want to see you suffering anymore. Tell me what happened. Please, Rhonda."

"It isn't a pretty tale."

When they sat beside each other on the sofa, Rhonda said, "I didn't blame Caleb for what happened. It was an accident. I knew that. He tried so hard to make it up to me. He took me home from church a few times. He talked me into going to a singing, but I was self-conscious, I didn't like people staring at me."

"So when did you meet David's father?"

A look of disgust flooded Rhonda's eyes. "He came

to our house. You remember him. He took me to the police station to make a statement about the accident."

"Drake Colburn? An *Englisch* officer of the law?" She hadn't expected that.

"At first, he was nice to me. He made me feel pretty again. I thought I was in love with him. I even considered running away to be with him. Then I found out he was married. He was only using me. I was such a fool."

"Oh, Rhonda, I'm so sorry you went through that. Did Drake know you were pregnant?"

Rhonda's eyes widened. "He doesn't know David is his. He can't know. Don't you see? David is proof of what he did. He could take my son away. He has the English law on his side. His wife was never able to have children."

"Rhonda, I don't believe he could take David from you."

"I can't risk it. Don't you see that?" She choked back a sob.

"Why say Caleb was the father? Was it because you blamed him for what had happened to you?"

"I thought if I told Caleb what had happened that he would marry me and make everything right. He had been so kind."

"So Caleb knew?"

"*Nee,* I had so much morning sickness that *Mamm* guessed what was wrong before I had a chance to tell Caleb. She and *Daed* confronted me. I panicked. I told them Caleb was the father. I was too ashamed to admit what had really happened. *Daed* was so angry. He made me go with him to see Caleb's parents that day and demand that he do the right thing."

"But Caleb wouldn't."

"When he denied it, I didn't know what to say. Once I accused him of being the father, I couldn't change my story. I surely couldn't tell *Daed* and *Mamm* the truth. I never expected Caleb to leave. I honestly thought that he would come around and accept that he had to marry me."

"No one believed him, and everyone believed you." Her sister had suffered a great wrong, but Caleb was a victim, too.

"When Wayne offered to marry me, I thought my nightmare was finally over. I knew I was breaking your heart, but you are so pretty, and you are so smart, I thought you would find someone else to love. Can you forgive me?"

"Wayne wasn't the one for me. I know that now. Does Wayne know about Drake?"

Rhonda clutched Leah's arm. "Wayne gave you up, he disowned his brother, all because of my lie. How could I tell him it was all for nothing? You can't tell him. Promise me you won't tell him. I couldn't bear to see him look at me with more contempt than he already does."

"It's none of my business, but it's clear that things aren't right between the two of you."

Rhonda pressed a hand to her cheek. "He can't stand to look at my face. He thinks I'm hideous."

Neither of them had heard Wayne enter the house until he spoke. "I don't find you hideous. It is my own guilt I can't abide when I look at you."

Startled, they both faced him. There were tears on his face.

"You heard!" Rhonda wailed. She sank to the floor and covered her face with her hands.

He crossed the room, ignoring Leah, and dropped to his knees in front of his wife. "I heard, and I would give anything to undo the pain you suffered. You are not hideous. Your face is beautiful to me."

"But I lied to you."

"I, too, have lived a lie, *mein lieb,* my own true love. I was the one driving the car the night of your accident. I thought I killed you. I ran home and Caleb found me cowering in the barn. I was so frightened I couldn't move. He raced to your side. He got help and saved your life."

Leah shook her head. "But Caleb took the blame for the whole thing."

Wayne looked up at her. "I tried to tell my father it was my fault, but the words stuck in my throat. I couldn't bear for him to know of my shame. Caleb was always in trouble. It was easy for everyone to believe he'd done such a reckless thing. My father shunned him. As the days went on, I grew terrified that Caleb would reveal the truth about that night. That's why I was glad he left and why I wanted him to leave again. I'm ashamed of what I have become. Rhonda, can you forgive me?"

"Now you know David has an English father, you must hate me."

He took her hands between his. "David is my son in every way. I could not love him more if I tried. Please believe that."

She gazed into his eyes. "I do. I pray you will some-day love me, too."

He gently pressed a hand to her scarred cheek. "We have much to learn about each other now that there are

no more secrets between us. If it takes me a lifetime, I will earn your love."

"It won't take that long, for you already have my heart."

He cupped her face and kissed her.

Leah left them alone and walked into the kitchen. She made coffee because she needed to do something. All Caleb had asked of her was to have faith in him, to trust him, and she had turned him away. She would tell him how wrong she had been and beg his forgiveness.

The outside door opened, startling her. Ike Mast came in, shaking the snow from his hat. He searched the room with his eyes and then focused on Wayne and Rhonda. "Is Joy here with you?"

Leah stared at him in shock. "No. How long has she been missing?"

"Maybe an hour. I'm not sure. She went to her room after supper. When I checked on her before I turned in, she was gone."

"Have you been to my house? She loves to visit the puppies."

"I came here first. I think she is upset because Caleb is gone."

Disbelief stole Leah's voice. A loud buzzing filled her head. No. Had she driven him away with her doubts? What had she done? Rhonda came to her side and put her arms around her. Leah leaned against her, thankful for her support.

Wayne stared at his father. "What do you mean, Caleb is gone?"

"He left two hours ago to drive back to Texas. I don't know why. I thought he had found peace with us."

* * *

Caleb paced the small confines of a service station waiting room just off Interstate 77. He had been on the road for only twenty minutes when his check-engine light came on. At least he'd caught a break when he found a place open on Sunday. Outside, the snow was picking up. He wanted to get on the road. The last place he wanted to be was stuck in Ohio in a snowstorm.

He carried his foam cup of lousy coffee to the window. Half the parking lot was blocked off by sawhorses with yellow flashing lights on top and *caution* written in black letters across them.

A fellow traveler came through the door. He stamped his feet on the worn rug. "Do you work here?"

Caleb shook his head. "I'm just waiting to find out how much it is going to cost me to drive out of here."

The shop owner came in from the service bay, wiping his hands on a pink rag. He patted his salt-and-pepper hair into place, scratched his grizzled whiskers and finished wiping his hands on his stained overalls. "What can I do for you, sir?"

"I think I made a wrong turn. Do you have a map?"

Caleb turned back to stare at the flashing caution lights outside. He saw the reflection of the two men behind him as they leaned over the map. The store owner jabbed a finger at the paper. "This is where you made your mistake."

Caleb heard the echo of his father's voice. *Caleb, you are making a mistake.*

The traveler leaned forward to examine the map more closely. "So how do I get on the right road?"

Outside the caution lights continued to blink their

warning. *Don't come this way.* Which way should he go? Caleb closed his eyes. *Which way, God?*

The shop owner said, "It's not easy to get there from here. You're going to have to go back a ways."

"I hate making mistakes. This is costing me so much time."

Mistakes are what I seem to do best, Dad. Caleb opened his eyes. If he knew it was a mistake, why was he leaving?

The shop owner took a pen and marked something on the map, then he pushed it toward his customer. "Jumping out of an airplane without a parachute is a mistake you can't fix. Most everything else just takes a little more effort to make it right. Go back about ten miles and follow this road. It will take you where you need to be."

The traveler thanked him and left. The shop owner looked at Caleb. "Mr. Mast, your truck is done. It was just a loose wire. I'm not even going to charge you for the time it took me to fix it." He held out the keys.

Caleb took them and stared at the Texas emblem on his key chain. What was there in Texas for him really? Nothing as important as the people he'd left behind. He would find a job. He would beg Leah to marry him, and if she didn't, he would still raise his beautiful daughter, as a good Amish father should.

"Where are you headed, son?" the man asked with a gap-toothed smile.

Caleb grinned, tossed the keys in the air and caught them again. "Home. I'm headed home. I just didn't know it until now."

Wayne quickly took charge. "We'll start a search for Joy. It's not a night for a child to be wandering around

the countryside. Leah, go to your house. Take David with you. If Joy isn't there, send David with a message to Eli Imhoff to meet us at *Daed*'s house. He'll send word for more men. I'll saddle David's pony and tie him behind your buggy."

"Where is David?" Rhonda asked.

"He came back to the house some time ago," Wayne replied.

Rhonda looked surprised. "I didn't see him come in. I'll check his room." She hurried away.

Leah looked at the men. "We should get a message to Caleb."

Ike nodded in agreement. "If Joy isn't at your house, stop at our neighbor's farm and use their phone. Caleb left us his cell phone number." He handed her a card.

Leah took it and tucked it in her pocket. She quickly pulled on her coat and tied her bonnet under her chin. "Don't worry, Ike. I'm sure she is with my puppies."

Rhonda burst back into the room, her eyes wide with panic. "David isn't in his room. He never leaves without telling me where he's going. Where could he be?"

Leah could think of only one thing that made sense. "He must be with Joy."

Wayne drew his frightened wife into his arms. "David is a smart and resourceful boy. He will take good care of Joy if they are together."

Leah said, "Wayne, come with me. Rhonda, stay here in case they come back. Ike, I think you should go home. I know Maggie must be out of her mind with worry. If they have returned, you can bring word to Rhonda. We'll coordinate the search from here."

Leah prayed for the safety of the children as she and Wayne scrambled into her buggy. Ten minutes later,

she pulled up in front of her own house. The windows were dark.

"Joy, are you in here? David?" She rushed through the front door and nearly tripped over Trixie. The dog ran outside, barking furiously.

Wayne came in behind Leah. "Are they here?"

"Nee."

Trixie stood on the front porch, barking into the night. Something was wrong. Leah lit the lamp she kept by the front door. The soft glow illuminated the empty kitchen.

"I will check the barn," Wayne said.

As he went out the door, Trixie came back in and went to her box. She whined as she nosed her litter. Leah quickly checked the rest of the house. She came back to the kitchen just as Wayne returned. She looked at him hopefully. "Anything?"

"Nee. The snow is coming down hard now."

"Do you think they might have gone to the school?"

Trixie barked sharply. Wayne glanced her way. "What's wrong with your dog?"

"I don't know. She's not usually like this." Leah crossed the room. She held the lamp over the whelping box. Only two puppies were snuggled together in the corner. "Pickles is missing."

She quickly checked the room, but Trixie's behavior told her the puppy wasn't close by. "I think the children took the puppy with them."

"At least we know that they came this way. You go to Eli's place and send the others here."

She blinked back tears. "It will take so long to gather everyone."

"Have faith, Leah. Our children are in God's hands. They always have been."

As they started out the door, the lights of an English car turned into the yard. Leah thought Ike must have gone to the English farm and called for help. Now they could gather the neighbors quickly and begin the search.

She realized almost immediately that it wasn't a car. It was a pickup. The same kind of pickup that Caleb drove. The truck stopped. Her knees almost buckled when she saw him get out.

"Thank You, God, for bringing him back." She flew into his arms.

He held her tight. "Your forgiveness is enough. I will never ask for more. I can't face a life without you and my daughter in it. I can't."

"I love you, Caleb. I know the truth. I'm so sorry that I doubted you, but darling, Joy is missing. She and David have run away."

Caleb's mind went numb with shock. "How long has she been gone? Is anyone looking for her?"

Wayne approached them. "It's good to see you, brother. We think they've been gone about two hours now. We are getting up a search party. Can you drive us to alert our neighbors?"

"Of course. Get in. Where were they last seen?" Caleb held open the door as Leah climbed in. Wayne quickly went around to the passenger side.

"We know that they came here and took one of Leah's puppies with them. Do you have any idea where Joy would go?"

The instant Wayne shut his door, Caleb stepped on

the gas. "The Christmas tree. We should check there. She wanted to show the puppy her tree."

The truck fishtailed briefly in the snow. Caleb slowed down. He couldn't find his daughter if he wound up in the ditch. "I never should've left. This is my fault."

If anything happened to Joy or to David, he would never forgive himself.

It took only a few minutes to reach the place close to Joy's tree. Caleb parked on the side of the lane and raced into the woods, calling her name. Only silence answered him.

Leah and Wayne joined him. Wayne held a flashlight he had taken from Caleb's glove box. He scanned the ground. "I don't see any fresh tracks in the snow. I don't think they have been here."

"Now what?" Leah looked to both of them.

Caleb raked a hand through his hair. He'd never been more frightened in his life. Wayne laid a hand on his shoulder. "We should let our folks know you have returned. The children may already be there."

Caleb nodded. If they weren't, he would gather men to help him search if he had to drive to every farm in the valley.

They returned to the truck and drove to the house. His parents hurried out to meet them. Caleb could see by their faces that the children weren't there. His mother threw her arms around him and held on tight without saying a word.

He gently pulled her arms down and held her hands. "We'll find them."

"I know you will."

The sound of muffled hoof beats reached Caleb. He turned to see a horse and cart coming into the yard. A

burly man in a knitted cap and long coat got down and lifted a bundle of blankets from the backseat. David climbed down from behind him. Caleb's heart stopped beating.

Leah said, "It's Carl King."

Maggie and Wayne rushed to embrace David. Carl nodded to Caleb. "Are you missing a couple of naughty children?"

"We are," Caleb managed to say past the lump in his throat.

Carl handed his bundle to Caleb. He pulled back the edge of the blanket. Joy's eyes fluttered open. "I fell asleep."

Her eyes opened wide and then scrunched with happiness as she grinned at him. "Daddy, is that you?"

He sat down in the snow and held her tight. "It's me, baby."

"You're squishing me, again."

"Too bad. You will get squished a lot from now on. Get used to it." *Thank You, dear Lord, for delivering her safely into my arms. Thank You so much.*

Carl shoved his hands in his coat pockets. "She came to scold my dog for not visiting his puppies. Called him a deadbeat dad. You're gonna have your hands full with that one, Caleb Mast."

Joy wiggled until she had her head free. "Where is Pickles?"

Carl went back to the cart and produced the puppy from a basket under the seat. He handed her to Joy, who held her close.

"*Danki,* Mr. King."

"*Du bischt wilkumm.*" He walked back toward his cart.

Caleb handed Joy to his father and went after Carl. He held out his hand. "Thank you."

Carl looked at Caleb's hand and then at his face. Quietly, he asked, "Are you a baptized member of the Amish?"

"I will be soon."

"After that, you cannot shake my hand."

That meant Carl had been excommunicated by his congregation. He was under the *Meidung,* shunned. Caleb kept his hand outstretched. "Then I need to thank you now."

Carl shook Caleb's hand. He got in his cart and drove away into the swirling snow. Caleb wondered briefly what mistake had driven the man into such a position. He turned back to where his family and Leah were gathered. He had his own mistakes to right.

It was after midnight before Wayne and Rhonda gathered their sleepy son from Caleb's room and took him home. Earlier, David told them he had been on his way to the house when he spotted Joy walking alone through the woods. He went after her but couldn't convince her to return home, so he went along with her to make sure she was safe.

Leah waved to her sister and Wayne as they left, and returned to the living room, where Caleb stood by the fireplace. His parents had gone to bed an hour before.

Caleb held out his arms. "Come here."

She snuggled up beside him. He draped an arm around her shoulder and pulled her close. It wasn't proper behavior for a schoolteacher, but Leah didn't care. There was nowhere in the world she would rather be and no one she would rather be with.

"It has been quite a night," he said and kissed the top of her head.

"Now that everyone's story is out in the open, I know the healing will start."

He lifted her face so that he could look into her eyes. "God did a wondrous thing when He brought me back to you and to my faith. I plan to be baptized as soon as possible so that I may experience all of His grace in this life and in the next."

"I'm so glad. I know this is what He wants for you."

"Have I told you how much I love you?"

"You have told me a little, but I don't think you told me enough. You might have to write it on the blackboard one hundred times."

He laughed. "What if I give you one hundred kisses instead?"

She pretended to think it over. "That will be acceptable."

His lips met hers and he proceeded to make her forget everything that had once stood between them. It lasted long enough to leave her breathless and hungry for more. He drew away slightly. "One."

"I'm ready for two."

"So am I, but I have one question to ask you first."

"What is that?"

"Will you marry me?"

"I should hold out until at least kiss five or kiss six."

"You do know how to torture a man. Okay."

He cupped her face in his hands and gave her five quick pecks on her cheek. "What is your answer?"

She moved away and folded her arms. "I've forgotten the question."

"Leah, you make my heart sing. You are going to be a wonderful mother for Joy."

"I can't wait for the day." It was the truth. She was about to have a special child, a special gift, courtesy of God and Caleb Mast.

He moved close and brushed his fingers along the edge of her *kapp*. "I can't wait for the day that I will see you with your hair down. You are so beautiful."

She trembled at the thought of what marriage to him would mean. "You're getting ahead of yourself. I haven't said yes."

"You have hit your limit of six kisses. Not another one until you say you will marry me."

She cupped his face between her hands. "You drive a hard bargain. Very well, I will gladly marry you."

His next kiss lasted longer than the first. A small voice that broke them apart. "You guys, I had a bad dream."

Leah tried to step away, but Caleb held on to her. "You have lousy timing, Joy, but come here and tell us all about your bad dream."

He moved to sit on the sofa and pulled Leah down beside him. Joy crossed the room and sat in between them. "I think it's gone. I don't remember what it was about."

Caleb brushed her hair away from her face. "In that case, I think you need to go back to bed. It's very late."

Joy tipped her head to the side and looked at him. "If you marry Leah, will that make her my *aenti?*"

He shared a sheepish grin with Leah. She said, "*Nee,* it will make me your new *mamm.* Will that be all right with you?"

"*Ja,* that will be *goot!*"

* * *

On Christmas Eve, Leah took the stage at the end of her students' final song. "And now we will have a play that isn't listed on your programs. This is a special presentation written and narrated by Anna Imhoff with Joy Perry Mast, David Mast, Kyle Troyer and Noah Imhoff as the players."

Anna walked out onstage. "A long time ago, in a land far away, there were shepherds tending their flocks in the hills near the little town of Bethlehem."

Leah stepped behind the curtain as David, Noah and Kyle walked on. They all carried shepherds crooks and wore long robes. They stopped and began to lay sticks together as if they were going to build a fire.

Kyle said, "Do you hear that? It sounds like singing."

"I don't hear anything. It's just the wind," David replied.

"And, lo, the angel of the Lord came upon them, and the glory of the Lord shone round about them. And they were sore afraid." Anna stepped away from the center of the stage.

Behind the curtain, Leah gave Joy a little push. "That's your cue."

Joy walked out to the middle of the stage. The paper wings pinned to the back of her white dress fluttered gently.

She paused and looked toward Leah. Leah nodded. "Go ahead."

Joy stood tall. "Fear not—for, behold, I bring you good tidings of great joy." She smiled at the audience. "My name is Joy."

Anna whispered, "Which shall be…"

Joy grew stern. "Which shall be to all people. For unto you is born this day in the city of David—"

She stopped and pointed at the shepherds kneeling before her. "This is my cousin. His name is David, too. For unto you is born this day in the city of David, a Savior, which is Christ the Lord. And this shall be a sign unto you. You can find him wrapped in swaddling clothes, lying in a manger. That's a cow feeder."

A ripple of suppressed laughter came from the audience. Anna stepped onstage again. "And suddenly there was with the angel a multitude of the heavenly host praising God, and saying..." She held her hand toward the children lined up along the wall.

They shouted as one. "Glory to God in the highest, and on earth peace, goodwill toward men."

Anna looked out over the audience. "And it came to pass, as the angels were gone away from them into heaven..."

"Oh, I have to leave." Joy waved at everyone and left the stage.

Anna composed herself. "The shepherds said one to another, Let us now go even unto Bethlehem, and see this thing which is come to pass, which the Lord hath made known unto us. And they came with haste, and found Mary, and Joseph, and the babe lying in a manger. And when they had seen it, they made known abroad the saying, which was told them concerning this child. And all they that heard it wondered at those things which were told them by the shepherds."

Anna held one hand high. "In this way, the good news of our salvation began to spread, thanks to the shepherds in the fields."

Joy rushed out onto the stage. "I have more good

news. My daddy is going to stay here with me. He is going to marry my teacher, Leah. She's not going to be my teacher anymore. That makes me sad, but she is going to be my *mamm,* and that makes me happy. Oh, and Pickles is gonna be our dog. *Frehlicher Grischtdaag,* everyone. That means Merry Christmas!"

Joy hurried off the stage to Leah's side. "How did I do?"

Leah caught Caleb's amused and loving smile from the audience. She put her arm around Joy and grinned at the child of her heart. "Darling, that was an unforgettable performance."

* * * * *

AN AMISH PROPOSAL

Jo Ann Brown

For Elizabeth McIntyre
Thanks for keeping us on track.
And herding writers is
definitely harder than herding cats…

For all people will walk every one in the name
of his god, and we will walk in the name of the Lord
our God forever and ever.
—*Micah* 4:5

Chapter One

Paradise Springs
Lancaster County, Pennsylvania

When the night sky opened and it started raining, Katie Kay Lapp stopped by the side of the road, covered her face with her hands and began to cry. The cold downpour was the final insult in a day that had begun badly and gotten worse with each passing hour. How had she gotten to this point? Months ago, she'd been the center of attention of young men at any gathering. They'd vied for time with her and for the chance to take her home in their courting buggies. Now she was abandoned and afraid and had no place to go.

You could go home.

Ach, it was easy for the little voice in her head—the one nagging her endlessly about doing the right thing—to say that. But she'd burned her bridges behind her and in front of her and around her. She couldn't go home. Her sisters would welcome her, but *Daed* would insist on knowing every detail of what she'd done since she

ran away. He'd want to pray with her and ask her to repent for any sins she'd committed.

And she'd committed a bunch. Some intentionally and others by accident. In the eyes of Bishop Reuben Lapp, what she'd done would need to be repented for with prayer before it could be forgiven.

She moaned aloud when she imagined telling her *daed* about her fear that she was pregnant. Many plain women her age were married with one or more *bopplin*, but she hadn't been ready to settle down and lead an Amish life, the only life she'd ever known until she left home four months ago to find out what the rest of the world was like. It hadn't been a carefree *rumspringa* decision. Instead, she'd made the choice with care and a lot of deep consideration.

Or so she'd thought at the time.

Raindrops slid beneath her T-shirt and down her spine like a cascade of ice cubes. October could be a beautiful month in southeastern Pennsylvania or unforgiving like tonight.

Straightening, Katie Kay looked around. She wasn't sure where she was. Somewhere in rural Lancaster County, she knew, but not exactly where. She hadn't paid any attention. She'd been surprised when Austin, whom she'd described to others as her *Englisch* boyfriend because she'd foolishly believed he cared about her, had driven her and a couple of other *Englischers* out of Lancaster City, but she hadn't watched where they were going. Rain had been falling, and the streetlights had glittered on the windshield, disguising any landmarks in splattered light. She hadn't expected she'd need to know. She'd thought she was returning to the apartment she shared with Austin and their friends.

Not her friends, she knew. Neither had protested when Austin snatched her cell phone from her purse and ordered her out of the car. Maybe Vinnie and Juan, his *Englisch* friends, had been as astounded as she'd been, never guessing he'd drive off and not come back for her.

She kept walking. She didn't have any other choice. The country road was two narrow lanes that curved and rose and fell over the rolling hillsides. It was edged on both sides by harvested fields. She peered through the darkness, but the lights she could see appeared to be a mile or two in the distance. Was she somewhere without many houses? Or were there ones between her and the distant lights? Amish houses wouldn't be lit this late in the evening because the people living in them usually rose before the sun and were in bed soon after sunset.

Two cars raced toward her. If the drivers saw her, they gave no sign, not swerving to the middle of the road to make sure they avoided her as they passed. The tires of the second sent a shower of dirty water over her.

"It's not fair!" she cried out. Nothing had been fair since her *mamm* died five years ago. Everyone had expected her to step into the role of housekeeper for her *daed*. After all, her half sister had when *Daed*'s first wife died. But Priscilla was the perfect Amish daughter and now was the perfect Amish wife and *mamm*. Katie Kay had been the one who questioned everything and was too curious to accept things just because someone told her so.

But look where curiosity had gotten her. A part of her wanted to pray, but she silenced that longing as she had for four months. Reaching out to God seemed like admitting she couldn't survive on her own among *Englischers*.

And why would God want to hear from her after she'd turned her back on Him and the life He'd given her? Another bridge she'd burned and wondered if it could ever be rebuilt.

A familiar sound came from behind her. Metal wheels on asphalt accompanied by iron horseshoes clip-clopping in a steady rhythm.

Katie Kay knew the source of those sounds. They'd been a part of her life since her earliest memories. Stepping off the edge of the road, she considered going down the slope toward a shadowed hedgerow until after the buggy had passed. An Amish person wouldn't go by her without stopping as the cars had, but she needed to avoid plain people until she figured out where she was.

Her feet refused to move. Her own body rebelled against standing a moment longer than necessary in the cold rain. Maybe she should try to hitch a ride with the buggy, so she could find shelter before the rain turned to sleet. Who would recognize her as the wayward daughter of Reuben Lapp, a beloved bishop?

The clatter of the wheels began to slow, and she knew she'd been seen in the lights connected to the buggy. Again, she was torn between running away and running toward it. How could she have gotten herself to this point? A few months ago, she'd been the pampered daughter of a respected Amish bishop. Now she was cowering by the side of a country road, left behind like a discarded kitten dropped by a heartless owner.

Which wasn't far off from the truth. Austin hadn't tossed her out of the car, but he'd raised his hand when she hesitated to follow his orders. Though he'd never struck her, she'd seen him flatten a man a head taller

than him with a single blow. Again she told herself she shouldn't have been honest with him about her suspicion she might be pregnant until she was absolutely sure. Austin Moore prided himself on being a man without a single obligation to anyone or anything, and she should have known he'd refuse to take responsibility if she'd conceived. She wasn't sure, though signs pointed in that direction. By now, he'd be at the apartment in Lancaster they'd shared with two other *Englischers*, and he'd be watching sports and drinking whatever was in the fridge. He wouldn't spare her another thought. It wasn't as if he loved her.

And that realization was the most painful of all.

A voice called from the buggy that had pulled alongside her while the rain fell relentlessly on her bare head. "Katie Kay? Katie Kay Lapp, is it you?" Surprise lifted the deep voice several notches, but she recognized it.

Micah Stoltzfus!

Out of everyone in Lancaster County, why did *he* have to be in the buggy?

Micah had taken her home—several times—from social events, and she'd even let him kiss her. She'd decided she liked him well enough, and she'd enjoyed his kisses, but she wasn't interested in someone who kept talking about the future. She'd been happy focusing on the present, when there were a lot of *gut*-looking guys eager to take her home.

Why not enjoy what was going on and let tomorrow worry about itself?

That had been her motto, but now she was being forced to see where such a shortsighted plan had left her.

Alone.

Possibly pregnant.

And about to have to beg help from a man she'd told to get lost a year ago.

The petite woman standing beside his buggy bore little resemblance to the vivacious beauty he'd admired for years, but Micah Stoltzfus knew he wasn't mistaken. Though she didn't answer him and confirm her identity, he recognized Katie Kay Lapp's oval face and very large blue eyes. Her blond hair was no longer pulled back beneath a white organdy *kapp*. It'd been cropped short with bangs above her tawny brows and hung around her shoulders, weighed down by the rain. He guessed the strands which had been silken when they escaped her bun and brushed his face would, when dry, bounce with each step she took. Instead of a simple dress, she wore blue jeans and a black T-shirt that looked as if it'd been ruined before she'd stood outside in the storm.

He wanted to ask her where she'd been and what she'd been doing since she had left her *daed*'s house after a big argument. Reuben had been troubled about her vanishing, fearing what might happen to his naïve daughter. Katie Kay had left behind a message stating she was going to live with an *Englisch* friend. She hadn't said which one or where or when she might come home. The burden of not knowing had bent Reuben's shoulders, and Micah believed only his plans to marry Wanda Stoltzfus, Micah's *mamm*, and his strong faith had kept the bishop from being ground down completely. Reuben was a shadow of the vibrant man he'd once been.

Instead of asking the questions taunting him, Micah

called through the open door on the driver's side of his buggy, "Don't you want to get out of the rain?"

She nodded, biting her lower lip.

For a moment, he wondered if he was wrong about her being Katie Kay Lapp. The Katie Kay he knew never had been abashed or quiet. Instead she'd had a quick retort and an easy laugh. This pale wraith might look like the woman he'd known, but where had her bright sparkle gone?

He was being silly. The woman was Katie Kay Lapp. She was walking in the direction of Paradise Springs, where both her family and his lived.

"*Komm* in," he said as he reached across the buggy to open the passenger side door. He shut the one on his side while she hurried around the buggy. The rain was falling harder, and he didn't want to get soaked before he reached home. He would have been there by now if he and his business partner, Sean Donnelly, hadn't needed to meet with a new client tonight.

He hoped he and Sean would get the job installing solar panels for a new client. Otherwise, it would have been a waste of an evening and a slow, cold ride home. Sean's wife, Gemma, had asked Micah to stay at their house overnight, but he hadn't wanted his family to worry when he didn't return to the farm.

And Katie Kay would have been left to walk along the road connecting Paradise Springs and Ronks in the heart of Lancaster County. He hadn't seen another vehicle, other than a couple of cars driving at an unsafe speed along the twisting road. Certainly no buggies, because any person with sense would be inside on an inclement night.

When Katie Kay climbed in and slid the door closed,

she sat as far from him as possible in the small buggy. Which wasn't very far. If they both put their hands on the seat between them, their fingers would overlap.

As they used to when he took her home after a singing.

That's over and done with, he reminded himself. She'd made it clear the last time he took her home in his courting buggy that if he disappeared from the face of the earth, she'd be fine. Instead, she had gone away, jumping the fence to live with *Englischers*.

She didn't look at him or speak, but in the glow from the buggy's lights, he saw she was shivering.

"Here." He stretched his arm behind the seat and pulled out a towel he kept among his tools. He used it when he washed up after a hot day of working on a roof while installing solar panels.

"Thanks." She hesitated as if he'd be upset her first word to him wasn't in *Deitsch*, the language of the plain people, and he'd order her out of the buggy. Before he could ask why she acted like a beaten pup, she added in not much more than a whisper, *"Danki."*

"Sounds like you've gotten used to talking to your *Englisch* friends."

"They aren't my friends," she snapped and then turned away to dry her dripping hair.

At last! A glimpse of the self-assured Katie Kay, though he wished he hadn't had to be irksome to get her to respond. When they'd first started walking out together, he'd admired that aspect of her. He'd thought then that she could be the special one for him. When she'd selected him from among her admirers, he'd believed it meant something. What a fool he'd been!

Taking the reins, he slapped them on Rascal's back.

The horse was the same dark gray as the storm clouds overhead. Rascal stepped on the road. Micah didn't need to convince him to a faster pace. The buggy horse was eager to get home and dry.

Katie Kay didn't say anything as they drove through the night. From the corner of his eye, he saw her squeezing water out of her hair and into the towel. She never glanced in his direction. He might as well have been invisible.

He pulled on the left rein to turn Rascal onto the road to the Lapp farm. The horse resisted.

"Let's go, Rascal," Micah said past clenched teeth. He couldn't let his irritation with the woman beside him make him upset at the buggy horse. Rascal wanted to go right to reach his dry stable.

A damp hand settled on his left arm. He hated the tingle erupting out from where Katie Kay touched him. After a year, she had the same effect on him. He was a bigger fool than he'd thought.

"Go some other way," she ordered. "Any other way."

"This is the fastest way to your house."

"No! You can't take me home."

"Of course I'm taking you home." He frowned. "Where else did you think I was taking you?"

"I don't care. Anywhere else." Her voice broke, and her whisper was raw. "Just not home. Please, Micah. Don't take me home."

He didn't bother to hide his shock. What had happened to her? He'd never heard her beg anyone for anything.

"You need to go home, Katie Kay. Your family has been beside themselves with worry about you. I'm taking you home."

"No, you're not!" She grabbed the passenger side door. "If you think I won't jump out of this buggy, then you're wrong."

"Don't be silly. You could hurt yourself."

"I didn't before," he thought he heard her mutter, but before he could ask if he'd heard her correctly, she said, "If you're going to be like that, Micah, stop and let me out."

"I'm not leaving you out here in the middle of a stormy night."

"And you're not taking me home." Again her voice broke. "I'm not ready to face them. Not yet."

Hardening his heart to her was impossible. They'd known each other all their lives. He'd counted her among his *gut* friends before he'd fallen for her. Her *daed* was marrying his *mamm* in a month.

Was that why Katie Kay had returned? For the wedding? If so, Reuben and *Mamm* would be overjoyed to see her. But why didn't she want to relieve her *daed*'s fears? Too much didn't make sense.

"Micah," she said softly, "please take me somewhere else."

"Where?"

"I don't know."

"Do you have any money? One of the hotels out on Route 30 might not be completely booked on a weeknight."

She rolled her eyes. "I don't have enough to pay for a room." Opening her soaked purse that sat in a damp spot on the seat, she gasped.

"What's wrong?"

"He took my money! I thought he was just taking my cell phone."

Micah's hands tightened on the reins. "He? Were you robbed?"

"Not exactly."

If she was trying to be baffling tonight, she was succeeding. Maybe if he tried a different approach...

"Katie Kay, I don't want to have to lie to Reuben when he talks about wondering where you are."

"I'm not asking you to lie. I'm asking you not to say anything about seeing me."

"That's splitting hairs."

"Maybe it is." Again she looked away. "But I can't face my family right now."

It was the second time she'd said those words. He wanted to ask why she intended to avoid her family, but she looked dejected and lost, so unlike the girl he'd known. He pushed aside his objections. The Bible taught that they were supposed to help one another. Yet it also was at the very heart of God's commandments that the duty to honor one's parents must never be set aside for any reason.

He drew in the horse and sat with his elbows on his knees as the buggy slowed to a stop by the side of the road. He knew what he should do. He should haul her at top speed to her family's house. But that might do more damage than *gut*. She obviously needed time to prepare herself before she spoke to Reuben. Letting her have a day or two wouldn't make a big difference, and granting her a favor might be the very thing that kept her from jumping the fence again. At least until after she and Reuben had a chance to meet. Not knowing where she was had been hardest on the bishop. If they could reconcile, perhaps it would smooth over the situation, even if she chose to leave again.

"All right," he said, hoping he wasn't making a complete mess of everything and praying both Reuben and God would understand. "I may know someone who can put you up for tonight."

"Not among the *Leit*. The news would reach my family before dawn."

That was true. The Amish didn't use phones or email except for business, but nothing stayed a secret long in their tight-knit community. Jokingly referred to as the Amish grapevine, gossip and rumors flew faster than anything in cyberspace.

"These people are *Englischers*." He glanced at her clothing. "I'm sure you're accustomed to folks who aren't Amish. I'll ask my friends Sean and Gemma Donnelly to let you stay with them tonight."

"*Danki*, Micah!" Her frown eased for the first time since she'd gotten into the buggy, and his heart did a crazy little flip as it always did when she smiled at him. But, this time, he ignored it. He wouldn't make the same mistake of thinking she cared for him as much as he'd cared for her. He wouldn't make that mistake ever again!

"Don't thank me yet. I'm not helping you unless you agree to do what I ask."

At his stern tone, her smile faltered.

Micah plunged forward with what he knew he had to get her to agree to do. "I will help you find a place for tonight and won't mention to anyone you're here, but only if you agree to speak with your *daed*. Not tonight," he added when she started to protest. "Within a week."

"That's too soon."

"Then tell me how long you need."

"I don't know."

"I told you what I think is long enough. Tell me what you think is long enough before you speak with Reuben." He couldn't relent on this, though he wasn't sure she'd honor any agreement. The Katie Kay he used to know would have, but the one sitting beside him was a stranger.

"A month."

He sat straighter. "What? A whole month? Why do you need a month?"

"You don't need to know why. I need time to be sure about things. A lot of things." She raised her face toward him, and he could see the glitter in her eyes. Determination to get her way or tears or both? "If you'll find me a place to stay, Micah, I'll talk to my *daed* before a month's gone by. Agreed?"

He considered her words. If he said no, that wouldn't change anything. She wasn't going to talk to her *daed*. If he said *ja*, there was a chance she might do as she said. He owed Reuben that much.

Turning the horse's head back in the direction they'd come, he said, "Agreed."

She thanked him, but he paid no attention as he stared out into the darkness. He'd made the best decision he could have under the circumstances or the worst. He wasn't sure which.

Chapter Two

Micah assured Katie Kay while they drove through the darkness that his friends would be willing to take her in for the night. As to what she'd do tomorrow night, she wasn't sure. Maybe one of her *Englisch* friends would let her stay at her house. She must have one who wasn't afraid of Austin.

But most of her *Englisch* friends had been Austin's friends a lot longer than they'd been hers.

She'd never felt more alone. Her whole life, she'd been surrounded by friends, both female and male. As she grew up, the male friends became admirers, and she'd had fun flirting with them. Soon, if her suspicions that she was pregnant were true, none of them would be interested in her.

Though she'd glowered at Micah, he hadn't backed away from his insistence she speak with her *daed*. He'd always been stubborn, but she'd usually persuaded him to change his mind. Not tonight. She recognized the set of his square jaw, identical to his twin brother's, except Micah didn't have a cleft in his chin. His black hair fell into his startlingly blue eyes that saw so much and re-

vealed so little. His days spent in construction work
had broadened his shoulders and knotted muscles in his
arms beneath his work coat. She couldn't believe some
girl hadn't snagged him as her husband in the past year.

And you should be glad for that. She hated listen-
ing to her conscience, but she couldn't argue with it. If
he hadn't been out tonight, she wasn't sure where she
could have found shelter without resorting to knock-
ing on doors.

But Micah couldn't understand why she didn't want
to talk to her *daed* and she couldn't tell him the truth.
She needed to know if she was pregnant or not. And if
she was… With a sigh, she admitted she didn't know
what she'd do.

The house where Sean and Gemma Donnelly lived
was closer to Ronks than Paradise Springs. Katie Kay
was relieved because the two districts her *daed* oversaw
as a bishop didn't reach that far west. The Donnellys'
single-story house was close to the road, and, unlike
the plain houses they'd passed, bright lights glowed in
the windows. Electric wires ran high over the drive-
way, where a pair of vans, one with lettering on the
side, were parked. She couldn't read what was painted
on it, and she didn't care.

All she wanted was to have a place to sleep and to
wake in the morning to find tonight had been noth-
ing but a nightmare. It had to be. Austin wouldn't have
treated her heartlessly, and her heroic knight in a gray
buggy wouldn't have been Micah. What a joke on her!

Drawing in his horse, Micah stopped the buggy next
to one van. She saw a hitching post nearby and won-
dered why it was there. Maybe the people inside pro-
vided a service to the plain community. He lashed the

reins around it while she stepped out with the towel over her head to hold off the rain.

"This way," Micah said, walking along flagstones to the front door.

She followed without saying anything. When he knocked a couple of times and then opened the door, she knew he must be a regular visitor. Amish people walked in without knocking but not the *Englischers* she'd met. They'd been horrified the first time she entered without waiting for someone to open the door. She'd been mortified, not realizing then how many more mistakes she had ahead of her.

"Is something wrong, Micah?" asked an *Englischer* as he entered the narrow hallway on the other side of the door. He wasn't as tall as Micah, but he wore similar work clothes. His hair was red and tightly curled both on his head and in his thick beard and mustache.

"We didn't expect you back tonight." A woman followed the man into the hallway. She was plump and wore her dark hair in a ponytail. Dressed in a flowery bathrobe and fluffy slippers, she looked ready for bed. "Are you okay? Is Rascal all right?"

"We're fine. I left him tied out by the driveway," Micah answered, and Katie Kay realized Rascal must be his horse. An odd name for a buggy horse, but maybe the beast wasn't plodding and slow when the weather was *gut*. "Sean and Gemma Donnelly, this is my... friend. Katie Kay Lapp."

Did the others hear his hesitation? It made her sad, though she wasn't quite sure why. She'd treated him poorly, so she should be grateful he attached the word *friend* to her name. She needed a friend.

"Come inside," Gemma said with a welcoming smile.

"What a horrible night to be out! Can I get you something hot to drink? I think there's cocoa left in the cupboard."

"Perfect," Katie Kay said at the same time Micah replied, "No, thanks, we don't need anything."

He frowned at her, and she wanted to ask why. Gemma had offered, and she'd accepted. She understood when Gemma turned, revealing the unmistakable outline of a very pregnant body. In a few months, she could look the same. Her fingers went to her belly. Was it as flat as it'd been a few weeks ago?

"Actually," Katie Kay hurried to add, "I'm fine. Being inside and warm is helping. I'll skip the cocoa." She hoped her stomach wouldn't growl and betray the fact she hadn't had anything to eat since noon, when she'd finally been able to hold down food. All morning, she'd been sick…as she had for the past week. She'd had to accept the possibility she was pregnant.

"Are you sure you don't want anything?" the woman asked.

"Ja." The *Deitsch* word slipped out as it hadn't in months. She was exhausted. That had to be the reason. It couldn't have anything to do with the brooding man beside her.

Such a description of Micah astonished her. Micah usually had been the one getting everyone to laugh. He and his brothers always teased each other, and if they could draw others into their sport, all the better. Yet, he stood like a disapproving Old Testament patriarch, not a hint of humor on his face.

The red-haired man asked, "What's up, Micah?"

"Katie Kay needs a place to stay tonight. Can she stay here with you?"

Questions flickered across both *Englischers*' faces, but she was relieved when, after a glance was exchanged, Gemma said, "Certainly. There's an extra bed in Olivia's room." She smiled at Katie Kay. "Olivia is our four-year-old daughter. I don't think she'd mind sharing her room as long as you're okay with sleeping with a chatterbox. She talks all day, as well as half the night in her sleep."

"That will be fine." What else could she say? She'd rather sleep in the rain? No, she was glad for the chance to be under a roof and warm. It hadn't been warm the past week in the apartment she shared with Austin and his friends. There hadn't been money to pay for heat, so they'd used what blankets they had and hoped the winter wouldn't be bad. "Is Olivia your only child?"

She ignored the look Micah fired at her when she didn't use the common *Deitsch* word for child. Why would she say *kind*? The Donnellys weren't Amish, and she had no idea how much of the language they understood. Probably some, because they were Micah's friends.

"No," Gemma replied with another warm smile. "We have two sons. DJ, which is short for Sean Donnelly Junior, is going to turn six in January, and Jayden is almost two." She laced her hands together over her distended belly. "And this is son number three. Dylan. He'll be here in a couple of months. His due date is Christmas, but he'll come when he wants. As they all do." She laughed, but a hint of fatigue slipped in. "Sean, why don't you help Micah get her bags?"

"I don't have any," she said.

"Oh." Gemma regained her composure. "Well, then we won't have to worry about Sean clomping up the

stairs and waking the kids. Come in and sit down. We just finished watching the news."

As they walked into a comfortable living room with bright green-and-white wallpaper on one wall and a fireplace on another, Micah glanced at Katie Kay, this time with an expectant expression. What did he want? *Ach*, he wanted her to thank his friends, and he believed she'd left her manners behind in Lancaster. As she started to express her gratitude to Gemma, feeling the familiar ripples of rebellion rising at his silent chiding, her hostess waved aside her words.

"We're more than happy to help any friend of Micah's," the woman said but glanced at him with an unsteady smile.

No doubt, Gemma wondered what Micah, so Amish with his broadfall pants and straw hat, was doing with a woman who wasn't wearing plain clothes and who had no luggage other than a drenched purse.

"We appreciate that," Micah said, saving her from having to explain. "When I come in the morning, we'll figure out what she'll do next. Okay, Katie Kay?"

Regarding her without a speck of emotion, he held her gaze. She might as well have been a plank of wood or a shingle. A shiver ran along her as she wondered if he despised her as much as he acted. Tears clogged her throat. She was more alone than she'd ever been.

She looked away first. She didn't want him to see her eyes fill. She wasn't going to cry as she had out on the road. Somehow she had to be strong. If not for herself, then for the *boppli* she might be carrying.

Though Katie Kay hadn't replied to Micah's question, everyone acted as if she had. Micah took his leave, and Gemma showed her to her daughter's room. Her

hostess explained that Micah and her husband owned a company together, so Micah came over every morning to catch a ride with Sean to work.

Trying to act as if she'd been in a house like this many times before, she knew the *Englisch* habits she'd tried to adopt still looked unnatural on her because Gemma asked if she was familiar with how to switch on electric lights in the nearby bathroom. Austin had teased her about being too "dumb-dumb Dutch"—his derogatory term for plain people—each time she made a mistake. She had tried to appear sophisticated and *Englisch* in the hope he'd notice her.

He had one night, the one she didn't recall much about. The result of it was the reason he'd thrown her out of his car and his life.

Why didn't she remember more of what had happened a couple of months ago? She'd been drinking, as she often did with the roommates, but she usually was careful, never having more than one drink because even that could make her head swim. The others would have can after can of beer until they passed out. She hadn't. Having finally gained a little control over her life, she didn't want to chance losing it again.

But one night she hadn't been cautious because she wanted to forget the bad day she'd had at work waiting tables at a diner. Nothing she'd done had been right, and when she got back to the apartment, she'd given into Austin's urging to keep drinking. Now she was paying the price for believing he wanted to comfort her. She couldn't blame him for her stupidity, but she did for his callous expulsion of her from his life.

Taking the nightgown Gemma loaned her as well as a toothbrush, she skipped the hot shower she wanted des-

perately. The Donnellys were ready to call it a day, and she didn't want to keep them up. She thanked Gemma, slipped into the little girl's room and got ready for bed.

It was far softer than any bed she'd slept on since leaving her own comfortable bed at home. Instead of a handmade quilt, the blanket and freshly laundered sheets were covered by an afghan. Its extra warmth would be welcome.

From the other bed, Olivia mumbled something. Katie Kay moved to check the *kind* and bumped into the table between the beds. Something fell off it and bounced on the floor. She realized it was an inhaler. She looked from it to the *kind*. Olivia must have asthma.

She put the device on the table and moved to Olivia's bed. In the faint light from a night-light shaped like a princess, the little girl's curly hair looked dark, but Katie Kay guessed it was as red as her *daed*'s. Her cheeks were as full as a well-fed squirrel's, and she clutched a well-worn, well-loved stuffed kitten to her pajamas that were decorated with more princesses.

Another flurry of tears threatened to fall as Katie Kay smoothed the covers over the sleeping *kind*. Olivia didn't resemble Sarann, but Katie Kay remembered tucking in her youngest sister before getting into her own bed. Sarann hadn't lived to be any older than this little girl; yet that had been far longer than any *kind* with her birth defects should have lived. Every day of her life, she'd had a smile in spite of the pain she must have suffered.

If Katie Kay had been half as courageous, maybe she wouldn't have taken the easy way out and left Paradise Springs. *Daed* had been patient and loving with Sarann,

seeing her as a special gift from God. No different from any of his *kinder*, as he'd said on many occasions.

Why was she remembering that now? She'd let her anger at him banish the memory. Well, it was too late to change anything, and she couldn't return home. Not when she was unsure if she was pregnant. Not when she hadn't made up her mind about being baptized and becoming a member of the Amish community. Not when she was confused about so many things.

Including Micah Stoltzfus. She'd changed a lot in the past four months, but she hadn't expected him to be different, as well. How many times had she joked that nothing ever changed among the plain people?

Something else to add to the long list of things she'd been wrong about.

Going to the other bed, Katie Kay slipped under the covers. Her hair was damp and fell against her face as she turned her head on the pillow to stare out the window at the rain.

In the morning, Micah would be back. She needed to make a plan for what she was going to do.

She wished she knew what that might be.

Guarding every word he spoke the next morning was almost more than Micah could handle. He sat at the breakfast table with his married brother, Ezra, and Ezra's wife, Leah, and her young niece, as well as *Mamm* and his other unmarried brothers. His twin, Daniel, and their older brother Isaiah both were getting married later in the fall. Daniel had built a house beyond the barn where his fiancée already lived, and Isaiah spent most of his time down the road with his late friend's family that had become his own.

Nobody had spoken of anything connected to Katie Kay. Even so, he couldn't think of anything other than the blonde who'd returned to Paradise Springs after living somewhere with the *Englisch* for almost four months.

Only four months? From the lines dug into Reuben's face by his unrelenting worry, the bishop looked, when Micah had last seen him on Sunday, as if Katie Kay had left years ago. But it'd been June when she left, and now it was October.

He shouldn't have told Katie Kay he'd say nothing to anyone about her return. That was wrong, and he intended to tell her so as soon as he saw her at the Donnellys' house this morning. But what if she reneged on her side of the bargain, too, and left without ever seeing Reuben? How could Micah face his bishop knowing he could have taken Katie Kay—willing or not—to her *daed* last night?

He'd get to the Donnellys' house early. Sean wasn't a morning person, something Micah had learned since the two of them had become partners about three months ago. Daniel, Micah's twin, had invited him to join Stoltzfus Brothers Construction, the company Daniel had started earlier in the year. However, for a couple of years, Micah and Sean had been talking about working together every time they were at the same construction site. They'd pooled their savings and started Plain and Simple Solutions, an alternative energy company.

"You're plain, and I'm simple," Sean had said with a laugh when he suggested the name.

"I've noticed that," he'd replied with a chuckle of his own. Sean was anything but simple. He was a brilliant carpenter and a great salesman, finding client after cli-

ent, so they never were idle. However, the name was perfect for what they did. Simple, green solutions to help *Englischers* cut their power bills and to enable plain households to get electricity that didn't come from the grid.

One after another, his brothers prayed silently before they rose from the table and went to their various jobs. Leah and her niece disappeared down cellar, probably to get canned vegetables and meat for the evening meal.

Micah barely noticed them leaving as he wondered if Katie Kay would keep her side of the bargain, even if he'd kept his. He wished he could trust her, but he couldn't.

For the past year, his brothers had teased him for not asking if he could take her home. They believed he was too shy to talk to her. None of them had any idea of the truth. He'd asked her, driven her home several times and then she'd told him to go bother some other girl and waved him away as if he were as annoying as a gnat.

He had collected the pieces of his broken heart and prayed God would help her see she'd made a mistake. If God had, she hadn't listened to Him. Last weekend, he'd taken Isaiah's late wife's sister Tillie Mast, home from a youth event...to get his brothers off his back. She was sweet and well-known as a great cook. He'd learned, however, contrary to the old adage, that the way to his heart was not through his stomach. He doubted he was giving her a chance, but he'd promised himself he wouldn't make a fool of himself over a woman again.

"Micah?"

He looked up from his scrambled eggs and fried potatoes when *Mamm* said his name in a tone that suggested she'd already repeated it more than once. *"Ja?"*

"Is there someone special you'd like to sit with at the wedding supper?"

The old tradition of pairing off the singles for the evening meal to give them a chance to get to know each other better was one he wished *Mamm* and Reuben would skip. Forcing a smile, he said, "No one in particular."

"Not Tillie Mast?"

"You'd do her a big favor by matching her with someone else." He wasn't surprised his *mamm* knew about him taking Tillie home. Eager eyes at the end of an evening noted who left with whom. Because he and Katie Kay had been careful, at her insistence, nobody had noticed them together.

"I'm sorry to hear that, Micah." She patted his cheek. "You're a *gut* boy, and you deserve someone special in your life."

"I trust God will send her along eventually."

Mamm picked up her empty cup and carried it to the stove to refill it with *kaffi*. Holding the cup to let the fragrant steam rise into her face, she said, "Reuben had hoped you and Katie Kay might sit together."

"What?" He sat straighter and berated himself for not leaving at the same time as his brothers had.

"I hear how Daniel teases you, and I've learned there's a nugget of truth in the jests you two throw at each other." She took a sip and lowered her cup. "*Ach*, it's impossible anyhow, but I keep hoping that girl will come to her senses and return home. It would mean the world to Reuben."

"I know." Guilt stabbed him. As soon as he reached Sean's house, he was going to get Katie Kay and drive

her home, whether she agreed or not. He didn't want to be caught in the middle of this mess any longer.

"Do you know where she might be, Micah?" His *mamm* went on as he tried not to choke out the truth. "Listen to me. Why would you know where she is? Though the two of you were *gut* friends when you were younger, things changed." Sorrow dimmed her eyes. "If you know someone who might know where she is, pass the word along that she is missed."

"I will." He intended to tell Katie Kay himself. Bowing his head and saying words of gratitude for the meal while he hoped the Lord would forgive him for his haste, he got up, gave his *mamm* a hug and hurried out before she could say more.

By the time he had Rascal hitched to his buggy and was on his way to the Donnellys' house, the sun was turning the eastern sky from black to layers of gray clouds. He practiced over and over what he'd say to Katie Kay. Last night, asking her to be sensible hadn't worked. In fact, he'd probably insulted her by suggesting she wasn't acting rationally.

"She isn't," he mumbled to himself as he turned onto the road leading toward Ronks. "Why would she return if she didn't intend to mend the fences she's jumped over?"

He was missing something important, but what?

The Donnellys' house was dark except for a light in the kitchen. Micah parked his buggy behind the lime-green antique Volkswagen van that Gemma drove. He stepped out and around the more modern van Sean had painted with their company's name and phone number, which Gemma answered in the house. Having her help had been a big step toward getting the company

going, but Micah wondered if they should hire an answering service. Gemma would be overwhelmed with three young *kinder*, a *boppli* and handling the calls. He'd have to talk to Sean about it. His friend was hesitant to make changes that didn't have an impact on Micah, too. For once, Sean needed to be a bit selfish and think of himself and his family.

Especially after Micah had selfishly left his problem with Sean and Gemma last night. While Gemma had settled Katie Kay, Micah had given his partner an overview of the situation and realized how little he knew about what had brought Katie Kay to Paradise Springs. He planned to get answers today.

"Come in, Micah," said Gemma, meeting him at the door.

She didn't usually do that, so he asked, "Is everything okay? Has Katie Kay been—?"

"Sit down, Micah."

"What's wrong?" He couldn't miss the underlying tension in her voice. He'd been about to ask what Katie Kay had done to upset the household, but he restrained himself. Bringing her to the Donnellys' house had been wrong. He'd transferred his problem to his best friends.

"You should sit down, Micah."

"Just tell me." How much trouble had Katie Kay caused?

Gemma took a deep breath and then let it out with a sigh. "I think your friend is pregnant."

"Pregnant?" He groped for a chair and sat as he stared at her. "That can't be true!"

"Because her father is a bishop?" She shook her head with a grimace. "Don't fool yourself, Micah. Her running away was already aimed at hurting him and toss-

ing aside everything she'd been taught. Getting involved with some man wasn't much of a step further."

He couldn't help thinking of Katie Kay saying someone had taken her money along with her cell phone. Was it the man who was the *daed* of her *boppli*? He felt his temper rise but pushed it down. Getting angry wouldn't solve anything. In fact, it might make things worse.

"Where is she?" he asked, relieved his voice sounded close to normal.

"Throwing up." She looked behind her as Sean came into the kitchen.

For once, his friend wasn't complaining about the early hour and how work should begin at noon. Instead, he looked from his wife to Micah and sighed. "I guess it's obvious why she didn't want to go home. What do you want to do?"

"I want you two to go to work," Gemma said before he could answer. "I've got an unused pregnancy test kit. I'll take care of her today. You take time to think about what you want to say, Micah." She gave him a sad smile. "I know you two used to date."

"I took her home a few times."

"Which is dating among the Amish." She wagged a finger at him as if he were as young as her *kinder.* "Don't try to pull the wool over my eyes."

"You sound like *Mamm.*"

"And you sound like you're trying to change the subject." Her *gut* humor fell away as she added, "Katie Kay needs to confirm if she's pregnant or not before she has to face anyone, including you." She sighed. "Maybe especially you. I can see she respects you a great deal."

He snorted his disagreement.

Gemma frowned. "Stop acting like a sulking teen-

ager and listen to me. She's a young woman in a bad situation. She doesn't have anyone she can turn to."

"The *boppli*'s *daed* can—"

"I don't think he's in the picture any longer. She hasn't said, though she opened up to me a bit more this morning. Or maybe she slipped up and spoke without thinking. She mentioned something about him chucking her out of his car last night like litter."

The curses the other construction workers used raced through Micah's head. He pushed them away and sent an apology to God, but the *gut* Lord surely understood.

How could a man get a woman with *kind* and then abandon her in an icy rain?

Gemma put comforting fingers on his arm, but it wasn't any solace when he recalled how Katie Kay's same motion had sent ripples of sensation coursing through him. Why did he have feelings for her? He didn't want to get enmeshed in her charms again. His heart didn't need to be broken once more.

"I know what you're thinking, Micah," she said, "because I feel the same way. Any good Christian would. However, we must deal with what *is*, not what we would like it to be."

The sound of *kinder* came from upstairs. Gemma motioned for him and Sean to go and kissed her husband before hurrying to collect the youngsters.

Sean opened the door so Micah could lead the way out. When his friend didn't ask any questions, Micah was grateful. Everything was changing. Gemma was right. He needed to take time to think because he was less sure now about what he should do than he had been the night before.

Chapter Three

Concentrating on work wasn't easy, and more than once during the day, Micah was glad he wore the safety rope that kept him from tumbling off the roof. He wasn't watching where he was stepping. He was also grateful he and Sean and the two men they'd hired to assist them were preparing the support framework to hold the panels being installed on the newly constructed house. With his mind elsewhere, he didn't want to be responsible for carrying the expensive twenty-five-pound panels up the ladder and setting them in place.

The end of the workday arrived, and Micah came to the realization his plans hadn't changed from that morning. He needed to talk to Katie Kay and insist she decide. She had to make up her mind and go home or go away.

But if she chose the latter, how would he ever explain to Reuben that he'd abetted Katie Kay? He prayed God would give him the words. She'd been too distraught last night to make a *gut* decision. But now she'd had a day to think about her future.

Micah stowed his tools in the rear of the van and got

in on the passenger side. Sean was already behind the wheel. Reaching for the key, he started the engine as Micah hooked his seat belt in place.

Neither of them spoke as they left the subdivision that soon would consist of nearly twenty new houses. Each would have solar panels, so he and Sean had several weeks of work ahead of them.

"How are you doing?" Sean asked, breaking the silence.

"If I knew, I'd tell you."

His friend gave him a sympathetic grin. "You'll feel better after you get this conversation with Katie Kay over with."

"I hope so." He didn't mean to give terse answers, but he wasn't sure what else to say.

Sean glanced at him and then back at the road. "I think it'd be a good idea if I get Gemma and the kids out of the way so you can talk to Katie Kay without us."

"Sean—"

"I promised them I'd take them out to a restaurant across from the Rockvale Outlets. It might as well be tonight."

"You're a *gut* friend."

"And you're a good partner. If you fall and break your neck because you aren't paying attention to the job, I'll have to find and train another." He looked away from the road again and gave Micah a brash grin. "I know how long that takes because, after all this time, I've barely got you trained."

Micah appreciated his friend's attempt to tease him out of his somber mood, so, though he didn't feel the least bit like laughing, he did. "I think you've got it backward. *I* have been training you. You didn't know

which end of the panel went where when I first met you."

"Yeah, yeah. Keep telling yourself that if it gives you comfort."

He listened as Sean continued jesting and tried to laugh at the appropriate times. The truth was, however, that nothing could make him feel better about talking with Katie Kay. No matter what the results of the pregnancy test had been, there still was the issue of her refusal to see her family.

When Sean pulled the van into the driveway, Micah tried to breathe slowly. This wasn't going to be easy, but he had to convince Katie Kay to do what she should and go home. If she was pregnant, she needed her family more than ever.

Micah gave his friend a brief smile when Sean clapped him on the shoulder as they walked to the front door. As always, Micah let Sean open the door. As always, a whirl of *kinder*, looking more like a dozen than three, surrounded Sean. Their young voices told him about their day at the same time, each trying to talk over the other. No matter how many times Gemma or Sean urged them to take turns, they were too excited to have their *daed* home at day's end.

Standing aside to let the loving assault run its course, Micah couldn't help envying his partner. Having a house filled with cute *kinder* and a loving wife who somehow found a way to stand on tiptoe and kiss him over the heads of the excited youngsters would be a true blessing. After seeing his siblings marry and begin to raise families, he'd known it was something he wanted for himself.

As if he'd spoken out loud, the *kinder* threw their

arms around him next, spewing out more of the stories they'd started telling their *daed*. To them, he was Uncle Micah, though two-year-old Jayden could manage only Mike. He hugged each one in turn, not wanting his anxiety to ruin their happiness.

The kids cheered when Sean announced they were eating out. Gemma smiled, too, but hers was as taut as Micah's felt. When she glanced at him, she didn't say anything. It wasn't necessary. He could tell from her strained expression that the pregnancy test had been positive.

He helped get the *kinder* into their coats and hats. When he offered to help put them in their seats in the car, Sean shook his head.

"We'll take care of them. You take care of her." He gripped Micah's arm and then herded his wife and *kinder* out the door.

Micah closed it. Once he heard the car back out of the drive, he went into the living room. Where was Katie Kay?

As if in answer, he heard dishes rattling in the kitchen. He went in.

Katie Kay wore the same jeans, but they'd been washed. Her battered T-shirt had been replaced by a black sweater. It brought out the gold in her hair, which she pulled back with clips that must have belonged to Olivia. One was topped by a red dog and the other a blue cat that was the exact same shade as Katie Kay's eyes. She had only socks on, and he wondered if her shoes had been ruined in the rain.

"Oh, it's you," she said as she closed the cupboard door.

"Hello to you, too." He put his straw hat on the is-

land and undid his stained work coat. "Sean is taking the family out for supper. A treat for the *kinder.*"

"Gemma said he might." Her voice was as unemotional as his. "She told me there are leftovers in the fridge and to help myself. Do you want something before you go?"

"I want to talk to you."

Her eyes narrowed with suspicion. He'd known he couldn't fool her with casual conversation. "What about?"

"You."

"I don't want to hear how disappointed you are in me or how you believe I should go to my family's house." She reached into the refrigerator and pulled out a plastic container with a bright green top. "You've made yourself clear on that."

"*Gut*, then we can talk about something else. Do you want to talk about you being pregnant?"

Color washed from her face, and the container fell out of her fingers to bounce on the kitchen floor. She grabbed the edge of the counter as he picked up the plastic box and set it beside his hat. Red sauce was leaking out. He pulled a section of paper towel off the roll by the sink and stuck it under the container. He wanted to give her a chance to find her voice, so it wouldn't feel like he was interrogating her.

"You know about that?" she asked.

"This morning, Gemma told me what she suspected. She's worried about you."

"About you, you mean." She crossed her arms in front of herself in a protective pose.

"You know Sean and Gemma are my friends. Of

course they're concerned about me, but she's worried about you, too. She's that way."

Katie Kay's shoulders lost their rigid stance. "You're right. She cares a lot, though I'm a stranger."

"You're someone who needs help. That's all she and Sean have to know. They're usually among the first to help anyone in the community, whether the person is plain or *Englisch*." He gave her a wry half smile. "She told me this morning because she wanted me to help you, too."

"This morning, I didn't know for sure." As fast as her face had bleached, it reddened.

"But you used the pregnancy test and found out you are."

"Do you know all my secrets?" she cried, flinging her hands in the air and storming past him. "I thought I could trust Gemma to keep her mouth zipped."

For a moment, she acted as if she intended to stamp out of the kitchen, and he was prepared to give chase because they couldn't postpone this conversation, especially since a *boppli* had been added to the mix. When she turned and faced him, he hid his surprise. In the past, Katie Kay had run away from whatever bothered her. Tonight, she held her ground. Another sign she'd changed.

But for the better or the worse?

"Gemma didn't say anything," he assured her. "I could tell by how worried she looked." He looked her steadily in the eyes. "I am concerned, too."

"I don't need you worrying about me. I got myself into this situation. I'll deal with it myself."

"How?" he fired back, his frustration escaping.

She froze at his sharp question, and, for one moment,

it was as if she were a balloon and his words a pin cutting into her. She deflated, and he crossed the room and took her arm before her knees folded beneath her. By the time she tried to pull it away, he'd sat her at the table.

He leaned one hand beside her and caught her gaze again. He was awed by the intensity of the pain and fear in her eyes, but he saw her resolve, too. As he watched, a quiet strength submerged the despair.

"How?" he asked. "How are you going to deal with this by yourself, Katie Kay?"

That *was* the question, Katie Kay admitted. Trust Micah to get to the heart of the matter. Her *daed* admired his frankness, which Micah had inherited from his own *daed*. It was a *gut* question, and she wished she had an answer. She and Gemma had talked most of the day when they weren't entertaining the *kinder*. DJ went to kindergarten in the morning, and the numbness left by the results of the pregnancy test had started to wear off for Katie Kay by the time the youngster got home.

"Your family will want to help you," Micah said.

Raising her eyes to his deeper blue ones, she could see he believed what he said. Most likely, he was right, but if she went home, everyone would expect her to fit into the constraints of an Amish woman's life. Gemma Donnelly had shown her *Englischers* could be as giving and compassionate as a plain person. Katie Kay had started doubting that when she went to live with Austin and his friends after her nearby *Englisch* friend's parents made it obvious she'd worn out her welcome. They'd been fine with her visiting, but they had Amish friends they hadn't wanted to upset by letting her stay longer.

"It's not that, Micah."

"Then what is it?"

How could she explain to a man who'd already been baptized and joined the Amish community? Micah always had an eye on the future, making plans for what he hoped to do. Her *daed* had mentioned it to her, probably in hopes of convincing her to do the same. But taking such an irrevocable step meant turning away from the wider world.

She wasn't like Micah. She wasn't focused on what could happen tomorrow. She wanted to savor today and the exciting things it might contain. What if she did get baptized and there were amazing things in the *Englisch* world she never had a chance to experience? She didn't want to miss out.

Austin and his friends had a word for it. *FOMO.* Fear of missing out. It described her feelings, but, when she looked at Micah's handsome face—and he'd gotten better-looking in the past year—she doubted he'd understand. Somehow, he'd found a way to strike a balance between the plain and *Englisch* worlds. She was still trying to find her way.

"I have to think of the *boppli*," she said, selecting the easiest excuse she could devise. "When I see this family, I know I want that for him or her."

"The *boppli*'s *daed*—"

"Isn't it pretty obvious he doesn't want anything to do with either of us?" She hated the bitterness in her voice, but how could she have misjudged Austin so completely?

"I'm sorry, Katie Kay."

His sympathy almost undid her. She wasn't going to cry again. Austin wasn't worth her tears. If she'd seen

that right from the beginning, instead of thinking he was much cooler than the guys she'd grown up with because he had a car and an apartment, she wouldn't be in the situation she was in. She couldn't change the past, but it was time to stand up for herself.

"Danki." She gave him the best smile she could manage.

"What can I do to help?"

She shook her head. "I don't think there's anything you can do. Gemma has invited me to stay as long as I need to."

"I didn't realize that." His tone made it clear he wasn't happy with his business partner's wife making the offer.

"You didn't think she'd toss me out, too, did you?"

"No. I know Gemma too well."

"But you don't want me to take advantage of your friends, ain't so?" The Amish phrase fell from her lips as easily as if she'd never been away.

"I didn't say that."

"You didn't have to." She stood. "Your opinion is splashed all over your face. Micah, I don't need your help. There's nothing you can do to help me."

"I can marry you."

Katie Kay stared at him in disbelief. He couldn't have said what she thought he'd said. Not after what she'd done, both in Paradise Springs and after she left. He knew too many of her faults, and if he'd ever cared about her, she'd squashed any hint of love by telling him to get out of her life.

He must have forgiven her, because he was trying to help her. But that, she knew, was the Amish way. Forgive others for their mistakes and move ahead as

if the transgression had never happened. She'd never managed to make it work herself, though she'd tried over and over.

When she didn't reply, Micah folded his arms over his chest and looked at her with a glacial expression she found impossible to decipher. "You should know one thing before you answer, Katie Kay. I didn't offer to marry you because of feelings I have for you."

"Y-y-you d-d-didn't?" she sputtered, shocked.

"No." He picked up his hat from the counter. "I offered because I admire your *daed*, and I don't want to see him and *Mamm* hurt."

"What does Wanda have to do with this?" She considered Micah's *mamm* a bit of a *buttinsky*—a word she'd learned from Austin's friends—and an inveterate matchmaker.

He stared at her, and emotion returned to his face. It was disbelief. "You really don't know?"

"Know what?"

"Your *daed* and my *mamm* are getting married next month."

Katie Kay sat again, so hard the chair rocked. She tried to wrap her mind around the idea *Daed* was marrying Wanda Stoltzfus. They'd been *gut* friends for years. Wanda often sent a *snitz* pie home with *Daed* when he went to the Stoltzfus farm for one reason or another. Apparently he'd really had only a single reason for going to visit. He'd been courting Micah's *mamm*.

"I can't believe it," she whispered.

"They decided after you left. Reuben has been praying you'd return for the ceremony, so all his *kinder* will be there."

She looked at her flat abdomen. "I'm not sure he'll want me there."

"If you apologize to him and are married—"

"I'm not marrying you, Micah Stoltzfus! Didn't I make that clear last year?"

"You did." He put on his straw hat and buttoned his coat. "And don't worry. I won't bother you by asking you again. You've made yourself clear tonight. *Guten owed*, Katie Kay." Without another word, he walked out of the kitchen. Seconds later, she heard the front door open and close.

She didn't move as the sound of buggy wheels rolling after a horse faded into the night. She'd handled it wrong. She should have thanked Micah for his offer before she turned him down. He'd been candid when he told her that he was asking her to protect their parents from pain.

Maybe you should have considered his offer. He might not have feelings for you, but you have plenty for him.

"Shut up!" She jumped to her feet and ran into the living room. Turning on the television, she kept pushing the volume button on the remote until the sound of voices and laughter were so loud her ears hurt. But it was useless. Nothing drowned out the truth. She may have lost her best ally as she faced the future alone.

Chapter Four

Slowly Katie Kay sank to sit on the Donnellys' front-porch step. She'd come outside after the family had returned home. She didn't want to ruin their excitement after their fun evening out, and she was too distressed to try to pretend she was all right.

The chilly evening wind was overwhelmed by the cold sinking deep within her as Micah's words replayed through her mind. *Daed* was getting remarried? Why hadn't someone told her? She wasn't under the *bann*. She hadn't been baptized yet, something she'd avoided discussing each time her *daed* had brought up the subject, so leaving wasn't a reason to shun her. Why hadn't one of her sisters let her know about this astonishing event?

Maybe because she hadn't written to any of them after she left Paradise Springs and moved to Lancaster. They wouldn't have known how to reach her.

She hid her face in her hands. While she'd been gone, it'd been easy to convince herself nothing would change here. Wasn't that one of the reasons she'd gone? Be-

cause everything stayed the same day after day while the outside, *Englisch* world buzzed by at warp speed?

But she was back. If she was in Paradise Springs when the wedding was held, should she attend? Her hand slipped over her abdomen. It was flat. With the right dress, she shouldn't have to reveal the truth in a month. She could go and see her friends and enjoy a bit of flirting and…

Those days were over. She'd put an end to them when she left Paradise Springs and sought the brighter lights and faster pace of Lancaster City.

And Micah knew the truth. He wouldn't spread it, but it would be only a matter of time before someone else discovered she hadn't come home alone.

Again she wanted to ask God why He had arranged for Micah to be the person whose path crossed hers. Was she being punished for being headstrong and curious about the *Englischers*? Hadn't *Daed* taught that their Heavenly Father forgave each of them as He asked them to forgive each other?

The cold air finally drove her inside. She was relieved to discover the family had gone to bed, but loneliness riveted her. Nobody told her their plans, which was a painful reminder that she wasn't part of this family or any other.

Tears stung her eyes. She kept them from falling as she turned off the light in the living room before creeping up the stairs. Refusing to look in the mirror over the sink, she got ready for bed. She tiptoed into Olivia's room. The little girl was asleep, her slow, deep breaths loud in the silent room.

Katie Kay crawled into her borrowed bed. The sheets were cool, but the drops running down her cheeks

seared her skin. Pressing her face to the pillow, she gave up the battle to hold in her grief.

She was alone. She and the *boppli*.

God is with you always. How many times had she heard that? But why would God offer her comfort when she'd turned away from the life He'd given her?

Once released, her grief and fear refused to be contained. The cotton beneath her cheek grew damp, then wet, and still her tears fell as she mourned for everything that had gone wrong in her life.

A gentle breath brushed her face in the moment before Olivia whispered, "No sad, Kay-Kay." Her tiny hand patted Katie Kay's arm. "No cry, Kay-Kay. Please."

Katie Kay was startled. She hadn't heard the little girl get up. Olivia must have been woken by her sobs. Another mistake to add to her long list.

Rolling over to face the *kind*, Katie Kay whispered, "Aren't you supposed to be asleep?"

"You sad. Wanna hug? A hug makes it better." She held up her short arms.

Suddenly Katie Kay couldn't imagine anything she wanted more than comfort from one small *kind*. Olivia's solace was offered with no strings attached other than her heartstrings, which had been touched by Katie Kay's weeping.

Katie Kay swung her legs over the side of the bed. Picking up the little girl, she set Olivia beside her. Holding out her own arms, she gathered the *kind* close. The aroma of Olivia's flowery shampoo swirled through her senses as she welcomed the hug.

"Danki," she murmured into the *kind*'s silken red hair.

"That means 'thank you,' doesn't it?" Olivia stared at her. "You talk like Uncle Micah."

"I do…sometimes."

"Will you teach me to talk like you?"

"If your *mamm*—your mother—says it's okay." She brushed her tears aside as a smile edged along her lips. Spending time with the inquisitive little girl would help her to stop thinking about her troubles…she hoped.

"*Mamm.* Mommy. *Mamm.* Mom." Olivia giggled and then clamped her pudgy hands over her mouth. Whispering again, she said, "Sounds the same."

"The words do, don't they?" She lifted the *kind* off the bed. "You should get back to bed."

"Mommy sleeps with me when I've gots a bad dream. I stay with you."

Katie Kay bit her lip to keep it from trembling as a new storm of tears filled her eyes. She watched Olivia run to her own bed and collect her pillow. The little girl put it next to Katie Kay's before clambering to sit beside her.

Lying down, Katie Kay blinked hard when the little girl embraced her again. She closed her eyes as she leaned her head on the *kind*'s soft hair. She wasn't sure which of them fell asleep first.

The hope that things would be better after a *gut* night's sleep had been as unreasonable as Katie Kay's expectation that Austin would do the right thing and apologize. Though Olivia's kindness had allowed her to find sleep, reality reared its ugly head again the next morning.

Nothing had changed.

Katie Kay woke with a groan. She heard sounds of

the household getting ready for another day. Olivia had returned to her bed sometime during the night, but she was already out of the room. Alone, Katie Kay was tempted to pull the pillow over her head and stay in bed until everyone else left.

Facing Gemma and Sean after last night was impossible. Their acceptance seemed to make the whole situation worse. Everyone was being kind to her. Even Micah, though he'd been blunt about why he'd proposed. But he'd been trying to be nice to her. He hadn't wanted her to have any illusions about why he was proposing.

She couldn't stay in bed. Getting up, she dressed in the clothes Gemma had lent to her. They didn't fit well, and Katie Kay knew—sooner or later—she needed to return to Lancaster and collect her things from Austin's apartment. She wasn't sure when he'd be there. He hadn't worked in the past month. Not like Micah who was successful in his business with Sean Donnelly.

She crossed her arms in front of her as she stared at Olivia's empty bed. She didn't want to think about Micah. It was easier to be angry at him than to wonder what she'd do now that she hadn't accepted his proposal. There had to be someone who'd help.

Because you're cute and a flirt, but you'll soon be fat and nobody will want to flirt with you.

She hated her conscience, but she wouldn't be forced into a loveless marriage. Maybe, before she had told Micah that she didn't want to spend time with him anymore, it might have been possible for her to accept his offer.

Not now.

Not after the cruel and taunting words she'd fired at him.

"Good morning, Katie Kay," called Gemma from the bedroom doorway. She held a bundle of dirty laundry in front of her. "How are you feeling this morning?"

"Fine," she replied, but her stomach roiled as she stood, countermanding her words. Putting her hand over her mouth, she ran to the bathroom.

It was almost ten by the time Katie Kay got downstairs. She glanced toward the kitchen, but the idea of breakfast was nauseating. She'd wait for lunch, and maybe her stomach would have settled by then.

Gemma smiled when Katie Kay came into the living room. "Just in time. You can join us."

"Us?" She glanced around the room, which was empty except for her and her hostess.

"My young mothers' prayer group." Gemma hurried on, warning Katie Kay that her pulse of dismay had been visible on her face. "It's okay. There aren't any plain women among my prayer group friends. I doubt any of them know folks from your district."

"I don't want to intrude."

"You won't." She smiled. "And lurking around in the kitchen will rouse their curiosity. Why don't you join us?"

Katie Kay was tempted to be honest and state she was uncomfortable joining an *Englisch* prayer group. She bit her lip. Until she made up her mind where she intended to live and how, she shouldn't close any doors or alienate anyone, especially the Donnellys, who'd welcomed her as if they'd been friends for years.

She helped Gemma put out plates of cookies and make coffee and tea for the members of the prayer circle. She watched Olivia, hoping the little girl hadn't said anything to her *mamm* about Katie Kay's tears last

night. Olivia seemed focused on playing with her little brother, Jayden, as they built buildings out of wooden logs and filled them with plastic horses in the most outrageous pastel shades. They giggled and jumped around as if they were riding the horses.

Gemma paused in her preparations when Olivia dropped her plastic pony and began to cough. Pulling an inhaler out of the pocket of the shirt that was taut across her belly, she inserted it into a tube. She held the tube to Olivia's mouth and told her daughter to breathe deeply. Pressing the inhaler, she calmed the little girl as the medicine hissed into the tube and was drawn into Olivia's mouth and lungs. They repeated the procedure a second time before Gemma led her *kind* into the kitchen and had her wash her mouth out with clean water.

"She has asthma," Gemma said when she caught Katie Kay watching. "When she plays too hard, sometimes she has an attack. Thank the good Lord, her inhaler takes care of it as long as we get to her fast."

"Do you always carry an inhaler?"

She smiled. "Always, and Sean keeps one in the truck." She continued chatting as she finished getting everything ready for her guests.

Katie Kay wanted to tell Gemma she understood what it was like having a special needs *kind* in the house, but such a discussion would have to wait.

The other five women began arriving just before eleven, and each of them seemed to accept Gemma's explanation that Katie Kay was a guest from out of town. The women ranged in age from younger than Katie Kay to their midthirties.

Sitting in the living room, she listened as they spoke about the challenges they faced as mothers. Would she

be confronted with the same problems? Not the ones where the women were concerned about their husbands, who were struggling, too, to understand the changes a *boppli* could bring to their lives. When the women bowed their heads to pray, so did Katie Kay, but her heart remained closed. She wasn't sure what would happen if she opened it to God. Would He turn His back on her as Austin had? And as Micah had when she turned down the proposal he'd made out of obligation?

She was surprised that Micah's actions bothered her more than Austin's. It had to be a sign she was too distraught to think clearly.

Katie Kay breathed a sigh of relief when the women turned to the refreshments and conversation. She had the excuse to bring coffee and tea to serve to Gemma's guests. They thanked her and tried to make her feel welcome, but she sensed the questions they didn't utter. She kept up an easy patter to defuse their curiosity.

When everyone was served, she took her chair again and selected a chocolate chip cookie from the plate on the coffee table. Suddenly she was starving. A *gut* sign because her hunger should mean the day's nausea was over.

Gemma's youngest, Jayden, toddled to his *mamm* and climbed onto her lap. Gemma continued her story without a pause but drew the little boy close to her. When he seemed to reshape himself so he could lean against her distended stomach, Katie Kay was startled by her surprising sense of longing.

Would the *boppli* inside her ever reach out to her with such innocent love as Jayden did?

"Mommy gots baby." Jayden patted her stomach and grinned while everyone chuckled.

Sliding off her lap, he went to the brunette whom Katie Kay thought was named Roberta. He tapped her belly as he had Gemma's.

"Gots baby?" he asked.

That brought more laughter, because Roberta looked ready to go into labor at any second.

He started to move to the next woman, who held her hands in the air and laughed, "No, Jayden. I don't 'gots baby.' Not yet anyhow."

"No baby?" His pudgy face dropped as he turned to Katie Kay.

As she tensed, Gemma scooped him up and cradled him as if he were a *boppli*. "That's enough, young man."

Katie Kay hoped nobody heard her soft sigh of relief that Gemma had halted him before he asked if she had a baby. Too many people already knew. She trusted the Donnellys and Micah to keep her secret, but the more people who discovered she was pregnant, the greater the likelihood that they'd slip and word of her condition would reach her family.

They couldn't know until she told them.

Whenever that might be.

Micah doubted he'd ever understood how deep guilt could go until, that evening after he drove home, he saw a buggy and a familiar horse near the barn on the Stoltzfus family farm. The handsome bay belonged to their bishop, Reuben Lapp.

Katie Kay's *daed*.

For a moment, he was tempted to turn his buggy around and drive in the opposite direction. He pushed that thought aside, knowing that, like Katie Kay, he couldn't avoid her *daed* forever. He drew Rascal to a

stop. As he stepped out, he saw his future stepfather emerging from the *dawdi haus*.

Reuben looked every bit the Amish bishop he was. His gray beard hung to the middle of his chest, and his eyebrows were so bushy they seemed to arrive ahead of him. His dark suspenders matched his broadfall trousers and scuffed work boots. In addition to his duties as their bishop, he oversaw his farm, more and more with the help of his son and son-in-law. When he called out a greeting, his deep voice resonated off the nearby barn.

"How goes the solar panel business?" Reuben asked as he waited for Micah to reach him on the lawn beneath a tall maple reaching the apex of its scarlet glory.

"Well." He hated having to force a smile, but he had to. A genuine one wouldn't come because he had to fight to keep from being honest about knowing where Katie Kay was. "Almost too well. A lot of folks, both plain and *Englisch*, want to get panels on their roofs to help offset heating costs this winter."

"The almanac says we could have a snowy winter this year. Will that be a problem?"

"No. Snow melts fast off the panels because they continue to gather the sun's heat through a few inches of snow. With a heavier storm, most homeowners won't have to do more than clear off a corner of a panel. That'll start the snow melting."

Reuben smiled. "They seem to be a true blessing for any of us who don't want to be connected to the grid." He raked his long beard. "Any chance I could pull strings as a soon-to-be family member and get on your schedule to have a couple put on my roof?"

Micah gave in to his laugh. It felt *gut* not to have to weigh every word and expression. "I think Sean and I

can squeeze you in, if you don't mind us spreading the job out over a few Saturdays."

"Your partner's wife is going to have a *boppli* soon, ain't so?"

"*Ja*, but not for a couple of months, so we should have plenty of time to get the panels on and hooked up for you."

The bishop's brows lowered. "I didn't realize you did the electrical work, too."

"I don't." He understood what Reuben wasn't saying. A plain craftsman seldom worked with wiring, except to take it out of an *Englisch* house where an Amish family planned to live. "I leave that to Sean. It's his specialty. Mine is getting the panels at the best angle to capture the most sunlight. There's no sense going to the expense of having them installed if the household can't get the most electricity out of them."

"No wonder you're such *gut* partners." Reuben's face cleared, and his easy smile returned. "I'm glad you've worked out your jobs as you have."

"Ja," Micah said again and then waited for the bishop to go on. Reuben wouldn't have brought up the topic if he didn't have something he felt he needed to say about Micah's work with an *Englischer*.

Reuben was blunt. "There have been worries about our young people who are working off their family farms. Any skill a man or woman can learn that is useful in a plain life is welcome, of course. However, some of our young ones are learning things that won't be of any use to them once they're baptized. *Danki* for not sneaking around as others are, Micah."

He nodded but avoided Reuben's steady gaze. If his future stepfather had any idea what Micah was hiding,

he wouldn't have given Micah a friendly clap on the shoulder and a cheery farewell before continuing toward his buggy. Reuben waved as he drove away.

Micah watched him go. How much longer was Katie Kay going to quibble over whether she should let her *daed* know where she was? Keeping the secret was eating him from the inside out.

God, You could have put anyone in her way that night. Anyone would have helped her. Why did You choose me? What am I supposed to do? She refused my proposal. What else can I do?

He ignored his conscience, which reminded him how coldly he'd spoken to Katie Kay when he asked her to marry him. But he'd wanted to make sure she knew right from the get-go that he wasn't asking because he loved her. She'd wound him around her little finger once, and he wouldn't be foolish again.

"Are you going to stand there all evening, son?" called *Mamm* from the *dawdi haus* porch.

Pasting another smile on his face and hoping it looked more natural than it felt, he turned to answer her question. He hoped it would be the only one she asked tonight. "Not if you have cookies or pie waiting."

She laughed. "And ruin the supper Leah has cooked for us?"

"A cookie or two has never hurt my appetite."

Again *Mamm* chuckled, and he did, too, though it wasn't easy to make it sound genuine. What would *Mamm* think if she learned of how he had abetted Katie Kay in her secrecy?

Something had to change.

Right away.

Chapter Five

The next morning, at the Donnellys' house, Micah accepted Gemma's invitation to come inside and have a cup of *kaffi* while Sean finished his breakfast. Glancing around the kitchen, he saw no sign of Katie Kay.

"She's been sick every morning," Gemma said when she noticed him looking around. "As I've told her, morning sickness should pass in a week or two."

"I hope she realizes how blessed she is to have you," he said as Jayden crawled in his lap.

The two-year-old wanted to show off the plastic cow he'd found at the bottom of the toy box. Because the little boy hadn't seen it in a few weeks, he was as excited as if it were a brand-new toy.

Across the table, DJ was eating his cereal as if afraid someone was going to snatch it away from him. Drops of milk clung to the table, his chin and the napkin stuck in the neck of his shirt. Olivia nibbled delicately on her toast, and Micah smiled. There was something extra precious about a little girl amidst her rowdy brothers.

A no-longer-unexpected throb of jealousy cut through Micah. He'd hoped to have a family like this—

or at least be beginning one—by now. If Katie Kay had been the woman he'd once believed her to be, maybe they would have been working together to have the life Sean and Gemma had.

He pretended to be enthralled with Jayden's black-and-white plastic cow. He realized he was overdoing it when Sean shot him a curious glance. His partner knew him too well, but Sean didn't know the whole truth about how Katie Kay had humiliated him.

As if his thoughts had summoned her, Katie Kay walked into the kitchen. She faltered and gasped when she looked at him.

"I thought you'd left already. That is, I heard—" She fled out of the room.

Setting Jayden on his feet, Micah stood and followed her. He stopped in front of her. If she pushed past him or edged around him, he wouldn't halt her, but he hoped surprise would pause her in her tracks.

It did, and she gave him the frown he was familiar with. The frown told him she didn't want him in her life any longer. Well, too bad. As long as she was living under his friends' roof, she was going to have to put up with seeing him. He'd rescued her from beside the road, so he was responsible for her...as he would have been if she'd been an abandoned kitten. And he couldn't ignore her unborn *boppli*.

"Are you going to keep running away forever?" he asked.

She blanched, and he regretted the words. As he started to apologize, she waved his words aside. "I don't want you lying to me, Micah."

"I don't want to lie either, but I could have been nicer."

"You could have." A faint smile played at the corners of her mouth. "I'm assuming you have something to say to me other than less-than-nice questions."

"*Ja*. When are you going to see a *doktor*?" He shook his head. "Knowing you, I guess that's not the question I should be asking."

Her whisper of a smile weakened. "No, it's not."

Before she could tell him—again—that he needed to stay out of her life, he hurried to say, "The question I should be asking is, have you seen a *doktor* yet?"

"I just found out I'm… I'm going to have a *boppli*." Color rose in her cheeks with the vibrant pink hue that had fascinated him from the time they were *kinder*. She'd been brimming with excitement back then, and he'd been drawn to the shade like a rabbit into a snare.

Telling himself to focus on the present and forget the past, he said, "You should see a *doktor* or a midwife right away. There's a birthing clinic in Paradise Springs. I'll take you there."

Her face seemed to thin as it paled once more, as if life had been sucked out of her. "I can't go to a clinic in Paradise Springs. Not yet."

He jammed his hands into the pockets of his work coat so she wouldn't see how they curled into frustrated fists. "Stop thinking only of yourself! You need to make sure your *boppli* is growing well."

"I'm not thinking only of myself."

"No?" He was pushing her, but she had to be sensible. Hiding at his friends' house was preposterous. He'd guessed she'd stay with the Donnellys for a night or two and then go home to her own family.

She walked to the front window. When Gemma hurried past them with DJ, making sure he wasn't too late

to catch the school bus, Katie Kay didn't turn to look at them or him.

The moment the door closed behind Gemma and her son, Katie Kay said, "All I've been thinking about is the *boppli*. I'm trying to figure out what's best for him or her."

"Keeping the *boppli* away from its family is…" He amended what he was about to say, knowing she wouldn't take it well. "It can't be right."

"I know. It should be simple, but it's not, Micah." She looked at him.

He wondered if he'd ever seen such honest emotion on her face. It revealed the uncertainty she was wrestling with. He was crossing the room to her before he realized what he was doing. He pulled her into his arms and wasn't surprised when his shirt dampened with her tears.

Lord, he prayed, *it hurts to see her brought low. I know she is too proud, but please lift her up so she can see the right way to go.*

A throat was cleared behind him, and he glanced toward the kitchen door to see Sean and the younger kids there. His friend looked concerned, but Micah couldn't guess if his anxiety was for Katie Kay's tears or because Micah was trying to comfort her. Should he have avoided trying to ease her pain?

With a sigh, he knew Katie Kay wasn't the only one who needed to make tough decisions…and stick with them.

Katie Kay wasn't sure how Micah had arranged it, but the following morning, he told her he'd set up an

appointment for her in two days at the birthing clinic in Paradise Springs after it closed for the evening.

"That way, nobody will see you go in or out," he said as he held out the page where he'd written the name of the midwife she would meet with.

Beth Ann Overholt, she read.

"Do you know her?" Katie Kay asked. "Will she say anything to anyone?"

"Beth Ann is a professional and doesn't gossip about her patients. She's delivered several of the *bopplin* for our family." He shook his head. "How did you get suspicious of everyone and everything?"

She looked again, ashamed of what she had to admit. "The hard way. People I trusted turned away from me."

"People? What people other than your ex-boyfriend?"

Astonished, she raised her eyes, and the intensity of his gaze seared her. "Isn't that enough?"

"I don't know."

"Then why are you asking?"

"Because if you keep acting as if you expect to be ambushed any minute, you're never going to fit into our community." He raised one hand to halt her before she could retort. "Don't say it. I know you haven't decided to return to the plain life."

"I haven't."

"But what are your plans if you don't go home?"

Katie Kay was glad when Sean called out from the kitchen to let Micah know he was ready for work. Sean had been avoiding her since he'd witnessed Micah trying to console her yesterday. Her host hadn't said anything, but she caught his glances, swiftly disguised, in her direction. He wanted to make sure she didn't hurt his friend again.

How much did Sean know about what had happened between her and Micah? Enough so he felt protective of his partner.

She should find another place to live, but where? Micah's question echoed in her mind. What *were* her plans if she chose not to return to her *daed*'s house?

Katie Kay knew she couldn't put off making the decision much longer. To do so, she needed to come to terms with her past. Not just with Micah, but with Austin. Being around Micah made her feel confused because he was her sole connection with the life she'd lived until a few months ago.

But it was time to move forward. She owed the *boppli* that much. Hoping she wouldn't regret it, she picked up the telephone and called Austin's number.

"Eyes on the job, Micah," Sean warned.

Micah knew his friend was half joking. All day, he'd been distracted, replaying the conversation he'd had with Katie Kay over and over. The memory of their sharp words matched the tempo of the drill he was using to prepare the roof for the solar panel frames.

When he'd given her Beth Ann's card, she'd seemed… What was the word he was looking for? Not quite relieved, but that was the closest description he could come up with.

If only Sean had waited a couple more minutes before they left for work. Micah had hoped he'd get an answer from Katie Kay about her future plans. He knew he was getting too mixed up in her drama, but how could he walk away when her *daed* was going to marry his *mamm*? And there was the *boppli* to consider. He knew she was in shock about being pregnant, but he couldn't

let her risk the little one while she came to terms with her changed life.

"Sorry," Micah said, realizing he'd wandered off into his dilemmas again. "Lost in my thoughts, I guess."

"No need to ask you whom you're thinking about." Sean adjusted the belt they used to keep them safe on the roof. "Be careful, Micah."

"I'm trying to be."

"Are you? You're getting more involved every day."

"I know." Micah drove the screw into the framework and checked to see if it was square. He hoped Sean didn't push further. In fact, if they weren't standing on a roof, Micah would have found an excuse to walk away and put an end to the conversation.

Sean meant well. Other than his brothers, Sean was the man he trusted most in the world. Yet, Katie Kay was one subject he wasn't ready to talk about with anyone, not even his best friend.

However, Sean didn't seem to feel the same. Shifting the metal framework an inch lower, he asked, "Do you think she'll leave again?"

"I have no idea what she'll do. I learned that last year." He hated the bitterness in his voice, but he'd always been honest with his partner. He wouldn't let Katie Kay's reappearance change that.

"When she dumped you?"

He paused as he was about to screw in the next bolt. Looking at Sean, he asked, "How do you know she dumped me?"

Sean gave a derisive snort. "Man, you've got the truth written all over your face. Every time you see Katie Kay, you either have a lovesick puppy expression or look like you wished you were a million miles

from her." He set the bolt he held into the metal beams to connect them together. "Even if I didn't know you'd dated her, I'd know there had been some serious history between you two."

"History is in the past." He said that as much to convince himself as Sean.

And he failed, because his partner said, "But she's here. It's got to mean something."

"Ja." He couldn't argue with that, but he wondered if she would have ever returned if her former boyfriend hadn't forced her out of his car and into her old life.

Micah struggled to keep his mind on the day's tasks. Every hour seemed to drag until it felt like a year. He was clumsy, and more than once, he had to dig another nut or bolt out of his pocket because his numb fingers had dropped the one he held. It wasn't only his fingers that were numb but every inch of him.

The break for lunch didn't help because, as he took a bite of the sandwich with the roast beef his *mamm* had made last night for supper, guilt flashed through him. He'd kept his promise to Katie Kay and hadn't told anyone about her return, but each time he thought about Reuben, he recalled how sad the older man looked whenever someone mentioned his runaway daughter.

"Why don't you come to supper tonight?" Sean asked as they threw their lunch trash into the dumpster in front of the house and put their lunch boxes in the van.

"You don't have to feed me every night."

"I know we don't, but Gemma likes to have a chance to see you, and you know the kids adore you."

"Tell Gemma some other night. *Mamm* mentioned she wanted to discuss her wedding plans with us tonight."

Sean screwed up his face. "Be grateful she doesn't want you to wear a rented monkey suit for the big event."

Micah chuckled because he knew Sean was trying to jest him out of his dismal mood. He played along the rest of the afternoon, but he doubted Sean believed his joking and easy talk about sports and future jobs they had waiting for them.

Why should Sean believe that when Micah didn't?

Chapter Six

Gemma burst out of the house as the Plain and Simple Solutions van pulled into the driveway just past noon the following day. Sean had forgotten his lunch, and Micah wanted to check on Katie Kay. He hadn't seen her that morning before they left for the job site.

Sean muttered something under his breath, and Micah understood when he saw dismay blossoming on his friend's wife's face. Sean didn't like Gemma getting upset now that she was so far along in her pregnancy. Or was his partner distressed because Gemma was running? Micah knew she should be more cautious not to bring on premature labor.

Then he noticed the other side of the driveway was empty. Had Gemma decided to put the family van in the garage with thunderstorms in the forecast?

Throwing open the door, Sean jumped out. "Gemma, is everything okay? Are the kids okay?"

"We're fine." She put her hand on his arm, glancing at Micah as he came around the work van. "My van is gone!"

Micah wondered if his face was as gray as Sean's became.

"Gone?" Sean asked. "Stolen?"

Gemma waved aside his words as ridiculous and then put her hand against the side of her rounded belly. She grimaced.

Sean lifted her as if she weighed no more than one of the pebbles beside the driveway.

Micah hurried to the front door and held it open. When the kids—including DJ, who must have just gotten home from school—crowded into the hall, he shooed them aside. Sean needed to carry Gemma in without tripping over one of the *kinder*.

Once Sean and Gemma had passed him, he shut the door and then rushed to make sure no toys were in Sean's way. Sending DJ for an afghan and Olivia for a pillow, he scooped up Jayden to keep the little boy from being underfoot. He set the toddler on the nearby recliner and motioned for him to stay there. The older *kinder* quickly returned with the items he'd requested. Putting the pillow against one arm of the couch, he stepped back so Sean could set Gemma down. She was protesting that she was fine and she could walk on her own two feet, thank you, but Sean ignored her. He placed her on the cushions as if she were made of precious china. Micah handed him the afghan, and Sean draped it over her legs.

"Mommy!" cried Jayden as he jumped from the chair and ran to her.

Micah halted the *kind* by swinging him into his arms. The little boy giggled, distracted.

"Do I need to call the doctor?" Sean asked.

"No." Gemma rolled her eyes. "Stop overreacting

to everything I do or say, Sean. It's not like you're a first-time father. I got a stitch in my side. I haven't run much lately."

"Are you sure?"

"Positive." She squeezed her husband's hand before she looked at Micah. "It's okay. Jayden, come and sit with me." Smiling at her other *kinder*, she motioned for them to join her.

As the youngsters climbed up beside her, Sean said, "As long as you're okay…"

"I am."

"Let's start over. Where's the van, Gemma?"

"I'm not sure." Her gaze shifted to Micah again. "I think Katie Kay has it."

Micah sank to the recliner's arm. "Why do you think that?"

"For one thing, she's not around, and I did tell her the first day she was here that she should feel free to borrow it. I wasn't sure when she planned to see a doctor or if she would want to get some things for herself. She has nothing but the clothes she was wearing and an empty purse. I told her she could use the ready cash in the smallest canister if she needed to buy something." She sighed. "She thanked me and showed me a driver's license, so I figured she knew how to drive. But I also figured she'd let me know before she took the van."

"When did she leave?"

"It must have been while I was taking a morning nap along with the kids. I didn't know the van was gone until DJ got home."

Before he could halt himself, Micah said, "I guess she didn't want to disturb you." He regretted the words as soon as he spoke them because he saw the weight of

worry in Gemma's expression. She was less worried about her van than about why Katie Kay had taken it. "I guess she could have left you a note."

"Yes, she could have." Gemma rubbed her forehead. "I'm sorry. I didn't mean to snap at *you*, Micah."

"You've got every right to be annoyed with me. I'm the one who brought her here. I'm sorry to get you caught up in her turbulent life."

"She's mixed-up and scared and feeling alone."

He nodded, agreeing. He'd never imagined Katie Kay Lapp feeling alone. All her life, she'd delighted in being the center of attention, and that had ended. At least for now.

Sean asked, "Could she have gone home?"

"I doubt it," Micah answered. "She's been insistent that she needs time to decide what to say to Reuben, though I don't know why it's taking her so long to realize she doesn't need to say anything other than 'I'm sorry' and 'Forgive me.'" Looking at Gemma, he asked, "Have you reported the van missing?"

"Of course not! If Katie Kay has it, and I'm sure she does, I don't want her being pulled over by the cops. I know you Amish don't like having police involved in your problems, Micah."

He understood what Gemma was trying to avoid saying. She was most worried about upsetting him. Wanting to thank her and reassure her that nothing Katie Kay did was a surprise any longer, he went into the kitchen to get Sean's lunch box. The Donnellys needed time to talk without him there.

As he picked up the battered box, he wondered how Katie Kay could have taken Gemma's van without asking. He hadn't thought Katie Kay was that selfish. What

was so pressing she couldn't wait long enough to let someone know she was borrowing it?

The search for answers taunted Micah the rest of the day. He tried to concentrate on work, because he could see Sean was having a tough time doing the same. When the distant rumble of thunder signaled they had to get off the roof, they collected their tools and scurried down the ladders. Micah sent up a silent prayer of gratitude.

They gathered the ladders to put them onto the rack on top of the van. As they were loading the last ladder, Sean's cell phone rang with the melody that meant Gemma was calling. Micah froze and then shoved the ladder into place. He lashed the bungee cords around it while his partner answered the call.

"It's Gemma," Sean said unnecessarily and then continued to listen to his wife. "She's back."

Hoping he wasn't misunderstanding, Micah asked, "Katie Kay?"

He got a nod in response.

Sean ended the call and motioned for Micah to get in the van. A few raindrops struck the windshield, but the storm went north as they sped south toward the Donnellys' house. Sean said nothing, and Micah did the same though curiosity taunted him.

Where had Katie Kay gone? Why? Was she back to stay? Was she ready to go home and face the rest of her life? Or was she there only to return Gemma's van and planned to leave for *gut*?

He was shocked at how the thought of losing her again was more painful than he'd expected. His efforts to banish her from his heart hadn't been as thorough as

he'd bragged to himself. After accusing her of having too much *hochmut*, pride had misled *him*.

Sean was out of the van the moment he thrust the shift into park. He started for the house and then paused.

"What's wrong?" Micah asked.

"Someone hit the van." He bent to run his fingers along a dent in the bumper. Straightening, he raced to the house.

Micah wanted to follow him and get answers, but he knew the couple needed a minute or two to talk before he burst in. He knelt by the van and examined the damage. Running his fingers along the dent as Sean had, he smiled grimly. It was minor. The dent could be knocked out easily. It wouldn't need much more than a little chrome paint to touch it up, and nobody would ever notice the difference.

He hoped he could say the same for the harm Katie Kay might have done to herself in the Donnellys' eyes.

And his.

Was she always going to be thoughtless and selfish?

He pondered that as he entered the house just in time to hear Gemma sigh.

"I don't know what happened," she said as he joined her and Sean in the kitchen. "She didn't say a single word to me or the kids. She didn't look hurt. Not physically anyhow. When I went out to talk to her, I saw the damage to the van. By the time I'd finished examining the dent, she was gone."

"Gone?" Micah asked. "She ran away again?"

Gemma aimed a frown at him. "Why must you think the worst of her, Micah?"

"Me?" He was shocked she'd turned her frustration on him. "She busted your van."

"It's a teeny dent. Nothing more. I thought you'd be more forgiving."

"Because I'm Amish?"

Her scowl deepened. "No, because you once were in love with her. She went to the swimming hole. I think she wanted to be alone to think."

A glance out the window over the sink revealed that Katie Kay still stood by the pond Sean had dug out a few summers ago to make a swimming hole for his kids. He'd stocked it with small fish the *kinder* could catch and release.

"As long as nobody was hurt," Sean said as he held out his arms.

As Gemma threw herself into Sean's embrace, Micah knew he should be somewhere else. Making sure he had his irritation with Katie Kay under control, he left the kitchen and crossed the yard toward her. The thunder was fading over the hills, and the air hung with a clammy dampness that suggested more storms were heading their way. He doubted they could be stronger than the one inside him.

He thought she was tossing pebbles into the water, but, as he got closer, he saw she was shredding a bright orange leaf. She must have heard him approach through the crackle of the fallen leaves, but she didn't look at him.

Stopping beside her, he remained silent. He bent and picked up a flat stone. He sent it skipping across the pond that reflected the gray sky. When she didn't react, he chose a second and then a third and watched them skim the water. The pond rippled, though he knew it was quiet beneath.

The opposite of Katie Kay who appeared calm, save

for a faint quiver in her fingers as she ripped the leaf to smaller and smaller pieces. She hunched into herself.

"You owe Gemma an explanation," he said when he couldn't endure the silence any longer.

She looked at him. "Don't, Micah. I don't need you yelling at me."

"I'm not yelling. I haven't raised my voice."

"Maybe not, but you're angry."

His brows lowered as he wondered how she expected him to feel when she'd acted outrageously. "Of course I'm angry. Gemma agreed to let you use her van. Not only did you take it without letting her know, you dented it."

"I would have told her, but she was taking a nap, and I didn't want to disturb her. I didn't realize I'd be gone so long." She clasped her hands in front of her as she added, "And for your information, I didn't dent the van. Someone ran into it while it was parked."

He believed her. Katie Kay had never lied to get herself out of trouble. "Where did you go?"

"Where else? Lancaster."

Astonishment ripped through him. She'd gone to the city? Back to the man whose name she seldom mentioned? Was she, as he'd thought earlier, at the Donnellys' only to say good-bye?

Katie Kay watched as Micah closed his mouth that had become a circle of surprise. He was trying to keep his promise that he wouldn't yell at her, but anger blazed from his eyes.

"Go ahead," she said when he didn't speak.

"With what?"

"Your questions about why I went to Lancaster."

"I don't need to ask. I think it's pretty obvious. You went to see the *daed* of your *boppli*, didn't you?"

"I did." She didn't let her eyes shift away from his intense gaze.

He took a single step toward her, but she wouldn't let him intimidate her. The thought startled her. When had Micah become her enemy? Their friendship had been destroyed when she stopped walking out with him, but he'd never been her foe.

Not as Austin had become.

No! She wasn't going to let either man unsettle her more. Nothing had gone as she'd hoped, but she'd done her best. Yet, just as when she'd tried to take care of *Daed*'s house, her best hadn't been *gut* enough.

"You've changed, Micah. You used to give me the benefit of the doubt. Now you assume I'm irresponsible."

"It's not that."

"No?"

A flush rose out of the collar of his work coat. She'd made her point, but she didn't feel any triumph.

His mouth grew taut again. "No, Katie Kay, it's not that."

"Then what?"

"How would you feel if someone you were responsible for went missing and you had no idea where he or she was?"

"You're not responsible for me."

"I'm not talking about me." He gestured toward her middle. "What if your little *boppli* vanished and you didn't know where to begin to look?"

Each word struck like the thunder resounding over the hills. She clasped her fingers protectively over her

abdomen. The thought of losing the *boppli* made her stomach twist. Realizing what she was doing, she let her hands drop to her sides. She mustn't give Micah—or anyone else—a clue to her greatest fear. The fear that, despite him not wanting anything to do with her or their *kind*, Austin might demand she turn their *boppli* over to him. What if he decided having a *kind* of his own made him look cool in his friends' eyes?

"I'm sorry. I should have told Gemma. I'll tell her I'm sorry, Micah," she said in a cool tone she hoped he'd misunderstand.

When he did, she was torn between relief and regret. Relief that she'd refocused the conversation on the van instead of the *boppli*, but regret that he seemed eager to see the worst side of her.

"I'm not sure Gemma will ever trust you again," he said.

"I know."

"What was so important you couldn't take time to jot a note to let her know where you were going?" His eyes narrowed. "Why were you eager to see the man who dumped you on the side of the road?"

She flinched. Micah said what he thought, but his comments used to be softened by her knowing he never meant to cause hurt. Today, she wasn't so sure.

"I found out Austin was at home. I know I was a fool to rush to Lancaster to try to get my things. When I got there, he agreed to talk to me, but he didn't let me into the apartment." She lowered her eyes, not willing to see the pity in Micah's.

She wasn't going to tell him how embarrassed she'd felt to stand in the dirty hallway and beg for her possessions. Nor would she reveal how Austin had refused

to give them to her. Vinnie, one of his friends, had sneaked down the fire escape with a small bag of her clothes. Not everything, and she guessed the rest had been claimed by others. Nobody had wanted the plain dress she'd brought with her from Paradise Springs, so it was at the bottom of the plastic bag.

"You hoped he'd ask your forgiveness for his outrageous behavior, ain't so?"

"I don't know. If I did, I was disappointed. He didn't apologize, and then everything got worse." She wrapped her arms around herself. "No, it went from worse to worst."

"Why?"

For a second, she hesitated; then the words spilled out of her. "He told me if I wanted to get rid of 'the kid'—that's what he calls the *boppli*—he'd be willing to give me money to hire a lawyer to arrange for an adoption." She couldn't keep her rancor out of her voice as she added, "He said it was my fault so I should pay for most of it. Before he slammed the door in my face, he said if the *boppli*'s new parents gave me any money, he wanted half."

"Is giving the *boppli* up for adoption what you plan to do? Or have you given that any real thought?"

For the first time, she met his eyes steadily. "Do you think so little of me, Micah Stoltzfus? This *boppli* is my responsibility, and I'm going to make sure it has the best life possible." She released a terse laugh. "Besides, I know Austin was lying. He'll never send me a penny for anything. I left and went back to the van. That's when I found the dent in the front and the policeman."

"It was hit while you were parked?"

She nodded. "The officer said the kid who hit it was

going too fast in the wrong direction along the one-way street. When he saw another car pull in to the street, he panicked and tried to turn around. He hit the van. The officer said if Gemma had a more modern car, the whole front end would have been smashed like the kid's car. Instead there's a small dent."

"Was the other driver hurt?"

"Not according to the policeman. I guess the *gut* Lord was watching over us." She was astonished by the warmth surging through her at the thought. Was it possible God still cared about His lamb who had strayed so far from the flock?

As if she'd asked that aloud, Micah said, "None of us should ever doubt that, Katie Kay. No matter what we do or where we go, God is just a prayer away. You're never alone."

"It didn't feel that way when I was talking to Austin." She flung the remainder of the leaf into the pond. "I should have known he wouldn't change his mind. He's as stubborn as…"

"You?"

She glanced at his face, hoping to see the charming smile he had worn when he walked out with her. Instead he remained as serious as a deacon facing a miscreant who'd ignored the *Ordnung*.

"Ja," she said with a sigh. The conversation wasn't going as she'd hoped. She hadn't expected Micah to take her in his arms and console her as he had before, but why did he have to be stonyhearted? "One thing I know for sure is that I can close the door on that part of my past."

"Are you sure? He is your *boppli*'s *daed*."

"Didn't you hear what I said?" she asked, feigning

irritation to conceal her deep fear that Austin would decide to claim the *kind* and take it away from her. "He wanted me to get rid of it. He doesn't care about the *boppli* or me."

He arched his brows. "People change their minds."

"If you're trying to scare me, Micah, don't bother. I'm scared enough already."

For a long minute, he didn't answer. He sighed and said, "Let's go. It looks as if it's going to storm any minute." He turned to leave.

She didn't move. "Micah?"

"Ja?" He halted but didn't face her.

Just as she hadn't turned to him when he came to the pond. The barriers between them were growing thicker and more impossible to cross. Maybe he realized that, too, which was why he kept his back to her.

"Please," she said as she walked to where he stood, "don't tell Gemma and Sean what I was doing in Lancaster."

"The van—"

"I'll explain to them how the van was dented. I've got a copy of the accident report so they can contact their insurance company. That's what the policeman told me to do. I don't want them to know…"

"How your *boppli*'s *daed* shut you out of his life?"

"Ja." It was humiliating. "Promise me, Micah, you won't tell them."

"I won't." Finally he looked at her. "I'll leave that for you to do."

As he strode away, she remained where she was and watched him go. He always seemed to know exactly what to do. Meanwhile, she was foundering. She'd considered Micah's well-mapped-out life to be boring. For

the first time, she guessed there must be a lot of comfort in being prepared for what lay ahead.

Was it too late for her to find out? She hoped not.

Chapter Seven

The birthing clinic was in a low, white building that looked as if it had been built as an *Englisch* ranch house. Shutters the color of pine needles flanked the windows, but the flower boxes were empty. A wreath of autumn leaves and miniature plastic pumpkins was centered on the yellow door. To its left, a small plaque was etched with Paradise Springs Birthing Center.

Katie Kay sat in Micah's buggy and stared at the clinic's front door. She didn't want to look at him. Was he thinking as she was of the night he'd told her about the future he envisioned with her? A future when they were married and had a family. Had he imagined himself bringing her to the midwife when she became pregnant?

How earnest and eager he'd been as he outlined every day of the life he wanted them to have together! So earnest and eager he hadn't noticed her reaction. She'd been horrified. How could she be certain she wanted to spend her life with Micah Stoltzfus when there was much she hadn't experienced? What if she missed wonders she couldn't even imagine?

She'd interrupted him and asked him to take her home. Though he'd been startled, he'd complied. He'd loved her then. She'd known that, which had unsettled her more.

Once she got home, she'd told him they were through. He'd asked why, and she'd just said she'd decided she didn't want to walk out with him any longer. It hadn't been the truth. She hadn't wanted to break up, but the only thing she'd been sure of was that she needed to sample what else life might offer her.

For days afterward, she'd tried to forget the pain on his expressive face when he turned without another word and climbed into his buggy and drove away. She'd wondered if she'd made the biggest mistake of her life but convinced herself the worst error she could make was always to question if a plain life had been right for her. Once she was baptized and married, there would be no escape without being shunned and losing contact with her family and the community.

But isn't that what you've done to yourself? She wished the faint voice of honesty would leave her alone, but it was true she'd self-shunned by not letting her family know where she moved to in Lancaster.

Again the idea of her mapping out her future flitted through her head. Could she? Should she? If she set a plan in stone as Micah seemed to, what if something marvelous popped up in her life? She didn't like the idea of having to pass it by because it wasn't part of "The Plan."

"The longer you sit there," Micah said, breaking into her thoughts, "the more likely it is that someone will drive by and recognize you."

His words jolted her, and she climbed out of the

buggy, almost tripping over her own feet. As she regained her balance, she was startled to discover gentle fingers on her arm. How had Micah gotten around the buggy so fast?

"Danki," she whispered as she stepped away from his touch, which scrambled her thoughts like a bowl of eggs.

Her hopes that he hadn't noticed the tremor in her voice faded when he said, "It's going to be okay." He flashed her a smile.

She was astonished by the warmth stirring in her stomach. Lost in her despair, she'd failed to see how much power his easy grins still had to move her. They weren't flirtatious, but seeing one made her think about how they'd laughed together after singings. Laughing was something they'd done a lot, and she realized how much she missed that simple delight.

Something else she'd thrown away when she tossed him out of her life.

"Tell me the truth, Micah," she blurted. "Why are you helping me?"

"Why wouldn't I? You're pregnant and—"

"But you could let others help. You don't have to feel obligated because you happened to be the one who found me."

He shook his head, sadness dimming his eyes. "After all this time, Katie Kay, I thought you knew me better than that."

She winced. His quiet, sorrowful words hurt as much as if he'd yelled them. She realized how much her question had wounded him. It hadn't been intentional. She wanted to know the truth about why a man whom she'd treated poorly would step up to help her.

No, it was more than helping. He wanted to be certain she and the *boppli* were taken care of and remained healthy. He was a *gut* man. A better man, she acknowledged, than she deserved, because she wasn't sure that if their situations were reversed, she would have been as forgiving.

He didn't say anything else as he opened the door and motioned for her to go inside ahead of him.

Katie Kay was relieved to see the waiting room was empty. It was long and narrow with six plastic chairs along each side of the space. A desk at the far end by a closed door was empty, but she guessed the receptionist usually sat there. Everything about the room exuded happiness and excitement. Too bad she didn't feel either. Uncertainty was the one emotion roiling within her.

When Micah closed the door, he drew the curtain over the window. The others were shut, she noticed with relief. Nobody driving by and looking into the clinic would see them.

"We might as well sit," he said. "Beth Ann told me we'd have to wait while she finished the day's paperwork."

She chose a red chair. "There must be paperwork for me to fill out. Do you know where it is?"

"It's been handled."

"What?"

Taking the chair beside hers, he leaned toward her. "When I explained the situation to Beth Ann, she assured me you could take the paperwork with you and fill it out before your next visit. It's not as if you have health insurance as *Englischers* do." His brow threaded in bafflement. "Or do you?"

"No. My jobs in Lancaster were part-time and paid

under the table because I didn't have a social security number card."

"I assume you don't have any savings then."

"Nothing." She looked at her clasped hands. "I know it's not cheap to pay for a midwife. That's why I'm going to talk to Beth Ann about how long it'll be safe for me to wait on tables."

"You're planning to get a job?" He regarded her with narrowed eyes.

"Of course. The costs of these visits and the delivery will be my obligation, and I need to repay Sean and Gemma for the damage to their van."

"I can fix it. It'll take just a few minutes. Don't worry."

"But it's my fault." Waving aside his argument before he could speak it, she added, "Besides, I've worked all my life, Micah. I'm not doing anything other than helping Gemma keep the house clean, cook a few meals and watch over the kids."

"Which the Donnellys appreciate. Gemma has told me the house has never looked better."

But it wouldn't meet her older sister's standards. She sighed as she imagined Priscilla's comments about the mess Katie Kay found herself in. Her exacting sister held everyone up to her ideas of perfection, and Katie Kay had longed to meet them, so her *daed* and the rest of the family didn't have to worry about the house. She'd failed time after time.

Not wanting to admit that to Micah, she said, "Maybe so, but the tasks at the Donnellys don't keep me busy enough."

"No matter how busy you get, you can't escape your thoughts."

She stared, stunned. Was that what she was doing? Working hard so she was exhausted enough to sleep the instant her head touched the pillow? Focusing on tasks to keep her mind from wandering to her troubles? She had thought her yearning for a job was so she could pay for what she and the *boppli* would need during the next nine months.

Now she wasn't sure.

She was relieved when the door across from the empty desk opened, and a woman stepped out. She didn't have to reply to Micah's too-insightful comment.

The woman introduced herself as Beth Ann. Much taller than Katie Kay, she wore a Mennonite *kapp* like the ones Katie Kay had seen at the Central Market in Lancaster when she went to get fresh vegetables for Austin and his roommates on the few occasions when she had money for such luxuries. Beth Ann's dark blue dress reached below her knees but didn't hide the plastic brace she wore on her right leg. She walked with a hint of a limp as she asked Katie Kay to come with her.

"I'll wait here," Micah said.

Words failed Katie Kay when she stood. For a moment, she wanted to ask him to come with her. Talking to a midwife made the *boppli* real, something she couldn't pass off as a bad dream she'd soon wake up from.

"It'll be fine, Katie Kay," he continued in the same gentle voice. "*You* will be fine."

Was the emphasis to reassure her, or was he talking about both her and the *boppli*?

She had to stop trying to find ulterior meanings in every word everyone around her said, especially Micah. Easier said than done.

Following Beth Ann through the doors, she thanked the midwife for staying late.

"I don't mind," Beth Ann replied. "But I can do this only once in a while because I've got a daughter at home who frets if I'm late often."

Katie Kay nodded. She hadn't expected that Beth Ann would see her after regular office hours every time, but what she said complicated matters. Coming during the day meant being seen by someone who knew her or her *daed*.

You could go home.

The words were as clear in her mind as if Beth Ann had spoken them, but the midwife was silent until they paused by a set of scales with a digital readout. Katie Kay stepped onto them. Beth Ann noted the number and also ascertained her height before motioning to come farther along the silent hallway.

Going into an examination room painted a warm cream, Beth Ann pulled on a white coat and settled a stethoscope around her neck. She smiled as she motioned for Katie Kay to sit.

"On the table?" Katie Kay asked.

"*Ja*, while I check your heartbeat and the *boppli*'s. After that, you can sit on a chair if you'd rather. This appointment is for us to get to know each other, so you're comfortable with me when it's time to give birth. I'll also have to take blood for a few tests."

"Will they show if the *boppli* has any birth defects?"

Beth Ann rested one hand on the table. "Are there many *bopplin* in your family born with defects?"

"One I know about. My youngest sister died when she was almost four years old. She was born with multiple handicaps, and my parents considered it a bless-

ing she survived as long as she did so we could have her in our lives."

"Tell me about the problems she was born with."

Katie Kay began to list the challenges Sarann had endured. Her little sister had never learned to sit by herself and had to be fed through a special tube in her stomach. Someone had to be with her always. Katie Kay had treasured her times with Sarann because the one thing her little sister did well was smile. Nobody knew if Sarann understood anything said to her, but it didn't matter. Seeing her brilliant smile was like beholding the face of their Heavenly Father shining through her.

Their *mamm* had never once uttered a word of complaint about the long hours of caring for a *kind* who couldn't do anything for herself. Instead, *Mamm* had made sure Sarann shared every experience with the rest of the family. *Mamm* took Sarann to church Sunday services, at least for the first hymns because the little girl seemed to be soothed by the *Leit* combining their voices in slow unity to praise the Lord.

Katie Kay had adored her little sister, and she'd feared her heart would never heal after Sarann's death. *Mamm*'s passing a few years later had changed everyone in the family more than any of them wanted to admit. *Daed* had thrown himself into his work on the farm and as bishop. She'd struggled to meet the high standards set by her older sister and tried to oversee her younger sisters, who were having as much trouble with their grief as she was.

Mamm had been strong while dealing with Sarann. Katie Kay wondered if she could be the same. No, she couldn't. *Mamm* had *Daed* and the rest of the family—as well as a powerful faith—to hold her up. Katie Kay

was alone, though she hoped God would eventually welcome her among those He loved.

You are among those He loves. Go home to be with them.

Ach, how she was coming to hate her conscience that spoke at the most unexpected times! It made everything sound simple. Go home as she had the other times she'd left to stay with her *Englisch* friend, but it wasn't straightforward this time.

The problems she'd left behind were waiting for her to face them. She couldn't deny that. She hadn't figured out how to deal with Micah. It would have been much easier if his glance didn't cause a once-familiar ripple of emotion to reach to her toes and fingertips.

Odd that she'd never felt anything similar with Austin.

What was she doing? She should focus on what the midwife said.

"Is it possible this *boppli* will be born with the same problems Sarann had?" she asked.

"Anything is possible, Katie Kay. That's why we must put our faith in God. He—and He alone—can see beyond this moment. He knows and loves your *boppli*. He will never—"

"Don't say it!" Katie Kay was sorry for her outburst the moment the words were out of her mouth, but she'd been unnerved by how Beth Ann's words matched her own thoughts.

The midwife looked at her as if she'd turned into a wild beast. "Say what?"

"God will give us nothing more than we can handle."

Beth Ann frowned. "I wasn't going to say that."

"Oh, sorry. I thought—"

"What I was going to say is God won't ever give us more than we can handle with His help."

Katie Kay bit her lip, not wanting to retort that she didn't want to hear that either. Getting off on the wrong foot with the midwife who'd done her such a great favor by seeing her after-hours would be ludicrous.

She submitted to the examination and listened to Beth Ann's instructions for what to expect as her body changed. She agreed to make an appointment to return in two weeks for a more thorough exam but otherwise spoke only when Beth Ann asked her a direct question. The midwife believed God stood beside Katie Kay. How she wished she could believe that, too!

Chapter Eight

I n Katie Kay's opinion, every adult at the table that evening deserved an award for their acting. She'd learned about movie award shows from Cherokee, Vinnie's girlfriend, who was fascinated with everything Hollywood. Katie Kay doubted those excellent actors and actresses would have been able to show such feigned enthusiasm for the stilted conversation at the table as the Donnellys, Micah and she did. Everyone acted as if nothing out of the ordinary had happened.

She'd played her part. She'd bowed her head while Sean said grace. That he spoke aloud was something she found disconcerting, because it was a reminder of how different this household was from the one where she grew up. Her *daed* had bowed his head in silent prayer before and after each meal, and the family did the same.

Yet it was nice to share prayers. While she lived in Lancaster, she'd seen the curiosity aimed in her direction when she bowed her head before she ate at the restaurant where she worked. She wasn't the only one who thanked God for a meal, but everyone there knew she'd been raised Amish. They watched what she did to see

if it matched what was on reality shows about people who claimed to be plain.

As the evening meal progressed, Katie Kay smiled when one of the *kinder* told a silly story, and she passed the serving bowls whenever anyone asked. She insisted on clearing the table and putting the dishes into the dishwasher, so Gemma could have time with her husband and *kinder*.

When Katie Kay lingered rinsing out the cooking pots, nobody came to ask what was taking so long. Tears welled into her eyes when she heard the laughter from the other room. The Donnellys were a family, loving each other and spending time together each day. Micah had become part of their family, too, the *onkel* who offered a knee for a *kind* to perch on. Once, she'd had that sense of family; then her *mamm* died and she'd gone from being a *kind* to a surrogate *mamm*.

How had her older sister, Priscilla, made the transition when *Daed*'s first wife passed away? Katie Kay had hoped in the days after *Mamm*'s funeral that Priscilla would give her hints of how to manage, but her sister had acted as if the answer should be obvious…if Katie Kay worked harder. She'd tried but never matched her older sister's skills at cleaning a house or canning garden vegetables or making a cake.

Another failure.

She wiped away dampness from the corners of her eyes. Beth Ann and Gemma had warned her tears were a common side effect of pregnancy, especially in the early months. She was glad—for once—to be alone.

Micah listened to his friends talk and laugh, but his ears strained for the sound of Katie Kay's footsteps.

She was taking too long to clean up after the meal. He guessed she was trying to avoid them. All of them or just him? On the way home from the birthing clinic, she hadn't said more than a handful of words, and those had been to thank him for making the appointment and driving her there. She hadn't looked in his direction through the whole meal. He worried when she became taciturn.

Then he heard the soft sound of her sneakers. He didn't look over his shoulder, not wanting to spook her.

Instead he listened as Gemma laughed. "As you know, Micah, Sean and I have had a long discussion about what we'll name the baby. A very long one."

"Which she won as always, so the new baby will be called Dylan." Sean patted his wife's hand. "A wise man knows when the route to victory is surrender."

As they continued to tease each other, Micah risked a glance toward where Katie Kay stood in the doorway between the living room and the kitchen. Her face was blank, but she had laced her fingers together and leaned forward as if she wanted to absorb the love swirling around Sean and Gemma. That, he could understand.

How many times had he wondered what it would be like to have someone love him as Gemma did his partner? Only he and his brother Jeremiah remained unattached among the Stoltzfus siblings. He was very happy his brothers and sisters had found love but yearned for the same for himself.

Once upon a time, he'd thought he'd found true love with Katie Kay. No longer. When she'd tossed him aside as if he were last week's newspaper, he'd closed his heart like a shop shuttered and out of business.

Yet, when he saw her in his friends' living room, he couldn't help feeling sorry for her. She was so alone

and too stubborn to admit that she didn't need to be if she returned to her own family.

When Katie Kay sat in a chair behind his, Olivia scrambled down from Sean's lap and crawled into Katie Kay's. Gemma and Sean exchanged a look. Were they worried about their daughter getting attached to Katie Kay or glad that Olivia eased her obvious loneliness?

Again he wondered what would have happened if he'd insisted Katie Kay let him take her home that rainy night. She was impetuous, but he found himself thinking he'd given in to her because he wanted to spend more time with her.

As soon as Gemma announced it was time for the *kinder* to go to bed, Olivia gave Katie Kay a hug before going with her parents. The boys followed.

Before Katie Kay could disappear, too, Micah said, "Let's talk outside while they get the kids ready for bed."

"I thought—I mean, it's late, so I assumed—"

"I'm going to be heading home, if that's what you're trying to ask, but I thought we could talk a few minutes." He stood and motioned toward the kitchen. "It's a nice night. Let's talk while I get Rascal hitched to the buggy."

He thought she might refuse, but she said, "What do you want to talk about?"

"You choose."

He could tell that startled her, because her steps faltered as they went into the kitchen. She hurried past him and pulled the windbreaker Gemma had lent her out of the closet by the back door. As she slipped it on, she said, "Okay. We'll talk about you."

"Me?"

"Sure. Tell me about how you got into installing solar panels."

He shrugged and picked up another cookie as he walked out with her. Gemma's baking wasn't as *gut* as his *mamm*'s, but he never passed up her chocolate chip cookies...or anyone else's.

The night was cool but not cold as the past few had been. The threat of a hard freeze had passed temporarily. Despite that, he glanced at Katie Kay to check her coat was zipped. He buttoned the top button on his own coat as he followed her down the steps.

Light from the waxing moon glittered off the dew scattered across the lawn. The silhouettes of the garage and the two vans concealed his buggy and Rascal, who must be eager to return to his warm stall.

As they walked on the wet grass, he said, "I feel like I'm serving God by helping others use the gift He created on the very first day."

"You're talking about light." The edge had left her voice, and he guessed he'd surprised her with his answer.

"*Ja.* There's something wondrous about light, which has shone since the beginning and hasn't abated once. It's waiting for us to use it as a precious legacy from the earliest moments of Creation." He grinned. "At least you aren't laughing."

"Why would I laugh? God gave Adam and Eve dominion over His creation and urged them—and their descendants—to use what He'd created. A gift that keeps on giving." She smiled and then laughed. "Something I heard *Englischers* say at the Central Market in Lancaster, and I liked it."

"I like it, too. A gift that never runs out. Sunlight is that, so I can't think of a reason not to use it."

"Especially since the bishops have approved solar on plain houses."

"Not all of them, but many are seeing the light."

When she groaned at his pitiful pun, he chuckled. He was relieved they could laugh together again. After she'd been silent on the way back from Paradise Springs, he hadn't been sure if they could salvage their fragile friendship.

He almost laughed again, but this time with regret because their relationships had teetered on the brink of disaster. And he had to admit, as he hadn't wanted to before, that the uncertainty hadn't always been her doing.

When he whistled, Rascal appeared out of the darkness. Sean had set aside a pasture for the horse and the pony he kept promising Olivia. Micah guessed his friend would want his help finding a gentle-spirited one that wouldn't bite the *kinder*.

"Before you go," Katie Kay said as he led Rascal to the buggy, "I'd like to say something."

"Go ahead."

"I appreciate—no, that's not right. I *needed* to hear what you said before we went into the clinic this evening. You've done so much for me. *Danki*."

As he set Rascal into place and secured him to the buggy, he said, "You don't have to thank me for doing what friends do."

She glanced at the house, which was brightly lit upstairs. "I am grateful to the Donnellys, too."

"They're *gut* people."

"*Ja*. They try to make me feel like family."

As he watched, the window of the boys' room went dark. "That's their way."

"But not everyone's." She wrapped her arms around herself as he stepped from the buggy and faced her. "It's special to have the chance to be with a loving family again. I've missed that."

He frowned, though he wasn't sure if she could see his expression in the moonlight. "If you miss being around a family, why don't you go home to yours?"

"I told you I need time to figure out what I'm going to do."

"You're going to go or you're going to stay, ain't so?"

She stepped away from him. "It's easy for you to say, but it isn't that easy for me to decide, Micah."

"Why not? You need to do what's right for your *boppli*."

"I am! I don't need to explain myself to you, Micah Stoltzfus!"

Before he could say another word, she whirled and ran into the house. He expected her to slam the door in her wake, but she closed it quietly. Because she knew the *kinder* might already be asleep?

He sighed. It wasn't for him to judge her and her intentions. That was God's task.

"You're being really tough on her," said Sean as he emerged from the shadows by the garage.

"You heard?"

"Yeah. I didn't mean to eavesdrop, but..."

Micah waved aside his words. "It wasn't as if we were whispering."

"One thing I've learned is the most even-tempered woman can be volatile when pregnant." He glanced in the direction of the van Katie Kay had borrowed.

"Katie Kay hasn't had a great week." He put his hand on Micah's shoulder. "If you want my advice, give her a break. Yourself, too."

"Me?"

"You've apologized to me at least two dozen times about a tiny dent, and I've told you every time it's okay." He gave a half laugh. "You Amish don't have a monopoly on forgiving others."

Micah sighed at the truth in his friend's words. "Or being grateful for forgiveness when it's offered." He stared at the house. "Or wondering why it hasn't been offered."

"Micah, if you want my opinion, you've gotten too wound up in Katie Kay's problems. She's made it clear she doesn't want your help when it comes to reconciling with her family. Why don't you back off until she figures out what she wants to do?"

"You're right, and taking your advice is the least I can do after you've taken her in, Sean. I never intended for her to stay here past that first night."

"Gemma told me how she appreciates having company during the day. Someone who discusses something other than *Sesame Street* and what color was used in kindergarten that day."

"I'm glad." He rubbed the bridge of his nose. "I need to let her get over visiting the midwife, as well as whatever happened in Lancaster." He almost revealed what Katie Kay had told him, but he wouldn't break the promise he'd made to her.

Sean gave him a half smile. "Another thing I've learned through Gemma's pregnancies is to avoid arguing with her when her hormones are raging. You're

smart to let Katie Kay come to terms with being pregnant."

Micah flinched as he did each time someone spoke of the baby who belonged to Katie Kay and her unfeeling *Englischer*. "I see your point."

He did, though he wished Katie Kay would ease Reuben's worries about her. Yet, he knew she needed to make the decision for herself.

Why don't you help her see what's right instead of pushing her to do what you *think she should do?*

That thought surprised him. Why wasn't he helping her discover what God's will was for her? Wasn't assisting one another what the *gut* Lord taught His *kinder* to do?

"Good," Sean said, interrupting Micah's musings. He turned toward the house, and Micah heard a tapping at a kitchen window. "Looks like Gemma's ready to call it a day, too." He started to leave and then paused. "By the way, I forgot earlier. She wants to know if you're planning to join us a week from Saturday at the harvest festival in Exton."

"Wouldn't miss it."

"Glad to hear it." Sean clapped him on the shoulder. "Safe drive home. See you in the morning. We should be able to finish the house by the end of tomorrow. It'll be good to move on to the next, and Gemma told me a couple more people have called and want to talk to us about installing solar panels. Will you have time tomorrow if she can set up appointments for us?"

"*Ja*. I'll let *Mamm* know I'll be late for supper tomorrow night."

"Plan on eating with us." He raised his hands. "Don't

say it. Gemma likes having you here to keep the kids occupied."

"In that case, I accept. *Gut nacht.*"

Sean hurried into the house, and Micah climbed into his buggy. As he drove along the moonlit roads toward his family's farm, he realized he hadn't asked Sean if Katie Kay was also joining the family at the harvest festival. He hoped so. Only to the moon and to God would he admit he looked forward to spending more time with her to learn about what she wanted and needed in the future for her and her *boppli.*

He knew what he wanted. He wanted to hear her laugh again as she had when they walked out together. Would her eyes sparkle as they used to when he teased her? He couldn't wait to find out.

Chapter Nine

Why did they run out of parts at the worst possible moment?

Groping in his tool belt pocket for another bolt, Micah appraised the metal structure that would support the solar panels on Reuben's roof. He and Sean had started working at the bishop's house early that Saturday morning. They wanted to get as much done as possible because they wouldn't be able to return next week. The harvest festival would eat up their whole day. When Micah had explained this to Reuben a couple of days ago, the bishop had accepted the delay.

"All things happen in God's time," Reuben said, "including harvest festivals." His grin had been bright through his gray whiskers. "Enjoy yourself with your friend and his family. The panels will be done when they're done."

The bishop's generous words and kind smile had added to Micah's guilt at not mentioning one important fact—Katie Kay would be going to the harvest festival with him and the Donnellys.

This morning, his stomach had twisted around and

around on the drive over in his buggy to meet Sean at the Lapps' house. Facing Reuben and not being able to tell his bishop the truth about Katie Kay had kept him awake most of the night. The fear Sean might accidentally mention Reuben's daughter had prevented him from sleeping the rest of the night.

He'd been able to breathe a bit easier when he discovered Reuben was visiting a family in his other district and would be gone most of the day. Before Sean arrived with their equipment, Micah had spent a few minutes speaking with Marnita and Ina Sue, Katie Kay's two younger sisters. They were excited about the young people's singing planned for the following evening and talked of nothing else.

It was odd to think that not long ago, he anticipated youth events with the same eagerness. That time, which was simple in retrospect, seemed like someone else's life.

Once he had climbed onto the roof with his partner, Micah had tried to lose himself in his work. Instead he kept losing the bolts and nuts he need to assemble the framework.

Looking over at Sean, he asked, "Do you have more of those small bolts? I'm out."

"That makes two of us," Sean said after checking the pockets of his work apron. "Guess it's time to run over to the hardware store and replenish the supplies. I should have gone yesterday after work, but our house guest made her delicious chocolate cake and I didn't want to risk having it all eaten by three kids and one pregnant wife before I got home." He bent and gave a gentle tug on the framework. "It's not going anywhere. We'll get back to it next weekend."

"*Ja.*" He was accustomed to his partner stating the obvious. Shortly after they'd begun working together, Micah realized that talking aloud was Sean's way of reviewing the next steps on a project.

After they'd collected their tools and climbed down, Sean carried a length of the metal framework to the van. They'd need it to make sure they got the right-sized bolts. Micah followed, pausing to let Reuben's daughters know he and Sean were done for the day.

"We'll be back the Saturday after next to finish the work," he said, though Reuben knew already.

"*Danki*, Micah." Ina Sue, who must be almost twenty, smiled at him. "You're nice to do this for *Daed* and for us."

"Sean is helping, too." He sounded idiotic, but he hadn't expected Katie Kay's sister to regard him with an invitation to linger.

"Will you be at the singing tomorrow night?"

"I don't think so." Most of the kids who joined in the youth events were too young for him. The guys were interested in pushing the envelope of their plain lives and trying to get a girl to drive home. A few had jobs beyond their family farms, but they hadn't decided what to do with their lives.

Telling the girls he'd see them at church in the morning, he strode to the van. He was walking a narrow line between his Amish life and the *Englisch* world where he worked. Every step had to be made with care.

Did Katie Kay feel that way, too? Or was she more comfortable among the *Englischers*? She continued to wear *Englisch* clothing but had begun to cover her head when she was doing housework. Was it a sign she was considering a return to her family? He'd heard her tell-

ing Sean's *kinder* about the school she and Micah had attended. The wistfulness in her voice had given him hope, but he cautioned himself not to be overly optimistic. She might not intend to resume her life among their people.

Micah was glad that, while they drove to Sean's house, they made a list of items they'd use the following week for the work on Reuben's house. He wrote down each part and the quantity they needed, adding in the ones he thought of while Sean called out others. Focusing kept him from thinking about Katie Kay.

For a few seconds anyhow.

As they entered the house, he heard the rumble of the vacuum. The kids came running, and the loud noise turned off. While Sean greeted his *kinder*, Micah watched Katie Kay lean the vacuum against a chair.

She went to the sofa and assisted Gemma to her feet. Gemma put her hand to her side, grimacing, but her smile returned while she thanked Katie Kay.

Waddling to the entry hall, one hand under her distended belly, Gemma asked, "What's brought you home early, Sean? Not that I'm complaining."

"We've got to run to the hardware store for some parts. I wanted to see if you needed anything from Strasburg while we're over that way."

"Pumpkins!" shouted DJ.

"Let Mommy answer." Sean gave his eldest a chiding frown.

DJ wasn't cowed. "But, Daddy, you promised to take us to get pumpkins the next time you went to the hardware store. Big, medium and small."

When Micah saw Katie Kay's confusion, he said, "Sean started a tradition a few years ago of making

pumpkin people. Because the cold can cause Olivia to have an asthma attack, she can't build snowmen. They solved the problem and got a jump on the cold weather with pumpkin people. They use carrots for noses, though a hole has to be carved out to fit the carrot in. The kids help set them up and then they paint clothes and faces on them out in the front yard."

"With the paint they don't splash on themselves," Gemma added with a tired smile.

"Can we go?" asked the *kinder* in unison.

Micah smiled at how the Donnelly kids could be of one mind when they wanted something.

Sean hesitated. "I know I promised, but Mommy is tired."

"I can go," Katie Kay piped up. "Micah and I will help to keep an eye on them while they pick out their pumpkins. That makes one *kind* for each adult. It should be simple." She glanced at Micah. "Ain't so?"

He nodded because he could see how exhausted Gemma was. Having the kids whining because of a broken promise would upset her. She needed her rest and peace and quiet.

"Thank you." Gemma's grateful smile was aimed at them. "I think I will—"

"You will sit and watch TV or take a nap." Katie Kay put her hands on the other woman's shoulders and steered her to the couch. "While Sean and Micah help the kids get their coats on, I'll make you a cup of herbal tea to sip on while we're away."

"But supper—"

Again Katie Kay interrupted. "Don't worry about that. I'll take care of it later. Enjoy your quiet time. You know it won't last long."

Micah said nothing as Gemma nodded, her every motion heavy with fatigue. She trusted Katie Kay with her *kinder*. The two women had grown closer as they spent more time together. He was tempted to ask Gemma how that had happened. Every attempt he made to heal the wounds between him and Katie Kay failed.

Because you keep pressuring her to make a decision instead of letting her find the way with God's help.

He was getting really annoyed with his conscience. At the same time, he had to be grateful for its guidance. It hadn't steered him wrong in the past, so he should heed it now.

Helping three small *kinder* into their coats was like trying to capture newborn piglets. They wiggled and jostled and reached in front of one another to collect hats. Three *kinder* seemed like a dozen. Micah wasn't surprised that Katie Kay had already returned from the kitchen with a cup of steaming tea by the time they finished getting the youngsters dressed.

When Jayden announced he needed to go to the bathroom, she took his hand and motioned for Micah and Sean to take his siblings out.

"We'll be there before you get them strapped in," she said, leading the little boy to the downstairs bathroom.

Micah had no doubts about that. DJ and Olivia ran in circles around him and Sean as they went outside. They bounced like a pair of rabbits and asked questions without giving him or Sean a chance to answer.

"We'll take Gemma's van." Sean grinned. "It's easier than moving their car seats. I already put the structure piece from Reuben's house in the back. Do you have our list, Micah?"

"I'll get it." He strode to the work van and opened the

passenger door. His clipboard had fallen on the floor, so he shook dirt off it as he returned to the other vehicle.

He was glad, when he got back, that Katie Kay was sitting with the *kinder* and helping Jayden into his car seat. The ancient Volkswagen microbus had a bench seat in the front with seat belts for three adults. Sitting next to Katie Kay during the ride to the hardware store would be exquisite torture.

His fingers itched to caress her cheek, which he knew was silken-soft. His arm ached to curve around her shoulders as it had when he'd drawn her to him in his courting buggy. His senses recalled the sweet scent of her shampoo.

Micah forced the memories away as he climbed into the front seat and didn't turn to look at her and the *kinder*. Whenever he remembered what he and Katie Kay had shared—for such a brief moment—in the past, he couldn't imagine a future without her.

Though she'd given him no sign she felt the same. Fool!

That was what he was. The biggest *dummkopf* ever.

Yet, knowing that, why couldn't he put her out of his mind? He needed to find an answer right away.

The hardware store in Strasburg was set behind its narrow parking lot. Unlike the fancy outlet mall on the Lincoln Highway in Ronks or the shops in Intercourse and Bird-in-Hand, this store focused on service for local farmers rather than tourists. A large sign painted Hardware was set atop the roof of the front porch running the length of the building. On the concrete floor was a variety of items, some on sale and others, seasonal clearance. Dried cornstalks were stacked on either side of

the door, and pumpkins were heaped beneath a lean-to shed to the far left side of the building. A pair of horses waited with their plain buggies near a hitching rail.

Micah was glad to hear Katie Kay insist that each of the *kinder* must hold a grown-up's hand before they started across the almost empty parking lot. Cars and trucks often zipped in and out.

It took about five minutes—far less time than Micah had expected—for the *kinder* to pick out the pumpkins they wanted. Sean lifted their choices onto a flatbed cart. He let his *kinder* "help" pull the cart toward the outside register, where they paid for nine pumpkins.

After putting the pumpkins into the van, they went into the store to look for the parts they needed. Sean asked Micah to help Katie Kay with the youngsters.

"I will get what we need," Sean said with a grin. "And I'll do it much faster without small fingers exploring what's in the bins."

Something about how his partner's eyes twinkled warned Micah that Sean had an ulterior motive for sending him with Katie Kay and the *kinder*. He was tempted to tell Sean that matchmaking could undermine their friendship, but he knew it wouldn't. And Micah couldn't be certain that leaving him with Katie Kay was Sean's primary motivation, especially when they were chaperoned by three imps who demanded all their attention.

After nodding to Sean, Micah looked at the kids. "What shall we look at first?"

"Need paint! For our pumpkin people," announced DJ. "Black paint."

"And white," added Olivia.

Jayden refused to be left out. "And bluenette."

"Bluenette?" Micah asked.

"For a pumpkin lady's hair."

Micah remained puzzled until Katie Kay whispered, "I think he means *brunette*."

He had to pretend to cough so he didn't laugh as they walked along an aisle. Jayden selected a small can of paint with a bright blue lid and announced he was painting his pumpkin lady with bluenette hair. Arching a brow at Katie Kay, Micah took the can from the little boy.

"Bluenette, it is," Micah said as he collected the white and black cans from the other two *kinder*. "Let's go and pay for these."

He had taken two steps when he realized Katie Kay wasn't following. Did she need something else? He couldn't imagine what she might be shopping for at a hardware store. Turning around, he was astonished to see her holding on to a shelf, her face as gray as the labels on the paint cans beside her.

"Are you okay?" he asked.

"Shhh!" She put her finger to her lips.

He raised his brows in a silent question.

"It's your brother," she whispered.

"Which one?"

"Your *twin* brother."

"Are you sure?"

"*Ja*. Daniel looks just like you."

Micah frowned. He should have remembered that coming with Katie Kay close to Strasburg was a risk. For the past six months, Daniel had been overseeing a massive project on a farm outside the village. His brother was a skilled carpenter, but he'd been challenged since he was hired by an *Englischer* to repair an old stone-end farmhouse and its half dozen outbuildings.

As Daniel had said more than once, the only thing holding up the structures were the termites.

He wanted to ask Katie Kay if she was sure about what she'd seen; then he heard Daniel's laugh and the low rumble of his brother's voice that others told him were much like his own. Hoping both he and Katie Kay were wrong, he peered around the end of the row to confirm their suspicions.

Daniel was talking to the store manager at the rear of the store. He couldn't have seen Micah or any of them. So far, so *gut*.

Micah said in not much more than a whisper, "I'll distract him while you slip out the door. Get in the van and keep yourself and the *kinder* out of sight until I join you."

She nodded, and he realized how distraught she was. Shrinking along the aisle and drawing Sean's kids with her, she motioned for him to hurry.

Micah hoped she'd be sensible. He almost laughed aloud at the thought. If she'd done the sensible thing and gone home, she wouldn't have to skulk through the store. Maybe this encounter would persuade her to reunite with her family.

As if he didn't have a care in the world, Micah sauntered around the end of the aisle. He set the three cans of paint on the counter and greeted his brother.

Daniel grinned. "What are you doing down here? I thought you were working on Reuben's house today."

"We are, but we needed to stock up on a few things." He glanced into the basket his brother carried. "More drywall screws? I thought you had the walls up."

"In the main house. Mrs. O'Neill has decided she

wants to use the old stable as a guesthouse, though there are five guest rooms in the big house."

Micah congratulated himself on changing the subject. It was his brother's first large project as a general contractor, and Daniel was enjoying every minute of being his own boss, a goal he'd set for himself when they were teens.

Trying not to be obvious, Micah glanced toward the front door several times. Why hadn't Katie Kay slipped out yet? He could keep his brother chatting, but eventually Sean would be done.

His brother stopped in the middle of a word and looked past him. "Did you see her?"

"Her?" He was glad Daniel wasn't looking at him, because he guessed his face revealed his anxiety.

"By the front door."

Micah turned around, holding his breath as he prayed he wouldn't see Katie Kay at the door. When an elderly man walked into the store, he looked at his brother. "Have you thought about getting glasses? That guy doesn't look like a *her*."

"Not him. A woman just left. She looked a lot like… Okay, you're going to find this strange. She looked a lot like Katie Kay Lapp."

"Did she?" Micah wouldn't lie to his twin brother. If Daniel asked him if he'd seen Katie Kay, he'd give his brother an honest answer. "I didn't notice any plain women in here."

"She didn't look plain. She looked like Katie Kay would if she were *Englisch*." He grinned. "Maybe I do need glasses. What would she be doing here?"

"Who knows?"

"I sure don't." His smile widened. "You dodged a bullet there."

"*Dodged a bullet*? Where did you learn that saying?"

Daniel's grin became a laugh. "Believe or not, from *Grossmammi* Ella. She learned it from one of the therapists who help her hold on to what memory she has left. For someone who has trouble recalling names, she can remember bizarre phrases and uses them over and over until the rest of us pick them up."

"How's she doing?" Micah was again relieved that Katie Kay was no longer the subject. *Grossmammi* Ella was the great-grandmother of Daniel's fiancée, Hannah, and Daniel had a great deal of affection for the cantankerous, headstrong old woman who sometimes, while lost in her memories, believed he was her late husband.

"Better than we thought a few months ago. The memory exercises she's doing seems to be stabilizing her Alzheimer's. We know it's not a long-term solution, but we count each day she's able to recognize us a blessing."

Micah paid for the paint and then stepped aside to let Daniel check out. When Sean walked toward them, Micah waved him back. Renewed guilt bore into him, and he knew only one way to ease it.

Katie Kay needed to go home, and he had to help her see that. He prayed God would send inspiration to show him how.

If the *kinder* thought she'd lost her mind as she hurried them to the van and helped them in, Katie Kay didn't try to persuade them otherwise. Instead she made a game out of keeping hidden in the van. She heard them whispering together about surprising their *daed* and Micah with cries of "Boo!"

Daniel's buggy was on the other side of the parking lot, and he wouldn't hear the *kinder* from there. He might, however, notice the little ones moving about the van, so she devised excuse after excuse, each one sillier than the one before, for them to crouch between the seats.

"I want to see my pumpkins," DJ announced, a sign he was bored with the game. He started to scramble over the seat as the unmistakable sound of metal buggy wheels and iron horseshoes sounded on the asphalt.

She grabbed the little boy by the heels and pulled him down beside the rest of them on the floor. Before he could protest loudly enough to be heard outside the van, she began making goofy faces at the three *kinder* and dared them to do the same. As they distorted their features into every possible shape, they laughed. She kept up the game until she knew the buggy must be gone.

Looking out, she saw Micah and Sean walking toward them. She started to get up, but this time the *kinder* reminded her to stay out of sight because they wanted to "scare" their *daed* and Micah. As she joined in with their game, she wondered how much longer she could avoid making the inevitable decisions about going home…and about Micah.

Gemma was asleep on the sofa when Katie Kay walked into the living room. Before she could ask the little ones to be quiet, they ran to their *mamm* and began chattering about the pumpkins they'd found. Half-asleep, Gemma gathered them to her and listened to their excitement, though her face was pale and she winced when she sat.

"Stay where you are," Katie Kay urged. Looking

over her shoulder, she added, "Sean, sit and enjoy your family while Micah and I make supper."

"I don't cook," Micah protested.

She laughed at his shock at doing what was considered among the Amish women's work. "Then it's time you learn. With Wanda getting married soon, you may be on your own to prepare your supper."

"Leah usually—"

"*Ja*, I know you depend on your sister-in-law to cook for you when you're not eating here. However, it won't hurt you to flip grilled cheese sandwiches while I make soup."

Sean grinned as he took the bag of paint cans from Micah. "She's got you there, my friend. I think your masculinity will survive giving her a hand making one meal."

"You're no help," Micah tossed back but grinned. "Show me what you need me to do, Katie Kay."

In the kitchen, she was pleased to discover he wasn't as inept as he'd complained. He followed her directions and got bread out of the drawer, as well as butter and cheese from the fridge. Spreading the ingredients across the table, he left her the small area by the stove to cut vegetables into a soup she was making with leftover chicken from earlier in the week.

Neither of them spoke of her near encounter with his twin brother at the hardware store. She wondered if he was relieved to focus on cooking and let everything else go. She was, because she could talk and laugh with him without having any of the issues plaguing them intrude.

During supper, Katie Kay enjoyed the calm within herself. She had to make decisions but not at that moment. She listened as the three youngsters told their

mamm—again—about their trip to the hardware store and their plans for the pumpkins. Gemma's lips twitched at Jayden's intention to paint "bluenette" hair on his pumpkin person tomorrow after church. He didn't notice because he was excited. It would be his first time to help with the painting.

Katie Kay, along with Sean and Micah, insisted Gemma rest after the meal. When Micah offered to help clean up, Katie Kay was pleased. It was lonely in the kitchen while she listened to the family enjoying each other's company in the living room.

Taking the plates and bowls from the table, Katie Kay set them on the counter. She frowned at the solidified cheese sticking to the top one. It needed to be removed before it could be washed.

"I'll scrape," she said, "if you'll load the dishwasher, Micah. You do know how to do that, don't you?"

"Gemma taught me long ago."

She chuckled as she handed him the first plate, and he put it in the proper part of the dishwasher. As they were finishing, Olivia ran in and gave her a hug. Jayden did the same. She wished them a *gut nacht*, which made them giggle as they did whenever she used *Deitsch*. She edged aside as they embraced Micah and ran back into the living room. Hearing the Donnellys heading upstairs to put the *kinder* to bed, she reached for another plate.

"The kids like you," Micah said.

"They are sweet and funny."

"I wasn't sure at first if you liked *kinder*."

She halted with the final plate held over the trash can. Setting it on a nearby counter, she asked, "What gave you that idea?"

"You never offered to watch the little ones during church services."

"I spent every waking hour, except those few at church every other week, taking care of my younger sisters. To be able to sit and listen to God's word and not have to worry about someone sticking a finger into the washer's wringer or trying to see the bottom of the well was *wunderbaar.*"

Resting his hand on the counter, he faced her. "I didn't realize that."

"I know. I didn't want to shame *Daed* by whining."

"Why not? All of us kids complained about our chores at one time or another."

"But you weren't the bishop's *kind.* We're held to a higher standard so other *kinder* can strive to do as we did."

When he didn't reply, she finished the plate. She handed it to him along with the rinsed bowls. He put them into the dishwasher.

As he snapped the door shut, he said, "I guess I should have known how it would be for you, but I never thought about it."

"It was all we were allowed to think about." She didn't add that Priscilla had mentioned the need for them to be role models at least once a day before she married. After that, her older sister had repeated the words each time she arrived for a visit and every time on her way out the door.

"Can I tell you something I've been wondering about?" he asked.

"What?"

"Something that isn't any of my business."

She sat at the table and looked at him with a gri-

mace. "Which means it's something to do with me and the *boppli*."

"How did you guess?"

"Because you act as if you're tiptoeing through a rattlesnake nest whenever you want to talk about the *boppli*."

He pulled out the chair next to hers and moved it so their knees were only an inch from each other. Abruptly she was aware of him as she hadn't been since they walked out together. No, that wasn't true. She was always vividly connected to his voice, where his hands were, what he was looking at. It was the only way she could keep the barriers up between him and her heart, which teased her to reconsider what she'd said to him when she'd ended their relationship, not guessing then that she also had rung a death knell over their friendship.

When he took her hands and folded them between his, she was so stunned she didn't jerk them back. And then it was too late because the heat seeping from his fingers to hers was delightful, and she didn't want to put an end to it.

Ice froze her next breath when he said, "I've been pondering this question for a while. Do you intend to keep your *kind*, or are you planning to give it up for adoption?"

Words vanished from Katie Kay's mind. Usually she had a quick answer for any question, whether it was a gentle word for a *kind* or a scathing one for someone who annoyed her. Now she couldn't come up with anything to say as he asked about the subject she'd avoided thinking about.

"I haven't decided what I'll do when the time comes." That was the truth.

He sighed with relief. "I'm glad to hear that because I thought you had."

"Why?"

"You say *the boppli*, never *my boppli*."

Did she? She hadn't noticed that. Was it a habit, or did the choice of words have a deeper meaning? She cringed when anyone mentioned the *boppli* was Austin's, whether she was among *Englischers* or the Amish. But she hadn't realized she never spoke of the *kind* growing within her as hers.

"I've been praying for guidance," she said softly.

"You have?"

"Why do you sound surprised? I didn't leave Paradise Springs because I wanted to get away from God."

"Then why did you leave?"

For a moment, she considered giving him the same excuse she'd used whenever anyone asked her the question. She'd been honest with him. Why not continue?

"I needed to see what else the world had to share with me. I left because I felt caged."

It was his turn to be speechless. She took advantage of his astonishment to slip her hands from between his and hurry out of the kitchen before he could ask another question that made her face what could become a bleak future.

Chapter Ten

The following Saturday, Katie Kay sat between Olivia and Jayden on the rearmost seat of Gemma's van. As he'd promised the Donnellys, Micah had pounded out the small dent in the front bumper. Only a few dark spots on the bright chrome remained as a reminder of the damage.

She wished she could pay for the chrome paint. She'd seen what the small cans cost at the hardware store. Her plan had been to select one and ask Micah to buy it. She'd reimburse him when she could. That, along with giving Gemma a break, was why she'd gone to the hardware store, but all her plans had gone out the window when she'd seen Daniel Stoltzfus. All she'd thought about then was slipping away without being noticed.

Her heart beat double time whenever she thought of how close discovery had been. If Micah hadn't assisted her by distracting his twin brother, she wouldn't have been able to get out of the hardware store unobserved. She was thankful for that.

But her heart pounded harder when she thought about holding hands with Micah in the Donnellys' kitchen.

When they were walking out, she'd been overwhelmed by the intense attraction between them, but the memory of the few times he'd taken her hand then seemed to pale in comparison with the powerful sensations that had swept through her while they sat facing each other.

Today she was also grateful the two *kinder* had pleaded for her to join them at the back of the van. Their request allowed her to avoid going through the awkward motions of not sitting beside Micah and DJ on the middle bench. She could have insisted on riding in the front with Sean and Gemma, but it would have been crowded with three adults—one of them *very* pregnant—on the bench seat.

She hoped she wouldn't get carsick. She had once while riding in the back seat of Vinnie's car, but he'd been making wild turns from one of Lancaster's streets to another, laughing when the rear end slid and the tires squealed. He hadn't wanted to stop until he realized she was serious she was about to throw up. He'd pulled over just in time for her to get out of the car and be sick on the curb.

It didn't seem to be a problem with Sean behind the wheel. She couldn't help noticing how much more smoothly he shifted the vehicle than she had. It didn't bounce like a jackrabbit as it had when she tried to downshift the first few times on the way to Lancaster.

When they arrived almost an hour later at the farm where the harvest festival was being held, traffic was backed up for more than a mile. Ahead of them, cars drove through an open gate into a field past the stone farmhouse and the circular red barn decorated with Pennsylvania Dutch symbols she'd heard called hex signs. She'd been asked about them while she lived in

Lancaster, and each time she'd said she didn't know anything about them. She wasn't surprised by the questions because many people assumed the terms *Pennsylvania Dutch* and *the Amish* were identical. The Amish were one group among the many German speakers who'd settled in southeastern Pennsylvania in the eighteenth century.

Olivia and Jayden, like their older brother, peered out the windows as the van inched forward. Finally it was their turn to edge onto the dirt road leading to a man wearing a bright yellow vest and holding a baton with a red flag at the end, who motioned them toward a long row of parked cars.

The kids laughed as the old van bounced on the uneven ground.

"Ouch!" groaned Micah when the wheels hit a deeper rut. He rubbed his head, and the *kinder* giggled. He gave them a fake scowl, which made them laugh harder when he asked, "Do you think it's funny my hat might be cracked?"

"As long as it's not your head," called Sean as he parked the van between two pickup trucks. "If that hit the roof, you might punch a hole right through it with your hard head."

Katie Kay joined in with the laughter as she helped Olivia and Jayden loosen the seat belts woven through their car seats. Another item she needed to get before the *boppli* was born. She suspected they were very expensive.

You won't need one if you go home, her conscience reminded her. Amish women usually carried their *bopplin* in their arms when someone else was driving the buggy. If she were driving it herself, she could keep the

boppli on her lap or make a nest of blankets and quilts on the floor to keep the little one safe.

She nodded her thanks when Micah offered his hand to help her from the van. Then she released it so she could lift the younger two Donnelly *kinder* out. The little ones acted as if they'd replaced their bones with bedsprings; they bounced around the adults, unable to restrain their excitement. She understood how they felt, because a thrill of anticipation raced through her, too.

Families and groups of teenagers walked between the rows of parked cars, and everyone seemed as eager as the Donnelly kids. Everyone was chatting and laughing, and Katie Kay let those *gut* spirits wash over her like a cleansing rain. Today was for having fun, something she didn't want to forget how to have.

Aromas of fried dough and hot dogs, as well as peppers and onions, welcomed them into the festival's midway. Booths lined either side of the wide walkway, where the grass had been ground into the dirt. At each one, *kinder* waited for their opportunity to win a prize.

However, DJ, Olivia and Jayden had one destination in mind. They wanted to take a hayride, especially Jayden who'd been too young last year to go. Until they did that, they weren't interested in anything else, though Micah whispered he'd prefer to wait until he could get a sausage sandwich with those delicious onions and peppers.

When they reached the field where the hayrides were under way, a hand-painted sign announced rides were available, first-come, first-served. The teenage girl selling tickets leaned her elbow on one of the uprights, looking bored.

Gemma exchanged a glance with her husband, and

Katie Kay knew she shouldn't try to catch its meaning. It was, however, obvious. Gemma wanted to let the *kinder* ride, but she didn't feel *gut* enough.

"We'll take them," Katie Kay said, cutting her eyes toward Micah. "That way, you two can rest and have something to eat. And get Micah a sausage sandwich before he fades away from hunger."

"You don't have to do that." Gemma's protests were halfhearted.

"We'd be glad to do it." She turned to Micah and asked, "Aren't we?"

She was glad when he didn't hesitate. "*Ja.* C'mon, kids. Let's get in line so we can take our turn."

"A sandwich will be waiting for you," Sean said, laughing. "What about for you, Katie Kay? Do you want one, too?"

"No," Micah answered before she could. "Katie Kay will want fried dough with plenty of powdered sugar and cinnamon on it." He smiled at her. "Ain't so?"

"*Ja.* How did you know?"

"I heard your stomach rumble when we walked by. It's true actions speak louder than words." He laughed, and the kids did, too, as if it were the funniest thing they'd ever heard.

Sean gave a feigned groan. "You see what I have to put up with every day."

As Gemma checked to make sure each *kind* had his or her coat buttoned, Katie Kay looked at the man beside her.

Micah was grinning as widely as the youngsters. He was a *gut* friend to the Donnellys. She wished she could say he was her friend, too. Or did she? Was friendship all she wanted with him?

The question unsettled her, and she pushed it away. She didn't want to think about such things while they were at the festival. She wanted to have fun.

"*Danki*, Micah," Katie Kay said as they walked toward the girl who was selling tickets to an *Englisch* family. "I know riding around on a flatbed wagon isn't a big treat for someone who grew up on a farm."

"You grew up on a farm, too."

"*Ja*, but…" How could she explain to him that in her few months away from the countryside she'd missed the open fields and the cool sensation of freshly turned earth between her toes and the rich scents of plants and animals and a *snitz* pie cooling on a windowsill? More than once, she'd considered leaving Lancaster just to rediscover what she'd left behind. If she had, she might not be pregnant.

She refused to think that way. She wanted to enjoy the day with the *kinder*, their parents…and Micah. Today was for happiness and fun. Trouble would return soon enough.

As they reached the front of the line and Katie Kay began helping the two littlest ones onto the wagon, Sean pulled Micah aside and said, "Thanks for taking the kids." He'd already said it a half-dozen times. He must have been really worried about Gemma getting overtired. As Katie Kay had, his partner said, "I know riding around on a horse-drawn farm wagon isn't a big treat for you, but it is for my kids."

"Riding around on a horse-drawn farm wagon and not having to spend the whole day sweating out in the field *is* a big treat for me." He laughed and was glad when Sean joined in.

Micah bent to hoist DJ up but paused long enough to sneak a glance at Sean, who had his arm around Gemma. Sean was worried about his pregnant wife. A flush of something that felt like sorrow flowed through him. Katie Kay wouldn't have anyone to be concerned for her when she was as rotund as Gemma. The *daed* of her *boppli* had cut any ties with her in the cruelest possible ways. Nobody would stand beside her as Sean did with Gemma, encouraging her and celebrating the new life with her. She alone would have to choose her *boppli*'s name.

He tried not to think of that as he put his hands on Katie Kay's still slender waist and lifted her to sit beside DJ. Climbing on himself, he pointed to one of the bales in the center. "You boys sit here, and, Olivia, you sit—"

"With Kay-Kay," the little girl announced as she settled herself on one of the bales and patted the hay. "Come and sit with me, Kay-Kay."

"How could I resist such an invitation?" She sat beside the *kind* and put her arm around Olivia's narrow shoulders. "You will hold on to me so I don't fall off the wagon, won't you?"

The little girl nodded so hard her braids bounced like a pair of reins along her back.

Though the ride was around an open field with the horses plodding at a pace barely faster than the *kinder* could walk, the Donnelly youngsters were thrilled with the experience. They talked without seeming to take a breath.

Micah relaxed and listened as they discussed the wagon, the horses and the harvest festival in specific detail. Now that they were enjoying their ride, their next thoughts were for lunch.

Or the boys' thoughts were.

Olivia was absorbed with a different matter. "I needs a bonnet. Girls on TV have bonnets."

"Which girls?" Katie Kay asked.

The little girl began to chatter about a show about a family that lived on the prairie. "They wears bonnets when they ride in a wagon. Mommy says girls always wears bonnets long ago."

"That's true," she replied as if the matter was the most serious one in the world.

Olivia pointed to the line, where others waited for their turn to get on the wagon. "See? They gots pretty bonnets."

Instantly Katie Kay stiffened. He could read her thoughts as if she spoke them aloud: Were there Amish at the festival? She should have known that they could encounter plain people there.

He scanned the line again and smiled. The girls in the blue-and-white-checked bonnets were *Englisch*.

"I see," she said to Olivia, and he noticed her shoulders relax.

"I wants a bonnet." The *kind* looked up at Katie Kay with innocent eyes. "Where can I gets a bonnet?"

Katie Kay glanced at Micah. He shrugged. He had no idea where an *Englisch* girl would obtain a checkered bonnet. Were they sold in stores, or were the brightly colored bonnets homemade? *Mamm* had made the far simpler bonnets she and his sisters wore.

"Where's your bonnet, Kay-Kay?" asked Olivia, obviously not ready to let the subject drop. "Uncle Micah says Amish girls wear bonnets to school and to church. You're Amish, aren't you?"

He waited to see how Katie Kay would answer. Did

she still consider herself Amish? She used *Deitsch* words often and wore a kerchief over her hair when she worked around the house. But both might be habit more than anything.

"Ja," she replied with a smile. "Amish girls do wear bonnets to school and church."

Olivia wasn't satisfied with Katie Kay's evasion, and neither was Micah. He listened as the little girl asked again, "So where's your bonnet, Kay-Kay?"

"At my *daed*'s house." Katie Kay started to add more, but Olivia sneezed once, then a second, then a third time.

"Gesundheit," he and Katie Kay said at the same time.

The youngsters giggled, and they began to talk again about the horses pulling the wagon. Micah wished he could figure out a way to return the conversation to bonnets and ask if Katie Kay planned to wear hers again.

He wondered if she'd finally faced the future and had made up her mind about what she intended to do with the *boppli*. Surrendering a *kind* was unusual in the Amish community, but it happened. A family beyond the biological parents' districts would be found for the little one. It would be adopted by a plain couple who would love it as if the *boppli* had been born within that family. But the choice had to be Katie Kay's.

The only decision he needed to make was if he wanted to sample at least once more the delight he'd rediscovered when he held her hands last night. His aim had been to offer her comfort while he posed such difficult questions. Then pleasure had skittered up his arm, and he'd found himself wanting to look into her eyes for the rest of his life.

Be careful, he warned himself as the wagon completed its circuit. He jumped off. Helping the others down, he thought about the *Englisch* saying Sean used often with a laugh. What was it?

Fool me once, shame on you. Fool me twice, shame on me.

That was the one, but he didn't feel the least bit like laughing. If he let himself be taken in by Katie Kay again, the resulting pain in his heart would be his own fault.

The boys ran to the gate where Sean and Gemma waited. Olivia sneezed again and again. Was she allergic to hay? It seemed unlikely because there were fields on every side of the Donnellys' house. Katie Kay gave the little girl a tissue so she could blow her nose.

"She may be getting a cold," Gemma said as they walked toward the midway. "I hope not. Once one gets sick, they all do."

"At least you don't have as many *kinder* as in my family." Micah chuckled. "*Mamm* used to dose each of us as soon as one got sick. We'd catch the cold or whatever but not as hard."

"A good idea." Gemma hooked her arm through her husband's. "Sean, I do believe you owe Micah a sausage sandwich."

They laughed as they picked out what they wanted for lunch and found a picnic table to enjoy it while they watched the other festivalgoers. Micah listened to the *kinder* plan what they wanted to do after they ate. A single glance at Gemma told him she hoped to sit at the table for as long as possible. The only way she'd do that was if he and Katie Kay amused the youngsters.

"What do you think about doing the corn maze?"

he asked her softly enough so the chattering *kinder* wouldn't overhear.

"I've never done a corn maze. Have you?"

He shook his head. "But I've been curious about them. It's got to take a lot of skill to carve a cornfield into a pattern that looks like a giant table with a turkey dinner spread across it."

"A pattern?"

Pulling out the pamphlet he'd taken from a stack near the parking lot, he opened it. "See? This is what the maze looks like from overhead."

"It is a turkey!" Olivia cried as she peeked over his arm and poked the page. "Mommy, can we do the turkey?"

Gemma said, "I don't know. That's a long walk."

"We'll take them if you'd like," Katie Kay said. "I know you want to spend time with them, too, but if you'd prefer to relax, we'll take them through the maze."

"And get them tired out." Micah winked at Gemma. "That way, they'll go to sleep right away when they get home."

"That sounds lovely," she said before looking at her husband. "Sean?"

"If Micah and Katie Kay want to wrangle three scamps through the maze, I say go for it."

Micah nodded as he saw Sean's thankful expression. "It's a deal. Just make sure you have plenty of fried dough—"

"And popcorn," added Jayden.

"And popcorn," he repeated with a smile. "According to the brochure, it takes on average a little over an hour to complete the maze."

"A feast will be waiting upon your return from van-

quishing yon corn maze," Sean said so seriously they laughed.

Leading the kids and Katie Kay, Micah went to the booth to buy tickets for them. They were asked to wait to the left of the entrance, because guests were spaced out to make it impossible to follow someone else around the twisting maze.

When it was their turn to go in, the man at the entrance said, "Have fun. When you smell pumpkin pie, you will be right close to the exit."

Olivia giggled and grabbed Micah's hand and then Katie Kay's. DJ took his other hand while Katie Kay offered hers to Jayden. Together, they entered the maze.

Around them, the dried corn leaves rustled with the slight breeze they had hardly noticed before. The kids stared around, wide-eyed, but giggled at each other's trepidation. The ground was well worn under their feet. Voices, disembodied and distorted by the stalks, reached them in snippets.

The kids asked to go ahead to the first intersection of the paths. Agreeing not to turn in any direction until the adults reached them, they skipped away. Olivia stopped to sneeze twice and then cough, but she shook her head when he asked if she needed her asthma medicine. She hurried after her brothers.

"Do you have her inhaler, Micah?" Katie Kay asked.

"No." Dismay shot through him. "I forgot to get it from Gemma."

"Then we should hurry. Maybe her coughing is nothing, but I don't want her to have an attack."

He nodded and matched her steps as they followed the *kinder*.

"While they're out of earshot," Micah said, "I wanted

to tell you, Katie Kay, I'm sorry for pressuring you. When you called your little one 'the *boppli*,' I thought you'd already made up your mind about what you would do with him or her."

"I haven't. I don't want to. Not yet. Can you understand that?"

"Ja." He smiled at her as they went together to where the *kinder* waited impatiently.

She conferred with them about which direction they should choose. They decided to go left and ran toward the next intersection, where people could be seen walking both ways. The five of them kept to the same pattern over and over with the *kinder* racing to the turn ahead of them, sometimes reaching a dead end and having to turn around.

As they retraced their steps a second time back to a branch of the maze, Micah reached out for the *kinder*'s hands, but when his fingers closed around slender fingers, he knew he hadn't caught either Olivia or DJ. Instead he was holding Katie Kay's hand.

Drop it! The warning was like a fire siren blaring through his head, but he couldn't make his fingers uncurl from around hers. Not even when other people going through the maze edged around where they stood in the middle of the path.

Drop it!

He couldn't. He'd waited for the chance to hold her hand again. As he did, the months since the last time he'd taken her home from a singing melted away like frost on a sunny morning.

When she raised her eyes to meet his, he couldn't mistake her expression. She was as pleased and as uneasy as he was. In spite of that, she didn't tug her hand away.

He drew her to the side of the path, stopping though the kids waved for them to catch up. The sharp edges of a corn leaf brushed against his ear, and he edged a single step away.

"This is the most fun I've had in a long time," he said.

"The kids are excited, and that's fun."

"Being here with you is fun for me." He ran his thumb along her palm. "I've missed our friendship."

"Me, too." She squeezed his fingers as her smile grew soft. As soft as her lips would be, he knew.

His rebellious heart leaped within his chest. He'd never wanted to kiss her—not even the first time—as much as he did now. Would friendship be enough for him with this woman he'd once loved?

An hour passed and then a second one, and yet Katie Kay remained lost with Micah and the *kinder* in the maze. She wouldn't have worried except that Olivia coughed more. Was it a cold, or was she having an asthma attack? Olivia seemed to be breathing okay, but Katie Kay wasn't sure how an attack progressed. She knew Micah was apprehensive about the little girl's situation, too, because he picked the *kind* up and carried her when she lagged.

Katie Kay did the same with Jayden. DJ was no longer running ahead, and he complained on every step he was thirsty, though he'd had a full bottle of water when they entered the maze.

When they reached what seemed like the thousandth intersection in the maze, Micah pointed to the right. "I think we're supposed to go that way."

"No, this way," DJ argued, gesturing left.

"Why do you think so?"

"I've seen a bunch of people go that way, and I haven't seen them backtrack."

"That's *gut* enough for me." He held out his hand, but she gave DJ a gentle shove in Micah's direction. The little boy grasped his fingers and began to ask another barrage of questions.

They kept walking. Others passed them, obviously eager to get out of the maze, too.

"You are a *gut* man, Micah Lapp," she said as Olivia's head dropped onto his shoulder. The little girl still coughed fitfully as she slept. Jayden had fallen asleep fifteen minutes earlier.

"I try to be." He gave her a cockeyed grin. "Glad to know I'm succeeding at least some of the time."

"I meant what I said. You're a *gut* man." *Too* gut *for me*, she added to herself.

Micah deserved a *wunderbaar* woman who hadn't ever treated him like dirt beneath her shoes. He should have a wife who was as devoted to a plain lifestyle as her sister, Priscilla, and who could make him a fine home.

The thought sliced through her like a blade, and she bit her lower lip to keep it from trembling. She didn't watch where she was going and stumbled over a stone, gripping Jayden more tightly so she didn't drop him.

Micah caught her arm. "What's wrong, Katie Kay? You look sick. Are you feeling bad?"

"I'm okay." She stepped away from him. For a moment, she wished he'd refused to let her go, because she'd felt safe with his wide hands curving along her arms. *Don't let your fear betray you.* "Let's keep going."

What did she want from him? He'd been worried

about her and the *boppli* when he drove her to the midwife's clinic. As well, he'd taken care of her when he discovered her wandering along the road, but wouldn't he have done the same for anyone he encountered? There was no question that he was a fine man. She'd let her heart lead her to him once, and that had been disastrous. So what did she want from him *now*?

Did she want him to treat her like he used to before they walked out together? That had been such an easy time between them. He'd made her laugh and feel special without putting her on a pedestal as other guys did. Sometimes, back then, that had annoyed her because she'd liked when the young men admired her and told her how splendid she was. As Austin had until the night he'd persuaded her to drink too much. How stupid she'd been dumping Micah when he treated her with kindness and respect and honesty. And then she'd let herself be beguiled by a man who had never really cared for her.

Suddenly Katie Kay caught her breath when she saw familiar silhouettes on the other side of the stalks. The straw hats and *kapps* told her who they were.

Grabbing DJ's hand, she sprinted in the direction they'd come. She ran until she came to another dead end, paying no attention to the *kind*'s questions. She gasped for breath and fought not to cry.

When Micah came around the corner and stared at her, she blinked hard to hold in her tears. He set the abruptly wide-awake Olivia on her feet as he asked, "Why did you flee, acting as jumpy as oil on a hot griddle?"

"I saw people who looked like our neighbors." She wouldn't say the word *Amish* aloud for fear of being overheard.

His eyes widened a moment and then narrowed. "So you ran in the opposite direction without bothering to identify them?"

"I couldn't let them see me." She glanced at Olivia, who was clinging to Micah and coughing again.

"You're going to encounter someone else who knows you eventually, Katie Kay. How long are you going to try to play hide-and-seek?"

"I don't think I—"

"There's the gist of the problem. You don't think things through."

She raised her chin. "I don't need you lecturing me, Micah Stoltzfus."

"No, you need—" He halted as the little girl doubled over with her coughing. Scooping Olivia up, he held one hand out to DJ. "C'mon. What *we* need to do is find our way out of here and take Olivia home so she can get warm again. So we all can get warm. You and I can talk later, Katie Kay."

She nodded. She wanted to groan when she saw lazy snowflakes drift onto them. She'd wondered how it could get any worse in the corn maze, and now she had her answer.

As if she'd said that aloud, Micah mused, "If it keeps snowing, at least we can see other people's footprints and follow them."

She trudged after Micah, holding Jayden close and hating the sound of Olivia's coughs. Keeping her head down, she resisted peeking out from under her eyelashes to look for any plain folk.

A sweet and spicy aroma tickled her senses, and she said, "Micah, wait! Don't you smell it?" As Micah

sniffed, she added, "The guy at the entrance said when we smelled pumpkin pie, we'd be close to the exit."

"*Right* close. We need to keep going right until we find the way out."

"I hope you're right... I mean, correct."

He didn't smile at her attempt to ease the tension. She hadn't expected he'd laugh out loud, but she thought his scowl might ease.

In a couple more turns, they reached the exit. Sean rushed forward to take Olivia, who was coughing hard again. As Gemma pulled out the *kind*'s inhaler, Katie Kay felt the overwhelming urge to say something, but she wasn't sure for which mistake she should apologize first.

Chapter Eleven

As the week started out, Katie Kay kept herself busy with work at the Donnellys' house. Monday and Tuesday and Wednesday mornings, she oversaw breakfast, getting DJ ready and out the door in time to get on the bus, cleaning the kitchen and doing laundry. For the first time since she'd come back to Paradise Springs, she hadn't lost her breakfast within an hour of eating it. Her stomach was queasy but didn't roil as it had since she'd become pregnant. The fear she'd have morning sickness for the full nine months eased.

Though Katie Kay's nausea had lessened, as each day passed, Gemma seemed to have a tougher time moving because she was gaining weight at a surprising speed. Her doctor had suggested she do less and rest more, a fact she hadn't mentioned.

Katie Kay knew only because Sean had explained what Gemma's obstetrician had said. "Can you keep an eye on her, Katie Kay, and suggest she stay in bed?"

"Ja." She didn't add that she intended to do more for the generous woman who had welcomed her into her home as if she were a long-lost sister. In fact, Gemma

was more accepting of Katie Kay than her real older sister had been.

She didn't need Sean's hints that she would have to be subtle or Gemma would keep working as she had… to prove she could, despite the burgeoning belly that suggested she was carrying more than one *boppli*. Tests had said otherwise, but Katie Kay knew they weren't always right.

By midmorning, Gemma had gone into the bedroom she shared with Sean to rest.

Katie Kay decided to make cookies so the *kinder* could help. That way she could keep an eye on them and they'd stay quiet. Maybe Gemma would be able to sleep.

However, Olivia, who'd had a runny nose and a hacking cough until yesterday, acted as if climbing onto a chair took too much energy. She made one attempt, slipped and began crying.

Hushing the little girl, Katie Kay assured her that she didn't have to help bake the cookies. Olivia agreed, shocking her. The little girl was usually the first one to volunteer whenever something was baked. Now, the *kind* continued to cry on and off until Jayden looked at his big sister with the same anxiety Katie Kay felt.

Katie Kay realized Olivia might be sicker than she'd been the night before. Her own younger sisters had made the same sounds that were halfway between a sob and a whine when they hadn't been feeling well. Putting her hand on the little girl's forehead, she frowned when she felt the unmistakable heat of a fever. She'd thought Olivia was getting better this morning. The *kind* hadn't coughed once during breakfast.

Picking Olivia up, Katie Kay placed her on the sofa. She set a pillow behind the little girl's head before tak-

ing a bright blue afghan off the back and spreading it over the fussy *kind*. Olivia turned her face toward the cushion and continued to sob. No, she wasn't crying, Katie Kay realized, appalled. Olivia was gasping for breath.

When two applications from Olivia's inhaler didn't help, Katie Kay looked from the little girl to the stairs. Should she disturb Gemma? If Olivia had a cold, as they'd suspected earlier in the week, keeping her *mamm* away would be wise.

But Katie Kay's mind was made up for her when Olivia coughed so hard she almost vomited. After giving the little girl a spoonful of honey to ease her sore throat, she ran up the stairs, taking two at a time.

She opened the door but didn't wait for Gemma to reply. Throwing it open, she said, "Gemma, I'm sorry to disturb you."

Pushing herself awkwardly to sit on the mussed bed, Gemma rubbed her eyes as if she were no older than her daughter. "You don't need to apologize. What's wrong?"

"It's Olivia. She's feeling worse than yesterday."

"There's another bug going around the school. DJ probably brought it home to her, and with her resistance down, she caught it. Let me check her."

"If it's contagious, maybe you should stay away from her. You don't want to get sick, too. Not at this point in your pregnancy."

"I've been exposed already."

Katie Kay nodded, realizing Gemma was right. She helped Gemma out of bed and then followed her into the living room. Locking her fingers together in front of her, Katie Kay murmured an almost-silent prayer that Olivia was already taking a turn for the better.

She knew her prayer hadn't been answered when Gemma put her hand on the little girl's forehead and gasped. "She's burning up."

"We need to call your *doktor*. What's his name?"

Without looking up, Gemma said, "Dr. Stafford! His number is on the wall by the phone."

Rushing into the kitchen—which was splattered everywhere with the eggs, sugar and flour Jayden was continuing to stir on the table—Katie Kay grabbed the phone and punched in the number circled in red on the paper tacked to a bulletin board. The phone was answered on the second ring, and a computerized voice asked her to choose a prompt. The first choice was to push three if it were an emergency. She pressed the button.

Another voice came on the phone. This time a real woman's voice.

Katie Kay said as she hurried into the living room, "I'm calling for Gemma Donnelly. Her daughter, Olivia, is running a very high temperature. Here she is." She thrust the phone in Gemma's hand.

Going to the sink, Katie Kay dampened a clean cloth. She placed it on Olivia's head while Gemma spoke to the *doktor*'s office. The little girl was too quiet except for the rasps as she struggled to draw in another breath and let it out.

Gemma ended the call and then made another. This one to Sean, Katie Kay guessed when Gemma said the *doktor*'s office had told her to get Olivia to the closest hospital's emergency room right away.

Everything became a blur as Katie Kay packed a small bag with snacks and drinks and Olivia's favorite stuffed toy. Jayden kept asking what was wrong, and

she paused long enough to open the bag of chocolate chips and tell him to pour them into the bowl. That occupied him while she bundled Olivia into her warmest coat, giving Gemma time to get her own on.

Then the Plain and Simple Solutions van squealed into the driveway. Sean rushed in. He and Gemma took Olivia and left at a speed that wasn't safe on the twisting road.

Katie Kay sent prayers after them and closed the door. She kept praying while she helped Jayden stir the cookie dough and put the first tray into the oven. When she realized she'd forgotten to turn the oven on, she pulled out the sheet and set the oven to preheat. She turned on *Sesame Street* for Jayden; then she began trying to mitigate the damage a two-year-old with a spoon and a bowl of flour could do to a kitchen when nobody was supervising him.

She was rinsing the dishcloth for the umpteenth time to get wet flour out of it when the front door opened. She wasn't surprised when she heard Micah's voice. Drying her hands on a dish towel, she hurried into the living room.

Micah was giving Jayden a hug but looked at her and asked, "What's happened? Sean got a call at the job site and left. He shouted that he'd explain later. He couldn't then because it was an emergency. The next thing I know, the van is tearing up the road. What's happened?" He glanced around the otherwise empty living room. "Is Gemma okay?"

"She's fine. Olivia's sick. We called their *doktor*, and they told Gemma to take Olivia to the hospital."

"Hospital?" His face became ashen. "What happened?"

Katie Kay shrugged. "I'm not sure. As you know, she's been coughing the last couple of days, but it stopped late yesterday, so Gemma thought she was getting better. So did I until Olivia started having trouble breathing. That's why Gemma was told to get her to the hospital as fast as possible." She wrapped her arms around herself, wishing he'd hug her as he had Jayden. "Micah, they told her not to wait for 911 to respond because they were concerned there would be too much of a delay in the EMTs arriving."

"Ach!" He dropped to sit on the nearest chair. "I didn't realize it was serious."

"Sean told you it was an emergency."

"I know, but…" He raked his fingers through his dark hair. "I guess I didn't want to believe it."

That was the truth. Micah hadn't wanted to imagine something horrible happening to the family he felt as close to as his own. Having the *doktor* tell Gemma to get Olivia to the hospital faster than the ambulance could was frightening. No wonder Sean hadn't paused to explain what was going on.

Poor little Olivia.

As Katie Kay had, he'd thought the little girl had caught a cold on Saturday. He smothered a shudder as he thought of how he, Katie Kay and the *kinder* had gotten lost in the corn maze for hours. If they'd gotten out faster, would Olivia now be playing with her little brother and asking her customary dozens of questions?

God, be with her and with her family. And with those of us who love her, so we can be strong for her and her family. Please…

"How did you get here?" Katie Kay asked, interrupting his prayer.

Her face was so pale the flour on her cheek was barely visible. Her hands shook as if she were sick, too, but she guided Jayden to the sofa and gave him his favorite picture book to read.

Standing, Micah followed her into the kitchen where she began to scrub the flour-sprinkled table with the dishcloth. "I hitched a ride with one of the men on the construction crew working on another house. He dropped me off at the crossroads, and I hoofed it here as fast as I could. What can I do to help?"

She opened her mouth to reply but halted when the phone rang.

Micah reached it in a pair of steps. Clicking it on, he said, "Hello. This is the Donnellys."

"Thank the good Lord, Micah!" came Sean's voice through the phone. The connection was clear, so Micah could hear the quaver in his friend's words. "I'm sorry I had to leave you—"

"Don't worry about it. How's Olivia?"

What Sean had to say was to the point. The *doktors* had diagnosed her with pneumonia, which was complicated by her asthma, but they wanted to run more tests. "From what we're being told, they'll be keeping her here overnight."

"Don't worry," he repeated. "Katie Kay and I will watch the boys. How are you and Gemma holding up?"

"I wish she'd be more careful, but she's refused to leave Olivia's bedside. The staff has brought in a recliner so she can put up her feet because her ankles are swelling, and that's a bad sign in a pregnant woman."

"What can I do?"

"Pray, my friend. Pray."

"I'm already doing that."

"Don't stop. We could use all the prayers we can get right now."

He hung up the phone after his friend told him that he'd call back with any updates. Micah felt helpless, but thanked the *gut* Lord for the *doktors* and their knowledge.

By the time he'd finished telling Katie Kay what Sean had reported, the school bus was stopping in front of the house. DJ jumped out. She went to welcome the little boy home and explain his *mamm* had taken Olivia to see the *doktor*.

Amazed how she shared enough of the truth so DJ wouldn't panic, Micah watched while she listened to the boy talk about what he'd done at school. She acted as if nothing were more important than what he had to say. While she made lunch for them, Micah couldn't stop pacing. The boys ate, but he couldn't sit still.

Katie Kay halted him by stepping directly into his path. In not much more than a whisper, she said, "Go and be with your friend. Don't hurry back if you want to stay late at the hospital." She raised her voice so the boys could hear her say, "I can order pizza for supper. We'll be fine."

DJ and Jayden cheered at the idea of having pizza, and Micah knew she'd found the perfect way to distract them.

From him and his worry.

"I know you will be fine." His fingers rose before he could halt them and cupped her cheek. "I'm glad you're here, Katie Kay."

He'd expected her to pull away, but she smiled as she

said, "Me, too. Sean and Gemma have done so much for me. I hope I can repay them a bit now. Go on!" She gave him a playful shove.

His arms reached out and encircled her before he had a chance to think. But as soon as he drew her to him, he couldn't think of anything but how her blue eyes glowed with astonishment. That he'd been bold, or at the instantaneous sparks arcing between them?

"Katie Kay..." Her name was the second sweetest thing he could imagine on his lips. Her actual lips would be the very sweetest.

"Go to your friends, Micah," she murmured. "They need you."

"But we need to—"

"We'll have time for everything else later." She plucked his arms off her and eased away. "Plenty of time, but you're going to regret even a minute lost when you could be with Gemma and Sean."

She was right. He knew that, but it took every ounce of his will to leave her standing there while he went to the phone and dialed the number of the *Englisch* driver his family used. After Gerry told him the van would be there in less than five minutes, he hung up.

"You never learned to drive?" Katie Kay asked.

"I did, but it's been so long I don't want to chance getting into an accident on the way to the hospital."

Did she believe him, or did she suspect the truth? He was too distraught to get behind the wheel of an unfamiliar vehicle. Either way, she nodded and went to refill DJ's glass with milk.

As promised, Gerry's van reached the house minutes later. Micah glanced back as he lifted his coat off the peg and pulled it on. With a strained smile, she mo-

tioned for him to hurry so he didn't keep Gerry waiting. She was trying to be brave, but he knew she was as heartsick as he was that Olivia had to spend the night at the hospital.

He wanted to tell her it would be okay, but he wasn't sure if it would.

Chapter Twelve

Though it was beginning to get dark, the porch light was on when Micah climbed out of the van in front of the Donnellys' house, thanked Gerry and headed up the walk past the three pumpkin figures the *kinder* had started. They didn't have any faces yet, and he wasn't sure when Sean would be able to help the boys finish them.

Micah moved as if he'd aged a hundred years in the past few hours. When he discovered the door was locked, he fumbled in his coat pocket for the ring of keys that included the one for the Donnellys' door. He hadn't expected he'd need it. He was glad he had the key because otherwise he would have had to ring the doorbell. Sean and Gemma never locked their door. In fact, nobody he knew did, but he guessed Katie Kay had picked up the habit while she lived in Lancaster.

Was she trying to keep out strangers, or did she fear someone she knew might come to the house while she was alone with the *kinder*? He wished he could meet Austin, the *boppli*'s *daed*. No, not meet him. Observe him from a distance. Micah wasn't sure if he could

withhold his opinions if he came face-to-face with the man who had no intentions of honoring his obligations to her and her *boppli*.

He grimaced. Thinking about Austin made him feel lousier…if that was possible after the visit to the hospital room where little Olivia was hooked to oxygen, straining for each breath. Her face had been colorless, and her parents' had been almost as gray.

There were a half-dozen double rooms in the pediatric wing of the hospital, and most had at least one *kind* in it. Seeing sick *kinder* was discouraging, but he'd said a prayer for each as he walked along the quiet hallway. The nurses' hushed voices and the incessant beeps of medical machines had been the loudest sounds.

Opening the Donnellys' door, he winced when a hinge squeaked. The noise would have been muffled in day-to-day life with three active youngsters, but in the hush it was as loud as a cat screeching after having its tail trod on.

Katie Kay was sitting on the couch, rubbing her eyes as he walked into the living room. Her tousled hair fluttered around her face, and there was a mark on her left cheek where the button on a pillow had been pressed against it. She must have been resting. *Gut.* They couldn't forget in the midst of the emergency that she was pregnant and needed her rest, too.

Looking past her, though he wanted to let his eyes linger on her adorable mussiness, he was surprised to see the boys coloring at the kitchen table. They waved to him and went back to their crayons.

"They're being quiet," he said as he shrugged off his coat and hung it before entering the living room.

"There's a first time for everything." She tried to stifle a yawn but failed.

Should he stay overnight to help her with DJ and Jayden? That might cause more trouble for Katie Kay. A young unmarried woman, even one who was pregnant, should not have a bachelor in the house with her. They wouldn't be alone, but two little boys wouldn't be considered adequate chaperones. It wasn't as if Sean and Gemma had a *dawdi haus* attached to their home that would offer countenance to the circumstances.

But he couldn't leave her alone. He wasn't going to be like her ex, who'd left her with the tough task and gone merrily on his way.

"How is Olivia?" she asked before he could figure out what to do.

"She's a sick little girl." He sat on the arm of the overstuffed chair. He didn't trust himself to sit closer to her. The yearning to hold her echoed through him with every beat of his heart. "As Sean told me earlier, they're pretty sure it's pneumonia, but they want to make certain there isn't something else wrong because she went downhill so fast. Even for someone with asthma."

"Poor, sweet *kind*." Pushing her hair behind her ears, she asked, "Will you pray with me, Micah?"

"That's the best idea you've had in a long time."

She slid off the couch and turned to fold her hands on the cushion as if it were a church bench. Kneeling beside her, he bowed his head and continued the prayer he'd been repeating over and over on the way home from the hospital. *Heavenly Father, please bring Your healing to Olivia and let all of us who love her know the comfort of Your presence.* Until Katie Kay put her hand over his, he didn't realize he'd spoken his request aloud.

"I'm sorry if I intruded on your prayers."

"Don't be sorry," she whispered. "What you said was perfect. *Danki*."

She got to her feet as the boys argued over which one of them got to use the red crayon next. Settling that debate, she opened the fridge. "How about I heat up some cider?"

"It's late," Micah replied.

She glanced at the clock on the wall beyond the television set. "It's only 5:30."

Micah wondered how the day could have gone so slowly. "I feel like I've lived a full week today."

"I know. Waiting slows a clock's hands to a standstill. The day my *mamm* died was one I thought would never end." She shook herself and forced a smile. "Would you like some warm cider?"

"*Ja.* Sounds like a *gut* idea."

Minutes later, she handed him a steaming cup. She put an ice cube in each plastic glass of cider before she gave them to the boys. When she picked up her own cup, he gestured toward the living room. She went in with him and sat on the rocker beside the sofa.

Neither of them spoke as the steam from the cups rose in front of their faces. He didn't need to see her expression to sense her melancholy. He understood too well, because he loved his partner's *kinder* as if they were his own and he'd seen Katie Kay grow close to the whole family.

"I'll call in the order for pizza," she said. "It'll probably be ready in about a half hour."

"I'll get it. The Pizza Palace isn't far from here."

"As long as you can be quick. I don't want the boys staying up late. Jayden's already been asking when his

parents will be coming home. I'm not sure either boy believes me when I say Gemma and Sean will be here as soon as they can."

"It's the truth."

"But not the truth they want to hear." She took a sip and then sighed. "I hope they will go to bed for me. They've done it before when Gemma's been tired, but they knew she was here."

"I can stay and help."

"Isn't Sean planning on you doing his work as well as yours tomorrow? You need to get your rest."

He laughed tersely. "I'm not going to sleep while I'm waiting to hear the news about Olivia. I might as well walk the floor here as at home, where I'll keep *Mamm* and the rest of the family awake."

"I can't argue with that." Looking into her cup, she said, "This isn't the time, but I don't know when we'll have any quiet again. I wanted to talk to you about what you said the day we went to the hardware store. You mentioned I always say *the boppli*, not *my boppli*. Remember?"

"Ja." He waited for her to continue because he wasn't sure why she'd brought up the uncomfortable subject now.

"The answer is simple. I'm afraid to love the *boppli*."

He hadn't expected her to say that. "Why?"

"Because if I love the *boppli*, what will I do if I have to give him or her up?"

"You've decided to surrender your *boppli* for adoption?" He almost choked on each word. Why hadn't she told him that she'd made the tough decision? He'd thought she trusted him enough again to discuss the future of her *kind* with him.

"No, but I've got to face the facts. Austin is the *daed*. If he wants custody of the little one, an *Englisch* judge could decide in his favor."

"But I didn't think he had a job to provide for a *kind*."

"He does. Off and on." Her mouth hardened. "Now that he can't depend on my tips and paycheck, he'll have to get a steadier job. His roommates won't let him sponge off them for very long." She blinked, and he realized she was struggling to hold back tears. "Even if it's not great, if he has any job at all, it's more than I have."

"But you're the *boppli*'s *mamm*. And Austin abandoned you on the side of a road in the dark on a rainy night."

"I don't know if a judge would take that into consideration."

"Why not? You and the *boppli* could have died if someone hadn't seen you or if you had caught a cold as Olivia has and become sick." He put his cup on the end table with such a thump the boys stopped talking in the kitchen. "I wish I could tell your Austin—"

"Not mine. Not anymore."

As if she hadn't interrupted, he kept going. "I'd like to tell him what I think of him." He shoved himself to his feet. "Face-to-face, man-to-man." He snorted a taut laugh. "Man-to-lizard, because no decent man would abandon his *boppli* as he has."

She jumped to her feet. "Don't joke about that, Micah."

He was taken aback. Was she defending the cur who'd treated her and her *kind* with such cruelty?

He realized how wrong he was when she added, "He isn't a man you can talk sense to, so please don't joke about it."

"I'm not joking. I would like to tell him what a mistake he's made."

"No, Micah! Promise me you won't do that." She grasped his arm. "Austin likes nothing better than to beat someone up. He bragged about the fights he got into." Stepping closer, she gazed with entreaty at him. "Promise me, Micah."

"Plain folk don't take pledges."

She copied his derisive snort. "Really? I've heard you tell Sean's kids you'll do something for them the next time you come over, and you do."

"Don't worry, Katie Kay. The chances of Austin and I meeting are pretty slim." Not giving her time to answer, he said, "As for tonight, Sean has an air mattress in the attic. I'll use that. I won't sleep much anyhow. Sean said I could check in on Olivia every few hours by calling his cell phone, and I'm going to do that."

"That sounds *gut*. If—"

The doorbell rang, and Micah glanced out the window. Who could it be? As far as he knew, The Pizza Palace, the village's sole pizza restaurant, didn't offer delivery. And they hadn't ordered yet.

His eyes widened when he saw a gray-topped buggy parked in front of the house. Not his. It was in the driveway. Who…?

Another vehicle was pulling into the driveway and stopping by his. When a woman stepped out of the first buggy, she was carrying a large basket and a padded container. Both were filled with food, he knew. It was the Amish answer to any crisis. *Komm* to offer assistance and prayer and bring food. No birth or funeral or wedding or church Sunday passed without women delivering food to share.

But that was among the plain folk. Why were these two women—no, make that three women because two women emerged from the second buggy—coming to the Donnellys' house with food? The Amish helped their *Englisch* neighbors in the midst of a disaster like a fire or a flood, but he hadn't expected to see his neighbors coming to his partner's door tonight.

They must have heard about Olivia being taken to the emergency room at the hospital. He was amazed at how fast news spread among the Amish, even without phones or internet or social media, but that didn't explain why they were at the Donnellys' house.

"Katie Kay—"

"No!" She rushed into the kitchen and toward the laundry room. "I can't answer the door. If one of them sees me, they'll recognize me."

"You've been hiding long enough. You need to make up your mind one way or the other."

"I can't." Her voice broke. "Not yet. Not when these *kinder* need me."

He started to retort that she was using the boys as an excuse, but then, as he looked at her strained expression, he knew she was speaking the truth. She hadn't always since she returned from Lancaster; yet she was being honest now. Another change. Was she being changed by her time with the Donnellys and him? He'd like to think that, but he didn't want to fool himself about her again. Sean's favorite *Englisch* saying raced through his head over and over.

Fool me once, shame on you. Fool me twice, shame on me.

The doorbell rang again, and Micah knew he couldn't stand there until she saw sense. Grumbling at her stub-

born inability to decide, he walked to the door. He heard the laundry room door closing as he opened the front one.

He'd recognized the caramel-colored horse pulling the buggy parked in front of the house. And he knew the woman standing on the steps, offering him a covered dish wrapped in pale blue towels.

"Do you want to come in, Cinda?" he asked.

Cinda's husband, Atlee Bender, was a minister in the district where Micah lived. "I must get home to my family," she said, "but I heard about the sick *kind* and how you're helping. I hope your friend's boys will enjoy these noodles as much as mine do."

"Danki," he said as he took the warm casserole from her and the basket redolent with the aroma of freshly baked bread. "It's kind of you to deliver this."

"You're welcome, Micah. We will be praying for the little girl." Not giving him a chance to say more, she raised her black shawl over her bonnet of the same color and walked away into the windy evening. As she climbed into her buggy, another was pulling into the driveway.

For the next hour, Micah was kept busy answering the door as, one after another, the members of the *Leit* arrived at the house with food. Some brought one dish; others delivered food from themselves and from their extended families. DJ helped him carry the gifts into the kitchen. Even Jayden lent a hand when Micah could entrust him with something that couldn't break if dropped. The fridge was soon full, and bowls were stacked high on the kitchen table and counter. As he thanked each person for their time and the food, as well as for their prayers for Olivia's health, he didn't

keep track of who had brought what. He would see the dishes were returned on a church Sunday, and each family would collect their own. No one expected praise for their generosity or the food he was certain would be delicious.

Darkness fell, and the last buggy was rolling toward Paradise Springs as Micah closed the door with his shoulder. He balanced a pie in one hand. *Snitz*, by the aroma of apples and cinnamon. In the other he held a basket covered by a miniature quilt. He guessed, though the food had been delivered by his neighbor Fannie Beiler, the pie had been made by *Mamm* and the little quilt sewn by his sister-in-law, Leah.

His eyes widened when he saw Katie Kay behind him. She held out her hands, and he handed her the food. When DJ stood on tiptoe to see into the basket, she tilted it enough so he could see the blueberry and cranberry muffins beneath the tiny quilt.

"Can I have one?" he asked.

"Me, too!" Jayden wasn't able to peek into the basket, but he wanted whatever his brother was getting.

"Supper is soon," Micah began.

"You might as well start," Katie Kay said with a warning glance at him, "by choosing one muffin each. Just one. Okay?"

The *kinder* cheered, and he knew she'd made the right decision. The little boys needed to have something to help take their minds off why their sister and their parents weren't there.

She gave him the pie as she knelt so each *kind* could select a treat from the basket. The boys pondered the decision as if the rest of their lives depended on it.

Micah remembered times when he and his twin had

been presented with a similar choice. They could spend five minutes or more trying to decide between a chocolate cupcake with white frosting and a white cupcake with chocolate frosting. *Mamm* never rushed them, letting them choose on their own.

Exactly as Katie Kay was doing with Sean's boys.

When DJ and his little brother were perched on their chairs, eating their before-supper treat, Katie Kay began to sort out the food. She put dishes in the fridge, rearranging what was already in there to make room. Others she stored in the freezer. Another few she set on the counter, but she didn't have enough space, so she had to stack others on top of dishes that could support them.

Micah looked around in astonishment. "I didn't expect them to bring this."

"You didn't?" She faced him, her face bright with a smile. "You have been spending too much time among the *Englischers*. You know the *Leit* never fails to appear with food or whatever else is needed when a family has troubles."

"But they came here. To an *Englisch* house."

She laughed. "Maybe you don't get it because you weren't raised in a bishop's house, but reaching out to those in need isn't based on whether the recipient is plain or not." She took his hands in hers and looked at him. In her eyes for the first time since she'd returned from Lancaster, he saw joy and contentment. "Don't you understand? Though the Donnellys are *Englisch*, Sean is your partner. It makes him a part of your community, and the *Leit* consider them part of their community, too, because you are one of them."

"Not a part of *your* community?"

She dropped his hands. "Let's enjoy this moment for

what it is, Micah. Can't you, just this once, think about now and stop worrying about the future?"

"I don't worry about the future much."

"You talk about it all the time! When we were walking out, you spoke constantly about the life you had planned for yourself. You only stopped talking about that when you began outlining the life you'd planned for us."

He stared at her, shocked. "I didn't realize. I was excited at the idea of what the future could hold."

"But if you look solely to the future, you're going to miss what's right in front of you. The life you have with your friends and your family now. You don't want to look back at this time and wish you'd treasured it more, ain't so?" She sighed. "Let me get supper for you and the boys. Why don't you go and bring down the air mattress? The boys will like watching you inflate it. Then we'll have our meal and see what the rest of the day brings, one minute at a time. Does that work for you?"

"*Ja.*"

"*Gut.*"

As she turned away, he didn't move. Again he was astonished at the realization that he was beginning to trust her enough to listen to what she had to say. Had he lost his mind? He'd asked himself that over and over, but this time he didn't have an answer.

Micah went to get the air mattress out of the attic and then checked that his horse was set for the night, while Katie Kay let the boys pick out which food they would have for supper, though she insisted they select a casserole, as well as dessert. Her own mouth watered while she watched them try to choose between the spice

cake and one of the half-dozen pies arranged in a double row on the counter between the stove and the fridge.

At last the boys settled on a cold spaghetti salad made with pepperoni and green peppers. She selected rolls and warmed them in the oven. DJ helped her set the table while Jayden went to watch for Micah.

The little boys chattered about the food they were going to have. She wondered if they'd be able to sit still long enough to eat. Most of the afternoon, the boys had been like balls bouncing in every direction and never coming to a complete stop. She'd been surprised they'd colored as long as they had.

When Micah entered the kitchen, bringing cold air with him, DJ and Jayden scrambled to get in their chairs and booster seats. She waited until Micah had taken off his coat and hat and scarf and hung them up. Once he was seated, she put a basket with the rolls in the center of the table and took her chair. The empty ones were a blatant reminder of the missing members of the family.

"Micah, why don't you say grace so we can get started?" she asked.

"*Say* grace?" He frowned, clearly questioning if she'd forgotten the Amish tradition of thanking God in silence.

"*Ja.* I think saying grace aloud tonight would be nice." She glanced at the two boys before looking at Micah again.

He nodded. "Very nice. DJ, Jayden, will you bow your heads while we thank the Lord for this *gut* food?"

Both boys complied. When Jayden reached out to take Katie Kay's hand and his brother's, hot tears filled her eyes. His short fingers trembled, and she wondered why they were trying to pretend nothing was wrong.

Micah took her other hand, and she raised her eyes to meet the worry in his. She wanted to remind him that God was with the Donnellys at the hospital, as well as with the four of them at the house, but saying that when the boys were listening might upset them more.

"*Danki*, Lord," Micah said, "for bringing us here tonight to enjoy the generosity of our neighbors. Let them know in their hearts how welcome and blessed their gifts are to this family. Watch over each of us tonight and bring us together again as soon as possible. Amen."

Katie Kay echoed, "Amen."

From the boys, she heard a smothered sniff and a half sob. She squeezed Jayden's hand and whispered, "Pass it on."

She saw DJ brighten when his little brother pressed his hand. Not giving them a chance to get lost in fear again, she scooped out servings of the cold spaghetti salad for the youngsters. Micah buttered them each a roll, and soon the kids were focused on eating.

Katie Kay did the same and found she was hungrier than she'd thought. She hadn't had more than a handful of crackers at midday. She didn't need the midwife telling her to eat wisely. She offered a silent apology to the little one inside her.

When Micah got up at the end of the meal and searched the counter, she asked what he was doing. "I thought we'd have my *mamm*'s *snitz* pie."

She stiffened. "Wanda was here? She didn't see me, did she?"

"She didn't come herself but sent a pie over in a cooler along with what her next-door neighbor and a couple of the other ladies along our road prepared." He

leaned one hand on the counter as he lowered his voice so the boys wouldn't overhear. "You can't hide forever."

"Now isn't the time to discuss this." She cut her eyes toward the table where DJ and Jayden were watching them, eager for dessert.

It was easy to see the reluctance clinging to Micah as he nodded. She longed to tell him she knew that he was right. She'd known it when she went to hide in the laundry room, but the words wouldn't emerge past her lips. Her emotions were as tangled as a basket of yarn.

Jayden didn't ask about his *mamm* and *daed* until Katie Kay had tucked him in after listening to the boys say their prayers. She tried to comfort him when he began to cry. She sat on his bed and put her arms around him. At the same time, his big brother, DJ, began to sniff and his lower lip quivered.

Micah didn't hesitate. He hugged the little boy and spoke so softly Katie Kay couldn't hear what he'd said. What mattered was that DJ did, and in a few minutes he wiggled beneath the covers.

Once Jayden saw his brother was willing to sleep, he stretched out, too, and Katie Kay drew the blankets over him again. She gave each boy a kiss on the cheek and promised to wake them when their parents and sister came home. She guessed they would be up at first light, long before the hospital released Olivia.

Making sure the night-light was on in the hall and the other one in the bathroom, she drew the bedroom door almost closed. She stood outside the room for a few minutes, but neither boy rushed out. Soon it was silent inside, and she hoped they'd found comfort in sleep.

She motioned for Micah to lead the way down. *"Danki,"* she said as she reached the bottom of the

stairs. "I'm not sure I would have been able to convince them to settle if you hadn't come in."

"You would have."

"Maybe." She paused with her hand on the newel post. "You're going to be a *gut daed*, Micah Stoltzfus."

"And you will be a *gut mamm*, Katie Kay Lapp."

Her fingers went to her slightly rounded abdomen. "Do you really think so?"

"Fishing for compliments?"

"I'm not looking for compliments. I'm looking for the truth." She sat on the sofa and looked at him. "I'll be truthful and say I'm not sure I'll be able to take care of this *boppli*. I left home in part because I was tired of tending to everyone else."

"I didn't realize that until you started mentioning a few things. I hope, if you go home, you'll find the situation easier to bear."

If you go home. Before this, Micah had insisted she should go home. Now he acted as if he doubted she'd make the choice.

The sudden urge to weep swept over her. There had been disappointment in his words. And why shouldn't he be disappointed in her? She was in herself.

Chapter Thirteen

If Micah had any lingering doubts about Katie Kay being a *gut mamm*, they would have vanished when she kept the boys to their normal schedule the next morning while she also got the laundry started. She didn't give them false assurances about their sister but also acted as if she believed everything would turn out for the best.

It wasn't an act, he realized, when she helped DJ put on his windbreaker and backpack. As Gemma did each day, she urged him to have a *gut* time at school and to listen to his lessons.

Suddenly DJ looked upset. When Katie Kay asked what was wrong, he motioned for her to bend toward him. He cupped his hand and began to whisper in her ear.

She hooked a finger in the kerchief she wore over her hair and drew it aside so she could hear him. When he finished, she smiled. "Don't worry. I'll take care of that, DJ."

The little boy gave her a grin and a hug that almost knocked her off her feet. As she went with DJ to the door, Jayden followed, asking for a hug of his own. She

lifted him and blew a kiss in his hair. He giggled and wrapped his short arms around her neck. With the little boys, Katie Kay went out to wait for the school bus.

Curious what DJ had whispered in her ear, Micah refilled his cup with *kaffi* before going to a window with a view of the front yard. Wind blew through the few leaves remaining on the trees and tugged at the black sweater Katie Kay wore over her jeans. She put up one hand to keep her navy kerchief from flying off.

The way she dressed matched how she stood between two communities—the plain one and the one inhabited by *Englischers*. Glancing around the modern kitchen with its electric stove, refrigerator and dishwasher reminded him how he spanned those two worlds himself, though he was committed to his Amish life. But he'd miss his interactions with the Donnellys and other *Englischers* if the *Leit* decided to change the *Ordnung* and prohibit a plain man from working with a non-plain man. That wouldn't happen, but it did show him that he wasn't different from Katie Kay in many ways.

With red lights flashing, the school bus stopped by the driveway. DJ hurried to get on board.

Katie Kay set Jayden down and held his hand while they waved to his brother until the bus rumbled to a start. When she walked with Jayden to the house, she swung their hands between them.

Micah edged back so she didn't catch him watching them. One thing was clear. All of Katie Kay's thoughts were focused on the *kinder*. Where was the proud woman who had insisted on commanding everyone's attention wherever she went? She wasn't the same person she'd been a year ago. With a wry laugh,

he acknowledged he wasn't the same person he'd been then either.

Katie Kay came into the kitchen accompanied by the sound of one of Jayden's favorite educational shows.

Micah couldn't restrain his curiosity longer. "What did DJ tell you?"

"He wanted to remind me that today was his turn to bring snacks."

"Snacks?"

She smiled. "Didn't your *mamm* ever send treats to school for the scholars?"

"*Ja.*"

"Gemma told me it's the same in *Englisch* schools. The parents take turns sending in a healthy treat for snack time."

"*Mamm*'s treats were sweet rather than healthy."

She laughed. "I think DJ's classmates would prefer Amish cookies or cupcakes or pie squares, but his teacher insists on healthy snacks. The last time Gemma went shopping, she got grapes and celery and carrots for him to take in. Once they're cut up, they'll make great finger food snacks for the scholars."

"I'll drive you over to the school."

"*Danki.* I was going to ask how to get there. DJ's directions were pretty confusing."

Whatever Micah might have said was forgotten when the phone rang. Reaching for it, he heard Sean's exhausted voice on the other end. There was nothing new to report because Olivia's condition hadn't changed. Gemma wanted to let Katie Kay know it was DJ's turn to bring snacks.

"All taken care of," Micah reassured his friend.

Relieved, Sean said he'd call later in the day to

give them an update. When Micah told his partner he planned to stop by the hospital again that afternoon, he heard gratitude in Sean's voice.

"You are a *gut* friend," Katie Kay said when he hung up the phone. "Sean and Gemma are blessed to have you." She opened the fridge door before he could reply he wasn't the only one they were depending on, but he wasn't sure how Katie Kay would take his words. The girl who had coveted compliments was a woman who seemed embarrassed by them.

Within the hour, Katie Kay had the fruit and vegetables prepared. She helped Jayden with his coat while Micah hitched Rascal to the buggy.

The little boy squirmed on the seat, excited about riding in the buggy to his big brother's school. He let out a cheer when the low, red brick building came into view. Katie Kay warned him to be quiet when they went inside, and he pretended to zip his lips closed. Micah wondered how long the *kind* would remember his promise.

Checking in at the office, they were directed to a room a couple of doors down the hall. Micah opened the door, and every student in the room turned to stare at the door. DJ ran to them. Taking them by the hand, he tugged them into the room.

He turned and announced, "This is my daddy's friend Micah and his friend Katie Kay."

Micah hid his chuckle when he saw Katie Kay's cheeks flush a pretty pink as speculation bloomed in the teacher's eyes. She should recall if a kindergarten teacher took everything a *kind* said as the truth, then the teacher was going to have to swallow a lot of tall tales.

"This is the first time we've ever had our morning snacks delivered in a buggy," said the teacher as

she came to collect the trays covered with aluminum foil. "Thank you for bringing them. Will you be picking DJ up? I know his parents have given you approval to do so."

"No," he said. "He should come home on the bus."

"All right." She hesitated and then said, "DJ told us his little sister is ill."

"*Ja*, she is," Katie Kay replied. "That's why we brought the snacks instead of Gemma. We'll let her know you were asking about Olivia."

"Thank you." The teacher opened her mouth, then closed it and gave them a smile before turning to her students. "Let's tell DJ's brother and his friends thank you for bringing us snacks."

"Thank you," said the scholars as one.

Jayden was reluctant to leave. His gaze focused on an easel with paints beside it. Micah herded the little boy ahead of him out of the room. As soon as they emerged into the crisp day, Jayden began chattering like a blue jay about everything he'd seen and asking when he could go with DJ to school.

Katie Kay answered each question until the *kind* became fascinated with watching cars and trucks pass the buggy. He jerked his arm up and down, and he grinned when one of the tractor-trailers blew its horn. Fortunately Rascal wasn't bothered by the noise.

"DJ's teacher seems nice," Micah said as he turned them off the main road. He didn't have to watch for the big trucks so he glanced at Katie Kay. "But I could tell she wanted to ask us a bunch more questions."

"*Englischers* are curious about plain folk." She smiled. "Otherwise, there wouldn't be so many of them

spending their vacations in Lancaster County. You must get plenty of questions from your clients."

"Not really." He rested his elbows on his knees and held the reins loosely. "Most of them, whether they're Amish or *Englisch*, are interested in getting the work finished. That's what I get questions about. Is it okay if I drop you off at the house and then head over to the hospital?"

"Of course." Her smile warmed. "I don't think I could stop you from being with your friend."

He looked away. She wasn't right. He could think of a reason to remain with Katie Kay, but he'd be a fool to kiss her again and risk his heart once more.

Fool me once, shame on you. Fool me twice, shame on me.

When, the following day, Micah said he wasn't going to work again, Katie Kay was relieved. Throughout the night while she tried to get the boys to go to sleep, she worried about Micah being on a roof when his thoughts were elsewhere. A single wrong step, and he could have been heading to the emergency room, too.

Only an hour before dawn, Micah had convinced the little boys to sleep on the air mattress with him. She doubted he got any sleep, because his eyes were shadowed with deep gray arcs. She'd snatched less than an hour herself before getting up to make breakfast.

As they were finishing the meal, sharing more of the freshly made bread delivered to the house, Micah asked the boys if they wanted to help him clean out the van after he pulled it into the garage. She was pleased that he realized the wind was too strong and cold for the little boys to spend much time outside. Nobody spoke

of DJ going to school because the *kinder* were dragging with exhaustion.

She waited until the little boys had followed Micah outside and then she found the phone number of the school. The woman who answered said that if DJ stayed home more than a couple of days, they would make arrangements to get his lessons to him.

"Tell Gemma and her husband that we're praying for them and their little girl," the woman said before hanging up.

Katie Kay's fingers lingered on the phone as she set it in its cradle. Those simple words offered such comfort, and she'd make sure she passed them on to Gemma and Sean. Katie Kay hadn't caught the name of the woman on the phone, but she guessed Gemma would know.

Hoping that working with Micah would calm the boys enough so they'd take a nap later, Katie Kay did the breakfast dishes and cleaned the house. She was surprised how much she enjoyed taking care of a home when she wasn't being criticized for missing a cobweb or leaving dust on a table. For the first time, she began to imagine what it would be like to have a house and family of her own like Gemma did.

And a husband, too, to complete the happy picture?

A sigh drifted from her as she stopped the vacuum and began to reel up the cord. Who would want to marry her when she carried another man's *kind*?

Micah had offered, and she'd turned him down. He'd told her he wouldn't ask her again.

What a mess she'd made of her life! All her hopes of experiencing things she couldn't while among the *Leit* taunted her. She'd gotten her wish but in ways she'd never reckoned.

Katie Kay flinched when the doorbell sounded through the house. Who could it be? She glanced out a nearby window and didn't see a buggy. Inching closer to another window with a view of the porch, she gasped when she saw the tall redhead reaching to push the doorbell again.

Rushing to the door, she threw it open. "Cherokee! Come in. What are you doing here? Why didn't you call to let me know you were coming?"

"Because I don't have a phone number for you." Cherokee wrapped her in a warm embrace.

Curvy was the best description of Cherokee Smith, who dated Austin's best friend Vinnie. Though Cherokee had never said, Katie Kay suspected she came from a wealthy family. The redhead never seemed to wear an outfit more than once, and her clothing was in the latest style from the fashion magazines she'd shared with Katie Kay while the men were watching sports or sitting on the stoop to smoke.

Today she'd draped gold bangles around her wrists, as well as a trio of necklaces over her black turtleneck sweater. Her earrings were large and gaudy with bright gems that might be costume or real. Katie Kay had no idea.

"How did you find me?" Katie Kay asked.

"Vinnie saw the license plate on the van you were driving." Cherokee winked as she added, "I had a friend do a little digging, and he found this address."

Katie Kay suspected Cherokee's friend wasn't involved with any type of law enforcement, but decided she didn't want to know why he had access to such information. She motioned toward the living room. Her friend began talking as fast and nonstop as Jayden had

in the buggy yesterday. Unlike the little boy who'd been positive about the idea of going to school like his big brother, Cherokee listed every reason she had to be miserable.

Sitting on the sofa after she'd moved aside the afghan as if it were a soiled diaper, Cherokee said, "The biggest problem is you aren't around to keep Austin under control."

"I never was able to do that."

"Maybe you didn't think so, but he acted less immature when you were around. Until he found out you were..." Her gaze focused on Katie Kay's abdomen. Looking away, she added, "Then he became more of a jerk than ever."

"I'm sorry."

"*You* don't have anything to be sorry for. I wish Vinnie would spend less time with him and more time with *my* friends. He says they don't want to talk about anything interesting, and they don't like him because he drinks too much and yaks about sports all the time."

Katie Kay tried to relate to such problems, but it was impossible. She hadn't realized how far behind she'd left her life in Lancaster and the group of young adults who could hardly be called friends. They quarreled and made fun of others when they weren't around. She'd felt uncomfortable but hadn't defended anyone. Shame flooded her while Cherokee continued to complain about people Katie Kay knew and some she didn't.

When Cherokee halted in the middle of a word, her mouth dropping open, Katie Kay started to ask what was wrong. The eager voices of DJ and Jayden burst into the room as the boys ran to where she sat on the rocker. They talked at the same time, each trying to be

heard, about Micah letting them help him sort out the nuts and washers stored in the van.

But the boys weren't who had caught Cherokee's attention. Behind them, Micah leaned one shoulder against the doorway. His gaze was focused on his partner's sons, and Katie Kay couldn't mistake the expression in his deep blue eyes. He wanted little ones of his own, *kinder* he could teach as he was Sean's boys.

"Who's that?" Cherokee asked, and Micah pushed away from the wall, his easy pose vanishing.

Katie Kay stood. "Micah, we have company. *Komm* and let me introduce you."

Micah walked toward her. She ignored the questions visible on his face because she couldn't answer them while Cherokee and the boys were listening.

"This is my friend Cherokee," she said, hoping her voice didn't shake. "Cherokee Smith."

If Micah was as shocked by the woman's name as Katie Kay had been the first time she'd heard it, nothing showed in his smile. "Nice to meet you, Cherokee."

"Nice to meet *you*." Cherokee eyed him with candid admiration before giving him a slow, appreciative smile.

Katie Kay curled her fingers so tightly her fingernails cut into her palms. She almost gasped at the strength of her irritation at how Cherokee was flirting with him. Cherokee had a boyfriend. She didn't need to intrude on…

Intrude on what? her rational mind demanded. It wasn't as if she and Micah were a couple. Still, she couldn't halt the jealousy searing her veins like liquid flame.

And the guilt. When she'd flirted with guys, had Katie Kay irritated other women as Cherokee was her?

She'd never considered how other girls felt. Probably because she knew her flirting didn't mean anything.

Maybe Cherokee's didn't either. Thinking that failed to ease the fire of jealousy within her. She had no idea how to douse it, and it made her uneasy. Only someone in love could be jealous, ain't so? And she wasn't in love.

She gulped as she glanced at Micah, and their gazes collided. The heat in his eyes urged her to melt right into his arms.

No! No! She couldn't be in love with him. She'd told him *twice* she didn't want to be involved with him. *Twice*! And now…

But she couldn't ignore how quivers raced through her each time his hand brushed against her, even just in passing. And his eyes, which could alter from storm-blue to the crystalline of a summer sky, invited her to find out if her memory of his kiss was as *wunderbaar* as she remembered.

She was grateful when Cherokee spoke again, freeing Katie Kay from her thoughts.

"Are these your little boys, Micah?" Her friend's grin broadened.

"No," he said. "Their parents are at the hospital with their sister, who has pneumonia."

Cherokee instantly grew serious. "Oh, I'm sorry. Is she going to be okay?"

"Ja," Katie Kay said, aware of the little boys listening to every word.

Micah excused himself and the *kinder*, so he could put an end to the conversation. She was glad when they returned to the kitchen to grab pie squares before heading to the garage.

Cherokee walked to a window. She whistled. "I understand why you didn't bother to come back, Katie Kay. Don't tell Vinnie I said this, but you've traded up. Your buddy Micah is swinging a heavy tool belt into the van as if it doesn't weigh anything. Nice muscles on that farm boy."

Katie Kay sat on the rocker, hoping Cherokee would take the hint to return to her chair. As her friend sat across from her again, Katie Kay asked, "Why did you drive here by yourself? I've heard you say too many times to count the countryside gives you hives."

"Why am I here?" Cherokee's eyes widened. "I thought it was obvious."

"It probably is to someone who's had more than three hours sleep total for the past two nights. Micah's keeping the boys busy in the hope they'll sleep tonight and not wake up every few minutes calling for their parents."

"Poor little kids." Clasping her hands on the knees of her stylish jeans, she smiled as her bangles clattered together. "I came out here to see how you're doing. Austin treated you really, really bad. I couldn't believe it when I heard what he did to you. I didn't think he would be low enough to abandon you in the middle of nowhere."

"It actually wasn't far from my family's house."

She waved aside Katie Kay's words. "That doesn't make any difference. Austin was a jerk. Vinnie thinks so, too."

"Vinnie was with us that night."

"I know." Her mouth tightened into a straight line. "I didn't talk to him for two days after I heard, but then I realized he was scared Austin would do something to him, too. If he gets kicked out of the apartment, he

doesn't have anywhere else to go except to his parents' house and they won't let him come back."

Katie Kay lowered her eyes. What if she returned home and *Daed* and her sisters and brother turned her away as Vinnie's parents had him?

"Tell Vinnie not to bother arguing with Austin," she said to her friend, so she could ignore her own thoughts. "He'd be wasting his breath. I'm done with Austin."

"I'm glad you finally wised up."

"Wised up? I thought you liked Austin."

"I *love* Vinnie, and, unfortunately, Austin comes along as part of the package." Her mouth twisted. "If I could think of a reason Vinnie would listen to, I'd convince him to dump Austin. Austin is a spoiled brat who thinks only of himself. A real user and a loser, but I don't have to tell *you* that."

Had Katie Kay been any better when she'd fled Paradise Springs and gone in search of everything she thought she was missing out on? She'd heard opposites attract, but she and Austin had been too much alike.

Had been.

She dared to believe that while he lived in his extended childhood, doing as he wished and wheedling others to do what he didn't want to do, she'd grown up. Six months ago, she wouldn't have been willing to take care of someone else's *kinder*. She wouldn't have felt satisfaction in putting a *gut* meal on the table or cleaning up after the family.

"So…" Cherokee leaned forward. "Are you and cute Amish guy an item?"

She hoped that explaining how Micah had found her walking along the road in the rain would satisfy her friend's curiosity about him. But Cherokee kept ask-

ing questions. How long had Katie Kay known him? How had he gotten those great muscles? Had he asked Katie Kay out?

Katie Kay should have expected it, because her friend was obsessed with everyone's relationships, including movie stars she'd never met. Any attempts to change the subject were fruitless until Katie Kay happened to mention the plans her *daed* and Wanda Stoltzfus had made.

"Your father is getting married to Mr. Cutie-Pie Amish Guy's mother?" Cherokee sighed. "Does that mean he's off-limits to you? That would be a shame." Her grin returned. "You could grab him right now and find a justice of the peace and get married."

"I'm not getting married now."

Her eyes widened. "Oh? Because of the baby? Vinnie told me that Austin said you two agreed you were going to give it up for adoption."

"I haven't decided yet." The words tasted like sawdust in her mouth, and her stomach twisted at the idea of abandoning her *boppli*.

"You're going to need to. After all, the kid has got to be a complication when you're in love with a man who's not the baby's father."

"Who said anything about love?" she snapped and then wished she hadn't.

Cherokee chuckled. "Nobody, but I'm not stupid, girl! You never looked at Austin—not once—like you look at Mr. Cutie-Pie Amish Guy."

"His name is Micah!"

"I know, and you're quick to jump to his defense. That's proof you're in love with him."

Katie Kay hadn't ever realized Cherokee was so

perceptive. Usually she hung on to every word Vinnie spoke and didn't seem to have a single thought in her head. There were depths to the young woman that Katie Kay hadn't guessed existed.

"Is your dad having a big wedding? He's some honcho, isn't he?" Not giving her a chance to answer, Cherokee smiled and added, "Maybe you'll catch the bouquet and your Cutie-Pie Amish Guy will take the hint and propose."

"We don't throw a bouquet at an Amish wedding. There isn't a bouquet, though sometimes there are flowers on the tables during the wedding meal. More often, there are vases filled with celery." She smiled. "That's one of our most cherished wedding traditions."

When Cherokee asked about other traditions, Katie Kay was relieved. They talked a half hour longer before her friend had to leave so she could return to Lancaster at the time she'd told Vinnie.

"He gets worried if I'm late," the redhead added. "Isn't that sweet?"

Katie Kay made a sound Cherokee must have taken as an affirmative because her friend stood, gave Katie Kay a hug and went to the door. With a wave of her fingertips, she was gone.

Silence fell on the living room. Cherokee may not have intended them to, but her words reminded Katie Kay that *Daed* was getting married, and he would have a much bigger family to worry about. She didn't need to cause him extra distress. It was time for her to face her mistakes.

Long past time.

But how? She bowed her head and began to pray, hoping God would listen to her heart, which was con-

fused about everything in her life. About going home. About having the *boppli* on her own. And about what she was going to do, because Cherokee was right. She was falling in love with Micah.

Chapter Fourteen

Micah grabbed DJ and Jayden by the hands as Gemma's familiar van turned into the driveway later that afternoon. The boys yelled in their excitement at seeing their parents after two long nights apart, but Micah didn't release them until the van had stopped and the doors opened.

He smiled as Sean stepped between the boys and their *mamm* so they didn't hurt Gemma or the *boppli* in their enthusiasm. Hugging them both, Sean listened as they tried to tell him everything at once.

"We'll talk inside," Sean said, ruffling their hair. "Go with Mommy while I get Olivia."

Stepping forward to help, Micah waited until Sean lifted a swaddled Olivia out of her car seat. Micah shut the van's doors as the family surged as one toward the house. His hope to catch a glimpse of Olivia's face to see how she'd improved was foiled by the blanket.

The front door opened. Katie Kay's face was as bright with elation as the autumnal sunshine. She ushered everyone inside and then moved out of the way to let Sean carry Olivia to the couch.

The little girl looked weak, and she rasped as she

breathed, but she gave a weak smile at her brothers and Katie Kay and Micah.

While Sean set her down as if she were made of flower petals ready to blow away at the slightest breeze, Katie Kay assisted Gemma with her coat and getting to a comfortable chair. Katie Kay picked up another afghan as Sean covered Olivia with the one on the sofa. Draping the afghan over Gemma, she tucked it around her from waist to toes.

Feeling useless, Micah went into the kitchen and made *kaffi*. He brought two cups in and gave them to Sean and Gemma.

"Hope it tastes okay," he said with a weary smile.

"You made this?" asked his partner, not trying to hide his astonishment.

"Ja."

"Things have changed a lot since we've been gone, honey." Sean winked at his wife. "Who would have guessed we'd ever see an Amish man working in the kitchen? Katie Kay, how did you convince him to do that?"

Micah became uneasy when Katie Kay didn't answer.

To fill the silence that seemed oppressive to him, he said, "She made it clear if I wanted *kaffi*, I could make it myself while she was getting DJ off to school."

"I'm going to have to try that with Sean." Gemma laughed, but fatigue tainted the sound.

Katie Kay smiled but didn't speak while she watched the little boys go back and forth between their sister and their parents, happy to have them home again. When Sean put out his arms to keep Jayden from patting Ol-

ivia's cheek for the third time, Katie Kay wrapped her arms around herself and bit her lower lip.

What was she thinking? She'd been happy when Gemma and Sean had arrived with Olivia. Now Micah sensed a barrier like the one she'd thrown up the night she'd decided not to walk out with him any longer. That night, he'd been hurt and angry at how she shut herself off from him.

She was doing it again, and he had no idea why. This time would be different. He was going to find out the truth.

Just not today. He'd have to be patient, he told himself as he listened to the happily reunited family and thanked God that Olivia was alive and home.

As he sent up that prayer, he glanced toward Katie Kay. She was gone. After everything she'd done to help this family, why wasn't she celebrating with them?

Another question he didn't have an answer to. But Micah's plan got turned inside out, because just before dark, Katie Kay walked into the garage, where he was touching up the paint around the dent on Gemma's van. He rested the paintbrush on top of the open can and stood.

Without a greeting, she said, "Micah, I believe it's time."

Time? For the *boppli*? How could that be? Her stomach was so barely rounded that anyone who didn't know she was pregnant wouldn't suspect it. It couldn't be time for the *boppli* to be born.

"What?" He couldn't manage more than a single word as he wondered if he needed to call 911. Swallowing hard, he tried again. "The *boppli*—"

"It's not time for that." Her smile appeared and fled

so quickly that it might have been his imagination. "It's time for me to go home."

"Home?" He sounded like he was half-asleep, repeating her words without understanding what they meant.

"*Ja*. I want to go home to my family."

He wasn't certain if she or he was more shocked when he asked, "Are you sure?"

"You've been insisting I need to reconcile with *Daed* and the rest of my family. Why are you hesitating?"

"Because I want you to be sure you're ready for what may happen."

"I'm not. I can't be, but it's time. I saw the expressions on Sean's and Gemma's faces when they came home to their boys, and I knew how much they'd hated being apart from their *kinder*. How painful it was for them!" Her voice lowered almost to a whisper. "And how painful it was for DJ and Jayden to be without them." She shook herself and squared her shoulders. "I've put my family through enough. I figured I'd go over there tomorrow and let them know I'm nearby."

"You don't plan to return home for *gut*?"

"I don't know." A faint smile eased her taut lips. "You asked me to make a decision, and so far all I've decided is I need to tell them where I am. I haven't thought beyond that."

"Why?" He'd thought the toughest choice would be deciding to go home, not whether she'd stay or not.

"The problems I left behind are still there."

He was delving into what wasn't his business. Or was it? Her family was soon to be attached to his. "Problems?"

"Mainly one. The fact I'll never meet the standards

set by Priscilla, something she reminds me every time we've talked since my *mamm* died."

"Priscilla? Is she the reason you left?"

"One of them. I got tired of her lambasting me about everything I did or didn't do."

Taking her by the shoulders, he looked into her sorrowful eyes. "Do you think you're the only one who's been the target of your sister's judgmental comments?"

Her head jerked up, the sadness replaced by amazement. "You, too?"

"*Ja*, and half the people our age in the district. She's careful to say nothing when Reuben's around, but she acts as if she's the sole authority on how everything should be done."

"I didn't realize that." Tears glistened on her lashes. "I thought I was the only one—"

"Trust me. You're not." He laughed. "Remember that when we go to Reuben's house."

"You're going with me?"

He brushed her soft golden hair from her face and framed her cheeks with his hands as he leaned toward her. "I wouldn't miss it for the world, Katie Kay. I always enjoyed taking you home."

Her lips parted to speak, but he silenced her with his mouth on hers. Maybe it was the right time to kiss her. Maybe it wasn't. Either way, he wasn't going to allow the moment to escape him again.

He thought she'd push him away, but she softened against him, and everything disappeared but her fingers sliding up his arms to encircle his shoulders. Time eclipsed to the last time he'd kissed her; yet it was as if he held her for the very first time as happiness envel-

oped him. She fit perfectly in his arms, as if she'd been made just for him.

She drew herself back, letting her fingers glide down to entwine with his. They stood face-to-face for a moment, and then she stood on tiptoe and kissed him on the cheek.

"I always enjoyed you taking me home, Micah," she whispered.

"Then—?"

She gave him no time to ask the obvious question: Why had she stopped walking out with him if she felt that way? She slipped her hands out of his and hurried out of the garage, leaving him more confused than ever.

Micah said nothing as Katie Kay worked hard to take care of the Donnelly family the next day. She'd spent the early part of the morning getting DJ off to school and making sure breakfast was ready for the rest of the family. Both Sean and Gemma stayed close to their daughter, checking her constantly until she got cranky at their smothering attention. At that point, Katie Kay insisted that they eat a sturdy breakfast before they sickened, too. She'd guessed, quite rightly, that neither Sean nor Gemma had eaten much at the hospital. Both of them looked almost as wan as their daughter.

While the hours unfurled and she prepared the midday meal and served it, Micah wondered if Katie Kay was using Olivia's homecoming as an excuse to defer her own. He hid his surprise—and his relief—when Katie Kay asked, late in the afternoon, if he'd be ready to leave in a half hour. When he assured her that Rascal and the buggy would be set whenever she wanted to go, she went upstairs.

He wasn't sure what she was doing until she came back down. He heard smothered gasps from the Donnellys and swallowed his own. Katie Kay was dressed in plain clothing.

Sean's and Gemma's surprise was because they'd never seen her wearing an Amish cape dress, but Micah had forgotten how pretty she was when she dressed plain. Her blond hair was in a miniature bun held in place by a handful of bobby pins beneath her *kapp*, and her cheeks were almost the same color as the warm pink dress she wore with a black apron that concealed her baby bump. Beneath the white *kapp*, her blue eyes seemed brighter. Instead of the jeans she'd worn since her return, her legs were covered in modest black socks, and she wore scuffed, black sneakers.

He said nothing as she thanked Sean and Gemma for welcoming her into their home. Both of them gave her a hug and wished her well before the *kinder* embraced her, as well.

Nodding his own thanks to his friends, he held the door for Katie Kay and followed her to the buggy. She climbed in without his help and remained silent while he got in, picked up the reins and gave Rascal the command to go.

The horse was eager to return to his warm stall, so he trotted along the road leading toward Paradise Springs. The Saturday traffic was light on the back roads, and Micah kept to them instead of risking the rush of cars and trucks on Route 30.

Almost ten minutes after the Donnellys' house had disappeared past a curve in the road, Katie Kay spoke for the first time. "*Danki*, Micah, for driving me."

"It's the least I could do, seeing as I didn't take you home a few weeks ago."

She glanced at him and away as the buggy wheels crunched leaves that had fallen from the trees by the fences. Smoothing her apron over her dress, she reached up to touch her *kapp*. "I shouldn't have cut my hair, but…"

When her voice faded, he looked at her. She appeared so nervous that, if he hadn't known the truth, he would have guessed she was going somewhere she'd never been before. His fingers settled on her hand to calm her.

"Reuben is going to be pleased to see you. He won't care you cut your hair."

"I hope you're right."

"I *know* I'm right, and so do you. Your *daed* lives the life he preaches."

"I know that, too." Her voice sounded dull, and he took his gaze from the road to check her again.

The last of the color had drained from her face, and she sat as tense and unsure as the night he'd discovered her walking along the road. Had something he said caused this change?

"What is it?" he asked, not willing to let her hide behind the wall she'd raised between them again.

"*Daed* does live the life he preaches. I've never been able to. It's another of the reasons I had to leave, Micah. I couldn't be the bishop's perfect daughter. I'm not quiet and proper and a role model for other daughters in my *daed*'s districts. In fact, I'm the opposite. Where I go, instead of peace, there's chaos."

"You're right about that." He didn't let his smile fall away when she glared at him. Resting his elbows on his knees as Rascal continued along the familiar road,

he glanced at her again. Longer this time. "Katie Kay, I've heard you talk many times about your little sister Sarann."

"She was the light of our family."

"But she was also a challenge for your family."

She frowned. "You know we didn't think of her that way. She was a blessing from God."

"Aren't you the same?"

"I'm not handicapped."

"No, you're not. At least not outwardly, but, like Sarann, you've been a challenge for your family. Do you think they love you any less than they loved Sarann?"

"Ja."

His shock at her answer must have been visible because she seemed to shrink into herself. Was this how she saw herself? Unloved by her own family? How could she think that when her *daed* had spoken well of her and was distraught when she left home?

Another bolt of astonishment struck him. Maybe she didn't know how Reuben loved each of his *kinder*. The bishop spoke of them often, admitting he couldn't hide his pride in his four living daughters and his son who helped him on the farm. Had Reuben told her that? Even if he hadn't, how could she miss how much her *daed* adored her and the rest of his family?

Realization struck him. She knew Reuben loved her siblings. She couldn't bring herself to believe he felt the same about the family's wandering lamb.

"Katie Kay Lapp," he said, "Reuben doesn't love you less than any of your siblings."

"I never said *Daed* doesn't love us."

"Then who?"

"Micah, it's not something I should be talking about beyond my family."

"But we'll soon be family. When *Mamm* marries your *daed*."

"Maybe, but we aren't family yet, and I've already said too much."

He had to accept her gentle chiding. It was true he was poking his nose where it didn't belong. He wondered if *Mamm* knew of this underlying cause for Katie Kay jumping the fence. Was it more than her older sister's pressure for her to be perfect? Curiosity about what had happened to sour Katie Kay on her family teased him, but he refused to ask. She was right. It was none of his business.

But that wouldn't stop him from trying to persuade her to tell him the truth.

Katie Kay was sure she'd forgotten how to breathe as Micah's buggy turned toward her *daed*'s house.

Toward home.

Her youngest sister, Marnita, was bringing in the laundry from the line that ran from the house to the main barn, and in the distance her brother, Lester, drove a team of five mules through a field. As the buggy drew to a stop by the white house, she saw Ina Sue, her other younger sister, walk past the kitchen window.

Where was *Daed*?

As if she'd shouted, *Daed* came striding from the barn. His bibbed denim overalls and knee-high rubber boots were covered with bits of hay and sawdust, a sign he'd been fixing something. He called a greeting to Micah, and she knew he'd recognized the buggy by the horse pulling it.

Micah took her hand and squeezed it, but he said nothing.

Katie Kay pushed open the door on her side. She climbed out and walked toward where her *daed* had stopped.

"*Daed*, it's…" Every word she'd practiced over and over fell out of her head as her *daed* stared as if he couldn't believe his eyes.

He looked old. Older than she remembered, as if she'd been gone for years instead of months. The lines in his face were gouged a bit deeper and his shoulders bent more. Was that a tremor she saw in his hands? The hands that had held the family's large Bible and had cradled a newborn as gently as a spring zephyr.

"Daed," she began again, trying to remember what she wanted to say first.

He strode forward and swept her into his arms and held her. She drew in the scents that had been a daily part of her life until the past few months. The smells of fresh air, hard work and the laundry soap the Lapps had used for as long as she could remember.

She clung to him, her eyes closed. If she opened them or moved a single muscle, the wonder of the reunion might disappear like the dreams she'd had of this moment. In the distance, she heard Marnita yelling for Ina Sue to come out of the house. Pounding feet rushed toward them and other arms were flung around her. She savored the embrace of the family she'd thought might be lost forever.

Daed stepped back but kept his eyes on her as the wrinkled planes of his face eased into a smile. Tears ran along his cheeks, falling into his beard. Marnita used her apron to wipe away her own, and Ina Sue leaned against her younger sister before whirling to pull Les-

ter into the family circle as he came running to learn why they were shouting.

"Katie Kay…" *Daed* whispered her name as if it were a prayer.

She realized it was, because he was thanking God for bringing her home. "*Daed*, I'm sorry. Please forgive me."

"There is no need to ask for forgiveness, my dear daughter. As Jesus told us in His parable of the man with two sons, when the prodigal son returned home, the whole family celebrated because the one who had been lost was found." He embraced her again. "Now *you* have found your way home, and you're here with your family, where you belong."

Her siblings joined into the group hug. She squeezed them, not wanting to let go of this moment or them.

"*Danki*, son," she heard *Daed* say and realized he was talking to Micah.

Katie Kay's sisters led her toward the house as Lester went to unharness the team and join them. Both of her sisters talked at the same time, reminding her of DJ and Jayden. As they stepped onto the porch, she glanced over her shoulder.

Happiness, greater than when she'd been in her *daed*'s arms, swept over her when she saw *Daed* with his arm draped over Micah's shoulders as they followed. Both of them were grinning like cats with a fresh bowl of milk.

She hated ruining their *gut* cheer, but she paused and turned to face them. She waited until they reached where she stood with her puzzled sisters. Watching her *daed*'s face, she whispered, "I'm pregnant, *Daed*."

"Your *boppli* is as welcome as you are here," he said

as if she'd announced she was making his favorite pie for supper.

Tears burst out of her as his words touched the part of her heart that had ached every hour she'd been gone. When he hugged her again, she heard the house door open and close. She saw her siblings had gone inside.

Micah started to do the same, but *Daed* put up his hand to halt him.

Realizing what *Daed* wanted to know, she said, "The *boppli* isn't Micah's." She pushed the rest of the truth out. "The *boppli*'s *daed* is *Englisch*."

"And where is he?" His voice was calm, but she heard the thunder of anger resonating beneath his words.

"Out of our lives, *Daed*."

He took a deep breath and let it out in a long, slow sigh. "Is this your decision, Katie Kay?"

Was it? Austin had thrown her out of his car and his life once he knew she was going to have a *boppli*. *"Ja, Daed,"* she replied, knowing it was the truth. "I made a mistake, but that doesn't mean the *boppli* needs to suffer its whole life for it."

"No *boppli* is a mistake." He cupped her chin and tilted her face so she met his eyes. "Each one is God's gift to us and the future."

"Danki, Daed. I needed to hear that."

He glanced again at Micah. "I'm sure I'm not the first one to tell you that."

"You're not," she whispered.

Without another word, *Daed* went into the house, leaving her alone with Micah.

Katie Kay wasn't prepared for the rush of shyness flooding her. She'd never been timid with Micah, but she was now.

He must have sensed that because he said, "I'm glad everything went well."

"You knew it would."

He grinned. "If I say *ja*, you'll think I'm saying 'I told you so.'"

"You have every right to."

"No, I don't." He became serious again. "I'd prayed for a *gut* homecoming for you, but only God knows for certain what's to come. We can only hope and pray."

"You are a *gut* man, Micah Lapp," she said as she had before. "And I'm glad you are my friend."

"Is that all we are? Friends?"

Through the early twilight, she felt the intensity in his eyes. She wished she could unsay her unconsidered words. What must he think of her calling him a friend when she'd kissed him so eagerly yesterday?

Before she could say anything, he walked to his buggy, climbed in and drove away.

She stood and watched as the buggy faded into the darkness, knowing she had hurt him worse today than she ever had in the past.

Chapter Fifteen

The bench wagon was parked in the yard when Sean dropped Micah off at the Stoltzfus farm the following Monday. Thanking his partner, Micah got out and waved as the van turned around before driving toward the road. The wagon must have arrived earlier. With most Amish weddings celebrated from late October until the end of the year, the bench wagon would be making many stops in addition to the homes where church Sunday services were scheduled to be held.

Inside it were the benches for the service, as well as extra dishes and flatware for feeding the *Leit* after worshipping. That wouldn't be enough for the large number of guests *Mamm* and Reuben had invited. He suspected most people would be at the house bright and early on the wedding day to enjoy their bishop's wedding.

But he could think of only one person who'd be attending.

Katie Kay.

He knew he shouldn't have stomped off when she called him her friend, but he felt as if he was reliving the past. As before, she'd kissed him and then she'd told

him she didn't consider him more than a friend. Well, it wasn't quite the same as before. Last time, she hadn't even wanted to remain friends.

He might be a coward, but he wasn't going to put his barely patched heart on the line and let her squash it like a bug.

Sean had been curious about what had happened, and Micah had told him how Reuben had welcomed his wayward daughter home. Nothing else. His partner had given him odd looks. Sean knew there was more to the story but respected him enough not to ask. Gemma was as circumspect.

Another barrier between him and the people who were important to him, and he hated it.

As he approached the wagon, he saw two of his brothers there. His twin, Daniel, and their older brother Jeremiah, the only Stoltzfus sibling besides Micah who didn't have a spouse or plans in the next few weeks to marry. Micah called a greeting, though he would have gladly walked past and sought the sanctuary of the room he soon wouldn't share with Daniel after a lifetime together.

"We figured helping Ezra get ready for the wedding was the least we could do," Jeremiah said with a smile.

Daniel added, "Which is why we're doing it."

Laughing along with his brothers and surprised he could pretend to be happy enough to laugh, Micah set his tool belt on the front porch. He opened the rear of the long wagon and began pulling out the benches. He handed benches, two or three at a time, to his brothers, who toted them into the upper level of the white bank barn. In a couple of weeks, they would be repeating the motions at Isaiah's house, a short distance down

the road. Isaiah's plans to marry Clara Ebersol and become the *daed* to two sets of irascible twins had been published the previous church Sunday. It hadn't been a surprise for anyone, because he and Clara had been taking care of the *kinder* since their parents' tragic deaths earlier in the year.

Daniel and his Hannah would be having their wedding before Christmas, giving the bride's relatives time to travel from New York State and other settlements to the west. They planned to keep the number of guests to a minimum because too much excitement would overwhelm her great-grandmother.

Micah would have been glad to work in silence, but his twin brother wouldn't have it. Daniel was happy to be in love, and he wanted everyone around him to feel the same.

"Have you talked to *Mamm* about whom you'll have the evening meal with?" Daniel asked as they toted a trio of stacked benches into the barn.

One of the favorite Amish traditions among newly married couples was arranging for their unwed guests to come into supper two by two and sit together through the evening. Courting couples dropped hints, so they would be matched. The rest were put together in the hope that the matchmaking would lead to them falling in love.

"No," Micah said in a tone he hoped his brother would realize meant the subject was closed.

Daniel either missed it or wanted to have his say. "You should talk to *Mamm* if there's someone special. Who knows? You could fall in love and get married, too."

"Love?" Micah sniffed his derision. "As far as I can

see, there's not much difference between that and in-fatuation."

"Really?" Daniel grinned at him. "You haven't fig-ured out the difference between them?"

"When did you?" he fired back, hating the envy puls-ing through him that Daniel had won the woman of his dreams and Micah had failed twice.

"About ten seconds after Hannah slipped into my heart." His expression softened as he spoke of his fi-ancée. "Is this about Katie Kay?"

"You know we aren't supposed to talk about the per-son we're walking out with."

"You aren't walking out with her, though the two of you spend more time together than some married cou-ples. When are you going to stop being a scaredy-cat and ask her to let you take her home?"

Knowing he had nothing to lose since Katie Kay had announced she wanted no more than friendship with him, he said, "I did. Last year."

Daniel's easy grin withered. "You never told me."

Micah realized he'd hurt his brother with his ret-icence. Growing up, the two of them had never had secrets from each other, and Daniel had been very up-front about falling in love with Hannah and her little sister and outspoken great-grandmother. Why hadn't he turned to his brother at the darkest point in his life?

"You were happy," he began and then halted himself before Daniel could reply. "No, that's not why I didn't say anything. I was humiliated when she told me to get lost. I didn't want to admit she'd dumped me."

"Because it would have made the breakup feel more final?"

"Ja." He sighed. "I've learned why pride is de-

nounced. It leads a man to do things he normally wouldn't."

"You are beginning to grow up, bro."

"Bro?"

"You *are* my brother, aren't you?"

"You've been spending far too much time with *Englischers*."

"And you've been spending a lot of time with Katie Kay from what I've heard. Why are you moping around? Because she's carrying another man's *boppli*? That didn't keep Joshua from marrying Rebekah."

Micah wanted to argue their oldest brother's situation had been very different. Rebekah's late husband had been Joshua's best friend, and Joshua had promised to look after her if something happened to Lloyd.

"It's complicated, Daniel," he said.

"Love is, but turning away from it is stupid. If you want it, you have to be willing to sacrifice everything to obtain it." Daniel walked out of the barn, leaving Micah to mull over his words.

The wedding was everything Micah could have wished for. It celebrated the love shared by *Mamm* and Reuben. All their *kinder* and *kins-kinder* were in attendance. A neighboring bishop listened to their vows to be with one another for the rest of their lives. Around the room, smiles broadened as the bride and groom returned to their seats after they were pronounced man and wife.

During the short wedding ceremony and the three-hour church service surrounding it, he'd been careful not to look in Katie Kay's direction. Envy wasn't an appealing emotion, and he didn't want her to see it on his

face. Yet he couldn't help wishing he'd been the one, instead of Reuben, pledging to love one woman forever.

Don't be pathetic, he chided himself as he had often in the past week. Even if Katie Kay was ready to stay in their community, she had plenty of choices for a husband. He'd heard whispered comments from other bachelors while they waited to go into the house for the service. Some of the remarks had been unworthy of a God-fearing man because they derided Katie Kay's jumping the fence and then returning without having to be called to account in front of the *Leit* for her sins. Those fools needed to remember that that happened when a baptized member left and was put under the *bann*. The shunning wouldn't end until that person atoned for breaking his or her covenant with the Lord and with the congregation.

Most of the unmarried men, however, had announced they would willingly overlook Katie Kay's sojourn among the *Englischers* if she were to give them the slightest sign she was interested in one of them. None of them, of course, knew how she'd walked out with Micah and the single *wunderbaar* kiss they'd shared then.

Or the latest one.

With a sigh, he acknowledged nothing had changed. Katie Kay remained the focus of men's attention wherever she went. She wasn't ready to settle down, or at least not with him. If the other guys knew she was pregnant, would they change their minds?

You didn't. The small voice of truth answered him swiftly. But, for once, the little voice was wrong. He *had* changed his mind about Katie Kay since learning she was going to have a *boppli*. Not because of the un-

born *kind*, but because he'd learned she was more than the flirt she'd portrayed well.

When the service was over, Micah gave *Mamm* a kiss on the cheek and shook Reuben's hand before moving aside to let others do the same. He glanced around the yard, where leaves had fallen to replace the ones they'd raked yesterday. Suddenly he felt more out of place than he had on the few trips he'd made with Sean into the city to meet with vendors.

He walked away from the happy guests, knowing he needed time to get his thoughts under control before he celebrated with friends, including the Donnellys, who'd been invited to the wedding dinner, and family...and Katie Kay.

The kitchen was busy with a half-dozen women who'd been asked to oversee the final preparation of the food for the wedding meal after the ceremony. Another group would step in and warm the leftovers for the evening meal. It was an honor to help for either meal, and Katie Kay was glad Wanda had picked her to work in the kitchen. It allowed her to keep a low profile.

If the other women had questions, they kept them to themselves as they worked to get food ready in time to serve three hundred guests. A few had been in the Stoltzfus kitchen since before dawn. Others, like Katie Kay, had joined them slicing bread and stirring chicken and stuffing after the exchange of vows.

Katie Kay was unwrapping sticks of butter to put on small plates, which would be placed on the tables by the young men and women acting as servers during the first seating. With so many guests, there would be at least three different servings.

"Let me help you," said a familiar voice in its usual icy tone.

Looking up, she saw her oldest sibling, Priscilla, carrying several more boxes of stick butter. Katie Kay said nothing as Priscilla set them on the table. They worked together in silence for several minutes.

Then Katie Kay said, "I owe you an apology, Priscilla. I haven't been fair to you."

"To me?" Her older sister stared at her in surprise that evolved into suspicion. "You've never worried about my feelings before."

"You're right. I've never worried about anyone's feelings but my own, because I was too wrapped up in my unhappiness to see beyond it."

"Why were you unhappy? Every boy in Paradise Springs and beyond wanted to walk out with you. Most of them probably still do. You don't have any reason to complain."

Katie Kay almost retorted that she wanted only one man to court her, but that was impossible now. She'd made such a muddle of everything. Micah had been honest with her the night she'd discovered she was pregnant. That night he'd told her he'd never ask her again to marry him. And why should he when she'd turned him down again?

She couldn't help pondering—for a moment—how different her life might have been if last year, she'd welcomed Micah's plans for their future instead of worrying about everything she might miss by spending the rest of her days with him.

Her sister didn't need to know how he'd planned a future with Katie Kay twice. Two very different futures but ones where they would have been together. As much

as Katie Kay ached to heal the wounds between her and her far-too-perfect sister, there were embarrassing matters she had to keep to herself. She wanted to believe the best of Priscilla, but her sister enjoyed gossiping. Katie Kay wasn't going to give Priscilla more fodder by telling her about the biggest mistake of her life.

No. Not one mistake.

The *two* biggest mistakes of her life.

"I was unhappy," Katie Kay said in the same near-whisper, "because I knew I couldn't ever be you."

Priscilla opened her mouth to retort, but no sound came out as she stared at Katie Kay in disbelief. Swallowing hard, she managed to say, "I don't understand."

"I think you do. You made everything look easy, and you were never satisfied until whatever you were doing was perfect. How could I hope to emulate that after *Mamm* got sick and died? I can't cook as well as you. I can't sew as well as you, and I can't keep house as well as you."

"I thought you weren't interested in doing anything but having fun."

"I wanted to help *Daed* and the rest of the family." She heard the stove timer go off. She opened the oven door and lifted out a tray of rolls and tilted it so the rolls fell into one of the baskets beside the plates of butter. Setting another tray in the oven to warm, she added, "But I knew everyone was comparing me to you, and I was well aware how far I fell short of being the bishop's model daughter."

"Just as I did." Priscilla's voice lost its hard edge.

"You? You were perfect."

"Far from it. I know how everyone expects the bishop's

kinder to be shining examples for their own families. Do you know why I tried hard to be perfect?"

"No." She'd never heard her older sister talk like this. "You made it look simple."

"It wasn't simple, but I learned how to pretend it was because I got tired of making mistakes and having everyone know. Maybe I've got too much *hochmut*, but I didn't want *Daed* to be disappointed in me like others were."

"I can't imagine anyone being disappointed in you."

"Do you think you're the only one who has gotten disappointed looks and tsk-tsks from people who think, no matter how hard you've tried, you can't measure up?"

Katie Kay stared at her sister. "Why didn't you say so after *Mamm* died and the responsibility for the house fell on my shoulders?"

"Because I was jealous of you," her sister answered as she opened another box of butter sticks.

"Of me? Why? I wasn't much more than a kid."

"You were filled with so much light and life you drew people to you like a moth to a flame. I used to be *Daed*'s precious little girl. That changed when you were born."

Katie Kay shook her head. "You're wrong. *Daed* doesn't have a favorite among us. If he did, it wouldn't be me because I've caused him many sleepless nights and heartache."

"You're asking me to explain something I don't understand myself." Priscilla stopped working, one of the few times Katie Kay had ever seen her hands idle. "Maybe I got lazy and didn't try to change a bad habit. Maybe I was resentful I had to leave behind my childhood when *Mamm* passed away, and everyone expected

me to do the same again when your *mamm* died, though I was a new bride with a household of my own." Priscilla sighed before giving her an ironic smile. "I've been praying, Katie Kay, to discover why I reacted as I did after your *mamm* died. I wasn't ready to repeat those unhappy years in my life. I was sure there must be more—"

"Out there to experience," Katie Kay finished, hardly believing the words as she spoke of them.

"*Ja.* How did you know?"

"Maybe we were more alike than either of us has ever wanted to admit. I tried to be perfect...like you. And you wanted to find out about a life beyond the one you'd known as the bishop's daughter...like I did when I jumped the fence."

"Have you jumped back?"

"*Ja.*" She put her fingers over her burgeoning abdomen. "I've got to think of someone else besides myself."

"Do you realize our *bopplin* will be born within weeks of each other?"

"You're pregnant?"

Priscilla nodded, her face brightening. "I found out yesterday. I plan to tell *Daed* and Wanda tomorrow. Today is for them. But our little ones will be cousins and can grow up together if you stay here."

"That would be *wunderbaar.*" Katie Kay hugged her sister and meant it for the first time in longer than she could remember. Maybe her whole life. It was sad to think of the times they might have had together if they had talked years ago as they were now.

As the day unfolded, Katie Kay couldn't help looking for Micah. She spoke with his brothers and his sis-

ters and their spouses and *kinder*, but each time she saw him at a distance, he was gone before she could reach the spot. Was he avoiding her? She couldn't blame him, but she'd thought he would give her the chance to apologize. At least one more time.

She found him among the young people gathering to be matched to eat supper together. It was a tradition those who were walking out together loved and everyone else endured. She wondered what Micah was feeling when he was instructed to stand by her side.

He said nothing, so she struggled to find a way to break the silence between them. Anything she could think of to say sounded insipid in her mind. Taking his hands in hers and pleading with him to let her explain her poor choice of words was impossible when other people milled around them.

By the time they were seated at one of the tables, she still hadn't found the right words. She was relieved when Micah asked without looking at her, "It was a nice wedding, ain't so?"

"A wedding where two people are in love with each other is a reason for celebration." She fought not to frown at her words, which were as trite as his. Not wanting to let the silence smother them again, she asked, "Did the Donnellys enjoy themselves?"

"As much as they could when most of the people around them were speaking *Deitsch*. I arranged for them to be part of the first seating, because the kids aren't used to waiting to eat as ours are."

"I had barely enough time to say hi to them. Olivia looks better, don't you think?"

"Sean says she's tired of not being able to run around with her brothers. If she does too much, the cough re-

turns. The *doktor* wants her to take it easy for another week." At last a smile pulled at his lips. "Gemma says she doesn't know if she can put up with Olivia's complaining that long."

"I let Gemma know she can ask me to babysit whenever she needs a break."

"That's generous of you, Katie Kay."

"It's nothing compared to what they did for me."

He rested his elbow on the table and leaned toward her. "Does this mean you're staying in Paradise Springs?"

Before she could answer, the roar of a car without a muffler exploded through the evening. The black car sped up the farm lane and squealed to a stop behind the rearmost buggy. Katie Kay's sharp intake of breath sounded like a shout in her ears, but only Micah seemed to notice. He put his hand over hers beneath the table as everyone stared at the car and the brown-haired man getting out of it.

Her whisper was as loud as a shout in the shocked silence. "Austin!"

Chapter Sixteen

Katie Kay gripped the table. She continued to stare at Austin, whom she'd hoped never to see again. If she'd imagined talking to him another time, it certainly wouldn't have been in the midst of *Daed*'s and Wanda's wedding supper.

He was dressed in casual *Englisch* style. Well-worn blue jeans, his favorite cowboy boots he wore though she doubted he'd ever been on a horse, and a dark blue T-shirt beneath his gray hoodie. His brown eyes scanned the crowd as he paused in the barn's doorway, and he began to smile when his gaze found hers. Strolling toward her as if he were the master of everything around him, he preened beneath the stares.

Her heart contracted in dismay and fear at what he might say and do. Why did he have to come and chance ruining *Daed*'s wedding? Was his arrival a horrible coincidence, or had Cherokee mentioned something to Vinnie, who then blabbed to Austin?

She wouldn't put such grandstanding past him, but she shouldn't paint him with misdeeds he hadn't done... yet. She needed to keep him from having the oppor-

tunity to make one of the scenes he loved. Could she convince him to talk to her privately? That way, he wouldn't intrude further on the wedding.

"You know him?" her *daed* asked as he came to stand next to her chair.

"Ja." She wanted to look at Micah to see his reaction, but she didn't dare to pull her eyes from Austin's broadening smile. Instantly she knew he was hoping to cause as much trouble as possible.

"You don't look happy to see him."

"It's all right, *Daed*," she said. "I'll handle it."

"You know him?" asked Ina Sue from the other side of the table. She put her hand over her mouth as comprehension bloomed in her eyes and the eyes of everyone else who knew about the *boppli*.

Wanda reached over and took her hand and gave it a gentle squeeze as she whispered, "God is with us always, my dear daughter. Don't forget that. You are never alone."

"I know." A strength that came from the depths of her heart, the part she'd kept closed, startled her, but she was grateful for how it allowed her to straighten her shoulders and raise her chin. Not in pride, but in knowing she was loved by the Lord and her family and her community. All of them were holding her up as she crossed the barn toward Austin.

"Hey, baby," he said as she came closer. "You're looking pretty good for—"

Putting her hand on his arm, she didn't let him finish because she was sure he'd use one of his crude terms. He considered plain folk backward and too stupid to become part of the twenty-first century.

Suddenly she was ashamed. Not for herself, but for

Austin, who believed, in order for people to notice him, he had to create trouble wherever he went. No wonder she'd been drawn into his life after they first met. She'd enjoyed attention as he still did. They were an imperfect match, the *Englisch* slacker who felt the world owed him a living and the Amish girl who'd believed the wider world owed her a whirl of excitement.

"Let's talk somewhere private," she said.

"I don't want to—"

Her fingers curled around his arm. "Either *komm* with me or leave."

"Hey, you're sounding Amish again. Did you forget how to talk good English?"

Before he could say more to insult her family and their friends, she tugged him away from the tables and out of the barn so what they said wouldn't be heard by others. Even if he threw a tantrum as he'd done more than once.

Austin made a pretense of protesting and then went along. Why wouldn't he when he was getting what he wanted? He had her full attention.

Leaning against the stone foundation of the tall barn, he chuckled. "Honey, I know you want to get me alone. Out behind the barn?" He gave her a wink.

"What are you doing here?"

"Cherokee told Vinnie you hadn't decided yet to get rid of the kid after it's born, so I figured I'd come out and see your glow of impending motherhood. And I thought I'd make sure you remembered you need to give me my share of whatever money the adoptive parents give you." With a coarse laugh, he said, "I hear you country girls like to entertain in the hayloft. Want to show me?"

She ignored the coarse words he obviously thought were seductive. It was impossible not to compare him to Micah, who was always solicitous of her. Micah treated everyone with kindness and respect. He'd been as concerned about Gemma's health while Olivia was in the hospital as Sean was.

"Austin, I think you should leave."

"But I just got here. You're not going to send me away without a plate of that great-smelling food and a piece of the wedding cake, are you?"

"You weren't invited."

He waved aside her words. "Don't split hairs with me. How many times did you tell me about how the Amish share what they've got to eat with anyone who stops in at mealtime?"

She started to answer, but a deeper voice said from around the corner of the barn, "She's asked you to leave."

Whirling, she saw Micah walking toward them. To judge by his easy pace, he was mildly perturbed, but she saw anger snapping in his eyes. She wanted to caution him about Austin's temper. Anything he said could make the situation worse...if that was possible because the very air seemed to hum with tension.

"Who's this loser?" sneered Austin.

"I'm Micah Stoltzfus," he said before she could answer.

Austin glanced at her. "Your ex?"

"*You* are my ex, Austin," Katie Kay said, trying to copy Micah's cool serenity. "You became my ex when you pushed me out of your car on a cold, rainy night after stealing my money and cell phone. I should have sent the police to arrest you." In spite of her efforts,

her voice began to tremble with the emotions she was struggling to control.

A gentle hand settled on her waist, out of Austin's sight. Micah's touch offered her strength. Though she longed to turn and throw her arms around him and ask him to forgive her for how she'd hurt him, she continued to look at Austin.

"It was a mistake," he said in the whining tone he used whenever he tried to get what he wanted.

She wasn't going to be taken in again. Her voice was steady when she replied, "Finally something we agree on."

"We can have good times again, Sweetie-Kate," he said, using the nickname he seemed to recall whenever he wanted to wheedle her into going along with his latest scheme. "I've got almost enough money to buy the motorcycle I told you about. We can head anywhere we want." His nose wrinkled as he glanced at Micah. "You don't have to stay around this place that reeks of cow manure and dumb-dumb Dutch."

She was tempted to tell Austin he was wrong if he thought trying to offend Micah would get the usual reaction. Micah wasn't going to answer with either words or fists.

"No, thank you," she said. "My family and my life are in Paradise Springs."

"But I know you want to see the world. You said so yourself a dozen times. I'll get the bike, and we'll hit the road and see it."

"What about our *kind*—our child?" she amended when she realized he wouldn't recognize the *Deitsch* word.

Austin waved aside her question. "If the kid is a problem," he said, "we'll figure something out. There are

always people looking for a baby, no questions asked."
He smiled as if he'd come up with the perfect solution.

Behind Katie Kay, Micah took a deep breath to re-
strain himself from reaching out and grabbing the loud-
mouth by the front of his T-shirt. Never had he been
so furious. Not even when Katie Kay told him to be on
his way and not return.

*Stay with me, Lord, and help me remember nothing
is solved by losing my temper.*

A gentle peace settled around his heart, easing the
tightness that had tormented him since he last walked
out with Katie Kay. All that time, though he'd tried to
deny it, he'd been angry. But anger solved nothing. It
only separated him from God. He had to let go of the
rage and begin to offer forgiveness.

Offer forgiveness to himself and to Katie Kay. He
had to forgive himself for pushing her too hard and too
fast…as Austin was. And forgive her for pushing back
as she fought to discover what she wanted. Not what he
wanted or what Austin wanted or her *boppli*, but what
life she wanted. He'd made the decision for himself, and
she deserved the same chance to choose.

Using only words an *Englischer* would understand,
he said, "A baby isn't something to 'figure out.' A baby
is a precious gift from God, and he or she should be
treasured, not seen as an inconvenience."

"Why don't you stay out of this, farm boy?" He jut-
ted his chin toward Micah in a candid invitation to take
a swing. "It's none of your business."

"You're right," Micah said in the same composed
tone, not taking the bait. He was aware of the many eyes
witnessing this confrontation from a distance. Most of

the guests, including his brothers and brothers-in-law, had moved to where they could watch. A single signal from him, and they would step forward as a unified force, but he didn't want that. He wasn't tempted to sink to Austin's level. There was desperation in the man's voice, and Micah wasn't going to feed that. "It is none of my business, except for the fact that Katie Kay is part of our community, and so is her *boppli*. Her baby."

"You don't know she's going to stay." His voice rose in volume on every word as if he could intimidate Micah by yelling.

The man was a bully.

Micah looked at him without replying. Anything he said would be thrown in his face and prolong the conversation.

When Austin realized Micah wasn't going to retort, he poked a finger in Katie Kay's direction. "You escaped from this straitlaced world once, Sweetie-Kate. Let me help you put it behind you forever."

"Forever?" When she widened her eyes and batted her lashes, Micah had to struggle not to laugh. He'd seen her do the same when an overly eager young man tried to impress her after a singing. "Are you proposing, Austin?"

The *Englischer* choked out a curse and shook his head like a dog coming out of water. "I didn't say anything about marriage."

"No, you didn't. And why would you? You don't want to grow up and take on a man's responsibilities. You want to have fun while you convince your friends to support you, as you convinced me to do. I was a fool, but I'm not going to be a fool any longer."

Quietly, too quietly for Austin to hear, Micah mur-

mured, "Fool me once, shame on you. Fool me twice, shame on me."

She took his hand. When he laced his fingers through hers, he watched as her shoulders rose as if she'd rid herself of a heavy burden.

"I think you should leave, Austin," Katie Kay said. "Leave and don't return."

"Oh, I'll be coming back." He pointed at her stomach. "It's *my* baby! Don't think I'm going to let you keep it! You wait and see."

When she didn't answer, he strode away, his feet pounding the ground as if he could make his footsteps echo across the valley. The wedding guests parted like the Red Sea to let him pass, but nobody spoke when he snarled at them. He got in his car and disappeared into a cloud of leaf debris and dust.

He was gone.

At last.

Micah saw Katie Kay shaking, and he wanted to help her, but wasn't sure what to say. Would Austin try to take her *boppli* from her? Maybe he thought Amish people didn't use attorneys. They didn't often, but when a *kind*'s life was at stake, he knew Reuben would give permission to hire legal assistance.

When his fingers settled on her shoulders, he was startled. She wasn't trembling with fear or with anger.

She was *laughing*?

As if he'd asked out loud, she smiled at him. "Well, you got your wish. You got to meet Austin and give him a piece of your mind."

"He needs more than a piece if he thinks he can threaten to take your *boppli* from you. A couple of

my brothers have adopted *kinder*. The attorney they used—"

She put a finger to his lips. "Let's not look for trouble before it arrives."

"That sounds like the old Katie Kay, the one who didn't want to think beyond the moment she was in."

"No, I'm thinking beyond the moment, but nothing is going to happen until after this *boppli* is born in about six months." Folding her hands behind her, she looked into his eyes. "Until then, I plan to stay in Paradise Springs. It's the best place for me and my *boppli*."

"It's a big change of heart, Katie Kay."

"*Ja*, it is." A smile drifted outward from the corners of her lips. "I've had several changes of heart in the past few days. You may not believe it, but Priscilla and I have come to an understanding."

"You have?" His eyes widened. He hadn't expected that after many years of acrimony between them.

"She's my family, and after seeing how Sean and Gemma and their *kinder* treasure each other, I realized I wanted to treasure my family, too."

"Your *boppli* needs a family, Katie Kay."

"I know, and he or she will have one. *Daed* and Wanda have shown me how eager they are to hold my little one in their arms."

"*My* little one? It's the first time I've heard you say that."

"Maybe because I've come to see I would be a fool to miss a moment with my *boppli*. My *mamm* is with the Lord and watches over me, but since I've learned I'm going to have a *kind* myself, I know she would have been grateful to have more time with my sisters and me." She curved her hand over her belly, where

her *boppli* was growing, before looking at him again. "I know you've been curious about the main reason I jumped the fence."

"Ja."

"It was because I was in love with you."

He was about to laugh and then realized she was serious. "In love?" He pointed at her and then himself. "You were in love with me? You sure had a strange way of showing that."

"I was scared, Micah. Scared of how I felt when I was with you."

"How did you feel?"

Her eyes glowed with powerful emotions. "As if, with you, I had everything I ever wanted or needed."

"But…"

She put her finger to his lips to silence him. "I was scared because I wondered if there was something more for me out in the *Englisch* world. I didn't want to come to regret that I had never found out if there was."

"And what did you find?"

"I was a fool to worry about missing out on something I couldn't name when you were offering me everything."

He drew her into his arms and rested his cheek on top of her *kapp*. "I'm sorry, Katie Kay, for pushing you into a corner."

"What do you have to be sorry for? All you did was make me fall in love with you."

Could he be any happier than he was at the moment when she told him she loved him? He got his answer when she smiled and said, "I love you, Micah Stoltzfus. Will you marry me?"

He chuckled. "You, the girl, are asking me, the boy?

You never do things the way other people do them, ain't so?"

"Ja." Her fingers swept along his cheek and into his hair, her touch gentle and yet sending shivers through him that threatened to buckle his knees. "You said that you'd never ask me again. I love you and want to spend my life with you and have you be my *boppli*'s *daed*, so I'm asking you. Marry me, Micah. Do you love me?"

"With every bit of my heart. *Ja*, my love, I will marry you." He pulled her into his arms and found her lips with the ease of months of longing to hold her.

She jerked back and gasped, "Oh!" Her fingers were splayed across her abdomen.

"Katie Kay, are you all right?"

Joy glowed from her as she whispered, "I felt the *boppli* move."

"You did? What does it feel like?"

She grasped his hand and pressed it against her. A faint sensation fluttered against his palm.

In awe, he cupped her face and bent to kiss her, knowing it would be the first of many kisses they'd share in the years to come.

Epilogue

Snow fell outside, but the cozy kitchen was warm. Katie Kay leaned over the cradle and smiled at the tiny bundle in it. Soft curls were so blond they appeared white, and the little girl's blue eyes were closed while her mouth worked as if tasting the air.

"You are *wunderbaar*, Sarann," she whispered. She didn't want to wake the *boppli* named for her beloved younger sister.

Unlike her sister, her daughter, Sarann, appeared to be healthy in every way. Beth Ann had insisted on having a *doktor* present at the birth at the house Micah had purchased a couple of months after he exchanged vows with Katie Kay. *Doktorfraa* Montgomery had checked Sarann and pronounced she showed no sign of any genetic disorders or other problems. When Sarann had let out a loud cry at that moment, they'd laughed.

Including Micah, who'd offered to be with Katie Kay for the delivery, giving her back massages to ease the labor pains. No one mentioned that the *boppli* wasn't his, and he'd been thrilled with the little girl. He'd cra-

dled her while Beth Ann tended to Katie Kay, and he mumbled nonsense like any new *daed*.

And he was Sarann's *daed* in everything but name.

"We are blessed, little one, to have such a man love us."

She looked around the kitchen, awed by the gifts heaped upon her by their loving God. The room had been painted a light blue with white wainscoting before Sarann's arrival, while Katie Kay still had been able to go up a ladder. The gas stove was a hand-me-down, but the refrigerator was new, a gift from her *daed* and Micah's *mamm*. Dishes that once had belonged to her own *mamm* were drying in the rack by the sink.

The house needed work, but it had five *gut*-sized bedrooms and three bathrooms as well as an artesian well in the cellar and storage in the attic. A chicken coop was close to the stable, which was large enough to hold two horses and the family buggy Micah had traded his courting buggy for after their wedding.

Peeling wallpaper and chipped paint would be taken care of. Between Micah and his brothers and Sean, who insisted on giving a hand now that his new son was almost six months old, the house was already much more livable than it'd been when Micah and Katie Kay had first seen it.

The door opened, and cold air and snowflakes floated in. Micah shook snow off his hat before he hung it on the peg by the door.

"How's our girl?" he asked.

Standing, Katie Kay smiled. "She's doing great. Sleeping like a pro."

He chuckled and then grew serious. "I stopped at the mailbox. Here."

She took the manila envelope he held out to her. When she saw the official return address, she eagerly turned it over and opened it. She pulled out a thick collection of papers. Paging through, she found the one she was looking for. She plucked it out and let the others fall on the table beside her. She found Austin's signature scrawled at the bottom.

"Is it settled?" Micah asked.

"Austin signed his parental rights away, as I'd prayed he would." She raised her eyes to Micah's, knowing they could complete the paperwork for him to adopt Sarann and become her legal *daed*. "You don't look surprised."

"I'm not. As soon as your friend Cherokee told you Austin had bought the motorcycle he was talking about, I knew he wouldn't want to be slowed down by a *boppli*."

"What about you, Micah?" She tossed the page on top of the others, knowing she'd read every word later. "Are you afraid of being slowed down by Sarann and me?"

"No, because no matter where we go and how we get there, we'll always be side by side. You and me and our daughter and any other *kinder* the *gut* Lord blesses us with."

She put her arm around his waist as he slid his around her shoulders. Together they looked at the *boppli*, knowing they both had the life they'd wanted, despite their roundabout way of discovering it. They had a life filled with love.

A life together.

* * * * *

WE HOPE YOU ENJOYED THIS

LOVE INSPIRED®

BOOK.

If you were **inspired** by this

uplifting, **heartwarming** romance,

be sure to look for all six Love

Inspired® books every month.

Love Inspired®

www.LoveInspired.com

LI1HALO2017R

Love Inspired®

Save $1.00

on the purchase of ANY
Love Inspired® book.

Available wherever books are sold,
including most bookstores, supermarkets,
drugstores and discount stores.

Save $1.00

on the purchase of ANY Love Inspired® book.

Coupon valid until February 28, 2019.
Redeemable at participating retail outlets in the U.S. and Canada only.
Limit one coupon per customer.

52616121

Canadian Retailers: Harlequin Enterprises Limited will pay the face value of this coupon plus 10.25¢ if submitted by customer for this product only. Any other use constitutes fraud. Coupon is nonassignable. Void if taxed, prohibited or restricted by law. Consumer must pay any government taxes. Void if copied. Inmar Promotional Services ("IPS") customers submit coupons and proof of sales to Harlequin Enterprises Limited, P.O. Box 31000, Scarborough, ON M1R 0E7, Canada. Non-IPS retailer—for reimbursement submit coupons and proof of sales directly to Harlequin Enterprises Limited, Retail Marketing Department, 22 Adelaide St. West, 40th Floor, Toronto, Ontario M5H 4E3, Canada.

U.S. Retailers: Harlequin Enterprises Limited will pay the face value of this coupon plus 8¢ if submitted by customer for this product only. Any other use constitutes fraud. Coupon is nonassignable. Void if taxed, prohibited or restricted by law. Consumer must pay any government taxes. Void if copied. For reimbursement submit coupons and proof of sales directly to Harlequin Enterprises, Ltd 482, NCH Marketing Services, P.O. Box 880001, El Paso, TX 88588-0001, U.S.A. Cash value 1/100 cents.

5 65373 00076 2 (8100)0 12399

® and ™ are trademarks owned and used by the trademark owner and/or its licensee.

© 2018 Harlequin Enterprises Limited

LICOUP94823